Dedication

To Melissa Cure- my first reader. Your help with the editing was of supreme importance to me. And to Nikki Cure, who turned me on to this genre many years ago. Thank you both for your contributions to this book.

THE DUCHESS OF BRISTOL
BY ANNE ODOM

Copyright © 2015 by Anne Odom

All rights reserved. No part of this publication may be reproduced, distributed, or transmitted in any form or by any means, including photocopying, recording, or other electronic or mechanical methods, without the prior written permission of the publisher, except in the case of brief quotations embodied in critical reviews and certain other noncommercial uses permitted by copyright law.

ISBN **978-1515258445(EPUB)**

The Duchess of Bristol

By Anne Odom

Prologue

England 1827

Diana Westmoreland the Dowager Duchess of Bristol was discontented. She didn't really know why or what to do about it. As a widow, albeit a very young one at twenty-eight, she was not constrained by the tenets of society as tightly as an unmarried woman. Because of her title and her incredible wealth, Diana was invited to any number of social events held by the *ton*. She had very little interest in those events, although she did attend the ones she felt she couldn't get out of. The events and the people who attended them bored her to tears. Since she was very wealthy, still quite young and exquisitely beautiful, she was sought after by both the bachelors, widowers, and some of the married men of the *ton*, which exasperated her to no end. Society men, whether titled or not, also bored her to distraction and the married ones disgusted her. She was truly at loose ends with no relief in sight.

Of course, she could travel, but to where and with whom. She could travel alone with her maid and good friend, Barbara, but knew society and her late husband's distant relatives would frown upon such a venture. However, she was an independent woman with a mind of her own. She had done what society and her family demanded of her for many years. Now it was time for her to do what she wanted to do. If she could only decide exactly what that was.

Therefore, since she had no close relatives, if she did choose to travel alone there was no one to say her nay. As Diana looked around her bedchamber, her eyes lit on the painting of her estate in Scotland, Ainsley Glen, where she had been born. The manor house was not especially large or beautiful. It was more utilitarian. However, the many acres surrounding the house were beautiful.

It sat in a glen in the Highlands, surrounded by huge oaks and alders with the incredible peaks of the Highlands behind it. The house was painted with the light of the noonday sun shining on it with the loch in the distance. This brought a smile to Diana's face for a brief moment. As Diana gazed at the painting, she felt a momentary urge to see her home again. It had been almost two years since she traveled there, but the urge to go to Ainsley Glen again was fleeting and soon gone.

The house held many happy memories, but also some intensely sad ones. But going home was not what she wanted either. She owned several large estates in England she could adjourn to, but she was not English. She had never really felt completely at home in that country. As Diana eyes again turned to the painting of Ainsley Glen, her mind traveled back in time.

Chapter 1

Scotland 1815

Diana had been born in Scotland, the daughter of a Scottish laird, Earl Fergus MacDonald and the love of his life, Lady Morna MacPherson MacDonald. Diana's mother died when she was ten of a debilitating fever. Diana had been groomed from an early age to take her place in Scottish society as the lady of the manor. When she was 16, her father had arranged a marriage for her with another Scottish laird's son, whose father owned the adjoining property. She had known Ian MacAllister all her life. She wasn't in love with him, but she did love him. However, it was more like the love she would have had for a sibling. She also knew that Ian wasn't in love with her, he loved another.

The one he loved, Alana Campbell, was not a laird's daughter. As a matter of fact, her father was the village drunk. Ian would never be allowed to marry Alana, something Ian, Alana and Diana knew, only too well. When their fathers arranged their marriage, Ian and Diana had no say in the matter. Diana, who was tractable and rarely rebelled against anything, would have reluctantly gone along with the arrangement if Ian wasn't so resentful. At nineteen, he was headstrong and rebellious. He was also completely and absolutely in love with Alana Campbell. And those feelings were very much returned by her.

Diana was racking her brain trying to think of a solution to the marriage issue while she curried her little black mare, Malmuira. Diana spent a lot of time in the stables or riding her beloved mare. She had been taught to ride at the age of two by her father. Riding was not only a hobby for her; it was her passion. Because she rode so much, her father had the keep seamstress make her several riding habits in different colors. Today she wore one of her favorites. It was a dark hunter green with a matching hat that sported a yellow feather which matched the blouse she wore under her riding coat. With Diana's red hair and green eyes, the habit was a perfect foil for her beauty.

The stable master, Edwin Burroughs, watched his young charge from the stall door. Miss Diana was the apple of his eye. Burroughs had been born at the keep, the son of Murtaugh Burroughs, the butler, and his wife, Agnes who had been an upstairs maid. He had risen to stable master at a young age because of his uncanny ability with horses. He was worried about Diana. He knew she wasn't exactly overjoyed about her impending marriage.

Since his father was the butler, young Edwin should have been groomed for the position of valet or head footman, later taking over for his father when Murtaugh saw fit to retire. However, Edwin had ever only wanted to be around horses. It was unusual for a servant to be allowed to ride a horse belonging to his master, other than grooms exercising them. However, Fergus MacDonald had never been a selfish or ungenerous man. He had noticed young Edwin hanging around the paddock and stables when he was just a lad of seven. After asking Murtaugh's permission, Fergus had taught the boy to ride. It was only a few years later, after Edwin had been a stable hand for a while, that Fergus noticed his affinity for gentling even the most recalcitrant horses.

Fergus kept a large personal stable and raised horses for market as well. When the young foals were old enough, the stable hands would walk them around in the paddock getting them used to a saddle on their backs. The horses were prepared slowly for a rider. Fergus didn't believe in rushing his young horses. He was well known for only selling horses that were spirited, but gentle enough they could be ridden even by a small child. The aristocracy in both England and Scotland came to him for horses for their families, especially their wives and children. It was very important that the horses he sold be easy to handle, but still have spirit. Edwin had an uncanny ability with the new foals. He would speak to the horses quietly and gently as he led them around the paddock, gaining their trust.

When it came time for the young horses to be ridden the first time, it was usually Edwin who took on the job. It was rare for him to be thrown. Most of the young horses knew him and loved him. He was kind and gentle with them and they responded to that part of him. When the old stable master became ill and eventually died, Fergus gave the position to Edwin although he was only two and twenty at the time. Fergus had never regretted that decision.

Edwin had been unbelievably successful training the young horses and overseeing the care of the others in the stable as well.

Fergus didn't fail to notice that Edwin took especially good care of Diana's mount and of her as well. She had been riding for fourteen years now, and it was Edwin who usually escorted her when she went somewhere in the neighborhood without her father.

Diana was very good about visiting the tenants on her father's property. She went at least once every week to the wee village near the keep to take gifts of food to the elderly and infirm. She would check on them to make sure they had enough fuel for their fires and make sure if medicine was required, it was obtained. Diana had taken over those responsibilities at a very young age because of her mother's ill health and Edwin had accompanied her on most every trip. She had been doing the calls on the tenants since she was eight, always with Edwin in attendance. He not only escorted Diana, he came into the homes of the tenants as well. If there was any heavy work needed, Edwin was there to take care of it. He looked on Diana as the little sister he had never had. He was an only child, as was she.

He had been helping Diana with her mare since Malmuira was a foal. He had broken the horse himself for his young mistress, trusting no one else with the job. Edwin was very protective of Diana. The impending match with Ian MacAllister weighed on his mind too and he was not happy about it. Diana had confided her feelings for Ian to Edwin. He knew she was very upset about being more or less forced to marry a man she saw only as a brother. Edwin was tempted to speak to his employer, but such a thing was unheard of. He had to keep silent on the matter, albeit unwillingly.

One night, a few weeks before the wedding was to take place, the three of them, Ian, Alana and Diana, met in the woods that separated their fathers' holdings. Diana, with Edwin's help, had slipped away from home alone for once. Without her knowledge, Edwin had followed her and was watching from a distance for her protection.

Ian was restless, pacing up and down before the two girls who were seated on a felled tree shivering in their heavy cloaks. Spring was close, but in the Highlands, it still felt like winter. Alana was also sixteen and she and Diana were best friends.

Diana said, "Ian, what can we do? Our fathers will never listen to us about this marriage. They think they know what is best for both of us, even though they are most definitely wrong."

"I have no idea. I just know I can't marry you, Di. I don't love you like that. You're like a sister to me. I love Alana, as you well know," said Ian with a note of desperation in his voice.

Alana, as was usual, was quiet. Her big blue eyes were drowning in sorrow with tears brimming and about to fall.

One more look at Alana and Diana knew she couldn't go along with the arrangement made by their fathers. She could not and would not be responsible for all three of them being miserable for the rest of their lives. Diana jumped up from the log and began to pace.

"You and Alana must run away and get married, " she stated baldly.

Ian and Alana turned toward her with very surprised faces.

"Tis the only thing you can do. If you are already married, then you cannot be forced to marry me. If you are already married, your father will have to accept Alana as his daughter," she rushed on to say.

"But how can we do that. I have no money. Where would we go, who would marry us," sputtered Ian.

"I have some money", stated Diana to the surprise of the other two.

"Where did you get money?" Ian demanded to know quickly.

"I've had it ever so long. When my mother died, my grandmother McPherson gave me the money and jewels that were in Mama's dowry. My father had never taken them. They were to be part of my dowry along with what my father will provide for me. I have had them put away all these years." Diana explained.

Alana grabbed Diana's hand, "We couldn't take your dowry, Diana. That would be ever so wrong."

"Pooh, it's not my whole dowry. My Da has much put away for me. Also, I will inherit Ainsley Glen since I'm an only child and it is not entailed to the earldom. I would not go to my wedding a pauper if you took what I have hidden."

Ian and Alana looked at each other with a glimmer of hope. Could they do it? Could they run away and get married using Diana's money?

"But where would we go?" Ian asked. "My father has friends all over Scotland that would be looking for us if we ran away. He would have our marriage annulled. We would be dragged back here in disgrace. Then he would make me marry you anyway."

"America," Diana exclaimed. "We're not that far from Inverness. You could be married there and catch a ship to America. No one would ever think to look for you there. I have enough money and jewels to set you up nicely in the new country. It's enough to buy land there. You know how to farm and keep sheep, Ian. You have worked along side your father and brothers for years. You would do well there, I know you would."

Ian mulled the idea over and over in his mind. He felt really terrible about running away from his father and his home, but his love for Alana could not be denied. The idea of living as Diana's husband, while loving another was more than he could handle.

Ian knelt down and grabbed Alana's hands. "Would you run away with me, lass? Would you get on a ship and travel all the way to the new land with me?"

"Yes, Ian," Alana said breathlessly. "I would follow ye anywhere."

Diana's face broke into a beautiful smile. "It's done then. I will get the money and jewels tomorrow from my hiding place. Meet me here just at dusk. Bring horses for both of you, Ian. Alana, I will pack some of my clothes for you. I know you wouldn't be able to bring anything with you from home. Ian, tell your Da you're going hunting and meeting your friends elsewhere. That way you can take your sword and guns, as well as food and some clothes. You can pack them on the extra horse, so taking two horses won't seem odd. Tell him you will be gone at least two weeks, hence the need for all the supplies. A last adventure before you marry."

"You have this all figured out, Diana. Have you been planning this for some time?" Ian inquired.

"No, I just have a quick mind, you twit. You should know that after all these years. Now, off with you both." Diana responded with a bright smile. The friends parted laughing at Diana's spirited reply.

The next day, Diana went about her usual duties with a light step and a lighter heart. She had finally found a way for her friends to be together and she would not have to suffer a loveless marriage for the rest of her days. After the evening meal, which was served around six, Diana went to the top of her father's keep to get her mother's dowry. She had hidden it years ago when her grandmother had given it to her, at the old woman's insistence. Her grandmother believed a woman should always have something hidden away to fall back on in hard times. As her grandmother had died only two years after the dowry was given to Diana, no one knew about it. Diana had never shared her secret.

Diana removed a stone from the corner of the solarium where the women went to spin wool. The small cask with the gold coins and bright jewels was covered in dust and spider webs. She wiped it off with her handkerchief and opened it slowly. She ran her hands over the many coins, stopping to pick up a very old-fashioned necklace set with large rubies and diamonds. She didn't know the prices of such things, but she thought this one item would be enough to buy land in the new country. It was only one of many in the cask. She felt wonderful that she had these things to give her friends for their future. Diana felt no emotional attachment to the jewels. The jewels had belonged to ancestors she had never known. Her father had kept her mother's jewelry for her, as part of her dowry.

Without another thought, she snatched up the cask and hurried down the stairs to her room. She opened the armoires where her gowns were stored. She had many gowns in many colors. Her father was wealthy and had always been most generous where his only child was concerned. Some of the gowns she had only worn once. With Alana's coloring in mind, blond hair and sapphire blue eyes, Diana chose gowns that would look well on her.

After she had put several gowns and a riding habit in a canvas sack that usually held wool for carding, Diana went to a trunk in the corner of her room and removed nightgowns, chemises and stockings to go with the gowns. Then she chose three pairs of shoes and a pair of riding boots that she thought would fit Alana. Luckily, her room's windows were at the back of the keep. She went to one of them, after adding the cask to the clothing, she dropped it out the window. She heard a soft thunk as the bag hit the ground. She watched carefully for a few minutes, but no one came to where the bag had fallen.

Now, to just slip out without being seen by any of the servants or her father. Diana was just heading out the door from the library to the garden when the housekeeper, Mrs. Gwen, came into the room.

"Where are you off to at this time of night, little one. The sun has already left the sky?" Mrs. Gwen asked.

"Just going out to catch the first scents of the spring flowers, Mrs. Gwen. I can hardly wait for everything to start blooming." Diana said blithely. She had prepared this answer on the off chance she was caught on her way out. Diana was well known for her romantic thoughts on the seasons, so Mrs. Gwen thought nothing of her reply.

Diana was careful to wander around in the few flowers that had already started to bloom, stopping here and there to sniff the blossoms, in case Mrs. Gwen was looking out one of the windows. After a few minutes, she slowly made her way deeper into the garden. When she was out of sight of all the windows, she followed the hedge to the back of the building and recovered her bag.

Diana had timed her departure just right. The servants had gone into the house for their dinner and the stable was empty. She saddled Malmuira and led her to the mounting block to reach the saddle. She rode the horse out the back of the stables into one of the paddocks and then let herself out the back gate. She had no idea that she was followed.

Edwin knew what she was about, but felt no need to stop her or report her to her father. He thought what the three young people were doing was the right thing for them all. He just wanted to make sure that Diana came to no harm.

When she got to their meeting place in the woods, Ian and Alana were already there. Ian had brought two fine horses. One was laden down with all manner of bags and sacks.

"Ian, did you bring everything you own for a hunting trip, lad?" Diana asked with a laugh.

"My Da had John Dougal help me pack. You would think I needed to feed an army with the amount of food he insisted I carry with me. I told him my friends would be bringing food as well, but he thinks all young men eat like he does. I also have a tent, cooking pots and several blankets. You would think it was the dead of winter the way he kept going on about how cold it is in the Highlands at night." Ian grumbled.

"Well, make room for one more. I have clothes for Alana and the dowry in this bag. You should hide some of the money on each of you, just in case. That way if one of you loses it, the other will still have some. Alana, you should change into the riding habit I brought you. Is there no saddle for her horse, Ian?" Diana inquired.

"Aye, I brought my mother's old sidesaddle for her. I snuck it out last night and hid it in the bushes at the back of the keep. It's in a bag hanging on the horse." Ian replied.

"Well, you will probably have to put some of that on your horse to get the saddle on hers. You get to it and we will go behind those bushes and I will help Alana change."

In just a very few minutes, the young lovers were ready to leave. Ian helped Alana up into the sidesaddle. She looked very beautiful in the sapphire blue habit Diana had brought for her. She had even remembered the matching hat. She looked the picture of a young lady out for a ride with her handsome escort. When she was helping Alana dress, Diana had tied a cloth around her waist with money and jewels tucked into it under her corset. Ian had done the same under his clothes keeping out only what he thought was enough to pay for their passage in Inverness.

They had all hugged and wished each other well. It was time for them to leave, and yet they hesitated. "Di, I don't know how to thank you for all you've done. Lass, I hope my running away doesn't end badly for you. You know how the gossips are around here. My actions could result in your father having trouble making a match for you. Some fool people may think I ran away because there is something wrong with you."

Diana hadn't thought of that, but it made no difference. Her friends were more important to her than some distant future husband or lack thereof. She had always assumed she would be married, but hadn't dwelt on the matter. Diana, though mature in many ways, was still naive about romance and marriage.

"Away with you, then. There is no need to worry about me. It's years before I will be considered an old maid. I am only just turned sixteen, you know. So be off with you now!"

At her final words, her friends turned their horses and headed in the direction of Inverness. Diana turned in the opposite direction for home. Unbeknownst to her, Edwin followed her home. He kept the other servants out of the stable long enough for her to put up Malmuira and slip into the house unseen by any but him.

The days went quickly by as others had in the past. Earl MacDonald went about his business on his estate and his daughter continued to run his household as she had since before her mother died when she was ten. The Laird's wife, Morna, hadn't been well in the last years of her life and Diana had been required to take over many duties she was too young for. It had matured Diana early, but the duties had never seemed to make her sad or unhappy. Diana, his beautiful red-haired daughter, was the apple of the laird's eye. She could do no wrong and he wanted only the best for her. His decision to wed her to his friend and fellow laird's son, Ian, was something he thought she wanted. The two had been close as thieves practically from the time they got out of swaddling clothes.

Fergus MacDonald never thought to ask his daughter what she wanted. Women were not usually consulted in the matter of marriage. A father did what he thought best and his children learned to live with it. Fergus wasn't unconcerned about his daughter's feelings, it just never occurred to him she wouldn't want to marry Ian MacAllister.

When a fortnight had elapsed and Ian hadn't returned to his father's keep, the elder MacAllister didn't think too much of it. Young men out on a hunt were apt to stay longer than the allotted time. But after a month and no Ian, Angus began to worry. The wedding was set in a couple of weeks time. He sent riders to the keeps of his son's friends with messages inquiring about Ian's whereabouts. The answers were none to his liking. None of Ian's friends had seen him in over a month. Inquiries around the village by the laird's men also brought no news of his son. However, there was news from the village that disturbed Angus deeply. The girl, Alana Campbell had also disappeared around the same time Ian had left home to supposedly hunt.

Angus had one of his men bring the girl's father before him. "Where has your daughter gotten off to, Campbell?"

As usual Dougal Campbell was well into his cups although it was only late morning. Or he had never sobered up from the evening before. His bleary eyes and rambling speech irritated Angus to no end. He ordered his servants to sober him up and bring him back. After a couple of hours, a somewhat sober Dougal was presented to the laird.

"Now, can you tell me where your daughter, Alana is? Has she gone to visit kin?" asked Angus impatiently.

"I don't know where she is. She just wasn't home when I woke up a while back and I haven't seen her since." Responded Campbell belligerently. "She's been after me to quit the drink, so maybe she just got tired of trying to make me quit and went somewhere else. I don't know and I don't care."

Angus was exasperated and disgusted by Dougal Campbell and had his servants send him away immediately. Angus was extremely irritated and worried by this point. He rode over to see his friend Fergus MacDonald to see if he or Diana knew where to look for his son.

Fergus greeted his friend and could tell immediately that something was drastically wrong. "What ails you, Angus? You look as if you've lost your last friend or your fortune, or both?"

"Tis worse than either of those. Ian is gone and I have nay idea where or with whom. He told me he was going on a hunt with some of his friends. He packed up and took two horses with him over a month ago. None of his friends have seen him. That Campbell girl he wanted so badly to marry has disappeared too. I fear they have run off together." Angus replied.

Fergus had had no idea that Ian wanted to marry another girl. He had thought both his daughter and Ian were reconciled to the choices their fathers had made.

"You are telling me that Ian didn't want to marry my Diana? This is the first I have heard of this. Why didn't you tell me he was taken with another girl? Blustered Fergus.

"I thought he would knuckle down and do as he was told. Joining our lands was a good thing and something we had been planning since they were bairns. I thought it was just foolishness on his part. I had nay idea he would just take off. Do you think Diana knows anything about this? Those two are thick as thieves and always have been. Maybe Ian told her something before he left."

Fergus had a servant go to fetch Diana. When she saw Angus, she looked disturbed, but unafraid. Ah, thought Fergus, she does know something.

"Diana," Fergus said, "Do you know where Ian has gotten off to? His father says he's been gone for over a month."

"Yes, Da," she replied. "He and Alana have gone to America. They were to get married in Inverness and then catch a ship to the new country."

All of this was stated baldly with no attempt to explain.

Angus began to stammer and shout, "What do you mean they have gone to America? Are you daft girl? Ian cannot go to America nor can he marry that worthless twit. How was he supposed to pay for their passage? He had no money of his own"

Fergus said, "Now calm down, Angus. It appears that the deed is already done. When did they leave, Diana?"

"About a month ago, Da. I gave them some money and jewels Grandmother MacPherson had given me when Mama died. They had plenty to book passage and start a new life in America. Please forgive me, Da, but Ian and I are like sister and brother. We could not marry. And besides, Ian loves Alana and she loves him. They belong together." Diana replied.

Angus and Fergus stared at her as if she was insane, but Diana felt no remorse about what she had done. She had helped two people she truly cared about find happiness together. What she did was nay wrong, it felt very right.

After Angus left, Fergus walked with Diana in the garden. He felt as if he didn't know his daughter at all. He was not an introspective man, nor a very sensitive one. He had thought he and Angus knew what was best for their children. Apparently, they had only been doing what was best for themselves, not their children.

Diana was unusually quiet on their walk. "Are you angry with me, Da?" she asked apprehensively.

"Nay, child. I am no angry. I am surprised and I feel sorry for Angus. He has lost his son."

"I didn't think of it as Ian being lost to his Da. He tried to tell him that he didn't love me, but Alana instead. His father would nay listen. He just kept telling Ian he had to marry me, that it was settled. Ian couldn't help how he felt about Alana. Should Ian and I have married, we all three would have been horribly miserable. Alana is my friend, as is Ian. I could nay hurt either of them that way." Diana said quietly.

"Why didn't you come to me with this problem, child?" asked Fergus, shaking his head.

"Da, would you have listened to me? I think not. I tried several times to broach the subject, but you just shooed me away. You aren't that easy to talk with, Da. I know you have much on your mind, so I don't fault you, but it would be nice to have someone I could talk to. I have always had Ian and Alana, but now that they are gone. I feel all alone in the world."

Fergus looked at his daughter with new eyes. He had always just taken for granted that she would do as she was told. He never thought about her feelings or desires. It was not the way of the world for children to be included in decision making for their own futures. Maybe that was wrong, he thought. Maybe, we should be asking their opinions instead of just doing what we feel is right. Now his friend had lost his youngest son. True, he had other sons to inherit his property and title and take over his laird's responsibilities, but he had still lost his youngest. Fergus believed that Ian had been Angus' favorite son as well. He was certainly taking the news hard.

Chapter 2

The days passed, as they are wont to do. Diana continued her duties as chatelaine of her father's keep. Her father continued his duties as laird. They rarely saw Angus MacAllister. Fergus heard that Angus was drinking a lot and had become surly and hard to deal with. He was sad to hear that his old friend was in that condition, but there was little he could do.

Several months later in August, Diana received a letter from Ian all the way from America, a place called Virginia.

> *Dearest Diana,*
>
> *I am writing to let you know how grateful Alana and I are to you for giving us this wonderful opportunity. We were married in Inverness two days after leaving you.*

We were lucky enough to catch the next ship sailing to America, the very day after we were married.

The voyage took a month and we landed at Wilmington, North Carolina safe and sound. We heard there was good land available in Virginia so we went there. I have been able to buy 400 acres of good land in the state of Virginia near Williamsburg. We have completed a small cabin on the bank of the river here for temporary shelter. We are planning to start the big house next year, as it will take that long to mill the necessary lumber. Alana will have our first child in a few months. If it is a girl, we will name her Diana in your honor.

I have hired several free men to work my farm. Free men are Negroes who are no longer or have never been slaves. We were shocked by the slavery in this country. Neither of us could ever condone owning another human being.

Diana, I have also written to my father several times prior to my letter to you. I have had no answer. I can only assume he has no interest in hearing from me. I feared his response to our leaving the way we did, but I could see no other way to live my life as I knew I must.

Please write to us and let us know how he does, as well as how you are faring.

*Yours affectionately,
Ian MacAllister*

Diana read the letter more than once. She was very pleased that her friends were doing so well. She was also ecstatic with the news of the baby. When her father came in for the evening meal, she handed him the letter to read for himself.

"It sounds as if Ian is doing well. You should be proud of yourself for assisting him in building this fine new life for himself and his wife. I wish Angus were a more forgiving man. I fear he will never reconcile himself to Ian's decision or to his choice of wife. I haven't seen him lately, but I have heard he is not himself. He is drinking too much and neglecting his duties as laird. It's good he has Robert to help him. He will make a fine laird when his time comes." Fergus said.

Diana had heard the rumors about Angus MacAllister as well. She was saddened to know her father's good friend wasn't doing well. She hoped he would be able to pull himself together for his own good and the good of his family and tenants.

Fergus handed back Ian's letter and pulled another letter from his sporran. "I also received a letter today. It is from the Duke of Bristol. He is requesting to come here to hunt stags and wild boar in two months time. He plans to stay for a month. I met him in England when your mother and I were there many years ago buying horses for your grandfather. I have not seen him since your mother and I attended his wedding a little later, although we have corresponded all this time. I am looking forward to seeing him again. He plans to bring his two sons with him and a great many servants. Will you be able to accommodate so many on such short notice?"

"Two months," Diana gasped. "That is not much time to hire additional help, air out the unused rooms on the second floor, have everything cleaned, and food prepared for that many people, Da. I had better get started right away. There is much to be done."

Fergus smiled at the shocked look on his daughter's beautiful face. He had no doubt that she would be able to accomplish everything that was needed for the visit. She was a wonderful chatelaine for his keep. All his tenants and servants loved her and would go to any lengths to see that she was happy.

The next two months passed in a whirlwind of activity for Diana. She hired extra maids from the village, oversaw the cleaning of the rooms for both their guests and their servants, and consulted with the cook and housekeeper on all that would be needed for a month's stay by their guests.

Diana also had to oversee the sewing of new draperies, servants clothing and additions to her own wardrobe. She had not replenished her wardrobe after giving so many things to Alana for their voyage. She hired extra seamstresses and wielded a needle herself for many hours. Diana was an expert at embroidery having been taught by her grandmother at a tender age. She wanted everything to be perfect for her father's guests.

Diana had no expectations for herself with this visit, as she didn't expect to be allowed to go on the hunts herself. She knew how to shoot and rode like a demon. She had been on hunts with her father and his friends many times. Since she was such an excellent horsewoman and shot, she would have loved the opportunity to go. However, she believed her father would expect her to stay home and make sure everything ran smoothly.

She was very surprised when her father appeared suddenly one day, entering the sewing room. "Da, is everything all right? It is rare for you to enter this room."

"Everything is fine, I was just wanting to inquire if you had prepared any new riding habits for yourself. I expect you to join us on at least the stag and pheasant hunts, if not the boar hunts. I know how you love it."

"I would love to do so. Will there be other ladies on the hunt?"

"I plan to invite some of our neighbors to join the later hunts, so I would imagine there might be a few of the younger ladies who will join us toward the end. On the initial hunts, you will be the only female present. Does that bother you at all, lass?"

"Nay, Da. I don't mind being the only one. I have hunted with you and your friends many times without another woman along."

Diana was well pleased with this information. She and her father had planned a ball for their guests from England. Some of the Scottish guests to the ball would also be coming to dinner earlier.

The entire keep had been refurbished in preparation for the visitors and the ball.

The day finally dawned when the English visitors were due to arrive. Diana was up before dawn to oversee final preparations for their guests. When she had completed all her tasks, Diana hurried upstairs to her bedchamber to bathe and dress. The guests were due to arrive in time for the evening meal.

Diana went to her wardrobe to choose her gown for the evening. With her coloring, dark red hair, creamy white skin and large green eyes, she had chosen her new clothes in shades of yellow, orange, green and blue. She decided on a beautiful pale yellow silk dress with a high waist, short puffy sleeves and a modest neckline. The skirt was not terribly full and almost touched the floor. She chose light yellow slippers to go with it. Since all the servants were so very busy, Diana excused Barbara to help Mrs. Gwen. She dressed herself and did her own hair. She piled her curls on top of her head and pinned them well. She encircled her head with a wide yellow ribbon that matched her dress perfectly.

Although, Diana's bust was generous, she was very reticent about wearing revealing clothing. She was after all, only sixteen. She knew some of her contemporaries had no such compunctions. She had been a guest at a house party some months prior and some of the young ladies, who were her age or even younger, were showing what she thought was a scandalous amount of skin.

When Diana was dressed, she went to her casket of jewels and chose a set of emerald earrings, bracelet and necklace presented to her by her father on her sixteenth birthday last March. When Fergus saw his lovely daughter coming down the stairs, his eyes lighted with admiration. She was the epitome of beauty, youth and good taste in his eyes.

"Do you think our guests will arrive on time, Da?"

"It is hard to tell about timing, my dear. We've had quite a bit of rain lately and the roads are not in very good condition. I hope the meal you have planned will hold in case they are not here in good time."

"Oh, yes, I took the nasty weather into consideration. Everything we are serving will hold well. Everything is prepared and just awaiting their arrival."

Just as Diana finished speaking, they could hear the dogs start to bark in the courtyard. Diana and her father hurried to the door, which was being opened by their butler, Murtaugh. Diana was surprised by the number of horses and riders in the party. There must have been at least ten of them as well as two wagons and a carriage. The horses in front were ridden by what she assumed must be the duke and his sons. The Duke of Bristol was an imposing man. He sat tall in the saddle of a huge black stallion. He wore an impressive black coat and buff breeches with a black waistcoat embroidered in silver. A very full cloak was around his shoulders, but tossed back as it was only cool this evening, not cold. His long black boots stretched almost to his knees. His face was lined and weathered, his dark hair turning gray, but he was still a handsome man. However, what Diana noticed first were his eyes. He had large, intelligent looking, dark brown eyes that glinted with good humor.

Diana's gaze next went to the sons riding on either side of him. One of them looked much like his father, but with light blue eyes. His eyes, however, were not glinting with humor. His eyes were very serious looking. He also wore somber colored clothing, but in brown. The other son, who was younger, was a complete contrast to his father and brother. He appeared to be tall, thin and fair. He had blond hair, darker blue eyes and a slim athletic build. His clothing was much more colorful than his father or brother's. He had a peacock blue coat in the latest style, a yellow embroidered waistcoat and tight buff breeches worn with tall black boots. His hair, a yellow almost the shade of his waistcoat, was curly and worn somewhat long in back with shorter curls around his almost pretty face. He had a sardonic smile upon his face as he looked around the keep with what looked like disdain.

Diana took an almost instant dislike to him. She was surprised by her feelings. She rarely disliked anyone, much less a stranger. As the guests started to climb down from their horses, the laird went forward to meet them. Diana remained on the landing by the front door. She felt timid and shy, but she smiled a welcome anyway.

"Welcome, your grace. I hope your journey went well."

"Other than all the rain and mud, it went just fine. May I present my sons? My elder, Geoffrey, the Marquess of Bradberry, and my younger son, Edward, Viscount Bradshear."

The young men bowed to the laird and he bowed back.

The duke looked up at Diana. "And this must be your lovely daughter, Fergus. She looks a lot like your Morna."
"Yes, that's my Diana. Diana, come and meet our guests."

Diana went down the steps toward the guests, moving with lithe grace. The Marquess watched her with hooded eyes. The Viscount, however, gave her hardly a glance. After being presented to the Duke and his sons, Diana and Fergus led them inside the keep.
"Your grace, if you will allow our butler to show you upstairs to your rooms, we will dine at your convenience. Will you be needing a valet, or did you bring your own men?" asked Fergus.

"Oh, we have our own, Fergus. If someone could just show Phillips the way, he will have our luggage unloaded and brought to our rooms. I'm fair starving and cannot wait to taste some of your wonderful Scots fare."

"Of course, your grace. Diana, will you have someone take charge of the duke's servants and see that their things are carried to their chambers right away."

As the duke and his sons followed Murtaugh up the stairs, Diana motioned for Phillips to follow her. Phillips was of an age with the duke and her father. He was tall and thin with a distinguished bearing. Two other men joined them. She assumed they were the valets of the sons. One was an older, unassuming man with a kindly face. The other was quite young and handsome and seemed somewhat full of himself, although he had a kindly smile..

Diana led the three men to the housekeeper, Mrs. Gwen. She took them to the kitchen, which held the servants stairs. Diana went back outside to oversee the unloading of the many bags and trunks from the wagons that had followed the horsemen. After the constant stream of men carrying bags and trunks finally ceased, Diana went back to the drawing room to await their guests.

When she arrived, she found her father standing in front of the huge fireplace holding a glass of whiskey. "Do you want a dram of something, Di?"

"Nay, Da, I will wait and have some wine with dinner. I am nay thirsty now."

They didn't have long to wait. The duke was the first to arrive. "Fergus, I like your home. It has character and warmth." The duke said, as he was served a glass of whiskey by one of the footmen, Hargis.

"Thank you, your grace."

"Oh, please no more of this your grace nonsense. Please call me Harold as you did in the days of our youth before I began to carry this heavy mantle of the duchy."

"My pleasure, Harold. I'm glad to see the years have been kind to you. You look hale. I was sorry to hear about your wife's passing. I only met her at the wedding, but your letters gave me a glimpse of the lovely woman she must have been. I take it you were happy in your marriage?"

"Yes, I was happy. It has been three years since Elizabeth died. However, I miss her still very much."

"As I miss my Morna. It has been six years since she left us. She was ill for several years before she passed. She was never strong, poor thing, as you know."

"I remember how delicate she looked when last I saw her in England, oh so many years ago. Your daughter has her coloring, but she seems to have her father's constitution."

Diana blushed under the Duke's scrutiny. Although, she had been to house parties in their region of Scotland with her father, she was too young to have had a season in London and was unused to being the object of such intense scrutiny.

The door to the drawing room was opened by Murtaugh to admit the Duke's older son, Geoffrey. He approached the group standing in front of the fireplace. As Diana had surmised, he was a tall and well-built young man. He looked to be in his mid twenties and had a very serious demeanor. He bowed to the Earl and then took Diana's offered hand and bowed above it as she curtsied. She blushed prettily as he held her hand a moment or two longer than was normal.

Diana felt flustered. Geoffrey was very handsome although very serious. She had just begun to regain her composure when the door was opened again for the younger son, Edward. Although the other two men had changed into dark evening clothes and looked very well indeed, they didn't hold a candle to Edward's costume. He wore a coat of gold with matching breeches and hose. Upon his feet, were dark blue dancing slippers. His waistcoat was a dark blue embroidered in gold to match his slippers. His hair had been left loose and curling around his shoulders. Diana thought he was probably the most beautiful man she had ever seen, but she felt wary of him. His eyes, she thought, had no life in them. They were a beautiful shade of blue, but the light she saw in them was strange. She couldn't determine exactly what she was seeing, but it disturbed her greatly.

After a half hour of drinks and conversation, the small party was ushered into the dining room for dinner. Diana, the cook and the housekeeper had spent hours on the menu for this first dinner and indeed for the duke's entire stay. The gamekeeper had brought several quail, a young deer, and several trout to the kitchen that morning. The meal started with a leek soup flavored with fresh sweet cream, herbs and sherry. As the soup bowls were taken away, a line of footmen began to bring in the main dishes. The quail were rubbed with fresh creamy butter then baked with herbs and served with roast potatoes, carrots and a dish of pease. Pease was a dish of yellow peas cooked down into an almost mushy consistency and flavored with onions, herbs, cream and butter.

Also served was a course of venison collops with mashed potatoes and thin toast. The fish course was sauteed with onions then poached in a buttery broth flavored with white wine. For dessert, there were three different flavors of syllabub, a bread pudding, and soft cheese and apples from their orchard. Wine was served with dinner. Diana had one glass of wine. However, she observed that Edward's wine consumption was prodigious.

Geoffrey watched as his brother became more and more animated throughout dinner. He, himself, rarely drank more than a glass or two of wine at dinner and rarely drank strong spirits at all. An occasional glass of brandy or whiskey was all he allowed himself. He disliked the fact that his brother's alcohol use was escalating more each day. He had spoken to his father about it. The Duke had reprimanded Edward, but it had little effect.

Geoffrey watched Diana surreptitiously all during dinner. He had rarely seen a more beautiful girl. Unlike most red haired girls, there were no freckles to mar her complexion. Her skin was a creamy color with pink highlighting her cheeks. Her hair was curly and had been pulled up into a fashionable knot on top of her head with curls cascading down around her face and neck. Her dress was pretty and appropriate for her youth. But it was her eyes that commanded most of his attention. They were the green of emeralds with flecks of gold throughout. Her lashes were dark, thick and long.

She had the kindest and sweetest expression on her face and that same kindness was reflected in her eyes. She seemed shy at first, but as the conversation drifted to tomorrow's hunt, Geoffrey observed Diana become more animated and lively. She obviously loved riding and hunting. Some of the girls of his acquaintance liked to ride, but very few came on hunts. Very few of his friend's sisters participated in either. Most preferred to pursue less stringent activities. He was glad that Diana would accompany them on the morrow. He was anxious to know her better.

Edward was also observing Diana. However, his opinion was quite different from his brother's. He saw a young provincial girl with no sophistication and very limited experience. She was attractive, he would admit, but that didn't really interest him. Girls weren't his cup of tea, so to speak. His interests lay in a different direction entirely. As he drank more wine, his thoughts drifted to his valet, Benjamin. Now there was someone who interested him completely. He was besotted with him.

Edward knew he shouldn't be drinking so much. He tended to forget himself when he was drunk. He didn't want to make a slip in front of his father. He was very careful to keep his proclivities to himself. He didn't want to be disinherited or arrested. Buggery was against the laws of England. Edward had no intention of ever being caught. He planned to marry some unsuspecting heiress to cover his tracks. He hadn't thought ahead to whom he would marry because he really didn't care. Once he was respectably married, he could relax. He never intended to consummate the marriage; it would just be a front. When the wine was offered again, he declined. Better to be safe than sorry.

The Duke watched the interplay of the young people at the table. He had thought Diana might make a good match for his youngest son when he planned this trip. He was very aware that Edward was an unhappy young man. He had no idea why. There were many young women in England who would have made suitable wives for Edward or Geoffrey. However, he had never forgotten

Fergus and his beautiful wife Morna. Morna had been the sweetest, kindest person he had ever known.

Harold had not been married when he became acquainted with Fergus and his wife. He had foolishly fallen a little in love with his friend's wife. Nothing ever came of his infatuation, of course, but he never forgot her either. Through Fergus' letters, he had come to know much about Diana and the type of person she had become. He devised this hunting trip on the chance Edward might also be taken in by her sweetness, as he had been by her mother's.

However, he noticed that Geoffrey seemed to be very interested in her instead. While Edward didn't really seem to care. He wanted his sons to have real marriages, not arranged ones. He had been very lucky that his parents had approved his choice. His Elizabeth hadn't been a duke's daughter, but a baron's instead. After his infatuation with Morna, it was his very good luck to meet Elizabeth about a year later. He had fallen deeply in love with her almost immediately. Some parents would have never approved their match because of the differences in their standing in society. However, his parents had married for love and wanted the same for their only son.

So few of his peers married for love, it was not usually even a consideration. They married to better their families, increase their lands and their coffers, and of course, to provide heirs. He and Elizabeth had been blessed with two sons, but he had always wished for a daughter as well. It was not meant to be. He had hopes that the women his sons married would become the daughters he never had.

Fergus watched his friend during dinner. Harold was up to something, he was sure. He noticed that he seemed to especially pay attention to Diana during the meal. He had a feeling Harold was sizing her up. When Harold had written to ask about the hunting trip, Fergus was mildly surprised. They hadn't seen each other in well over twenty years. They had written occasionally, but sporadically over those years. He still felt a special friendship for Harold however.

When Fergus had been sent to England by his father to buy a special stallion and a couple of mares, he had been unaccustomed to the ways of the English aristocracy. It was worlds different from the much more relaxed Scottish society. The hierarchy in England was very old and very insular. Although, he and Morna had received invitations to social events, neither of them was completely comfortable. They had met Harold Westmoreland at the first entertainment they had attended. They had all three liked each other immediately and spent much time together.

Harold Westmoreland had been friendly and extremely helpful in obtaining the horses Fergus had come for. Also, he had made it a point to introduce the couple to other young people with similar interests and personalities. Although, Fergus and Morna were a few years older than Westmoreland, he took to them instantly. He had eased their way into the center of the life of the *ton* for the month they had been in England so many years ago.

After Westmoreland took them up, the invitations increased to a flood. There were balls, musicales and theater parties almost every night. Morna, who was much less inhibited around people than Fergus, enjoyed the activities to the fullest. Never one to be shy in society, she soon captured the hearts and minds of society matrons, unmarried debutantes and of course a lot of the young men. She was not only beautiful; she was witty and charming as well. Fergus was so very proud of the way she had shone in England, but he was not at all surprised. She acted the same way at home in Scotland. Everyone there loved her as well.

When Westmoreland and Elizabeth had married a couple of years later, Fergus and Morna had attended the wedding. They had spent several weeks at Bristol Castle in Cornwall. They had been in need of a diversion and an English wedding seemed to fit the bill perfectly.

Morna had been pregnant several times since their marriage, but couldn't seem to carry any of the babies to term. They both wanted children very badly and were despondent. Morna, always the optimist, told Fergus they would have a child. She was convinced that at least one of her pregnancies would produce a healthy child.

Although, the local doctor didn't hold out much hope, Morna never gave up her dream to be a mother. When the couple was in England for Westmoreland's wedding, Morna saw a London physician who gave her hope. He prescribed total bed rest the next time she became pregnant. He also prescribed some tonics to build up her blood. Morna had been prone to illness since childhood and the doctor thought her weakened state contributed to her inability to carry her babies to term.

When Fergus and Morna returned to Scotland, Morna was anxious to try again to have a child. However, it was several years before she again became pregnant. She immediately took to her bed. She sent to London for more of the tonic and took it religiously. As Morna's pregnancy progressed, the couple became more and more hopeful. At last, after a very hard delivery, they held their tiny daughter in their arms and rejoiced.

Unfortunately, Morna never fully recovered from the birth. Her health steadily declined for the next ten years. Finally, when she contracted a bad cold and fever, her body just couldn't fight it off and she had died. Fergus had mourned her for the last six years. He never thought about marrying again although he was only in his late forties when his wife died. He was content to finish raising his child and hopefully to get a chance to know his grandchildren some day.

After dinner, Diana excused herself to the drawing room while the men had brandy and cigars. She seated herself at the pianoforte and idly touched the keys. She found herself playing a moody piece by Handel. Soon, she was lost in the music. She didn't hear the drawing room doors open. The men stood in the doorway captivated by her playing. Diana played with amazing skill and intense feeling. The music seemed to flow from her fingers with no real effort. She sat very straight on the piano bench with her head slightly cocked to the side as her body swayed to the music.

She had her eyes closed. After she finished, her eyes snapped open as she heard applause.

Geoffrey, who had been impressed before, was even more so now. Many of the young women of his acquaintance could play, but few played with such enthusiasm or feeling. He was really beginning to like this girl. He hoped he would have some time to get to really know her.

Geoffrey was in the army and was only on leave for three months time. He had already been home for six weeks and had only six weeks remaining. He was happy to return to his duties, but was a little reluctant to leave the country again now that he had met Diana.

Geoffrey had been leading his company in the fight against Napoleon on the continent. The Battle of Waterloo had been fierce. Geoffrey had lost a lot of his men and many of his fellow officers and friends in that battle. He, himself, had been wounded, although not critically. He had taken a deep saber cut to his left arm. It had healed, but still retained some stiffness.

The Duke had tried to persuade Geoffrey to not rejoin the army and sell his commission. As the eldest son, he would inherit the title and all it entailed. His father did not want Geoffrey to risk life and limb again. The Duke had been horribly worried while Geoffrey was on this last campaign. He loved both his sons, but he had no illusions about Edward. He was suspicious of his younger son's sexual proclivities though he had no real proof. He did not expect to gain an heir from Edward. And having an heir was uppermost in his mind.

The Duke was healthy, but men of his time rarely lived past the age of fifty and he was nearing that age now. He only wanted enough time to groom Geoffrey for the title. Not that he was ready to die, far from it, but he was a realist. He understood that Geoffrey had a strong sense of responsibility to his country. However, the Duke wanted to keep him home where he thought he belonged.

Geoffrey, on the other hand, felt his return to his regiment was of paramount importance. There was still the mopping up to be done after Waterloo, as well as the troubles in India. Britain was still at war, even if Napoleon had been defeated. Geoffrey hadn't received his orders yet, but felt strongly that he was going to be sent to India. His cavalry regiment would no doubt be needed to battle the Gurkhas in Nepal.

All these thoughts rushed through Geoffrey's head as he stood watching his father compliment Diana on her playing. Her face was flushed, whether from embarrassment or pleasure, he couldn't tell. Her cheeks were normally rosy, but now her whole face and neck was a charming shade of pink. Her beautiful emerald eyes were shining and she had a lovely smile on her face. He walked over to the pianoforte to add his comments on her playing. He was happy to see that his words seemed to increase her high color. With the urging of both fathers, she again began to play.

Geoffrey didn't recognize the tune, but it was lively and his toes started to tap. He loved to dance. This song really lent itself to a lively dance. Since Diana was the only female present and she was providing the music, dancing was out of the question. He could hardly wait for the ball that was planned. He wanted to dance every dance with beautiful Diana.

Edward, on the other hand, didn't really see what all the fuss was about. Yes, the chit played well enough, but so did many others. This type of music didn't hold the same fascination for him that it did for his father and brother. Since dancing was only done between males and females, that didn't interest him either. He found no pleasure in leading some young chit in a quadrille, nor did he want to hold them for the astonishing new dance, the waltz. Now if he could hold his beloved Benjamin close and dance around the floor, he would indeed love that.

Diana played a few more songs, then begged off saying she was overly warm and thirsty. Geoffrey made his way quickly to her side to escort her to one of the sofas in the room. The small drawing room where they were gathered was very cozy and well decorated. There were two sofas covered in a deep blue damask fabric flanking the fireplace as well as several chairs covered in the MacDonald plaid of red, blue, green and black. On the walls, paintings depicting pastoral scenes of the Highlands and hunting scenes were hung. There were several small tables in front of the sofas and beside the chairs. The tables were covered in a collection of bric-a-brac and candles. There were several candelabra around the room flaming with beeswax candles. The drapes were dark red velvet trimmed in silk tassels of the same deep hue. In front of the tall windows opposite the fireplace, a table and four chairs were placed for playing cards. Above the fireplace hung a very old and beautiful tapestry. The scene depicted on it was of the keep in the spring with flowers of many colors growing in the parkland grasses in front of the house.

Geoffrey took a seat next to Diana on the sofa as the duke and earl sat in chairs next to each other. This left Edward somewhat adrift. Seeing him glancing around the room, Diana offered him a seat next to her on the sofa. Geoffrey's face wore a slight scowl at the offer. However, Edward declined and sat in a chair near his father. In his father's company, Edward maintained a very low profile.

With his own friends, he was very outgoing. Constantly laughing and talking, he was the center of attention wherever he went. Not with his family, though. He had absolutely no intention of drawing attention to himself other than through his flamboyant clothing. Since many of his contemporaries also dressed as brightly as peacocks, he felt he could get away with his fashion flair. He had noticed the old earl looking askance at his evening clothes. The old man seemed to bridle somewhat at his gold ensemble. So what, he thought, people would hardly notice in London.

He had seen many more outrageous costumes at Almacks and private balls in the city. He, himself, owned many more colorful and outlandish outfits. He didn't wear them where his father was to appear however. His boring brother, he didn't care about. Geoffrey knew what he was and although it obviously bothered him, he never censored Edward for his lifestyle.

The evening wore on for Edward, but the other guests seemed to enjoy themselves immensely. Murtaugh offered wine, whiskey and brandy to the guests and family. Diana, who was truly thirsty after playing so long, asked Murtaugh to bring a tea tray. She didn't care for strong spirits and didn't think wine would quench her thirst.

When the tray arrived, she offered tea to the other guests, but only Geoffrey accepted. She had noticed he drank very little at dinner, unlike his brother. For some reason, that made her feel good. She had seen enough men too far into their cups at the house parties she had attended with her father. Most of them acted a fool. Fools were not something Diana suffered gladly.

She found herself to be more serious than her peers. At sixteen, she had been caring for her father and the keep for eight years already, four of them totally alone. Her mother had been almost bedridden for two years before she died. Her maternal grandmother had helped when she was in residence, but she hadn't lived with them. She had other children and divided her time amongst them all. They lived in a variety of places in Scotland. She spent a few months with each of her six children and numerous grandchildren. When she was with Diana, she did all she could to teach and help her with the myriad duties a chatelaine had to perform.

The housekeeper, Mrs. Gwen, had been a Godsend. She had been with the family since she was a young girl herself. Running the household was a huge job on its own, but she always found time to teach Diana what she needed to learn. Cook, Mrs. Allen, had always been a fount of information for Diana as well, especially when it came to herbs and medicines. She was an excellent cook and knew how to handle her kitchen with an iron fist, but with good humor.

Diana was very lucky that all the servants had been with the family since many years before she was born. They each knew their duties and did them willingly. The earl was a good employer, fair and kind. Even with all that help, Diana still carried the mantle of responsibility as chatelaine of the keep. It was a heavy burden for young shoulders, but Diana had grown into her position in a surprisingly small amount of time.

Diana rose at half past nine to bid the gentlemen goodnight. Surprisingly, both Geoffrey and Edward decided to turn in as well. They escorted Diana upstairs and left her at her chamber door. Their rooms were in the opposite wing across from each other.

The older men continued to sit and talk for another couple of hours. They had much to catch up on. Letters were fine to impart news, but a good visit between old friends was needed to really know the details of their lives.

"Diana has grown into a very beautiful and talented young woman." The duke remarked.

"Yes, unfortunately she had to grow up very fast when Morna became ill. She was only eight when Morna could no longer see to the day-to-day running of the keep. Diana took over with the help of Morna's mother. Of course, Mrs. MacPherson didn't live here all the time, so Diana had to learn much on her own with the help of the servants. I couldn't be more proud of my little girl."

"I can see that. That pride is justified. She seems a kind and serious young woman. A young man could do much worse than to take her to wife."

The earl looked at his friend musingly. Was he interested in Diana for one of his sons. Probably the younger one, Edward. Fergus didn't think Harold would want the daughter of a Scottish earl to marry his heir apparent. Surely he would be looking to the daughters of other dukes for a mate for Geoffrey.

Fergus didn't know Harold's sons, but from just this one evening, he didn't feel comfortable with the thought of Diana being wed to Edward. There was just something wrong about that boy. He went to bed in a somber mood. How would he refuse his old friend if he proposed a match between Diana and Edward?

Chapter 3

The next day dawned sunny and bright. Everyone gathered just after dawn in the dining room for breakfast. The sideboard held a wide array of choices. There was broiled haddock, Scotch eggs, oaten porridge, scones, toasted bread with butter and a variety of jams and jellies made from the native fruit blaeberries, strawberries and raspberries. Each of the party helped themselves to whatever they desired then sat together for their repast. There was a pot of hot chocolate, a pot of tea and a pot of coffee on the table. Diana noticed that only Edward drank the coffee. Coffee was not a taste Diana had acquired. She preferred hot chocolate in the mornings.

The younger men seemed surprised to see Diana dressed for riding. When Fergus noticed this he said, "Diana will accompany us on the stag hunt this morning. She rides well and really enjoys the chase. She will also come when we hunt pheasants. She doesn't care for boar hunts however, and won't be joining us for those."

Geoffrey smiled at Diana and said, "I'm very glad you are joining us, Lady Diana."

Edward made no comment, nor did he smile. He thought to himself, "I hope the chit doesn't slow us down." He had been looking forward to the hunt. He prided himself on his riding skills. He looked forward to riding to the hounds as they chased one of the big Scottish red deer through the bracken. Edward was always competitive with Geoffrey when they hunted, but not outwardly so. He knew his father frowned on that sort of behavior. Ever the sycophant with his father, Edward would never do anything openly, by word or deed, to undermine his father's good opinion of him.

When the party went out the large front doors, their horses were waiting in the courtyard. The earl had provided fresh horses for his guests, as their own horses were tired from the long trip.

Geoffrey was pleasantly surprised when he saw Diana mount a small black mare with the assistance of a groom. She sat in the sidesaddle with ease and handled her spirited mount with a firm hand. He noticed a rifle in a scabbard attached to her saddle.

"So," he thought, "She really does hunt. She doesn't just go along for the ride." Most of the young women of his acquaintance did not join hunts and if they did, they only came along for company. Apparently, Diana was a sportswoman as well as being beautiful and talented. Geoffrey was more and more interested in this young woman. He had no idea of her age, but thought she must be at least twenty from her comportment and abilities.

The keeper of the deer hounds brought the barking dogs around the corner from the stables. There were six of them, huge beasts with rough gray and brown coats. Their muzzles were long as were their legs. They looked to weigh around a hundred or more pounds and stood almost three feet tall. The duke and his party were used to the much shorter, smaller hounds used in fox hunting. They were surprised at the size of these dogs.

After an hour or so of riding, the dog handler loosed the hounds and the chase began. The terrain was hilly and wet from the recent rains. Mud flew from the hooves of the horses as they chased the hounds. The veil of Diana's pretty green hat blew in the wind generated by the rapid running of her horse. Her eyes sparkled and she had a grin on her face. She was in her element.

She had enjoyed hunting with her father and his friends since she had learned to shoot at the age of seven. Ever a precocious child, she had been one of the few girls in the neighborhood to do so. There weren't many girls her age in the area, most of her contemporaries were male. She had grown up somewhat a tomboy since she didn't want to be excluded from the activities of her friends. She and Ian had hunted with their fathers and alone with each other or other friends for years.

After what seemed a short chase to the Brits, the hounds had cornered a great red stag in the bracken at the base of a tall hill.

Fergus offered the duke the shot. Just as the duke raised his gun and fired, the stag broke away and took off again. He had been hit in the left haunch. The stag had still not gained his breath after the run. With his wounded haunch and little breath left, he gamely tried to get away.

A shot rang out and the stag fell about a hundred feet from the hunting party with a shot to the head. The men all looked around to see who had taken the shot. It was a magnificent shot to hit a running stag in the head at that distance. Diana had raised herself in her sidesaddle to almost a standing position to take the shot. Her rifle was still up to her shoulder when the men looked around. Realizing that she had taken the duke's shot, her face flushed crimson in embarrassment.

"I am so sorry, your grace, for taking your shot. I was so afraid the stag would suffer if the hounds caught him before the handler could reach them. I took the shot without thinking."

"No need to apologize, my dear. What a shot! I have rarely seen anyone, man or woman who could have made that shot. Fergus, you didn't tell us she was a crack shot. I have never seen the like."

"Diana has been hunting since she was a child. My Morna taught her how to use a gun. Morna was raised with only brothers and they taught her at a young age as well. I'm sorry you didn't get a stag today, but we will hunt pheasants tomorrow. I know you will bag a lot of them."

"No matter," said the duke. "We have plenty of time to hunt more stags while we are here. I am completely satisfied with the hunt today. It doesn't really matter who took the final shot," the duke said with a bright smile.

When the hunting party returned to the keep, they all parted ways to change from their hunting clothes for luncheon. They met in the dining room. The sideboard was used again. There were a selection of cold meats, rye bread, and plain loaf, several cheeses, and crocks of butter and jam.

When everyone had filled their plates, again, they sat around the table and conversed about the hunt. Diana was quiet as usual. She noticed that most of the conversation was between the two older men. They never seemed to lack for something to discuss. Edward sat a little apart and seemed to take no notice of the other members of the party. Geoffrey was also quiet, but she caught him looking at her several times. Finally, at the end of the meal, he asked, "Lady Diana, would you like to go for a walk this afternoon? It seems a fine day."

Diana raised her eyes from her plate to see a smiling Geoffrey. "I would be delighted." she answered quietly.

They each quietly quit their places at the table and left through the French doors leading to the back gardens. After several minutes of quiet, Geoffrey put his hand on her arm, stopping her.

"I am not normally so forward, but I cannot seem to think of anything but you. I have never met anyone quite like you. You seem to be so refreshing and different from the young ladies of my acquaintance. I would very much like to get to know you better, if you will permit?"

Diana was dumbstruck. She had given no thought to being courted by such a handsome young man. He was quite a bit older than she, but she didn't mind the age difference. He seemed so much a man of the world, she could not countenance why he would be interested in her. However, she liked the idea quite a lot.

"I do not know quite what to say, my lord," she stuttered.

"Just say I may spend some time with you while I am a guest in your home, please."

"Well then, yes you may."

A very happy smile appeared on Geoffrey's face. She gave him a tentative smile back and started to walk through the garden again.

As they went along, he asked questions about the types of flowers growing so abundantly in the garden. She explained that they grew hyacinths, iris, lilies, roses and many other species of plant and flower so easily because of the large amounts of rainfall they had each year.

As they wandered near the walled kitchen gardens, Geoffrey inquired as to what was behind the wall.

"Ah, that is Mrs. Allen's pride and joy, the kitchen garden."

Diana opened the gate and preceded Geoffrey into the walled area. An abundance of kitchen produce grew within. There was cabbage, onions, potatoes, radishes, beets, beans, and a complete herb garden. At the end of the garden sat a bench to allow a little rest for the weary garden workers.

"Would you sit a minute and talk to me" Geoffrey inquired.

Diana didn't respond directly, but she sat upon the end of the bench leaving room for him to sit as well. They sat in silence for a few moments enjoying the quiet of the enclosed space.

"My father told me you are in the army. Have you been involved in the war with France?"

"Yes, I am just back from the Battle of Waterloo. I took a small wound on the final day. I have been sent home to fully recover before my next assignment. I don't have my orders yet, but I assume my regiment will be sent to India. There is an ongoing conflict with the Gurkhas in Nepal."

"It hardly seems fair to send you right back into battle so soon after an injury. How long will you be at home?"

"I have another six weeks before I have to report to my commanding officer. I was anxious to get back, but now....."

"But now?"

"Well, we have only just met. I would very much like to spend some time getting to know you. I find you fascinating."

"Fascinating? Me? I'm the most ordinary person I know. I live a very quiet and ordinary life. You, however, have traveled and fought in a war. You are the one who is fascinating."

Geoffrey smiled at her and took her hand in his. She didn't perpetually wear gloves like all the young ladies in London did. Her hand was slender with long tapering fingers and soft skin. He felt an electric current when he touched her. From the small gasp she uttered, he thought she felt it too. She didn't take her hand away, but she did blush very prettily and look down, hiding her eyes.

They spoke of inconsequential things for another hour or so, all the while holding hands. Just as they were about to return to the house, it started to rain suddenly with no warning. Geoffrey threw his arm around her shoulders and started to run toward the house to try to stay dry. They both began to laugh, running as quickly as possible toward the French doors of the dining room.

Just as they reached the portico over the doors, thunder rolled and lightening flashed nearby. Diana jumped and issued a small cry of alarm. Geoffrey put both arms around her and held her close. She tilted back her head and looked at him with wide green eyes. Before he even realized what he was doing, he touched her lips with his. Again, that spark jumped between them. Diana gasped, starting to pull away. At the last moment, she leaned forward instead, melting against him.

What had started as a simple kiss of reassurance became a kiss of passion. Their lips were pressed urgently together. Diana had never been kissed. She had no idea, even how to kiss. She was shocked when Geoffrey's tongue touched her bottom lip. She opened her mouth to protest, but then his tongue came into her mouth. The feeling was so unexpected and wonderful; she didn't pull away. Instead, she reached out with her tongue and touched his, surprised at her own boldness.

When Diana's tongue touched his, Geoffrey uttered a low moan and tightened his grip on her lithe young body, crushing her to him. Her day dress was of soft, fine linen in a light green color. It was soft and not terribly full. He could feel her full breasts through the thin material crushed against his chest. He was drowning in intense emotions. He had never wanted a woman so badly, or so quickly. He knew if he didn't end the kiss, he would take it too far. Even as these thoughts rushed through his mind, his hand brushed against the bottom of her full, firm breast. Shocked, Diana pulled away staring at him with wide eyes in a very flushed face. They were both breathing hard and fast.

"I am sorry to take such liberties, my lady. I don't know what came over me."

"Whatever it was seems to have come over me as well."

Diana surprised him with her words. He had been worried he had frightened her with the intense kiss they had shared. Apparently, she had been as affected as he. A smile suddenly appeared on her lips and she said, "We had better get inside before we drown. This rain seems to have set in for the afternoon. I seem to be soaked and so are you. I must go change."

With that, she opened the door and hurried inside. He followed more slowly. He left the dining room just in time to see her hurrying up the wide staircase. At the top, she turned and smiled at him lifting her hand in a little wave. Then she ran down the hallway to her bedchamber.

Geoffrey was flabbergasted. He had expected recriminations, tears, a slap or something of the like. The fact that Diana had admitted she felt as strongly as he, was amazing and wonderful. He could not wait to see her again.

Chapter 4

Geoffrey didn't see Diana until dinner that evening. After their encounter, he had changed his clothes and sought out his father and brother. He had found them in the earl's library having a glass of whiskey and talking with the earl.

"Did you enjoy your walk, my son?"

"Yes, I enjoyed it very much until the rain. It came on most suddenly. Is it always thus in Scotland, my lord?" he asked Fergus.

"Oft times it is. We have much rain in our fair country. 'Tis what keeps it so green hereabouts. It makes for bad traveling, but wonderful crops," the earl replied with a twinkle in his eye. "Join us for a spot of whisky, lad. You probably need it after being rained on."

"Thank you, I believe I will." Geoffrey poured himself a small tot of the excellent whiskey the earl served. He noticed that Edward had a full glass in his hand. It was probably not his first drink from the high color in his cheeks. Geoffrey hoped his brother kept control of himself. He didn't want him to embarrass himself in front of their father or the earl. He had seen Edward out of control on more than one occasion and it was not a pretty sight. He was loud and obnoxious when he was heavily in his cups.

Edward felt Geoffrey staring at him and knew what his brother was thinking. He had no plans to embarrass himself on this trip. He knew just how much to drink to get the nice mellow feeling he was looking for. He was in a good mood. He had been able to spend some time with Benjamin after the hunt. His valet was good for a whole lot more than helping him dress and undress. Edward smiled to himself thinking of their short, but very intense session before luncheon.

After a pleasant dinner of fresh venison roasted with herbs over the kitchen spit, roasted potatoes, fresh bannocks cooked on the large stone in the kitchen fireplace, and trout cooked in butter with herbs, and for dessert, crumpets filled with raspberries and served with clotted cream, the men sat at the cleared table and had port and cigars.

Again, Diana went to the small drawing room to wait for them. She had brought her embroidery down before dinner leaving it beside one of the chairs, near a large candelabra. She needed as much light as possible to see the delicate stitches she was putting in the dress she was working on. It was the dress she planned to wear to the ball next week. The material was bronze silk. She was embroidering tiny flowers all over the skirt in shades of cream with dark brown stalks and green leaves. The dress was more daringly cut than any she had ever owned. The bodice was tight with short puffed sleeves and a low sweetheart neckline. The back laced up tightly making her waist look tiny. The underskirt was a deeper shade of bronze as was the bodice. The overskirt she was working on was a lighter bronze with reddish highlights. Her father had ordered the material from France for her trousseau when she was supposed to marry Ian MacAllister. Since she had no intention of marrying him, she had not used the material until now.

She wanted this dress to be perfect. The seamstress for the keep had cut and sewed the dress using a fashion plate from La Mode magazine. All that was needed to make the dress complete was the final embroidery. When Diana first started the dress, she had been somewhat apprehensive about wearing something so daring. Her clothes were usually much more modest.

After the kiss she had shared with Geoffrey this afternoon, she could hardly wait for him to see her in this dress. She knew the colors would go well with her red hair and green eyes. She planned to wear her mother's emeralds with the dress. Her father had presented them to her on her sixteenth birthday, but she had not worn them yet, as he had also given her a set of smaller emeralds of her own at the same time.

Diana was completing a row of the tiny flowers near the hem when she heard the men coming out of the dining room. She quickly put her sewing away. She didn't want anyone to have a glimpse of her dress before the ball.

When Geoffrey entered the drawing room, he noticed that Diana was a little breathless and her face was flushed a becoming shade of pink. She had a small secretive smile on her face. She looked as if she had just flung herself down in the chair moments before the men had entered. He wondered what she had been up to.

Crossing the room, he entreated Diana to play the pianoforte for them again. She agreed and took her place on the piano bench again. Edward came over to the pianoforte and started to look through her music much to her chagrin. Finding something that caught his interest, he handed her the music and asked if she could play it in the key of D. After looking at the sheet, she began to play softly. Suddenly, a beautiful tenor voice started to sing the words of the song, Take Back the Heart. Startled, Diana looked up into Edward's face as he stood to her left. The song was slow and sentimental, not one she would have expected Edward to know.

When the song was done, there was applause from the rest of the group. With very little prompting, Edward chose another song and asked Diana to sing along. Their voices blended very well. Diana's voice was contralto, which melded with Edward's tenor beautifully. By the time Diana was too tired to play more, they had sung every popular song she had music to play. Laughingly, she held up her hands in surrender.

"Edward, I have run out of songs for you to sing. You have a wonderful voice. Thank you so much for sharing it with us," Diana said as she rose from the pianoforte bench.

"You are most welcome, my Lady. Your voice is quite fine as well. I have enjoyed this evening very much," Edward said with a little bow.

As conversation started again between the two older men, Geoffrey offered his arm to Diana to escort her back to the sofa. As she sat in the middle, a brother took his place on either side of her. She was surprised that Edward had joined she and Geoffrey. On the previous night, he had not participated in the conversation much and had seemed moody. It was a pleasant surprise to have him include himself so charmingly.

Soon, Diana excused herself to go upstairs to her chamber. Again, as on the previous evening, the younger men also excused themselves and escorted Diana to her bedchamber. When Diana was alone she thought over all the events that had occurred that day. She thought of her walk with Geoffrey and especially that kiss....oh, that wonderful kiss. She had never felt such a sensation. When Geoffrey touched his lips to hers, she had felt weak in the knees. Diana was shocked at how she had responded to Geoffrey's kiss. Having no frame of reference, she didn't know what to do or how to act. She had just followed her instincts after the initial shock.

Chapter 5

Diana's maid, Barbara, woke her early the next morning for the pheasant hunt. After breaking their fast with scones, raspberry jam and clotted cream (and of course, the ever present tea, chocolate, and coffee), the company rode their horses several miles from the keep. They dismounted about a quarter mile from the broad meadow covered in tall grasses where they were to hunt. They climbed from their horses and unlimbered their shotguns from the scabbards on their saddles. They walked quietly abreast to the edge of the meadow with the dogs going in front.

The pheasants were creatures of habit. They generally rose from their roosts about two hours after sunrise feeding on insects they found in the long grass. Fergus had some fine pointer bird dogs. They would creep up on the pheasants and quietly point with their noses, with their tails out straight behind them, toward the pheasants. If the pheasants spotted the dogs, they would spring into the air calling a kok-kok-kok warning to their brethren.

As the hunters followed the dogs into the tall grass, Diana was reminded of an old poem she had once read by Alexander Pope.

> The whirring Pheasant springs, And
> mounts, exulting on triumphant wings: Ah!
> What avails his glossy, varying dyes, His
> purple crest, and scarlet-circled eyes, The
> vivid green his shining plumes unfold, His
> painted wings, and breast that flames with gold.

Just such a scene greeted the hunters on this bright sunny morning in October, 1815. The dogs quietly found a bouquet of pheasants pecking away. As the first pointer took his stance, a large male pheasant took flight sounding his warning call.

The hunters, who were spread out side by side, raised their fowling pieces and prepared to shoot. The noise was astounding as five shotguns fired almost as one. Birds rained down from the sky. The hunters quickly reloaded and fired again. The size of the bouquet was enormous. Finally after reloading three times, the last of the large birds was gone. The dogs rushed to find the fallen pheasants. They returned to the hunters several times with dead birds. Fergus had provided burlap sacks for the birds to be collected in, which were carried by the footmen who had accompanied them along with the gamekeeper.

"We will have a fine dinner tonight. Mrs. Allen can cook pheasant several ways and they are all delicious," Fergus said.

"Yes, our Mrs. Allen is a wonderful cook. I'm glad you have arrived at this time of year. Our tenants have been harvesting their crops and we have a bounty of fresh grains, fruits and vegetables. Our cook is a wonder indeed," added Diana.

Having tasted several meals made by the redoubtable Mrs. Allen, the Duke and his sons were quick to agree. The company soon walked back to their horses and mounted up. The footmen tied the bags of pheasants behind their saddles. Again, Diana had been a crack shot and had accounted for more than one bird per shot.

Geoffrey was in awe of the small girl with the beautiful auburn hair.

Was there nothing she could not do? He had seen her excellent riding, shooting, and musical ability in both playing and singing. He had also caught a glimpse of her fine needlework the night before. She was truly accomplished in every way that a man of the nobility would want his wife to be, he thought. "Wife", he thought,"where did that come from.?" Did he truly want this girl for his wife? He had only known her a couple of days, but he felt inexplicably drawn to her. Every time he saw her, he felt an electric tingle. When he touched her, there was a definite spark that flew between them. He wondered if she felt that spark as well. Then he remembered their kiss and was sure she felt the spark as strongly as he did.

Upon arriving at the keep, the company dispersed to change out of their hunting clothes. The horses and dogs were removed by servants, so too were the bags of birds. Mrs. Allen went into a frenzy of activity when she received the birds. She set the scullery maids to cleaning and plucking the large number of pheasants.

She took the giblets and stewed them in claret with sugar, pickled barberries and spinach. Then she boiled several pheasants in a cauldron over the fire. With these she made Queen's Potage with broth, fresh bread cubes, eggs, herbs, onions and minced pheasant which was then baked in an earthenware container in the huge kitchen fireplace.

She had scullery maids turning spits over the fire with several of the younger pheasants per spit. All in all, Mrs. Allen used twenty birds for dinner that evening. While she was engaged in the flurry of preparations for dinner, she also had to provide a luncheon repast for the company and her employer. She had been working on that meal since the hunters had departed. For luncheon, she served mutton meat pies filled with juicy pieces of mutton, carrots, onions and potatoes with a flaky, buttery crust, fish, fresh caught that morning from the loch, that were pan fried in butter with a delicate breadcrumb coating, and pickled cucumbers. For dessert, there were small fried apple pies. The crust was light and delicious, the filling full of apples and cinnamon, and having been fried slowly in butter, they practically melted in the mouth.

The men of the company partook of the luncheon repast with vigor. Being out in the fresh air and the amount of exercise they had while riding and hunting had made them all ravenous. Even Diana, who normally didn't have a large appetite, managed to eat a full helping of everything and two apple pies for dessert, as they were her favorites. She was very glad their apple crop had been so good this year. She knew she could look forward to her favorite apple dishes all fall and winter. Mrs. Allen had been able to have several barrels filled with apples this year from their trees. She had also made apple jelly, apple butter and cider.

After luncheon, the older men retired to the library for more conversation. Diana and the younger men adjourned to the small drawing room. A game of Pharo ensued with Diana acting as banker. Much laughter was heard by the older gentlemen as they rested and drank a glass of whiskey in the library.

"What think you of my son, Geoffrey?" asked the Duke.

"A fine young man from all appearances," replied Fergus. "He seems an honest and upright young gentleman. When you wrote that he had been wounded, I was worried about his recovery, but he seems fine now."

"Yes, his shoulder wound was not as bad as I had first been led to believe. He has recovered nicely. However, he is determined to return to his regiment in a few weeks time. I want to buy out his commission and continue his training to take his rightful place when it becomes necessary. I fear for him should he return to the army. The war in India is not going very well. They have been fighting for over a year with no end in sight."

"Does Geoffrey not want to stay at home?"

"No, he feels responsible for the men in his regiment. He doesn't believe the nobility should buy out their commissions when they are young. He believes that he should remain in his majesty's service for at least ten years."

"That is very admirable, but I can understand your concern. We are neither of us getting any younger and I am older than you by almost ten years. I have no son to take over my earldom, so it will revert to my brother's son, Robert, although this keep will belong to Diana. My property here at Ainsley Glen is not entailed to the earldom. It came to me from my mother. My sole concern now is to make sure Diana is well cared for. Money will not be an issue for her, but I fear she would be lonely here all alone. I had betrothed her to a neighbor's boy, but she would have none of it. He was in love with another and Diana only felt sisterly affection for him. She helped them run away together to America."

"How on earth did she accomplish such a thing?"

"Her MacPherson grandmother had given her the dowry I never took for Morna. She had squirreled it away somewhere. It was considerable and she gave the whole thing to the boy. He and the girl he loved were married in Inverness and took the next ship out. They have already bought several hundred acres and are making a good life for themselves in a place called Virginia.

At first, I was very upset with what she had done, but upon reflection, I now feel differently. I had mistaken her sisterly affection for Ian for love, but I was completely wrong. I was lucky enough to marry for love and would have the same for my daughter. The problem being that she has not met any eligible young man that interest her. I have been taking her to house parties and balls in the neighborhood lately, but she has yet to meet anyone to her liking. She is only sixteen, so there should be plenty of time, but we never know what the future will bring," mused Fergus.

"What would you think of my boy Geoffrey for a son-in-law?"

Fergus was very surprised and it must have shown on his face because Harold continued,

"I would have my sons marry for love as well. I, also, was lucky enough to have that kind of marriage. I know so many other members of the *ton* who can barely stand to be in the same room with their spouses. It is not what I wish for either of my sons. I have noticed how Diana and Geoffrey look at each other. I think with a little time, they might develop deep feelings for each other."

"I would not object if that were to come to pass. It would please me greatly for our families to be united. I am somewhat surprised that you would consider a mere Scottish earl's daughter for Geoffrey since he will inherit your title some day. Won't the *ton* find that unusual?"

"That they may, but to be honest, the *ton's* approval is not important to me. It really never has been. My parents were much the same. They didn't insist I marry a duke's daughter, they allowed me to find someone I truly cared for."

Chapter 6

As the afternoon waned, the fathers discussed their children's futures in detail. The children, however, spent the afternoon getting to know one another better. When it was time to dress for dinner, Geoffrey escorted Diana to her bedchamber while Edward joined the older men in the library for a drink before changing. As Edward neared the library door, he heard his father and the earl discussing a possible marriage between Diana and Geoffrey. He was surprised, but not displeased. He wouldn't mind having Diana in the family. She seemed not nearly so silly as the debutantes of the *ton* that he knew.

Suddenly, Edward was struck with a new thought. With Geoffrey safely married, his father might turn his attention to Edward's future. Edward knew that he would eventually have to marry, but didn't relish the idea. He had hoped for several more years of independence before he was saddled with some insipid miss. He didn't plan to change his ways one whit. Whichever poor girl he was stuck with would just have to learn to live with the fact that he would never be a "proper" husband to her. His only hope was to find someone not interested in having children who wouldn't want her husband under foot all the time. Surely, there was someone like that in the *ton*.

Later, after their wonderful pheasant dinner, the company repaired to the small drawing room again. On this night, Diana begged off playing the pianoforte because she was tired, instead suggesting that Edward might like to play. She had already ascertained the previous evening that he did, indeed, know how to play and enjoyed playing. After going through Diana's music, Edward found several pieces he liked and knew. Diana and Geoffrey again sat on the sofa while the older men took adjoining chairs near the fireplace. The evening was cool and there was a large fire for their comfort.

As Edward played and sang, Diana and Geoffrey enjoyed a quiet conversation. After Edward decided to stop playing, he, Geoffrey and the older men discussed the army and the political situation in India. Diana was disturbed to think Geoffrey would again be heading into a war. She hadn't known him long, but she felt incredibly close to him already. Diana was surprised that Edward seemed to know quite a lot about the political climate in India as well.

When she had first met him, he had seemed to be something of a dilettante. He had seemed bored with most of the previous conversations between the older men. Diana felt uncomfortable for judging him on his somewhat outlandish clothing and insouciant manner rather than getting to know him herself.

The next day dawned cold and rainy. The boar hunt was postponed to a better day. As Diana hadn't planned to go on the boar hunt, she had slept in. Barbara came to wake her at eight and found her already up and dressed. She was sitting by the window with a warm shawl around her shoulders working on her ball gown.

"The gentlemen didn't go hunting because of the weather and have all slept in as well. They will be breaking their fast shortly. Did you wish to join them, my Lady, or will you have a tray in your room this morning."

"I will go down and join them. Just let me finish this last row and I will be down."

Diana was halfway down the stairs when she heard steps behind her. She turned and saw Geoffrey coming towards her with a big smile on his face. After greeting her warmly, he escorted her to the dining room. They each took a plate and made their way to the sideboard to make their selections. Mrs. Allen had outdone herself this morning since she had so much extra time to cook. She had made Scotch eggs, one of Diana's favorites, as well as kippers and scrambled eggs, bannocks, and scones. She had set out three different pots of jam, raspberry, blaeberry, and strawberry, along with fresh creamy butter and clotted cream. There were pots of tea, coffee and chocolate as well.

Diana and Geoffrey were soon joined by the others. The conversation was sprightly in spite of the weather. There was a roaring fire in the dining room fireplace that brightened the room considerably. Mrs. Gwen had also made sure there were many fresh beeswax candles in the candelabras. The curtains were drawn over the windows and French doors to keep out the gloom and the cold. The company lingered over their meal, none too eager to leave the cheery dining room.

When they did finally depart, they all headed to the small drawing room. The rest of the morning was spent in conversation and cards. Diana and Geoffrey sat on the bench of the pianoforte together. Diana idly played some soothing old Scottish folk songs, while she and Geoffrey talked of inconsequential matters. Edward and the two older men played a game of whist.

A discussion of the ball came up. Geoffrey was very happy to hear that the musicians hired for the ball knew how to play the new waltz music that had become all the rage in London. Not long before he had joined his regiment for the Battle of Waterloo, he had learned to waltz at the balls in London. He very much looked forward to holding Diana in his arms again.

As Diana looked a little apprehensive at the news that the waltz would be played, Geoffrey asked her, "Do you not know the steps for the waltz, my Lady?"

"I have not had a season yet in London, so I haven't learned the latest dances. I can dance the country dances, but have never even seen the waltz performed."

Edward jumped up from the card table and cried, "That will not do, my Lady. You must have a dancing lesson. I don't waltz myself, but I know several of the waltz pieces. I will play while Geoffrey teaches you the steps."

Diana and Geoffrey rose from the bench as Edward rushed over. The older gentlemen along with a couple of footmen cleared out a space in the middle of the room for the young couple. Diana uttered a small gasp when Geoffrey encircled her waist with his left arm, taking her left hand into his right hand. She had felt that little spark again. She glanced up to Geoffrey and saw he had felt the same thing. He smiled down at her and began to move to the music. After a few missteps, Diana found the rhythm of the dance. Soon she and Geoffrey were twirling around the room with abandon smiling into each other's eyes.

The two fathers stood against the wall smiling benignly at their progeny. It looked as if things were definitely going the way they wished them to. Hopefully, by the time the visit had ended, the two young people would be in love.

Chapter 7

The days until the ball passed in a flurry of activity. Diana begged off hunting the last couple of days before the ball to help Mrs. Gwen and the other servants get the ballroom ready for the big day. The room had already been thoroughly cleaned before the advent of the company. However, there was still much to do before the ball.

Buntings were hung on the walls, chairs moved into position around the outside walls in groupings of three to five. Numerous candelabra, as well as the huge chandelier hanging in the middle of the room, were filled with new beeswax candles and placed on tables around the room. On the day of the ball, all the servants were busy either preparing food or gathering flowers to fill the entry hall, drawing rooms, dining room and the ballroom. Diana and Barbara spent hours arranging flowers in tall and short vases. She had gone through the garden and greenhouses the day before with Mrs. Gwen and the head gardener choosing which flowers were to be cut for the ball.

Fortunately, the gardener at Ainsley was an exemplary grower. Since Fergus had been planning to have a ball this fall anyway, he and Diana had met with the gardener, Mr. Fitzgerald, in May to discuss what flowers should be ready for the fall. There were two large greenhouses at Ainsley that were filled with blooming plants now.

There were several colors of fragrant roses, peonies, gladioli, pansies, and much greenery to complement them in the vases. When Diana and Barbara had completed the last vase of flowers and seen to its placement, they went to Diana's bedchamber to get her bathed and dressed. There would be additional guests for dinner this evening. Her father had invited the MacAllister, Bruce, and Cockburn families to sup with them prior to the ball at eight that evening. The other ball guests would arrive at ten.

Diana was excited. It was the first ball her father had hosted in many years. She knew he wanted her to meet someone to marry and balls were the best way for that to happen. Secretly, she was almost sure she had already met the man she wanted to spend the rest of her life with. Her heart hammered in her chest when she thought of Geoffrey. He was so tall and handsome. But more important, he was kind and intelligent. Being so much more mature than her age, Diana had little in common with the young men she had met at the balls and house parties she had previously attended. They all seemed to be interested in only horses, hunting, and dueling.

After Diana's bath, Barbara helped her don the beautiful new bronze colored silk gown over her corset, stays and several petticoats. She wore dark bronze silk dancing slippers on her small feet. The waist was tight, the bodice low cut, and the sleeves short, puffy, and off the shoulder. The underskirt was cut much narrower than the overskirt and was dark bronze like the bodice. The overskirt billowed over several petticoats skillfully hidden from view with an overlapping piece of the lighter colored bronze material. Diana had never worn nor owned a dress such as this.

Barbara dressed Diana's hair high on her head in a coronet of fat curls with ringlets cascading down over her shoulders. She placed diamond and topaz pins in her hair. When Diana was dressed and coiffed, Barbara lifted the topaz necklace and placed it around her neck. The large topaz centerpiece was set in gold and surrounded with diamonds. Small topaz stones were set in gold in a spider web pattern around the larger center stone. The earrings were medium size topaz stones with diamonds between them. They hung down almost two inches from Diana's ears accentuating her long slim neck. Around her wrists were coordinating bracelets made of three strands of topaz interspersed with diamonds. On the center strand, in the middle, was a large topaz surrounded by diamonds. Diana had decided the topaz set that had belonged to her mother matched her dress much better than the emeralds.

When Diana looked at herself in the large Cheval mirror in the corner of her room, she hardly recognized herself. Who was this creature with the shining green eyes dressed in this beautiful dress and jewels? She twirled around the room in excitement.

There was a knock on her door. When Barbara opened the door, Fergus stepped through and stopped abruptly. His child stood before him a woman. He had always thought Diana beautiful, but she had never been lovelier than she was this night.

"Diana, lass, you are a vision to behold. You so remind me of your mother. You have the look of her from the shape of your great emerald eyes to your shining red hair. You are Morna made over. Ah, lass, if she could only see you this night," Fergus said with a hint of moisture in his eyes.

"Oh, Da. Do I really look like my mother? So many people have told me how beautiful she was when she was young. I'm so sad I only really knew her when she was ill. She was still beautiful to me though."

"Aye, she was always beautiful and so are you. You will truly be the belle of the ball this night. The young men won't be able to take their eyes off you all evening."

At those words, Diana blushed and lowered her eyes.

"Would there be one young man in particular that you might be anxious to dance with this evening? I have noticed that you and Geoffrey seem to spend a lot of time together."

"Oh, Da. I…..I think I love him."

"Do you now? Well, I think that's fine, but I want you to take your time and be sure. Marriage is forever you know."
"Marriage??? Do you think he would want to marry me?" Diana asked breathlessly. "We're not exactly on an equal footing socially. His father probably wouldn't want me for him. He probably wants him to marry a duke's daughter at the least."

"Harold wants him to marry someone he loves, just like he did with Elizabeth and I did with your mother. Your title is unimportant. Only how you and Geoffrey feel really matters."

Diana's heart sputtered in her chest. She had never thought to hear those words. She had been constantly worried since she had admitted to herself she was in love with Geoffrey. She thought he felt the same for her although he had never spoken the words. He looked at her with such tenderness; she just had to believe he loved her as well. They had known each other such a short time. She could hardly believe their feelings could be so strong so quickly. However, she knew how she felt and the emotion was true. He lit up her life. There was no other way to put it. When Geoffrey was around, there was no one else in the room.

Fergus escorted his beautiful daughter down the stairs to stand in the entryway to greet their guests for dinner. They were soon joined by the Duke and both his sons near the front door. They all looked resplendent in their dark evening clothes. Even Edward had foregone his usual peacock look for an evening suit of dark blue velvet. His only concession to his usual way of dressing was a flaming red cravat instead of the usual white one.

Geoffrey and Diana only had eyes for each other. Harold and Fergus watched them watching each other with smiles on their faces. Earlier in the evening, Harold had gone to Geoffrey's chamber while he was dressing. He asked Geoffrey about his feelings for Diana. Geoffrey had haltingly told him he loved her even though they had only known each other for a short time.

"It was the same with your mother and I. We met at a country dance while I was hunting in Devonshire. I knew immediately that she was the one for me. We were married just a few months after we met."

"Father, you and I have never really discussed my marriage. I had assumed you would want me to court a duke's daughter or someone with a huge dowry. Is that not what you had planned?"

"My son, I want you to be happy. That is my only consideration and has ever been so. I was blessed with a happy marriage and hope the same for you. It matters not whom you marry as long as it is someone you truly care for."

"I am so relieved to hear you say these words. I have been so very worried that I would have to go against your wishes to have my

Diana. I am ever so grateful that there will be no dissension between us on this subject. I have always tried to be a good and obedient son, but I would have asked for Diana's hand no matter what. I have never felt anything for another woman. Diana is the first to touch my heart."

"That is truly music to my ears, Geoffrey. I know that Fergus feels the same as I, so there should be no impediment to your suit. As long as Diana shares your feelings, I see no reason you cannot marry, and soon."

"I only have four weeks until I have to report for duty. There isn't time to pull together a wedding before I leave. I may be gone for more than a year this time. My regiment will not be coming back from India until the troubles are settled for good this time."

"I would counsel you to resign your commission to stay home and wed Diana. I know you feel very strongly about your service, so I will not say another word on that subject. I would suggest though, that you speak to Diana before you make a decision that will affect both of your lives so much."

"I don't think there will be much opportunity to speak with her tonight, but if the opportunity does arise, have no doubt, I will ask for her hand. If not tonight, on the morrow for sure."

As Geoffrey gazed at Diana in all her splendor, he thought of the conversation with his father earlier in the evening. He was much relieved that he didn't have to fight his father for the right to wed the woman he loved. He had no doubt that Diana would consent to be his wife. The light of love shined brightly out of her beautiful emerald eyes.

The dinner guests were arriving. It seemed they had almost come together, so closely did they arrive. The MacAllister's were first. Angus came with his oldest son, Robert, and Robert's wife, Mary. Angus looked years older than the last time he had visited their home. Both Fergus and Diana were shocked at his appearance.

His hair, once so blond and thick, was thin now and gone completely gray. But it was his face that shocked them the most.

He had deep grooves in his forehead, cheeks and around his mouth. His eyes were sunken into his head and there were dark circles around them. He had lost weight and walked slightly stooped. Fergus took one look at him and turned his eyes to Robert in shock. Robert only shook his head and moved to help his father further into the house to a bench in the entry hall. He sat heavily and bowed his head.

Fergus was horrified at the changes in his old friend. It had only been a few months since Ian had left. Surely, that was not enough time to have wrought such horrible changes in a man. Where Angus had once been vital and filled with life and laughter, he now looked like a shell of his former self.

Diana felt instantly guilty. She had had no idea Ian leaving would have had this affect on his father. She was completely contrite. She thought, "I must write Ian and tell him he has to come home, at least for a visit. Maybe that would make Mr. MacAllister feel better and help him to heal of whatever malady has struck him down so quickly." She promised herself she would not wait, but post a letter to America tomorrow.

Fergus and Diana's attention quickly moved to their next guests as the Cockburn's were admitted by Murtaugh. The Cockburn family were their neighbors on the other side from the MacAllisters and had been friends with the MacDonald's for many years. Viscount Dale Cockburn and his wife, Alice, were getting on in years now. Their children were grown and married, living in several different areas of Scotland. Only their oldest son, Adam, lived at home with his parents. He and his wife, Agnes, would be taking over the property when Mr. Cockburn passed away. They were a large, friendly, gregarious family. There was much laughing and talking during the introductions to the Duke and his sons.

The Cockburns were still standing near the doorway when the Bruce's arrived. Sir Donald Bruce, his wife, Adelaide and their only daughter, Beatrice, also lived in the neighborhood, but a few miles further down the glen from the MacDonald's estate. Sir Bruce was a laird and a viscount. He was very involved in Scottish politics and was not at home much. Fergus hadn't seen him in several months and was glad to have the opportunity later to speak to him about affairs of the government.

Sir Bruce's daughter, Beatrice, was a lovely blond girl with very fair skin and light blue eyes. She reminded Diana of a china doll. She was tall and slim with a lovely heart shaped face. Her dress tonight was the same color as her eyes and complemented her coloring perfectly. Although, Beatrice was close to Diana's age, being eighteen, they were not close. Diana thought Beatrice silly and Beatrice thought Diana too shy and ungainly to command her attention.

Beatrice had ambitions to marry very well and leave Scotland once and for all. She had set her sights on marrying an English duke or at least an earl. She wanted to live in London and go to parties every night and wear beautiful clothes. Nothing else really mattered to her. She had absolutely no intention to remain in the country of her birth if she could help it. She felt Scotland was backward and provincial. These feelings had been instilled in her by her mother, Adelaide, and fostered from an early age.

Adelaide MacMillian Bruce felt she had married beneath her own social status. She was the youngest daughter of a Scottish duke who had come upon hard times by the time Adelaide was of an age to marry. She had no dowry to speak of, but Donald Bruce hadn't cared, he had a good income of his own. He had his eye on a political future and was not above using his future wife's connections to get him what he wanted. Their marriage had been arranged, as many marriages of the time were, for the advantages each could bring to the match. An influx of Sir Bruce's cash to the financially strapped duke was made quietly when Sir Bruce asked for Adelaide's hand. She had had no say in the matter. After twenty years of a cold, barren marriage resulting in the birth of only one child, Adelaide was determined for her daughter to do better. Adelaide always felt she was treated shoddily by society for her lowly marriage.

When Sir Bruce had received the invitation to dinner and the ball from Fergus, Adelaide had been enormously pleased and insisted they attend. Since she knew the duke had two marriageable aged sons, she started to immediately groom Beatrice to hook the older of the two. As soon as she got a look at Geoffrey, she started to scheme on how she could get he and Beatrice seated next to each other at dinner. Not only would he be a duke, but he was very handsome as well.

When the company went into the dining room, Adelaide was very upset to see that she and her family had been seated at the end of the table, all on one side, near the earl. The Duke was seated at one end of the table and Fergus at the other. This was highly unusual, but since the earl had no wife, it wasn't totally unheard of. What upset Adelaide the most was Geoffrey was seated beside Diana with the other son, Edward on her other side. Adelaide could hardly change the seating arrangements, but it frustrated her to no end that Diana was seated between the sons and near the duke while her family was at totally the other end of the room so far away from her target.

Diana felt Lady Bruce's antagonistic stare from down the table. She had no idea what had prompted the woman to stare at her with such animosity. She hardly knew the lady. The entire family was not too often in the neighborhood. Sir Bruce was usually in Edinburgh, not only because of politics, but because business kept him there. Lady Bruce didn't entertain much at their country place. She enjoyed the society in Edinburgh much more. There was little to hold her interest in the country as she felt herself so very far above her neighbors.

Harold looked down his friend's long dining table and intercepted a particularly vicious look from both Adelaide and Beatrice toward Diana. "Aha", he thought, "That madame has set her sights on one of my boys for her daughter." Harold was well aware of Bruce's political ambitions. He knew marriage to one of his sons, especially Geoffrey, would open doors to Bruce that would remain closed otherwise. He didn't know Bruce personally, but he knew his reputation, which was far from exemplary. He had no intention of either of his sons falling into the trap that was apparently in the making by Lady Bruce.

After dinner, the ladies repaired to the large drawing room while the gentlemen had their brandy and cigars. Diana offered sherry, wine or tea to her guests. After they had stated their preferences, she rang for Murtaugh. Murtaugh returned shortly with a laden tray. The ladies were seated on the couches and chairs closest to the fireplace as it was a very cool evening. Diana went to Mrs. Cockburn, who seemed to be cold, and offered to send for her shawl.

"That would be wonderful, my dear. So kind of you to think of it. I am a bit chilly this evening. Age, you know. Once you get to my advanced age, the cold just settles into your bones and 'tis hard to ever be really warm after summer has gone."

Diana rang for Murtaugh again and requested Mrs. Cockburn's shawl. She had asked the other ladies if they wanted their wraps as well, but all declined. When Murtaugh returned, Diana took the shawl and wrapped it around Mrs. Cockburn's shoulders.

"Thank you, my dear. You so remind me of your dear mother. She was always the kindest little dear. You have her ways and of course you look very much like her. You have her coloring, though I do see some of Fergus in you around your eyes. Your mother had blue eyes, you have the MacDonald green."

"Thank you for saying so, Lady Cockburn. I miss my mother so. It has been six years since she left us, but it seems like just yesterday. It is sometimes lonely here without her. My father has tried his best, but a young lady needs her mother sometimes."

Lady Cockburn smiled at Diana and patted the couch beside her. "Come, my dear, sit beside me and tell me what you have been doing. I'm sure with such grand company, you have been busy."

"Yes, we have been busy, both with our guests and getting ready for the ball tonight. We have been hunting several times. We have had a most enjoyable time."

"Tell me about the duke and his sons. What are they like?"

"The duke is not what I expected at all. He is very friendly and kind. He is very interesting to speak with. His sons are wonderful young men. The Marquess of Bradberry is in the military and has just come back from the war with Napoleon. He fought at the Battle of Waterloo and was injured. He is also extremely kind and nice. Viscount Bradshear is a very talented singer and can be quite amusing as well."

Lady Cockburn noticed that Diana's whole countenance changed when she spoke about the marquess. Her eyes shined with a softer light and the smile on her pretty lips was different than when she spoke of the duke or his other son. "Aha," she thought, "The marquess seems to have made quite an impression. I hope he doesn't dally with my Diana. Her little heart will be broken if he doesn't return her affections. I must watch out for my sweet little motherless dove."

Soon, the men rejoined the ladies. After a couple of rounds of drinks, it was time to begin greeting their ball guests. Diana stood between her father and the duke in the hall. As Murtaugh opened the door and ushered the guests to the receiving line, Diana's face started to become tired from all the smiling she was doing. She was glad when the last guest had been greeted. She took both her father's arm and the duke's when they made their way into the ballroom, followed by Geoffrey and Edward.

Chapter 8

Traditionally, Diana and her father led the first dance, a country reel. As soon as that dance was over, Geoffrey claimed her for the next dance, a waltz. As they spun around the floor, Diana had never been happier. She smiled up into Geoffrey's eyes.

"I wish to have every dance with you tonight, my Lady. I suppose that won't be possible as beautiful as you look though. Every young man here will be flocking to your side as soon as this dance is over."

"I really have no wish to dance with anyone but you. However, I'm afraid it would cause a scandal. I was told by my grandmother that I was not to dance with any one man more than three times."

"That is true of unattached ladies, unfortunately. Diana, I had a chance to speak to your father this afternoon. There is something I want to ask you. Will you take a turn in the garden with me after this dance?"

Diana's heartbeat sped up to an almost painful cadence. "No, it wasn't possible. Did he mean to ask her to marry him?" she wondered.

When the dance ended, Geoffrey folded her hand over his arm and walked to the large French doors leading onto the terrace. It was a chilly night, but Diana did not feel it. All she felt was her heart slamming against her ribs in expectation.

Geoffrey led her away from the doors to a quiet corner of the terrace. He took her into his arms and said, "Diana, my love, I know we have not know each other long, but I have never felt about anyone the way I feel about you. I love you and want you to be my wife. I have spoken to your father and he has agreed, as has mine. You have only to say yes."

Diana gasped in wonderment, "Yes, Geoffrey, I will marry you. I was so worried that your father would object to such a match. I am not a social equal to you, nor is my family equal to yours. I expected the duke to arrange a marriage for you with someone in the *ton*, a duke's daughter at the least."

"My father wants me to be happy. You make me happy. I know we will have a wonderful life together. When the time comes, and

I hope that will be many years in the future, you will make an exceptional duchess. You are kind and intelligent and beautiful beyond my dreams. I have seen how your father's tenants dote on you and you on them. I know you will do the same for the tenants on our holdings as well." Geoffrey's lips claimed Diana's for a long soul stirring kiss. When his lips released hers, he said, "I cannot imagine my life without you. I am ever so grateful you have agreed to be my wife. Come, we have to tell our fathers. I believe your father wants to announce our engagement tonight."

Diana practically floated into the ballroom on Geoffrey's arm. As soon as she saw her father standing in front of the fireplace with the duke, she practically beamed at both of them. Their faces carried identical smiles in return.

When the young couple stood in front of their respective fathers, Geoffrey said, "Diana has made me a very happy man tonight. She has consented to be my wife. When I get back from my tour in India, I will resign my commission and we will be married. Then we can commence our lives together. I truly wish there was time for us to marry before I leave, but I only have a very few weeks before I must report."

"I will wait for you Geoffrey. There is much for me to accomplish before we can be married, much for me to learn. I wish to be a good wife to you."

Both fathers were very happy with the news. Fergus would have his little girl for another year and then she would be wed to someone she truly loved. Harold was very pleased that his son had found the love of his life. His only regret was that Geoffrey would wait to resign his commission until after his tour of duty in India. He had hoped he would resign now. He had a nagging feeling of impending doom concerning his oldest son, but hoped he was wrong.

Fergus walked to the orchestra leader and asked him to stop playing after this song. He walked back to the fireplace to stand with his friend and their children. When the song ended, he raised his voice to be heard over the ball guests.

"I have wonderful news to share this evening, my friends and neighbors. My daughter, Diana and the Duke of Bristol's son, Geoffrey, Marquess of Bradberry, are to be married. Please join the duke and I in congratulating our children. We wish them a long and happy marriage."

The happy couple was inundated with congratulations and good wishes from the ball guests. All but one that is. Lady Bruce was beside herself with anger. She had wanted the duke's first son for her own daughter. That little upstart Diana was not worthy of such an honor. Only her own daughter was good enough, in her opinion, to wed a duke's first son. She very soon went to her husband and daughter and wanted to go home. Neither her husband nor her daughter, Beatrice, were inclined to do so.

Beatrice was not happy about the engagement announcement either, but there was still the younger son. He wasn't firstborn and wouldn't inherit the title, but he would be an Earl. Beatrice knew the Bristols had a lot of money. If she couldn't be a duchess, being the wife of a very rich earl would do as well. Besides, the duke's second son was very handsome. Beatrice was cold-hearted when it came to choosing a marriage partner, but she wasn't averse to having a handsome young husband. After all, she might have had to marry an old man to get the amount of wealth she required and the title she felt she deserved.

Edward stood at the edge of the crowd of well-wishers gazing at the happy couple with hooded eyes. "So," he thought, "Geoffrey is not a complete cold fish. From the way he is looking at the little chit, he could eat her up. Well, it is of no consequence to me. I know I will have to marry some day, but I had no designs on one such as Diana. She is much too innocent for me. I need someone with absolutely no aspirations for motherhood and a loving husband, as I can provide neither."

Harold watched his son and future daughter-in-law with a broad smile on his face. He was so happy for his son. He had seen the way Geoffrey looked at Diana and vice versa. He recognized the signs of a deep love beginning between them. He was content that his first born son would soon be happily married and hopefully producing heirs. Now, to just get Edward settled before the grim reaper came calling.

Harold had not felt entirely well recently. There was nothing he could pinpoint, nothing he could tell his physician in Harley Street. Just a feeling he couldn't shake that his time on earth was drawing to a close. Maybe it was a premonition, he didn't know, nor really much care. Since his Elizabeth had been gone, the true joy of life had seemed to go with her. He wished for Geoffrey and Diana even a fraction of the happiness he had known with his beloved wife.

Fergus also watched the young couple with a smiling face. However, his eyes were sad as he thought of his Morna and how she would have rejoiced to see their only child so very happy. She would have liked Diana marrying Harold's son. She had told Fergus after their first visit to London that Harold had exhibited signs of a crush on her. When he married Elizabeth not too much later, she was very happy for them both. It would have made her even happier to see their daughter and Harold's son married.

Fergus was also sad because he knew his daughter would be leaving him and Scotland once she was married. The young couple would live in London part of the time and on one of the Bristol estates the rest. He feared he wouldn't see his daughter much in the future. His duties as laird to his tenants would keep him in Scotland most of the time. He could visit he knew, but it wouldn't be the same at all. "Ah," he thought, "This is how it should be. Children grow up and marry, and move away. Especially daughters. They go to live with their husbands in their own homes. It is the way life goes"

Since Fergus had no son to inherit his title, he had known all her life that Diana would probably move away some day. That was one of the main reasons he had been so enthusiastic about a marriage between Diana and Ian MacAllister. Since Ian was not a first son, he and Diana would have lived at Ainsley Glen. Fergus could have kept her close until he passed away.

These lands were not entitled, he had inherited them from his mother. Diana would inherit the lands and all his money when he died. She would be a wealthy woman on her own. One of his brother's sons, Robert MacDonald II, would become the new earl. When Fergus married Morna, before he became the earl, he had chosen to live on the lands he had from his mother, not his father's lands. He had left those to be overseen by his younger brother, Robert, who had been born second. The younger Robert already lived on the MacDonald estate as Fergus' brother had died many years ago.

As these thoughts ran through Fergus' head, he happened to see Angus MacAllister in the crowd. His countenance was thunderous. He looked ready to explode. Fergus was instantly contrite. His daughter's happy news must have been hard for Angus to swallow since his son had been betrothed to her not all that long ago. Fergus started toward Angus, but Angus turned and stomped toward the door with his son and daughter-in-law in tow. They were gone before Fergus could make his way through the large crowd of well-wishers.

Diana and Geoffrey stood for quite some time accepting the congratulations of the ball guests. Finally, the orchestra began to play again and people began to dance. Geoffrey swept Diana to the dance floor for another waltz. She had never been happier as she spun in the arms of her smiling beloved. She had never expected to feel this way about anyone. Now she understood how Ian had felt about Alana and why he could not have married anyone but her. Diana could not imagine herself married to anyone except Geoffrey. She was ambivalent, however, about the marriage being at least a year and maybe more in the future.

She knew that there were myriad things she needed to have accomplished before she left to become Geoffrey's wife. She was well versed in running a household, but was apprehensive about running a duke's household. The keep at Ainsley Glen was large, but it would not compare in any way to the estates owned by the Bristol family. And there was also the large house in London she would be expected to be chatelaine of as well. It was overwhelming to her. After all, she was only sixteen.

"Nonsense," she thought, "I can learn whatever I need to know. Geoffrey will help me as well as the duke. After all, Geoffrey won't inherit his title for many years. The duke is still young and hearty. I will have years to learn all I need to know."

With those happy thoughts, Diana spent the rest of the evening dancing with Geoffrey and thinking of their future together.

Lady Beatrice Bruce wasted no time in insisting her father escort her to the group Edward was a part of near the dance floor. She turned her brightest, most angelic-looking smile on Edward as she flirted shamelessly with him. Edward, who was used to this type of behavior, paid scant attention to her at first.

After a few minutes, he studied her more closely. Maybe, this beautiful young woman with the ice-cold blue eyes could be the answer to his problem. It was obvious she was after him. It was also obvious to him that she felt no real affection for him. She was after the money and the title.

Beatrice Bruce was exactly the type of young woman he was looking for to be a cover for his own activities. That she was of the Scottish nobility was good as well. She would be unknown to the London *ton* and that would be in his best interests. She wouldn't know anyone to tell about his proclivities if she found him out. If she became a problem to him, he could always send her home to Scotland to visit her parents for a very extended stay. He doubted she would be interested in producing heirs or having a devoted husband. Yes, he might just pursue her or more aptly let himself be caught since she was already in hot pursuit herself.

Chapter 9

The next two weeks rushed by. Diana and Geoffrey spent every minute together they could. When the Bristols arrived back in London, Geoffrey would be reporting to his regiment a few days later. Diana was consumed with the thought that she wouldn't see him again until he came home from the war in India.

While Diana and Geoffrey only had eyes for each other, Edward spent quite a lot of time at the Bruce estate nearby. He was bored to tears listening to Beatrice and her even more irritating mother, Adelaide. However, he was a very patient man and was willing to play the part of the love struck swain at least until he was married to the little chit. Then he would leave her with her mama and set up an apartment in Inverness or even Edinburgh with his valet to use when they were not in London.

During the last week of the duke's visit, Diana couldn't sleep for worry that something would happen to Geoffrey in the war. Or that he would change his mind and not want to marry her when he came back. She would pace the floor in her bedchamber until she was exhausted. Falling into bed, she would try to sleep. Her dreams were chaotic and frightening. She dreamt that Geoffrey was in the middle of some terrible battle and was struck down by a saber blow. She would wake from this type of dream crying.

Some nights she would dream she was coming down the stairs at Ainsley Glen when Geoffrey walked through the door. He looked at her with cold eyes, shook his head and walked out the door again. Somehow she knew in the dream that he no longer wanted to marry her and was leaving her forever. Again, she awoke with tears streaming down her face.

Diana's eyes soon had dark circles beneath them. Her father was worried she was sickening with something as she was also losing weight. Geoffrey tried on several occasions to learn what was bothering her, but she kept mum on the subject.

One night, after a particularly vivid nightmare, Diana could no longer stay in her bedchamber. She felt the walls were closing in on her. She grabbed her robe and quietly went down the servant's staircase. She exited the kitchen door and ran to the stables. The stable was dark and quiet. She crept into Malmuira's stall. The mare rubbed her nose against Diana's hand. Diana stood with her arms around the horse's neck as she cried in anguish from the dream.

Geoffrey had heard Diana's door open. He had been awake worrying about her. He knew she loved him. He could not understand what was bothering her so much. He was also worried she might be ill. He opened his door just in time to see Diana turn into the servant's stairwell. He decided to follow her and try to talk to her one more time. He and his family were leaving in two days. He had to know what was wrong now.

When Geoffrey came into the stable and heard his love sobbing, it broke his heart. He went to her quietly and took her into his arms.

"You have to tell me what the matter is, Diana. You are breaking my heart with your sadness. Are you sad to leave your father? Do you not really love me? Please, you have to tell me what is bothering you."

"Oh, Geoffrey, I love you too much. I keep having waking thoughts that I am not fit to be your wife or that you will change your mind or that you will not return from India. These horrible thoughts go on and on in my head. And then when I finally do fall asleep, I have very frightening nightmares along the same lines. I can get no rest awake nor asleep."

"Diana, my love, those worries are for naught. You are most fit to be my wife. I love you and only you. You are kind, intelligent and loving. What more could a man want? As for my not returning, if Napoleon couldn't kill me, I do not think a few Gurkhas will cause me harm. As for me not wanting you anymore, that is the most foolish of all. I love you with all my heart, Diana. That will not change because of time, or distance, or anything. You are my heart, my soul, my life."

Geoffrey held Diana close and kissed her lips softly. The kiss started chastely, but because of their deep feeling for each other, the kiss deepened into passion quickly. Geoffrey hadn't really noticed that Diana was only wearing her bed gown and a light robe at first. As their kiss deepened and he held her even closer, he could feel her body through the thin night clothes she wore. His body responded immediately. He didn't want to frighten her, as he knew she was completely innocent. Soon, as Diana responded to his kiss with even more alacrity, he lost his head and ran his hands over her back to her buttocks, pulling her even closer than before.

He heard her gasp and started to let her go when she flung her arms around his neck and pulled him even closer than before. His hands again found her small round buttocks and pulled her even closer to his swelling manhood. His lips trailed from her lips down her neck to the opening of her nightrail. Removing one of his hands from her adorable little bottom, he began to untie the ribbon at the top of her gown. Instead of stopping him, Diana rubbed her chest against his hand. It was more than Geoffrey could handle. He quickly untied her gown and found her breast with his hand. Her breast was warm and round, the nipple puckered and hard. He slid his lips from her neck to her nipple and suckled softly at first.

As Geoffrey heard Diana gasp, he thought he had gone too far. He started to raise his head, when her hand came to the back of his neck to pull him closer still. He needed no other encouragement. He took her nipple between his lips and suckled harder than before, lightly grazing it with his teeth. Diana moaned and moved her lower body against his in an age-old rhythm. Soon they were both far gone in their passion for each other.

Diana was lost. She had never felt such sensations before. Geoffrey had kissed her deeply several times in the past days. She had felt an electric tingle in her breasts and in the secret place between her legs. She had enjoyed those kisses very much. She had been around breeding horses and other animals all her life and knew the rudimentary facts of life. However, with no mother to talk to, she had no concept of how a man could affect a woman or vice versa.

Suddenly, Diana's knees felt weak. It seemed Geoffrey was supporting her full weight with his hands under her buttocks pulling her close to his lower body. She felt the large bulge in his breeches pressed against her pubis. It both frightened and fascinated her. Geoffrey lowered her to the soft hay in her mare's stall, lying partially on top of her. The horse had moved away from them into a corner of the large stall.

Geoffrey's hand moved under the hem of her nightrail sliding slowly up the inside of her thigh. When his fingertips barely touched her most private of places, Diana again moaned. When one of his fingers slowly parted her core and touched the small nub there, Diana almost lost her mind. She had never experienced this type of sensation before. She felt that small touch all over her body like an electric shock. Without her volition, her legs parted and her knees drew up. As Geoffrey's finger moved slowly against her nub, her hips began to rotate on their own. Diana's head rolled from side to side and her eyes were shut tight. She could hear herself moaning, but could not stop for the life of her. The feeling was so intense she had to have some form of release. She felt something building inside of her. It started where Geoffrey's lips and tongue were touching her breast and spread like wildfire to the spot his fingers were touching between her legs.

She wanted something, but in her innocence, didn't know what it was. She only knew that if she didn't have whatever it was, and soon, she would burst. Suddenly, waves of pleasure hit Diana like a landslide. When the pleasure peaked, she issued a small scream and shuddered against Geoffrey's hand. She couldn't stop shaking. She had never felt anything like this in her short life. When she stilled, she opened her eyes and looked at Geoffrey in the gloom of the stable. He had the most beautiful smile on his face.

Diana was both dismayed and overjoyed by her reaction to his ministrations. She felt she should be ashamed to let Geoffrey touch her this way, but she didn't feel that way at all. Instead, she felt wonderful. She reached up and touched his face with her hand.

He smiled down at her and she smiled back. No words were spoken between them, none were needed.

Geoffrey began to move his lips from one breast to the other as his hand again touched Diana between her legs. This time, he inserted a finger into her and moved it slowly in and out touching her little nub each time with his thumb. The sensation this time was different, if anything, it was even better. When Diana was again moaning and moving her hips against his hand, Geoffrey loosened his breeches and slowly moved between her legs. Diana's knees rose on their own and her legs fell further apart. Geoffrey very slowly began to enter her.

"This will hurt, my darling, but only for a little while and only this once. I'm sorry, but it is the way of things."

Diana squeezed her eyes shut as the pain exploded in her. She couldn't stop a gasp of pain from escaping her lips. She wanted him to stop, to go away from her now. Suddenly, he did stop. He lay quietly on top of her with his manhood inside her. Very slowly the pain subsided. When Geoffrey saw Diana's eyes open, he slowly slid out of her and slowly, back in. He began to suckle her breasts again skillfully and gently, using his teeth as well. He slipped his hand between them and gently rubbed the small nub that brought her so much pleasure, as he slid in and out of her body.

Soon Diana was feeling the intense pressure inside again. She felt it mount in waves until she could no longer stand it. Her orgasm burst inside her like fireworks. She felt herself tighten and shudder against Geoffrey time after time. His movements sped up and then she felt his body stiffen. He slammed into her body one last time and lay there shuddering as well.

Time had lost all meaning to the young couple in the stable. They were lost in a world completely their own. Neither of them realized that they had been discovered. Neither of them knew that their secret was not their own any longer.

Edward quietly left the stable smiling sardonically. He had sneaked away from the house much earlier to have an assignation with his valet, Benjamin, in the woods. He didn't dare enjoy the attentions of his valet in the keep as he really liked to with all the nosy eyes and ears around. He had his valet meet him in the woods near the keep at midnight. Since the weather was still nice, it wasn't a hardship on either of them. They could have their fun and no one the wiser. Edward had taken a couple of bottles of wine with him this night to enhance their encounter.

He didn't dare leave the wine bottles behind in the woods for fear of discovery by the earl or one of his servants. He had been hiding them in the stable to be disposed of later when he heard his brother and Diana. Edward was much amused by the interlude he had witnessed. "So," he thought, "dear Geoffrey has put the cart before the horse this night. What would father think?" Edward chuckled to himself as he considered how he might use this information to his advantage. He was in no hurry to expose his brother and his fiancé, he would wait to see what happened next. Edward got a lot of pleasure out of knowing the secrets of other people. He had found it very convenient to know things in the past. He had used his knowledge countless times to get out of sticky situations or gain an advantage over someone. He would be patient and see what this information could gain him.

When Diana came down the next morning, she found both Geoffrey and Edward in the dining room already. She blushed when she saw Geoffrey, but hardly noticed Edward at all. She and Geoffrey had talked some last night after they made love, but she was still very shy and embarrassed. She knew that what she and Geoffrey had done was considered wrong by society, but she couldn't feel badly about something that had given them both so much pleasure. It just felt right to love Geoffrey in every way. The thought that she may have become pregnant had hit her as soon as she awoke this morning. The idea both thrilled and frightened her. She would love to have Geoffrey's child, but he was going away for at least a year. What would she do if she discovered she was with child while he was in India?

These thoughts and many others assailed Diana as she filled her plate and sat next to Geoffrey at the dining table.

"Where are our father's this morning, Geoffrey? Did they go hunting on their own?" Diana asked.

"I believe they have already broken their fast and gone to look over some of the new horses in your father's herd."

"And how did you sleep last night, Lady Diana," asked Edward with a strange smile on his face.

"Fine, thank you. And you, my Lord?"

"Wonderfully, thank you very much." With those enigmatic words, Edward excused himself and left the dining room. However, he only went a few feet and quietly returned to eavesdrop on the young lovers.

As soon as Geoffrey thought Edward was out of hearing range, he took Diana's hand in his and kissed it. "I love you so much, my darling. Last night was incredible. Our lives together will be so wonderful. I can hardly wait for us to be married."

Diana was thrilled with Geoffrey's words, but the worry about bearing a child out of wedlock weighed down on her. Geoffrey saw at once that she was not herself.

"What is wrong, my love? Do you regret what we did last night? Please tell me you do not. It was the most beautiful night of my life."

"No, Geoffrey, I do not regret making love with you. I am, however, worried that there may be consequences to our actions. You are going away for quite some time. If I am carrying your child, what will I do? You couldn't leave the army in the middle of the campaign. I would be ostracized by society and it would also break my father's heart. We are not the only ones concerned in this situation."

In the heat of the moment, he had not thought of their actions bearing such fruit, Geoffrey was instantly contrite. How could he not have thought of Diana becoming pregnant with his child? He made up his mind to resign his commission immediately, instead of after his tour in India, so they could be married right away if necessary.

As he turned to Diana to give her the news, their two fathers walked into the dining room. They both immediately picked up on the strange atmosphere between the young people. Harold thought, "What now? Are they having an argument already?" However, there didn't seem to be any animosity between the two. Diana looked sad and Geoffrey looked resigned. What could have happened?

"Father, I was just about to tell Diana I have decided to give up my commission now instead of going to India. Neither of us wish to wait so long to marry. When we go back to London in two days time, I will offer my resignation to my commander at once. That way, we can begin to plan our wedding right away."

"My boy, that is wonderful news. I have been so worried about your return to the army after you were wounded during the last battle with Napoleon. I will sleep much better knowing you are safe. Fergus, you and Diana must come to London right away so we can plan for the wedding. There is so much to be done, so many decisions to be made."

"Yes, we will come in a fortnight. I have things to put to rights here before I can travel, but it shouldn't take any longer than that. We do have much to consider." Fergus stated.

Diana was shocked by Geoffrey's announcement. She had not wanted to force him to give up his commission because she knew how he felt about his regiment. However, she couldn't say she was disappointed.

Later that afternoon as Geoffrey and Diana were walking in the garden, they discussed their ideas for their wedding.

"Do you want to be married in Scotland?" Geoffrey asked with some trepidation.

"It really doesn't matter to me, one way or the other. Would you prefer to be married in London?"

"Well, I wasn't really thinking of myself. I feel that father would probably prefer us to marry in London. How would your father feel about that?"

"I honestly don't know. I will speak with him. We have never discussed such a thing. We both always assumed I would marry a Scot."

"Are you sorry you aren't marrying a Scot?"

"No, Geoffrey. I cannot imagine being married to anyone but you."

Geoffrey caught her hands in his and pulled her close to him. His head bent slowly down to hers. His lips touched hers gently at first. As the kiss deepened, a soft moan escaped Diana's throat. Upon hearing that moan, Geoffrey pulled her even closer running his hands down her back. His hands moved to her hips and down again to softly caress her backside. Diana gasped and pulled away quickly, but she smiled at him sweetly.

"We must be careful, my love. It is the middle of the afternoon and we aren't exactly in a private place here in the middle of the garden."

"You are right. I am sorry. I just cannot seem to keep my hands off you. I love you so much, Diana. I can hardly wait until I have the right to touch you anytime and anywhere."

Diana's cheeks blushed a deep pink. The tip of her tongue stole out and wet her dry lips. The sight was almost more than Geoffrey could stand. He caught one of her hands and pulled her gently along the path toward the house. He must not compromise her again, he thought. He must control himself until the wedding. The wedding had better be soon though. He didn't know how much longer he could wait to have his darling Diana again..

Chapter 10

The day of the Bristols departure dawned bright. The weather had been unusually good while the duke and his party had been in residence. Usually the Scottish autumn was much cooler and much, much wetter.

Diana had risen well before dawn. She wanted to look her best when she bid her beloved Geoffrey goodbye. When she entered the dining room, she was a vision in a dark hunter green silk day dress. The waist was high and the skirt full. The sleeves were long and trimmed in a mauve pink ribbon. The same color ribbon was woven into her deep auburn curls. On her small feet, she wore matching hunter green silk slippers.

Geoffrey looked up from his plate upon her entrance and smiled broadly. She was a vision, his beautiful Diana. He couldn't wait to show her off to his friends in the *ton*. They would be jealous of his good fortune. When they got to know her, they would be even more jealous. She was so very different from the usual London debutante. She was intelligent and had no trouble expressing her opinions in a very articulate fashion. He admired that about her so much.

The duke and earl were watching the young people with smiles on their faces. They were extremely happy about this match. Their two families would now be united for all time. Edward, on the other hand, had a smirk on his face that he quickly changed to a smile when his father looked his way.

"From the amount of visits you have been making to the Bruce household, I wonder will we be having another wedding to a beautiful young Scottish miss soon?"

"You can never tell about me father, but anything is possible." Edward said with a strange smile.

Soon, the London visitors had departed leaving Diana and her father alone for the first time in a month.

"We must make arrangements to visit London in a fortnight. There is much to be done before the wedding."

"Father, do you mind if we marry in London instead of here at Ainsley Glen?"

"Not at all, my dear. I love our keep, but honestly, I don't believe we could accommodate the amount of guests required to be invited to the wedding of a future duke."

"How many guests are we speaking of, Da?"

"The duke told me there will probably be close to four hundred from their side alone. We must invite all our relations here, as well as most of our neighbors. Then there are my political friends from Edinburgh and your mother's family. That will be around another hundred or more. The duke and I discussed this very soon after the ball. It only makes sense to have the wedding in London. It will be much easier for a hundred people to travel to London than for four hundred to travel here."

"Five hundred people??? Da, that's impossible. How can the duke know that many people?"

"It is not that he's personally close to that many, but family connections and politics will warrant that a lot of people be invited who aren't close to the family at all. Harold is directly related to the King. It is the way of the world you will be living in soon. That is another reason we need to go up to London as soon as possible.

You will need to meet a lot of people. You will also need a whole new wardrobe made in London. The fashions there are nothing like what we have here at home. Your wedding dress, especially, will take some time to make. I plan to take some horses with me to the market and our regular buyers there as well. We can combine business and pleasure that way."

"Ah, Da. Combining business with pleasure? That is always the way with a Scot. Heaven forbid, to take a trip without some profit to it somewhere." Diana teased with sparkling eyes.

Fergus had always been thrifty, but not cheap. She wasn't surprised that he wanted to use their trip to deliver some of their orders. They had had a really good crop of foals this year, so they needed to sell some of the two year-olds to make room. There was much to do to prepare for their trip.

"Da, how long will we be in London, do you think?"

"I would suppose we will be there until the wedding. Have you and Geoffrey set the date as of yet?"

"No, but Geoffrey wants to get married as soon as possible. And so do I."

Fergus smiled to himself. He had felt the same about his Morna.

In less than two weeks , Diana received a letter from Geoffrey.

> *My dearest Diana,*
>
> *I know that it has only been a few days since I saw you, however, it feels as though it has been a year. I miss you more each day. I have decided I cannot wait to see you again. I am coming to Ainsley Glen in two days time to escort you and your father to London.*
> *I know your father plans to bring some horses and I can help him ready them for travel. However, that is not*

the main reason for coming. I simply cannot stay away from you any longer. My father finds my impatience amusing and I believe Edward thinks I have lost my senses. I care not.

I have resigned my commission much to the chagrin of my commanding officer. I do not regret this move in the least. You are more important to me than an army career or anything.

I eagerly await our next meeting. Know that I love you more than life itself.

With all my love, Geoffrey

Diana looked at the date on the letter. Her heart beat rapidly as she thought of seeing her love again so soon. He should arrive in just a few days if all went well. She rushed to tell her father and to have Geoffrey's room gotten ready.

The day Geoffrey was expected dawned rainy and cold. Diana had breakfast with her father and they discussed the timing of their trip to London. They decided they should be ready to leave in early the next week. With Geoffrey's help with the horses, as well as the grooms they were already taking, they should reach London in about a week to ten days. Diana was both excited and apprehensive about going to London. She had never been out of Scotland. She honestly had never thought she would leave her home country. She found herself daydreaming constantly of what her life would be like when she and Geoffrey were married.

As the day progressed, the weather became even worse. The rain turned to sleet and the temperature dropped even more. As Diana went from room to room making sure all the fires were burning brightly, she tried not to worry about Geoffrey. She felt as if a dark cloud were hanging over her head though. She couldn't shake the feeling that Geoffrey was in trouble.

When the time reached seven in the evening and Geoffrey had still not come, Diana paced the floor of the drawing room. She had been unable to eat a bite of her dinner. Fergus watched her in concern.

"Diana, darlin'. Geoffrey has probably been delayed by the weather. He may have even decided to stay overnight in an inn and come on tomorrow when the weather lets up."

"Do you think so, Da? You could be right. The weather is ever so terrible this night. The rain and sleet are pouring down and it is so very cold."

Finally, at midnight, Fergus insisted that Diana go up to bed. She had just donned her nightgown and Barbara was brushing her hair when she heard a disturbance downstairs. Thinking Geoffrey had arrived at last, she grabbed her robe and headed down the stairs at a run.

Murtaugh had opened the door just as she reached the bottom stair. The sight that greeted her made her lose her breath momentarily. Geoffrey's valet stood there holding a bleeding Geoffrey up. There was blood all over the front of his shirt. His face was so pale, he looked almost lifeless. Diana rushed forward to help Murtaugh and the valet to carry Geoffrey into the drawing room.

"Hurry, Murtaugh, fetch Da and Mrs. Gwen . Have someone ride for the doctor. We will need hot water as well as bandages." Diana looked at Geoffrey's valet, "Please help me get his jacket and shirt off. What has happened to him? Was there an accident?"

"My young master has been shot, my Lady. We were attacked several miles from here on the road. The blighters shot him from ambush. When he fell from his horse, I took a shot at the woods where I thought they were. We always travel with our pistols ready in case of highwaymen. I heard a yelp and then a couple of horses running away. I got off another shot, but I do not think I hit anything. I picked Lord Geoffrey up and got here as fast as I could."

"You did well. I thank you for all you have done, oh, I'm so sorry, I don't know your name."

"It is Wilson, my Lady. Here let me get his lordship's boots off so we can put his feet up on this sofa."

Fergus rushed into the room. He had been about to undress when one of the footmen knocked on his door. He had rushed downstairs as fast as possible. Almost on Fergus' heels, Mrs. Gwen came in carrying a pan of warm water and an armful of bandages. Between the four of them, they got Geoffrey's coat, waistcoat and shirt off. There was a hole in his chest on the left side. To Diana, it seemed huge. Blood welled from it very quickly. Mrs. Gwen very quickly took a pad of bandages and pressed down on the hole firmly. Geoffrey groaned at the pressure. He had not regained consciousness, which worried Diana to no end.

Mrs. Gwen had Diana wet a cloth and wash Geoffrey's face. His face was already hot and flushed. The wound in his chest was still bleeding profusely even with all Mrs. Gwen could do to staunch it. The women worked over Geoffrey steadily trying to ease his suffering and stop the bleeding. His skin was so white and his breathing so shallow, Diana didn't see how he still lived. He had lost so much blood. Tears began to gather in her eyes, but she willed them away. Time enough for crying later, she thought.

Diana had all but given up on the doctor arriving when there was a knock on the front door. Murtaugh rushed to admit the doctor. Mrs. Gwen and Diana continued to assist the doctor as he examined Geoffrey.

"The bullet is still in his chest and it must come out, but I fear he will not survive the surgery. He has lost so much blood and has developed a fever as well. We need to get him upstairs to a bed as soon as possible." The doctor said.

Fergus had Murtaugh summon some of the footmen and between the six men, Fergus, Murtaugh, Wilson and three footmen, they picked up Geoffrey as gently as possible and bore him up the stairs to a bedchamber. The fire had burned down. One of the footmen was quickly dispatched for more wood while another stirred the embers. Candles were brought quickly and placed all around the bed to give the doctor more light. Fergus shepherded Diana out of the room to give Wilson and the doctor a chance to remove the rest of Geoffrey's clothes. The doctor wouldn't allow Wilson to dress Geoffrey in his night robe, but had him just leave his smalls on instead.

After a few minutes, Wilson opened the door and Fergus and Diana rushed back into the room. Diana immediately went to Geoffrey's bedside across from where the doctor was working on him. She took a cloth and wrung it out, placing it on Geoffrey's forehead. He was even hotter than before and so deathly pale and still. Diana's fear escalated intensely. The blood still welled from the hole in Geoffrey's chest, but not as quickly as before. At first, Diana thought that was a good sign and said so to the doctor.

"Nay, lass. I am afraid, tis not a good sign at all. He has lost so much blood there just is nay much left to come out. I fear for this young man's life. I am doing all I can for him, but I fear this wound is mortal."

Diana would not, could not believe that her Geoffrey was going to die. He was too young, too virile to succumb like this. She looked at her father for assurance, but saw from the look on his face, that he agreed with the doctor. The tears tried to start again, but she would not let them fall. Somehow she felt if she gave in to her grief, the unspeakable would happen. Geoffrey might really die.

The night wore on as the doctor, Mrs. Gwen and Diana worked feverishly over Geoffrey. The wound finally began to clot around dawn, but Diana feared it was too late. Geoffrey had not moved nor made any noise since they had placed him in the bed.

"Da, you must send for the duke at once. Geoffrey will want him here. He needs to be here for Geoffrey."

"Aye, I will send Burroughs with one of the footmen and extra mounts. They will fly like the wind."

Fergus rushed off to get the men on their way. He scrawled a hasty note to his old friend urging him to come with all haste. He gave only the bare essentials as to what had happened to Geoffrey, but made sure the duke knew the situation was very serious.

As the day progressed, Geoffrey's fever rose higher and higher. He became restless and delirious. Diana never left his side. She could not be persuaded to leave for more than the few minutes it took for her to change out of her nightrail. As soon as she was dressed and her hair pinned up, she was back. She drank some tea, but would not eat. Fergus despaired of her health as well. Finally, he brought a tray of food into the room himself and insisted that she take at least a few bites.

She ate the food given to her without ever taking her eyes from Geoffrey's face. She neither wanted nor tasted it. She only ate it to lessen her father's distress. All her energy was focused on willing Geoffrey to live.

The doctor also only left Geoffrey for short periods of time. He was astonished the young man had lasted this long. He must be a very strong individual. Any other man would have succumbed to the blood loss hours ago.

As the day waned, Geoffrey again became very still. The doctor had given him powders for his fever and it seemed to lessen somewhat much to Diana's relief. Diana sat by his side bathing his face and holding his hand in between. She didn't know if he even knew she was there. Since he hadn't been conscious since he had arrived, she wasn't sure he even knew where he was.

Around midnight, Geoffrey opened his eyes for the first time. Diana was sitting beside him with her head resting on her left hand while her right hand held his. She looked like an angel with a red halo. Her curly hair had escaped some of its pins giving her a rosy glow. He smiled and squeezed her hand. Her head jerked up immediately.

"Oh, thank God, Geoffrey, you are awake. I have been so afraid for you, my love."

"Diana, my sweet one. How did I come to be here? I don't remember anything. Wilson and I were riding in the pouring rain. That's the last thing I remember. Did I fall from my horse, what happened?"

"You were shot from ambush, my love. Wilson shot back at them and probably saved both your lives. They ran away. He brought you here last night."

Geoffrey could hardly keep his eyes open. He was so very tired. He wasn't in pain, but felt as if he was floating. He tried to hold on, but he could feel himself slipping away. Just as he was about to lose consciousness, he whispered, "I love you Diana."

"Oh, Geoffrey, my love, I love you too with all my heart."

Diana was not sure he heard her, but he had a slight smile on his lips as he slipped away again.

Several days passed with Geoffrey never again regaining consciousness. Diana had lost all hope by the time the duke and Edward arrived. She sat staring dully at Geoffrey's wasted face. The doctor had informed she and Fergus two days ago that he held out no hope for recovery and the end could come at any time. He was completely amazed that Geoffrey was still alive after so much time. It was as if he were waiting for something or someone to finally let go. His wound had gone septic with the bullet still lodged in his chest. He had never recovered enough for the doctor to remove the bullet. The doctor was convinced that doing so now would hasten the end.

The duke and Edward entered Geoffrey's bedchamber quietly and went to stand by Geoffrey's bedside. They were both utterly shocked by Geoffrey's condition. Geoffrey looked wasted. His skin was pale, his body slack, unresponsive, and burning with fever. The only color on his body were the bright red fever spots on his cheekbones. He looked as if he had lost three stone in just the week since the shooting. His cheeks were sunken and he had huge black circles around his eyes. His breathing was labored and very shallow.

Diana didn't look much better. Always slim, now she was skeletal. Her eyes were sunken in her head as well, with matching black circles around her eyes just like Geoffrey. But it was her eyes themselves that stopped Harold in his tracks. They were so desolate, so completely devoid of feeling. It was as if she had ceased to live herself. It took her a minute to even realize that Harold and Edward had entered the room. She rose and came to stand beside the duke. He put his arm around her shoulders and pulled her tight against him to try to comfort her. She didn't speak at first. Then she slowly turned to the duke.

"He is going to die. We have all tried everything in our power to save him, but he's going to die. How will I go on with him gone, sir? I love him more than life itself."

"Geoffrey would not want you to grieve overmuch for him. He would want you to go on with your life if his is forfeit. I know my son, and I know that he loves you as much as you love him. Is there no hope at all, then?"

"The doctor says not. At first I didn't believe him, but Geoffrey hasn't responded to anything he has given him. The bullet is still in his chest. He lost so much blood he was not strong enough at first to have it removed. The doctor feared removing the bullet would kill him in the beginning. Since the wound has gone septic, now there is no need to risk the surgery. It is too late to remove the bullet. There seems to be nothing else to be done for him."

"My dear, I am so very sorry. I can see how very much you love my son."

Harold worried for his good friend's child. She spoke in a monotone and seemed on the edge of collapse herself.

"Now that we are here, why don't you try to get some rest? Edward and I will sit with Geoffrey. We will wake you if there is any change."

"No, I cannot leave him. I have not left him for more than ten minutes since the beginning. I feel if I leave him, he will let go and I will have lost him forever. I cannot go. My father has tried repeatedly to get me to leave this room, but I just cannot do it."

Diana moved back to her chair and again assumed her vigil. Harold and Edward stayed in the room for several hours until Fergus came in to tell them dinner was served. Diana didn't even look up when her father entered the room. Fergus looked at her with pity and trepidation. He feared for his daughter's sanity and even her very life. She was a ghost of the beautiful girl she had once been. Her lost eyes and pale face pulled at his heart, but there was nothing that could be done. He had tried so many times to get her out of this room, but she would only leave to relieve herself and occasionally to bathe. Every time, she rushed back to Geoffrey's bedside hoping there had been a change, but there never was.

Fergus led Harold and Edward down the stairs to the dining room. He had lost weight himself and felt years older than he had a week ago. Geoffrey's predicament brought back memories of his wife's illness and subsequent death. He remembered how lost he was when his Morna had died. He wished there was something, anything he could do for his beloved girl.

As the men were finishing their meal, they heard a shriek from upstairs. Diana was screaming over and over, "No, no, no."

They rushed up the staircase and into Geoffrey's bedchamber to see Diana collapsed on the bed, her arms around Geoffrey's torso crying hysterically. Fergus went to her and pulled her forcefully off the bed and into his arms. He could tell that Geoffrey was no longer breathing. The valiant young man had finally lost his battle with the mortal coil. Diana was inconsolable.

The doctor had been getting some much needed rest and rushed in when the commotion started. He quickly mixed some laudanum in a glass of water and practically poured it down the girl's throat. Even though he had given her a large dose, it was some time before she became quiet. Her eyes became heavy and she slowly became limp. Fergus picked her up and carried her to her bedchamber. Her maid, Barbara, took over and got her undressed and into bed with the help of Mrs. Gwen.

Chapter 11

When Diana awoke two days later, she just lay in bed and stared up at the bed hangings. She was too emotionally spent to even cry. Mrs. Gwen had been sitting with her. She stepped out the door to alert Fergus that Diana was awake at last. He had been sitting in a chair in the hallway catching a nap. Fergus entered the room, but Diana didn't look in his direction.

"Oh, Diana, my sweet girl. I am so very sorry about Geoffrey. I know that you loved him very much."

Diana did not respond. It was as if she were in a catatonic state. She was vaguely aware that her father was in the room and speaking to her, but she felt too drained to respond. She had been up for so many hours, under such tension; her nerves had finally played out.

Fergus tried for some time to get a response from his daughter to no avail. Finally giving up, he retreated to below stairs to speak with Harold.

"Diana is finally awake, but she won't speak nor even look at me. I don't know what I am going to do, Harold. Could you possibly speak to her? I hate to ask. I know you are grieving for Geoffrey too. I just don't know what else to do."

"Of course, Fergus. I will be more than happy to try. I don't know her well, but I care for her. She loved my boy as much as I did myself. How could I not want the best for her?"

Harold entered Diana's bedchamber quietly nodding at Mrs. Gwen who sat by her bedside. Mrs. Gwen slipped out the door. Harold stood for a moment looking down at the girl who would have been his daughter-in-law in just a few weeks. He would have welcomed her into the family with open arms. Not only because of his relationship with her father or because of the love he had once felt for her mother, but for the girl herself.

She had been so fresh, so alive, so beautiful when they had first come to Scotland. He had relished the fact that Geoffrey had fallen in love with her. Her love for Geoffrey had shone from her big emerald eyes almost from the beginning. Having fallen in love with his wife just as quickly, he could understand the depth of feelings between Diana and Geoffrey even though they had known each other such a short time.

"Diana, my dear. Will you speak with me? I know you are in dire pain as I am myself. Losing Geoffrey is a blow like no other. He was such a good and kind man. I was proud to be his father. But your father feels the same about you and he is very frightened that he has lost his daughter. Please won't you say something?"

At first, Harold didn't think Diana would respond. Slowly, she turned her eyes toward him. In the saddest voice Harold had ever heard she said, "If I did not believe I was carrying Geoffrey's child, I would die myself. But I know he would not want his child to die. He would want his child to live and grow into the kind of man his father was. Unfortunately, he will grow up a bastard with no true future. I have lost my love and now I will lose everything else. My father will be ashamed of me when he finds out, society will reject me, and I will raise a child who may some day hate me."

Diana turned her eyes once more to the bed hangings and said no more.

Harold was in shock. A child, Geoffrey's child! Oh what a blessing that would be. To have a small part of his son to carry on when he, Harold, was gone. It did not bear thinking that this baby would be branded a bastard. He could not allow that to happen. He must think of a solution as quickly as possible.

Harold went downstairs to talk to Fergus. He felt remorseful having to tell Fergus about the possibility of a baby, but he knew they had to put their heads together and find some way to protect the child and Diana. He knew she couldn't be very far along. No more than 4 or 5 weeks at most. Suddenly, the solution was literally staring him in the face.

Edward was standing at the bottom of the staircase looking up. Edward would be the duke when Harold died. Edward must marry Diana. That was the perfect solution. Geoffrey's child would still become the duke in time unless Diana and Edward had a son. There would be no stigma attached to his birth. Many babies were born "early". Some might gossip, but there was no way to prove the date of conception. Diana could go to one of his country estates for her lying in. No one in the *ton* would ever know. The perfect solution. Now he only had to convince Edward.

Surprisingly, Edward needed no convincing at all. Once he heard the reasons for a swift marriage, he readily acquiesced. He was perfectly content to marry his dead brother's fiancée. He knew that Diana would neither want nor need his love or affection. She had loved his brother very much. Edward had not been unaware of the depth of feelings between the two of them. Although he had never felt the least affection for any female, other than his mother, he had loved, and understood the emotion perfectly. Also, she would be having a baby, so for the next several months, according to his father, she would have her confinement at one of the country estates. So much the better. He would stay with her. He wouldn't miss town much. There was plenty to keep him busy in the country. To all appearances, he would be the doting husband. He would have Benjamin with him. It would be perfect.

When Diana was informed of the plans for her future, she hardly batted an eye. She simply didn't care. She was glad that her baby wouldn't be born a bastard, but her grief for Geoffrey was the only emotion she was capable of at this time. She steeled herself to get through the funeral. Normally, Geoffrey's body would have been taken to Bristol Castle, the family seat to be buried in their family crypt, but because of the baby, all involved decided he would be buried in the small cemetery where Diana's mother rested.

Edward was surprisingly supportive during the ordeal. She wondered at first if he grieved for his brother at all, but when she saw the anguish in his eyes when his brother's casket was lowered into the ground, she understood. He had loved her Geoffrey too.

For the next few days Diana's maid Barbara and Mrs. Gwen were busy packing her things. She was to take everything with her. She and Edward were to be married in a quiet ceremony at Ainsley Glen next Monday. Since Scotland did not require banns before marriage, the traditional wait could be avoided. They would then depart from Scotland to Cornwall, the Bristol family seat. Diana took very little interest in any of the arrangements. She was still trying to recover from the ordeal of Geoffrey's death and slept a great deal. All involved encouraged Diana to eat and rest.

Surprisingly, Edward seemed able to convince Diana to partake of more food than the others put together. He exhibited extreme patience with her. He would sit with her in the drawing room for hours, not really doing anything. They didn't talk, just sat quietly together on the sofa. He was not bothered at all by her lack of interest in him or their marriage. For Edward, it was the ideal situation.

The duke and Fergus decided that society would be told that Edward and Diana had been married the week before Geoffrey's death. Normal mourning was twelve months and convention decreed no exceptions to that rule. There had been no formal announcement in London about Geoffrey's betrothal to Diana. They had only been home a few days when Geoffrey left to return to Scotland.

The people who had been at the ball were all Scottish except for the duke and his sons. Fergus decided to very quietly let his closest friends know that Diana was now married to one of the duke's sons without revealing which one.

By lying about the date of the marriage, the twelve month rule about weddings could be avoided. The duke had not informed anyone of Geoffrey's shooting before he left Town. He had simply left immediately for Scotland when he got the news. He knew there might be questions, but there was no way for anything to be proven. The duke planned to spend his time of mourning at another of his country estates in Lancashire. No one in the *ton* would be any the wiser at the end of the mourning period. Edward, Diana and Harold would return to London soon after the mourning period for Geoffrey was over. Harold had informed his barrister and man of business about Geoffrey's death and Edward's wedding in the same letters.

With Diana's condition, waiting a year was out of the question. She had begun to feel sick in the mornings. As soon as she rose from her bed, she would feel the first stirrings of nausea. After the first time, Barbara was waiting with a basin and a wet cloth. After she threw up, Diana would lie back down for a short time. When she arose again, she felt weak, but no longer nauseated. She was not looking forward to traveling all the way to Cornwall. It was a trip expected to take up to two weeks by carriage. Barbara would be accompanying the young couple along with Edward's valet, Benjamin. The servants would travel in a separate coach. There would be three coaches in all. One for the newlyweds, one for the servants and a third for the luggage.

Edward hadn't brought much in the way of luggage on this very hurried trip to Ainsley Glen. However, his father had sent a runner to their home in London to have his and Edward's belongings packed and transported to Cornwall and Lancashire. Since it was a much shorter trip from London, their belongings should arrive well before they did.

Monday dawned overcast and cold. The weather reflected Diana's mood. She had begun to speak a bit more, but only in answer to questions directed to her. She volunteered nothing. She had mostly been quiet in company, but now she was always quiet. Even her beloved father could not bring a smile to her face, although he constantly tried.

The priest arrived at Ainsley Glen from Ainsley Chapel promptly at nine in the morning. Diana and Edward were to be married at ten followed immediately by a wedding breakfast attended only by their fathers and the minister. They would then leave for Cornwall. Their wedding night would be spent at an inn some ten miles away. They would start early the next day and try to travel twenty miles a day. Considering the condition of the roads this time of year, the twenty miles might be wishful thinking.

Since Fergus had traveled extensively all over Scotland, he made a list of the decent inns and public houses in several towns along their route. When the duke and his family had originally traveled to Ainsley Glen, they had been on horseback and had made good speed. However carriages were much slower and required a change of horses. Edwin Burroughs had volunteered to accompany the new couple to their destination in Cornwall to oversee the extra horses required for the trip. Most people who traveled did so by trading their horses at the different inns and public houses along the route.

Fergus did not want his horses traded for inferior ones. His stock was very well bred and expensive. Because of that, a herd of horses would precede the coaches on the trip. Since they would be carrying no loads, they would be well enough rested overnight to change places with the horses that had pulled the coaches on that particular day.

Since it took four horses to pull each coach, Edwin and his two assistants would be trailing twenty-four extra horses plus Diana's Malmuirra. They would not drive the horses in a herd, but would have them tied to each other. Each man would be responsible for eight horses. Because of the danger of highwaymen during this time, there would be outriders with the coaches and the extra horses. All tolled they would be a party of almost thirty people for the long trip from Ainsley Glen to the Bristol castle on Cornwall's coast.

As Edward waited for his wedding to begin, he reflected on the circumstances that had brought him to this day. He and Geoffrey had not been close since they were small boys, but he had loved his brother. Edward was surprised at the amount of pain he felt on the loss of Geoffrey. Also the thought that he, Edward, would be required to take over the ducal duties one day was an unpleasant one for him. In fact that thought terrified him. He had enjoyed being the second son. All the money he needed and none of the responsibility had seemed perfect to him. Now he would be required to be groomed for his future responsibilities, he would be a married man, and he would, in the eyes of society, be a father. It was overwhelming.

Diana was also thinking unpleasant thoughts on this day. Her wedding day. What a difference this day would have been if Geoffrey were the one she was marrying. She would have been filled with joy to think of spending the rest of her life with him, raising their child together in a home filled with love and laughter. Diana doubted she would ever laugh again. Her heart was so filled with anguish she could hardly breathe. How would she make it through this ceremony?

As Fergus took his place in the small drawing room with Harold, he could not help but feel trepidation. He had liked Geoffrey very much, but he did not particularly care for Edward. There had never been anything specific that had happened. It was just a feeling that all was not right with Edward. Something in the look in his eyes sometimes when Fergus saw him observing Geoffrey and Diana, almost a look of derision. Fergus understood that this marriage was the best solution to a terrible problem, but he could not reconcile himself to feel good about the union.

As Harold looked at Diana and Edward standing in front of the minister, he felt the loss of Geoffrey tenfold. This day should have been filled with joy, not sadness. Geoffrey had loved Diana so much and she him. Harold felt they would have had a wonderful life together. Now Geoffrey was dead and Diana was carrying his child. That fact alone had made life bearable for Harold since Geoffrey had died. His grandchild, oh to think a part of Geoffrey would live on. Harold had been surprised Edward was so tractable about this marriage. He didn't feel as if he truly knew his younger son. Edward had been a happy little boy, but upon reaching puberty he had become someone Harold hardly knew. Now at the age of twenty-one, Edward was almost a stranger. Harold worried that Edward would not take enough interest in his duties as a duke or as a husband and father to Geoffrey's child.

When the priest spoke the words you may kiss your bride, there was a significant pause. Edward's face showed a combination of fear and something near disgust for just a moment. Then he gave himself an imperceptible shake and bent his head to Diana's. His lips barely brushed hers and even so, Diana visibly shuddered. Not a very auspicious beginning to a marriage, the priest thought. This certainly didn't seem to be a love match. Oh well, he thought, most of the marriages he performed were not love matches. As a matter of fact, such matches were rare.

Mrs. Allen had tried to make the wedding breakfast special. She had prepared several delicacies for the meal. She and everyone in the household knew the true reason behind this very quick marriage between her beloved Diana and the duke's younger son. The servants had all liked Mr. Geoffrey very much, but had ambivalent feelings toward Edward. He had never treated them badly; it was more that he had ignored them completely, as if they were invisible. Mrs. Gwen also had a very uncomfortable feeling about this marriage. She was very worried for her little sprite going so far away from home with this young man. Diana was in a terrible state, as it was, with the loss of Mr. Geoffrey, as well as knowing she had to marry because of her child, Mrs. Gwen was convinced she would never see her darling girl happy again. Thank goodness Barbara was going with her. She would have at least one person with her she could depend on, no matter what happened.

Diana barely touched her food, only drinking several cups of tea. She sat with her eyes downcast with her hands in her lap. She rarely spoke during the meal, only answering questions when put to her. Edward's appetite also seemed to be somewhat lacking. He did manage to eat a little of the delicious food, but what he really wanted was a good stiff drink. Since this was a wedding breakfast, no spirits were served. There was ale, but that wasn't strong enough for his purposes. He had indulged in a couple of glasses of whiskey while Benjamin was dressing him, but he could use a lot more.

The enormity of his situation had just hit him this very morning. He was going to be a married man and a father, even if the child didn't belong to him in the biological sense, it would be his legally. He would be responsible for the child and for Diana. He had never been responsible for anyone before. It terrified him.

Edward had never had to buckle down to accomplish anything in his life. His studies at university and before at Eton and Oxford had come easily to him. Nothing concerning the duchy had ever been asked of him because he was a second son. He had been left to his own devices once he had come down from university and that was the way he wanted it. All of this was supposed to be Geoffrey's responsibility. Damn his brother for dying. Suddenly, he was angry, angry with his brother, Diana, his father, everyone and every thing.

Diana happened to glance up. She gave a small startled gasp when she saw Edward's face. He suddenly looked so very angry. When Edward heard her, he looked right into her eyes. What Diana saw in Edward's eyes frightened her. She involuntarily started to rise from her chair. She felt she had to get away from him immediately.

Seeing the expression on Diana's face brought Edward back to his senses. He couldn't afford to alienate Diana. He would need her compliance if he was going to be able to live the life he wanted. He forced a smile at her and lay his hand on her arm gently. Diana settled back into her chair, but leaned as far away from Edward as possible.

"It will be all right, Diana. Every thing will be all right." Edward said in a very low voice.

Diana didn't respond, but she allowed him to keep his hand on her arm. She had gotten used to Edward being with her almost constantly the last few days. She had been cognizant of his presence and it had been comforting to an extent. She really didn't know Edward at all. The time he and his family had spent at Ainsley Glen, she had been consumed with Geoffrey. She remembered she had been ambivalent about Edward at their first meeting and for the first couple of days of their stay. After that, all her attention had been focused on Geoffrey.

Soon the wedding breakfast was over. It was time for the young couple to be on their way. The trunks and bags had been loaded earlier that morning. All they had to do was climb into the coach and be off.

As they were about to go out the door, Fergus stopped Diana. Fergus put his arms around his daughter and held her close. Speaking where only she could hear, he said, "Diana, if you need anything, don't hesitate to send me word. I will come immediately. I will be there when your time comes, but if you need me before, send a letter or one of the servants. I will ride like the wind to you if you should need me."

"Thank you, Da. That is a comfort to me. I must admit I am frightened to be going so far from you and all I have ever known, but it is the best way to protect my child. That has to be my main concern. I will not have him known as a bastard. Geoffrey's child deserves so much better than that. I know I did wrong to be intimate with Geoffrey, but wrong or not, I do love this child growing in me."

"I know you do, lass. I know you will make a wonderful mother, just like your mother before you."

Chapter 12

With those final words, Fergus released her and she followed Edward through the door to the coach. Edward assisted her into the coach and then climbed in himself. He took the opposite seat from her and she was relieved.

Diana didn't wish to seem ungrateful for what Edward had done for her and her child, but she was uncomfortable with him after seeing his face at breakfast. She thought he must regret their marriage now. She regretted it too, but only because she still loved Geoffrey with all her heart and soul. She couldn't even imagine trying to be a "real" wife to Edward. She hoped and prayed he would not expect to avail himself of his marital rights too soon. She had made up her mind that eventually, she would have to be a real wife to him, but she couldn't find it in her heart to even think about it right now.

The first part of the journey passed in silence. Edward seemed to have much to think about. As for Diana, she was exhausted. Before she knew it, she had fallen asleep with her head leaning back on the cushions of the seat. The swaying of the coach lulled her tired body and mind.

Edward sat staring at his sleeping wife. Wife, what a strange thought. He had a wife. Marriage was something he had always known he would have to face eventually, but he had thought to put it off for many more years. A lot of the men of the nobility didn't marry until they were well into their thirties. At only one and twenty, he had thought he had many years of freedom left to him. He had hoped to travel the continent with Benjamin and maybe a couple of his like-minded friends. Well, there was nothing to stop him from still doing that, he thought happily. For propriety's sake and his father's, he would have to wait until the child was born and the mourning period had ended. After that though, a belated honeymoon would not be looked at askance by his father or society. He could ensconce Diana and the child in a country villa in Italy while he did the grand tour without her.

The more Edward thought about his future, the more content he became. Nothing really had to change all that much. He could continue his relationship with his beloved Benjamin with no one the wiser. Every gentleman travelled with at least his valet, if not several servants. Yes, it would be fine. With those happy thoughts, Edward leaned back in the seat and went to sleep as well.

When the coach stopped, Edward and Diana awoke simultaneously. He smiled at her and she gave him a small tentative smile back. The footman opened the door of the coach and announced they had reached the inn where they would be spending the night. Edward got down and offered his hand to Diana. She allowed him to help her from the coach. He kept her hand in his and lead her into the inn.

As Edwin and his grooms had left well before the newlyweds, he had already made arrangements for rooms for all of them and accommodations for the stock. He was waiting in the taproom of the inn when they arrived. He immediately went to Diana.

"Miss Diana, are you well, you look very tired?"

"I am all right, Edwin. How is Malmuira? Did she travel well? I was worried about her. She is not used to going so far in one day."

"Ah, that filly is fine. She is not even tired. Still as spirited and ornery as ever." Edwin said with a laugh.

"That is truly wonderful news. I can rest easy knowing she will make this long trip with ease, then. Have we rooms? I really would like a good wash and some tea. Although I slept most of the way, I seem to still be very tired."

"Of course, Miss Diana. I will have the innkeeper show you to your room right away."
Edward had just stood at Diana's side during this conversation. He had no intention of sharing Diana's room, but knew he must escort her there. When they reached the room, he saw it was not large,

but it was clean and the bed at least looked somewhat comfortable. Diana's maid, Barbara, had preceded them upstairs and was building up the small fire burning in the fireplace. Diana took off her cloak and bonnet and dropped then into a chair.

She was uncomfortable. She didn't know if Edward expected to share the chamber with her. She turned to Edward with a questioning look.

"I will leave you to your maid then Diana. Perhaps you would like to take your meal in your room so you can rest. I will eat downstairs before I retire to my own room, if that is all right with you. I know the journey has exhausted you."

Diana thanked Edward for his concern. It was apparent to him that she was relieved he would not be sharing her room tonight. It amused him to think she may have expected him to want to consummate the marriage. He had no intention of ever consummating it, but she didn't need to know that yet. Time enough for that conversation after they arrived in Cornwall. He could use the excuse of her obvious exhausted state during the journey as to why he didn't join her in her room. She was still mourning Geoffrey as was he, so it would not seem unusual to her for them not to share a bed right now.

Edward made his way downstairs to question the innkeeper about his own accommodations. He was informed that his valet had already taken his things upstairs. He was shown to his room by a chambermaid. He asked for warm water to be brought for washing and a bottle of brandy as well. He not only needed, but deserved a good long drink after this day.

Edwin Burroughs was well pleased that Edward had adjourned to his own room this night. He had every reason to be concerned for Diana. He had seen Edward and his valet in the barn one night during the duke's visit to Ainsley Glen. It had been raining and he supposed they couldn't use their usual rendesvouz, the woods near the keep. He had seen them coming from the woods together on two separate occasions before the barn incident. He had thought they had slipped off to the village to drink at the pub the first times. However, what he had seen in the barn had convinced him otherwise. In his mind, it was unnatural for two men to be together that way. It had made him sick.

When Edwin had been told that Diana would be marrying this man, he had almost told the earl what he had seen. Once he heard from the kitchen gossip that the girl was with child, he had changed his mind. She had to marry someone and fast. He couldn't bear to have that wonderful girl despised and cast out by society.

He intended to keep a close watch on Edward, duke's son or not. He had volunteered to come on this journey just for that reason. He did need to look after his employer's stock, but the most important reason he came was to watch over his employer's daughter. He was much older than Diana. He had watched her grow from an engaging little sprite to a beautiful young woman. He had a brotherly interest in her welfare. No one would harm her as long as he was around.

The next day dawned rainy and cold. Barbara dressed Diana in a warm woolen gown with extra petticoats and two pairs of stockings. It would be very cold and damp in the carriage. She had one of the grooms take hot bricks to the coach just before they departed to put under her mistresses little feet. Diana was so small and had lost so much weight during her vigil at Geoffrey's bedside, Barbara hardly knew how she kept going. She encouraged Diana to eat a bowl of porridge and some toast after her morning sickness was over. Diana did manage to get down most of her breakfast. She knew she had to eat for her baby.

All her thoughts were now directed at delivering a healthy son for Geoffrey. Having a daughter never entered her mind. She somehow knew it was a boy she carried in her womb. Since she had suspected she was pregnant, she had tried to eat and rest more. She knew that eating and resting were supremely important for a healthy birth. From having been around her father's tenants families over the years, she was not unaccustomed to being around breeding women.

Edward came to Diana's door, when the coaches were ready, to escort her down. He smiled kindly at her and inquired if she was dressed warmly enough. She assured him she was and donned her heavy fur lined hooded cloak. Edward held an umbrella above her head as he led her to the carriage. After he had deposited Diana into the carriage, he joined her. There was a heavy rug on the seat which he spread over her legs wrapping it securely around Diana and the bricks beneath her feet.

The interior of the coach was very dim since there was little daylight to be had. There were lamps hanging on the wall near the windows. Edward asked one of the footmen to bring a taper to light them. They didn't provide much heat, but they did take some of the gloom away.

The carriage swayed and bumped along on the soggy road. Diana and Edward spoke little again this day. They had been on the road for less than 2 hours when Diana really began to feel the cold intensely. She began to shiver even with all the extra clothes and wraps. Edward had been absorbed in his own thoughts and hadn't noticed her discomfort at first. As soon as he heard her teeth chattering, he reached for her hands. They were ice cold. He chafed her hands between his. They were both wearing gloves, but the temperature in the carriage was so low, the gloves were almost worthless.

"What can I do to warm you, Diana? Let me put my cloak around you."

As Edward began to unbutton his cloak, Diana stayed his hand with hers.

"You will be cold yourself, Edward. If you could ask the driver to stop for a moment, I have an extra cloak in one of my trunks. Also, I believe Barbara packed several blankets for this type of emergency."

"Of course. I will take care of it right away. I should have thought to ask before we even started the journey today. I'm so sorry. I am not accustomed to having the care of anyone except myself. I will try to do better in future."

Edward knocked on the roof of the coach with his walking stick. The driver stopped immediately. One of the footmen opened the door. Edward relayed the message to him for Barbara. Soon, the extra cloak and two blankets were brought to them. Edward started to wrap the cloak and one of the blankets around Diana when she noticed that Edward was now shivering as well.

"Edward, I think it would be better if you sat beside me and we shared the coverings as well as the extra cloak and blankets."

Seeing the sense of her suggestion and being very uncomfortable in the cold, damp air, Edward moved to sit beside Diana. He managed to wrap the extra cloak and blanket around them both and settled the rug and other blanket over their legs. To get the coverings around them both, he had to sit quite close to Diana. Edward had, of course, touched women before while dancing, but he had never been this near to one for so long before. He feared he would be disturbed at being so to close Diana, but found after a short time, his uneasiness abated.

After a few hours, Diana's head began to bob with exhaustion and sleepiness. Edward was tired as well. The road was so very rough, he felt as if he had been beaten. He knew Diana must feel the same. As her head nodded again, Edward put his arm around her and drew her head down onto his shoulder. She was so tired and sleepy, she didn't object nor really even seem to notice. Soon, she was completely asleep. Edward soon joined her.

When the carriage stopped for the night this time, Edward and Diana found they were in front of a house when they alighted from the carriage. Edwin had found accommodations in a private home as there was no inn in the area. The house was not very large nor very clean. The home owner and his wife had several children of various ages and were obviously not well off financially. They ushered their guests into the large room that served as drawing room, dining room and kitchen.

The house was not really dirty, but was very cluttered. Diana supposed with so many people living in the small house, the poor housewife would be hard put to maintain much order. The fire was burning brightly in the hearth and something smelled delicious. After having only bread and meat for luncheon while they travelled, both Diana and Edward were quite hungry. The footmen and grooms were being housed in the barn and their food was taken to them by one of the older children. The rest of the party were seated at the families dining table on an assortment of stools and chairs brought from around the room. The meal consisted of a thick soup made of turnips, potatoes, onions, leeks, and herbs served with loaves of crusty bread with butter.

Diana thought she had never tasted anything quite so lovely. Finally she was warm and was putting hot food into her stomach. She watched with interest as Edward talked to the farmer and his wife. He was not disdainful as she had expected him to be in the circumstances. Before she had thought Edward to be arrogant, but tonight, he seemed just to be content to be out of the carriage and in a warm house. When dinner was over, Barbara helped the lady of the house and her older daughters clean off the table and wash the dishes. Diana also offered to help, but was shooed away to sit near the fire. Normally, she would have insisted on helping, but she was so very weary, she contented herself with just getting warmer.

While drowsing by the fire, Diana wondered where in the world they would all sleep. Edwin had already said he would sleep with the other men in the barn, but there was still Edward, Benjamin, herself and Barbara needing beds. The house had a second storey, but surely there wouldn't be enough bedrooms for everyone to have their own. She had no problem sharing with Barbara, but she didn't really want to sleep in the same bed as Edward. As she worried over this predicament, Barbara came to her.

"Lady Diana, if you will come with me, I'll get you ready for bed."

"But, Barbara where will we all sleep? " she whispered, "I fear we will dispossess these good people from their beds."

"We are to share a bedroom with two of the older girls. Lord Edward and his valet will share with two of the boys. The little ones who usually use those beds will sleep near the fire, here."

As Barbara led Diana up the stairs, she glanced back at Edward. He was standing in front of the fireplace with Benjamin. He glanced her way and gave her a small smile.

Upon entering the bedchamber, Diana was surprised to see two beds in the room. There was little room for anything else, but the beds looked clean and fairly comfortable. The girls were already there. They must have hurried upstairs and dressed for bed quickly for they were already beneath the covers on one of the beds. They were pretty girls, fair haired and blue eyed. They looked very much alike. They seemed to be around twelve and fourteen.

"Good evening, ladies. Barbara and I thank you so much for sharing your room with us. What are your names?"

After some giggling and shy glances, the older girl said. "I'm Sharon and this is Carolyn, my Lady."

"Well, again, Sharon and Carolyn, thank you very much for sharing your room. I am ever so tired and will really appreciate being able to lay down my head."

Barbara helped Diana undress down to her chemise. Then she pulled a heavy flannel nightgown over her head and helped her button it up. Diana crawled into bed and within a very few minutes, she was asleep. She didn't even know when Barbara came to bed.

After a breakfast of porridge, the party loaded into the carriages again for another long day of travel. Diana was gratified when she saw Edward hand a well-filled purse to the farmer. She knew the poor family could use the extra money. They had little, but were willing to share all they had. Because of the terrible condition of the roads, they hadn't been able to travel the hoped for twenty miles. It had stopped raining and was a trifle warmer, but not much.

Edward again sat beside Diana and they shared the wraps and blankets as they had the day before. Soon the days took on a certain sameness for Diana. She was rarely comfortable or warm during the day. Edward did his best, but circumstances just weren't conducive to comfort. Travel during this time period was never easy in Scotland. The roads were badly maintained and there was not always a public inn or alehouse from which to receive accommodations. Diana felt herself grow wearier and wearier as time went on. She slept a great deal in the carriage, but it was not a restful sleep. Without Edward's aid, she would have been tossed about the carriage like a rag doll. He held on to her as they were jounced and jostled by the road, trying his best to provide what comfort he could.

Chapter 13

Finally after over two weeks of misery, their party reached Cornwall and the duke's ancestral home. Diana had never seen a home so large. It was actually a castle built atop the cliffs right on the sea. There was always a breeze and more often than not, a very heavy wind blowing. The smell of the sea was invigorating to Diana. She had always lived inland, although she had travelled to Inverness on occasion. However, that city was on a river not the sea.

The travel party arrived at dusk on the fifteenth day after leaving Ainsley Glen. Diana had been unable to gain back any of her weight on the exhausting trip. Her appetite was not strong and the food they had been served had not always been tasty. Having been raised on Mrs. Allen's wonderful cooking, Diana's taste buds were less attuned to rough food. Edward had eaten everything he was served. As with most young men, his appetite was healthy and he could eat voraciously on occasion.

When their carriage drew up to the front of the castle, the great doors were opened by the butler, Edmonds. He ushered the young people into the castle and organized several footmen to help unload the carriages. The housekeeper, Mrs. Smythe, took charge of Diana and Barbara at once. She preceded them up the stairs to the apartments formerly used by the Duchess, Edward's mother.

There was a huge sitting room with a white marble fireplace on one wall with a roaring fire. The furniture was covered in a flower printed silk in shades of blue and mauve on a gold background. There was a sofa and two chairs in front of the fireplace, a beautiful escritoire in one corner with another chair covered in the same silk, and several occasional tables around the room. The tables were covered in beautiful ornaments, vases, and statuary in colors to match the rest of the room. The walls were hung with sky blue silk and the drapes were a rich mauve velvet picking up the pinkish color in the furniture. There were five windows in the room bathing it in soft twilight. Diana knew the chamber would be wonderfully bright during the day.

This room opened into a very large bedchamber with a huge bed. The bed hangings were of very sumptuous dark blue velvet. The drapes on the many windows were of velvet as well, but in a gold brocade with dark blue tassels and tie backs. The walls were covered in a silvery blue silk. The cushions on the chairs were embroidered in flower patterns in blues, golds, and pinks on a mauve background. It was the most beautiful set of rooms Diana had ever seen. In the anteroom next to her bedroom there was a dressing room and bathing chamber. Next to the dressing room was Barbara's room. It was also very nice and a good size. She would have Barbara near at all times. Diana really liked that part of the arrangement. She needed Barbara near. She was the only person in Cornwall that Diana felt she really knew.

Just as Diana and Barbara had completed their tour of the rooms, there was a knock on the door. Mrs. Smythe answered the door to admit Edward.

"Do these rooms suit?"

"These rooms are incredibly beautiful. Did they belong to your mother?"

"Yes. She took great pride in these rooms. She decorated them herself. They had been filled with heavy, dark colors and furniture when she became duchess. She had them totally redone immediately."

"She had a wonderful eye for color. The rooms actually tend to lift the spirit. But should I have these rooms? I am not a duchess after all."

"No, not yet, and hopefully, not for a long time. However, my father suggested you have these rooms. He felt they were being wasted with no one to inhabit them. He was very proud of the job my mother did on them. I am just down the hall in the rooms I have had since I was a boy should you need anything."

Edward walked to the door and then glanced at Diana over his shoulder. "You should get some rest. I know the journey was especially hard on you. If you would like to have dinner in your rooms tonight, I would be agreeable. I, myself would relish a good bath, a hot meal and an early bed."

"As you wish, Edward. And thank you so much for everything," Diana said with a special emphasis on the last word. Edward knew she was not just referring to his care on the journey. He surmised he meant for marrying her and giving her and Geoffrey's baby a name. He merely inclined his head and left the room.

After asking Mrs. Smythe to see that dinner was sent up for she and Barbara, she then asked that hot water be sent up for a bath. She had never had a bathing chamber and was looking forward to a good soak. There had been no bathing facilities for the entire long trip from Ainsley Glen. The ladies had to make do with washing in sometimes cold or lukewarm water at the inns or public houses where they stayed. At Ainsley Glen, a tub was brought to her room by a footmen and she bathed in front of the fireplace with a screen around the tub. The tub had only been large enough for her to sit upright with her knees bent.

This bathing chamber had no windows to allow drafts to come in and a small charcoal brazier to warm it. There was a huge white tub with flowers painted on the side in shades of yellow, red and blue. There was enough room in the tub for Diana to stretch out completely and still have room to spare. There was a large painted silk screen to be placed around the tub to keep in the heat. The painting on the screen was similar to the painting on the tub. The walls were not hung with silk in this room, but plastered and painted a rich, lively yellow with white trimmed woodwork. In the corner of the bathing chamber, there was a washstand with a built in white basin that matched the tub. A pitcher with the same flower print sat on the edge of the washstand. There was an armoire in the corner filled with large linen towels and wash cloths. Diana had never seen such luxury. She was not sure she would ever get used to this opulence.

Diana luxuriated in the bath until the water was tepid. Barbara had washed her hair with soft soap that smelled of lavender. Then she had relaxed against the back of the tub in water up to her neck. She felt some of the tension from the journey drain away as she lay there. Finally, she called Barbara to help her get dried and dressed for bed. They had their dinner on trays before the fireplace in the drawing room in their nightgowns. Diana was pleasantly surprised by the quality of the meal they were served. There was a delightful beef consomme to start, followed by roast partridge with carrots and onions served with delicious saffron buns with butter. For dessert there was a strawberry trifle topped with clotted cream. For the first time in what seemed a long time, Diana was actually hungry and ate heartily much to Barbara's delight.

Soon after she had dined, Diana went to bed. She was very tired, but her mind would not allow sleep. She thought back over the past few weeks. Tears ran down her face as she thought of Geoffrey. She had loved him so much and did still. The thought of his child growing in her belly was a comfort, but it was bittersweet. She knew that he would have cherished this child as did she. They had discussed children of course, when they had decided to marry. He had wanted several. Now there would be only one.

That is unless she were to become pregnant with Edward's child when they consummated their marriage. She had very ambivalent feelings about lying with Edward. It just didn't seem right. She could not imagine being that intimate with him. She felt absolutely no attraction to him. In fact, she had only just started to feel a sisterly affection for him, much the way she had felt about Ian MacAllister.

Diana was grateful for Edward marrying her for the baby's sake and for her own. She was also very grateful for the care he had shown her on the torturous trip from Ainsley Glen to Cornwall. He had been a gentleman in every way. The only time he had touched her, in any way, was to offer her the warmth of his body in the carriage and to assist her in and out of the carriage. They had never shared even a sitting room on the journey, much less a bed.

These thoughts and many more whirled about in Diana's head, but soon her exhaustion won out and she slept deeply. The sound of the drapes being pulled back from the windows woke Diana late the next morning. She opened her eyes to see sunshine coming through the many windows in her bedchamber. However, there was a brisk wind blowing and Diana could actually feel the cold coming through the windows. It had been very cold when they arrived last evening. It seemed even colder today. Diana was very grateful for the briskly burning fire in the fireplace in her bedchamber. Getting out of bed would have been much more uncomfortable otherwise. Diana wondered at the extreme cold. It had been quite cool in Scotland, but not nearly as cold as here in

Cornwall. She determined to ask Edward about it when next she saw him.

In the meantime, she instructed Barbara to close the drapes to keep out as much cold as possible. Just as Barbara had finished her hair, there was a knock upon her door. Barbara opened the door to admit Edward. He was looking much better rested and had returned to his former sartorial splendor. He wore a bright yellow coat and breeches with a white ruffled shirt and purple waistcoat. On his feet, he wore slippers that matched his waistcoat. When she entered the drawing room, Diana was surprised by his ensemble.

Diana herself was clad all in mourning black. She had worn nothing except black since Geoffrey's death. Edward had also conformed to proprieties at Ainsley Glen and on their journey. It was something of a shock to see him returned to his usual peacock state.

When Edward noticed the surprise in Diana's eyes, he did a small pirouette in the middle of the drawing room floor.

"Well, what do you think? I simply could not stand to wear black another day. Don't get me wrong, I still mourn my brother, but all that black was depressing me. We will not be receiving guests here because of our state of mourning, so I see no reason to wear black as long as I don't go out. And neither should you. You are only sixteen years old, Diana. You should wear clothing that matches your age."

"I wouldn't feel right wearing bright colors so soon after Geoffrey's death. I don't mind that you do, but I just could not."

"Ah, well, suit yourself. Were you ready to go down to the dining room for breakfast? It is usually served at nine of the clock when the family is in attendance here."

"Yes, I am ready. I suppose I should meet the staff today and speak to Mrs. Smythe and cook this morning as well. I am anxious to take up my duties here. It will give me something to occupy my mind."

"If you feel up to it, that would be fine. There is no great rush to take over the household duties however. Mrs. Smythe manages quite nicely. She has run the household alone since my mother's death three years ago. Bristol Castle sits right on the sea, so we experience a lot of inclement weather here. Usually we are only in residence here a few months a year. We generally leave Town in late August and come here to escape the heat. Then after the new year, we go to one of the other estates the family owns in the Midlands or Suffolk or Kent, somewhere to escape the extreme cold. In March, we go back to Town to ready ourselves for the Season. Parliament is also in session during that time, so father must be in Town for political reasons as well. Of course, this year we will not be participating in the Season. We will be in mourning until late October"

After Edward had revealed all this to Diana, she was distressed. She had lived all her life in one place, Ainsley Glen. Yes, she had travelled with her father to houses near their home for balls and house parties, but she had never been out of Scotland or actually no farther than twenty miles from home. She was not sure she could grow accustomed to different homes several times a year. Well, she would just have to get used to it.

She would have her baby in July if Mrs. Gwen's calculations were correct. The normal lying in period for the nobility was two months time. That would bring them to September before she could travel at all. Hopefully, she would have gotten used to the idea of multiple homes by then.

As Edward and Diana descended the staircase into the main hall, they were greeted by the butler, Edmonds, and Mrs. Smythe. Once ushered into the dining room, Diana was amazed by the size of the room. The table would seat forty comfortably. It was of a dark, highly polished wood with matching chairs. The seats of the chairs were covered in striped silk in differing shades of gold. The frescoed ceiling was painted with clouds and frolicking cherubs in shades of blue and white similar to a real sky. The walls were hung with red silk above wainscoting that was finished in the same dark hue as the table and chairs. At one end of the dining room, there was a huge fireplace with a dark mantle that rose to the ceiling which must have been twenty feet tall. The fire was made up of large logs six feet long. Diana had never seen a fireplace that huge. However, even with the roaring blaze, it was still cool in the dining room.

The windows looked out on the sea. Diana's attention was immediately caught by the spectacle of the sea. She had never seen it before. Somehow, she was drawn to it. She wanted to walk outside and down to the edge of the cliff so she could see it better. However, she did not relish being out in the cold.

There were two places laid at the end of the table nearest the fireplace. The table was so wide, there was room for two large chairs at each end. Edmonds pulled out Diana's chair. She sat and folded her hands into her lap. Edward took the other chair directly beside her. Edmonds, pulled a bell rope and footmen began to enter from another door in the rear of the room. They carried several covered platters to the table and arranged them in front of Diana and Edward.

As the platters were uncovered, Diana was amazed at the array of food. There were two platters of eggs, one coddled and one fried, a platter of bacon, one of sausages, and another of kippers. Three kinds of bread were served as well as several pots of jams and jellies and mounds of rich yellow butter. Another footman entered carrying a tea tray, while another came bearing coffee and hot chocolate. Diana was overwhelmed by all the choices and hardly knew what to pick.

Edward, on the other hand, had no problem at all. He took helpings of fried eggs, bacon, sausages and kippers. He buttered a slice of bread and covered it with a good quantity of strawberry jam. He indicated to the footman that he would have coffee. When his coffee was poured, he added cream and sugar to it in abundance.

When Edward realized Diana still had nothing on her plate, he turned to her.

"Are you not hungry this morning? If you do not see anything you like, perhaps cook can prepare something else for you."

"It is not that I do not want what is before me, it is just that there is so much it is hard to make a decision."

"Well, then let me make it for you." At that Edward picked up Diana's plate and added a coddled egg, several slices of bacon, a sausage and a slice of bread to her plate. He buttered her bread and asked which of the jams she preferred. When she indicated that strawberry would be fine, he put a healthy portion of it onto her bread.

"I believe you prefer chocolate in the morning, do you not?"

"Usually yes, but I think I would prefer tea today, if you do not mind."

One of the footmen poured her tea adding sugar and set it beside her now filled plate. Diana felt pampered. With a smile and a thank you to Edward and the footman, she began to eat. Diana didn't really know what to make of Edward. They had been married two weeks now, but he had shown no interest in her, except a polite consideration for her comfort. They had not actually discussed their marriage or what his expectations were. During the long two weeks of their journey, they had spoken little, and then only of mundane subjects, never anything personal.

Diana expected to fulfill her wifely duties to Edward at some time, but she was inordinately pleased that he didn't seem to be in any rush for their marriage to be consummated. Her love for Geoffrey and the grief at his death were still much too fresh in her mind to consider much else. That and the baby growing inside her consumed all her attention.

Edward was grateful that Diana didn't seem to expect much from him. He really had little to give. He had been raised to be polite and considerate to everyone, especially ladies, so seeing to her comfort was second nature to him. He had no illusions about the type of marriage they would have. He hesitated, however, to inform Diana of his true nature. He still held some fear that she would inform his father of his inclinations.

Edward had absolutely no desire for his father to be privy to his proclivities. Especially not now. With Geoffrey dead, he would have to be trained to take over his father's position as duke. He hoped with all his heart that his father remained in excellent health for many years to come. He loved his father, although his father didn't understand him. Also, Edward enjoyed his freedom and in point of fact, was lazy. The thought of having to learn estate business as well as politics made his head ache. Since his father hadn't intimated when his training would begin, Edward assumed it would wait until after the baby's birth when they returned to Town. Geoffrey had been groomed from a very young age for the duties of the duchy. Edward had much to catch up on.

Chapter 14

The duke of Bristol, at that exact moment, was planning the training of his youngest son. He had no allusions about Edward's laziness. He had watched his younger son skate through life without much effort. He knew that Edward had exceptional intelligence, he had just never had to use it. That was all about to change. The Bristol family owned nine estates, three of them huge. Edward would have to become acquainted with the managers on all of them, and soon. He would have to meet with the duke's man of business and his solicitor. He would also be required to sit in with his father when Parliament resumed in the spring. There was so very much to teach him.

Harold was worried he wouldn't have time to teach Edward everything he needed to know. He had been to see his doctor when he reached Town. The tightness in his chest had increased with Geoffrey's death. It had not lessened much afterwards. The doctor had told him his heart was damaged. The prognosis was not good. There had been no way for the doctor to give him a timeline, but he had cautioned Harold that he might not have a lot of years and possibly not many months before he succumbed to his heart ailment.

When Harold received the prognosis, he immediately sent a letter to Fergus. He wanted his old friend to know his situation and to be prepared. He also wanted to assure Fergus Diana would be well taken care of. After drafting the letter to Fergus, Harold visited his solicitor. He made provisions in his will for Diana to inherit his largest estate that was not entailed, the one in the Midlands. The provision also stated that her first born child would inherit that estate regardless of sex. He knew Diana would be Edward's duchess, but he wanted to be absolutely sure she would always be provided for, no matter what happened to his own estate. Her child, if a girl, would not be in line for the duchy. He wanted to be sure that child, Geoffrey's child, would always have a home and an income.

If Geoffrey's child was a boy, legally, he would be entitled to the duchy. However, if Edward and Diana had a son together, Harold wasn't sure how Edward would feel about Geoffrey's son inheriting the title and all that went with it. There were so many variables in the situation, Harold tried to think of every way he could to protect every one involved. He knew he would not be around to take care of these matters in years to come. He had to solve as many of the issues as he could before he was no longer able to do so. His doctor had told him his life might end quickly, or he might become very weak and slowly slip away. Again there was no way to be sure.

When Fergus received Harold's letter, he was shocked. He had no idea his old friend was in ill health. He was somewhat relieved to know that Diana would have an estate of her own. Fergus was still very uncomfortable about her marriage to Edward. There was just something about that young man that hit him as wrong. He couldn't put his finger on the issue, it was just intuition. Something in his eyes, the way he observed people, but rarely participated, put Fergus' nerves on edge. Fergus knew that Diana would inherit Ainsley Glen and all his personal money, so he wasn't worried that she would be destitute even without the duke's generosity. However, it was always heartening to know his little girl would never need to worry about a home or money.

Fergus missed Diana even more than he had thought he would. She had done so much at Ainsley Glen, especially for his tenants. It was impossible for him to keep up with his own duties and hers. He thought he must delegate Diana's duties to someone, but he was hard pressed as to who that should be. Just as he was contemplating this issue, Edwin knocked on his door.

Edwin, of course, he thought. He would be perfect to handle the tenants. Mrs. Gwen could handle the keep, but he really needed someone he could trust to take care of the tenants. He broached the subject with Edwin. At first Edwin was hesitant about taking over the task along with his horse training duties, but with some persuasion from Fergus, he agreed.

With that problem taken care of, Fergus could concentrate on Ainsley Glen and the family estate that his nephew and heir lived on. He could also continue his horse breeding and training without the guilt of his tenant's welfare hanging over his head. Fergus wrote a letter to Diana with the news. He knew she would be pleased that Edwin would be handling her beloved tenants. Fergus knew that Diana and Edwin had a special relationship and had since Diana was a small girl.

Edwin, too had misgivings about Diana's marriage to Edward. As he left the keep, he thought of the long journey they had been on a few weeks before. He couldn't fault Edward as to his treatment of Diana on their journey. However, since Edwin knew about Edward's sexual proclivities, he wasn't surprised at their lack of intimacy. What he was so very worried about was Diana's reaction when she found out. And knowing her intelligence, youth, and strong moral sense, he feared for her emotional well being as well.
Only time would tell, he supposed.

There was another party upset at the marriage of Diana MacDonald to the duke's younger son. Adelaide Bruce was beside herself. None of her carefully laid plans had worked out. When Diana had become engaged to Geoffrey, Adelaide had been furious. She had planned for her daughter, Beatrice, to marry him. Then, when the younger boy, Edward showed interest in her daughter, she formed a plan to make Beatrice a duchess.

She had a trusted servant who had been with her family for many years. In fact, that servant was the manager at their Scottish estate and had been Adelaide's lover for several years. Her husband was always in Edinburgh for his political career so she was free to do whatever pleased her. Sleeping with Horace pleased her very much.

Shortly after the duke and his sons left for London so did Adelaide and Beatrice for a shopping trip. They were accompanied by Horace. Adelaide had him hire someone in London to do away with Geoffrey. They were to make it appear cutthroats had accosted him in the streets to steal his purse and had killed him for it. That would leave Edward in line for the duchy and her Beatrice would be a duchess.

When Geoffrey decided to ride back to Scotland after only a week, it looked like Adelaide's plan would work out even better than she originally hoped. The roads were notorious for highwaymen. People were robbed and killed on a regular basis on the roads going out of London. The two men Horace hired were none too smart however. They tried on two occasions to accost Geoffrey and his valet, to no avail. Finally, when they were almost back to Ainsley Glen, they got their chance. Geoffrey was shot, but so was one of the miscreants. He perished as well as Geoffrey.

But then, everything went wrong. Instead of marrying her beloved Beatrice, Edward had quickly married Diana and taken her away to Cornwall of all places. Adelaide could not believe she had spent so much time and money on her plan, only to have it fall through so bitterly. Now Diana MacDonald would be a duchess and her poor baby would have to settle for someone of lesser nobility. Adelaide felt absolutely no remorse about having Geoffrey killed. What she and her daughter wanted was all that mattered to her. Of course, she hadn't told Beatrice about her plan. Only Horace was privy to what had really happened to Geoffrey. He would never let a word slip from his lips. He had also silenced the other thug he had hired when he got back to London. Horace had handled it himself, so there was no one to ever know how Geoffrey had really died. Adelaide couldn't for the life of her figure out why Diana had married Edward when it was Geoffrey she had been engaged to. Adelaide finally decided Diana was only interested in being the Duchess of Bristol and she didn't care which brother she had to marry to become the duchess.

Chapter 15

For Diana, the weeks passed by very slowly. She had, after the first couple of days, met with Mrs. Smythe and the cook, Mrs. Evans. She found, just as Edward had told her, that Mrs. Smythe had the castle well in hand. About the only thing Diana was needed for was her input on the menus based on her personal likes and dislikes. After consulting with Edward, she found that he would basically eat anything. Therefore, she went over the daily menus with Mrs. Evans each morning and usually made few changes.

She, herself, was not eating much these days. Her morning sickness had now manifested itself to both morning and afternoon. She would rise in the mornings and be sick. After about an hour, she would be able to eat a light breakfast, but again in the afternoon, soon after luncheon, she would be ill again. Another hour would need to pass before she was truly feeling herself. Barbara was wonderfully kind to her during these times, never leaving her side.

Edward, on the other hand, kept his distance during the daytime. Diana was not sure if the sickness bothered him or the pregnancy itself. Since she mostly kept to her rooms during the day, she didn't see much of Edward. They would have dinner together each evening, then spend some time in one of the smaller drawing rooms. Their conversation was inane and dealt with only the most mundane topics. Edward, like Diana, was a great reader, so they discussed books or music. There was an incredibly beautiful pianoforte in the drawing room they used. Some nights, Diana would play and Edward sang. Other nights, Diana would play and Edward would just listen. Sometimes they sang together. He seemed to be in good spirits, but kept his distance from her emotionally.

As ill as Diana felt during the days, she was grateful to be left alone. She had never been sick a day in her life, so she was impatient with what she saw as her body's betrayal. Having no basis for comparison, she had no idea whether what she was feeling was normal or not. Barbara had never been married or carried a child, but she had been the oldest child in her family. After having been privy to her mother's several pregnancies, Barbara did have some experience. However, her mother had not suffered the same complaint as Diana, so she was really not a lot of help with what was going on right now.

During the Regency era, women were usually attended by a midwife at the time of the birth. Doctors were not normally called unless there were complications. There was no such thing as prenatal care in the nineteenth century.

When almost four months had passed, Diana began to experience some lessening of the daily illness. As her stomach grew larger, she began to feel better and take more interest in her surroundings. Her weight began to slowly increase as did her appetite. The weather had been so cold, she had not ventured out of doors since she had arrived at Bristol Castle. Now that it was nearing March, the weather, though still cold, was not so devastatingly impossible to go out in.

Edward still kept his distance. He and Diana had continued to share dinners until she began to feel better. After she started going down to breakfast and luncheon, she and Edward shared all their meals. On most days Edward appeared in one of his colorful outfits. This morning he appeared in a black coat and breeches with a white frilled shirt, and long black boots.

"Are you going somewhere today, Edward?"

"Yes, I am going to the local village to pick up some supplies and to gather the post. Would you care to join me? I don't believe you have left the house since you've been here. Surely, you must be longing for some fresh air after all this time."

"I am. Thank you for asking me. I would be very glad to accompany you. I have some letters to post myself."

"Wonderful. I was planning to leave after breakfast. Does that suit?"

"Yes, I will have Barbara bring my cloak and bonnet. Edmonds, will you please direct Barbara to bring my things down while we complete our breakfast, please?"

"Yes, my Lady. I will do so at once."

Diana had not gotten to know Edmonds very well. He was an austere man who said little. He did his job remarkably well. The household ran impeccably between he and Mrs. Smythe. Diana had not really gotten to know anyone in the household very well. Since she had been more or less confined to her chambers since her arrival, she hadn't even had a real tour of the house. So far, she had seen her chambers, the small drawing room, the front hall and the dining room. The castle had over fifty rooms she was told by Edward. She looked forward to exploring more since she was feeling much better.

Edmonds had the coach waiting at the front door when they had completed their meal. Edward took Diana's cloak and bonnet. He handed her the bonnet, then draped the cloak over her shoulders. After she tied her bonnet, Edward pulled her cloak snugly around her and buttoned it. It was the closest they had been in weeks. She glanced up at Edward and saw he was smiling down at her. She returned his smile.

The trip to the village took less than thirty minutes. During that time, Diana and Edward exchanged pleasantries about the weather and the dinner they had enjoyed the night before. As usual, their conversation was impersonal. They could have been any two strangers in a carriage travelling anywhere. Again Diana was struck by the strangeness of their marriage. While she had been ill, she had not expected, nor even wanted, Edward's attention. She had only wanted to be left alone in her misery. Since she was feeling better however, she longed for someone to really talk to.

After their errands had been accomplished in the village, Edward instructed the driver to take the coast road back to the castle. Diana was amazed by the majesty of the Cornish coast. The weather was sunny today and the wind was pleasant, not the usual gale blowing off the water she had become accustomed to.

"Edward, I have been meaning to speak to you."

Edward's face took on a closed expression as if he had been expecting this and dreading it.

"Yes, Diana. What was it you wished to speak to me about?"

"Well, this is rather embarrassing. I don't really know where to start or what to say exactly."

"I think I may be able to help you somewhat. You are curious about our marriage and what I expect of you, are you not?"

Diana was surprised by his astuteness. "Yes, that is it exactly. We have been married for several months, yet I don't feel as if I know you at all. I realize we have both been mourning Geoffrey and I have been quite ill. However, since I am now feeling much better I feel we should discuss our relationship."

"Well, Diana, there is not much to discuss in all reality. You are carrying my brother's child. I married you to keep that child from being a bastard. It was my father's wish and I complied. I expect nothing from you other than what you have already given. I have enjoyed our discussions on books and music. I enjoy singing to your accompaniment and hearing you sing and play. As a matter of fact, what I received in the post was some new sheet music I ordered for us to learn."

"Edward, do you not expect a real wife from this arrangement?" Diana asked as she blushed a very bright pink.

"By real wife, I assume you are referring to conjugal relations?" Edward was almost as pink as Diana.

"Well, yes. I went into this marriage on the assumption that someday we would have such. I don't mean to embarrass you, but I truly would like to know what kind of life we are going to live together."

"Diana," Edward looked down at his hands clasped tightly in his lap. Then he looked directly into her eyes. "I, I am not like Geoffrey. I, well, I don't have the same desires and needs he had. I will never be the kind of husband Geoffrey would have been to you. You and I will never consummate our marriage in the conjugal sense. My affections are otherwise engaged. Our marriage is much like a business arrangement. You will have your memories of Geoffrey and your child. I will have my freedom and never have to worry about how other people may judge my choices."

"Oh, Edward. I am so very sorry. I had no idea you loved another woman. Why didn't you say so. We could have found some other way to protect the baby. I feel terrible that you are bound in this marriage and cannot marry the woman you love. Does your father know you love someone else?"

"Diana, I don't love another woman. I love a man."

With those words, Diana almost stopped breathing. She looked at Edward with a shocked expression. She had heard whispers about that sort of thing, but had never known anyone who was homosexual. She didn't even know what that type of relationship entailed. At almost seventeen, Diana was innocent in so many ways.

Edward saw the look on her face and knew he would have to be even more open with her.

"Diana, I am in love with my valet, Benjamin. He and I have had a relationship for several years. Our love is illegal in this country and almost every other country. My father must never know what I have told you today. No one must know. I could be arrested and thrown into prison and even hung just for loving another man. My father could and probably would disinherit me as well. I have taken a great risk telling you this, but I feel a friendship has developed between us these last months. I am hoping that friendship will be enough to insure your silence on this matter. That is all I really am asking of you, just your silence and friendship."

Diana was silent for some time. Edward had begun to really worry when she said,

"Edward, I honestly don't know what to say. I am almost relieved. I know that sounds terrible, but I could not face having physical relations with a man I did not love. I was so worried about that I have been unable to sleep well at night. I like you very much. You have been very kind to me. But I don't feel any sort of attraction to you as a man. What I feel is more a sisterly affection and concern for you. Your secret is safe with me. I hope we can become very good friends. I need someone I can talk to and I think you may need the same. Let us agree to be very good friends to each other from now on."

Edward was shocked by Diana's reaction. He had expected recriminations and possibly hysterics. Instead, he had received an offer of friendship. This girl was remarkable and mature beyond her tender years. This farce of a marriage may well turn out to be the best thing ever to happen to him.

After dinner Diana and Edward adjourned to their usual small drawing room. They talked for hours. Edward was able to unburden himself about his homosexuality and Diana was able to speak about Geoffrey as she had never been able to do before. She had had no one to share her feelings with since she had no siblings nor close friends near her own age since Ian and Alana had left. They both felt a huge sense of relief.

Over the years Edward had developed a hard shell over his emotions. His fear of discovery and the constant worry attached to it had hardened him to a degree. However, with Diana, he discovered he could be truly himself. He didn't have to act at all. He found he could speak to her about Benjamin just as she could speak to him of Geoffrey. He had been somewhat contemptuous of Diana and Geoffrey's relationship at the beginning. Now, he felt an even more intense grief for the loss of his brother after seeing him through Diana's eyes. She had adored Geoffrey and saw in him qualities his own brother had not seen. Their conversation was an awakening for Edward.

Diana also learned much she had never known. She learned that Edward's feelings for his Benjamin were not so very different from hers for Geoffrey. Edward was very open about his feelings and his fears. Since she and Geoffrey had only been intimate once, she couldn't quite comprehend the passion Edward felt for Benjamin, but she did understand the love. When she told Edward that she and Geoffrey had only been together once, he admitted that he had known. He explained why he had come into the stable that night. Diana was upset that she and Geoffrey had been heard, but not angry. The fact that Edward had been with Benjamin on the same night was somehow comforting to her. She could not explain that fact, even to herself, it was just how she felt.

After that evening, Edward and Diana were pretty much inseparable. They spent their days and evenings together, but never their nights. Edward's nights belonged to Benjamin. Many evenings, Benjamin would join Diana and Edward in Diana's private drawing room. She would send Barbara downstairs to socialize with the other servants while the three of them enjoyed an evening of cards or charades.

Diana had never played either game, but the two men thoroughly enjoyed teaching her whist and the ins and outs of charades. They found her take on charades amusing. They discovered Diana was a born actress with a flair for the dramatic she had not known of herself. For the first time in months, Diana could laugh again.

As Geoffrey's baby grew inside her, she felt closer to him than ever. She could hardly wait for the baby to be born. Edward had told her of his plans to tour the Continent after their mourning period was over. She was enthusiastic about travelling, but a little apprehensive about taking a newborn on such a trip. Edward assured her they would take plenty of servants and take their time travelling for her convenience. He suggested a wet nurse, but Diana was adamantly against that. She wanted to feed her child herself. She knew society would frown upon this practice, nevertheless, she planned to feed her own child.

Possibly an extended trip to the Continent would help insure Diana's strange ideas about motherhood would not be the fodder for gossip it would be if they stayed in London, thought Edward. He had such a fear of discovery, he had always been extremely careful to adhere to all society's rules. He knew he could relax now, but still found it hard to get used to. Marrying Diana had turned out to be such a wonderful answer for he and Benjamin. They were all the best of friends now. He could be completely open around her. He had never experienced that type of freedom and it took some getting used to.

Edward thought that one day Diana might feel the desire or need to take a lover. He had absolutely no objections to that. He would encourage her if she made that decision. Right now, her baby was the entire focus of her life, other than her friendship with he and Benjamin, but he didn't expect that to be the case forever.

Chapter 16

The months passed and Diana became very heavy with child. She was very small, but this baby was quite large. Barbara was extremely worried for her friend and mistress. Edward was concerned as well. He wrote to his father who in turn wrote to Fergus. They both converged on the castle the same day bringing the duke's personal physician.

After examining Diana, Dr. Baker met with Edward, Fergus and Harold in the drawing room. His expression was grim making the three men very apprehensive.
"Lady Diana is carrying a very large child. Being as small as she is, she may encounter problems with the delivery. There is no way to be sure now, as she is not due for another month. She should not travel at this stage or I would have her come to London so I could be on hand. Is there a reputable physician nearby?"

The duke shook his head in the negative. "There is a physician some distance from here, but no one in the village. The closest would be inhi St. Ives some twenty miles distance. I would prefer that you stay here with Diana until she delivers. I will make whatever compensation you require."
"I will need to have one of my fellows take over my practice while I am gone. Can a message be sent today? I only arranged to be away for a few days." Dr. Baker said worriedly.

"Of course. Let me escort you to my office so you can write your missive. I will have one of the footman take a swift horse and ride for London right away."

The three men were much relieved that Dr. Baker would be staying for the duration. After Dr. Baker's note had been sent, they adjourned to the drawing room. Diana joined them after a time.

Fergus went to her side immediately. "My dear, should you be out of bed in your condition?"

"Oh, Da. I am not an invalid. I feel fine. It is just cumbersome to move about much, but I will be fine. Oh, Dr. Baker, you are still here. I would have thought you would have started back to London by now. I know you must be very busy."

"I will be staying until your confinement, my Lady. I will be at your disposal the entire time."

Diana was surprised to hear this. She looked at Edward and he looked worried as did her father and the duke.

"What are you not telling me, Dr. Baker? You didn't mention any problems when you examined me."

"I don't want to upset you my Lady, but you may have some complications with your confinement because of the size of the child. Your bone structure is such, you are so smally built, there is a possibility of your needing a physician instead of a midwife for the birth."

Diana was suddenly very apprehensive. She was not worried about herself. If anything happened to her baby, she didn't know how she would survive the loss. She looked to Edward. He immediately came to her side and put his arm around her shoulders.
"Not to fret, Hin. You will be fine. I know you will. We are just taking precautions. You are so precious to us, we felt the need to make sure you had every advantage. Dr. Baker is my father's personal physician and is very well known in London circles for his fine work. I'm sure you will be fine. Please don't worry."

Diana took comfort in Edwards reassurances. Both her father and the duke joined him in reassuring her as well. Her worry certainly didn't go away, but it did lessen somewhat. After a good dinner, Diana was feeling tired and decided to go upstairs. Edward escorted her to the staircase and assisted her up the stairs. Barbara was waiting in her bedchamber and helped Diana get ready for bed.

Lying in the huge bed, Diana again felt a terrible premonition that something was going to happen to her baby. The baby was very active and rolled and tumbled almost constantly now. Diana took comfort from the fact that he was so active. That must mean something she thought. It was several hours before sleep overcame Diana.

The days seemed to drag by for Diana and the three men who cared for her. Each day she found it harder to make it up and down stairs. Finally, two weeks before she was due, Dr. Baker told her she shouldn't make the trip again until after the birth of her baby. Edward spent much time with her trying to keep her entertained. He could see the worry eating away at her. They had become so very close, like brother and sister. He was very worried about her.

Finally on a fine morning in the middle of July, Diana awoke with her back hurting. She had been very uncomfortable for the last couple of days. As the day progressed, the pain moved from her back to her stomach. At first the contractions were several minutes apart and although uncomfortable, they were not painful. By six that evening, Diana was in labor in earnest. Her contractions became closer and closer until she was in constant pain, one contraction would end and another begin.

Barbara and Dr. Baker were in constant attendance. Edward, Fergus and Harold paced the floor in Diana's drawing room. There was little conversation between the men. They were all too worried about Diana to waste energy on words. They could hear Diana's moans and cries through the door. It seemed an eternity that they waited.

Inside Diana's bedchamber, Dr. Baker watched Diana closely. Barbara was behind her on the big bed holding her shoulders up while she labored to push the baby from her body. Diana was exhausted. She had been at this for hours and her strength was waning. Just as she thought she couldn't push again, she felt her baby's head between her legs. She cried out. Dr. Baker forgot modesty and threw back the covers. Diana's small body was stretched to the maximum and it was still not enough. Dr. Baker took his scalpel and cut her to make more room for the baby's large head. Blood gushed from the incision. When Diana pushed again, the head eased out another couple of inches. Dr. Baker encouraged her to try again.

"It's almost over, my Lady. One or two more good pushes and your child will be born. I know you are weary, but you must make the effort. Now, now push with all your might."

Diana took a big breath and bore down with all that was left of her energy. She felt a ripping sensation and an agonizing pain. She continued to push anyway. Suddenly, she felt her baby gush from her body along with a rush of blood.. She fell back completely exhausted and almost lost consciousness. Then the lusty bawling of her child brought her back. She opened her eyes to the most incredible sight. Dr. Baker was holding her son up for her to see. He was screaming and covered in mucus and blood, but he was the most beautiful sight she had ever seen. Tears flooded her eyes as she beheld her little miracle. Geoffrey's son. She had done it.

Dr. Baker quickly handed the baby to one of the maids who was assisting he and Barbara. Diana was losing a great quantity of blood not only from the incision the doctor had made, but from the great tear to her peritoneum the baby's large head had made. Dr. Baker must get her stitched up immediately to staunch the flow of blood, but first he had to deliver the placenta. Again he asked Diana to push and again she bravely complied even though she was weak almost to the point of passing out. Once the placenta was out, Diana did lose consciousness which was a blessing.

Dr. Baker quickly stitched Diana up. Ordinarily only a few stitches were required in these cases, but Diana required seventeen stitches to repair the damage. He had rarely seen a woman that torn who survived. This young woman was very strong though. She had managed to deliver a very large child. The baby was not overly fat, but was long and had a large head.

Having delivered both Edward and Geoffrey, Dr. Baker was not overly surprised by the size of the child. Both the boys had been large, but their mother was not a small woman. She had been tall with broad hips made for birthing.

This poor child, however, was very small with narrow hips. He didn't think she should try to have another child. She might not survive a second birth if the child was equally as large. She was still not out of the woods yet. Only time would tell if all the bleeding would stop. Even after the stitches were put in, there was still blood seeping from her wounds. Dr. Baker packed her with clean rags and left her to Barbara and the maids to clean up.

When the door of Diana's drawing room opened, Dr. Baker was faced with three very worried men.

"The child is a boy and it was a very difficult birth. The child is fine. The mother, however, had a very hard time. I have done all I can for now. Only time will tell whether she will make a full recovery. Right now she is resting and that is the best thing for her."

Edward clutched the doctor's arm. "May I see her? I just want to make sure she is all right."

"She would not know you were there. She is completely worn out. I don't believe she will wake for many hours. I will stay with her the entire time. There is still some bleeding I am worried about. You can see her when she wakes up."

Edward was not happy with this information. He needed to see Diana himself, but he had to comply with the doctor's wishes. The maid walked out the open door with the baby in her arms. He was no longer crying, but was not asleep. The men crowded around to look at the baby. Edward had never entertained any ideas about fatherhood. He had never expected to be around a newborn. He was surprised at the feeling of love that washed over him as he beheld Geoffrey's son. He was a fine looking baby. He had a large head of fine dark hair and light blue eyes just like Geoffrey's. He appeared quite large for a newborn, almost filling the maids arms.

Harold looked at his grandchild in wonder. He looked much as Geoffrey had looked when he was born. The same coloring, the same shape to his face. However, his nose was not like Geoffrey's, but like Diana's small and well shaped. Something about his eyes reminded him of Diana as well. Not the color, but the shape was very similar.

Harold looked at Fergus to see him studying his grandchild as well. Fergus walked closer and reached for the baby. The maid lay the child in his grandfather's arms. Fergus gazed down at the child with wonder. He could hardly believe his little girl had given birth to this beautiful, but large child. He was ecstatic and at the same time, very worried.

Dr. Baker asked that tea be sent up and returned to Diana's bed chamber. She was sleeping peacefully at the moment. He asked Barbara if the bleeding was still as heavy. She affirmed that when they cleaned Diana there was still a lot of blood. Diana's skin was very white and her breathing was shallow. She had lost entirely too much blood. Dr. Baker checked the rags between her legs and saw they were soaked again. He called for more rags and packed them tightly again. Diana did not stir during his ministrations.

All during the long night, Dr. Baker changed the rags. Each time, there was less blood. Finally around daybreak, he checked Diana again and found the rags dry and clean. He was much relieved. Sitting in a chair by the side of the bed, Dr. Baker finally succumbed to a few minutes of sleep. It had been a long day and night for his patient and himself.

Barbara kept watch while the doctor slept. She was so very worried about her little mistress. She had watched her mother give birth several times, but had never seen anything like this birth. So much pain and so much blood. She hoped to never go through something like this again.

The baby lay in it's cradle near the fireplace. One of the maids sat in a rocking chair nearby. Suddenly, the baby began to move about and cry. The poor little thing was hungry. The sound of her baby crying roused Diana. She opened her eyes and frantically looked for her child. Barbara saw her distress.

"The bairn is fine, my Lady. A big lusty boy. He's just hungry. The doctor has sent for a wet nurse. She should be here soon and then he'll be happy."

"No, no wet nurse. I will feed my child myself." Diana said as she struggled to sit up.

Dr. Baker awoke. "My Lady, you are too weak to nurse your child. A wet nurse will relieve you of that burden."

"I do not see feeding my child to be a burden, sir. I see it as a privilege. Please bring me my son."

Seeing the fire in her eyes, Barbara knew better than to argue with Diana. Her mistress was even tempered and very easy to get along with, but when she made up her mind to something, there was no changing it. Barbara picked the baby up and took him to his mother. Diana was so weak, she had trouble loosening her gown. Barbara helped her with it and lay the baby in her arms then piled more pillows behind her to raise her head and shoulders.

Diana's face was wreathed in smiles as she beheld her son for the first time. He looked like Geoffrey. She watched his little mouth latch onto her breast for the first time. The tugging sensation was not unpleasant, though slightly painful, as her nipples were very tender. Barbara had told her some new babies had trouble feeding the first time, but not this one. He seemed to know by instinct exactly what to do. He sucked greedily on her breast for some minutes. Barbara then picked him up and moved him to the other breast. When she first pulled him away, he started to cry, but quickly stopped when the other nipple was offered to him. Again, he suckled greedily and finally fell asleep when he was satiated.

Barbara took the baby from Diana and carried him back to his cradle by the fire. Diana was exhausted, but happy. Dr. Baker had turned away while she fed the child, but now turned back to check her over. He was surprised she had awoken so soon. He was also surprised to see her color was better. So far, there was no fever, but it still might come. He cautioned Diana to get more rest as she was far from well yet.

She was only too happy to follow the doctors orders. After some beef broth and tea, Diana settled against her pillows and closed her eyes. She swiftly drifted off the sleep. When Diana awoke, Edward was sitting on the edge of her bed holding her crying son.

"Is he all right?"

"Yes, he just woke and I believe he's hungry. Do you feel up to feeding him? If not, I can get the wet nurse. She has arrived and is downstairs."

"No, I will feed him. I feel much better. Have I been asleep long?"
Diana struggled to sit up, but gasped as she felt the pain in her lower regions. She hadn't noticed Barbara sitting near the cradle, but saw her as she lept from the chair to help. Barbara pulled the pillows up behind Diana so she was in a half reclining position. Edward handed her the baby very carefully. Then turned to go.

"Edward, will you come back when he's done. I would enjoy your company."

"Dr. Baker told me to only stay a few minutes that you need your rest. I would love to stay with you awhile though."

"Just let me get little Geoffrey fed, then come back. I am hungry myself. Barbara, will you see that a tray is sent up. Something more than broth and tea, please. I could happily eat one of my father's prized stallions."

Barbara and Edward both started to leave the room laughing. When Edward reached the door, he turned back. "So, you are naming the baby Geoffrey? He would be so pleased."

"Yes, Geoffrey Edward Benjamin Fergus Westmoreland. Since your father's middle name is Geoffrey, he is covered as well."

Edwards face was covered in a huge smile as he walked from the room. She was naming the baby after every one she loved, how like Diana, he thought. He hoped the baby would be able to grow into such a long name.

Diana spent several very enjoyable minutes holding her son and feeding him. Dr. Baker had gone to get some much needed rest and Barbara had gone down to get her food. For a few blessed moments, she was alone with her son for the first time. As she gazed at his sweet face, her heart filled with such love it was almost overwhelming. She saw Geoffrey in his little face and dark hair, but she also saw something of herself in the shape of his blue eyes and his nose. She was glad he hadn't gotten her red hair, but she would have liked for him to have looked just a little like her father. It looked like Geoffrey's blood had been the strongest if looks were any indication.

Barbara came back with a tray laden with food and took the sleeping baby back to his cradle. After Diana had feasted on eggs, bacon, buttered toast and jam with two cups of chocolate, she felt much better. She was horribly sore and still felt weak, but she didn't feel ill at all. When she moved she felt the pull of her stitches quite strongly. She needed the chamber pot, but when she tried to swing her legs over the edge of the bed, the pain made her so weak, she collapsed onto the pillows. Barbara and one of the upstairs maids brought the screen and the chamber pot near the bed and helped her onto it.

Barbara had tried to carefully pull the rags away from her lower body while she was still lying down, but they had stuck to her skin with dried blood. When Diana was seated on the chamber pot which was fitted into a chair with no bottom, Barbara poured warm water over her to loosen the rags. They finally fell off into the pot beneath. The warm water had made Diana urinate and the pain from that was almost overwhelming. Barbara and the maid,

Glenda, had to support her on each side to keep her from falling from the chair. It was some minutes before Diana gained enough strength to try to get back into bed. While she was resting, the maid stripped the bed and made it with freshly ironed sheets. Barbara helped Diana into a fresh nightgown and brushed her hair, rebraiding it into a long braid down her back.

Just as Diana was about to try to return to her bed, there was a knock on her drawing room door. Barbara hurried to answer it. Fergus stood in the doorway looking ten years older than he had the day before. The lines of worry and fatigue stood out glaringly on his face. He asked about Diana. When she heard his voice, she called for Barbara to show him in.

When he saw Diana sitting on the commode chair in her nightgown, he thought she looked as she had when she was a little girl, her rich auburn hair hanging in a braid down her back and wearing a frilly white nightgown. Except her face, he thought, her face looks like a woman's face. She was still pale, but some color was returning.

"Come in Da. I was about to try to get back to bed. I can wait though if you want to see your grandson first."

"Nonsense, lassie. I will put you to bed myself."

With that, Fergus strode to the commode chair and lifted Diana easily in his strong arms depositing her in her bed. Barbara pulled the covers up and plumped her pillows into a semi-sitting position. Fergus sat down on the edge of her bed and stared at her.

"Well, Da, do I look different? You are staring at me."

"Sorry, lassie. I was so very worried about you last night. The doctor was alarmed about the amount of blood you lost. However, you don't look really ill. How do you feel?"

"I am fine Da. I am that sore, but I will be right as rain in a few days. Have you seen my Geoffrey? Is he not the most beautiful bairn you have ever beheld?"

"He is a fine young lad, but no, you were the most beautiful bairn I ever saw. And you are still my beautiful bairn." Fergus said with a hint of moisture in his eyes.

Diana was alarmed at how much her father seemed to have aged in just the few months since she had last seen him. His sandy hair was more gray than blonde now and the lines in his dear face had deepened so much. Sometimes she forgot that her Da was not a young man. Diana had been born when her parents were somewhat older than most parents of the period. They had tried for years to have a baby and had almost given up hope when Diana had been born.

"So, you have decided to name the bairn after his father? It's a fine name and one he shared with his own father."

"Aye, I know. His full name is Geoffrey Edward Benjamin Fergus Westmoreland What do you think of that?"

"Well now, that is quite a mouthful. I am that proud that you have included my name among the others. It is a rare honor and one I most assuredly appreciate with all my heart. Your mother wanted to tack Fergus on to you if you had been a boy, but I hadn't wanted the confusion, so she had chosen Fergus as one of the other names just as you did. She would have been so proud of you and her grandson. I wish with all my heart my Morna was here this day."

"So do I Da. I miss Mama so much. It hardly seems seven years have passed since she left us. It seems strange that I have turned seventeen this March and we lost her in April just after my tenth birthday."

"Aye lass, seven long hard years without my Morna. You were a great blessing to me when she passed and ever since. I have not told you what you mean to me, Diana, in many years. I love you with all my heart, lass."

"I know Da. I know. And I love you. You have always been the best father a lassie could want. I would wish my child to have a father half as good and strong as my own."

"Ah, speaking of fathers. How do you think Edward will fare as a father to little Geoffrey? Has he been a good husband to you?

"Edward will make a wonderful father. He has become my best friend. He has been very supportive and kind during this whole time. I do not love him as I did Geoffrey, but we are well suited."

Fergus got the feeling his daughter was being evasive about her marriage to Edward. They had been married several months now and Diana seemed content. Fergus was still uncomfortable around Edward and he didn't know why. It had been obvious the night before when she was in danger that Edward cared for her, but he seemed to feel more brotherly affection than the love of a husband.

Well, Diana had been pregnant the entire time they had been wed. Mayhap, Edward did not fancy bedding a pregnant woman. Some men in society left their wives strictly alone when they were breeding he knew. He had not been of that mind set and he doubted Geoffrey would have been either. Ah well, it was not for him to question his daughter about such things. She seemed content and that would have to do for now. Maybe in the future she would develop feelings for Edward and he for her. It was Fergus' wish for his daughter. He hated to see her in a loveless marriage.

After visiting with Diana for a short time, Fergus could tell she was fatigued. He walked over to the cradle and peered down at the bairn lying there sound asleep. He was a fair bairn, no doubt of that. Fergus was a proud grandda for sure.

When he turned again to Diana, she had fallen asleep. Her long dark lashes lay on her cheek. She had one hand curved around her wee head and the other laying over her still swollen belly. She looked so very sweet and beautiful as she slept. Fergus nodded to Barbara, who had taken up her place in the rocking chair near the cradle, as he made his way out of the bedchamber.

Fergus went in search of Harold. They had been up most of the night worried for Diana, each of them seeking their beds when the doctor told them he was guardedly optimistic about her as she was doing better. Fergus had only been able to sleep a few hours before worry roused him. Now that he had seen Diana and knew she was doing well, he felt a great weight had been lifted from him.

Fergus found Harold and Edward in the small drawing room the family seemed to favor. He had been directed there by Edmonds when he came downstairs. The day was warm so no fire was burning, but Edward stood in front of the fireplace with one arm resting on the mantle. He looked tired too, as did Harold. Only Harold also looked ill to Fergus. He had no idea if Harold had confided in Edward about his illness, so he didn't bring attention to his friends health.

Fergus gave them an update on Diana's condition. Edward seemed very pleased by this information, as did Harold.

"Now son, since Diana is doing better, shouldn't you get some rest yourself. I know you didn't go to bed when we did because Edmonds told me you spent several hours in Diana's room with the baby after we retired."

"I couldn't just go to bed not knowing for sure that Diana was going to be all right. I sat in her room and held little Geoffrey until he awoke. When Diana was so adamant about feeding him herself, I knew she was going to get well. I have been too excited to sleep thus far. Perhaps, I will go up and try to rest awhile since Diana and Geoffrey are both asleep now. I will have Benjamin check with Barbara periodically and let me know when they are both awake again."

With that, Edward left the room. Harold looked after him with a bemused expression on his face.

"I am not sure what I expected of Edward, but his devotion to little Geoffrey and Diana comes as something of a surprise to me. His behaviour throughout this whole ordeal has been confusing to me. He seems to really care for Diana, but I can't help but feel the affection is more brotherly than anything else."

"That is exactly what I was thinking just minutes ago. Diana told me she is content and that she and Edward are well suited. However, there was no love light in her eyes when she spoke of him. That light still shines for Geoffrey and for Geoffrey's child. Do you think we may have doomed the two of them to a loveless marriage for the rest of their lives? I certainly hope not for both their sakes."

"Who knows what the future will bring, Fergus. Many good marriages have started with a lot less. Only time will tell if we made a terrible mistake insisting they wed. Edward didn't seem to have given his affections elsewhere, so maybe there is hope for them."

"Speaking of hope, what does Dr. Baker say about your condition? Have you informed Edward yet?"

"Dr. Baker says I may have another year, but not much more than that. I feel more run down and weaker all the time. I am only able to sleep a few hours at a time, so I am always tired. When I lie down I feel a terrible weight on my chest. I am getting my affairs in perfect order before I inform Edward. I fear he will not take the news well. He has never aspired to be a duke nor has he been trained for that responsibility. I must cram several years into less than one to prepare him for the duchy and all it entails."

"I am more than sorry, my friend. I always thought, since I am some years older, that I would be the first to go. It saddens me that I will be losing one of the best friends I have ever known."

"Ah, do not get maudlin on me, Fergus. Let us have a spot of brandy and talk horses or hunting. I have no wish to dwell on my own demise."

Chapter 17

And so they did. For several hours the two men drank brandy and discussed many things, but never Harold's health. When Edward came back downstairs later, he found them still in the drawing room talking away, each with a glass in their hands. Edward had not been drinking at all since he and Diana had become such good friends, not even wine with dinner. Wine had been hard on Diana's stomach during her pregnancy, so Edward had Edmonds stop serving it with dinner. He had not missed it, he found.

Before his confession to her about his lifestyle, he had felt a great deal of pressure from their marriage. He didn't know how to handle being a husband and was uncomfortable in Diana's company as a result. He had taken to drinking in the evenings with Benjamin in his rooms, after Diana went to bed. He knew he was drinking too much, but couldn't seem to sleep without it. He had had too many worries to settle into sleep, so he drank himself to sleep every night. Benjamin had tried to talk to him about it, but Edward was in no mood to listen. His drinking had even begun to cause problems between he and Benjamin because he became so foul when he drank so much.

Then, when Diana had been so accepting of his love for Benjamin and of Benjamin himself, that pressure had disappeared. Once again, Edward fell asleep almost immediately without the aid of alcohol. The three of them had developed a very close relationship in the last few months. Benjamin had even been excited about the baby. He came from a large family and babies had been commonplace in his home.

Edward had met Benjamin Jenkins at Eton. He was not of noble birth, but his father had made a fortune in coal mining in Cornwall making Eton a possibility for his sons. Unfortunately, a mining accident had claimed his father's life leaving Benjamin's older brother, Rupert, in charge. Rupert had run through the family money in short order. Soon Benjamin had to leave Eton and go home.

When Edward had learned of Benjamin's difficulties, he had written asking him to become his valet when he went up to Oxford. It was very soon after that, the two of them fell in love. They had been devoted to each other since. Edward depended on Benjamin completely emotionally. Benjamin was the stronger of the two and tried to keep Edward's more volatile nature in check.

Benjamin was as fond of Diana as Edward was. He had been up all night too, although he couldn't wait with Edward as he would have wished to. He had stayed in their rooms walking the floors waiting to hear some news of his friend, Diana. He had been elated when Edward brought the news that Diana was going to be all right.

He was anxious to visit her, but knew it would turn heads if he did. Valets didn't visit their employer's wives in their bedchambers. It just was not done. The fact that he spent so much time in Diana's drawing room with Edward had not gone unremarked by the other servants in the castle. He knew the relationship the three of them shared was fodder for gossip below stairs, but as long as the duke was not in residence, they had gotten away with it. While the duke was here, they would have to be circumspect in all ways.

When Edward had visited Diana after awakening from his nap with Benjamin, he had been impressed on how much better she was already. When he went into the room, she was about to nurse Geoffrey again. He started to leave, but she stopped him.

"You may as well come in. I will be doing this several times a day from now on. I don't expect you to get up and leave every time the bairn is hungry. You will be running back and forth constantly. He is eating every two to three hours. I cannot seem to fill him up." she said laughingly. "Just let me get him started and then I will cover his head with a blanket so I don't embarrass either of us."

Edward turned his back and when she was done, he turned around. His heart overflowed as he watched Diana gaze down at little Geoffrey. She had so much love in her eyes they absolutely sparkled. How he wished his brother was here to see this scene. Geoffrey would have been so proud of his son and Diana. Though he and Geoffrey had not been close as they grew older, they had been inseparable as boys. He had hero worshipped Geoffrey who was always smarter, stronger and better at everything than his little brother, Edward.

Diana glanced up at him and smiled. "Where is Benjamin? I want him to see our Geoffrey. I feel he belongs to the three of us, not just me."

"He wants to come, but is afraid of what the gossips would make of it. As you know, our evenings have not gone unnoticed below stairs. He does not wish to make waves, especially while my father is here."

"Nonsense. We cannot leave him out. We will just have to figure some way for him to come without anyone knowing." Diana thought a few moments and said brightly, "Oh, I know. That door over there. Doesn't it pass through to the chambers set aside for the duke? Is your father using those rooms while he is here?"

"No, he has taken rooms near your father for his stay. He asked me why I hadn't been using the rooms myself last night. And yes, that door opens into the bedchamber."

"Well, that solves it then. You must move into the rooms next door. Benjamin would be the one moving your clothes and things. I will send everyone else away on some excuse or another and Benjamin can come visit me and little Geoffrey whenever the coast is clear. And he can continue to come because he will be staying in those rooms from now on"

Edward laughed at Diana's enthusiasm. He was intrigued by her ability to work through problems so quickly and easily. Her mind seemed to be so nimble and quick. It was one of the things he admired most about her, her intelligence and her generosity. She had welcomed Benjamin into her life with open arms. She had accepted that he and Edward loved each other and had never issued one word of condemnation to either of them. Edward did not know if her being raised more or less out of society had contributed to her having an open mind, but he was very pleased that she did.

Edward rushed to his rooms to advise Benjamin of Diana's plan. Benjamin immediately began to gather Edward's clothes and personal items for the move. They agreed on a signal of two knocks on the adjoining door when the coast was clear for Benjamin to visit. In less than an hour, there were two knocks on the door and Benjamin stuck his head around the door. Diana bade him come in and give her a hug. Benjamin hurried to the bed and gently put his arms around Diana giving her a loving hug.

"Oh, Benjamin, you have to go and see Geoffrey. He is such a little pig. He ate for over thirty minutes and then went straight to sleep. Go get him, he sleeps like a rock. You won't wake him up."

Benjamin walked to the cradle and picked up the sleeping child.

"Ah, Diana, what a wonderful thing you have done. You have brought a new life into this world. And such a bonny sweet bairn as you would say."

Diana laughed. Shortly after the three of them had formed their friendship, Benjamin had begun to tease Diana about her Scottish brogue. He and Edward spoke with impeccable accents, but Diana used a lot of Scottish idiom in her speech. Her accent and expressions had become fodder for a running joke between she and Benjamin.

"Aye, he is a bonny wee bairn though, is he no?" she said with an even broader accent than usual.

Laughing, Benjamin said, "That he is my sweet, that he is."

Edward joined them shortly through the connecting door. The three friends had a wonderful visit and made plans for when Benjamin could come again. They had found the perfect solution to their gossip problem, thanks to Diana.

The next day Dr. Baker pronounced Diana well on the way to recovery and with the duke left for London. Edward and Diana were disappointed that the duke had to return to Town so quickly. He requested that they join him at the house in Town as soon as Diana was able to travel. He made it sound very important that they come as soon as they could, which they both found odd.

Fergus planned to stay for a couple of weeks before travelling back to Scotland. He knew he wouldn't get another opportunity to visit with Diana for several months. Since he was privy to Harold's diagnosis, he also knew that Edward would be extremely busy for the next few months learning how to handle the ducal responsibilities that would regrettably soon be his.

Chapter 18

After just three days, Diana was up and around. She had been told to stay in bed for a full two weeks by Dr. Baker, but simply could not stand to do so. She had always been energetic and having a baby hadn't changed that at all. She had also found lying down made her more sore than moving around. None of the tenants wives had stayed in bed for so long. Some of them were up the same day they gave birth. She didn't see why she should lie abed when she felt so well. When no one was in the room with her, she would get up and walk slowly around her room. She felt much better for the exercise.

Geoffrey continued to thrive. He ate more and more each day and started to put on weight and fill out. He was a good baby and rarely cried except when wet or hungry. Diana wanted to spend every minute with him when he was awake. She would hold him and speak to him about his father. She planned to tell him, when he was old enough, that Edward was not his father, but his uncle. She wanted him to know what kind of man his father was. She told Edward this and he was agreeable. Surprisingly, Edward doted on the baby also. He spent many happy hours in Diana's bedchamber with her and the baby, as did Benjamin.

Benjamin and Edward both encouraged Diana to take the baby out into the castle's beautiful garden every day. The garden had high walls and was protected from the constant wind coming off the sea. The three of them would gather up all the needed paraphernalia for Geoffrey and spend hours in the garden in the sunshine.

Fergus would join them on most days. He did think it odd that they were joined by Benjamin, but since Benjamin carried most of the needed baby items, Fergus didn't think too much of it. The young people seemed to enjoy each other's company and that was good enough for him. Never having stood on ceremony himself, he was not surprised that Diana paid little heed to strict societal rules of conduct. She had not been raised with the usual constraints put on people of noble birth because she had been raised in an isolated location at Ainsley Glen. With Morna being ill for so many years, they had not entertained much.

Diana had led a very sheltered life, making friends with the tenant's children when she was very young as well as Alana Campbell from the nearby village. She also counted her maid, Barbara as a friend. When she was older, her friends had been Alana, the tenant's wives and older daughters as well as a few children of the neighboring nobility. Fergus could not think of one young lady of noble birth that Diana truly counted as a friend. He was somewhat worried she would find the constraints of life in London little to her liking. He took it upon himself to warn her of what she might face living there.

"Lass, there is something I need to speak to you about. When you and Edward go to London next month, there will be certain expectations for your behavior. The ladies of the *ton* will eat you alive if they know you entertain Edward's valet in your private drawing room or take him with you on outings. I see nothing wrong with it myself, but I have a more egalitarian turn of mind than those old biddies do. I would hate to see you ostracized by them for the company you keep."

"Oh, Da, I know. Both Edward and Benjamin have been telling me about the ogresses of Almacks and the snooty dowager duchesses. They have warned me I will have to watch what I say and do every minute we are in the public eye. Neither Edward nor I plan to attend many social functions if we can keep from it. We will still be in mourning until late October, so we won't have to go anywhere until then. Personally, I find the whole social hierarchy tedious. You have never stood on ceremony at Ainsley Glen and we are none the worse for it."

"Aye, lass, but then I am only a Scottish earl, not an English duke. The rules for them are far more strenuous than they are for the likes of me. I never thought you would be marrying into a family such as this or I would have tried to prepare you better. I had thought for many years, you would be marrying Ian and living at Ainsley Glen the rest of your life. By the way, have you heard from young Ian?"

"Yes, I received a letter right before the baby was born. In all the excitement of Geoffrey's arrival, I forgot to mention it to you. He and Alana are doing very well. Their child was born, it was a boy. They named him Angus after Ian's Da. They have their new home almost complete and will be moving into it before winter. I wrote to him as soon as I reached Bristol Castle to let him know I was married and where to write me."

"Ach, I am that glad the boy is doing well. Every time I think of what you and he pulled, I am tempted to laugh. Although what it did to Angus is no laughing matter. He is still not doing well at all. Has Ian written to his Da?"

"Yes, he has written several times, but had no response. He has been writing to his brother Robert and he has received answers to those letters. I am sure Robert has been telling his father how Ian is doing. I am that surprised that Laird MacAllister has not seen fit to respond to Ian's letters. It seems he would have gotten over his disappointment by now."

"You would think so, but Angus is a hard man. Even as a lad, when he didn't get his way, he would hold a grudge for a long time. It is my hope he will relent and contact Ian, and soon."

To Diana it seemed Fergus' visit came to an end much too quickly. On the day he was to leave, Diana, Edward and little Geoffrey stood in the courtyard at the front of the castle to bid him goodbye. Fergus swung himself up into his coach and waved his hat out the window until he was across the great bridge over the moat. He had brought several outriders with him for the hazardous journey all the way across England from Scotland. He also had his driver and four footmen for added protection. Highwaymen made the roads unsafe for all but well protected travellers.

Chapter 19

For the next two weeks, there was a flurry of preparation for Edward and Diana's trip to London. They had been instructed by the duke to bring all their belongings. Apparently, they were not coming back to the castle any time soon. Diana, Barbara and the castle seamstresses had spent the weeks prior to Geoffrey's birth making blankets, caps, dresses and all manner of booties and little socks so he was well outfitted.

Diana, however, needed a new wardrobe. Her body had changed with her pregnancy. Her bosom had never been exactly small, but now was much larger. Most of her chemises were too tight across her chest as were her gowns. She still had several months of mourning, so all her new clothes would need to be black. She was lucky with her coloring, black was very becoming to her. Diana and Barbara went through all her clothes and found only two gowns that she could still wear in comfort.

Edward informed her that she wouldn't need many gowns at first. He had decided to take her to a modiste he had heard of in London for the clothes she would wear after her mourning was over. He wanted to outfit her in beautiful colors to bring out her flashing green eyes and lovely auburn curls. Being a proponent of Beau Brummel himself, he could hardly wait to see his good friend tricked out in bright, rich colors like copper, sapphire blue, emerald green and gold.

He planned to have a new wardrobe made for himself and Benjamin as well. Edward still wanted to take the Continental tour he had been planning. Now, it would be even more exciting because Diana and Geoffrey would be along. They would have such fun, he thought. He could hardly wait to show Benjamin and Diana all the sights in Rome and Paris. He and his brother, Geoffrey, had been taken by their parents when they were younger to see all the usual sights in France, Italy, Greece and even Germany. He relished his role as tour guide to the two people he loved most in the world.

Finally, the whirlwind of sewing and packing was done. The day dawned for them to start their trip to London. They would have four carriages this time. They needed almost an entire carriage for all the equipment needed for the baby and his nursemaid, a carriage for Barbara and Benjamin, one for their luggage and of course the one they would ride in themselves. With all the outriders and footmen necessary for safety, their party would number thirty-one. Diana's mind was boggled at the thought of finding lodging for that many people every night. It would take at least five days to reach London if the weather held.

They would be travelling on one of the new Turnpike roads that had been built to help convey miners and their products to London and beyond for sale. The roads charged a toll for each wagon or pack mule that crossed it. There were toll houses built at each end of the road and toll takers were housed in them. The houses had an octagonal front wall with windows looking up and down the road for travellers. There were usually two toll takers per house as they were open twenty-four hours a day. One could sleep while the other collected tolls.

Edward convinced Diana that accommodations should be no problem as there were plenty of inns and public houses on the new roads. Since mining was a huge business in Cornwall, the roads experienced heavy traffic moving coal, hence the need for plenty of good accommodation along it.

Edward handed Diana into the first carriage. She was surprised and very pleased to see that a small cradle had been fastened between the seats on one side for Geoffrey. Unlike many Regency mothers, Diana did not want her child to travel with his nursemaid in a separate carriage. She could not bear to be away from her bairn for hours on end. Also since she was nursing him herself, it was necessary for him to ride with she and Edward.

As Edward climbed into the carriage, she smiled at him and thanked him for his foresight and kindness.

"Well, you are very welcome. However, I cannot take credit for the cradle. That was Benjamin's idea. He and the carpenter worked on the design for three days. It is sturdy and safe. Geoffrey should be quite comfortable for this journey."

"I must thank him right away," Diana said and started to the door of the carriage. Just as she reached the door, Benjamin's head appeared. He was carrying Geoffrey and a bag of clothes and nappies.

"Oh, Benjamin, I was just coming to thank you for the cradle. It was so thoughtful of you. I really appreciate your kindness."

"Well, I couldn't be having our little duke or his lovely mother being uncomfortable, now could I? My Lord, could you take the baby so I can stow his bag of necessities away before we leave, please?"

Edward took Geoffrey as Diana seated herself. Edward handed her the sleeping baby and took the bag from Benjamin placing it on the seat beside him.

"I believe, my Lord, you will find the bag will fit under the cradle perfectly. I fear it may slide off the seat and hit the little duke while he is sleeping otherwise."

Edward stowed the bag under the cradle and they were finally ready to depart. Diana lay the sleeping baby into the cradle. She noticed that the cradle was somewhat deeper than the one they had packed in with the nursemaid. She assumed that was for safety's sake as well. In the jostling of the carriage, there was no chance that Geoffrey might be thrown out of the cradle. Benjamin had thought of everything, as usual. She thanked him again and gave him a bright smile.

Finally, the four carriages were loaded and ready to leave. Diana settled back into the seat across from Edward and tried to compose herself for the trip. She had bad memories of the long arduous journey that had brought them from Ainsley Glen to Bristol Castle. She hoped this trip would be an easier one. At least it would be a shorter one.

At the end of the first day, Diana was exhausted. Geoffrey had slept the first two hours, but then had awakened fussy. She had changed and fed him, but nothing she did seemed to satisfy him. It was the first time he had been fussy like this and she was worried. As a new mother, she worried all the time. Since she had never been around small babies on a daily basis, she had no frame of reference to depend on. She had read all the available pamphlets on child rearing, but they had been sparse and not very enlightening. She did know there were any number of causes for a baby to be fussy, she just didn't know enough about the distinct signs to tell what Geoffrey's real problem was.

When the party stopped for luncheon, Diana had Edward bring the nursemaid, Bertha, to their carriage to get advice. Bertha looked

Geoffrey over, felt of his little head, and then put her hand under his dress to check his stomach.

"I believe the poor little mite may have the colic. His wee tummy is swollen and tight. The way he pulls his little legs up when he squalls may mean his tummy is hurting him."

"What can we do, Bertha? He just cries and cries."

"He needs some onion broth. Though I don't know where we are going to get it here on the road."

"Onions for a newborn? That doesn't sound right."

"Yes, my lady. That's what we always gave me brothers and sisters when they were colicky. Ye boil the onions and then give them the broth. It seems to settle them down right well, it does."

"Thank you Bertha. We will have to just wait until we stop for the night. We will have some made at the inn we will be staying at."

Edward was as worried about Geoffrey as Diana. He had grown very attached to his nephew. After luncheon, Edward took Geoffrey so Diana could rest for awhile. He tried rocking him to no avail. Finally, Diana asked Edward to sing to him. Although he protested he knew no lullabies, she said it didn't matter, any song would do.

When Edward started to sing a slow love song in his beautiful tenor voice, Geoffrey became very quiet. He stared up at his uncle with his light blue eyes so like his father's. After three songs, Geoffrey finally went to sleep. Edward lay him down in his cradle. Edward was most pleased with himself that he had been able to stop the babe from crying. He looked up at Diana and smiled. She had drifted off the sleep herself.

The peace lasted for about two hours and then Geoffrey was crying again. Diana changed and fed him again, but that only stopped the crying for a short time. She did as Bertha had and checked his little stomach. Sure enough, it felt swollen and hard. She could hardly wait until they arrived at the inn so she could have some onion broth prepared. She had high hopes for its efficacy, after all Bertha was experienced and she was not.

As soon as the party arrived at the inn, Diana inquired of the landlord about the onion broth. Being a father of six himself, he was familiar with the concoction. He called to his wife in the kitchen. A short, stout woman with dark curly hair and a smiling face came around the counter. Diana explained what she needed.

"No problem, my lady. I'll get it on right away. Ye go on up to your rooms and I'll have my daughter bring it up as soon as it cools. Do ye have the means to give it to the babe?"

"Well, no. I thought I would try to give it to him with a spoon. Is there some other way?"

The older woman looked at the young mistress with a smile.

"Aye, ye can use a rubber nipple on a glass bottle. I have just what ye need in the kitchen. Never ye worry, now. We will get ye fixed up right soon."

After thanking the landlord's wife, Diana tiredly mounted the stairs. Edward, Barbara, and Benjamin were already above stairs sorting out the rooms. Diana, Barbara and the baby would share a room with the nursemaid, Bertha. Thankfully it had two beds. Barbara and Bertha would sleep in one and Diana in the other. Edward and Benjamin would share the other. They also had a small sitting room between the bedchambers. Shortly after they had all gotten settled in, there was a knock at the door. Barbara opened the sitting room door to admit a very pretty dark haired girl of about twelve. She had a tray with a napkin covering it. On the tray was what looked like a smaller version of a wine bottle with a rubber nipple covering the opening. The bottle contained a somewhat cloudy broth that smelled decisively of onions. Also on the tray was a flask filled with the broth.

"Me mother said to tell ye she will make more of the broth for ye to take with ye on yer journey tomorrow." the girl said with a curtsy.

Diana thanked her and proceeded to try to get the crying baby to drink the broth. It took Geoffrey a bit to get the hang of the rubber nipple, but after a few tries, Diana was able to get a few ounces of the broth into him. He continued to cry for a few more minutes then he burped very loudly and became quiet. All the adults were instantly relieved. The crying had worn on every one's nerves, but especially Edward's and Diana's as they had been alone in the carriage with him for hours. Bertha took the baby and sat in a rocking chair near the hearth. After only a few minutes of rocking, Geoffrey was finally sleeping peacefully.

After a good meal of roasted beef, potatoes, root vegetables and bread, the weary travelers took to their beds. They all knew this was just the beginning of their long journey to London Town. The next morning all rose before dawn to get ready for the day's travels. After breaking their fast with fresh meat pies and tea, they were ready for whatever the day might bring. The landlord's wife had filled their picnic baskets for them. There would be no need to try to find a place for luncheon, they would have it with them. The flask of onion broth was included as well, much to every one's relief.

The next days seemed to pass much as the first. The biggest difference was Geoffrey. After the first two days, his colic seemed to disappear much to every one's surprise. He became his usual eating ,sleeping, making nappy messes little self. Geoffrey was almost six weeks old and had grown substantially in that short time. The dark fuzz on his head was thicker as was his little body. His eyes were so much like his father's that Diana received a small frission of pain each time she gazed into them. It had been almost a year since Geoffrey had been killed, but the pain had only slightly subsided, it definitely was not gone.

Chapter 20

At last the travelers arrived in London. Diana was aghast at the sights and smells that made up London. She had never been in a city like it. Inverness was a very small village in comparison. She had only been to Edinburgh once and that was when she was a small child, but it too was nothing in comparison. These London streets were crowded with every type of vehicle and person. She saw everything from small children begging on street corners to society dames accompanied by their servants going from shop to shop. The noise was incredible to her as was the smoke in the air. The air was almost palpable. It was as if she could reach out and touch it. She could feel her throat closing as she tried to breathe it in. She thought it must be very bad for her baby and covered his little face with a blanket. Thankfully, he was sleeping and didn't seem to notice.

They went directly to the duke's mansion in Mayfair. Diana, after living in the castle, was not surprised that the house was huge. Edward told her it had sixteen bedrooms not including the servants quarters. The house was four stories tall and had beautiful mullioned windows on every floor. It was made of light colored stone and built in the Gothic revival style with several spires on the gabled roof.

The grounds were fenced and gated, with two guards in a little house to one side of the gate. As soon as they recognized the duke's crest on the first carriage, the gates were swung wide. When the carriages pulled up in front of the imposing structure, the door was opened and several footmen and maids along with the butler, Forbes, came out of the house. Soon, the duke emerged as well.

Diana and Edward were taken aback when they saw the duke. They had seen him only a few weeks earlier when Geoffrey was born, but he looked so very frail now, they were immediately concerned. Edward was the first to alight and immediately went to his father.
"Are you well, sir? You seem a bit pale."

"No, Edward, I am not well. That is why I have insisted that you come to London as quickly as possible. We have much to discuss. But let us go into the house. Ah, here is our pretty Diana and my grandson."

Diana had been assisted from the carriage by Benjamin, who then reached into the cradle and handed her the sleeping baby. She hurried to the duke's side and they all entered the huge foyer without further ado. She noticed right away how thin and pale the duke appeared, as well as how slowly he moved.

"Your grace, have you been ill? You should have sent for us. We would have come sooner had we known." Diana gently chided the older man.

"Come, come. Let us go into the library. We will have tea served and then we will talk. There is much I must tell you both."

After a maid had brought a tea tray and everyone was served, Edward again asked his father about his health.

"I don't really know how to tell you this, so I will be blunt. I have something wrong with my heart. The doctor tells me I may only have a few months, maybe a year, to live. I have known for some small amount of time, but didn't want to worry you when I saw you last. There was enough going on with the birth of this fine baby." The duke looked at the sleeping baby in Diana's arms with great sadness. "I was so looking forward to watching this young one grow up. I am sorry to break the news to you both in this fashion, but we have so little time and there is so very much to tell you both."

Edward was in shock. His father had always seemed larger than life. So strong and sure. He had always been the rock Edward leaned on emotionally. He had never felt his father understood him, but his father had always been there and that was enough. Edward's thoughts pitched headlong into fear. If his father died, he would have to take over all the duties of being the head of the family and the Duke of Bristol. He didn't know how to be a duke nor how to take care of other people. He had never been responsible for anyone except himself and he hadn't done a very good job of that until Diana had come into his life. He had thought this day would not come for many years into the future. He was consumed with panic. All he really wanted at this stage in his life was to take the planned trip to the Continent and have a good time with his lover and Diana who was his good friend and his wife.

He had been doing so well these last months. He had his drinking totally under control. Benjamin had tried for years to curb Edward's carousing and drinking to no avail. Diana and the baby had had a wonderful settling influence on him. He hadn't over indulged with alcohol since he and Diana had reached their understanding. As a matter of fact, other than an occasional glass of wine with dinner, he had drunk no alcohol. His mind had been settled and he had been very happy these last few months for the first time since he was very young. Now this, what was he to do, he thought.

Diana was similarly disturbed by the bad news. First Geoffrey and now the duke. What was happening? She did not consider herself close to the duke, but he was Edward's father and her son's grandfather, and she liked him a great deal. She loved Edward dearly, but she had a sinking feeling he was not up to taking over the duchy at this point in his life. He was still so very immature. Although he was some years older than her, at two and twenty, she often felt the older of the two. He just wanted to have fun. That was his whole outlook on life, how to have fun. Diana wished Benjamin had been able to join them. He was a stabilizing influence on Edward. Edward desperately needed him now.

The look of stark terror on Edward's face made the duke realize that Edward was in no condition to hear anything about his future duties. He had feared the boy wouldn't take the news well. He was young, even younger than his two and twenty years. He had never had a strong will, preferring to drift through life having a good time. This news would bring that aspect of his life to a screeching halt. Harold decided to give the boy as much time as he could to get used to the idea. However, his own time was so limited, he couldn't afford to give Edward much. Edward would have to pull himself together and soon.

As Harold glanced at Diana, he saw her watching Edward closely. Now, there was someone with maturity beyond her years. Her intelligence and good sense were abundantly clear in the way she had handled herself after Geoffrey's death. Yes, she had been distraught, but she had pulled herself together and gotten through the marriage and the journey to the castle with aplomb. She had also, somehow, become a good influence on Edward. Harold had noticed how much better he was when he visited at the birth of the baby. He had immediately noticed Edward's lack of alcohol consumption and been very happy for it. He didn't think the young couple were in love, but he did see affection and caring between them and was very pleased. He thought Diana had been a steadying influence on his son and that pleased him as well. Edward would need her now. Harold hoped she was up to the demands the future would bring. He felt more confident in her abilities than in his son's at this particular point in time and that made him very apprehensive and not a little sad.

When Edward and Diana were shown up to their rooms on the third floor, Diana lay the sleeping baby in his cradle. The bedchamber was magnificent. The color scheme was ivory and peach and very feminine. The huge bed had an ivory velvet headboard and was housed in a gigantic wooden alcove with hand carved wood and scrolling. There was a matching dressing table and washstand. The armoire took up almost an entire wall and was made of the same wood with the same elaborate detail. The bed hangings and drapes were a soft peach color trimmed in ivory lace. The cushion on the vanity chair was an ivory and peach stripe. On the other chairs in the room, the upholstery was flowered in the same shades with accents of three shades of green. If Diana hadn't been so upset at the news about the duke's health, she would have loved to explore the room more.

After leaving the baby in Bertha's care, Diana went through their connecting drawing room. She knocked on the connecting door on Edward's side of the drawing room. Benjamin opened the door and drew her quickly into the room. This room was much more masculine in shades of blue, but just as opulent as hers. Just as she feared, Edward was slumped in a chair with a glass of brandy in his hand. From the looks of it, it wasn't his first and they had only separated ten minutes before.

Diana immediately went to Edward and kneeled by his chair. "Edward, my dear. Would you like to talk about your father's news? I know you must be very upset."

"Talk, what good will talk do. My father is dying, what good will talking do. I'm going to drink myself insensible. That's what I am going to do." Edward's voice had risen steadily and was almost a shout on his last sentence.

Diana and Benjamin looked at each other in trepidation. It was as Diana had feared. Poor Edward was not strong enough to handle this situation. Whatever were they to do? She tried to reason with Edward as did Benjamin, to no avail. He just continued to drink until he was almost insensible. Benjamin told Diana he would put him to bed and then come speak with her later.

Just as Diana exited through the connecting door, she heard Geoffrey begin to fuss. After a change and a feeding, Diana handed him over to Bertha so she could get out of her traveling clothes and have a bath. The road had been hot and dusty and she knew a good bath and clean clothes would improve her outlook.

Dressed in a sober black evening dress, Diana sat at the mirror watching Barbara brush her hair. Barbara put the long auburn curls into a simple knot on the top of her head with tendrils hanging around her face and neck. She didn't bother with jewelry other than the wedding ring Edward had given her. Soon she heard a knock on the connecting door from Edwards room. It was Benjamin.

"He's asleep. I got him into a bath and convinced him to lie down before dinner. Oh, Diana, I so feared this would happen. I noticed his Grace didn't look well when Geoffrey was born, but I didn't want to say anything in the hope it was a temporary condition. What are we to do?"

Sitting in chairs before the hearth, Benjamin and Diana spent quite some time discussing what they could do to help Edward deal with the news of the duke's impending death. Neither of them could come up an idea of how to get Edward to curb his alcohol intake, but both agreed to try their best to speak to him when he woke up. It would soon be time to go down to dinner and Edward was still sleeping off his excess from earlier in the afternoon. Benjamin went back next door to see if he could rouse him and get him dressed. A maid came to fetch Diana when it was time for dinner. She knocked on Edward's door. Benjamin opened the door and with a sad smile, ushered her into the room.

Edward was bathed and dressed, but he already had a glass of brandy in his hand. He hardly looked sober even after his nap. Perhaps he hadn't slept off the effects of his earlier drinking, but Diana couldn't know how much he had drunk after he awoke. She dreaded the evening. Again, she wished Benjamin could have dinner with them to help her with Edward, but she knew that sort of thing was just not done.

Diana didn't know whether to try to speak to Edward before they went down to dinner about his drinking or whether that would just exacerbate the problem. She stood staring at him for some minutes. Finally, she walked over to him and took his hand.

"Edward, we need to talk. You cannot just stay inebriated. You are going to have to deal with the very unpleasant fact that your father is dying. There is much for you to learn about your responsibilities when that happens. You cannot absorb all the information if your mind is clouded with brandy. I don't mean to badger you, but you must get hold of yourself. If not for me, then do it for your father. He will need you to be strong during this time."

"But I am not strong, Diana. I am weak." he said jerking his hand from hers and rising. "I have always been weak. Geoffrey was the strong one and he is dead. Now my father will be dead and there is nothing I can do about it. Please do not expect me to be strong for you or my father. I cannot." With that declaration, Edward picked up the brandy decanter and poured himself another glass.

Diana insisted that Edward accompany her down to dinner. Finally after much persuasion from she and Benjamin, he did escort her to the dining room. The duke was already at the table when they entered. Diana was struck again by the changes in him. He must have dropped two stone and his skin was a sickly grayish color.

Harold took one look at Edward and knew immediately he was drinking. His eyes were glassy and his lips had a loose look. Harold's heart sank. How was he to educate the boy on his duties, when he drank like a fish? "Well," he thought, "the boy will just have to stop this childishness at once." Harold knew better than to try to talk to Edward when he was this deeply in his cups, but he planned to have a talk with him first thing in the morning.

Dinner was a very uncomfortable affair. Edward did not eat a bite, but drank glass after glass of wine. He became louder and more unruly as the meal progressed. Harold looked at his younger son with disgust. Finally, when she could stand it no longer, Diana excused herself and Edward and practically dragged him back upstairs.

Benjamin heard Edward singing at the top of his lungs long before they reached the door to Edward's room. He had the door open when they got there. He looked at Diana with such sadness in his eyes, her heart broke. Benjamin loved Edward very much, but he really had no control over him and never had. Geoffrey had been the only person who had at least a modicum of influence over Edward. With him gone, Benjamin held little hope he and Diana would be able to contain Edward's behavior.

Benjamin dreaded the duke's reaction to Edward's obvious inability to hold himself together. He knew the duke had threatened to have Edward committed to a sanitarium at one time before because of his drinking. Geoffrey had spoken to Edward and he had slowed down considerably. After Geoffrey's death, Benjamin had again been worried that Edward would turn to drink, and he had at the beginning. Benjamin considered Diana's acceptance of he and Edward's relationship as the reason Edward had again pulled himself together. The last few months before the birth of the baby, Edward hadn't drank at all. Benjamin didn't know if the duke would again consider the sanitarium, but Benjamin knew that Edward would not do well in that setting. He had heard about those places. They sounded dreadful. He didn't believe his beloved Edward would survive such a place.

Diana came into Edward's room with him and helped Benjamin get him seated on the edge of the bed. Edward was so far gone, he didn't even realize where he was. Diana helped Benjamin remove Edward's coat, cravat and waistcoat, then left him to complete the job and get Edward into bed.

Diana went through the connecting door into the drawing room she and Edward shared to find the duke sitting in front of the empty fireplace with Geoffrey in his arms. He looked up with such pain in his eyes, she went to him and dropped to her knees in front of him.

"What are we to do, Diana? Edward obviously cannot handle the duties of a duke. He can't even stay sober his first night home. Has he been this way at Bristol Castle?"

"Nay, my lord. Edward has been doing wonderfully. He hasn't had anything at all to drink in months. Since he and I....well, since we became friends, he has done very well. He and... he helped keep my spirits up when I would become despondent over Geoffrey's death. He taught me to play cards and charades and made me laugh when all I wanted to do was cry."

"That type of unselfish behavior hardly sounds like Edward. I feared Geoffrey's death would send him into a drunken frenzy. Edmonds did tell me he drank at first, but then seemed to come to grips with the situation and behaved like a man. He seemed honestly concerned about you during little Geoffrey's birth and after. I was surprised to see him take such an interest in the babe. That was not like him either. I do not want to pry, but what exactly happened between the two of you to change him."

"Edward and I came to an understanding about our relationship and our marriage. We became friends. We don't have a conventional marriage. We feel towards each other like siblings. I am like the little sister he never had and he is my big brother. I will always love Geoffrey and he understands that. Though sometimes, I feel like the older of the two of us. Edward does not believe he is strong, but he can be if he makes his mind up to it. He was very good to me and for me after my bairn was born. It is because of him that I became well so quickly. Your son is a good man, he just does not believe it himself."

"When you say you are like siblings, I assume you mean you do not have an intimate relationship? There will be no other children? I'm sorry, my dear, I shouldn't pry. I suppose, because of my illness, I am more distraught than usual."

"It is not surprising, my Lord. I do not mind answering your question. No, there will be no other children." Diana said with dignity.

Harold felt terrible about the situation. Diana and Edward were so very young to be trapped in a loveless marriage for the rest of their lives. He had hoped, with time, they might feel an attraction to build a relationship on. Obviously, that was not to be. If they had only familial affection for each other, there was little hope for a love match. The guilt Harold felt was numbing. He had forced the issue and felt much remorse. However, in the circumstances, he could not think of another solution to the problem of young Geoffrey's legitimacy.

"I am so very sorry, Diana. That kind of marriage is not what I or your father wished for you. I feel responsible. What can I do to make it up to you?"

"There is nothing to make up, my Lord. I loved your other son with all my heart and soul. No one could ever take his place. If not for my bairn, I would probably never have married. I would have stayed on with my Da going on as before I met Geoffrey. But there was a bairn and I could not in good conscience let him grow up as a bastard. Edward was very kind to marry me and give little Geoffrey a name. I do not regret our marriage in the least. Please do not despair on my account. I am content with my lot."

The duke was not convinced Diana would always feel this way. She was very young and had many years ahead of her to always be alone. Yes, she had the baby, but babies grow up and go away. She would be only 32 when the boy went up to university. What would she do with her life then?

The next morning, a footman knocked on Edward's door at eight with a note to meet his father in the library immediately. Being much the worse for wear from the evenings over imbibing, Edward was not yet even awake. Benjamin ordered water for a bath and started trying to wake him. After almost forty-five minutes, he was finally able to at least get Edward out of bed and into the bath. By then the water had cooled appreciably, but Benjamin made no effort to warm it up. He hoped the cool water would help to bring Edward around sooner. It did seem to help somewhat as Benjamin was able to get Edward bathed and dressed in less than an hour. That time was much sooner than usual after a night of heavy drinking.

When Edward was arrayed in one of his black outfits, he was able to stand on his own, but was quite wobbly. Benjamin didn't dare give him a drink to steady him as he was meeting with the duke right away. However, he did accompany Edward down the stairs to make sure he made it and also to make sure he actually went directly to the library, not the drawing room to drink.

The duke was sitting behind his massive mahogany desk working on correspondence when Edward knocked on the door. He was admitted by one of the footman who was waiting to take the duke's letters to the post. He looked horrible. His skin was pasty and his whole body appeared to be trembling. He looked ten years older than his twenty-two years. Harold dismissed the waiting footman and sat for several minutes just looking at his son.

"Edward, I know the news about my eminent demise has greatly upset you, but you really must get control of yourself. There is much you must learn in the next few months. You cannot learn it if you are always in a drunken state."

"But, you see father, that is indeed the problem. I do not wish to be a duke and learn all these facts you are speaking about. I was very content to be the second son and never have to concern myself with any of this..this.." Edward stopped upon seeing the look on his father's face.

Harold jumped up from behind his desk in a rage. He could not believe those words had just issued from his son's mouth. How dare he feel this way. Geoffrey was dead, Edward had to take over the duchy. There was no choice in the matter.

When the duke rose so abruptly from his chair, Edward knew a moment of real fear. His father's face was almost purple with rage. Edward flinched in his chair and put his hands to his head in despair. He began to cry in great racking sobs, his entire body quaking with grief.

Harold had no idea what to do. For a grown man to cry like that just was not done. Men didn't blubber like small children! He had no idea what to do either to his son nor for him. He abruptly sat back down in his chair and waited for the storm to subside.

It seemed hours, but was actually about ten minutes before Edward was able to contain his emotions. He took a handkerchief from his sleeve and wiped his face and blew his nose.
When it was apparent he was in control of himself again, Harold spoke.

"Edward, this will not do. It just will not do. You are a man of two and twenty, you cannot give way to your emotions as if you were a small child. In just a few months, you will bear the title of the Duke of Bristol with all that entails. You will sit in the House of Lords and vote on important legislation that will affect the entire empire. You will hold the actual lives of hundreds of people in your hands. This family owns several titles and huge estates that support many, many tenants and their whole families. We have interests in shipping, mining, farming and horse breeding all over the country. The Prince Regent himself will ask your opinion on matters pertaining to state. How in the world will you be able to manage all of these responsibilities in a drunken state? You must control yourself."

Edward just stared at his father with haunted eyes. He had no answer for him. He knew he could not do any of the things his father had just enumerated. He was not strong like his father and Geoffrey. He was weak and always had been. Right now all he wanted was to drink himself into oblivion and have Benjamin hold him while he cried. He jumped out of his chair and ran for the door.

"Edward, come back here this minute. I demand that you not leave this room."

Edward ignored his father's words and ran out of the room and up the stairs to his bedchamber. He slammed the door and ran into Benjamin's arms already sobbing. Benjamin held him tightly and rubbed his back speaking soothingly to him.

Diana rushed in through their connecting door. She had been waiting for Edward to come back. Benjamin had come over and informed her of the duke's note as soon as Edward had left. She rushed to Edward and put her arms around him as well.

"Edward, poor dear, please do not take on so. It will be all right. We will manage somehow. Benjamin and I will help you in any way that we can. Between the three of us we can do anything. Is that not correct, Benjamin?"

"Of course, it is my Lady, of course it is. Edward, no one expects you to know everything right away. We will learn your duties together. Whatever you learn, you can come and tell Diana and I and we will remember it for you. I know your memory is not always what it should be, but we both have excellent memories, do we not Diana?"

"Yes, we will remember for you. I will ask the duke if I may sit in on your lessons with you to take notes for you. That way, I will be learning everything too. I can share the notes with Benjamin and then we will all know what to do in every situation. You will see, everything will work out splendidly."

After quite some time, Benjamin and Diana were finally able to quiet Edward and get him back to bed. They were both in hopes that some more sleep might help him immensely. Thankfully, he didn't ask for anything to drink. They were both surprised and relieved on that score.

Diana went downstairs and knocked on the library door. When the duke bade her enter, she went to stand in front of his huge desk. She hadn't been in the library yet and was very impressed. The room was huge and filled to overflowing with books of all types. If she hadn't been there on such a sad errand, she would have loved to roam the shelves for hours. The room had shelves on three walls from floor to ceiling. The ceiling was at least thirty feet tall. There were rolling ladders to reach the top shelves. A huge fireplace was behind the gigantic desk with a very large portrait of a lovely lady wearing a beautiful blue dress hanging above it. She immediately saw the resemblance between the lady and Edward and assumed it was his mother. The wall hangings and upholstery on the comfortable sofas and chairs was a rich ruby red with gold accents.

Harold looked at Diana with such sorrow in his eyes, it almost took her breath away.

"Oh, your Grace, please don't despair so. Edward will come around. I know he will. I will do anything in my power to help him learn his responsibilities. I have had an idea I wish to broach to you. What would you think if I attended your meetings with him to take notes on all you say? I did the same for my father for years when he would meet with his tenants and would be pleased to do the same for Edward. My father, like Edward, does not have a very good memory. With the notes I took, he had a point of reference when he had forgotten some important point or the other. I truly believe Edward's lack of memory is one of the reasons he is so filled with fear concerning his future responsibilities. With me there, that fear could be relieved."

"My dear, that would be highly irregular. Ladies do not usually concern themselves with business nor politics. I fear some of my men of business would not take kindly to having you present. I am not sure how I would feel about it myself."

"I understand, my Lord. Perhaps I could be concealed behind a screen or some such in a corner of the room. I would only need a small table with parchment, ink, and quills."

"Ahem, well Diana, sometimes the language at these meetings is hardly fit for a lady to hear. I meet with all sorts of people, you know. I would be embarrassed for you to have to hear some of the things that are said. As far as the meetings between just Edward and myself, I see no problem with those."

"Oh, please, your Grace, do not concern yourself on my account for that reason. I have dealt with Scottish tenants and horse breeders for years. When my father travelled to deliver the horses, I managed quite well on my own with them. A few harsh words will certainly cause me no harm. Please let me do this for Edward. I truly believe it will bolster his confidence to have me there. If you feel the men you are meeting with will be terribly upset if they learn of my presence, perhaps Benjamin, Edward's valet, could take over for me on those occasions. He could act as Edward's secretary in those instances. No one would think much of having a secretary present."

"Well, my dear, you may actually have something there. I know that Benjamin is a well-educated young man from a good family that has fallen on hard times. I am sure he could handle a secretaries duties as well as those of Edward's valet. Let me think on this and I will let you know. I had planned to start today, but in light of Edward's, shall we say, indisposition, we will begin on the morrow. I will think on this the rest of the day and let you know my decision at dinner."

"Thank you, your Grace. I am truly convinced this is the answer for all of us."

With that, Diana curtsied and left the room. She quickly ran upstairs to check on Geoffrey and finding him awake and hungry, fed him and rocked him to sleep. When the baby was resting sweetly, she went into the drawing room between Edward's bedchamber and hers. She found Benjamin there pacing the floor looking terribly worried.

"I think his Grace will allow one of us to be in the room with Edward when he is learning his new duties. He is thinking about it and will let me know at dinner. If he does agree, we will begin tomorrow. If I am busy with the baby, you will go and act as Edward's secretary taking notes. If the meeting is with men his Grace believes would be upset by my presence, then you will take over in that instance as well. Oh, Benjamin, this has to work."

"Diana, it will work. We just have to assure Edward that he won't have the full responsibility on his own and he will be fine. He just does not have enough confidence in himself to face this alone. Between the two of us, I just know we can get through this difficult time."

That evening at dinner, the duke agreed to allowing either Diana or Benjamin to always be with Edward when he was being taught whether by the duke or his men of business. Diana was much relieved, as were Edward and Benjamin, when she gave them the news. Edward had slept most of the day. When he woke in the late afternoon, Diana and Benjamin had explained their plan to him. He was almost pathetic in his relief. He still was not calm enough to go down to dinner so he and Benjamin had a tray in their room and then played with Geoffrey until his bedtime.

The next day, Diana arose early to make sure Geoffrey was taken care of before collecting Edward and heading to the library. Diana was very glad the duke treated Edward kindly and made no mention of the former day's hysterics. Edward hadn't drunk anything the night before and looked much better. He was subdued, but he was attentive and put in a sincere effort to absorb the information his father gave him concerning their estate in Cornwall where Bristol Castle was situated.

The estate encompassed several hundred acres and was comprised of several farms and mines. Some of the tin mines extended underground well out into the sea, some were near the castle itself. The copper and tin mines constituted the largest part of the income from that estate and employed hundreds of men. The mines had managers who took care of the day to day running of the mines, as well as overseeing the transport of the ore to London and other ports for exporting. Cornwall was the largest producer of tin and copper during the Regency era. The mines accounted for a large part of the amazing amount of wealth held by the Bristol family. Diana was surprised at the extent of the fortune Edward would be overseeing in the very near future.

When it was time for luncheon, Diana hurried upstairs to attend to the baby and had a tray in her drawing room when she was done. Edward and Benjamin joined her and they discussed what had been learned that morning. Both Edward and Benjamin were amazed at how quickly Diana had caught on to the business side of the estate. Neither of them had really known how involved Diana was with her father's business. They were both very aware of her intelligence, but her diligence and ability to retain information about the businesses surprised them both.

Edward began to feel much better about the situation. He was still terribly upset about the thought of losing his father and having to take over the duchy. However, he didn't feel so paralyzed by fear as he had. He began to believe, with Diana and Benjamin's help, he could attain some degree of knowledge and actually not destroy the entire family fortune in a few months. His greatest fear was letting down all the multitudes of people who depended on the Bristol family for their daily bread. It would just be easier to crawl into a bottle of brandy and not come out, but it didn't look as if his father, wife or his lover were going to allow him to do that. He looked at Diana and Benji with affection as they sat discussing the morning's lessons.

Chapter 21

After luncheon, Edward and Diana again joined the duke in the library. It was more of the same. There was just so much to learn and such a short time to do so. All the days thereafter followed the same routine. If the daily lessons were with the duke alone, Diana accompanied Edward. If there were others involved, Benjamin assumed the position of secretary and took the notes. Harold was amazed how well the arrangement was working out. He had been petrified at first that Edward would continue to drink, but with the support of his wife and friend, he seemed to be getting along splendidly. After luncheon, most days, Diana would bring the nurse and little Geoffrey to the library for an hour or so to visit with his grandfather.

Increasingly, Harold was amazed at how much attention Edward paid to the baby. He could coax smiles from Geoffrey with very little effort and truly seemed to enjoy holding the baby on his lap and talking to him. Harold noticed the softness in Diana's eyes when she watched Edward with her child. At first, he had hoped that feeling would grow into something more, but as the days went by, he understood that Diana's feelings for Edward truly were platonic. She truly loved him like a brother. Harold's guilt and remorse at saddling Diana with a loveless, sexless marriage continued to plague him, but there was little he could do. Eventually, he had to accept that the young people seemed to be content, at least for now.

The days flowed into weeks and the weeks into months. Harold's physical condition very slowly deteriorated as his doctor had told him it would. Finally there came a day when he simply didn't feel well enough to get out of bed. He insisted that the lessons continue in his bedchamber. Diana and Edward consulted the doctor and were told to go on as before as it would make very little difference in the outcome. They were warned that the end was near and keeping the duke from trying to complete Edward's education would do more harm than good.

Now Diana brought Geoffrey to the duke's chambers in the mornings, as well as the afternoons. Geoffrey was now seven months old and crawling everywhere. It made the duke smile for the baby to be allowed to crawl all over his huge bed. Geoffrey would sit beside his grandfather and play with his little toys while his mother and Edward listened to the duke and took notes on all he said. When Harold would tire, Diana would tell he and Edward tales of her life in Scotland. Harold would lie back on his pillows and listen to her melodious voice as she described riding her horse in the Highlands and the valley where Ainsley Glen sat. She would describe, very humorously, some of her dealings with the tenants on her father's estate.

Diana would have them laughing about Granny Cameron who was seventy years old and had not a tooth in her head. Granny still liked to eat however, being a short, stout lady, and would have one of her granddaughters mash all her food with a large fork as for a toddler. When her granddaughter was put out with old Granny, who was a bossy one, she would over salt her porridge and only half mash her food. Unable to move very fast, instead of trying to chase the girl down to punish her, Granny was given to throwing things at her. Diana told of coming to their house one day to find items like socks, cups, pewter forks and spoons all over the floor.

On each succeeding day, their study time became shorter and shorter as Harold had less and less strength. Finally the day came when the duke began to sleep most of the days and nights. Diana and Edward knew the end was very near. Diana and Benjamin watched Edward very closely for fear he would begin to drink again, but he did not. As the months had slowly gone by, Edward had grown in many ways. His confidence in his own intelligence and abilities was so much improved, it was as if he was a different man.

In some ways, he was very much the same. He was still light hearted most of the time, teasing Benjamin and Diana unmercifully. He still loved his bright colored clothes and wanted the newest fashions. Because of the duke's illness, they had not gone out much when their mourning ended in October. But on the occasions when they felt impelled to attend some event of the *ton*, Edward was resplendent as a peacock.

Diana felt she paled beside her husband. Her taste did not run to bright colors or the newest trends. She loved clothes and enjoyed wearing pretty things, but that was not her main focus in life as it was for many society women. Her child and her family were her main focus. When she attended a ball with Edward, she always chose a gown that complemented her coloring and didn't clash too badly with whatever wild color Edward chose to wear.

When the duke had taken to his bed, Diana had written to her father and advised Fergus to make the journey to London as soon as he could. Within a few days, Fergus arrived and was much upset to see his old friend barely hanging on. He stayed with them and was a great comfort as the duke lapsed into a coma in his last days. Diana and Fergus were sitting with Harold on the last day of his life. The duke's family had not left him alone and had been taking turns sitting with him twenty-four hours a day since his coma had commenced.

Diana was amazed to see Harold's eyes open. He hadn't been lucid in three days. He reached out his hand and Diana took his hand in hers and squeezed his fingers gently. His eyes turned to Fergus and a slight smile appeared on his face.

"Diana, would you get Edward please?" he asked weakly.

"Of course, I will go right away."

Diana hurried from the duke's bedchamber to the dressing room next door where Edward was catching a nap. She could hear the rumble of the duke's and her father's voices as she ran to rouse Edward.

When the young people came back into the room, they saw Fergus standing beside the bed gripping Harold's hand in his. There were tears in Fergus' eyes as well as the duke's. Edward rushed to his father's bedside. Harold took his hand from Fergus's and reached for his son's.

"Edward, I just want to tell you how very proud I am of you. You will be a fine duke. I can leave this world in peace knowing you and Diana are here to take over my place. Take care of Diana and little Geoffrey for me. I love you Edward."

With those final words, Harold, Duke of Bristol, closed his eyes for the last time. Tears began to fall from both Edward's and Diana's eyes when they heard the duke take his final breath. Edward dropped to his knees beside the bed sobbing. Diana went down on her knees beside him and wrapped her arms around him. He turned to her and embraced her crying into her shoulder.

Fergus was somewhat disturbed at the emotional display, but not really surprised. He had never taken Edward for a strong man. He had hoped that Edward had grown up during his father's illness, but was now not so sure. Fergus had never really trusted Edward. There was nothing in particular that he could put his finger on, but there was just something "wrong" about him. As Fergus watched the two of them, Benjamin came into the room. He immediately went to the young couple. He helped them both up and Edward flung his arms around Benjamin's neck and clung to him as Benjamin guided him out of the room.

Diana looked at the two men sadly, then followed them out of the room. It struck Fergus like a physical blow. Edward wasn't a man at all. He was one of those "lavender aunts" Fergus had heard spoken of. Oh, his poor darlin' lass. Married to a man who was not a man at all. He wondered if Harold had known. He emphatically hoped not.

Fergus quietly drew the sheet up over his old friend's face and left the room. He went to Diana's drawing room and knocked on the door. Barbara, her maid answered the door and told Fergus Diana was feeding Geoffrey. Fergus was too agitated to leave and told Barbara he would wait. When Diana had finished with Geoffrey she left him to Bertha to put to sleep and joined her father in the drawing room.

One look at his face and she instantly knew something more than the death of his friend had upset her father. She was frightened to see him like this. Having just lost her father-in-law, now she worried if her father was ill as well.

"Da, are you well? You look, well, you look even more upset than you were a few minutes ago. What has happened?"

"Diana, there is something I must speak to you about and I actually don't know how to even begin."

"Da, please, you are frightening me. Just tell me what the matter is, please."

"Diana, there is something wrong with your husband. He, he is not normal. He, well, I don't know any other way to put this, he is not a real man. Do you have any idea to what I am referring? I know you have led a very sheltered life, but you must have realized how effeminate Edward is."

"Oh, Da. Are you talking about the love that Edward and Benjamin share? Yes, I am very well aware of it. I have known for many months that Edward will never be a true husband to me, nor do I want that. I have no illusions about Edward or our marriage. He has been most honest with me. Our arrangement suits me fine. I still love Geoffrey and believe I always will. Edward is good and kind to me and my bairn. He and Benjamin are the best friends I have ever had. We have a good life together, the three of us."

Fergus looked at Diana with horror. "The three of you. How can you be so complacent about something that is so morally and legally wrong? Edward and Benjamin both could be hanged for the type of relationship they have. This type of aberration is against the laws of God and man. Can't you see that lass?"

"Da, what Edward and Benjamin feel for each other is beautiful. It is much the same as what I feel for Geoffrey. They sincerely love and care for each other. Without Benjamin Edward would be lost. And truthfully, so would I. Benjamin has been a rock for both of us from the very beginning. He helped both of us through the horror of Geoffrey's death. He was there for me through the worst of my lying in. He loves little Geoffrey with all his heart, just as Edward and I do. I cannot make myself believe that he or Edward are evil just because they love each other instead of some woman."

Fergus looked at his daughter as if he had never seen her before. She spoke with the wisdom and understanding of a woman far beyond her nearly eighteen years. He was still appalled at the situation she found herself in, but he could see that she had come to terms with it and was content. He didn't believe she would always be content. Geoffrey had been gone less than two years and Diana was very young. Someday, he felt, Diana would want to fall in love again. He felt sure that his daughter would not take a lover. Many women of the *ton* did just that, married or not, but he could not see his lass putting herself in a position that could lead to scandal. Fergus was horrendously upset about the situation and very worried for his only child's happiness.

Chapter 22

The funeral for the Duke of Bristol was held three days later. The service was held in the evening as was the custom for royalty and nobility. The official funeral was held in Westminster Abbey and attended by hundreds of Society's best, as well as the Prince

Regent and many members of the royal family, as befitting a blood relation to the King. Harold's solicitor, secretary, and main man of business had taken care of all the arrangements with the Prince Regent's agents. Before his death, Harold had stipulated exactly the type of funeral he wanted. He had told Diana privately that he would really rather be taken to Cornwall and buried at the castle where he had grown up with just family and close friends.. However, tradition demanded his body lie in state in London until the funeral service. He would be buried in Cornwall at the family tomb however. Only close friends and family would attend the actual burial.

Edward was not doing well, but Diana had expected nothing less. He was torn by grief and fear of failure and had begun to drink on the day his father died. Between she and Benjamin, they got him sober, bathed and dressed on the evening of the funeral. Diana wasn't sure how they were going to keep him sober until after the burial, but they were going to try. Diana instructed the staff to put away all alcohol, even the normal ale and beer served with meals. They, along with Fergus, and the few remaining members of the family would depart for Cornwall early in the morning, after the funeral service.

Diana had never met most of Edward's family. He was not close to them as he only had distant third and fourth cousins. They were all considerably older than he and Geoffrey. As an only child, Harold had some cousins, but they were not close. The Napoleonic war had depleted the family ranks, as well as illness and deaths from childbirth, which were very common. Only a couple of cousins had visited the mansion during the duke's illness. He seemed to have little use for most of them, telling Diana they were money-hungry leeches on more than one occasion. She was not looking forward to the long trip to Cornwall in the company of some of the leeches, as well as a drunken Edward and a very lively baby.

As Edward and Diana went downstairs on the evening of the funeral service, they were met by Fergus and several of Edward's cousins. They immediately entered the various carriages for the ride to Westminster Abbey. Diana had a very bad feeling about how Edward would behave during the service, but he proved her wrong. He stared straight ahead, clutching her hand in a death grip during the entire service. When the service was complete, three hours later, Edward rose gracefully and turning to Diana offered his hand.

When Diana grasped Edward's hand, she could feel him shaking uncontrollably. She slipped her arm through his and offered what support she could as they walked up the long aisle of the church. Thankfully, people could see how upset Edward was from the expression on his face and did not delay their departure with platitudes. The trip back to the mansion took about thirty minutes and Edward maintained his silence and his display of fortitude until they returned home.

As soon as the door was opened by Forbes, Edward practically ran upstairs leaving Diana to attend to their guests. After what seemed an interminable time, the final guest departed. Diana looked at her father and issued a great sigh.

"I feel drained of all energy. I must see to Geoffrey and then go to my bed. I will see you on the morrow Da."

Fergus embraced his daughter and kissed her cheek. The lass was too thin and pale by half. He decided he would stay even longer than he had planned. With everything he had learned, he felt he couldn't leave his little lass in good conscience.

Diana checked on Geoffrey and he was fussing and hungry. After feeding him, with Barbara's help, she changed into her night dress and robe. Slipping through the drawing room, she started to knock on Edward's door when she heard him shouting. Without knocking, she opened the door. Edward was sprawled in a chair with the brandy decanter in his hand. He wasn't even bothering with a glass this time. Benjamin was across the room looking out the window. He turned when Diana entered and gave her a very sad smile.

"Di, old girl. Just what I need someone else coming to give me a lecture on my behavior and responsibilities. Please just leave off at least for tonight. I have to have some peace of mind and brandy is the only way I can obtain it." Edward exclaimed with tears running down his face.

"I did not come here to upbraid you in any way. I was only coming to tell you goodnight. We are both overtired and over wrought. We will talk tomorrow. Please allow Benjamin to help you get ready for bed. It is very late and this has been an extremely taxing day."

Benjamin gave her a grateful look and walked over to Edward resting his hand on Edward's shoulder in a sympathetic way. Edward shook off Benjamin's hand and tried to rise sloshing brandy on his clothes and the beautiful Aubusson carpet. He dropped back into the chair and took another swig of the brandy.

"I suppose I had better let him help me since I cannot seem to rise from this chair on my own." Edward said laughing uproariously. "But he better stop lecturing me. I won't have it. I am a bloody duke now and no one can lecture me ever again."

Dropping the brandy decanter on the floor, Edward dropped his head into his hands and sobbed like a small child. Benjamin picked up the decanter and put it on a table. Getting to his knees in front of him, he encircled Edward with both arms, rocking him gently to and fro. Diana quietly let herself out.

Early the next morning Diana had just finished changing and feeding Geoffrey when there was a knock on her door. Barbara answered the door to find Fergus standing there looking thoroughly upset.

"Da, what is wrong now?"

"It is Edward. I stopped by his room to speak to him a few minutes ago and it smells like a distillery in there. He is already drunk. How are we to make the five day journey to Bristol Castle with him in this condition?"

"Let me just go and see what I can do."

Diana went through the drawing room and knocked on Edward's door. Benjamin opened the door and Diana could see that the room seemed to have been wrecked and Benjamin had an angry red mark on his cheek. There was an overturned chair and several tables were upside down. Ornaments were strewn all over the floor. Edward's travelling cases were by the door.

"What has happened here, Benjamin? Did Edward do this to the room and to you? Has he totally lost control of himself?"

"Yes, I have lost control." Edward baldly stated as he came out of his dressing room.

Diana could tell he was extremely drunk. He swayed and his eyes were glassy and bloodshot. He had the ever present glass of brandy in his hand.

"Edward. We must leave immediately to accompany your father's body to the castle. You must get a hold on your emotions now." Diana said sternly.

"I am not bloody going. I am a bloody duke now and no one can make me do anything I do not want to do. So, my dear little wife in name only, what do you have to say about that?"

Diana looked at Edward as if he were a stranger. She looked at Benjamin and he sadly shook his head, whether in sadness or disgust, she could not tell.

"I may be your wife in name only, Edward, but I am still your wife. You may be a duke, but what I think you are is a horse's ass. You had better be downstairs in ten minutes and climb into that carriage with me and my father, or you will rue the day."

With that, Diana stalked out of the room and slammed the drawing room door. Edward had such a comical look of surprise on his face, Benjamin almost laughed, but caught himself in time.

"Did you hear her? She cannot speak to me in that fashion. I am a duke."

"Duke or not, Diana is your wife and can speak to you any way she pleases. Edward, please, your father would have been mortified at the way you are acting. You must go downstairs and get in that carriage. You can sleep the day away if that is what you want, but you must go. The scandal of your not attending your father's burial will never go away. Think of your father, if you care nothing for Diana, Geoffrey and I."

Edward hung his head. He knew his father would have been horribly upset at the way he was treating Benjamin and Diana. He just couldn't help it. What was he to do now? His father was really gone, dead, and would never be there for him again. His self-pity was boundless. Finally after a few minutes, he threw back the contents of his glass, tossed it into the fireplace with a crash, and went out the door with Benjamin following closely behind.

Chapter 23

Diana, Barbara, Bertha, Geoffrey and Fergus were already downstairs. Diana looked up and gave her husband a quick nod, but did not speak to him. She swept through the front door when it was opened by Forbes and made her way to the carriage. Benjamin hurried to give her a hand up. When she was settled, he handed her Geoffrey. Fergus followed soon after and settled himself across from Diana. Edward finally climbed into the carriage and plopped down on the seat next to Fergus. He glared at Diana as the carriage got under way, but she paid him no mind.

Finally, seeing his dark looks had no effect on his wife, he slumped into the corner and went to sleep, promptly beginning to snore quite loudly. Fergus looked at him with disgust. He had noticed the red mark on Benjamin's face and knew that Edward had struck him in a drunken rage. Fergus made up his mind if Edward ever raised a hand to either Diana or Geoffrey he would call him out. Husband or not, Fergus would not allow his daughter or grandson to be abused. He would take them home with him to Scotland if Diana would go. He gingerly broached the subject.

"Diana, I think you and young Geoffrey should come home to Ainsley Glen for a time. Edward is not in his right mind at present. Maybe it would be better if you were not in England right now. Everyone would love to see you and to see this fine bairn as well. Why don't you come home with me for a few months?"

"Da, I appreciate what you are trying to do, but I cannot leave Edward now or really ever. When I come back to Ainsley Glen it will be with my husband. Edward is having a hard time right now, but I believe between Benjamin and I, we can get him straightened out. He is just so full of fear of failure, that is all he can think about. We have to prove to him that he will not fail the duchy and all will be well."

"If you and Benjamin cannot aid Edward in this, will you then consider coming home?"

"I will not fail. I cannot think of failure. I can only think of success. It is imperative that Edward take over the responsibilities his father has spent his last months training him for. I will stay by his side every step of the way, as will Benjamin, and he will be fine. I know it in my heart."

"I hope you are right, lass, but I do not have your faith in Edward. I have no faith at all."

Diana regarded her father sadly. She could hardly blame him. He didn't know the good side of Edward like she and Benjamin did. He had only been around him once when he wasn't drinking when Geoffrey was born. She knew she and Benjamin could help Edward to realize his own worth. It would take time, but she was confident in their future together, a good future for all four of them.

After several hours of travel, the party, all seven carriages, stopped for luncheon at an inn. Geoffrey had been exceptionally good all morning, but was beginning to fuss from the confinement and had woken Edward who was not in a good mood. Since Geoffrey had started crawling, he was not happy unless he was scooting along the floor in search of a toy or his puppy. He had tasted that freedom for several weeks now and was not pleased at having it taken away. Diana asked the innkeeper if they might have a private room and was pleased that one was available.

As soon as Geoffrey was set onto the hearth rug, his fussing ceased. He raised his sturdy little body up onto his hands and knees and took off straight to Edward who had just walked into the room. At first Diana thought Edward would ignore the baby, but after looking down for a couple of minutes with a scowl on his face, he suddenly smiled and sat down on the rug with the baby. Geoffrey crawled up into Edward's lap wanting to play their usual game of peep-eye. Edward would cover his face with his hand and say, "Where's Daddy?" Geoffrey would howl with laughter when Edward removed his hands so the baby could see his face and say, "Here he is." Geoffrey never tired of this game that Bertha had taught him and Edward had quickly taken up.

In just a few minutes there was a knock on the door and a young serving girl delivered their luncheon of mutton and bread. She also brought a pot of tea. Diana had informed the innkeeper that she wanted no alcohol, not even small beer to be brought up. Edward glanced at the tray and frowned, but didn't say anything.

After Diana had fed and changed Geoffrey, they sat down to eat. Benjamin and Barbara were joining them for lunch, but Bertha was downstairs eating in the taproom with the drivers and footmen. The assorted "leeches" had been given a private room of their own as per Diana's instructions. Her father had graciously offered to dine with them so Diana could have some private time with her little family. Actually, he could not stand to be in the same room with Edward anymore than he had to at present.

Edward ate little, but drank three cups of very sweet tea. Diana made no mention of the condition she had found him in earlier nor did he. There was little conversation at the table at all. Diana was still very angry with Edward, especially for his having struck Benjamin. The red mark had faded, but was still obvious on Benjamin's cheek. Benjamin was very quiet as well. He took it upon himself to keep Geoffrey entertained during the meal. It made Diana very happy to know that Geoffrey had Benjamin in his life. He was wonderful with the little boy and had infinite patience with him.

When they all went downstairs to continue their trip, Diana was the one to pay the innkeeper while Benjamin made sure everyone was accounted for and gotten into the proper carriages. Edward had simply gone out the door and climbed into the carriage with the intention of going back to sleep. When Diana finally came out of the inn, Benjamin was there holding Geoffrey and waiting to help her into the carriage. Her father was not in the carriage, but Edward was already asleep.

"Do you know where my father is?"

"He decided to ride in one of the other carriages to give you both more room since you have the baby. He is riding with one of the cousins and his wife. I believe it is Percy."

"I am not surprised. Oh well, let us get started. Benjamin, please ride with us. Since Edward is determined to sleep the whole journey, I could really use your help in keeping Geoffrey occupied. He gets so restless being confined."

"Of course, your Grace, I would consider it an honor."

With that, Benjamin handed Diana into the carriage and passed her Geoffrey. He climbed in and sat across from her, beside Edward. After that, Benjamin rode in the duke's carriage for the rest of the journey. Edward slept the whole of the first day. When they stopped for the night, he immediately went up to his and Benjamin's room and went to bed without even eating. Benjamin and Fergus joined Diana in her small drawing room for their evening meal of bangers and mash. Geoffrey had been fed and Bertha had taken him into the bedchamber to rock to sleep. She would go down to the taproom later for her supper with Barbara.

Conversation was desultory. None of them wished to bring up Edward's very bad behavior, but it was like the elephant in the room. Finally Fergus could stand it no longer.

"Lass, what are you going to do? You cannot live forever with a man who acts like a small child who has not gotten his way. He is actually pouting like a three year old. I do not know how you can stand to ride in that carriage with him all day. Has he spoken with you at all?"

"No, but then neither have I spoken to him. I am still very angry with Edward. If I were to speak to him right now, I would say entirely too much. As it is, he is very aware that I am angry with him, have no doubt about that."

Fergus was beside himself with anger. He didn't want to say too much in front of Benjamin, however, before he could stop himself, he fumed. "There has to be something that can be done about Edward. Benjamin, do you have any ideas? You seem to know him better than anyone."

Benjamin looked up in alarm, but seeing the look on Diana's face, he had to assume that her father knew the truth about her marriage and about the relationship he and Edward shared. His face turned red to the roots of his dark hair. He looked down at his plate and then glanced up to Diana with a pleading look on his face.

"Da, Benjamin does what he can, but Edward is a grown man although he doesn't act like it. We cannot force him to accept his position in life with grace. All we can do is try to keep him from wrecking the duchy and himself in the bargain. Since the duke's death, Benjamin and I have handled all correspondence with the solicitor and the man of business. We will not allow Edward to harm anyone except himself if we can help it."

Benjamin could contain himself no longer. "Sir MacDonald, please believe me when I say I will do my utmost to protect your daughter and your grandson. I care very deeply for Edward, but I know what he is like. He is very immature and selfish, but he does have a heart. I don't believe he would willingly hurt either of them. He may not love Diana as a husband, but he does care for her deeply and he loves little Geoffrey with all his heart. He will get better. It may take some time and an infinite amount of patience on all our parts, but I have to believe he will eventually get a grip on his emotions."

"Well, for all our sakes, I hope it happens sooner rather than later." With that, Fergus rose from the table and left the room.

"Oh, dear Benjamin, what are we to do? If Edward keeps up this type of behavior, my father may not be able to contain himself much longer. I know my father's temper. If he loses his temper with Edward, I have no idea how Edward will react. He already seems on the brink of a breakdown. His drinking has escalated daily since his father's death. He will kill himself if he doesn't slow down. All he does all day is drink while we ride in the carriage. I don't know where he is getting it. I made sure that no strong spirits were packed for this trip. I have spoken to both the innkeepers when we have stopped so they would not provide any to him. Do you have any idea where the brandy is coming from?"

"I really don't know for sure. I packed Edward's bags myself and I certainly did not include any brandy. However, he seems to have a never ending supply. Every time I see him, he has a bottle in his hand. He finishes one on the morning ride and yet has a new one when we start our trip in the afternoons. I will speak to the drivers and footmen and ascertain that they are not providing the brandy. However, I cannot counteract his orders to them. I do not even know if they would allow you to do so."

"Oh, believe me, if they are providing brandy to Edward, they will answer to me. I am the one now paying their wages. If they will not do as they are told, they will be replaced with servants who will."

Benjamin had never seen Diana so determined nor so angry. He felt for any one who stood in her way when she was in this type of mood. Benjamin had learned how very strong Diana really was since the duke's death. She had taken every lesson taught to Edward to heart. She could run the duchy alone, Benjamin was quite sure.

He had looked over the letters from both the solicitor and man of business, but it was Diana who made the decisions they required. The grasp she had of the business side of the duchy was probably equal to the former duke's and was quite a bit better than Benjamin's own. She was miles ahead of Edward. He had grasped the rudimentary facts, but Diana knew every detail of every property and business owned by the duchy. Benjamin had no fear that as long as they could keep Edward from making decisions in the state he was in, the duchy would not only be fine, it would grow.

The next morning, Benjamin knocked on Diana's door very early. Barbara admitted him and Diana greeted him from the rocking chair in front of the fireplace where she was feeding Geoffrey. There was no false modesty between Benjamin and Diana. When she knew who was at the door, she simply pulled the baby's blanket over his little head.

"I have discovered the brandy culprit. It is the driver of the baggage carriage. He was newly hired for this journey. Edward has been paying him an exorbitant amount to procure the brandy for him. There were several bottles in the carriage with the trunks and cases. I have taken the liberty of removing them and actually sold them to the innkeeper here and added the money to the purse you gave me to pay for accommodations on this journey . Good brandy is still hard to come by even though the war with Napoleon is over. He was quite happy to take the bottles off my hands. The driver has been threatened with his job. I do not believe he will buy brandy for Edward again. How Edward is going to react when he finds the brandy gone, I cannot say."

"Thank you, Benjamin, for handling this situation for me. I will handle Edward. Do you know if he still has any brandy left from yesterday?"

"Yes, when he went to bed last night there was over a half bottle. He actually took it to bed with him. He has not awakened yet this morning."

"That is fine. Wake him up and help him prepare for the day. Let him have the brandy that is left in the bottle, but don't let him drink all of it. Try to get him to eat something since he didn't eat dinner last evening. He can take what is left of the bottle into the carriage with him. He will run out before we stop for luncheon. I will tell him at that time that there is no more and there will be no more.

I have written a letter to Edmonds at the castle instructing him to lock up all the spirits in the house, even the wine, and to not give Edward the keys. I sent a rider ahead this morning to deliver it. We must protect Edward from himself. When the internment is over, I will do my best to get rid of the cousins as quickly as possible. My father will help me with that chore. I will need you to assist me by making sure their carriages are ready the morning after the interment. I want them out of the castle as quickly as possible. We want to keep the scandal of Edward's behavior as contained as possible."

"Will we be staying at Bristol Castle for some time then?"

"Yes. I feel we can better control Edward there than in the city. Once he dries out, hopefully, he will come to his senses and take an interest in the duchy as his father planned. We can go back to London at that time. If not, you and I will just have to take care of things ourselves. We can use dispatch riders to carry letters to and from London. They can make the trip in two days using the new roads and only stopping to change horses when needed. We will stay at Bristol Castle as long as it is necessary. I also sent a rider back to London to have all our clothes packed and sent to Bristol Castle."

"You have thought of all contingencies already. Did you sleep at all last night?"

"Not much, but I am young and do not need much sleep. I can nap some today while Geoffrey and Edward are asleep. I will be fine."

Benjamin had no doubt that Diana would be fine. She seemed electrically charged this morning. Later as he was helping Diana into the carriage for the day's travel, he noticed a small smile on her lips. He wondered what was going through her head, but since Edward was standing nearby, he didn't ask.

The day went on as any other. Edward drank what brandy he had left in his bottle and then curled up on his seat with his head on Benjamin's leg and went to sleep. Benjamin took turns with Diana keeping Geoffrey occupied as best they could. Around ten that morning, Diana fed Geoffrey and rocked him to sleep. She lay him in the travel cradle mounted in the carriage and sat back with a tired sigh. Soon, she closed her eyes and the rocking of the carriage took her off to sleep.

Diana was brought abruptly from her nap by the sound of Edward quarrelling with Benjamin. She didn't immediately open her eyes, but listened to see what was being said.

"But, Benjamin, we need to stop now, right now. I need something from my cases immediately. I will not wait until we stop for luncheon. I want you to tell the driver to stop right this minute!" Edwards said loudly and petulantly.

"Edward, if you keep shouting, you are going to awaken Diana and the baby. We will be stopping in an hour's time. Whatever you need, you can get at that time. It makes absolutely no sense to stop twice." Benjamin said sternly.

Edward threw himself back against the squabs in frustration. He was still somewhat drunk, but not as drunk as he wanted to be. Benjamin and Diana both knew he was not likely to try to speak to the driver himself. He had never done such a thing for himself. He had always had someone to do everything for him.

Diana could not go back to sleep, but pretended anyway. She was trying to put off the inevitable as long as she could. When the baby started to fuss, she opened her eyes and leaned forward to pick him up. After a nappy change and a cuddle, Geoffrey was ready to play. He reached his little arms toward Edward and spoke his first words, "Dada."

Diana and Benjamin were delighted and even Edward had a slight smile on his lips for the child. Edward reached shaking hands toward the baby and took him upon his knee. He talked to him and kept urging the baby to speak again, but Geoffrey would just smile and play with Edward's watch fob and chain.

Before long, they would be arriving at the public house for luncheon. Diana knew she had to speak to Edward before they got there. Hopefully, she could keep him from creating a scene in a public place. She especially didn't want the cousins to witness such a spectacle.

"Edward, there is something I must speak to you about. I know you have been horribly upset about the death of your father. I have been as well. He was a wonderful man and he will be missed by everyone who knew him. However, your behavior since his death would have embarrassed and saddened him to no end. You have hardly drawn a sober breath since his passing. You must get control of yourself. There are many decisions about the duchy to be made in the coming days. You cannot make informed decisions when your brain is addled by brandy.

Benjamin and I have found the source of your brandy supply and I have stopped it. There is no brandy in the baggage carriage. No brandy will be purchased for you by Benjamin or myself for the rest of this trip, nor wine. None of the servants will buy it for you either. They have all been warned they will lose their places if they do so. I have advised Edmonds to lock up all spirits at Bristol Castle and to give the keys only to me. I am sorry to treat you in this manner, but you leave me no choice. If you cannot control your drinking on your own, then Benjamin and I will have to control it for you. We will stay at Bristol Castle until you have overcome this compulsion to drink to excess."

"You bitch, you cannot do this to me. I am a fucking duke." Edward was screaming at the top of his voice. He had forgotten he held Geoffrey until the baby started to scream as well. Benjamin reached for the baby at the same time as Diana. Diana got her hands on him first and pulled him into her arms cuddling him close and speaking reassuringly to him.

Edward continued to scream and curse Diana, his face becoming redder and redder. Finally, Benjamin grabbed Edward and gave him a good shake to pull him out of his hysteria. Edward collapsed in Benjamin's arms and cried as loudly as Geoffrey.

Diana was horrified at her husband's behavior. She had known he would be upset, but she had no idea he would totally lose control and speak to her in that fashion. He had never spoken to her with anything but kindness in the past. She knew he had taken out his frustrations on Benjamin before, but never on her or the baby. His behavior just hardened her heart for what was to come. She knew she must not weaken her resolve. She must be strong to help him stop drinking once and for all.

By the time, they reached the public house, Edward had stopped sobbing, but was still crying quietly with his handkerchief over his face. Diana looked at Benjamin. His face was a study in sadness. He still had his arm around Edward and was rocking him gently from side to side.

"I will go and get us a private room to dine in." Benjamin offered as he climbed from the coach. "Edward, pull the hood of your cloak over your head. It is rainy and cool so no one will notice if you do so. Wait for me here, both of you. I will be back to get you inside in just a few minutes."

Neither Diana nor Edward spoke a word to each other while they waited for Benjamin to come back. Diana crooned to the baby who had finally quietened. When Benjamin came back, he took Geoffrey and handed him to Bertha. He helped Diana from the carriage and then reached in for Edward. Edward stumbled from the carriage. Without Benjamin's support, he may have fallen. They entered the public house as quickly as they could, before the others could join them. Benjamin led them upstairs to a private room and left them to arrange for the meal and accommodations for the others in their party.

Edward slumped into a chair in front of the hearth still with his cloak on and the hood pulled up. Diana sat Geoffrey on the hearth rug and turned to Edward. Without a word, she pulled his hood down and took his cloak from his shoulders. He hung his head and didn't speak. Geoffrey crawled over to Edward and pulled up on his leg. Edward caressed the baby's head with one hand tenderly. Geoffrey babbled at him then surprised him when he called him Dada again. A hint of a smile flitted across Edward's face. It was the first smile of any kind Diana had seen from him since his father died.

After taking off her travelling cloak and bonnet, Diana sat in the other chair before the hearth looking at Edward with kindness.

He glanced up at her, then swiftly dropped his head to his chest once again.

"I am so sorry, Di. I should not have spoken to you as I did in the carriage. You have been nothing but kind to me in all this. I don't know what came over me. I am not normally so horrid, but I need a drink badly. I cannot stop shaking. Brandy is the only thing that stops the pain even a little bit. I have to have it, Di, I just have to."

"No, Edward, you do not have to have brandy. What you need is some food and a good cup of tea. You cannot go through your whole life drunk. Your father feared this more than anything. He spoke to me of you often before he died. He was so very worried that you would not be able to cope. I kept assuring him that you were stronger than even you thought you were. Look how well you did before Geoffrey was born. You didn't drink anything at all for months. You gained weight, your color was good. You were happy, I know you were. You can be happy again. I expect you to mourn your father, as will I, but you must mourn him without a brandy crutch. Benjamin and I will help you in any way we can. We both love you and want what is best for you."

"You don't understand, Di. I really am not strong like you and Benjamin. I am a weak and terrible person. I thought I would lose my mind after Geoffrey was killed, but I saw how very strong you were and I tried to be like you. I managed to fool even myself for a little while, but now with the death of my father and knowing all that I must do for the duchy, what little strength I had is gone. I would be better off dead."

Diana rose and put her arms around Edwards shoulders. "Do not ever let me hear you say that again, Edward. You might be better off, but what about me and little Geoffrey. And Benjamin, who loves you more than life itself. We love you too. You are Geoffrey's Dada. He depends on you for love and affection now while he's so tiny. And he will depend on you even more when he is older to teach him many things, like how to ride and shoot, and even how to shave his face. He needs you and I need you. You are my family in every sense of the word. You know I have never had a brother and you are that to me and more. Our world would be an empty place without you in it. I truly believe you are stronger than you know. Benjamin and I will be right beside you on any decisions you must make about the duchy. We have both studied all aspects of your properties and businesses. I dare say between the three of us, we will show an increase in profits at year's end. Just you wait and see."

Edward looked at the young girl whom he had married at his father's request. When had she grown into this beautiful young woman. It had been less than two years since they had married, but her maturity was many times her actual age. He knew he was not as intelligent as Diana, or Benjamin, for that matter. He wasn't as strong either, no matter what she said. Then he glanced down at little Geoffrey. He was looking up at him with his dead brother's bright blue eyes shining from his brother's face. The baby looked at him with love and trust. He might be able to disappoint Diana and Benjamin, but little Geoffrey was another thing altogether. He picked up the baby and held him close. His hands were still shaking, but maybe with the love of this child and Diana and Benjamin, he could pull himself together.

Chapter 24

Somehow, they all made it through the rest of the journey to Bristol Castle and the internment of the duke's body in the family crypt under the castle's chapel. Generations of Bristol dukes and their heirs had been entombed there, including Edward's mother. Between Diana and Fergus, they were able to take leave of the "leeches" in a short time, regardless of their grumbling about the shocking lack of hospitality. Diana explained to each of them that Edward was overcome with grief and needed to be alone with just his wife and child for quite some time. Since Edward had not shone his face except for the internment, the cousins had no choice but to leave the day after the burial.

Edward had a hard time for several days after the internment. At first he would not eat at all, then when he tried a couple of days later, nothing would stay down. He had trouble sleeping and would walk the floor of his bedchamber and the drawing room at all hours of the day and night. Not only his hands shook, but his whole body spasmed uncontrollably while he was going through the alcohol withdrawal. It took almost two weeks, but slowly he began to be able to eat and sleep again. After another week, he was almost back to his old self, though much quieter than before.

It was then that Fergus bid them adieu. He was satisfied that Diana and the bairn were no longer in any danger. He hardly believed the young man who came out to tell him goodbye was the same who had drunk himself through his father's funeral and interment. Edward did look some years older after his debacle, but otherwise was not the worse for it. Diana looked content as well. She smiled as she hugged her father goodbye. She noticed that Fergus was really showing his age now. The death of his friend and Edward's horrible behavior had taken a toll on him. She cautioned him to get some rest when he got home and to come again soon. Again, he waved his hat until he was across the moat and could no longer be seen.

The three friends soon established a routine. They would meet for breakfast after Diana had tended to Geoffrey in the drawing room between their bedchambers. All correspondence was delivered there by Edmonds. They would go over the correspondence and answer any needing immediate attention. Then they would go over the business and property accounts that needed it. By then it was time for luncheon. With the three of them working together, they were usually able to deal with all the business in the mornings and had the afternoons free.

The weather in Cornwall in May was glorious. The wildflowers were in bloom outside the castle walls and the castle gardens were spectacular. Every day that the weather was nice, the three friends would go riding. Diana had her beloved mare, Malmuirra, Benjamin rode a spirited gelding named Brutus, and Edward rode the large black stallion that had been his father's favorite steed, who had the incongruous name of Adonis. They were all excellent horsemen and enjoyed racing across the meadows at breakneck speed, laughing into the wind.

Edward still had bouts of melancholia, but could usually be jollied out of them by either Geoffrey or Diana. Benjamin's natural reticence didn't lend itself to joviality, but he made a great effort to help Diana alleviate Edward's moods any way he could. Since they would be in mourning until the next April, they were not expected to entertain or to go out in Society. That was all to the good. Diana wanted Edward to regain his equilibrium before he ventured out with the *ton* again. There were entirely too many n'er-do-wells in the *ton* who would be only too eager to steer Edward down the wrong path.

The months passed swiftly at Bristol Castle. Geoffrey began to walk and say a variety of words from Mama to horsey. He was a bright, happy little boy. A smile usually graced his little face. He was gregarious and everyone in the household loved him. Edward was especially taken with the little tot. Diana and Barbara with Bertha's help had converted the bedchamber on the other side of hers into a nursery. The traditional nursery was in a separate wing. Diana could not countenance having her baby so far from her.

After Geoffrey's first birthday in July, he was weaned from the breast. Since he had several teeth, he was able to eat solid foods. Diana and Edward decided he should come to the dining room for breakfast and sometimes luncheon. He had his dinner in the nursery and was put to bed before the adults went down to dinner in the evenings.

Edward would come into the nursery in the mornings and carry Geoffrey downstairs on his shoulders for breakfast. Diana knew they were seriously breaking protocol by having Geoffrey eat with the adults in the dining room, but she truly didn't care what Society expected of their children. She only knew she enjoyed her son's company and so did Edward and Benjamin. The child had a very good appetite and hardly met a food he didn't like. The cook still mashed or cut his food up very small, but he had no trouble eating it by himself in his little feeding chair that Benjamin had ordered from London for him. The chair was hand carved from mahogany and polished to a bright sheen by one of the downstairs maids every day. Benjamin had ordered Geoffrey's name to be carved in the back of the chair. Nothing was too good for the little duke to be.

Edward soon began talking about getting Geoffrey a pony, but Diana put a stop to that right away. He was entirely too young for a pony. She finally agreed that Geoffrey could have a pony for his fifth birthday. She and Edward both had received ponies at that stage in their lives, so she considered that the proper age for Geoffrey as well.

Fergus came to visit in late August. He couldn't stay away from his grandson any longer than that. Diana was shocked by her father's appearance on this visit. He seemed so much older than when she had seen him in April. It had only been four months, but he seemed ten years older.

On the first evening of his visit, he knocked on Diana's door just before dinner. Barbara was putting the finishing touches on Diana's coiffure when he came into the room.

"Lass, you are looking bonnie tonight. I take it from your appearance and Edward's that all is well at Bristol Castle."

"Yes, Da. I told you Edward would gain control of himself. He just needed our support and love. He is doing very well. He hasn't been drinking at all and is eating well and has gained back his weight. He is handling business matters every day with mine and Benjamin's help. I believe, barring any more family tragedies, we will all be just fine. How are you, though, Da? You don't really look well. Have you seen your doctor?"

"Yes, lass, I have seen him. Fat lot of good it did. You forget that I'm an old man now. I was not a young lad when you were born. Your mother and I had about given up hope of having a bairn when you finally came along. I will be sixty my next birthday and my body is tiring and becoming worn out. There is nothing in particular wrong with me. I just seem to stay tired. I have been thinking of having your cousin take over more of my duties for the earldom so I can rest more. I have even given the reins of the horse business to Edwin. I just don't have the energy to do all that travelling any more. He is younger and knows the business as well as I do."

Diana was amazed and worried. That her father was having his nephew and Edwin assume his duties was so out of character, she actually feared for Fergus' life. Later after dinner, she discussed her fears with Edward and Benjamin. They were also surprised at Fergus' appearance and his lack of energy.

As the days passed, Fergus seemed to be more rested and have more energy to play with Geoffrey. He spent a large part of each day with his grandson. Geoffrey loved all the attention and would sit quietly on Fergus' lap while he told him tales of waterhorses and kelpies. Though still a baby, Geoffrey loved to be told stories or read to. Diana was not sure how much he understood, but he seemed inordinately interested. Fergus had planned to stay a month, but as time grew near for him to leave, Diana convinced him to stay longer. He seemed so much better since he had arrived, she was reluctant to let him leave.

Finally, in early October, Fergus took his leave. He wanted to get home before the weather turned the roads into mush. Diana, Edward, and Benjamin waved goodbye as Fergus' carriage rolled across the moat bridge. The wind was very cold coming off the sea. Although it was early fall, the weather in Cornwall felt more like winter. Diana was not looking forward to another long cold winter in Cornwall. They had spent last winter at the castle and Diana remembered how many extremely cold, wet days there had been. They had been unable to go outdoors for weeks on end.

After turning one in July, Geoffrey had become very curious and was a bundle of energy. He ran Bertha and Diana ragged each day just keeping up with him. Now with Fergus gone, Edward and Benjamin helped to corral him as well. They had to keep all the doors closed because Geoffrey was fascinated by the staircases. If he got loose from one of his keepers, he would invariably head to the staircase. Diana was very worried about the stairs closest to their rooms.

Finally after much research, Benjamin found an advertisement for a gate that could be attached to the newel posts at the head of the stairs near their rooms. He immediately ordered it from London and it arrived two weeks later by special messenger. Diana felt much relief when the gate was finally installed. Geoffrey could look down the stairs, but the gate was much too high for him to try to climb over. It was very strong as well, so he couldn't push it open either.

Geoffrey was growing so quickly, they had trouble keeping him in clothes. He was still in dresses, but Edward was lobbying for breeches to be made for the little tyke. He told Diana he and his brother Geoffrey had each been dressed in breeches by age two. Diana thought he should remain in dresses for several more months. He was no where near being able to unfasten breeches with his little hands. He was just now, in January, at almost eighteen months, using the chamberpot on his own. Diana finally convinced Edward to give the tyke at least six more months in dresses to improve his dexterity before putting him in breeches.

Days turned into weeks and weeks into months. There were visits from the mining managers, the farm manager, the solicitor and the general man of business. The businesses were all running well, the tenants were enjoying good crops and there were no major problems to be dealt with. Edward continued to stay sober and became more and more like his old self, only better. He doted on Geoffrey as did Benjamin and Diana.

When the weather turned good again in late March, it was no longer just the three of them riding across the countryside. Geoffrey either rode in front of Edward or Diana. He would be two in July and was anxious for his breeches so he could be just like his Dada and Uncle Benjy. For the first time since Geoffrey's death, Diana was truly happy. She had her two best friends and her wonderful little son. She had recently received a letter from her father and he had assured her his health was no worse, no better, but no worse. She had also heard from Ian. He and Alana had another child, a girl, whom they had named Diana in her honor. She was supremely happy for them. All was right with her world.

As the end of their mourning period was drawing near, the friends started to make plans to return to London in April. There would be much to be done before they could re-enter Society. Diana was apprehensive about returning there. She had not especially enjoyed her few months of Society when she was in London the year before. She was looking forward to a new wardrobe however. After almost 2 years in black, she would be very happy to wear some brighter colors. Benjamin had ordered the latest ladies' and gentleman's fashion journals. He, Diana and Edward spent some merry evenings talking about the clothes they would have made. Diana had never been very fashion conscious, but she had discovered when she was last in Society that being dressed correctly was imperative.

The men were anxious to have the new trousers just coming into fashion made for themselves. Beau Brummel had introduced the new style and it was now all the rage. Men had worn breeches for hundreds of years both for daytime and evening wear, but the new style was taking over quickly. The new trousers were much more comfortable and warmer in the winter. Breeches were still worn for evening however. Both Edward and Benjamin could hardly wait to visit their tailor on Seville Row to choose fabrics and styles.

Chapter 25

At last the day came for them to start the five day journey from Cornwall to London. For this trip, they had only three carriages. Edward insisted they wouldn't need all their clothes as they were all getting new wardrobes very soon after their arrival. They had only their best clothes packed and gave the rest to the castle servants. Diana gave Barbara and Bertha first choice on her things. She was so much shorter than the other two women, they had to let down hems and add frills to be able to wear her dresses. Bertha was also much plumper, but since the Empire style had full skirts, fitted under the breasts, the bodices could be let out to accommodate her fuller figure. Both of the women were very grateful for the clothes. Not all mistresses were so generous.

Edward also gave his clothes to the servants. However, he found that only the very youngest would fit in them or were interested in them. The older servants could never see themselves wearing some of Edward's rather outlandish costumes. He also left some of his mourning clothes behind for the servants. He could hardly wait to become a peacock again.

The trip on the toll roads was uneventful. Since it was the fourth time they had made the journey together, they knew which inns and public houses were the best and which to avoid. Geoffrey was also a year older and needed a lot more distraction on this trip. Diana made sure to pack plenty of picture books, paper and charcoal for drawing, and toys for him. Benjamin had ordered him a set of lead soldiers from London and he spent hours playing with them. Edward had found a carved horse with tiny wheels attached to its hooves pulling a little cart for Geoffrey on a trip he had made to meet with one of the mine managers in St. Ives. He had bought it for Geoffrey's first birthday. Geoffrey would kneel on the floor of the carriage and roll the little wheels on the seat over and over.

When Geoffrey tired of his toys, he would climb into someones lap and ask for a story or a book. Usually after hearing a couple of stories, he would fall asleep for an hour or so in the afternoons. The cradle had been taken out of the carriage as Geoffrey was much too large to fit into it now. One of the adults would hold him or lay him next to Diana on the seat. Having him lie on the seat worried Diana. She feared he would fall if they hit a big bump or the carriage had to stop suddenly for some reason. She became so agitated that finally, Benjamin sat on a cushion on the floor of the carriage in front of the sleeping child in case he fell. After that, Diana was able to relax.

Finally after five long, exhausting days, they reached the house in Town. Forbes must have been watching for them, for the front door opened before the carriage came to a halt. Footmen and maids flowed out of the house to assist with unloading the carriages. Soon everyone was inside and upstairs in their rooms. Diana had sent instructions months prior for the bedroom next to hers to be converted to a nursery as had been done at Bristol Castle. Forbes had seen to everything.

The nursery was decorated as befitted a tiny future duke. The room had been painted a sunny yellow. It was furnished with the crib and other furniture from the nursery that Edward and Geoffrey had shared when they were small, all freshly painted white. There were new, filmy white muslin curtains at the windows that let in the light making the nursery a bright and happy place. There were also heavier dark green drapes that could be pulled at night or during the winter to keep out the cold. Diana was very pleased with the results. Bertha would sleep in the room with Geoffrey and a very comfortable bed had been moved in for her. She was also very pleased. She had never slept in such a fine bed. She loved her little charge very much and enjoyed being his nurse.

The next few weeks were busy indeed. Every day there were trips to the modiste and tailor, the glove maker, the shoe maker, the hat maker, the ribbon store and on and on. Diana was exhausted by the time Edward declared their wardrobes complete.

Diana now had ten day dresses with coordinating shawls, ten walking dresses with matching or coordinating spencers or pelisses, six new riding habits with boots and hats, and an even dozen evening gowns with all the necessary accessories. Since the fashions of the time were made from very thin muslin and silk she also had two dozen chemises and the same number of frilly petticoats. Being so slim, she didn't need corsets nor the new "divorce" to separate her breasts. As she was so young, her breasts were still high and firm, although somewhat larger after breast feeding for a year.

Edward would have dressed her in every color in the rainbow if she had not intervened. With her red hair and pale complexion, she felt she couldn't wear some colors well. Bright colors and patterns were just being introduced to high fashion and there was also an increase in the amount of trimming added to women's clothes. Diana was more comfortable with less rather than more and had instructed her modiste accordingly.

Her clothes were not drab by any means, but neither were they overburdened with an abundance of frills. She had chosen jewel tones for most of her evening clothes with a minimum of lace and flounces. Her day dresses were lighter colors, but still in shades of green, yellow, gold , blue and bronze with only such frills as were absolutely required by fashion. The same applied to her bonnets and caps.

Edward on the other hand, had a wardrobe to make a peacock jealous. He had plaid and striped trousers with matching coats and coordinating waistcoats in a wide array of colors. His cravats were waterfalls of frills and color. His evening ensembles were made of brocaded satins and silks in several colors. He had plain white shirts, colored shirts, and shirts with ruffles for evening. And more shoes and boots than any one man could ever need. With his fair hair and blue eyes, he could wear almost any color and he did.

Benjamin, being much more conservative, had chose more sombre colors, but had taken up the same new trouser suits and styles as Edward. They made a dashing pair when they went about town together. Benjamin now wore the title of secretary rather than valet, in the public eye. It was perfectly acceptable for a gentleman's secretary to accompany him around Town, where it would have been fodder for gossip if Edward took his valet with him everywhere.

The three of them had to become used to Society's rules now that they were back in London. The freedom they had shared at Bristol Castle was no more. Since their year of mourning was over, as soon as the word was out they were back in Town, the invitations began to flood in. Every day, there were more and more people coming to call. Edward had had cards printed for himself, Benjamin and Diana. It was unusual for a secretary to have cards with his own name, so Edward had his name put on them as well, with Benjamin's name under his with the title Secretary after his name.

They had to observe the proprieties in all things to avoid gossip. Talk had been bandied around about Edward before Geoffrey's death. It was mostly because of the company he kept at that time and his rather wild drinking habits. Since he was now a married man with a child, that talk had subsided. However, they all knew that ruinous rumors could be started for very inconsequential reasons.

Diana was reluctant to accept invitations for every day or night. She kept her activities down to three times per week. She didn't want to impinge on her time with Geoffrey nor with the time she spent with Edward and Benjamin on duchy business. She was the exception to the rule. Most ladies of the *ton* accepted more than one invitation per day starting with luncheon, then on to tea, then afternoon musicales, and balls, the theater, or entertainments in the evenings.

Being seen at only certain events, created a sense of mystery around Diana and Edward and even more invitations came. Also, since they only attended functions as a couple, they were the exception in Society. Most couples were only seen together on special occasions. Benjamin quietly spread the word, through other secretaries and valets that he knew, that they were very wrapped up in each other and their child.

This also added to the aura of mystery since most Society ladies hardly saw their spouses or children. The children were reared by nurses, or governesses when they were older. Most upper crust marriages of the time were marriages of convenience. The matches were made for either social position or to improve one or the other partner's financial status. There were a few love matches, but they were in the minority. The men of Society concerned themselves with their holdings, their hobbies, their clubs and their mistresses. The ladies spent their time with their wardrobes, their friends, their lovers and gossip.

Diana did take the time to attend some charitable events. She had a strong sense of community from her work with her father's tenants. She was appalled by the plight of the poor orphaned children in London. She worked relentlessly with other like-minded ladies to improve the few orphanages in the city and to raise money to build more. She was the youngest and usually the most attractive personage on those committees. Her peers were not interested in such things and didn't understand her interest either. However, her youth and beauty helped to bring contributions up and she was welcomed with open arms.

Also, instead of riding in a carriage in the park like the other ladies, Diana rode her mare between Edward and Benjamin. Some other ladies rode, but not every day like Diana. She enjoyed riding and had no intention of giving it up. Edward was supportive in this as well. He wanted Diana to be happy and if riding made her happy, then she would ride and he would accompany her. Edward and Benjamin also much enjoyed riding, so the situation was beneficial to all. The men's presence stifled what would have normally been juicy gossip and lent credibility to the rumors started by Benjamin.

Ladies of the time would pay calls in the late mornings. Diana rarely received her visitors. She had instructed Forbes to tell them she was out, although she was actually busy. She, Edward and Benjamin maintained their normal work times on duchy business in the mornings after their play time with Geoffrey. Most Society ladies and gentlemen kept late hours, not usually rising until after nine in the morning. Breakfast was usually around ten. In their household, Diana, Edward and Benjamin rose early, usually around seven. They would dress and meet in the dining room before eight. After breakfast, they would spend a couple of hours with Geoffrey in the library. When it was time for their work day to begin, Bertha would take Geoffrey into a corner and read to him or play with him while they worked, but he remained in the library.

They would have luncheon in the library with Geoffrey, giving Bertha some time off to have her meal with the other servants in the kitchen. After luncheon, if their work day was finished and they had no meetings, they would all go upstairs to the nursery and spend time with Geoffrey until he was ready for his nap. Bertha would take over and they would dress for their ride in the park. If the weather permitted, they rode every day. Diana had always ridden, rain or shine. Since it rained so much in Scotland, she found it amusing that ladies of the *ton* rarely set foot outside if there was more than a mist. Edward and Benjamin, who hunted in all weather, also had no problem riding in the rain. Unless there was a downpour, they could be found astride their horses every afternoon.

Their happy routine abruptly ceased when a letter came from Fergus asking Diana to come home to Ainsley Glen as soon as she could. In the back of her mind, Diana had been expecting that letter. Her father's health had seemed to decline rapidly in the last few months according to his letters. He wanted to see his daughter and grandson one more time he said. When Diana showed the letter to Edward and Benjamin, they immediately began to arrange for the journey. It would take about ten days to reach Ainsley Glen. Within two days, everything was packed and all arrangements had been made.

Chapter 25

On a cool dreary day in late May, four carriages left London for the Highlands of Scotland carrying some very worried people. Diana had requested that they take their horses on this trip. She knew it would be very difficult to keep Geoffrey busy for ten days in a carriage. He loved to ride and would be much happier and more easily entertained on the back of a horse with either she or Edward. She would also find the time easier to bear if she was riding. She couldn't begin to be able to face sitting in the carriage worrying about her father for ten days.

On the second day of the journey, the sun was shining brightly. Everyone was much happier that they could ride on this day. For safety's sake there were ten footman accompanying them, as well as the drivers for all five carriages. Highwaymen were always a problem and they wanted to be prepared at all costs. Geoffrey's death at the hands of highwaymen was ever present in their minds when they travelled. The footmen either rode on top of the carriages or on horseback. The ones on horseback would accompany Edward, Diana and Benjamin when they would ride ahead of the carriages as protection. All in all there were thirty-five people in their party so the trip was slow indeed.

One of the grooms and one of the footmen would ride ahead swiftly to find accommodations for luncheon and then for the night. They ate in public houses and inns for the most part, but sometimes stayed with acquaintances in whatever neighborhood they were passing through at the time. Three times, they stayed at properties they owned as they travelled north through England.

Although they were trying to make the trip as quickly as they could, they did take the time to meet, in the evenings, with their farm and business managers when they stayed on duchy property. They were able to accomplish quite a bit in those brief evening meetings. In the normal course of things, they would have visited these properties soon anyway, so there was some good that came of the journey.

The days seemed to drag by for Diana. She was so worried about her father, she found the slow torturous journey maddening. Fortunately it was June and the weather was fine for the first week on the road and they could all ride their horses every day. Then their luck changed and it began to rain steadily for the last three days of the trip. By the time the large party reached Ainsley Glen, they were all exhausted and tempers were frayed. Trying to keep a very active, almost two year old occupied while stuck in a carriage was much harder than they had supposed. Geoffrey was a normal, active, very curious little boy and it was quite difficult for him to be confined for long periods every day.

It was dusk when the carriages pulled into the long winding drive of Ainsley Glen. One of the grooms had ridden ahead, so they were expected. Mrs. Allen, Mrs. Gwen, Murtaugh and Edwin Burroughs along with most of the staff hurried out of the house as they arrived. Diana was enveloped in the arms of the two ladies almost as her feet touched the ground. They made a huge fuss over Geoffrey also. He was soon whisked off the the nursery by Bertha and one of the maids for a warm bath and dinner.

Fergus was not among the crowd that welcomed them. Instantly Diana was even more alarmed. Her father must be ill indeed if he wasn't able to greet her. She rushed into the house and she and Edward were directed by Mrs. Gwen to her father's bedchamber. Fergus was propped up on pillows in the huge old bed. Diana could hardly believe her eyes. Her once large vigorous father was a shell of himself. He was so thin his face appeared gaunt. His skin looked thin and papery and his hair had gone all white.

"Diana, lass, it is wonderful to see you. I have tried so hard to hang on until you arrived. I am afraid I have very little time left. It warms my heart to see you home again."

"Oh, Da, why didn't you write sooner. We would have come right away. Why did you wait so long?"

"Oh, lass, I haven't really been ill for long. I took a fall from my horse a few weeks ago. I didn't seem to be hurt badly, nothing broken. Then I developed a fever and couldn't hold down my food. I have gone down hill rapidly since. The doctor has been here several times, but he can't seem to find any medicine that works. I still cannot eat solid food at all. Even Mrs. Allen's good broths sometimes won't stay down."

Just speaking for even a short time seemed to tire Fergus terribly. Diana took her father's thin, white hand and smoothed his hair off his forehead.

"Just rest, Da. We are here now. Do not worry about anything, just rest."

Diana and Edward exchanged worried glances as Fergus drifted off to sleep. Neither of them could countenance the changes just a few short months had wrought in him. Diana knew immediately that her father was not going to survive this illness. She felt the specter of death hanging over Ainsley Glen once again.

It was very late. Diana had heard the clock in the hallway strike three as she sat beside her sleeping father. Edward had tried to convince her to go to bed and let one of the others sit with Fergus, but she would have none of it. Fergus hadn't awakened again. His breathing was labored and shallow. Diana feared he would never wake again. She so wanted him to see Geoffrey at least one more time before he was gone forever.

Sometimes she felt as if everyone she loved went away from her. It made her worry for the safety of her child. It seemed to her when she loved someone, they died. First her mother, then Geoffrey, the duke and now her father. So much loss for one so young. She was only eighteen and almost alone in the world. She loved Edward like a brother, as she did Benjamin, but hers was not a real marriage and they were not related by blood. She hardly knew her MacDonald cousins having been raised so far from them.

She sometimes thought wistfully of the kind of marriage she might have had with Geoffrey. They had talked of their future together, but somehow she had never been able to visualize how it would be. Now, as she looked back, she realized they had really had very little time together. A matter of a few weeks spent together, a couple of letters exchanged after he had left. That was all she really had of Geoffrey, except his son. When she looked upon her son's face, she saw his father. The same bright blue eyes and dark curling hair, even his smile was the same. She would never need a reminder of Geoffrey, she had a living one.

As Diana ruminated on her life and losses, time marched slowly on. Before long, she could see the first wisps of daylight through the heavy drapes that hung on the windows in her father's bedchamber. She gazed on her father's pale, gaunt face. As she was looking at him intently, his green eyes opened and he smiled gently at her.

"You really are here lass. I thought I had dreamt you."

"No, Da. I am not a dream. It is so good to see you smile. How do you feel?"

"I feel just fine, lass. I have no pain now. I will be with my Morna soon. I am very sorry to leave you, my sweet bairn, but it is my time. I wish I could leave this world knowing you were happy. That was always your mother's and my wish for you. We only wanted you to be happy."

"I am happy enough, Da. I have Geoffrey and also Edward and Benjamin. That is enough for me. I need nothing more except you. Are you sure you are leaving me? Do you not believe you will get better in time?"

"Nay, lass. I will not get better. Whatever is wrong with me, it is too much for my old tired body to fight. I have willed myself to live long enough to see you and Geoffrey. That is the best I can do. Please do not ask me to keep fighting. I just do not have it in me anymore."

"I will not ask it of you then, Da. I do not want you to suffer, though I will miss you more than I can say. You have always been my rock. You were there for me when Mama died and again when I lost Geoffrey. Without you, I am not sure I would have made it myself."

"Nay, Diana. You are much stronger than you give yourself credit for. You are the one who helped me survive when we lost your mother. Without you to cling to, I would not have been able to go on. As for Geoffrey, I wish I could have done more for you. I still regret allowing you to marry Edward so swiftly. At the time it seemed the only answer, but now, now…"

Fergus seemed so distressed, Diana rose and put her arms around him. "Da, please do not trouble yourself on my account. I am content. Edward is who he is. There is nothing to be done about it. We are married and will remain so. He treats me kindly and he loves Geoffrey with all his being. He is a very good father to him. I do not need anything more."

Fergus sighed deeply and closed his eyes again. He was soon asleep. Diana sat in the chair again and held his hand. Mrs. Allen came into the room after quietly knocking on the door.

"Diana, darling, why don't you let me sit with the Laird. Geoffrey is up and wanting his Mama. Maybe after you both have some breakfast you can bring him here. I know the Laird has been anxious to see you both. He has spoken of little else."

"All right, Mrs. Allen. If there is any change, please have me summoned."

Diana went directly to the nursery. When she opened the door, Edward was sitting in the rocking chair holding Geoffrey on his knee and reading him a book. They both looked up and smiled at her.

Geoffrey climbed down and ran to her. She picked him up and hugged him closely. She loved the feel and the smell of him. His dark curly hair was so soft and smelled so sweet. She never tired of holding his small body against hers. She knew absolutely, he was safe when he was in her arms.

"How is your father this morning, Di?"

"Not very well, Edward. I believe we got here just in time. I want to have some breakfast with you and Geoffrey and then take him in to see Da. We shouldn't waste much time."

Edward knew immediately that the old earl was not long for this world. He gathered his little family and escorted them down to the dining room. They ate quickly and hurried Geoffrey along as best they could. After calling for a maid to bring a wet cloth, they wiped him up and Edward carried him to see his grandfather.

When Diane, Edward, and Geoffrey entered the room, the doctor was there. Fergus was awake again, but his breathing was even more labored than before. Edward carried Geoffrey to the bed.

Diana went around to the other side and spoke quietly to the doctor for a few minutes. He could offer her no hope.

She turned her attention from the doctor to her father. Geoffrey was sitting on the counterpane holding Fergus' hand with one of his and petting him on the arm with the other. The child seemed to know instinctively that something was wrong. His normal exuberance was curbed and he sat quietly. Tears filled Diana's eyes as she watched the two people she loved best in the world comfort each other. She looked up and Edward was watching her with tears in his eyes as well. She went to the other side of the bed and sat softly behind Geoffrey laying her hand on her father's leg.

No one spoke, there was no need for words. The love they felt for each other was palpable in the air. The doctor very quietly left the room. There was nothing more he could do for his old friend, Fergus had the people he loved with him. That was all that was required now.

Fergus MacDonald, Earl of Ainsley, laird to his people and beloved father and grandfather died that day, just minutes after Edward took Geoffrey from the room. Diana sat alone with her father for quite some time. She shed many tears as she lay her head next to his on his pillow. He had been a good father to her and she had loved him with all her heart.

When Diana left her father's bedchamber, she immediately went downstairs and sent one of the grooms to notify her cousin Robert, the new Earl MacDonald. She asked Edwin Burroughs to come to the library next. They had not seen each other since he had escorted she and Edward to Bristol Castle just after they were married. Edwin had been her father's trusted employee, but also his friend. Edwin noticed right away that Diana had matured greatly since the last time he had seen her. She was more beautiful than ever, but she wasn't the green girl he had reluctantly left at Bristol Castle.

Diana was grieving for her father, but she was also taking care of everything that needed to be done. She informed him that her cousin had been sent for. She asked him to call a meeting of the tenants for the next morning. She knew that she would inherit Ainsley Glen and all the lands around it. This property had belonged to her paternal grandmother's family for many years, and therefore was not entailed to the earldom. Robert MacDonald and his family already occupied what was the MacDonald seat. Ainsley Glen had been given to her father when his mother had died. His older brother, Andrew, was still alive and the earl at that time. When Andrew died of pneumonia without a male heir, Fergus became earl. Fergus had decided not to move his family to the family seat. He left that property in the care of his younger brother Robert, but maintained control of the earldom. When Robert, died at a young age, he asked Robert's son to continue to live at the family seat. After all, he would inherit the title and the family seat, so Fergus asked him to live there and care for the land until he inherited it. It was an unusual arrangement, but Fergus had been an unusual and very generous man.

When Diana met with Edwin, she also informed him that she wanted him to be the new laird of Ainsley Glen. He protested, but she insisted she needed someone to look after her home and her people that she could trust implicitly. She explained that she had to live in England now with her husband, but needed to know everything would be taken care of correctly. Edwin was very proud that Diana saw him in that light. He had always cared very deeply for her and her father. He had been concerned for her welfare from the time she was born.

The next morning, Diana walked out onto the steps at the front of the keep. There was a crowd of men and older boys standing with their hats in their hands and their heads bowed. The earl had been very beloved by his tenants. He had always been more than fair to them as had his daughter. Most of them knew that Diana would inherit Ainsley Glen and its lands, but were concerned now that she had married and lived so far away.

Diana assured them all that things would go on as before. She gave them the news that Edwin would be the new laird, acting in her stead. This pleased the men. They all knew Edwin and knew him to be fair and honest. Diana also told them they would owe no rent for this quarter. They were astonished by this until Diana said she was doing it to honor her father. After her speech to the men, Diana had the footmen circulate with trays holding glasses of good Scotch whiskey. She took one herself and raised her glass high.

"To Fergus MacDonald, the best laird and father this world has ever known."

With that she raised her glass and drank it down as did all present including Edwin. There were few dry eyes in the crowd.

Later that day, Robert MacDonald, along with his wife and children arrived at Ainsley Glen. Diana and Edwin met with him in the library for several hours along with Fergus' solicitor and man of business. Diana had never felt close to her cousin Robert, but she respected and liked him. He was a large taciturn man with little humor. However, he was not unkind. Diana knew he would perform the duties of the earldom well, if with little imagination.

The funeral for Fergus was set for three days hence giving neighbors far and wide a chance to travel to Ainsley Glen. Edward watched his wife with amazement. He knew how much she had loved her father and how hard all this was for her. However, she never hesitated to do all that was required to establish the new earl and the new laird of Ainsley Glen. When he went looking for her at the end of the day, he found her in the garden sitting on a bench staring up at the sky. Edward didn't say anything, just sat beside her and reached for her hand. She turned to him and gave him a sad smile.

"Is Geoffrey already in his bed?"

"No, that's why I have come looking for you. He is wanting his Mama. Will you come up with me to tell him goodnight?"

"Of course. I haven't had much time to spend with him today or with you. There is much to be done here before we can return to England. I know there is much to be done on duchy business as well. I fear we will have to stay here another week or more after we bury my father to get all completed."

"We can stay as long as necessary. If there is pressing duchy business both our solicitor and man of business know where we are. They can send a runner if anything needs immediate attention. Any other matters can wait or be dealt with by post. Do not worry about any of that right now. How are you? You have not had much time to grieve for your father."

"I will have the rest of my life to grieve for my father. I am doing what he would want me to do. I am taking care of his land and his people. My father had all his affairs in order. He either had a premonition of his death or he was ill longer than anyone knew. He left everything spelled out exactly as he wanted it to be done. I am just the arbiter of his wishes. I thank him for that tremendously. Right now, I am not sure I would be able to make these decisions on my own. Because of his foresight, I don't need to."

"Your father loved you very much. If he had any inkling of his death, I am sure he would have wanted to spare you as much as possible. He and my father were much alike in that."

"Yes, they were. They both loved their children above all else. After having had Geoffrey, I can understand."

With that, Diana rose and taking Edward's hand, she went inside and up the stairs to be with her son.

The day of Earl Fergus MacDonald's funeral began with sunshine and ended with rain. Diana thought that was fitting somehow. Her father was buried in the cemetery on Ainsley Glen beside her mother. The headstone Fergus had chosen for his beloved wife was large enough for both of them and already had his name engraved upon it. All it was lacking was the date of his death. Diana would have to see to having that done before she left for London, she thought as she stood with the rest of the friends and family who had come for the service. She was trying to think of anything except her father being really gone. She didn't want to disgrace him by falling apart at his graveside.

Edward stood by her side with Benjamin on the other side. Edwin stood just behind her with his father and mother. The rest of the crowd was made up of Robert, his family, other distance relatives and Ainsley Glen's neighbors and friends. All the tenants were there as well, but stood a respectful distance from the gentry.

Diana was glad to see Angus MacAllister in the crowd of friends and neighbors when she had arrived. He looked better than last she had seen him. After the service, everyone returned to the keep. Diana made her rounds to greet everyone and make sure they had food and drink. She made her way to Angus's side as soon as she could.

"Laird MacAllister, how are you? It is good to see you again although for a very sad reason."

"Aye, lassie. 'Tis good to see you as well. I'm doing fine and I can see from looking at you that you are doing very well yourself. I understand you have a bairn. A wee braw lad, I hear tell."

"Yes, sir. My Geoffrey is almost two. He keeps me busy. Have you heard from Ian lately? I had a letter a couple of weeks ago. He seems to be making quite a life for himself and his family in America."

"Aye, I had a letter around then myself. He does seem to be doing well. You know, lass, I was some upset with you when you helped Ian and Alana go to America. But I have to say, it seems to have worked out fine. I should pay you back the money you gave them to leave on."

"No, no, my lord. That was a gift to Ian and Alana, not a loan. They are my friends and have been my whole life. It was my pleasure to help them in their time of need. You must be proud to know your name will continue in a new land what with Ian having two boys now."

"Aye, lass, it does. I would love to see those boys as well as little Diana. Ian has sent letters telling me all about them, but to actually see them, well that would be really something."

"Why don't you go to see Ian and his family, my lord? I know Ian would be ever so happy to see you."

"I have thought on it, but I just don't know about sailing all that way. It happens I have the seasickness. When I sailed to France in my younger days, I was sick the whole way there and the whole way back. And that's a short voyage. Going to American would take a month or more. I probably wouldn't survive."

"I'm so sorry, my lord, I didn't know. I've never been on a ship. If I ever do go on a voyage, I hope I don't have that problem."

Diana spent some more time speaking to Angus and his family, then moved on to the other guests. After what seemed hours, the last guests took their leave. Diana dropped into a chair in the drawing room in exhaustion. Just as she was about to go out to the garden for some well deserved rest, she heard the crack of lightening striking nearby. The rain began to come down very hard in sheets, with thunder rumbling loudly.

Well, thought Diana, at least everyone got away before the rain started. She was relieved. She had been so busy the last few days, she had hardly had time to even think of her father, much less to grieve for him. She needed some time alone. She tiredly climbed the stairs to her bedchamber. She had the room she had had since she was small, while she was at Ainsley Glen this time. Edward and Benjamin had rooms right down the hall and Geoffrey and Bertha were sleeping in her dressing room on a little bed that she had moved in just for them.

Diana loosened her stays and lay down on the bed to rest. The sound of the rain was soothing as she closed her eyes. Before she knew it, she was asleep.

Chapter 26

The next days passed quickly as she, Robert and Edwin met several times with the solicitor and man of business to complete the transfer of the earldom and the tenancy of Ainsley Glen. Finally, everything was done and Robert and his family left for the MacDonald ancestral home. Diana began preparations for the return to London. She knew they needed to get back as soon as possible.

The long journey was uneventful until the eighth day. The weather had been cooperative so Diana, Edward and Benjamin were on horseback, riding ahead of the carriages. Geoffrey was riding in front of Edward when suddenly his horse spooked and took off running through the woods at the side of the road. Diana, Benjamin and the footmen riding with them all took off in pursuit.

They could hear the horse crashing through the woods in a panic ahead of them. Diana was terrified for both Edward and her son. The woods were very dense with low hanging limbs and a lot of underbrush. Suddenly they heard the horse scream in agony. They could hear a loud crash as well.

Diana was in the lead of the group when she came to a deep ravine. She pulled Malmuirra up sharply to keep her from going over the side. At the bottom of the ravine, she could see Edward's big black stallion lying on his side, kicking his feet in terror. The more he kicked the more tangled he became in the underbrush at the bottom of the ravine.

Diana jumped off her mare and ran down the side of the ravine as quickly as she could. She saw Edward, but she didn't see Geoffrey. Edward was partially trapped under the horse. His left leg was wedged between the horse and the ground. He was unconscious, with blood running down his face from a cut on his forehead. Diana ran to him. He was breathing, at least.

Benjamin had reached them by this time and took over checking on Edward. One of the grooms got the horses head and quieted him. Diana and some of the footmen frantically looked for Geoffrey. Finally, they found his little body, broken and bleeding some distance from the horse and Edward above the ravine. Diana dropped down beside him and lifted him into her lap. She rocked her poor broken baby, wailing pitifully.

Diana didn't hear the gunshot that put the stallion out of his misery. She was totally oblivious to the sounds of the footmen and Benjamin pulling Edward from beneath the dead horse. They carried Edward up the ravine embankment. One of the footmen had ridden to meet the carriage hurrying them along. They lay Edward in the carriage on one of the seats. He had been blessedly unconscious so far.

Benjamin went to Diana and tried to console her, to no avail. She was hysterical and could not be calmed. They tried to take Geoffrey from her and she screamed and fought them. Finally, Benjamin picked her up while she still held her baby and carried them both to the waiting carriage.

Barbara came running with tears coursing down her face. She and Bertha had been told that Geoffrey was dead. Benjamin set Diana down on her feet. Her wailing had subsided into deep painful sobs by this time. Barbara wrapped her arms around her mistress and the baby and pulled her toward the carriages. Diana was unmindful of what was going on around her. She let herself be lead to a carriage and assisted in by Benjamin. She sat on the seat and slowly rocked her dead baby as she cried. Benjamin climbed into the carriage and knelt on the floor checking on Edward. He was still unconscious. Benjamin had instructed the driver to go as quickly as possible to the next town. He held Edward as steady as he could during the two hour trip.

When they arrived in Warwick, the driver went to the closest inn. Benjamin leaped from the carriage while it was still moving accosting the first hostler he saw to inquire on the whereabouts of a doctor. The hostler hurried to fetch the doctor while Benjamin went inside the inn to get accommodations for their party.

When Benjamin returned to the carriage, he again attempted to get Diana to give him Geoffrey. She would not give up her baby to him or anyone. Barbara climbed into the carriage next, but it was useless. Finally, Benjamin lifted Diana down, while she still held Geoffrey, and escorted her into the inn and up to their rooms. He settled her in a rocking chair in front of the fireplace with Barbara by her side. Diana had stopped crying finally, but it was worse somehow that she just stared down at her child with empty eyes as she rocked him.

Benjamin returned to the carriage and with the help of several of the footmen, they carried Edward inside and up to the bedchamber assigned to them. Benjamin was afraid to move him too much, but did remove his coat, waistcoat, and cravat. He feared Edward's leg was badly broken and didn't remove the boot on that leg, but removed the other one. He tenderly washed the blood from Edward's face. The cut had stopped bleeding so profusely, but continued to seep. Edward's breathing seemed fine, but he hadn't awakened since the accident. There was a huge knot on his head above and around the cut on his forehead. Edward's leg was swollen and blood oozed from more than one place. When Benjamin accidentally touched Edward's leg, he moaned, but still didn't wake up.

The doctor finally arrived. He examined Edward's head wound, then took a pair of scissors from his bag and began to cut his trousers off. Every time his leg was moved, Edward would groan and move his head from side to side, but he was still not conscious.

Barbara came into the room and spoke to Benjamin about Diana. The doctor turned from working on Edward's leg to inquire about her injuries. Benjamin explained that she was not injured, but her child had been killed in the accident. He also explained that they couldn't get Diana to give up the child's body. She had been holding him for hours. The doctor went to his bag and gave a small bottle to Barbara.

"This is laudanum. Drop three or four drops into a cup of tea and get her to drink it any way you can, even if you have to pour it down her throat. It will put her to sleep. You will be able to take the child then and get your mistress to bed. She should sleep until tomorrow. Then bring back to the bottle to me. Your master will be needing some of it very soon when I set his leg."

Barbara did as she was told. After the tea she ordered had arrived, she dropped four drops into it and took it to Diana. It hurt her heart to have to force her young mistress to drink the tea, but she managed to get most of it down her throat. Soon, Diana began to sway in the chair and then went to sleep. Her arms finally let go of her sad burden. Bertha took the child and lay him on the settle.

Between the two women, Barbara and Bertha, they were able to get Diana undressed and into the bed. Her clothes had been covered in her husband's and child's blood. When they finally got them off, Barbara put them in the fireplace to burn. She knew Diana would never wish to wear them again, even if they could be cleaned.

In the meantime, the doctor had Benjamin call up one of the footmen to help them. They got the rest of Edward's clothes off, but didn't bother putting a nightshirt on him. The doctor stitched up his head and bandaged it. Finally, it was time to try to set his leg. It had swollen so much, the doctor wasn't sure he could even pull it straight. He had asked if any ice was available and someone from the inn had gone to a nearby castle and asked for some. When they found a nobleman was injured, the duke in residence was happy to oblige. Benjamin had the ice broken into small chunks and he and the doctor had packed it around Edward's leg before the doctor started on his head.

The leg was broken in two places and the bone had broken the skin in both of them. The ice had taken down some of the swelling, but not all. The doctor instructed Benjamin and the footmen to hold Edward's shoulders while he tried to put the broken bones back into place. When the doctor pulled on his leg, Edward came to with a scream of pain. It was all Benjamin and the footman could do to hold him steady while the doctor worked on him. The pain was so intense that Edward soon passed out again. The doctor was able to marginally straighten the leg, but it would not be perfectly straight when it healed. He explained to Benjamin that he had done the best he could, but the injury was very severe and the elapsed time between the accident and their arrival, plus the subsequent swelling had impeded his ability to completely straighten the leg. He stitched the two wounds on the leg and immobilized it with boards, tying the leg to the boards with rags.

The doctor handed the bottle of laudanum to Benjamin with instructions to give Edward a dose whenever he woke for the next couple of days. Edward would need to remain as still as possible to allow the bones to start to knit and his pain would make that almost impossible. The best thing for him was to be kept unconscious as much as possible for at least two days.

Edward had roused before the doctor left and had been given a dose of the laudanum. The doctor assured Benjamin he would sleep for several hours. He also stated that Edward would need to remain where he was for several weeks before being moved home to London.

When the doctor left, Benjamin dropped into a chair at his bedside and held his head in his hands. He was exhausted and heart broken. He had loved little Geoffrey with all his being. He loved Diana as well and knew that the loss of her child would be difficult for her to handle, especially coming so closely after her father's death.

After assuring that the footman, George, would sit with Edward, Benjamin went to the room next door to check on Diana. He was glad to see she was asleep, but the sight of Geoffrey's small body lying on the settle was almost more than he could take. He knelt beside the small body and smoothed the dark hair off his forehead. Barbara and Bertha had washed the small body and dressed him in his best little breeches and coat. His long lashes rested on his cheeks as if he was simply asleep, but the pallor of his skin and his complete stillness put lie to that.

After leaving Diana and the baby, Benjamin went to make sure Edward was still asleep, then ventured downstairs to speak to the inn keeper about a coffin for the baby. Benjamin didn't know if Diana and Edward would want him buried with his father and grandfather at Ainsley Glen or taken to Bristol Castle to be buried with his paternal grandfather. Either way, the trip would be horrendous for all concerned. Edward would not be in any condition to be moved for some time. Benjamin didn't know if Diana would be able to make any decisions at all when she awoke the next day. He couldn't take it upon himself to make those decisions for either of them.

When Diana awoke the next morning, she didn't know where she was. She looked around the strange room and couldn't remember how she got there. She immediately looked for Geoffrey, but he was not in the room with her. Then she remembered. Her baby was dead. How could he be dead? He was the light of her life. He *was* her life in so many ways. She didn't want to live without him. She had lost everyone in her life she cared about. She turned her face towards the wall and quiet tears leaked from her eyes.

Benjamin soon knocked on Diana's door and was admitted by Barbara. He walked to the side of Diana's bed. He could tell she was no longer asleep, but she had not turned her head from the wall upon his entrance. He put his hand on her back and spoke to her softly.
"Diana, how are you this morning?"

There was no answer, but then, he hadn't really expected one. "Diana, Edward is in the room next to you. His leg is badly broken and he has a head injury. I know you are grieving terribly for Geoffrey, but I really must speak to you about something."

Benjamin waited a few minutes, but again there was no response. He tried again, "Diana, please turn over and look at me. I really must know what you want me to do regarding Geoffrey's burial.

Edward will not be able to be taken home for several weeks. Do you want me to take Geoffrey to Ainsley Glen or to Bristol Castle?"

Diana suddenly rolled over and stared with wild eyes at Benjamin. "You are not taking my baby anywhere. I will take him myself. I will bury him with his father and my father. I will leave today. You stay here with Edward. He needs you more than I."

With those few words, Diana scrambled from the bed and began issuing orders to Barbara and Bertha concerning their journey. She turned to Benjamin with such pain in her eyes, he felt a physical pain himself.

"Please make the arrangements to have the carriages readied. I will be needing all the footmen and drivers, but only two grooms since I won't be taking my mare or your riding horse. I will take only my trunks. Edwards and yours can stay here. I will take Barbara and Bertha with me as well. I don't know how long I will be gone or if I will even come back."

"Diana, what do you mean you may not come back? Edward is going to need you desperately. You know he loved Geoffrey as if he was his own. He will be grieving too. Also, he will be in a lot of pain and need a lot of medical attention and nursing."

"Hire someone to help you with the nursing and whatever else you need. I can't think about anything right now, but my bairn, my poor, poor wee dead bairn...."

With that, Diana was wracked by huge sobs. She stood in the middle of the room in her nightrail sobbing hysterically. Benjamin went to her at once and took her in his arms. She collapsed against him and began to beat her fists against his chest.

"Oh, Benjamin, he can't be dead. Not my Geoffrey. Now I've lost both my Geoffreys and I don't want to live without them. When Geoffrey was shot, I wanted to die, but I had to live for my bairn. Now my bairn is dead too. What do I have to live for now?"

Benjamin didn't know what to say to her. He, himself, was beset by a grief so deep he could hardly countenance it. Little Geoffrey had meant the world to him too. He knew Diana was deep in the throes of her grief and he feared she might do something foolish if she was left to her own devices. However, he couldn't leave Edward to go with her to Ainsley Glen. Benjamin was pulled in too many directions at once.

Benjamin finally convinced Diana not to start the journey to Scotland until the next day. He convinced her he would need some time to make all the arrangements. Actually, he needed time to come to a decision about whether to stay with Edward or go with Diana. Edward would be sedated for a couple of more days, but then he would be in pain and need someone with him constantly as he would be helpless. The trip to Ainsley Glen would likely take over a week to just get there. He wasn't sure how long Diana would stay in Scotland either. Arrangements would have to be made to bury the baby and that might take a couple of days.

Even if Benjamin came back to Warwick on horseback, alone, he couldn't possibly be back for probably at least two weeks. He couldn't leave Edward that long, but his conscience concerning Diana wouldn't let her go alone. Burying her baby alone would be the single hardest thing she had ever done. Benjamin was not sure her nerves could handle it especially coming so close to the loss of her beloved father.

Benjamin spent a sleepless night, but finally determined that he couldn't leave Edward. He knew that Diana and Edwin Burroughs were close. If he could send word to Burroughs via one of their groomsmen, Burroughs could ride hard and meet Diana in a few days. It was the best solution he could come up with. He knew it was not ultimately the best solution, but it was the only one he could find.

The next morning found Diana up and dressed before dawn. She hadn't eaten anything the day before and didn't want food again that morning. However, Barbara insisted she eat some toast with her tea. She harangued Diana until she finally ate a piece of toast just to hush her up. Diana's mind was numbed by grief. She had only one driving purpose and that was to take her baby home to Ainsley Glen as swiftly as possible.

Diana had visited Edward the afternoon before. He had been deeply asleep thanks to the laudanum left by the doctor. She was horrified by the way Edward had looked when she saw him. His head was heavily bandaged, his face was so white it was the same color as the bandages. His leg was propped on several pillows and not covered by the quilts. The doctor didn't want any more pressure on it than could be helped. The leg was hugely swollen and discolored.

Diana had spoken to the doctor when he visited Edward in the evening. He had informed her he feared infection setting in in the leg. If it did become infected, the leg might have to be removed. Diana looked at him in shock when he said Edward might lose his leg. She knew how vain Edward was. Losing his leg would possibly be more than he could handle along with the baby's death. Diana was torn between taking Geoffrey to Ainsley Glen for burial and staying with Edward.

However, in the end, her mother's heart won out. She could not even consider staying. Her baby needed her one last time and she would not let anything get in the way of her last duty to him. Diana told Benjamin what the doctor had said about Edward's possibly losing his leg. She told him to let the doctor amputate if that was the only way to save Edward's life. Benjamin reluctantly agreed.

Diana, Barbara, and Bertha, with the footmen, drivers, and grooms left just past dawn for Scotland. At first, Diana had insisted that Geoffrey's body ride with her in her carriage. After much persuasion, Benjamin convinced her to allow Bertha to ride with him in the second carriage while Barbara rode with her.

On their third day of travel, they were hailed by Edwin Burroughs and several footmen and grooms from Ainsley Glen. Benjamin had told Diana he had notified Edwin, so she was expecting him, but not so soon.

When the carriage door opened, Diana almost fell into Edwin's arms. Her tears had finally dried up the second day of travel, until she saw her old friend. The flood gates were opened immediately as she sobbed in his arms disconsolately.. Finally, getting herself under control, she climbed back into the carriage with Edwin at her side.

"It is so good of you to ride to meet us, Edwin. I didn't expect you until tomorrow or the next day though. Did you ride straight through?"

"Nay, lass, I brought extra horses and rode long hours. I knew you would need your old friend, so I hurried as best I could. I'm so sorry, lass, about your bairn. He was a lovely little fellow. Life is damned hard sometimes."

"Yes, Edwin, life is hard. When life takes everyone you love away from you, it doesn't even seem worth living."

"Nay, lass, don't you be talking that way. Your Da lost your mother and never did I see a man mourn so, but he kept living. He had people depending on him, just as you do. And you'll go on living for them, if not for yourself. There are many people who care for you, so you are not alone, although I'm sure it feels that way right now."

Diana knew Edwin was right, but at the present time, her tenants at Ainsley Glen and all the tenants on Duchy lands meant very little to her. She still had Edward and Benjamin, but the hole left by the loss of her bairn was too large for them to fill. She didn't think she would ever feel whole again. There was a place inside her that was empty, black, and lost and it was a huge place.

The next few days passed in great sorrow for Diana. She would wake in whatever inn they were staying, not remembering that Geoffrey was dead. Her dreams of him during that time were beautiful ones, not nightmares as she had expected. She dreamed she played in a meadow full of wild flowers with him. They ran chasing beautiful butterflies through the long grasses and multi-colored flowers. She would wake with a smile at her dream, but then the realization would hit her that Geoffrey was dead and the grief was new again. She wondered if she would ever wake with a bright outlook again. As the days progressed, she slept little and ate less. Each day saw her grow thinner and more quiet.

Finally on the seventh day, the sorrowing party reached Ainsley Glen. Fittingly, it seemed to Diana, it was raining. The entire household came out anyway. Mrs. Gwen and Mrs. Allen took turns holding a sobbing Diana. The tiny casket was carried into the drawing room and placed on a table there surrounded by candles.

Before he left Edwin had notified the priest at Ainsley Chapel that another funeral was needed. A groom went to fetch Father Andrews immediately upon their arrival. Father Andrews was new to the parish and didn't really know Diana. He had given last rites and officiated at Fergus's funeral, meeting Diana then.

When Father Andrews arrived, Diana was sitting vigil with Edwin, Barbara, and Mrs. Gwen in the drawing room. Father Andrews had never seen a sadder face than Diana's. His heart went out to her. She had only very recently lost her father and now to lose her only child in a terrible accident was horrific. He had been told her husband was also gravely injured and had to be left behind. His heart went out to the beautiful young woman before him.

When he went to console her, it was if she didn't hear him at all when he spoke. He looked at Edwin and the others and they just shook their heads. Diana was in a state of shock. She had been that way since they had brought the casket into the drawing room. She had neither spoken nor responded to any of them. She simply sat staring at the little box with the most heartbroken look on her face. Diana would not eat nor drink. Edwin feared for her sanity. He thought she might just have reached the end of her ability to deal with any more pain. She had lost too many people she loved in too short a time.

The funeral service for small Geoffrey was held the next day and his little body was buried beside his father and grandfather in the graveyard at Ainsley Chapel. Diana, again dressed all in black, stood beside his grave in the rain for hours after the service. No one could persuade her to leave. Finally Edwin sent everyone else away and he stood beside her holding an umbrella over her. When Diana's legs finally gave out, Edwin dropped the umbrella and caught her before she hit the ground. He carried her to the carriage and took her home to Ainsley Glen.

The next day, Diana would not get out of bed. She lay with her face toward the wall and would not answer when spoken to. She would not eat nor drink. Mrs. Gwen feared she would simply waste away if something wasn't done. She had eaten almost nothing for days, only sipping a cup of tea a couple of times. Edwin knew she had reacted the same way after the baby's father, Geoffrey, had been killed. This time there was no bairn growing inside her to give her a reason to go on. Nor a loving father to reason with her. No one knew what to do to help her.

After the third day of the same behavior, Edwin could stand it no more. Early on the morning of the fourth day, he threw the door to her bedchamber open and stomped into the room.

"Diana Isabelle MacDonald, you will get out of that bed this instant and get dressed. Your father would be ashamed of you for giving up so easily and so would Lord Geoffrey. The sun is shining for the first time in days and we are going for a ride. I have several horses that are in need of exercise and you are going to help me with them. I will not take no for an answer, so get yourself up and get into a riding habit right this minute. I'll meet you in the dining room in one half hour"

Not waiting for an answer, Edwin stomped out and slammed the heavy door. Barbara, who had been sitting beside Diana's bed, was shocked by Edwin's behavior. She looked at Diana and was surprised to see her feebly turning back the covers on the bed. Diana didn't speak, but she did rise and walk haltingly toward the wardrobe. Barbara hurried ahead of her and opened the wardrobe doors. Diana reached inside and pulled out a black riding habit, then laid it gently on the bed. She was so weak, she had to sit on the side of the bed to rest after only that smidgen of exercise.

Barbara didn't think Diana would be able to even walk down the stairs alone, but after she was dressed, Diana went slowly to the door and proceeded to the stairs. Barbara hurried to walk down beside her in case she stumbled or became faint. Although Diana held the balustrade with a white-knuckled grip, she managed to go downstairs on her own. Her whole body was trembling with weakness, but her head was held high.

Edwin was surprised when Diana entered the dining room. He didn't think his tactic had worked. She hadn't made it in a half hour, but she *had* made it. Edwin could tell Diana was in no shape to ride and didn't mention the horses again. He did however, insist that Diana eat something substantial and poured her several cups of tea.

After they had finished breakfast, Edwin took Diana's arm and escorted her to the library. He seated her behind the desk and came around to sit in a chair opposite her.

"Diana, hinny, we must talk. You cannot go on as you have these last few days. I know you have had a terrible blow, but you cannot give up. You are not yet even close to twenty and although right now you don't believe it, your life is nay over. You must find a new purpose for yourself. I have never mentioned this to you, but I know what your husband is or should I say is not. I know your marriage is in name only."

Diana looked at Edwin in total shock. "How did you find out?" she gasped.

"When the duke and his sons were here the first time, I saw Edward with that valet of his in the stable. I had been exercising a mare who came up lame. I was putting her in the stable when I saw them kissing and touching each other. They didn't see me, but I most definitely saw them"

"You never said a word."

"Nay, it was not my place to carry tails. When you married him, I had grave misgivings, but then I heard the maids talking in the kitchen about you carrying a bairn and I understood. That is one of the reasons I insisted on going with the two of you to Bristol Castle. I had to make sure in my own mind that he would nay mistreat you. I could see that he was nay the kind of man to hurt a woman after just a couple of days. Indeed, he was very considerate of you on the journey."

"Yes, Edward has always been most kind to me. He and Benjamin are like the brothers I never had. They feel the same about me. Edward always treated Geoffrey as if he was his own son and loved him very much, as did Benjamin. I know they are both heartbroken about Geoffrey. Edward is very ill from the accident. He was badly injured."

"Well, lassie, there you have it. You must return to your husband as soon as you can. He needs you now, and you need him."

Diana knew that Edwin was right. Although, she could hardly contemplate another long journey so soon, she knew it was what she had to do.

Chapter 27

It took another two days for Diana to regain her strength. On the morning of the third day, Diana, Bertha and Barbara climbed into the carriage together and left Ainsley Glen yet again. Edwin, along with several grooms from Ainsley Glen and the grooms and footmen Diana had brought, accompanied the women on the trip back to Warwick. They were able to make good time and had no incidents on the road. They reached Warwick, after seven long, hard days of travel, at dusk.

Diana had sent a groom ahead with a note for Benjamin. He was very relieved that she was back. Edward had regained consciousness, but was still in extreme pain. The doctor was still giving him large doses of laudanum, but not large enough to put him to sleep. Edward was burning with fever and his leg was festering at the sites of the wounds. The doctor hadn't yet said he had to amputate, but Benjamin feared it was only a matter of time before he would.

Benjamin was ashamed to admit, even to himself, that he was extremely relieved that Diana was back. He hadn't wanted to make the decision to remove Edward's leg. Edward himself was delirious and had been so almost from the beginning. He hadn't fully awakened and it had been over two weeks since the accident. Benjamin didn't know if it was the head injury, the fever, the broken leg, or possibly the laudanum, but Edward didn't seem to realize that Geoffrey was dead. He had tried to tell him when he called repeatedly for Diana and the baby, but Benjamin wasn't sure if he understood or not.

Diana immediately went to Edward's bedchamber when she arrived, not even waiting to change out of her travelling clothes. She was shocked at Edward's appearance. He was very thin. His face was deadly white, with bright red fever spots on both cheeks the only color in evidence. He was not conscious, but he wasn't resting easily either. He tossed his head from side to side and pulled at the covers on the bed with restless hands. His broken leg was still outside the covers and looked ghastly. The skin was swollen and discolored especially around the stitches.

The wounds were oozing yellow pus through the bandages and there was a horrible smell in the room. Diana went to the bed and placed her hand on Edward's forehead. It was burning hot. She turned to Benjamin with a question in her eyes.

"The doctor says the wounds are infected, but he hasn't mentioned amputation again….yet."

"Has he said whether he thinks Edward will recover the use of his leg, if he gets to keep it?"

"I asked him that, but he said he cannot tell yet. It will depend on how the wounds heal and how long the fever lasts. He told me Edward will need to stay here for some weeks to come. He cannot be moved right now at all. The Duke of Asbury, who has an estate here near Warwick, has come and offered his home for Edward's recuperation, but the doctor advised that he remain here for now. Maybe in a few weeks, he can be moved to Asbury Park, but not yet."

"Then that is what we shall do. We shall remain here until Edward is well enough to be moved. His welfare is all we should concern ourselves with at this moment. Have you arranged for rooms for me and my ladies?"

"Yes. I have a sitting room with an adjoining bedchamber for you next door to these rooms. Also, there is a room arranged near yours for Barbara and Bertha. I have been sitting up with Edward during the night and Harold, one of the grooms, has been sitting with him during the day so I can get a few hours sleep on the settle."

"Well, I'm here now. I will take the day shift or the night, whichever you prefer. And you must have a room with a proper bed as well. You look almost as thin and pale as Edward. You must keep your strength up Benjamin. I have had that drilled into my head by Edwin and Barbara for days, so now I will start to badger you in the same way." Diana said with a semblance of a smile. She walked to Benjamin and put her arms around him. She could tell that Benjamin's strength was about gone. He had been a rock for her and Edward during these last few weeks, but now he needed some rest and loving care too.

Benjamin, although much taller than the petite Diana, bent over to rest his head on her shoulder and wrapped his arms around her. It was so very good to have her back with them. She had ever been the more level headed of the three. She had an iron strength in her even she didn't know she possessed. Benjamin desperately needed that strength now. He had been about to the end of his rope when Diana returned. He hadn't known how much longer he could have gone on.

The next morning the doctor arrived early to check on Edward. Edward had been restless most of the night in severe pain. He had not truly been awake, but he had hardly slept either. Diana came into the room shortly after the doctor arrived.

"How is he this morning?"

"He is much the same as the last week. He has not been truly coherent since the accident. I am not sure as of yet whether the cause is the head injury or the leg injury. Both are quite severe. I am very glad you have returned, your grace. Decisions may have to be made soon as to whether the duke will be able to keep his leg or not. As you can see, the leg is infected at the wound sites. I cannot tell if the infection has spread to the bone yet, but I am watching it very closely."

"Is there not more that we can do for the leg ourselves? Would warm poultices help at all? I have used them on my father's tenants from time to time to draw out infection from serious cuts they received farming. Would there be an apothecary here in Warwick where herbs could be obtained?"

"Warm poultices would certainly not hurt. I doubt they would actually heal the wounds, but they may provide some relief from the pain of the infection. There is an apothecary on the high street. Perhaps one of your servants could fetch what you need?"

"Yes, I will send my maid Barbara with one of the footmen. She has helped me prepare the poultices before. Also, I was wondering if I could bathe my husband and change his clothes. The fever is making him perspire horribly. I know he would be more comfortable if he could be clean and have on fresh clothes."

"Again, my Lady, that is a good suggestion. I know that his valet has wiped him down a couple of times to try to cool him off, but a real bed bath would probably do him good. I will change the bandages on the wounds on his leg and head while you arrange for whatever you need to bathe him and make the poultices for his leg. The poultices can be applied over the bandages."

"Actually, doctor, might I apply them directly to the wounds instead. I have found that the direct application of the herbs is more efficacious for withdrawing the pus from a wound. I can re-bandage his wounds when I am done."

"As you wish, my Lady. I will just examine him now and only re-bandage his head wound. Would you care to leave the room while I examine the duke?"

"There is no need for that. After all, Edward is my husband. I will assist you in any way that I can."

The doctor was most impressed with the young duchess. She had a very level head and seemed to have some great experience in tending to wounds. He had honestly expected some society chit who would swoon at the thought of seeing suppurating wounds. She never blinked an eye as he unwound the bandages on the duke's leg. There were no red streaks yet, but the doctor feared they would appear at any time. The wounds were crusted with blood and pus. The odor was so bad even the doctor had a hard time keeping his gorge. However, the young duchess didn't so much as flinch. She stood close on the other side of the bed and watched intently as the doctor mashed on the wounds to expel as much purulence as he could. He wiped the matter away with a clean rag.

The doctor instructed Diana to change the bandage on Edward's head wound twice during the day and twice at night. There was no infection at that wound site yet, and the doctor wanted to keep it that way. He was treating the wound with honey which had natural antibacterial properties. Diana was very aware of the efficacy of using honey on wounds as she had done the same in Scotland for her father's tenants.

Benjamin had sat up with Edward all night, so Diana sent him to his room to rest. She asked him to have Barbara join her as soon as possible. When Barbara arrived, Diana dispatched her to the apothecary to purchase slippery elm powder and calendula to make the poultices. She also asked her to have the innkeeper send up clean rags, honey, and hot water.

While Diana was waiting for the supplies, she went to Edward's trunk and found a clean night shirt, his shaving mug, shaving brush and razor, and his hairbrush. She lay all these things on the bedside table. She knew she would need help turning him so she summoned Edwin to help her. Edwin had decided to remain in Warwick for a few days to help Diana in any way he could. He was still very apprehensive about her mental state. Although she had eaten and slept some on their journey to Warwick, she was still subject to fits of deep depression. It was only to be expected after the deaths of her father and child had come so closely together.

The water and rags arrived quite quickly and with Edwin's help, Diana soon had Edward bathed and shaved. They had been as gentle as they could, but they could both tell that even gentle movement was painful for Edward. Soon after they had finished their ministrations, Barbara came into the room with the ingredients for the poultice. Diana mixed a thick paste of the slippery elm and calendula. She spread it on a clean cloth that had been soaked in very hot water. She then lay it on top of the two wounds on Edward's leg. When the hot poultice touched his leg, Edward's eyes popped open. He stared wildly around the room, his eyes finally settling on Diana.

"Di, oh Di, where have you been? I have looked for you every night and every day, but you weren't here. Where is Geoffrey? I want to see our baby. Is he in the next room? Please bring him to see me."

Diana almost lost her breath at those words. Benjamin had warned her that Edward didn't seem to know that Geoffrey was dead, but somehow she hadn't really registered it with everything else that had been going on.

Diana went close to the bed and took Edward's hand in both of hers. "Edward, Geoffrey died in the same accident that you were injured in. I have been to Scotland. I buried Geoffrey with his father and mine at Ainsley Glen. I am sorry I could not be here with you, but I had to take care of our bairn." Diana said with tears streaming down her face.

"Dead, Geoffrey is dead? How can that be? We were just riding along, laughing together. He was riding in front of me. I had my arm around him holding him close and pointing out things on the sides of the road. He was trying to repeat every word I said. What happened? I don't remember anything after that."

"Your horse spooked, we don't know why. He took off through the wood. As far as we can tell, you were run under a branch. That is how you received your head injury. When the horse went off the ravine and fell, your right foot was trapped in your stirrup beneath the stallion, breaking your leg in two places. When Geoffrey fell from the horse, his little head apparently hit a tree and the blow broke his little neck. He died instantly. Oh, Edward, our bairn is gone, our sweet, sweet bairn is gone."

Edward's face was a study in sorrow. Tears ran down his face in rivulets. He sobbed in a heart rending way. Diana leaned over and put her arms around him. They cried together for quite some time. Edwin and Barbara quietly left the room giving the couple some privacy in their grief.

When their tears had finally dried, Diana explained everything that had happened since the accident to Edward. She was changing his poultice again when he suddenly went rigid and put his hands over his face.

"This was my fault wasn't it. If I had just held onto Geoffrey, he might still be alive. If I had just been stronger, our baby would still be here with us. Oh, Diana, I am so very sorry. I am so weak I couldn't even hold onto our baby. I am entirely to blame."

"No, Edward, you are not to blame. The doctor has told me that the blow to your head would have immediately rendered you unconscious. If your foot hadn't been trapped in the stirrup, you would have fallen off as well. There is no way you could have held onto Geoffrey. It was an accident, a tragic horrible accident. You must not blame yourself. There was nothing you could have done. We will probably never know what spooked your stallion. We had to put him down he was so badly injured."

"No, Diana, it was my fault. I'm just a weak person. I have always been weak. You know I'm weak. Look what I have put you through with my drinking. How can you not hate me?"

"I could never hate you Edward. You and Benjamin are the brothers I never had. Please don't place the blame for this on yourself. It is no one's fault. It is just fate. I have come to that conclusion after nearly losing my mind. I didn't want to live after I buried Geoffrey, but Edwin reminded me I have responsibilities. To you, to Benjamin, to my tenants and yours. We must find a new reason to go on."

Edward just shook his head and turned his eyes to the wall. He wasn't strong like Diana, he didn't have her will or her sense of responsibility. He had only ever really cared for himself, except for his father and brother, until he met Benjamin. Then, when his father had requested he marry Diana, he had come to care for and admire her immensely over time. But the one person he had ever loved completely and unselfishly was Geoffrey. That baby had meant the world to him. The way he felt about Geoffrey had taken him by surprise. The first time he had held him, he had felt such a strong bond he had been amazed. He honestly didn't know if he even wanted to live now that Geoffrey was gone. Why should he go on living when almost everyone he had ever truly loved was dead?

Diana worried about Edward as the days slipped by. He was in almost constant pain. His leg seemed to improve somewhat as far as the infection was concerned with the continued use of the poultices. The wound on his head began to heal and the swelling went down. He continued to have severe headaches and couldn't bear light in the room most of the time. They kept the drapes pulled tight and only used as much candlelight as necessary to change his bandages and see to his personal needs.

After five days, Edwin took his leave and returned to Scotland. His duties as laird wouldn't allow him to be gone for too long. He was worried about Diana, but even more so about how Edward's depression was affecting her.

She would sit with Edward during the day, trying to get him to eat and talk, taking care of his wounds, and even bathing him most days. When Benjamin would come in in the early evening, she would go to her sitting room and just sit in front of the fireplace and stare at nothing. It was summer and no fire was needed during the days, but this far north, the evenings were chilly. Diana never felt warm, day or night. She would have Barbara build a fire in both the sitting room and bedchamber every night.

Diana continued to eat and sleep, but did neither as much as she should have. She was very thin and pale. She never left the inn. She was either taking care of Edward or sitting in her rooms. Barbara, Bertha and Benjamin feared for her. They knew she needed to put some space between her and her problems to maintain her sanity, but didn't know what to do about it. They knew no one in Warwick. There was no one for her to visit and very few shops in the little town in which to shop. So in effect, there was nothing for her to do.

Finally, the day came when the doctor ruled Edward fit to be moved. The Duke of Asbury had renewed his offer of hospitality on several occasions by sending notes. When the doctor pronounced Edward well enough to move, Diana sent a note to the

Duke to let him know they would like to avail themselves of his hospitality if the invitation still stood.

The next day there was a knock on Edward's door. Diana went to open the door to find a liveried footman bearing a note from the duke. He had sent his own carriage to take them to Asbury Park. In a flurry of activity, Diana got everyone organized to make the move. They had all been living out of their trunks, so in effect, their possessions were already packed. After collecting the laundry the innkeeper's wife had done for them, they were ready to go.

It took eight footmen and grooms to move Edward down the stairs and he was groaning in agony almost the whole way even with a healthy dose of laudanum before the move was attempted. The doctor had fashioned a sling for his leg from blankets to avoid pressure on the sensitive areas of the broken bones and still healing wounds. Moving him down the narrow inn staircase was very difficult, but finally they reached the carriage waiting outside. Edward was ensconced in the duke's carriage lying on the well padded seat. Benjamin sat on the floor to steady him. Diana and her ladies rode in one of their carriages and the attendants followed in the other two carriages with the luggage. The extra horses trailed behind.

Chapter 28

Diana hoped the duke knew what he was letting himself in for. She had written him that she would leave her retainers at the inn, but he had insisted that all her party could be accommodated at Asbury Park with no difficulty. When the line of carriages started down the long paved drive, Diana could understand the duke's note much better. Asbury Park was even larger than Bristol Castle. Diana was sure there must be near a hundred rooms in the four story stone building. There was a huge central wing with even larger wings on each side and another wing at the rear of the building making a huge square. The interior courtyard was filled with flowers, trees, and fountains and was very beautiful.

The duke greeted his new guests by coming out of the imposing double doors with his butler and many of his staff. He was a man of middle years, somewhere in his late forties or early fifties from what Diana could tell. He was not terribly tall and a little rotund. He had a kind face and large soft brown eyes. His dark brown hair was graying at the temples, though still thick. He affected a thick mustache that was also turning gray. He smiled charmingly as Diana was handed down from the carriage by one of the footmen.

"Welcome, welcome, your grace. I am so sorry you have had to remain at the inn for such a long time. I truly wish you could have come to me much sooner, but I understand the extent of the duke's injuries would not allow it. I have spoken to his doctor and have made arrangements for him to have chambers on the ground floor. Therefore, he won't have to submit to the pain of being born up the stairs."

"Thank you so much, your grace. I appreciate your thoughtfulness and kindness more than I can say. It is very considerate of you to have had special chambers arranged for my husband. Will my chambers be near his as well? He still needs a considerable amount of nursing and prefers myself or his secretary to take care of him."

"Oh, yes, your grace. Your chambers connect with his by a drawing room. I have also arranged to have your maid and other attendants quartered in the same wing. You must be very fatigued from everything that has occurred recently. I was acquainted with the late Duke of Bristol. I wish to offer my condolences on his passing as well as your own father and child. I was sorry I wasn't able to attend Harold's funeral in London, but unfortunately I was burying my wife at almost the same time."

"I am so very sorry to hear that, my Lord. Our condolences on the loss of your wife. It seems sadness permeates this land lately."

"You poor child. I cannot even imagine the pain and sadness you have been feeling. I am so very sorry you have had so much sadness in your life. It doesn't seem that life has been treating you very fairly, does it?"

"No, my Lord, it hasn't."

The duke could see that talking about her recent losses was very upsetting for Diana, so he briskly led the way into his home changing the subject as quickly as he could. Diana was amazed by the sight that greeted her upon her arrival in the grand hall of Asbury Park. The ceiling was forty feet high and painted in scenes of Roman gods and goddesses. She had never seen anything like it in her life. The background of the painting was a pastoral scene upon which the gods and goddesses frolicked with abandon. They were all nude with a few leaves scattered upon their bodies in strategic places. The paintings depicted some very erotic scenes. It was all Diana could do not to gasp aloud or laugh. She had to wonder what type of place they had come to. Her host certainly didn't appear to be debauched, but his ceiling most definitely was.

When the duke saw the expression on Diana's face, he was at first unable to understand the reason. Then he glanced at the ceiling and began to laugh.

"Oh, your Grace, I am so very sorry. I should have warned you about my ancestor's folly. That is what we call this hall. One of my great-great grandfathers was a wastrel and a rake. He had this ceiling commissioned by an Italian artist over a hundred years ago. Unfortunately, he also placed a codicil to his will that it could never be painted over. Over the years, I have just learned not to look up. Please do not be alarmed, the rest of the house is quite ordinary, I assure you. Fortunately he ran out of money before he could have the rest of the house done over in the same style. Please, please come this way. I know you will want to get your husband settled. I believe they are carrying him in now."

Diana turned to see six men bearing Edward in the door. She hurried to him. She could tell he was in terrible pain from all the movement of the short journey. She and her entourage followed their host out of the grand hall into the wing on the right side of the massive house. The duke hurriedly opened a door half way down the hall and gestured for the men to carry Edward into the room.

The chamber was the drawing room the duke had mentioned to Diana earlier. It was elaborately decorated in several shades of green and gold. There was an enormous chandelier in the center of the ceiling, but thankfully, the ceiling was plainly painted. The duke led them to the already opened door on the right. The men bore Edward inside and very gently deposited him on the already turned down bed. The bed was enormous and quite high off the floor. The headboard was heavily carved with twining leaves and flowers. The bed draperies were a dark blue velvet and matched the window coverings. The bed covering was done in blue and gold stripes and there was gold and blue patterned upholstery on the chairs. The room was quite large and boasted not only the bed, but two tables on either side of it, several other tables and some chairs grouped around the fireplace. There was also an enormous armoire against the wall opposite the bed.

Diana could see that Edward was exhausted from the very short journey to Asbury Park. She quickly cleared the room so he could rest. Benjamin stayed with Edward while Diana accompanied the duke as he escorted her to her own bed chamber on the other side of the drawing room. It was also huge and was filled with approximately the same type of furniture. However, it was much more feminine in color and hue. The colors were a soft pink and a very light green with touches of a soft gold as well. The wood on the bed and other furniture in the room was a lighter finish than in Edward's chamber. The room was filled with vases of beautiful flowers. Diana was touched that the duke had gone to so much trouble to make her feel welcome.

Diana oversaw the maids and footmen who were bringing in their trunks and bags. She had them set Edward's belongings down in the drawing room outside his door. She didn't feel he should be bothered right at that moment with people coming and going in his room. Tomorrow would be soon enough to put away his clothing and personal items. Today, he needed to rest.

The duke could see Diana was anxious to go to her husband and excused himself after a few pleasantries. Diana was grateful to the man for his consideration and promised herself she would thank him for it later.

She left Barbara and Bertha unpacking her trunks and bags and went to Edward's room. Benjamin was sitting on the edge of Edward's bed holding his hand. Edward's eyes were glazed with pain. He was moving his head restlessly and groaning. It had only been an hour or so since his last dose of laudanum, but she could see the short journey had taken a toll on him. She pulled the bell and when the door was answered by one of the duke's maids, she requested a tea tray, some hot water and clean towels. The maid scurried away as Diana went to her open bedchamber door and asked Barbara to bring the herbs and cloths they used for poultices.

Diana didn't dare give Edward any more of the laudanum so soon, but she could at least try to make him more comfortable with the poultices. They seemed to relieve the pain to some degree. When she unwrapped his leg, she was upset to see that one of the wounds had started to seep blood and suppuration. No wonder Edward was in such agony. The wound had opened a little from the fragile healing that had been accomplished over the last few weeks. Diana was quite distraught by the sight. She carefully cleaned the area with warm water and then applied the poultice as usual. She replaced the poultices three times when they cooled before the bleeding clotted and the discharge stopped. She very carefully re-bandaged the leg with honey and went to stand beside Edward's head, next to Benjamin, smoothing his hair back from his forehead.

She and Benjamin shared a concerned look, but in a few minutes, Edward fell into an exhausted sleep. Benjamin moved two chairs near the head of the bed and sat down tiredly. Diana poured him a cup of tea and added extra sugar, then she joined him in the other chair. He needed a pick me up as did she. They sat in companionable silence drinking their tea and just resting. The past weeks had taken a toll on them both. They were all still grieving for Geoffrey, but had not had time to really grieve properly with all that had been going on with Edward's health.

Diana felt tired beyond any weariness she had ever experienced. The weeks since she had returned from burying her baby had passed in something of a blur. She had steeled herself not to dwell on her sadness although her heart literally hurt every time she thought of her poor wee bairn....and she thought of him many times each day and night. She still wasn't eating or sleeping as she should, but she was doing the best she could.

Benjamin was a tiny bit better since she had returned, but still looked worn to the bone. He was so thin. His once proud shoulders drooped under the load of his grief for Geoffrey and his anxiety for Edward. He looked like he had aged ten years since they left London. Diana felt she had as well. She no longer felt young in any way. Her true age might only be nineteen, but her heart felt as if she were a hundred years old.

She and Benjamin had managed to take care of all the duchy business as well as the Ainsley Glen business while staying at the inn, but it had taken a toll on them both. Diana was very glad she had Edwin to handle the bulk of the business for Ainsley Glen. She only had to read letters and send instructions occasionally when some question came up only she could answer. And of course, there always seemed to be papers to be signed for a solicitor or man of business for her estate in England.

The duchy business was more complex by far. The correspondence was heavy and decisions had to be made on a variety of subjects almost every day. While at the inn, their man of business had travelled there from London twice to get answers to immediate questions and signatures on documents. At first Edward was not well enough to even sign his name, but eventually, he had done so desultorily. He rarely asked what he was signing. He took no interest in the duchy business at all. He simply signed his name and attached his seal wherever he was told to do so.

Diana was very worried about Edward's state of mind as well as his physical health. He took little or no interest in anything anymore. He could barely be cajoled into eating. It was true the fare at the inn was not especially appetizing, but he didn't seem to care about that either. He hadn't asked for brandy, which was surprising considering the amount of pain he was suffering. Diana was worried about his consumption of the laudanum. She knew it wasn't good for him to have so much, but there didn't seem to be anything else that even dulled the pain for him.

Finally, Diana dragged herself out of the chair and went to bathe and change for dinner. She felt she must put out some effort to be pleasant to their host. It wasn't everyone who would have taken in the lot of them for an indefinite period as he had.

After bathing, Diana had Barbara help her dress in one of her black evening dresses and arrange her hair in a knot on top of her head, with the ever present curls hanging down her back and around her face. She took a quick glance in the full length mirror and stopped suddenly with an indrawn breath. She had not seen more than her face in weeks as the only mirror at the inn was above the wash stand in her bedchamber. She was so *very* thin. Her dress was hanging on her where the laces couldn't draw it up tightly enough. Her shoulders were scrawny looking. She had never been plump in the slightest, but she had been rounded where she should be. Now there was little roundness left on her at all. Even her breasts seemed depleted. They had been so much bigger after Geoffrey was born, now they seemed small and a little droopy without her corset and stays. She hadn't even noticed how very thin she was until this moment. She had taken no time for herself since Geoffrey had died. She had gone through the motions of living, but hadn't really been living at all. She and Edward had much in common.

With a deep sigh, Diana turned from the mirror and went out into the hallway to make her way to the dining room for dinner. Edward and Benjamin would have a tray in their rooms and the servants would eat in the kitchen with the duke's servants. She supposed it would only be she and the duke to dine this evening. Diana was surprised when she heard more than one male voice in the dining room.

The door was opened for her by one of the duke's footmen. There were two men already seated at the table. They both rose when she entered. Diana looked toward her host with a small smile. The duke came around the table to take her hand and lead her to her place beside him at the table. As she came around the table, she took notice of the other occupant of the room.

The man was very tall and quite broad as well. His evening clothes were immaculately tailored and fit him beautifully. He had dark wavy hair that he wore longer than was the fashion.. His eyes were large and an odd silver color, below dark brown winged brows. His eyes were fringed by long dark lashes. He wasn't classically handsome, but he was very attractive. There was something rugged about him that Diana hadn't seen in many Englishmen.

"Your Grace, please let me introduce you to my other guest. This is Viscount Lawrence Banbury recently come home from America. Sir Lawrence is my nephew through marriage. Lawrence, may I present her grace, Diana, the duchess of Bristol."

Diana dropped a curtsy as Sir Banbury bowed from across the table. They seated themselves and traded pleasantries for a few minutes before the meal began to be served. The first course was a very flavorful consomme of beef accompanied by buttered toast points. Diana was very appreciative of the wonderful flavors. She hadn't tasted really good food in weeks. She found her appetite revived after the first few spoonfuls of the lovely broth.

When the soup plates were cleared, a procession of footmen carried in dish after dish covered in silver salvers. The food was placed on a very long sideboard and one of the footmen took plates from a cabinet under the sideboard and began to serve the first course to the dinner companions. When Diana's plate was placed before her, she was delighted to see fillet of sole in an almond sauce.

After the first taste, she expressed her admiration for the duke's cook. "Your Grace, if I may I would like to express my gratitude to your cook. This is undoubtedly the best sole I have ever tasted. After eating the food at the inn for so long, I had forgotten what truly well cooked food tastes like."

"My dear, I am so glad you are enjoying your dinner. My cook, Mrs. Perkins, will be delighted to hear you enjoyed it. She so loves to have guests to cook for. I'm afraid I never do justice to her creations to her mind. But one man can only eat so much." the duke said with a bright smile as he patted his rounded stomach.

Diana was charmed by the easy going manner of the duke. She was even more grateful for his hospitality as the evening wore on. Sir Branbury was also a charming dinner companion. She couldn't quite guess his age, but thought he might be in his early thirties. He regaled them with tales of America and some of what he had seen there during his travels. He planned to return to America in a few months time. From the gist of the conversation, Diana understood he was a younger son of a duke and planned to move permanently to America to make his fortune.

During the course of the meal, Diana told the duke and Sir Branbury about her friends Ian and Alana MacAllister. Sir Branbury had travelled through Virginia during his stay in America and had ended up buying land not terribly far from Williamsburg. Diana was surprised to hear he would be so close to her friends. She offered to write a letter of introduction for him to Ian and Alana, if he so chose. He expressed his gratitude for her kindness as he knew no one there as of yet.

After several more very tasty courses, dinner concluded and Diana rose to leave the gentlemen to their brandy and cigars. The duke surprised her by informing her he and Sir Branbury would join her in the drawing room now rather than later. At every other dinner she had been to, the gentlemen always remained in the dining room for at least a half hour after dinner.

The duke explained he didn't necessarily stand on ceremony when he didn't have a large number of guests. Since she was the only lady present, he didn't want her left to her own devices especially on her first evening in his home. Diana was much impressed and pleased with his kind consideration.

They adjourned to a beautiful drawing room near the dining room. It was decorated in shades of red, but was by no means over powering. The drapes and some of the furniture was red velvet, but there were touches of silver and dark blue as well in the upholstery on the other pieces. The wood on the furniture was a very dark mahogany and gleamed with polish. In the corner of the room stood a beautiful pianoforte, which drew Diana like a magnet. She walked over to the instrument and ran her fingers lightly over the keys. It had been many weeks since she had touched an instrument. She missed her music. She and Edward had spent many long hours playing and singing with each other at the house in London as well as at Bristol Castle.

"Do you play, Lady Bristol?" asked the duke.

"Yes, I do, but it has been several weeks since I have had the opportunity."

"Please take this opportunity, if you would. We would be very pleased to hear some music this evening."

Diana sat down on the bench and looked over the music that was available. She found a piece she knew very well and began to play. Before long, she was lost in the music. She closed her eyes and without even knowing it, her body swayed gently to the melancholy tune.

Sir Lawrence Bradbury had never seen such a beautiful woman in his life. Her red curly hair gleamed in the candlelight. Her pale skin was almost translucent without a blemish or mark on it anywhere. It was true she was too thin, but after all she had been through lately, it was a mark of her tremendous strength that she was even still sane. The duke had acquainted him of her recent troubles. Yet, here she sat at the pianoforte coaxing such incredible music from it with seemingly little effort, it almost hurt his heart to hear it. Her face wore a peaceful look for the first time that evening as her small hands danced across the keys when the pace of the piece picked up some what.

Lawrence knew she was married, but he couldn't help wishing it was other wise. He wanted to meet someone like her some day. A strong, beautiful woman with a real heart. He had recently been disappointed in love. Before he went to America, he had been engaged to be married to what he thought was the love of his life, Lady Christina Waterbury. While he was gone, his beloved had eloped to Gretna Green with a marquis set on inheriting a dukedom. Apparently, a younger son, who would probably never inherit and held a minor title, was not good enough for her after all. The experience had hardened Lawrence's heart toward females in general. He didn't plan to make the same mistake twice.

As he watched the duchess play song after song, he was totally captivated. When she began to sing as well as play, his interest was peaked even further. Her voice was a deep throaty contralto, yet she hit the high notes as well, with no effort. He could listen to her all night.

After several pieces, Diana stood and left the pianoforte bench to sit in a chair near the gentlemen.

"Your Grace, I have so enjoyed your performance this evening. You have made an old man very happy to be listening to such wonderful playing and singing as you have given us tonight." the duke said.

"Quite right, that was truly marvelous. I don't believe I have ever heard music in a drawing room from a non-professional that was that compelling.", stated Lord Branbury.

"Thank you both, gentlemen. I have always enjoyed playing and singing. I didn't realize how much I had missed it these last weeks. Music seems to soothe my soul as does nothing else. I must ask you to excuse me now, however, I must check on the duke before I retire for the evening."

Both men were reluctant to see her go, but understood her concern for her husband. Diana quickly made her way to Edward's bedchamber. As she was about to open the door, she heard Edward shouting at Benjamin. She couldn't quite make out the words through the thick door, but she thought it was about Edward wanting more laudanum.

As soon as the door opened to admit Diana, Edward became quiet and turned his head away towards the wall.

"What is going on, Benjamin?"

"Edward wants me to give him more laudanum, but I just gave him a dose less than an hour ago. It's too soon, but he doesn't want to listen to me."

The pain in Benjamin's voice was almost more than Diana could bear. He looked so very sad and forlorn as he stood beside the head of Edward's bed, wringing his hands. Diana walked over and put her arm around his shoulders.

"Why don't you retire for the night, Benjamin. I will stay with Edward. He and I need to have a talk."

Benjamin looked at Diana in heart-wrenching relief. His eyes glittered with unshed tears. He simply turned and went to the door of his small room next to the dressing room. "I will leave you with it then. I am most dreadfully tired tonight." Benjamin said with a sob in his voice. With that Benjamin exited the room quickly, shutting the door softly behind him.

"Edward, you must stop badgering Benjamin for more laudanum. We are giving you the dose suggested by the doctor. We cannot give you more. I know it doesn't completely alleviate your pain, but the drug has some terrible side effects. You could become addicted to it if you take too much or even die."

Edward turned his head and Diana was surprised at the venom she saw in his eyes. "What difference does it make? My life is pretty much over anyway. I will never walk correctly again. Will never be able to ride, or hunt or do almost any of the things I have always enjoyed doing. My father and my son are dead and you have to hate me for not protecting Geoffrey. There is little for me to want to live for."

"Oh, Edward, you are so very wrong." Diana said emphatically. "I don't hate you, I love you. You are still the brother I never had, just as Benjamin is. Geoffrey's dying in the accident was **not** your fault. It was an accident, no more no less. Yes, it was a tragic accident and not a day goes by that my heart doesn't break again from the loss of our sweet bairn, but I don't fault you for it. Life is just sometimes very cruel. We have both lost the people we loved most in the world and in a very short space of time. However, we do still have each other and we both have Benjamin. You are breaking both our hearts right now."

With those words, Diana slumped into a chair, lay her head on the bed and choked back a sob. Edward reached his hand over and lay it on her head.

"I'm sorry Di. I don't mean to be such a horse's ass. I know you're hurting too and so is Benji. But I just lay in bed day in and day out with my leg hurting so badly, all I can think of is relief. I am a weak, selfish man as I have always been. Why you continue to put up with me, I just don't understand, but I'm glad you do."

Diana raised her head and saw tears glittering in Edward's eyes. He looked so remorseful she couldn't be angry with him. She reached for his hand and held it in both of hers.

"Things will get better, Edward. I know they will. We have to give it time. Time for your leg to heal, as well as time for our hearts to heal. I know patience has never been your strong suit, but please try for Benji and I. We both love you so."

"I'll try, Di. I will try."

The next few days were very hard for Edward. The move had impacted his healing more than even the doctor had foreseen. He developed a fever on the day after the move and the wound that had opened on his leg became suppurated badly again. The rounds of poultices several times a day began again. Diana sent Barbara and one of the footmen to Warwick to replenish their supply of herbs and honey.

Bertha took over the task of boiling the rags they used for poultices in the castle washroom daily, as well as the other laundry. After Geoffrey's death, Bertha had asked Diana if she should try to make her way back to Cornwall, but Diana told her she wanted her to stay on and help with Edward's nursing. She told Bertha she could stay with them as long as she wanted. Diana couldn't turn away the young woman. Although she had been hired as a nursemaid for Geoffrey, Diana couldn't in good conscience send her away. She was also grieving for the small boy whom she had loved very much. Diana knew there would always be a place in her household and her heart for Bertha.

Diana was concerned about her other retainers while staying at Asbury Park. She knew the grooms had little to do other than care for the riding horses and carriage horses. The footmen had nothing to do at all. After discussing the issue with Benjamin, she offered the services of her footmen to the duke. At first he was reluctant to use them, but when Diana assured him they would be better off busy, he had his butler find places for them among his staff. Since he had guests, there was enough work for all the footmen in the house. As for the grooms, he asked his stable foreman to find what work he could for them in addition to their regular duties which didn't take up much of their day.

Chapter 29

Soon all the Londoners settled in to their assigned duties. Diana and Benjamin nursed Edward. After about a week, his fever finally broke and his leg began to heal again.

After two more weeks, the doctor declared Edward ready to start getting out of bed for a few hours every day. He was extremely weak and the two or three hours he was up were very tiring for him. Gradually, he could stay up longer and longer. After he had been able to stay up most of the day for a week, the doctor brought crutches for him to try. He wanted Edward to start trying to put a little weight on his leg to strengthen the muscles that had been inert for so long.

The first time Edward stood with the crutches under his arms, his face turned white and he almost fainted from the pain of the blood running down his leg to his foot. Benjamin who was at his side, caught him under the arms and gently lowered him back to his chair. It was several days before they could convince him to try again. Finally with much reassurance from Diana and Benjamin, Edward stood and took a couple of steps. Diana could see the pain etched deeply into his face and didn't push him any more that day.

His leg had withered and was much thinner than the other one. Diana was very worried that he might never walk again, but slowly, he was able to put more and more weight upon the bad leg. The progress Edward made was very slow, but it was progress.

The leg had healed on the outside and the bones had knit together, although weakly. His leg was no longer straight, but had a decided curve to it at the point where it was most badly broken. It caused his gait to be off and the leg to be shorter than his other one. Each time Edward actually looked at his leg, it made him sick to his stomach. There were scars where the bone had broken through the skin as well as discoloration on the whole leg from constantly being swollen. The doctor assured him the discoloration would fade with time as would the scars.

During all this time, Diana had been most supportive of Edward as had Benjamin. They took turns keeping him occupied while he was sitting up in a chair. When he was finally able to take some steps, they walked with him up and down the hallway to help him strengthen his muscles.

Diana tried to get Edward to join the duke, Sir Branbury, and she for dinner, but he steadfastly refused. Sir Branbury was leaving soon to go back to America and Diana would be sorry to see him go. He had come to meet Edward and Benjamin not long after they had arrived at Asbury Park. He had become a friend to Diana in the weeks they had known each other at the Duke of Warwick's home and she would miss him, as would the duke.

Diana would not let herself think about the real reason she dreaded to see Sir Branbury leave. She found herself attracted to him and knew he felt the same for her. It could not be, of course. She was married, even if in name only. She was not one to take a lover even though Edward had suggested just such a thing when they were first married. She wanted no hint of scandal to mar the Bristol name.

Soon before Sir Branbury's departure date, Diana wrote a very nice letter of introduction to Ian and Alana for him. She knew they would get along well together and hoped her friends could help Sir Branbury become acclimated to America. He did not plan to come back permanently to England, but did say he might visit in a few years. Diana did not encourage him to contact her should he visit, however much she wanted to.

Diana was coping with her losses the best way she knew how, by keeping busy. She spent a lot of time with Edward, as well as hours on the duchy business every day. Her host also took up part of her day. The duke insisted she get out of the house occasionally for a ride in the countryside on her beloved mare. Although the duke didn't enjoy riding, Sir Lawrence did and would accompany Diana on her rides along with a couple of grooms for propriety's sake.

The duke also took her to visit the famous Warwick Castle built by William the Conqueror in the eleventh century. They were accompanied that day by Sir Lawrence. Diana was overwhelmed to think a building of that size had been built almost eight hundred years before and was still in remarkably good condition. She enjoyed her outings with the duke and Sir Lawrence, but also felt guilty because Edward was still so terribly miserable as was Benjamin.

The day finally came for Sir Lawrence to take his leave. At breakfast that morning, he had taken Diana's hand in his and bowed low over it, just touching it with his lips. Diana felt a sudden spark between them and hastily pulled her hand away. They stared at each other for what seemed like hours until the duke came bustling into the room to say goodbye. If the duke noticed anything untoward, he didn't mention it to either of them.

Diana was glad that Sir Lawrence was leaving and yet she would miss him very much. It had been a welcome distraction to have someone to talk to and ride with, but she knew her attraction to him was wrong and she fought against it with all she had.

When Sir Lawrence had bade his final farewells, Diana and the duke walked slowly back into Asbury Park arm in arm. Diana had become very attached to the older gentleman and would miss him when they returned to London.

It was now early fall. They had been away from London for four months. So far, they had been able to handle the duchy business from Warwick, but they would need to return home soon. There was much they needed to go over with the mine managers from Cornwall as well as the men of business for the estates in other parts of England. Diana and Benjamin began to make plans to return to London in a months time before the winter weather set in and made the roads even harder to travel. They hoped by then Edward would be well enough to tolerate the jouncing of the carriage. They knew they would have to travel for shorter hours and stop a lot more often.

They had been able to wean Edward off the laudanum for the most part, except to help him sleep, until he started to try to walk. The pain of using his injured leg was more than he could stand without some help. Diana discussed the dosage they should use with the doctor. He also suggested brandy to help with the pain, but Diana explained Edward's former dependence on alcohol and that plan was scratched.

When Edward first began to try to walk, he required a dose of laudanum every time he attempted to put weight on his leg. Slowly, they were able to back off on the size of the dose until he was able to walk several feet without any medicinal help. Diana felt that now was the time to go back to London. When she broached the subject with Benjamin, he was in agreement. However, when she brought it up to Edward, he showed little interest.

It had been that way with everything. He was completely apathetic about almost everything in his life. Edward only spoke when spoken to, took no interest in the duchy business, nor did he take any interest in Diana nor Benjamin nor even his clothing. He was just a shell of what he once was in so many ways.

When the bandages were removed from Edward's leg, he would look away. He couldn't stand to see the scars from his wounds nor the way his leg now curved in and his foot curved out from the badly healed break mid-leg. His leg was now about an inch shorter than his other and he had a very noticeable limp.

When the doctor suggested a cane instead of the crutches just before their journey back to London, Edward just looked toward the wall and didn't reply. Diana thanked the doctor and told him they would have a cane made right away. She thought a cane might help Edward feel more normal than the crutches did.

That night at dinner, Diana asked the duke to suggest somewhere to have a cane made for Edward. He was more than willing to loan her one of the canes he kept for himself, but she wanted to do something special for Edward, something uniquely his own. The duke suggested a woodcarver in the village.

Diana and Benjamin put their heads together and came up with a design for the cane. Since Edward and Benjamin were about the same height, they used Benjamin to measure the length the cane would need to be. While Edward was napping one afternoon, the duke took Diana and Benjamin into the village in his carriage to the woodworker's shop. They showed him the design and he measured Benjamin to get the correct length. They chose a sturdy piece of mahogany to have the cane carved from. Diana wanted it to be finished in a dark stain and have Edward's initials down the front with the family crest at the top of the shaft.

The woodcarver suggested silver for the cane handle rather than wood as it would be more comfortable to grip and much more handsome. There was a silversmith in the village and his shop was their next stop. The silversmith suggested that Edward's name be engraved on the handle of the cane instead of his initials on the front of the cane and Diana agreed. The silversmith said he would confer with the woodcarver for the size and specifications.

It took a week for the cane to be completed. Benjamin went into town and picked it up. When he returned he and Diana were very pleased with the end product. The shaft of the cane was beautifully carved with vines and leaves and had a gleaming dark stain. The ducal crest was on the front at the top of the shaft. The silver handle had Edward's name in beautiful script on the side of the handle and similar vines and leaves decorated the handle as well. All in all, it was a complete success, or so they thought.

When Edward was presented with the cane that afternoon after his usual nap, he looked at it, but had little to say. When he rose from his chair for his exercise session, he reached for his crutches, not the cane. Diana was hurt and disappointed, as was Benjamin, but neither of them said anything about it to Edward. After a few days, Diana did notihihice that Edward did start using the cane for at least part of his exercise each day.

Finally the day came for their return to London. Edward requested a carriage to himself. His excuse was that he needed to be able to stretch his leg out on the opposite seat from time to time. Diana found the excuse thin, but didn't argue the point. Edward had been steadily pulling farther and farther away from she and

Benjamin. He was severely depressed and Diana didn't know how to reach him anymore. Benjamin's feelings were hurt that Edward didn't want him to ride in the carriage with him, but Diana was a little relieved. She was becoming more and more uncomfortable in Edward's presence. He took no interest in books, music, clothes or conversation. It was quite difficult to spend time with someone so morose.

Diana hoped that getting back to familiar surroundings might help to alleviate his dark mood. He had grown up in the London house and hopefully, he could find some peace in it. The night before their departure, the duke had his cook prepare a feast. They started the meal with baked oysters. The oysters had been shipped at some expense packed in ice from the coast. They were baked in butter and herbs in their shells. The next course was a rich beef bouillon served with a piece of fresh trout caught from the Avon river nearby. The trout had been baked in wine and herbs and was very flavorful. The main course was a baron of beef served with turnips, carrots and potatoes. To finish the meal, the cook had outdone herself with four separate desserts, a warm, creamy chocolate pudding, a brandy syllabub, a very light lemony cake and a bread pudding served with a whisky sauce.

Diana thoroughly enjoyed the meal and complimented the duke and his superb cook several times. After dinner, she and the duke retired to the drawing room. The duke requested she play and sing for him one more time before she went home to London. Diana played and sang several songs. As she was playing a very sad and melancholy tune, she suddenly realized she had an audience other than the duke. Edward stood in the door of the drawing room leaning on his cane. His face was a study in sadness.

It was the first time that Edward had ventured to the drawing room. Diana was very surprised to see him. When she finished the piece, she rose and went to him. He looked at her with such agony in his eyes, it broke her heart. She put her hand on his arm and asked him to join she and duke. He complied and followed her to a sofa across from the duke's usual chair.

"Sir, I wanted to thank you for the kind hospitality you have offered to my wife, myself and all our servants while we have been here. Please, if you come to London, it would be an honor if you would stay with us while you are there. Our home is always open to you." Edward said stiffly.

"Thank you, your grace. I much appreciate that. I don't come to Town often, but when I do, I will gladly take you up on your offer. I don't keep a residence in London since I'm there so seldom. I usually stay in an hotel or with a distant cousin I have there, Lord Wilshire. However, Lord Wilshire is in his seventies and doesn't hear very well, so the visit is spent shouting into his ear trumpet. I did suggest he try one of the new mechanical hearing devices I had read about, but he is not a person subject to easy changes." the duke said humorously.

Though Diana tried not to laugh, she couldn't hide the smile that this image brought to her mind. Edward, however, never changed expression. It seemed all humour had gone out of his life. It made Diana very sad when she thought of the exuberant, slightly silly young man he was before Geoffrey's death and his own injuries.

Chapter 30

The morning dawned bright and sunny, much to Diana's relief. Finally everyone was loaded into the carriages or onto the horses and they began their journey. Since Edward preferred to ride alone, Diana and Benjamin decided to ride their horses for much of the journey when the weather permitted. At first, Diana was reluctant to do so thinking Edward might resent the fact that he could not ride as well, but it didn't seem to make any difference to him one way or the other.

After five long days of travel, many stops to allow Edward to exercise his leg, and a couple of days of bad weather, the weary travelers finally arrived at their home in London at dusk. Forbes and several footmen came out to greet them and help them unload and get settled. Edward was in a temper because his leg was paining him so badly. The weather had turned very damp and cold and that seemed to affect his leg tremendously.

After being helped up the stairs by Benjamin and Forbes, Edward was finally ensconced in his own room. Benjamin had helped him undress and was in the process of mixing Edward a dose of laudanum when Diana came into the room.

"Edward, are you in much pain?"

"Of course I am. I have been tortured for days. What do you expect?"

Diana was taken aback by the venom in Edward's voice. He had been surly for the past few days, but he hadn't been quite so ferocious. Diana and Benjamin exchanged worried looks across the bed.

Benjamin handed the glass of laudanum mixed in water to Edward. He downed it in one large gulp, then slumped against the pillows.

"I would appreciate it if you would both leave me alone. I wish to rest and I cannot do so with you hovering over me every minute." Edward said nastily.

"Edward, I don't feel we are "hovering" over you," said Diana patiently, "We are simply trying to see to your comfort and well being."

Well, I am not comfortable, nor have I been for months. I will probably never be "comfortable" again, so don't bother."

With that, Edward turned on his side and faced the wall. Seeing there was nothing else to be done for him, Diana and Benjamin left the room, going into the drawing room that connected Diana and Edward's bedchambers.

"What are we to do, Diana? He is getting worse instead of better. I had hoped when he was able to walk alone again, although still with a cane, he might begin to adjust to the situation somewhat. However, if anything, he seems to be getting more unhappy every day. I don't know what to do to help him. He will not talk to me."

"He doesn't talk to me either. It is all I can do to get him to answer when I ask a question of him. I don't know either. Maybe we should have a doctor come examine him. Maybe it's something physical. He is still so very thin and hardly eats enough to sustain a mouse. Maybe if Dr. Baker came. He knows him well and I know Edward respects him."

"That's a very good idea, Diana. I will send for Dr. Baker first thing in the morning. Maybe he can give Edward some type of medicine that will help him. Goodness knows, you and I have tried everything we know to no avail."

Around ten o'clock the next morning, Benjamin came to the library to let Diana know that Dr. Baker was in Edward's room examining him. She asked Benjamin to show the doctor to the library when he had completed his examination.

It was over an hour later that Dr. Baker was shown into the library by Benjamin. As Benjamin turned to leave, Diana asked him to stay. Dr. Baker raised his eyebrows at this, but Diana explained that Benjamin was not only Edward's secretary, they were old friends from school. Diana rose from behind the desk to greet the good doctor. The serious expression on his face made Diana nervous.

"First, your grace, allow me to extend my condolences on the loss of both your father and your son. I hardly know what to say about so tragic a circumstance."

"Thank you, Dr. Baker. It has been a very difficult time for all of us. The fact that Edward was so gravely injured in the same accident that took our son, has also been very difficult. His recovery has been extremely slow and very hard. Were you able to come to any conclusions from your examination of Edward?"

"After a very careful examination of Edward's body, I cannot find anything physically wrong with him except a very weakened state from many weeks abed and the after effects of a very badly broken leg and concussion. The concussion is completely healed and the leg is really in better condition than I expected after receiving a letter from Dr. Phillips in Warwick about the initial state of his leg. However, his emotional state is another thing all together. He seems to have a very tenuous hold on his emotions. Edward was never a strong person emotionally. This last incident, atop the loss of his father and brother so closely together, seems to have pushed him past the point where he can control himself."

"Is there anything we can do, medicine, some type of treatment?"

"I know of no medicine for emotional distress or melancholia as it is better known. If Edward does finally lose the very tenuous control he has, he may have to be institutionalized." Seeing the look of horror on both Diana's and Benjamin's faces, the doctor quickly went on. "However, that would only become necessary if he became violent. He can be treated at home for now. I would suggest you do whatever you can to help restore his confidence in himself."

Benjamin asked, "How do we go about doing that?"

"Compliment him on his strengths and try not to dwell on his weaknesses. That has long been Edward's problem. He has always thought himself weak, so he has acted as a weak person would. I believe he has an inner strength that has not been plumbed before. The task for you both is to find that strength and pull it forward. It will not be easy and I must warn you, it may not even be possible. However, that is the only way I know of to help pull him from this very deep depressed state he is now in."

After Dr. Baker left, Diana and Benjamin spent hours trying to come up with the best way to help Edward. Diana felt if she could get him to play the pianoforte and sing again, it might help. He had always found pleasure in music and he had a great amount of talent.

Benjamin determined to try to get him reading and discussing books again. Possibly even trying to interest him in having some of their old school friends as guests to stimulate his interest, would be a good idea. Diana agreed and Benjamin sent letters to several of their friends from Eton he felt might be good for Edward.

That evening, they both tried to cajole Edward into coming downstairs to dinner, but he was having none of it. He wanted a tray in his bedchamber and wanted to eat alone. Several times that day, both Diana and Benjamin had tried to enter into conversations with Edward about duchy business, books and music, to no avail. Edward simply wanted to be left alone. No matter what tact they tried, they were refused.

This went on for several days. Finally in frustration, Diana entered Edward's bedchamber just before luncheon and told him in no uncertain terms that his isolation had to end.

"Edward, I know you are unhappy and you have good reason to be. I am unhappy as well. Losing Geoffrey was the hardest thing I have ever faced, maybe even harder than losing his father and my own. He was the light of my life and I know you felt the same about him. However, you cannot simply stop living life while you grieve. If you do that, the pain will not lessen, it will just grow stronger. I have made a decision and I will carry it through no matter how much you fight me on it. I will no longer allow trays to be carried to your room for all your meals. I understand it is hard for you to get going in the mornings, so I will allow you to break your fast here, but for luncheon and dinner, you will come downstairs or into our drawing room if the stairs are too much for you. If you do not do this, you will not eat."

Edward stared at Diana for a moment, with what amounted to hate in his eyes, then turned over in the bed with his face to the wall and ignored her. Diana stood beside his bed for some minutes, then turned and left the room. She went downstairs and gave her orders to Forbes and the cook. No more food, except breakfast, was to go to Edward's bedchamber. They stared at her a moment in shock.

Then Forbes said, "Your grace, as I have always done, I will accede to your wishes as will cook."

Diana was sure they both thought her cruel, but she had no other way to compel Edward to get out of bed and at least make an effort to start living again. It was three days before Edward appeared in their drawing room for luncheon. He was even more gaunt than before and the lack of food had weakened him even further, but he did appear. His eyes were dark rimmed and sunken into his head, his dark mourning clothes hung on him loosely, and his blond curls were in need of a good wash, but at least he had made the effort to join Diana and Benjamin for their midday meal.

The meal was strained as Edward refused to join in the conversation and studiously avoided them both. He didn't even answer questions that were directed to him. Diana was not happy with his attitude, but she thought it was a start.

That evening, Edward again presented himself in the drawing room for dinner. During the day, Diana had the servants move a pianoforte into the drawing room from the music room down the hall. She saw that Edward noticed it the minute he walked into the room. He made no comment. Again, he did not participate in the conversation between Benjamin and Diana, not speaking to either of them the entire time he was in the room.

When dinner was concluded, Diana excused herself and walked over to the instrument and sat down on the bench. Her fingers drifted lightly over the keys, then settled into playing a piece by Handel that Edward had always liked. Edward abruptly rose from the table and shuffled his way slowly toward his room relying heavily on his cane. As he got to the door, he turned and glared at Diana with intense dislike before going into his room and slamming the door.

Benjamin immediately followed Edward to help him prepare for bed. Only a few minutes after he had entered the bedchamber, he came back with deep frown on his face.

"Edward has refused to allow me to help him undress and get ready for bed. He told me you and I were conspiring against him and he wanted nothing more to do with either of us."

"Oh, Benjamin, I am so very sorry. I was hoping he wouldn't take out his anger on you. I am the one who made this decision. Believe me, it was a hard decision and I have often doubted whether it was the correct one. However, I do believe that the fact he has at least come here for two meals is significant. Please try not to be too hurt by his attitude. He is striking out at the people who love him because he doesn't believe he deserves to be loved. We have to just keep trying to show him we do love him. I know it is very difficult, but I am willing to keep trying. I hope you are as well."

"Of course, I will keep trying. I love Edward with my whole being, although sometimes it is difficult to remember why." Benjamin said as he slumped into a chair before the fire.

Diana rose from the pianoforte bench and went to Benjamin. She knelt down in front of him and put her hand upon his where it lay on the chair arm.

"We must keep trying. I don't know what else to do. We can't just let him wallow in his grief and self pity forever. Something must be done to pull him out of this depression. I know it is very hard for you, as it is for me, but we must persevere."

With those words, Diana rose and went back to the pianoforte bench with a grim determination. She sat and played a dozen songs before she finally gave up and went to bed herself, leaving Benjamin sitting in the same position lost in his thoughts.

Every day for the next two weeks was much the same as the one before. Edward did appear in the drawing room for meals, but left as soon as he had eaten. He still refused Benjamin's help with his personal grooming. He became more and more disheveled and smelly. Finally, Diana enlisted Forbes' aid in finding a footman, Joseph, who could at least help him bathe and shave on a semiregular basis. Edward accepted Joseph's help grudgingly, but he did accept it. Perhaps his own odor had finally gotten to him.

Now at least when he appeared in the drawing room for meals, he was decently groomed and dressed. Edward had finally begun to gain back a little of his weight, although he was still far too thin. He had not been exercising as he should and his leg had stiffened even more. He hobbled about on his cane when he had to move from the chair before the fireplace in his bedchamber to be bathed or to the drawing room for meals. He had still taken no interest in duchy business nor had he been downstairs once since they had returned from Warwick. He seemed to have no interest in helping himself in any way.

Benjamin finally had a reply from three of their old friends from school. He arranged for them to come to dinner on a Tuesday night. Diana informed Edward a few days before the dinner party that there would be no dinner served in the drawing room that evening. If he wanted to eat, he would have to come downstairs to the dining room.

When Diana was dressed for dinner, she knocked on Edward's door. There was no answer, as usual, so she let herself in. Edward was sitting in his usual chair before the fireplace staring despondently at the fire. He was not dressed for dinner, in fact, he wore his dressing gown over his night shirt. Apparently, he hadn't gotten dressed all day. He did not look up when Diana entered the room though she knew he heard her.

Diana went over to him and knelt by his chair. She gently touched his face with her hand, but he jerked away from her immediately.

"Don't touch me. I know you hate me, so do not try to act otherwise." he said vehemently.

"Hate you? I don't hate you, Edward. I love you like a brother as I always have. Why do you persist in thinking I hate you?"

"Because it's my fault that Geoffrey is dead. I killed our sweet, innocent little baby boy."

"Oh, Edward, we have been over and over this before. It was an accident that took our baby. You were knocked unconscious by a limb when the horse spooked and your boot was caught in your stirrup when the horse went over the edge of the ravine. Geoffrey may have been knocked off your horse by the same limb, since we found him above the ravine some distance from you. You and the horse fell over the embankment into the ravine after Geoffrey was already off the horse. You cannot hold yourself responsible for something you had no control over. We will never know why your stallion acted the way he did. Perhaps he was bitten by a bee or smelled a wild animal. We will never know. The area we were in was very densely wooded. It could have been anything, but it was definitely not your fault."

Edward looked at Diana with a glimmer of hope in his eyes. "You truly don't blame me for Geoffrey's death?"

"No, Edward, I don't blame you. There is no one to blame and especially not you. I know how much you loved Geoffrey, as he did you. You would never do anything to hurt him. You were his Dada."

Edward dropped his face into his hands and sobbed pitifully. Diana put her arms around him and held him close while they both wept for their son. Benjamin opened the door and saw them grieving together. His eyes filled with tears as well. He walked over and put his arms around them both, consoling them gently.

Chapter 31

After that day, Edward seemed to actually begin to want to live again. He got up at a decent hour, allowed Benjamin to bathe and dress him, and went down to breakfast in the dining room. The first few days were very difficult for him. The stairs were hard for him to navigate, but he finally got the hang of it and soon could come down much faster.

On the day of the dinner party, Edward had Benjamin dress him in his best black evening clothes. The fashion of the day still called for breeches for evening wear, but Edward was obviously uncomfortable in them. He was concerned about the appearance of his injured leg in silk stockings. He had not worn breeches since the accident. Benjamin could see his hesitation when the breeches lay on the bed with his evening coat.

Benjamin decreed that they would start a new fashion trend and took out black trousers instead. When he said he would wear trousers as well, Edward gave him a look of gratitude and reached over to touch his hand. It was the first overt gesture of affection Edward had shown Benjamin since the accident. Benjamin had to turn his head quickly so Edward wouldn't see the tears that had come into his eyes. Benjamin had missed the intimacy that he and Edward shared.

When Edward and Benjamin were both dressed for the evening, they went through the drawing room to Diana's bedchamber to fetch her. Barbara opened the door and both men were delighted to see how beautiful Diana looked in her black evening dress. Her auburn hair was pulled into a knot on the top of her head with curls hanging down around her face and neck. She was wearing the Bristol diamond parure. The gems glittered at her neck, ears and on both wrists. She wore her wedding ring on her left hand and a beautiful diamond ring on her right.

Diana had lost a lot of weight after the accident, but she had started to gain it back when they were at Asbury Park and was now at her normal weight. She was still a small woman, but her figure had filled out with childbirth. She had always had an ample bosom, but now, her decolletage was quite impressive. She was still only twenty, but had gone through more tragedy than many women thrice her age. The sadness in her life was reflected in her large green eyes. There was a pained depth to them that hadn't been there just a few months prior.

She smiled at her two favorite men. "Don't the two of you look handsome this evening? I really like the look of the trousers with your evening coats. You would put poor Beau Brummel's nose out of joint, if he were to see you this evening."

Both of the men laughed then Edward said with a spark of his former wit, "Well, Beau did introduce the trouser. We're just showing him an even better use for them. But you are right, he would probably be upset he hadn't thought of it himself."

The three friends were actually laughing as they started down the stairs. Forbes was just going to answer the door for the first of their dinner guests. The first to arrive was the Earl of Ashworth, or Bernie to his friends. He was not very tall, but was some what round. He had very light blonde hair and sported a full mustache a couple of shades darker than his hair. When he looked up, Diana noticed he had very merry, startlingly blue eyes. His eyes were his best feature, but his smile was what Diana liked most. Bernie's smile lit up his whole countenance and was infectious.

They had barely had time to greet Bernie, when the next guest arrived. The Earl of Ithorne, or plain Michael to his friends. Michael was quite tall and dark. He had very dark hair, deep brown eyes and was quite well built. Diana thought he looked very athletic. His evening clothes fitted him perfectly and he affected a black satin cape-like cloak with a red silk lining. She thought him a dandy.

The company was just heading into the drawing room, when Forbes again answered the door. The last member of the party had arrived. The Earl of Wellesley, better known as Dickey, was also tall and well built, but there the comparison to Michael ended. He had dark auburn hair and slightly tilted green eyes. His skin was very pale, almost translucent, with a spattering of freckles across his snub nose. To Diana, he looked Irish to the core.

Benjamin had apprised her of a brief history on each man. She knew Bernie was in line to be a duke when his father passed away and didn't relish the job. Bernie was so very light-hearted and somewhat frivolous, a duke's duties were overwhelming to him.

Michael had only recently become an earl, on the passing of his father, and was just settling into his new duties, albeit, reluctantly. Michael enjoyed the company of ladies, many ladies. He was considered by his friends to be something of a lothario and his conquests were considered legion by them all.

Dickey had been an earl since the age of eleven when his father was killed in a duel over an insult to his Irish wife. The countess had been so grief stricken at the loss of her beloved husband, she had retired from life to reside at one of their country estates. Apparently, she had retired from motherhood as well. Dickey had been raised by a series of retainers and educated for his earldom duties by his father's secretary and his man of business.

All five of them had been at Eton. When Benjamin had to go home because of his family's loss of fortune, they stayed in communication with him as had Edward. When Benjamin joined Edward at university as his valet, they renewed their friendship with him then also.

It was a lively dinner party. After brief condolences when they first met, none of the guests mentioned their recent losses or Edward's terrible accident, although Diana knew they were acquainted with the details from Benjamin. She was grateful for their compassion and kindness in not bringing up painful reminders on this night that was supposed to be about renewing old acquaintances.

After dinner, Diana stood to retire to the drawing room as was the custom. All five men stood up and begged her not to go. She had been entertaining them all with tales of her life in Scotland as a child and they were loathe to lose her company.

"Ah, gentlemen, I must leave you to your brandy and cigars. I know you have "manly" things to discuss." she said with a twinkle in her eye. "I can continue my Scottish tales in the drawing room later."

With that, Diana left the men and entered the large drawing room they had planned to use that evening. She went directly to the pianoforte and started to go through the music there.

The men were indeed sorry to see her go. She was like a bright flame and drew them like a moth.

"Ah, Edward, you are a lucky man. Wherever did you find such a splendid girl to become your wife?" asked Dickey.

"We met while I was on a hunting trip with my brother and father. Diana's father was an old friend of my father's from their younger days. I am, indeed, fortunate to have her." Edward said with a slight smile.

At the mention of his father and brother, Bernie spoke up, "We were very sorry to hear about all your recent tragedy, old boy. You have had more than your share of trouble lately."

The others gave him a surprised look. They had agreed amongst themselves not to mention the deaths of almost Edward's entire family in a space of three years. But then, Bernie could never keep what ever was in his head from spilling from his mouth, they thought.

Edward took it well, considering, and only muttered a thank you in response. Benjamin quickly took up the conversation and asked Michael about his new stallion, Satan Michael always eager to talk about his acquisitions took the reins of the conversation, so to speak, and the moment was put behind them.

After a half hour of conversation around the dining room table, the men adjourned to the drawing room. Diana was seated on the pianoforte bench, softly playing a Scottish melody when they all walked in. She glanced up and was gratified to see that Edward was smiling at something the inimitable Bernie had said. She smiled brightly at them all and started to rise.

"Oh, please Di, play something for us. You play so beautifully. If we ask nicely, she might sing for us as well." Edward said, surprising Diana.

"I'll be happy to play and sing if you will join me Edward. I love the sound of your voice, you know." she replied with a smile.

With the encouragement of his fellows, Edward slowly walked to the pianoforte and sat beside Diana on the bench. In the old days, he would have stood, but his leg was paining him and standing was not an option.

The two of them mesmerized their company for two hours with their playing and singing. Finally, laughing, Diana rose from the bench and stated she needed some tea. She pulled the bell for Forbes and ordered tea for herself and port for the gentlemen. The conversation that ensued was merry and the evening was a success.

As the three guests were leaving, they all stated that they must do this again. Dickey went even further and invited all of them to his townhouse on Saturday evening. They all concurred they would be there.

Diana was much encouraged after their little dinner party. She and Benjamin had witnessed so much improvement in Edward, they were amazed. He was walking better, eating better, sleeping better and seemed well on his way to recovery.

As Edward's health improved, so did his attitude. Diana was surprised a couple of weeks later to see Edward arrive in the library while she and Benjamin were working on correspondence.

Smiling shyly, Edward said, "I decided I have been very remiss in not taking a part in the work for the duchy. After all, I am the Duke of Bristol and it is my responsibility. The two of you have been wonderful doing all this, but now, I plan to at least be here to help. I will have to be brought up to date on what is going on, but I plan to help from now on with whatever needs doing."

Benjamin and Diana saw this as another very positive step in the right direction for Edward's complete recovery. They smiled at each other over his head as he sat between them behind the huge desk looking over the correspondence they were working on. It became the habit for all three to meet in the study after breakfast to work on duchy business. Diana also accepted their help with the business for Ainsley Glen and her English estate when there was a lot of it. Mostly, she handled everything herself, but there were times when several situations arose at once and she appreciated their help.

Chapter 32

The three friends were still grieving for Geoffrey, but their lives soon took on a routine that didn't exactly bring them joy, but at least allowed them to derive some pleasure and sense of accomplishment from their days.

As they were still in mourning, they did not go out in society, but did accept invitations to dinners with their three friends, Bernie, Michael and Dickey. They only went if the dinner was at one of the friend's respective residences and if no other company was to be there.

The days turned into weeks and the weeks into months. The anniversary of Geoffrey's death arrived in June and found the three friends returning to Scotland in his memory. They were a somber group when they arrived at Ainsley Glen. Burroughs, as well as Mrs. Gwen and Mrs. Allen and a number of maids and footmen greeted their arriving carriages.

It was a bright, sunny day. The flowers in the glen were blooming brightly and the air was clean and pure from a rain the previous day. Diana's heart was heavy as were Edward's and Benjamin's.

Edward's leg had improved to the point he could walk unassisted by his cane across level floors, but always employed it when he was out of doors. Because Edward couldn't walk for a very long distance, the three friends, with Edwin Burroughs, went by carriage to the cemetery.

Diana had ordered a stone for Geoffrey in London and had it shipped to Scotland as soon as she was able upon her return. She had seen the stone when it was complete in London, but hadn't seen it since it was placed upon his grave. She had been too consumed with Edward's recovery and duchy business to travel back to Scotland before now.

When the party alighted from the carriage, Diana saw the stone at once. She had had the stone engraved with the usual name and dates, but also the image of a small boy wearing trousers and sitting astride a pony. The inscription simply read, "Marquess Geoffrey Edward Benjamin Fergus Westmoreland Beloved son of Edward and Diana and grandson of Harold and Fergus". Edward nor Benjamin had seen the stone at all. Diana had taken it upon herself to take care of that sad task alone.

When Edward read the inscription, he turned to Diana with tears streaming down his face. "Thank you, Di, thank you so very much."

Diana did not reply, but took his hand and then Benjamin's, who stood on her other side. Edwin walked away to give the three of them some private time to mourn their child. He had been very worried about Diana when he left her in Warwick, but her letters, especially recently, had seemed much more upbeat. She didn't appear to be happy, but she did seem content and less worried than she had been.

Edwin knew Edward's recovery had been very difficult, but he knew no details. However, he could read between the lines in Diana's letters and had known that it was not going well for several months. Diana, not being one to cast aspersions on anyone, had not told him or anyone else of the agonies she had gone through at that time, but the truth was in the deep shadow of sadness in her eyes.

Edwin wished that she could know the true joys of a loving marriage. He, himself, was just learning that joy. He had recently married a young widow named Hannah. She was the daughter of a laird nearby who's husband had died of consumption two years hence.

Hannah and Edwin had known each other for several years as her father bought horses from the former laird, Fergus MacDonald. Edwin was always the one to deliver the horses. Since Hannah had loved horses, she was often around when a new one was delivered. Edwin had admired her from afar, not thinking his circumstances would ever be such he could ask for her hand. Then she had married a man from another county and he hadn't seen her for several years. When her husband died, Hannah came home to her father's house to look after him when her mother had passed away. She and Edwin had renewed their acquaintance. That acquaintance had quickly turned to something so much more.

Hannah's marriage had been a happy one and she worked hard to make her new marriage the same. She and Edwin loved each other very much. They were looking forward to becoming parents in about five months. Her first marriage hadn't been blessed with children, but she was very thrilled that this one would be, as was Edwin.

Edwin walked back over to the grave after giving the three friends some time together. "It's a fine stone you picked out, lass. Your father would be that proud to see his name on it as part of the bairn's name and also as his grandda."

Diana thanked him with a teary smile. "I appreciate your having the stone erected as well as having the cemetery looked after. It helps to know you're here taking such good care of things for me. I don't know what I would have done without you Edwin. You have been a true friend."

"'Tis I who should thank you, lass. You have given me a position I never could have had without you. Because of you, I now have a wife and will soon have a child. I am forever in your debt. Should you ever need me for anything and I do mean anything, please just send for me."

"Thank you Edwin. That is a very comforting thought."

The three friends stayed in Scotland for a fortnight. Diana visited her tenants, went over the accounts and met with Edwin and her man of business on numerous occasions. She liked Edwin's wife, Hannah. She was a pretty young woman who smiled often and looked at Edwin with love in her eyes. Diana was very happy for her old friend. However seeing how happy Edwin and Hannah were, left a small ache in her heart for what she would never have.

While she was at Ainsley Glen, Diana visited the MacAllisters. She was very gratified to see that Angus was much better, almost his old self. He was even thinking about attempting a trip to America to visit Ian and Alana and meet his grandchildren. There were now four of them, three boys and little Diana.

Diana tried not to think about her own situation any more than she had to. She felt a deep sense of obligation to the duchy and did her best to make sound decisions about the different estates, the mines and the other interests that were a part of the estate. She knew that without her, the duchy business would have been in dire straits while Edward convalesced from his accident.

She also felt great affection for Edward and Benjamin. She had begun to have very friendly feelings for Dickey, Bernie and Michael. She didn't really have any female friends in London, or for that matter anywhere, except her maid Barbara who had been with her since they were children. She hoped now that their mourning was again over, she might find someone to call friend in London. Diana didn't hold out much hope of finding a really true friend among the matrons of Society. She planned to continue her charitable works now as well. She hoped to find someone to be her friend among the ladies with whom she worked on the orphan situation.

Chapter 33

The trip back to London was uneventful. As a kindness to Edward, she and Benjamin rode in the carriage with him rather than on horseback as he had still not mastered riding. His leg had been weakened so by the accident, he didn't feel comfortable on horseback since strong legs were required to ride well. When they finally reached London, in the late afternoon, they were all tired and sore. They went to their rooms to rest and bathe the travel dust from their bodies.

Later, they would meet for dinner downstairs in the dining room. Diana had rested for about an hour and then gone to the library to check on the correspondence that had piled up in her absence. When she saw there was a letter from Ian, she eagerly opened it first.

Dear Diana,

It was wonderful to hear that Edward is doing so much better. Alana and I would love for you and Edward to come to America to visit us. I know you are both busy with the businesses, but if you ever see your way clear to come, please do not hesitate. You are both always welcome here. I would really love for you to meet our children. We have another son now named Alec. He was born two months ago and is growing larger day by day.
The farm is doing very well. I believe we will have a huge crop this year, barring any natural disasters. I have been able to more than triple my (or I should say your) investment in the years since we have arrived here in Virginia. The land here is more fertile than any I have ever seen. I would like to send you back

your money, although you have told me in several letters that you neither need nor want it. Please reconsider, if you would please.

Alana and I have had the pleasure of meeting your friend, Lawrence Banbury. He has settled within five miles of us and is building his home, while living in a small cabin already on the property he bought. I was fortunate to be able to help him hire some freedmen to help establish his farm. I believe he intends to breed and raise horses mainly, but will also plant fields of hay and corn for feed. We have had the pleasure of his company on several occasions in the months he has been here. We find him a most pleasant and interesting companion. He speaks highly of you.

We feel so very much sorrow for you and Edward on the loss of your little son a year ago. Hopefully, you will have another child ere long. We know another child can never take the place of your Geoffrey, but children are such a blessing we cannot help but wish you receive such a blessing again soon.

Please write to us soon as we so look forward to your letters.

With love and affection,.

Ian

For several minutes after reading Ian's letter, Diana sat completely still in her chair gazing out the window. She was very glad her friends were doing so well. She was also extremely happy for the birth of their fourth child. She knew she would never have another child, but it didn't preclude her happiness for her friends.

She thought for a few minutes about Lawrence. She was disturbed at the way her heart had hammered when she read about him in Ian's letter. She had no right to feel that way about another man. She was a married woman. Even though her marriage was not traditional in any way, she was still married and would honor her vows.

Diana took the letter and put it in her pocket then got down to opening correspondence pertaining to duchy business until it was time to go into dinner.

The days passed quickly as they were all very busy. Edward had again determined that they all needed new wardrobes as they were re-entering society again. This year's season was almost over, but Edward was determined to go to a few entertainments before they adjourned to Bristol Castle for the fall.

When everyone was again outfitted to Edward's approval, they began to accept invitations to a few events. They went to balls, the opera, the ballet, and often to dinner with Bernie, Michael or Dickey, sometimes all three at once. Edward could no longer dance, but since he had never enjoyed it much, he was not unhappy.

He was happy to have his friends dance with his wife as well as other young gentlemen in the *ton*. Diana loved dancing and was very good at it. She soon became a much sought after partner. Diana was not yet twenty-one and grew more beautiful every day. Her auburn curls were dressed in the latest styles and because of Edward, her clothes were numerous and extremely stylish.

It wasn't long before certain young men, both single and married, began to make romantic advances toward Diana. She handled each with kindness and humor, but also a firm refusal. She had no intention of taking a lover, although Edward would not have minded and indeed tried to encourage her to do so. Her own morals would not allow such a thing. Word soon got around that the Duchess of Bristol did not play her husband false and the overtures declined, but didn't stop completely. There was always some young man who thought he would be the *one*.

The season ended and the three friends soon adjourned to Bristol Castle for the fall. They planned to travel to another of the Bristol estates in Suffolk in January when it became too cold in Cornwall. They had invited Bernie, Michael and Dickey to join them for the hunting season starting in late September.

The first few weeks in Cornwall were taken up for Diana with readying the rooms for their visitors and taking care of duchy business concerning the mines. Diana didn't travel to the mines for meetings with the manager, Edward and Benjamin took care of those. She did, however, usually make all the important decisions before and after those meetings. Edward had come to depend on her sharp business acumen when dealing with any of the duchy business.

Other men would have looked askance at Diana being at a meeting. They had no idea that the innovative ideas proposed by Edward were actually all Diana's. She was very adamant about increasing safety in the mines and increasing miner's wages so they and their families could live better lives. She used the same tactics her father had taught her when dealing with their tenants.

At first the mining managers were surprised and suspicious about some of the changes. They felt the miners were being molly coddled by the gentry. When production increased after the changes, they had to admit that the new practices were smart and had been much needed. The miners were much impressed by the new Duke and were very happy indeed with all the changes they thought he had wrought.

Edward often felt quite a fraud when he was congratulated by the mine managers, since the ideas had all been Diana's. However, he knew he could not give credit where it was due. Even the miners would have looked askance at a woman making policy for them.

Diana, however, could and did interact with the tenants at Bristol Castle regularly. They soon grew to love their young duchess and look forward to her visits. She never failed to remember their names and those of their children. She made sure every one had food to eat and coal to warm them. Whenever she found a tenant with some difficulty such as illness or trouble with another tenant, she was quick to find a remedy one way or the other.

The friends soon got into the routine of working on duchy business in the library in the mornings and spending their afternoons either in the garden or one of the drawing rooms if the weather was inclement. Benjamin had bought a lot of new music for Edward and Diana to learn. Although not musical himself, Benjamin loved listening to them play and sing both separately and together.

The day came, about two weeks after their return, that Edward decided to attempt to ride again. Benjamin and Diana had been missing their wonderful rides, but would not go without him. Their horses had accompanied them on this trip.

Since Edward's horse had been destroyed after the accident, Diana had Edwin specially train another for him. When they were in Scotland in June, Diana had picked out a two year old bay gelding with the amusing name of Freddy who had plenty of spirit, but also a very willing and easy nature. Edwin had one of the grooms deliver the horse to Bristol Castle in late July.

Edward didn't know about Freddy as he was to be a surprise. When Edward went down to the stable with Diana and Benjamin, he was surprised to see a horse already saddled for him with a red ribbon on his bridle. He had never seen this horse before. He had been content to ride any of the horses usually stabled there for the family and their guests.

Edward and Freddy took to each other immediately. Edward was gratified that Diana had thought to have such a wonderful gift ready for him should he decide to ride again. Her forethought and kindness was much appreciated by both Edward and Benjamin.

When Edward first mounted, he had difficulty using his legs to turn Freddy as he had been used to do before the accident. Diana told him this horse was different. He had been trained to be guided more with the reins than the knees. Edwin had trained him as he would have a ladies horse. Since ladies normally rode sidesaddle they controlled their horses more with their hands using the reins. Freddy was trained in that manner and responded beautifully to hand commands. Before long, Edwin got the hang of riding without using his legs much to guide his horse.

Soon the three friends were again galloping across the fields on the estate every afternoon when they were done with duchy business for the day. The exercise was good for Edward and he soon became stronger and healthier. Edward still had periods of depression if he was not kept busy, so Benjamin and Diana made sure he was occupied at almost all times.

Benjamin and Edward had finally been able to resume their personal relationship in the months prior to their trip to Scotland and were closer than ever. They were much wrapped up in each other. Benjamin often felt great sorrow to see Diana so alone in an intimate way. She was so kind, so young and so beautiful; Benjamin despaired for her. She had such sadness in her eyes since Geoffrey's death. Benjamin wished desperately there was something he or Edward could do to make her happier, but he had no idea what to do. Diana steadfastly refused to even consider a relationship with another man. She always said she was content the way they were.

The days and weeks rushed by and soon the three friends were joined by Bernie, Michael and Dickey. Diana rose early as always and took care of duchy business before the others came down for breakfast. Many times Benjamin joined her in the library to help, but Edward, not being a morning person, most often did not.

On one such morning, Dickey came down earlier than expected. When he was informed by one of the maids that Diana and Benjamin were in the library, he joined them there. He was surprised to see Diana sitting behind the desk and Benjamin sitting beside her answering correspondence at her dictation.

"I say, you two, what are you up to so bright and early this morning? Where is Edward, Diana? Isn't this his job?"

Diana laughed and stood to give Dickey a quick kiss on the cheek. "Edward is not a morning person, Dickey, as you well know. While Edward was unable to take care of this type of thing when he was so ill, we became used to doing it for him. I suppose old habits die hard."

"Some men have all the luck. A beautiful wife who is also very intelligent and hard working. Ah, if I could only find someone like you, Diana."

Benjamin said, "I don't think there is another like our Di. She's one of a kind." he said as he put his arm around Diana and gave a laughing Diana a hug.

Dickey was inclined to agree. He envied Edward his wife and his close relationship with Benjamin. He had suspected for years that Edward and Benjamin were closer than friends. When he heard that Edward had married, he wasn't surprised. He knew he would have to marry eventually to keep he and Benjamin safe. But, when he heard that Edward and Diana had a child, he was even more confused. When he saw the effect of little Geoffrey's death on all three of them, he was completely perplexed.

Neither had he expected Edward's wife to be so very beautiful nor so very exciting to be around. Diana was intelligent, well read, talented and well versed in the political intrigues that went on constantly in British politics.

Diana was much more than Dickey had expected and he found himself somewhat jealous of Edward. He seemed to have it all. A wife who was everything a man could want, but who also seemed to be close to his lover. It was a conundrum to Dickey. He found it hard to understand the relationship between the three of them. He could not make himself believe they were part of some type of threesome. Diana just was not that sort at all.

Benjamin knew their old friends were having a hard time figuring out the dynamics of their relationship. He had overheard Dickey, Bernie and Michael discussing that very subject not long ago. He had confided what he had heard to Edward and Diana. The three of them had decided they would try to explain their rather unorthodox relationship to their three London friends during this visit. They just hadn't found the right time to bring it up, but they would.

The next night after dinner, the six friends adjourned to the drawing room right after dinner as had become their custom. Since again, Diana was the only female, the men felt it only fair that they all go together rather than spend an hour with brandy and cigars. Instead of heading to the pianoforte as she usually did, Diana sat on one of the three couches grouped around the huge fireplace.

"What, Diana, no music tonight?" asked Michael.

"Not tonight, Michael. Edward, Benjamin and I wanted to speak to the three of you about something we know you have been wondering about." Diana responded.

Michael, Bernie and Dickey exchanged a somewhat worried look, then took seats themselves.

Diana turned to look at Edward and smiled. Edward remained standing by the fireplace with his arm leaning nonchalantly against the mantle. Benjamin came and sat beside Diana and put his arm around her.

Edward smiled at his friends and began, "First, please let me acknowledge that I would not be telling this tale if I didn't believe that the three of you were our very good friends and would keep what I tell you in the strictest confidence." Edward looked at Michael, Bernie and Dickey and saw them nod acquiescence to his request. He continued, "I am not only sharing my own secrets, but those of Diana and Benjamin as well. I know the three of you must have wondered about the relationship the three of us have. I don't doubt any of you were ever fooled by me bringing Benjamin up to school to be my valet. You must have known that we are much more to each other. That has not changed in all these years and I doubt it ever will." Edward said, sharing a special smile with Benjamin. "Diana was engaged to my brother Geoffrey. The child we had, who died so tragically was his. When my brother was killed just weeks before they could marry, my father asked me to marry Diana to give the child a name. Since I needed to marry at some point anyway, I was more than happy to do so."

"Not long after we were married, I was drinking heavily and Diana confronted me about it. In a moment of weakness, I told her about Benjamin and I. Surprisingly, although she was so very young and innocent I had to explain in some detail what I was trying to get across to her, she took it very well. She accepted our relationship with such kindness and generosity, she made it easy for the three of us to share our lives quite well."

"However, I had no idea how absolutely wonderfully the arrangement would turn out. Yes, we lost our dear baby boy, Geoffrey, to a terrible accident and we all three have grieved terribly because of it. We all loved him with all our hearts. But the almost two years we had him were the very best of all of our lives. I have Benjamin and Diana, especially Diana, to thank for coming back from that accident as well as I have. She kept the duchy running all those months I was laid up as well as making me get well in spite of myself. " Edward said with a laugh. Then Edward turned to Diana with a look of love and gratitude.

"I do feel that Diana has the very short end of the stick in some ways, but she assures both of us that she is content with our arrangement. She loves us both as if we were her brothers or maybe even more. I have encouraged Diana to seek a lover, but she has refused steadfastly from the beginning. I feel that she is being cheated somewhat, but she denies feeling that way." Edward concluded.

Michael, Bernie and Dickey looked at each other in wonder. In all their speculation, they had never considered that Diana was completely aware of Edward and Benjamin's relationship and condoned it. Of all the scenarios that had run through their heads, and there had been several, this one was not even thought of.

Michael spoke first, "I hardly know what to say. Yes, the three of us have known for years that you and Benjamin were lovers. It was obvious in the way you looked at each other and that you were rarely separated except for classes when we were at school. We like our valets, but we don't chum around with them. As for Diana knowing and accepting your relationship, we had not a clue. I must say Diana, you are a capital good sport to say the least."

Diana laughed and replied, "Thank you Michael. I love these two very much. They have both been there for me through thick and thin. Without them I don't know how I would have survived the loss of Geoffrey, especially when I found out I was carrying his child. Edward saved me and my family from a disastrous scandal, to say the least. But he also loved my bairn as if he was his own, as did Benjamin. That more than anything sealed the bargain we have with each other. When our little Geoffrey was killed, it almost killed all of us as well. Edward was very badly hurt in the accident, but the loss of the baby was harder for him than the fact he was no longer able to do some of the things he had enjoyed doing before."

Bernie spoke up, "But what about you, Diana? Don't you want a traditional marriage and more children?"

Diana looked at him with such pain in her eyes, he almost lost his breath. "No, I do not want that. I would have had a very happy marriage with Geoffrey, whom I loved more than life itself. We were perfect for each other. I don't really think I could ever feel that way about a man again. As for more children, well, the pain of losing my bairn was so bad, I don't think I could face that again either, ever. Also, I had such a hard time with Geoffrey's birth, the doctor doesn't think I will be able to have another child. Life is too unpredictable. I have lost everyone that ever meant anything to me in less than three years except Benjamin and Edward. I am content with things the way they are. I have two wonderful men in my life, my work on the duchy business and now three great friends to keep me company. I need nothing else." Diana said with finality.

"Now that we have dispensed with the personal business of the evening, I think it is time for some music. Edward, will you join me for some songs?" Diana said, rising.

Without answering, Edward walked to Diana and offered his arm. She accepted and they went to the pianoforte and sat side by side on the bench. For the next two hours they played and sang their hearts out. It was quite a sight, the small, beautiful woman and the tall, handsome man, both so talented and so obviously in tune with each other, not only musically, but in other ways as well. It was obvious that they cared deeply for each other.

Only Dickey hadn't said anything about what they were told that evening. He sat quietly and stared at Diana with a brooding look on his face. He felt himself falling even more in love with her than he had already been. He had kept his feelings strictly to himself, but he had been more and more attracted to his friend's wife almost from the first time they met. He had felt really horrible about it, until tonight. Dickey had no illusions about Edward's proclivities, but had accepted that maybe he was a true husband to Diana after all since they had had a child. To know the child was not Edward's and that he and Benjamin were still together in every way left Dickey in a quandary.

Should he speak to Diana about his feelings, or even to Edward? He had no idea what to do. He admired Diana greatly, but his more tender feelings were engaged as well. He thought about Edward having suggested she take a lover. He didn't want to just be her lover, he wanted to have her all to himself, as his wife. He wanted to take care of her and try to erase some of the sadness he saw in her eyes. He wanted her to be his forever, not just temporarily, but there was only one way for that to happen and he could not see Diana divorcing Edward or vice versa.

The only other way would be for Edward to die and Dickey cared for his old friend way too much to wish for that. So, it looked like Dickey would just have to admire Diana from afar. That thought made him quite despondent.

Chapter 34

The next weeks flew by. The six friends had a wonderful time riding and hunting; eating and conversing; and laughing and enjoying music together. Bristol Castle had not seen so much frivolity and good cheer since the last duchess had died. The servants were kept busy, but they were happy themselves to see everyone having such a good time.

As Christmas neared, Diana told her friends about an American custom she much admired called a Christmas tree. Ian had written to her about the custom some time ago. He and Alana had adopted it their first Christmas in America. She had read the letter to Edward and Benjamin and they had discussed it several times thereafter. However, they had been in mourning so much in the past, they had never erected such a decoration. This year, they decided to not only have a Yule log, but to also put up a Christmas tree at Bristol Castle.

The six friends rode their horses to a wooded area near the castle to search for the perfect tree. Three footman accompanied them with a farm cart to haul the tree back and to do the heavy work of cutting it down. Diana had a fixed idea what the tree should look like from Ian's detailed description of his and Alana's trees over the years. Since the large drawing room they were putting the tree in had an unusually high ceiling, Diana wanted a very large tree.

After a couple of hours, Diana finally found the perfect tree. It was a well shaped evergreen with plenty of room on the branches for decorations and candles. Diana also had the footmen cut ivy, holly and evergreen branches to decorate the rest of the castle. They had a full wagon load when they returned as they had also cut a huge tree for the Yule log.

Diana employed everyone, guests and servants, to help make decorations for the tree, the drawing room, the staircase and main hall. Bertha was an old hand at making wreaths and was put to work with a couple of the other maids making a huge wreath for the front doors as well as one for above the fireplace in the main drawing room where the tree would stand. Barbara and two of the other maids were busily making swags for the staircase of evergreen boughs dressed with bright red ribbon. They also made swags for over the windows and chandelier in the drawing room and main hall. Pots of rosemary were brought in from the garden as well as Christmas roses to add to the color and fragrance of the season.

Diana had brought materials from London to make bows and balls for the tree itself. She had written to Alana for patterns and instructions a few months prior. Finding that Dickey was artistic, she set him to painting the completed wooden balls in bright colors. When they were dry, she had Bernie tying bows on them to hang them from the tree branches. When he protested, she told him to pretend he was tying fishing flies as he loved to fish. With much laughter, and encouragement from Diana, the party finally was able to complete the decorations in preparation of raising the tree on Christmas Eve.

Christmas Eve finally arrived. Diana came down for dinner wearing a dress made of velvet in the design of the McDonald plaid. She had requested the material through Edwin Burroughs in Scotland and had it made up before she left London. She hadn't worn it, but waited for this special evening. The bodice was low cut, but not overly so. It was fitted to her small body perfectly and the skirt flared out over several petticoats with the top white lace petticoat showing at the hem of the dress for several inches . It was trimmed in small red bows and had a white lace inset in the skirt. With her hair pulled up on her head with ringlets hanging down the back and small curls around her face, she was a vision. She also wore the emeralds her father had given her.

All the men looked at her admiringly when she entered the drawing room. Edward went to her and took her hand leading her to one of the sofas flanking the fireplace. The men were having a before dinner drink, except Edward, he was drinking a cup of tea. Diana joined him for a cup and then they went into dinner.

Diana had ordered a feast for the occasion. She had also ordered a special meal for Epiphany as well. On Christmas Eve they dined on baked oysters just harvested off the Cornish coast, a goose stuffed with currants and root vegetables, a variety of vegetables from the fall harvest and for dessert, mince pies with clotted cream. There were three varieties of fresh bread with bowls of sweet creamy butter to spread upon them.

The friends stuffed themselves and then retired to the drawing room to trim the tree. Diana didn't exclude the servants from the fun either. Several of the footmen and maids helped to hang the decorations on the windows and chandeliers. The footmen also brought in the Yule Log and the tree. The Yule Log was placed in the fireplace on an already brightly burning fire.

The tree had been placed in a large tub of dirt and stood in a prominent corner of the room. A ladder was brought for decorating the top of the large tree. Diana, Barbara and Bertha had strung ropes of almonds, raisins and currants to string on the tree. These were applied in great loops all around it. Small clusters of sweets and nuts had been placed in small bags made of colored paper and were hung on the branches with fruit and the bows and ornaments made by she and her friends.

Lastly to go on were the candles. Diana had ordered small molds for the beeswax to be poured into earlier in the fall to make small slender tapers for the tree. Each was stuck with wax to a small saucer and sat upon the branches all around the tree. Diana had made a bow for the top of the tree. However, before it could be placed, Benjamin brought her a beautifully wrapped box.

"Di, when you started to talk about having a Christmas tree, I did some research and found that stars are sometimes fixed to the top of the tree to represent the star that hung over Bethlehem on Christmas Eve. I ordered this for you from London. It's from Edward and I. We really hope you like it."

After thanking Benjamin and Edward, Diana opened the box to find a beautiful solid gold star covered in small gems of different sizes and colors. It was one of the most beautiful things she had ever seen. There was a clamping mechanism on the bottom to attach it to the tree. She hugged Benjamin and turned to Edward holding out the star.

"Would you put it on top of the tree, Edward? It seems only fitting for the Duke of Bristol to add the crowning glory to our first tree."

"Of course, my dear Di. I would be most pleased to do so." Edward said taking the star. He gingerly climbed up the ladder with Benjamin and Michael steadying the bottom for him. He clamped the star to the very top of the tree and carefully climbed down.

One of the footmen lit the candles from the huge Yule Log in the fireplace. At last, their masterpiece was complete. Diana had most of the other candles in the room snuffed out so only the glow of the tree and the glow of the roaring fire illuminated the huge room. The three friends, their guests and most of the servants stood around the tree in awe. None of them had ever seen a Christmas tree, but all agreed they wanted to have one every year from now on.

Ian had also told Diana of the custom of giving Christmas gifts to the servants and each other. She had bought small gifts for all the maids and footmen as well as the housekeeper, the butler, and the cook. She asked the housekeeper to have all the servants gather in the main hall. She had Benjamin bring in the large box she had placed the gaily wrapped gifts in. Each gift had a small tag with a servants name on it. They were all individually chosen for that particular person.

For Barbara, Diana had bought a pair of fine kid gloves with a fur muff. She knew Barbara's hands were often cold when they were at Bristol Castle and wanted her to be comfortable. For Bertha, Diana had bought a small gold necklace with a miniature of Geoffrey in it. The nursemaid had loved her son almost as much as she had. When Bertha saw the small picture, her eyes filled with tears and she impulsively hugged Diana. There were tears in Diana's eyes as well.

For the maids, Diana had bought a length of fine cloth with lace and trimmings for them to make a new Sunday dress. Each received a color to complement her particular hair and skin colors.

Diana had taken a lot of time to choose these gifts and they were much appreciated. For cook, Diana had bought a warm wool shawl in bright green which she knew was cook's favorite color. For the housekeeper, a book written by Jane Austen because she knew she loved to read and for the butler, a bottle of good Scotch whiskey she had Edwin send her from Ainsley Glen. The footmen all received nice wool scarves, again in colors to complement their colouring.

After an outpouring of awed gasps and thanks, Diana told them they would all have the next day off. They could visit friends or family or do nothing at all if that was what pleased them. This was unheard of in this day and age. Servants usually had a day off, but never did they all have the same day off. The household had to be run. However, Diana had already made arrangements for all six of them to be gone the entire next day to a fox hunt and ball at a neighboring estate. They would leave early in the morning and not return until the day after.

The next day dawned cold but sunny. The six friends broke their fast on cold meat and bread then galloped away to the estate of the Earl of Cambridge. He was an old friend of Edward's father and held a fox hunt every Christmas Day. It was a short ride, no more than thirty minutes, and the friends arrived just in time for the hunt. After riding to the hounds in the cold weather, they were all more than ready to join the earl's other guests for warm drinks and a good luncheon.

Diana had been shown to a guest bedchamber after the hunt to change from her riding habit into a day dress. She had sent over clothes for all of them the day before by one of the footmen since they were riding and had no way to carry anything with them. One of the upstairs maids had been enlisted to help her dress and fix her hair. Diana chose a dress of pale yellow muslin with long tapered sleeves that fit tightly on her slender arms. The dress was trimmed in a deep forest green ribbon and a deeper yellow lace under the high bodice, around the neckline and on the cuffs. The maid wove a matching green ribbon into her auburn curls leaving a few curls around her face and down her neck. She chose very simple gold jewelry to go with her ensemble.

Just as she was ready to go downstairs, there was a knock upon the bedchamber door. The maid opened the door to find Edward waiting to escort Diana to the dining room for luncheon. He had also changed from his riding clothes into one of his trouser suits. The trousers made from a charcoal gray and navy blue plaid, his coat was cut high at the waist and was a solid navy. His waistcoat was red and his cravat was plaid to match his trousers. Edward had always loved bold clothing and had finally begun to take an interest in them again recently.

His eyes lit up when he beheld his beautiful wife. "Di, you do me proud. You always look fetching, but that color is wonderful with your hair. You should wear brighter colors more often."

"Thank you Edward, but you are the peacock of the family, not I." Diana said with a pleased laugh.

As they were proceeding down the staircase, they heard voices in the great hall. It seemed their friends had gotten there ahead of them. Diana and Edward heard Michael regaling the others about a fox hunt at his property the prior year as they headed into the dining room.

The four men had not yet been seated when Edward and Diana entered the room. All four looked at the handsome couple with smiling faces, but Dickey's smile was the widest. He thought Diana a vision in the yellow dress she had chosen.

If Benjamin had still worn the title of valet, he would not have been included in the hunt or taken his meals with the rest of the house party. He would have been expected to eat with the servants in the kitchen and waited for his betters to return from the hunt. As Edward's secretary, he was included in all the festivities much to Diana's delight. She never wanted Benjamin excluded from anything she and Edward were involved in. To Diana, he was on an equal footing with them in every way. He might not hold a title or be wealthy, but he was such a part of their everyday lives, she would have felt terrible if he had not been accepted by the *ton*. There were other secretaries present also, as they normally travelled with their employers to take care of business when they were away from their homes.

The luncheon was extravagant to say the least. There were four varieties of meat, roast beef, mutton and pork as well as stewed rabbits, a large selection of vegetables, three kinds of fresh bread and numerous sauces and condiments. For dessert there was a plum pudding, mince pies and two different syllabubs. The friends were seated near each other and enjoyed the good food and conversation for some time. The luncheon went on for over two hours.

After the meal, everyone adjourned to a large drawing room with a roaring fire at each end of the room. A Yule log was burning in both of them. The room had been decorated with fresh evergreens and holly as well as brightly colored ribbons. A large pianoforte stood in one corner of the room. Diana had never seen one with an inlaid design such as this. There was a landscape scene depicted on the front above the keys. It drew her like a magnet.

Diana ran her hand along the inlaid design. It had been painted to depict this very estate. The house stood in the center with the grounds stretching to the sides. It was definitely the most beautiful instrument she had ever seen. As Diana was looking at it, she heard a quiet voice behind her.

"Why don't you play something for us, Lady Bristol? I remember how very well you played on the last occasion I was lucky enough to be in your company." the old Earl said.

"It is a very beautiful instrument, my lord. I would very much like to try it out."

Diana seated herself on the bench and ran her long slender fingers over the keys. She began to play a hauntingly beautiful aria from an opera by the Italian master, Bellini. She, Benjamin, and Edward had seen the opera in London last season and Benjamin had immediately ordered the music. She had learned to play it almost at once, finding the long melodies much to her liking.

As Diana was playing, she felt someone slide onto the bench beside her. She looked up and smiled at Edward. He had also found the Bellini opera entrancing and had learned the music with Diana. Soon, he was playing the right hand notes and she, the left. They did this often at home and thought nothing of it since they were both so musical. When the piece ended, there was loud applause from everyone in the drawing room. Some of them even stood. Diana blushed and laughed as Edward stood and took a bow.

Soon they were playing popular songs as well as classical tunes. They stayed at the pianoforte for more than two hours. Finally, Diana tired and joined the rest of the guests leaving Edward playing alone. The earl's wife soon joined him. When he could finally break away, he left the Earl's wife playing and joined his wife and friends.

The rest of the afternoon was wiled away pleasantly until time for the guests to dress for dinner. Diana had chosen her new bronze colored evening dress for the occasion. The dress was in the usual high waisted style, but was made of velvet. The sleeves were short and slightly puffed and the bodice was low cut. There were flowers embroidered in silk all over the gown in shades of pale gold with sage green leaves. The bottom of the dress was embroidered with sage green leaves interspersed with the same gold flowers. The skirt was not overly full and just touched the tops of her gold evening slippers. Her gloves were the same shade of bronze as her gown, but made of silk and went above her elbows. She had the maid arrange her curls on each side of her head from a center part with silk flowers pinned at the top of each cluster of curls. She wore her topaz jewelry to complete her ensemble.

Again, just as her toilette was complete, there was knock upon the door. The maid opened it to admit Edward resplendent in a plum colored evening coat with a heavily embroidered waistcoat in gold.

He was wearing buff colored trousers and a white ruffled shirt. His cravat was gold silk to match his waistcoat. His blond hair was brushed to a sheen.

"You look wonderful, Edward. I really like that plum color on you. It is very becoming."

"Thank you, Di, but you are the one everyone will be looking at this evening. You are a vision in that dress. You may be right about not wearing really bright colors. Everything you have chosen lately has been a great success."

Smiling her thanks, Diana took Edward's arm as they proceeded to the drawing room to wait to go into dinner. The assembled company was attired in a plethora of colors and materials. Every lady and even some of the men seemed to want to outdo the others. There were dresses of every hue, some simple and some very ornate. Diana seemed to stand out among the other ladies, not only for her wise color choices, but also for her beauty. Her hair was glossy, her skin clear, and her beautiful green eyes shone.

They had a sumptuous dinner of eight courses which included baked oysters for the first course and a beef consomme flavored with wine. The second course was baked sole in cream sauce. The rest of the courses consisted of different kinds of meat and fowl served with many types of vegetables. The dessert course was actually two courses, one of puddings and the other of four different cakes. All that was followed with fruit, cheese and more wine. The Earl of Cambridge set a very fine table.

After dinner, the guests adjourned to the ballroom. In the gallery above the dance floor, an eight piece orchestra was already beginning to play. The earl and his lady had invited many of their neighbors to join their already large house party. More than a hundred people were in the ballroom when everyone had arrived.

Diana was kept extremely busy dancing that evening. She loved to dance and was very light on her feet. She had determined before the ball to dance waltzes only with people she knew quite well like

Benjamin, Michael, Dickey or Bernie. The reels, however, she felt free to dance with almost anyone. Because of his leg injury, Edward no longer danced and that suited him just fine. He had never really enjoyed the pastime and did not miss it at all. Instead, he spent his time in the card room playing whist. Gambling he did like and he was quite good at it.

Since Edward no longer drank, he had stopped losing at cards. When he was drinking heavily, he was also usually losing heavily. That had all ended now. He was rather proud of himself. It had been a very long time since he had imbibed more than a glass of wine or two at dinner. He never drank port after a meal, but had continued to develop his taste for coffee instead. Diana was still a tea drinker as was Benjamin, but Edward really loved the stronger taste of coffee.

Around two o'clock, Diana was tired of dancing and made her way to the card room to find her husband to say goodnight. She found Edward along with the rest of their friends seated around a table playing whist together. She put her hand on Edward's shoulder to get his attention. He smiled up at her.

"Are you tired, little hin? Did you get your fill of dancing already?", he asked with an indulgent smile.

"Yes, to both of your questions. I'm about to go upstairs to bed and wanted to wish you all a good night."

All the men at the table had risen upon her arrival. They all said their good nights and Dickey came around the table to Diana's side.

"I'll escort you to your bedchamber, Diana, if you like. I find myself a bit tired as well." Dickey said.

Benjamin, who had noticed Dickey's unusual interest in his friend's wife, also came around the table. "I believe I will join the two of you. It has been a long day and I am not having any luck with the cards tonight."

Benjamin noticed Dickey's scowl and was glad he was accompanying them. He didn't fear that Dickey would do anything untoward, but he didn't want Diana to have to deal with an unwelcome advance by their friend. Benjamin had noticed how Dickey stared at Diana much of late and had been watching for something like this to happen. He knew Dickey's reputation with the ladies and was eager to keep Diana safe from his charms.

Benjamin had no doubts that Diana was not interested in an affair with anyone. She had stated her thoughts on that subject several times. Her moral sense could not condone an extramarital relationship and that was all that was available to her. He felt sorry for her because she didn't share the intimacy with anyone that he and Edward had. He wished more for her, but knew her own morals wouldn't allow such a thing. Benjamin loved Diana like one of his sisters and felt very protective toward her.

The next day dawned cold and sunny yet again. The friends left the earl's estate right after breakfast and enjoyed a brisk ride home. After changing from their riding attire, they all met in the small drawing room to gather around a briskly burning fire for tea and coffee.
Again Benjamin noticed that Dickey singled out Diana for conversation and when they weren't talking, seemed to stare at her broodingly. He began to worry that his friend had fallen in love with Diana and determined to speak to him soon about his behavior.

Since it was Boxing Day, Diana had arranged for their tenants to come to the castle for their gifts in the afternoon. As tradition dictated, Edward passed out coins to the tenants and refreshments were also served to them in the great hall. Cook had been up for hours making huge bowls of wassail, cookies, candies and cakes. Each tenant arrived with their families for the celebration. Since Diana had given the servants the day off on Christmas Day, there was plenty of help to serve their Boxing Day guests. As Diana circulated among the tenants, their friends were surprised to discover she knew each tenant and his family members by name.

When all the tenants were assembled, Diana called all the children together and took them into the large drawing room to see the Christmas tree. None of them had ever seen a decorated tree set up for the holiday and watched the candles be lit with awe. Diana explained it was a custom in America and that she had friends there who told her about it.

She had one of the footmen bring a large box into the room. Inside were gaily wrapped packages for each child with his or her name on them. There was a cacophony of noise when the excited children unwrapped toy horses, whistles, tops and the like. There were pretty ribbons for the little girl's hair and warm gloves and scarves for many, as well as toys. Their parents gathered in the large doorway to watch their children's excitement with delight.

When all the tenants had finally left, the friends settled down in the small drawing room again for some peace and quiet. Edward sat at the pianoforte and played a quiet tune while Diana poured tea and served cakes and cookies to their friends. Benjamin again noticed Dickey's intense scrutiny of Diana. He was surprised she had not noticed it herself, it was so obvious to him. Benjamin decided to speak to Edward and Diana before he approached Dickey.

That evening when all were dressing for dinner, Benjamin and Edward came into their adjoining drawing room and knocked on Diana's bedchamber door. Barbara answered their knock. Diana had just completed her bath and was sitting at her dressing table while Barbara brushed her hair. She was wearing the new robe they had bought her for Christmas. It was a heavy velvet in dark green that complemented her hair beautifully.

When Benjamin broached the subject of Dickey, Diana surprised him. "Yes, I've noticed Dickey's preoccupation with me. I was hoping I was wrong about the reason, but I suppose I wasn't. It is unfortunate that he feels that way about me. I like him a great deal, just as I like Michael and Bernie, but I have no other feelings for him. You both know my opinion of affairs. I simply could not do that."

Edward spoke next. "Yes, Hin, we know how you feel about that matter. You have expressed your feelings to us before. We're not encouraging you to have an affair, but just letting you know you may be approached by Dickey. Benjamin feels he or I should speak to Dickey about this matter. What do you think?"

"I truly don't know if that is a good idea. If, or when, Dickey approaches me, it might be better if I handled it myself. That way, the only embarrassment he will feel will be from me. I wouldn't want to hurt his feelings in any way, although I cannot reciprocate his feelings or desires. If either of you speak to him, he would suffer more I think."

Both Benjamin and Edward were again surprised by Diana's compassion and insight into Dickey's reaction to her rejection of his affections. The three friends spoke a bit more on the situation and then let it rest.

It was several days later that Dickey found an opportunity to speak to Diana alone. He came upon her in the library while she was looking for a book. He had been trying for some time to catch her without the others around.

"Ah, Dickey, how are you this afternoon? I was just looking for a new book. I finished the newest Jane Austen last night and am in need of something new to occupy my time this rainy afternoon." Diana said when she noticed him at the door.

"Diana, I'm so glad to find you here. I have been wanting to speak to you for some days."

"Indeed, Dickey, is there something I can do for you?" Diana thought to herself the moment she had been dreading had come, but she knew she had to handle the situation as diplomatically as she could.

Dickey seemed nervous as he slowly came further into the room. Diana was standing on the far side of the huge library perusing the biographies on the shelves. She had turned toward the door when she first felt herself to no longer be alone. Dickey seemed to come slowly toward her in a rather meandering way. When he finally reached her, he reached for Diana's hands with both of his.

She let him take her hands and looked up at him expectantly with a slight smile on her lips. "Is everything all right, Dickey? You seem upset about something. Not bad news from home is there?"

"No, Diana, I've had no news from home. It's just there's something I've wanted to speak to you about and now that I've found you alone, I don't quite know how to start."

"Well, I have always found that starting at the beginning is helpful." Diana said with a broader smile

"I don't know that there is a beginning. I need to start by saying that I admire you greatly. I find you beautiful, intelligent and very, very charming." Dickey said as he tried to pull her closer to him.

Diana's smile went away. She pulled her hands away from his and backed up a couple of steps. "Thank you, Dickey. It's always nice when ones friends think highly of one. I appreciate the compliment. I enjoy spending time with you, Bernie and Michael very much. Edward, Benjamin, and I have really enjoyed your visit." Diana said as she chose a random book from the shelf and slowly started to walk away from Dickey.

"Diana, I don't think you understand what I'm trying to tell you. Oh bollocks, I'm making a mess of this. It's just that I find myself drawn to you like a moth to a flame. I can hardly think of anything but you." Dickey said chokingly.

"Dickey, are you saying you are attracted to me?"

"More than attracted, Diana darling. I'm in love with you. Hopelessly and completely"

"I'm sorry to hear you say that, Dickey. I'm a married woman. I made vows when I married Edward and I expect to abide by those vows for the rest of my life. I know our relationship, our marriage, is not a traditional one, however, it is a marriage. I could never take a lover nor could I divorce Edward. There is no future for you with me, none whatsoever." Diana said in a very firm voice. She didn't speak loudly, but she did speak very clearly. She didn't want there to be any misunderstanding between them.

Dickey looked stricken. "Somehow I knew you would say that, but I just had to tell you how I feel about you. I believe we could have a wonderful life together. You might even grow to care for me as much as I care for you over time. Oh Diana, won't you even consider us being together? It's not right for Edward and Benjamin to have each other and for you to have no one." he pleaded.

"No, Dickey, I won't even consider what I would consider a mortal sin. I am a Catholic. There will never be a divorce for me and my conscience would never allow me to accept a lover. I still love Edward's brother Geoffrey with all my heart and I sincerely believe I always will. There can be no future for me with any man except Edward. Please, Dickey, don't let's quarrel about this matter. Please just accept the fact that I am content with my life and let it go."

With those words, Diana turned and left the library. Dickey was beside himself with embarrassment and grief. He truly did love Diana, but he didn't want to upset her and he feared he had done just that with his declaration of love.

When Edward and Benjamin came to fetch Diana to go to dinner later that evening, they could see she was upset. She told them about the scene in the library earlier in the afternoon. She felt sorry for Dickey, but that was the end of it as far as she was concerned. She was not attracted to Dickey and even if she had been, she would not have acted on that attraction. Edward and Benjamin were sympathetic towards both Dickey and Diana. They understood both their viewpoints, but felt helpless for them both.

Benjamin looked at Diana with pity in his eyes. He felt much remorse for the situation she was in. There was little that could be done, it truly was a hopeless situation.

That evening, Michael and Bernie could tell something was wrong, but had no idea what it was. Dickey was very quiet, as was Diana. Benjamin and Edward tried to act as if everything was alright, but there was a definite pall over their company. Later, after Diana had gone up to bed, as had Dickey and Edward, Bernie asked Benjamin what was going on. He explained the situation. Bernie and Michael weren't entirely surprised. They had also seen the way Dickey looked at Diana. They had actually been hoping she would return his affection, but weren't surprised that she didn't. They both knew that Diana had very high moral standards, unlike many so called ladies of the *ton*.

The next day, Dickey decided he had better leave Bristol Castle because he just couldn't hide his feelings for Diana any longer. Diana, Benjamin, and Edward did a half hearted job of trying to persuade him to stay at least a few more days. but he demurred. Michael and Bernie decided to go with him as they had already been at the castle for several weeks and had things they needed to do. In any case, the three had only planned to stay a few more days, so their leaving wasn't too awkward, just a littler earlier than expected.

Chapter 35

The weather became wilder and colder as December ended. The three friends had decided to leave in January for the somewhat warmer climes of Suffolk and soon prepared to do so.
There was a flurry of packing by the servants and then once again they boarded the carriages surrounded by their outriders, footmen and grooms for the week long trip to the Bristol estate in Bury St. Edmunds.

The estate there was quite large, but had not been bringing in the income Diana thought it should. That was the reason she had chosen that estate for a prolonged visit this year. The principle crop was sheep, but the farms there also grew corn and hay for winter feed. The sheep herds had dropped off slowly, but surely, and to Diana alarmingly, over the past couple of years and Diana was interested to find out why. There had been no drought nor disease that she could find mentioned in the farm records. The manager of the estate, one Mr. Charles Crumbly, had answered her letters of inquiry rather desultorily without much detail as to why the sheep were not reproducing as they had in years past.

When the large group arrived at the Bristol estate named Brashers in honor of a distant relative who had built it, they found the small castle to be understaffed and not altogether clean. Diana and Edward were both surprised at the condition of the main house and the outbuildings as well. Mr. Crumbly was not at home when they arrived although he had been informed of the date of their arrival well in advance.

As soon as Diana had washed the travel dirt off and changed her clothes, she went directly to the study on the ground floor where the farm records were kept. Much to her surprise, the records seemed to be missing some pages and very sloppily kept, at least for the last two or three years. Before that time, everything had been shipshape. Diana, determined to get to the bottom of this mystery, rang the bell for the butler, Mr. Collins. When Mr. Collins arrived, Diana was comforted to see an older gentleman who was immaculately attired in his neat, if somewhat threadbare, black suit with his hair neatly brushed and his white gloves perfectly in place.

Ah, she thought, this gentleman at least seems to know how to do his job.

"Mr. Collins, may I ask if you know where Mr. Crumbly has gotten off to today? Was he not apprised of our arrival?"

"No, your grace, I do not know where Mr. Crumbly is. Yes, your grace. I delivered the duke's note to him myself over a week ago when I received my own orders to ready the house. I must apologize for the state of the castle, your grace. The maids do try their best, but this is a very old building without many modern conveniences and with so few staff, it is very difficult to keep it up as it should be."

"And why is that, Mr. Collins, the small staff I mean? Is there no one local who wishes to be employed at Brashers?"

"Oh, no, your grace. There are many willing and able servants for hire in this area."

"Well, Mr. Collins, can you tell me why none have been hired, then?"

"Mr. Crumbly let most of the servants go about a year ago. He kept only a very small staff. Just two maids of all work, two scullery maids, the cook and myself. Since the castle has forty six rooms all tolled, there is no way to keep it up to standard with that size staff. Again, your grace, I do apologize for the state of the house. I am embarrassed you must see it this way. Mr. Crumbly gave no reason for letting the staff go, he simply did it."

"Well, Mr. Collins, we must remedy that and immediately. The duke and I have brought several footmen with us, as well as grooms, my ladies maid, and another maid of all work, Bertha. She is an excellent laundress. I did not hear you mention a laundress on staff, did I?"

"No, your grace, we have no laundress as such. One of the scullery maids, Mary, does the laundry along with her other duties in the kitchen."

"I see, well we will put that to rights also. I would very much like you to go to town in one of our carriages, in the company of one of our footman, to hire enough staff to take care of the castle properly. I would think at least four upstairs maids, four downstairs maids, two more scullery maids, a laundress, and five or six footmen should just about do it. I also noticed that the grounds are in need of quite a bit of work. Are there groundsmen and gardeners on staff?"

"No, your grace, Mr. Crumbly let all the outside help go except for one of the grooms to take care of the limited number of horses left in the stables."

"Oh, dear, Mr. Collins, we cannot have that either. Please see to it that the stables are completely staffed as well as enough groundsmen and gardeners to bring the grounds back up to standard, if you please. Also, I will be raising your wages as well as all of the present staff's as well. You have been doing the work of two people here and deserve better pay than what I have found in the account books."

"Actually, your grace, none of us have been paid for the last three quarters."

"Oh, my, Mr. Collins, I must now apologize to you. I had no idea that things were going so badly here at Brashers or the duke and I would have taken care of this situation before now. I will have the duke's secretary take care of that immediately. If there is anything else that needs my immediate attention, please tell me now."

"Your grace, I believe several of the local tradesman haven't been paid for goods in quite some time either."

"We were lead to believe the estate was self sufficient growing their own vegetables and raising their own meat. Is that incorrect?"

"I am afraid, your grace, that you were mislead. I don't believe Cook has received any produce or meat from any of the farms in over a year."

Diana was shocked and appalled. Every accounting for Brashers she had seen showed the farms to be supplying the castle with meat, produce and grain in quite ample amounts. From the looks of the staff, they hadn't been eating very well and they certainly weren't dressed very well. It was Mr. Crumbly's responsibility to clothe and feed all employees as well as make sure the castle was maintained correctly. He had apparently failed abysmally on all fronts.

Diana soon met with Edward and Benjamin and brought them up to date on the state of Brashers. They were also very upset at what she had found. Benjamin set out immediately for Bury St. Edmunds with a list of the unpaid tradesmen, a list of needed supplies, and Mr. Collins, along with a couple of footmen and 2 carriages to carry the new servants and supplies. Diana furnished him with a large purse to take care of it all. She also made sure all the existing servants were paid their wages immediately including their raises.

Diana and Edward spent hours going over the household accounts and farm accounts. They soon discovered that Mr. Crumbly was not a very clever thief, but he was a greedy one. He had been siphoning off large amounts of coin from the farms as well as keeping much of the allotted household monies for himself, but had failed to cover his tracks hardly at all. After a meager luncheon of watery soup and fresh bread, Diana and Edward set out on horseback to the farms to see for themselves what was going on.

At the first large sheep farm, they spoke to the overseer, Mr. Clayton. He told them in detail what his farm produced and showed them his account books. The discrepancy between his books and Mr. Crumblys was enormous. Mr. Clayton showed an increase in his herds where Mr. Crumbly showed a decrease. When asked if he knew of Mr. Crumblys whereabouts, he did not, but allowed he had heard Mr. Crumbly maintained a house in a nearby village for his mistress. After visiting several other farms and finding the same circumstances, Diana and Edward decided to pay Mr. Crumbly's mistress in the village a call.

Following directions from Mr. Clayton, they left from the last farm for the nearby village. Upon reaching the house, Diana and Edward did indeed finally catch up with Mr. Crumbly. As a matter of fact, he answered their knock on the door. Diana felt an instant dislike for the man, which was very unusual for her. When apprised of their identities, he would not look directly at either she nor Edward, but seemed to have a particular dislike for Diana. He was a small, very nervous, and extremely thin man with a cocky attitude and shifty, darting eyes. When Diana began to question him about the discrepancies in the accounts, he wouldn't answer her directly, but addressed himself to Edward instead, not even deigning to look once at Diana. Edward soon put him in his place however.

"Mr. Crumbly, when my wife, the Duchess of Bristol, asks you a question, it would behoove you to answer it directly, truthfully, and swiftly. My secretary is in town right now alerting the magistrate to what we found upon our arrival at Brashers. Unless you have a very good explanation for not only the condition of the castle, but also the discrepancies in your accounting, you will be brought up on charges and sent to prison."

"Your grace,", the unpleasant little man sputtered, "I meant no disrespect to your lady. I am not used to dealing with women where business is concerned." Mr. Crumbly asserted with not a little disdain. "I am quite sure I can explain everything to your satisfaction. We have had a run of bad luck on the farms, that is all. I'm sure that will change soon. I didn't have time to get everything put to rights before your arrival. If you just give me some time, I'm sure I can fix things right up and the farms will turn a profit again."

"Mr. Crumbly, we have already visited every farm on the estate and looked over their books, herds and fields. We saw nothing to indicate a run of bad luck and the overseer's accounts are quite different from the ones we were sent." Edward stated with a severe look. "What say you of that?"

Crumbly suddenly lost his sullen manner and looked very distressed. He seemed at a loss for words. Apparently, he had not expected the duke to take the initiative to actually visit the farms himself. Seeing that he had been caught in his lies, he didn't know what to say or do. Crumbly had been the castle manager for some ten years and had been a fairly good employee for all but the last two years, only stealing a little. After he had met Mavis, his pretty young mistress, he had found his wages didn't stretch far enough to cover the house she demanded, nor the servants, coach, jewelry and clothes she deemed necessary for him to stay in her good graces. The first year, he had only stolen enough to keep her happy, but the longer they were together, the more it took to keep her happy, so the more he stole.

Not being particularly clever, Crumbly had been smart enough to take advantage of the duke's grief over the loss of his older son and his own illness to persuade him by post there was no need to visit Brashers as he usually did a couple of times a year. After the duke's death, Crumbly had not expected the young duke to take a personal interest in Brashers and he had become even more greedy. Because of Fergus' death, the accident and the loss of their child, Edward had not visited the castle either, so Crumbly felt fairly safe.

When he received word that the duke and his party would be coming to stay a couple of months at the castle, he had not worried overmuch. He had met Edward once and found him to be a silly young man who had little interest in his father's holdings. The young man who stood before him now was not the same man at all. He had a strength and maturity Crumbly had not seen before. Crumbly knew the jig was up and he was caught.

Diana watched the interplay of emotions over Crumbly's face. Finally his shoulders slumped and he suddenly began to confess his transgressions. The door of the house burst open and a plump, somewhat pretty, young woman came storming out. Apparently she had been listening just behind the door.

"Shut your stupid mouth, Crumbly." she shouted. "These nabobs can afford to lose a few coins where I cannot. If you go to prison, who's gonna pay for me house and me baubles?"

"Hush now, Mavis. I'm caught and that's all there is to it. I will go with the duke to the magistrate right now. There's nothing else for it. I'm that sorry girl, but I always knew this couldn't last forever. I should never have started this. It was madness."

Mavis face lost all animation. She turned without another word and stomped back into the house. Crumbly went to the horse tied at the side of the house and mounted without another word. The trio headed to Bury St. Edmunds and the magistrate's office straight away.

Diana and Edward were at the magistrate's office for a good two hours while Crumbly confessed to all. He had apparently started his criminal career by keeping some of the proceeds from the lamb sale on only one farm to induce Mavis, who had been a maid at the castle, to take up with him by buying her a bracelet. That escalated to the present situation where he had taken all of the profits from all the farms by the end of the first year. Then finally, the castle household accounts as well. He admitted he had fired all the servants except what he absolutely had to have to keep the house running at a minimum. He had even stolen the wages for the few servants left from the last three quarters. When all was said and done, Crumbly was a broken man. The cocky arrogance he had first exhibited had completely disappeared.

By the time Diana and Edward returned to Brashers late that afternoon, they were exhausted and starving. Benjamin greeted them amidst a flurry of cleaning in the house and frenzied activity on the grounds. Wonderful smells were coming from the kitchen much to Diana and Edward's gratification. Soon a tasty dinner was served in the newly cleaned dining room. A roaring fire was going in the fireplace and the room was very comfortable where before it had been cold and dirty when they had their meager lunch.

After dinner, the friends adjourned to one of the smaller drawing rooms on the first floor. They were all very tired from their days activities. Benjamin had been able to hire enough servants to really staff the castle and it's grounds as well as procuring all the supplies needed to clean the entire building and stock the larder.

He had visited the butcher and greengrocer filling the cooks list and paying old accounts.

When Diana and Edward were at the farms, they had requested that fresh meat and vegetables be delivered to the castle the next day. The overseers at the farms had been surprised that the castle was so poorly stocked as they had been sending the usual amounts each week. Crumbly had been intercepting those deliveries and either taking them to his mistress or selling them to the local merchants himself. He had left a broad trail of his deceptions and thievery.

It took two weeks for the castle to be completely cleaned and refurbished with new drapes, linens and the like. Diana made several trips with Barbara and Bertha into town to purchase fabrics, furniture, candles and other sundries to bring the castle back to its former splendor. The original building was very old having been completed in 1504 by the original Brasher. He was knighted and awarded his lands after showing exemplary courage at the battle at Blackheath in 1497. It took over five years to complete the original stone building. Over the years, more wings had been added and the castle was now quite large, but also quite primitive.

Diana, Edward, and Benjamin determined to spend their months at Brashers coming up with improvements to the castle and farms to achieve maximum comfort for them and their guests and efficiency and profit for the duchy. Diana was very good at listening carefully to the servants and tenants about what was needed to improve their holdings. She would listen to them and then make notes on what they needed, then come up with innovative solutions to their problems. She was a master problem solver and Edward and Benjamin had learned early on to listen to her suggestions without fail.

The months of January, February and March passed quickly for the friends. They were all very busy either looking for solutions to problems or implementing them when they were found. Several of the farms had fallen into disrepair under Crumbly's stewardship in the last two years. Diana, after listening to their tenants and also questioning other nobility in the area found the best builders and craftsman in the area. She, along with Edward and Benjamin, met with them and put forth the changes she wanted made. When it was feasible, she handled the negotiations herself, if not, she gave a written plan to Edward or Benjamin and they dealt with it.

By the time they were ready to go back to London at the end of March, Brashers was running smoothly and most of the renovations were finished. They had found a very good new manager, Mr. Cumberbatch, who had recently worked as an overseer on their largest farm. He had the reputation of being a very honest and hard working man and they were glad to elevate his position. He had been recommended by Mr. Collins, their butler.

Diana, in particular, had formed a solid relationship with the old man and found him a fount of information on practically everyone and everything in the neighborhood. They all felt really positive about leaving Mr. Collins in control of the castle and Mr. Cumberbatch in charge of the farms when they left.

Chapter 36

Before they knew it, the day arrived for the trio of friends to leave Suffolk for London. The trip to London from Suffolk was much shorter than from Cornwall to Suffolk. The weather stayed fine and they reached London in four days much to every ones relief. What had been thought to have been a restful stay at a country estate had turned into very much work and worry. They were relieved to arrive at the Mayfair mansion where nothing immediately required their attention except the refurbishing of their wardrobes and deciding which invitations to accept.

This was the first full season of the *ton's* entertainments the friends had experienced in almost four years. They had been in mourning for all or at least part of every season previously. Diana had turned one and twenty in March, Edward had turned six and twenty in February, and Benjamin would turn six and twenty in May. Diana was again reluctant to accept more than three or four invitations per week. She took up her charitable work for the London orphans again, Edward sat in Parliament, and Benjamin was kept very busy with his secretarial duties for Edward's political dealings and the duchy. Diana found herself handling more and more of the duchy business alone since Edward and Benjamin were so involved in Parliament this term.

With the death of poor, mad King George III, a new monarch, George IV, was to be crowned and a new government established. Edward, as a member of the House of Lords, was required to attend the convening of Parliament in late April. As a Tory, the ruling party at that time, and a direct relative of the king, Edward was much sought after for his support by different groups. Never having really been involved in the political arena before, there was an enormous amount for Edward to learn. Benjamin and Diana had always been interested in the political situation and were well versed in what was going on in the country at any given time. As usual, they advised Edward and offered their support when needed, which was almost constantly. Diana, of course, could not attend the Parliament sessions, but she was very instrumental in forming Edward's progressive and liberal opinions by writing his speeches with Benjamin's help.

Edward soon became known as a very forward thinking young man who wielded his family's power and wealth judiciously and fairly. He actually thought himself a fraud and a charlatan since a good portion of the ideas and innovations he was credited with were actually his wife's and his lover's. At first those thoughts really bothered Edward, but he soon adopted a different outlook and found the situation amusing instead, but never in public. When alone with Diana and Benjamin, he would make fun of several of the more austere members of Parliament with a very wicked sense of humor. He especially found Lord Westerly absurd and often made fun of his mannerisms and his bigotry.

As for the Prime Minister, Lord Liverpool, Edward had a profound admiration. They had similar liberal views and Liverpool was also much admired by Diana for his views on Catholicism.. Lord

Liverpool was often a guest in the Bristol household and never failed to make a positive impression on all assembled there.

Chapter 37

The days and weeks seemed to fly by. Soon it was August and time for Parliament to take a break. The weather had turned tremendously warm and humid in London. The trio of friends decided to take a trip to one of their country estates in Staffordshire to escape the smells, heat, and misery that filled London in summer.

Preparations were made and soon Diana, Edward, Benjamin, Barbara and Bertha as well as several grooms and footmen departed for the small Staffordshire estate owned by the duchy. As the estate was not far from Warwick, Diana wrote to the Duke of Asbury and asked that he join them for a house party. She also invited Dickey, Bernie and Michael. The three friends hadn't seen much of Dickey during the season. He had been called to Ireland to deal with some issues on his mother's estate and had only just returned to town. After his declaration of love for Diana, there had been some tension, but it had dissipated after the first few times they had all met.

Dickey had come to realize that Diana would never change her mind and reconciled himself to the fact that his love would remain unrequited. He had eventually given up the idea of having a relationship of any but the most platonic kind with her. While in Ireland, he had renewed his acquaintance with another beautiful red-haired girl named Maeve. She was the daughter of Earl Seamus O'Brien with whom Dickey had many business dealings as well as political ones. The two young people had actually met when they were children as the earl and Dickey's mother, an only child, had grown up together on neighboring estates. Dickey's mother, still a beautiful woman although in her late forties, had repaired to Ireland on the death of her husband and renewed her friendship with the O'Briens, her neighbors.

When Dickey's grandfather died late in 1819, Dickey was named the Earl of Kilkenny in Ireland. He was already a Duke in England so his responsibilities almost doubled in the matter of a couple of days. While Dickey was in Ireland becoming familiar with his grandfather's estates, he and Maeve were thrown together socially on a very regular basis. Maeve was tall and graceful with sparkling blue eyes and a sunny smile. She had light freckles on her little upturned nose and a sweet, biddable nature. Dickey was at first attracted to her because of her red hair, but soon her sweet personality outshone her small similarity to Diana. Diana was a strong, independent woman whereas Maeve had been raised to be just the opposite. She was very tractable and rarely expressed an opinion truly her own.

When Dickey received the invitation to the house party in Staffordshire, he wrote Diana and requested an invitation be sent to Maeve's parents to include them and her. Diana was only too glad to issue the invitation. Michael had also begun to court a young lady from the *ton* named Lady Mary Sheraton, so an invitation was sent to her family as well. When all invitations had been responded to, the house party numbered almost twenty not including the Bristols. Diana had soon hired extra staff for the onslaught of guests. Most of the party would bring their own valets or ladies maids, but extra kitchen staff was required as well as extra footmen for the fetching and carrying. Also some of the men were bringing their secretaries as well. Fortunately, the house had a wealth of bedrooms, thirty two in all and the servants quarters could accommodate the extras as well.

There was a flurry of preparation in the days prior to the arrival of the first guests. Diana had received a letter from the Duke of Asbury that he had a house guest of his own that she knew and asking if he could accompany him to her party. Lawrence was in England to attend the marriage of his sister and had decided to spend a few days with his uncle. Diana was ambivalent about seeing him again, but good manners dictated that she include him in the house party with the duke. She wrote by return post that Lawrence would be most welcome.

On the first day the guests were expected, Diana rose very early to take care of duchy business and conclude preparations for her guests. Since it was summer, there was no shortage of beautiful flowers to decorate the rooms. Diana, Barbara and Bertha spent hours making arrangements for all the occupied bedrooms and the downstairs common rooms. Diana also consulted with cook on final preparations for the cold luncheon and lavish dinner that would be served.

Maids and footmen were scurrying everywhere making sure all was in readiness for the expected guests. Finally, around eleven, Diana hurried to her room to bathe and dress. The first guests were expected around noon. As Barbara was putting the final touches to Diana's coiffure, Edward knocked on her door. He was dressed in a trouser suit of a deep rich purple with a yellow waistcoat and a lavender cravat. It was a spectacular costume even for Edward.

"Oh, my Edward. You will outshine all the ladies in that outfit. You will put them to shame."

Edward laughed, "But not you, hin, not you. That dress is perfect for you. Yellow is definitely your color, I think."

Diana's dress was a very pale, lemon yellow thin muslin with a high waist and short puffy sleeves. It was embroidered in tiny orange flowers on the sleeves and hem as well as the bodice. The leaves on the flowers were bronze, gold and olive green with twining vines between them in the green shade. She looked like a flower garden. Her silk slippers peeping from the hem of the dress were the same orange color of the flowers. She had ribbons running through her hair in bronze, orange, gold and green to match her dress. They were tied at the back of her head in a bow and cascaded down on her shoulders. She wore her small emerald set given to her by her father on her sixteenth birthday.

Edward believed that Diana was probably the most beautiful woman he had ever seen. If he had been attracted to women, he would have fallen in love with her immediately just from her looks. Knowing her as he did, he knew that any man would be very lucky to have her. She was not only beautiful, but she had an intelligence and business acumen very few men held. She also had very high moral standards and a very soft heart for the downtrodden. She was indeed the perfect woman in his eyes.

Soon, the young couple went downstairs to begin greeting their guests along with Benjamin. The first to arrive were Bernie, Michael and Dickey who had travelled from London together as it was their wont to do. They had travelled by horse with a carriage trailing after them with their valets, secretaries and luggage. They were all warmly greeted by Edward and Benjamin with much shaking of hands and manly hugs. Diana gave each of them a warm hug and a kiss on the cheek as well. She paid particular attention to Dickey's demeanor. He seemed his old jolly self and she was very glad. When she had received his request to include the O'Brien family, she has been very pleased. It seemed that Dickey had gotten over his infatuation with her and fairly quickly too.

As the other guests continued to arrive, Diana was beginning to dread the arrival of the Duke of Asbury and his nephew. She wanted to see Lawrence again, but was wary of her feelings toward him. It had been almost 5 years since her Geoffrey had been killed coming to fetch she and her father to go to London to make their wedding preparations. Much had changed since that tragic event. She had known the joys of motherhood and the horrific loss of her child. She had known much sorrow from the loss of almost every one she held dear, especially her father and her child, and that sorrow had matured her well beyond her years. There was still a deep shadow of sadness in her beautiful green eyes and she still suffered bouts of depression that she had to fight very hard to overcome.

Diana had carved a life for herself from those losses through strong will and determination. She was content being the Duchess of Bristol, with all the title's attendant responsibilities and perks. She enjoyed a wonderful relationship with Edward and Benjamin, but there was definitely a large hole in her life since her son, Geoffrey, had been killed. She was busy and enjoyed her life for the most part, but then she still wasn't truly happy and doubted she ever would be.

The moment she had been dreading was suddenly upon her as the butler announced the arrival of the duke and Lawrence. Diana hurried to her friend, the duke, and gave him a warm hug. They had not seen each other since they had stayed at his estate in Warwick during Edward's convalescence, but they had maintained a lively correspondence during that separation. The duke looked exactly the same. His cheerful smile and warm demeanor had not changed at all. He could see that his little friend was much better than she had been when last they met. There was still sadness in her beautiful eyes, but it was not fresh sorrow he saw there. She was more beautiful than ever. The thinness was gone, her figure had matured somewhat though she was still slim and graceful. She looked wonderful as did Edward and Benjamin.

When Lawrence stood before Diana at last, she gave him her hand. Even through her silk gloves, she felt the electric current pass between them and Diana gave a little gasp. Oh, no, she thought, nothing has changed in the almost two years since I have seen him. He still affects me the same. Her eyes, which had swept down at the contact, raised immediately to his. His grey eyes were staring into hers with an intensity that frightened her.

"Sir Lawrence, it is very pleasant to see you again. How goes your enterprise in America? My friend Ian has written me several times since last I saw you. He has mentioned that you live nearby and he and Alana see you often." Diana said. She was very proud that there was very little shake in her voice. There was a slight breathlessness, but it wasn't overly noticeable, she hoped.

"Your grace, Lady Diana. It is wonderful to see you again. In answer to your question, my American enterprise is going exceedingly well. I have managed to procure several hundred acres about five miles from Ian and Alana. My home is now complete, I have many acres under cultivation growing feed and hay, and my horses seem to enjoy the climate as they are multiplying nicely." Lawrence said with a smile. He did not relinquish her hand while he made these statements, much to Diana's chagrin.

She didn't want to create a scene by pulling her hand away, but she felt she must remove it or she would become lost for sure. She couldn't seem to take her eyes from his fathomless gray ones. She noticed that he was smiling tenderly at her. This would not do, no this would not do at all.

She turned to Edward, subtly, but firmly pulling her hand away from Lawrence, and touched Edward's arm. "Edward, dear, you do remember Viscount Banbury, don't you? You met him when we stayed with the Duke of Asbury in Warwick a couple of years ago."

Edward hadn't noticed the peculiar exchange between his wife and the tall, dark-haired man who now sketched him a bow as he had been exchanging pleasantries with the duke.

"Of course I do. Viscount, how have you been? I believe Diana told me you had immigrated to America. I would love to hear more about that country. Perhaps, we can spend some time while you're hear discussing it." Edward said with a bright welcoming smile.

Edward may not have noticed anything untoward, however, both the duke and Benjamin had. "Ah", thought Benjamin, "Diana has an admirer and she doesn't seem to mind at all." Benjamin was happy about the situation until he realized this tall man lived on another continent and was only in England for a short period. That wouldn't do at all. Diana deserved happiness, not more heartbreak. He would have to see about keeping them apart to protect Diana's feelings.

Finally all the guests had arrived and been escorted to their rooms to rest and change for luncheon. There was a flurry of activity as maids and footmen rushed up and down the stairs with freshly pressed clothes and hot water. Soon the guests began to trail down the stairs for luncheon.

Diana had decided to serve a cold luncheon as there was no way to be sure all the guests would have arrived near the same time. The fact that everybody had arrived before the appointed luncheon time was a boon for the kitchen staff and the cook. The guests all met in the large drawing room for tea or sherry while a line of footmen came from the kitchen bearing trays and bowls of food to lay on the sideboard in the dining room. Diana had the butler, Stephens, announce to the assembled company that luncheon was served. Diana took both Edward's and Benjamin's arms and lead the way into the dining room.

Taking a plate from one of the tall stacks at the end of the sideboard, she proceeded to fill it with a selection from the large array of cold foods. There were 3 kinds of cold meat, beef, chicken and smoked ham (though they weren't actually cold, just room temperature), small round sandwiches filled with potted beef , sliced green onions, and slices of good cheddar cheese, an English green salad, a beetroot and onion salad, a potato salad also made with beetroot, a selection of olives and pickles, pickled walnuts, three types of bread, both hard and soft cheeses and lots of fresh creamy butter. For dessert there were tiny iced cakes done in different flavors and colors. The sideboard was practically groaning under the enormous load of food.

Soon, all the guests had filled their plates and taken their seats at the enormous dining table which could easily seat fifty. The dining room was decorated in creams and golds. The seats of the dark wooden chairs were covered in a gold damask material with cream roses. The backs were carved with a rose pattern. The table linens were cream colored with gold damask napkins at each place setting. The plate was good Staffordshire china made in the region and was a beautiful cobalt blue. The drapes were a matching cobalt blue and the wallpaper was cream with gold cabbage roses on it with thin stripes of cobalt blue. Since the day was sunny and warm, the large French doors leading onto the terrace were open as were the many windows to let the breeze blow through.

Diana was seated at the foot of the table and Edward at the head. Diana had placed the elderly duke on her right and Bernie on her left. On Edward's right was Lady O'Brien and on his left, Lady Sheraton. The other guests were seated male, female down the length of the table. Diana had been sure to seat Michael next to Mary Sheraton and Dickey next to Maeve O'Brien in the middle of the table across from each other and quite a distance from either of their parents. She wanted them to have ample opportunity for private conversations if they so wished. She had also made sure to seat Lawrence on Edward's end of the table between Lady Sheraton and her other daughter, Abigail, who was also unmarried and quite lovely.

Diana carried on a sprightly conversation with the duke and Bernie. Bernie, being much like the duke in temperament, was a perfect luncheon companion choice. The two got on famously as Diana knew they would. They were a lively party. There were more men than ladies, but with all the secretaries who had arrived with the gentlemen, it couldn't be helped. A ball had been planned for the end of the week. Diana had invited more young ladies than young men to the ball for that reason. Now that everyone had arrived, the party numbered twenty-six. Diana knew she might be hard pressed to entertain that many people all with different interests, likes and dislikes. She was depending on Edward and Benjamin a lot in that area. This was the first house party she had ever been the hostess for and she wanted it to be perfect.

Having attended several of this type of affair when she was much younger in Scotland, she knew entertainments had to be planned for everyone. She had spent a lot of time closeted with the housekeeper, Mrs. Clyde, since arriving. Mrs. Clyde had been with the family for over twenty years and had helped with innumerable parties such as this. She gave Diana many good ideas and was gratified that the young duchess came up with several wonderful ideas on her own. A good time should be had by all.

As the luncheon wound down, Diana stood and addressed her guests. "I know some of you may be quite fatigued from your journey, so I haven't planned any formal entertainment for this afternoon. Please avail yourselves of our gardens, our library, our stables or whatever takes your fancy. There are card tables set up in the small drawing room if any of you would care for a game. There is also a music room here with a variety of instruments if any one would care to play or sing. Or if you would rather go to your rooms to rest, please feel free to do so. Dinner will be at eight this evening with drinks at seven in the large drawing room. I do have something I believe you will enjoy planned for this evening, so don't wear yourselves out." Diana said with a laugh. "Please enjoy yourselves in whatever way you wish this afternoon."

The guests started to leave the table and gather in small groups to make plans with each other for the afternoon. Edward and Benjamin both came to congratulate Diana on a wonderful luncheon and her thoughtfulness in allowing their guests to choose their own entertainment on this first day. Many of the older guests headed up the stairs for a nap or to just rest from the rigors of travel. The younger ones soon broke into groups to stroll the garden, play cards or peruse the library.

Diana, herself, was much too busy seeing that everyone else was enjoying themselves to worry about what she would like to do. She and Edward drifted from room to room and group to group making sure everyone was occupied doing something they liked. Finally around five in the afternoon the hosts climbed the stairs to have a short rest before dressing for dinner.

Diana was pleased by the way the party was progressing. She had planned a treasure hunt for after dinner. She had enlisted several of the servants and even Edward and Benjamin to help with the treasure maps and hiding the treasures throughout the house in the days preceding the party. Benjamin had turned out to be a wonderful map maker and she had left that chore entirely to him. The "treasures" were little gifts of Staffordshire pottery. There were tiny animals figurines, snuff boxes, porcelain balls painted with bright designs, and even tiny brandy kegs, filled of course with good French brandy from the castles cellars.

Barbara helped Diana disrobe down to her chemise so she could rest for half an hour before she bathed and dressed for dinner. She hadn't planned to sleep, but she was really exhausted and almost immediately fell asleep. It seemed she had just closed her eyes when Barbara woke her to bathe. Barbara let her sleep an extra few minutes while the water was carried to her bathing chamber and Diana was grateful for even those few extra minutes.

Diana didn't linger in her bath. She wanted to be dressed and downstairs before her guests began to descend. Her dress for the first dinner of their party was not a color she usually chose. It was actually white, a color she hadn't worn since she was very young. When her modiste in London showed her the fabric though, she couldn't resist. The fabic was sheerest silk from China. It had been embroidered with exotic birds, their plumes in shades of emerald green, deep sapphire blue and deep red. The bodice was tightly fitted with a diamond shaped inset in the center. The entire top of the dress was pure white with white lace on the short puffy sleeves and around the low vee neckline. The skirt, below the inset, was made of the embroidered Chinese silk. The birds cavorted on a jungle-like background that spread across the skirt front and back. The bottom of the dress was trimmed with the same lace as the bodice and sleeves. Diana had chosen white silk evening slippers overlaid with white lace. Barbara wove white lace through an elaborate braided coiffure tying the ends in a bow at the nape of Diana's neck.

Diana chose sapphires to wear with her ensemble. Edward had gifted her with a parure of sapphires for her twenty-first birthday in March. The parure included two bracelets, a necklace, earrings, and a pin. The design was very different from anything else Diana owned. The center sapphires were large and cut in a square shape with smaller round sapphires on the top and bottom. The chain for the pendant on the necklace was about a quarter of an inch wide and paved with diamonds. Both of the bracelets had the same type of chain, but narrower and the sapphires were mounted on the tops instead of hanging in a pendant style. The earrings were pendants like the necklace. Diana chose not to wear the pin that evening because she really couldn't think of place to put it.

When her toilette was complete she went through the private drawing room to Edward's room. After knocking, she was admitted by Benjamin. He was already dressed for the evening in a dark evening suit with trousers and a snowy cravat. Edward, however, looked quite the peacock in a royal blue coat and trousers, a waistcoat of yellow with royal blue embroidered roses, and a yellow cravat atop a snowy white ruffled shirt. His evening slippers were the same vivid yellow as his cravat.

"Edward, I don't know where you come up with the ideas for these outfits, but you have outdone yourself this time. You, my dear, are a vision!" Diana stated as she walked around him in awe.

"No, hin, you are the vision. Wherever did you get that fabric. It is exquisite. I would love to have a waistcoat from that silk. I'd have it made up in a coat, but even I couldn't get away with that." Edward said with a laugh.

"No, Edward." said Benjamin, laughing, "Not even you could carry that off."

Still laughing uproariously, the trio started down the stairs. They didn't notice Lawrence coming down the hall of the right wing, but he saw and heard them. He was gratified to hear Diana laugh. She had rarely even smiled when he had known her two years ago. The death of her father and her child, as well as Edward's horrendous accident had only very recently occurred and she was not only in deep mourning, she seemed to be almost in a state of shock. Lawrence was happy to see her looking so much better and more at peace. He had noticed that she still had a deep shadow of sadness in her beautiful green eyes, but that was expected after all her losses.

Lawrence couldn't help how he felt about her, but he would not act upon it in any way. He felt the almost electric shock when he touched her and knew she felt the same. However, she appeared to have a good marriage and he would do nothing to cause her more pain. She had experienced more than her share already.

Lawrence soon joined the trio and some of the other guests who had already gathered in the drawing room. Drinks were passed around and he soon found himself sitting on one of the sofas with his uncle and one of the other guests, Miss Abigail Sheraton., who had been his luncheon partner. She was a pretty blond girl, but she was so very young and immature. Her conversation was inane and uninteresting. She stuck to subjects like the fine weather they were having and the terribly tiring trip in her father's carriage from Berkshire. Lawrence was bored to tears.

He excused himself and went to stand near the empty fireplace with a glass of brandy in his hand. Before long, Edward joined him and started a conversation about America. He asked many intelligent questions about the farming there and made some references to Ian and Alana MacAllister.

"I've never met the MacAllisters, but I feel like I know them from the way Diana talks about them. She reads all of Ian's letter to me as soon as they arrive. They all grew up together in Scotland and were very close. We even adopted some of the American Christmas traditions at Bristol Castle this past year to great success. Neither I, nor any of our tenants had ever seen a Christmas tree. It was a sight to behold. We owe much to the MacAllisters for a wonderful new tradition. Of course, it was all Diana's doing. She's wonderful with our tenants. She knows all their names and the names of their wives and children too. It's amazing to me how much information is stored in that little red head." Edward said with a laugh.

Lawrence made some noncommittal reply. He was wondering at the tone the duke used when speaking of his wife. It almost sounded as if he was speaking about a cherished little sister instead of his wife. Lawrence saw him look over at Diana and his face wore an indulgent smile, but it was not the smile of a man who was in love with his wife. The smile Diana returned was very similar. It seemed the Bristols enjoyed an easy camaraderie, but Lawrence saw no romantic passion from either of them.

Edward and Lawrence were soon joined by Edward's secretary, Benjamin. He was shocked to see Edward's eyes light up with love for the other man and it was definitely reciprocated from the look on Benjamin's face. He quickly looked at Diana, but she was smiling at both of them with a look of sisterly love and pride.

Lawrence was shocked. He, of course, knew that some men preferred the company of other men, he wasn't an innocent. But to find out that Diana was married to one of them was very shocking indeed. They had had a child together and he had witnessed how all three of them had been almost out of their minds with grief at the death of that child. He simply could not understand the situation. It made him very uncomfortable.

Soon, the butler announced dinner and the party broke into couples to proceed to the dining room. Diana walked out with Benjamin on one side and Edward on the other. Again, Lawrence was mystified. He couldn't believe Diana was part of a menage a trois or that she would or could condone her husband being in love with someone else, especially another man. He was determined to find out what was going on. He felt very concerned for Diana.

Dinner was a long affair with nine courses. The seating arrangements were the same as for luncheon. Diana had been happy with the way the arrangement had worked and kept the place cards the same. The first course was oysters broiled in their shells with butter, cayenne, and lemon juice. The second course was an English salad with a variety of fresh greens dressed in a vinaigrette sweetened with honey. Then the meat courses started to arrive. There was baron of beef, leg of lamb and a haunch of venison. These were served with glazed carrots, potatoes a la duchesse, and pickled onions. There were also fresh tiny peas from the castle garden cooked in a butter cream sauce. Several kinds of bread were served with mounds of creamy butter. For dessert, currant and raspberry cream molded and served with whipped cream in the center, sponge cake with blackberry preserves under a royal icing that had been dried and decorated with sugared violets, and a selection of cheese and fruit from the orchards and hothouses. There were different wines with each course.

When the final course had been consumed, Diana rose from her chair and lead the ladies back to the drawing room. The men remained for their after dinner brandy and cigars. Lawrence noticed that Edward had coffee instead of brandy. He had also noticed he only had a single glass of wine with dinner as had Diana and Benjamin. Another curiosity. Most British nobility were known to imbibe much, much more. Edward didn't partake of cigars either, but quietly sipped his coffee and conversed with all his guests on many subjects.

The ladies filed into the drawing room. Almost immediately, Mary Sheraton asked Diana to play and sing. Apparently, Michael had spread the word of her talent. The other ladies also insisted they wanted to hear her so Diana sat on the bench and began to play. As usual, when she played, she closed her eyes and swayed with the music.

For some reason she was feeling nostalgic for Scotland tonight and played several Scottish ballads, singing in her rich contralto voice. Then she thought of a story her Da had told her about Helen of Kirkconnel. In the burial ground of Kirkconnell, near the English border, is the grave of Helen Irving, recognised by tradition as Fair Helen of Kirkconnell. She is supposed to have lived in the sixteenth century. It is also the grave of her lover, Adam Fleming – a surname that once predominated the district. Helen was beloved by two gentlemen at the same time. The spurned one vowed to do away with the successful suitor. Watching for an opportunity, he found the happy pair sitting on the banks of the Kirtle. Helen perceived the desperate lover on the opposite side, and in an effort to save her favorite, jumped in front of him receiving the arrow wound intended for her beloved She fell instantly and expired in his arms. He instantly avenged her death; then fled into Spain, and served for some time against the Infidels. On his return, he visited the grave of his unfortunate mistress, stretched himself on it, expiring on the spot. He was interred by her side. A cross and a sword are engraved on the tombstone, with 'HIC JACET ADAMUS

FLEMING'; the only memorial of this unhappy gentleman, except an ancient ballad which records the tragic event. The men returned to the drawing room in time to hear the last verses of Helen of Kirkconnel as written by Sir Walter Scott in 1803.

O that I were where Helen lies!

Night and day on me she cries;

Out of my bed she bids me rise,

Says, "haste, and come to me!"

O Helen fair! O Helen chaste!

If I were with thee I were blest,

Where thou lies low, and takes thy rest,

On fair Kirconnell Lee.

I wish my grave were growing green,

A winding sheet drawn ower my een,

And I in Helen's arms lying,

On fair Kirconnell Lee.

I wish I were where Helen lies!

Night and day on me she cries;

And I am weary of the skies,

For her sake that died for me.

When the last melancholy note died, there was tremendous applause from the assembled guests. Rarely had they heard a more beautiful voice or more emotional playing. Diana had a remarkable talent. Having been so immersed in the music, she was at first startled by the applause and then embarrassed by it. Her fine white skin blushed a charming deep pink.

Seeing her embarrassment, Edward quickly joined her on the bench and started to play a rollicking modern song Benjamin had recently been able to obtain the sheet music for. They had seen a play at the Savoy Theater this season where this particular song was sung by the lead actress. Edward played and sang with gusto taking the focus off Diana with ease. She looked at him with a smile on her lips and gratitude in her eyes.

Lawrence watched this interplay, still wondering what kind of relationship the Duke and Duchess enjoyed. They seemed close, but not intimate. The situation was very much a conundrum to him.

Edward played a couple of songs singing alone and then with Diana. Their voices melded beautifully. The party could tell they had played and sung together many times. Their harmony was almost perfect.

At the end of the third song, Diana rose and spoke to her assembled guests. "Edward and I have a little entertainment for you tonight. No, it isn't our singing," she said laughingly when the guests started to applaud. "We are going to have a treasure hunt. Small items have been hidden all over the bottom floor of the house, in every wing. You will separate into teams of three and search for all twenty items that are hidden. There are enough of you to make eight teams with one extra gentleman. I will assign that lucky man to a team of three ladies. When you find your first treasure, you must bring it back here to the drawing room before you can have clues for the next one. If you are very quick, you could find several treasures. The team with the most treasures will win the prize."

It wasn't long before one of the all male teams returned with a tiny blue elephant. They were summarily given another set of cluesThe guests immediately set up a clamor to know what the prize was. Diana would not reveal the prize until the end of the treasure hunt. There was much laughing and jesting as Diana dramatically pulled a list from Edward's pocket and read off the names of the team members. She had placed Dickey with Maeve and Lady Sheraton, Michael with Mary and Lady O'Brien, Lawrence with the duke and Abigail Sheraton, Lady O'Brien with her son, Rory, and one of the secretaries, and Bernie with three young ladies of the *ton* who had been invited at the request of either Lady O'Brien or Lady Sheraton. Two of the last teams were all male, but that could not be helped. Diana had tried to make sure that all propriety had been kept by assigning a more mature person with the Sheraton girls and Maeve O'Brien.

Diana, Edward and Benjamin had a chance for some much needed rest and quiet time while their guests were running helter-skelter all over the house laughing. Edward looked at Diana with laughing eyes.

"I know what you are up to. I noticed that both Dickey and Michael were paired with their little turtle doves, but without the corresponding parent. Very ingenious my dear. You've given them a tidbit of privacy, but with that privacy tempered by a completely legitimate chaperone. Aren't you the clever little hin?"

"Oh Edward, they do need some time to get to know each other without their dear Mama's breathing down their necks every minute. I have noticed both of the ladies are just a tad bit over protective, so I thought I would help out just a bit." Diana laughed.

and set off again. At last all twenty of the treasures had been recovered and the winners declared. As Diana had expected, the winning team was made up of all males, two noblemen and a secretary. Edward presented them with three pairs of tickets to the Savoy theater for the first production of the next season and they were much pleased. The tickets were for the Bristol box. Diana and Edward rarely used the box, but the duchy had owned it for years, so Diana felt good about having it used for some of her guests.

Later in the evening Lawrence had occasion to speak to his uncle, the duke privately. "What do you know of the marriage of the Duke of Bristol and his lady? I saw very little of him when I met them in Warwick two years ago. He was still very ill at that time and stayed in his rooms almost the entire time they were at your home."

"I, myself knew very little of Edward at that time as well, other than seeing him occasionally with his father when he was a child. The only information I could at first glean from my conversations with Diana was that they had been married almost three years and she had just lost her son, who was not yet two years old. That tragedy was part of her husband's accident and happened just a very few weeks after she had lost her father in Scotland. She seemed devoted to her husband regaining his health and strove daily to that end."

"From all appearances, they are no different than many other young noble couples with the exception that they appear every where together, neither of them is ever seen at an event alone. This fact has occasioned some gossip, but it was bandied about by one of their friends that they were very devoted to each other, so the gossip ceased. Also, Edward's secretary, Benjamin, is never far from either of their sides. Diana told me Benjamin took excellent care of Edward when she had to travel to Scotland to bury her son and had taken very good care of her as well."

"Benjamin was also very instrumental in Edward's recovery when they stayed with me. He went several times into town for herbs with Diana's maid, was always part of the consultations with the doctor, and spent many hours with Edward while he convalesced. He and Diana worked in her drawing room every day on business correspondence delivered to my home either by post or by their man of business. He seemed very involved in the business although that is not completely unexpected as he is Edward's secretary. However, I got the impression, he and Diana had been handling the duchy affairs together for some time."

"He accompanied Diana and I to have Edward's cane made and contributed several ideas upon the design of it, which Diana acted upon without question. That in itself is odd, most servants have no input on such things. I got the feeling that Benjamin is not considered a servant, but a member of the family."

" A member of the family," mused Lawrence. "I have known many members of the nobility in my life and have never seen a secretary entrusted with that amount of latitude."

"Lawrence, please watch your heart where Diana is concerned." said the old duke touching Lawrence on the arm. " I wasn't going to say anything, but I fear I must. I have noticed how you follow her with your eyes. I noticed the same two years ago and I have to admit Diana seems to reciprocate at least some of your interest. However, you should know that she confided something to me one day when she was especially distraught that leads me to believe she will never divorce Edward, as she is Catholic, nor will she take a lover. Her strong moral sense simply would not allow it. I cannot reveal what she said, but just so you know, nothing can ever come of your attraction. I would hate to see either of you hurt."

"I believe I know what Diana confided to you. I have observed a certain intimacy between Edward and Benjamin when they think no one is watching. I believe they are lovers and have been for some time. And the strangest thing is, I believe not only does Diana know, but she somehow approves of, or at least condones their relationship. That is what is driving me crazy. I just cannot see her as part of a menage a trois, she seems much too moral for anything like that. I just don't understand how she can sanction such a relationship between her husband and his secretary"

"Well," said the duke slowly, "Since you have deduced a large part of what I was told and you seem unwilling to let this go, I suppose I will have to break a confidence to allay at least a part of your turmoil. Yes, Diana knows about their relationship and she is fine with it."

"She's fine with it!!! How can that be? I do not understand that attitude at all. They are unnatural. It is disgusting to say the least and against the laws of God and man. How can she be fine with it? She actually became pregnant by him."

"Lawrence, you must calm yourself. There is more to the story than you know. The child she lost was not Edward's, but his brother Geoffrey's. Geoffrey was killed by highwaymen just before they were to marry. Edward, although his affections were otherwise engaged with Benjamin, married Diana to give the child a name and save her from disgrace. She didn't know about Benjamin when they married, but when she found out some months later, she was surprised at how their feelings mirrored the ones she still held for Geoffrey. It made it much easier for her to be accepting of the situation. Also, she was only sixteen years old when all this took place. I sometimes think she sees Edward as both her saviour and a younger brother she must protect and care for."

"That poor girl. She lost every one she loved at such a tender age. And now she is saddled with a marriage that is not even a real marriage. She is trapped for the rest of her life in an untenable situation. My heart goes out to her"

"As does mine," the old duke said sadly. "But there is nothing to be done. Diana has made the most of a bad situation. She has a close, loving relationship with both Edward and Benjamin. For Diana, it is much as if three siblings are living together. However, in some very important ways, it leaves her much apart from the other two. They have a loving intimate relationship. From something she told me, I believe she and Geoffrey were only intimate once. So they have something she has never had and believes she never shall. It is a very sad situation and I grieve for her."

The next day Lawrence saw Diana in a different light. He felt an even stronger attraction to her than before if that was possible. He had realized from the first that she was trying to avoid him as much as she could and still be polite. He had noticed that he was not seated near her at meals, nor did she seek him out for conversation as she did others in the party. He was determined to find a chance to speak to her before the two weeks were up and he had to leave again for America. It seemed he only ever saw her when he was in transit.

The next few days were filled with day trips to the River Trent for a boating excursion, a picnic at the small lake on the estate, a horseback trip to the local pottery factory, a trip to see the Swarkestone Bridge which had been built in the thirteenth century and was considered a marvel of English bridge architecture, and all manor of games like croquet and lawn tennis. The guests were kept busy and entertained to the best of Diana's ability.

The only time they stayed the entire day at the castle was on the two days the weather was rainy and dull. On those days, Diana had arranged for games of charades, cards and musical entertainments. Knowing English weather, she had been prepared for rainy days.

On the second of those rainy days near the end of the two week time allotted for the house party, Lawrence finally found a chance to speak privately with Diana. He had been coming downstairs when he saw Diana slip into the conservatory alone. She was carrying a book. He hoped she had found a few minutes to herself to read.

When Lawrence entered the conservatory a few minutes later, he found Diana just seating herself on a rattan sofa upholstered in white with a red cabbage rose design. She looked startled when she first saw him, then seemed to give herself a small shake and managed a smile. "Lawrence, come join me. I thought I would steal a few minutes to enjoy the rain through the glass walls of the conservatory. I have always loved rain. Good thing since I was born and raised in Scotland where it rains all the time." Diana said with a bright smile.

Lawrence sat across from Diana on a chair covered in the same fabric. "Diana, I am glad to have found you here. I have been wanting to speak to you for several days. My time here is almost up. I will travel back to Warwick with my uncle and then almost directly proceed to Liverpool to catch my ship back to Virginia. I have actually been away longer than I had planned. While here for my sister's wedding, I have also been required to deal with some properties left me by my father a few years ago. I have sold all my holdings in England. I do not plan to come back for many years. I have made a new life for myself in America."

"I am glad to hear that your plans for America have come to such successful fruition. I know my friends the MacAllisters love it there and they enjoy having you for a neighbor. From their letters, it seems you see a lot of each other."

"Yes, we do. Ian, Alana, and their children have become something like family to me I'm happy to say. We spend much happy time together. Ian's knowledge of the countryside had been a tremendous help to me. He has advised me on everything from the right people to hire to what crops to plant. I believe he had a like mentor in Mr. Marcus Benefield when he first arrived there five years ago. Mr. Benefield has also been a considerable help to me."

"I do believe he has mentioned Mr. Benefield several times in his letters. I am so very happy for he and Alana. They seem to have a very full and comfortable life in Virginia. It is good to see my friends doing so well."

"And what of you, Diana, are you doing well?"

"I am doing quite well, thank you. My life is busy and I am content."

"Content, but not happy? I see such sadness in your eyes still. I know you must still grieve for your son and your father. Do you plan to have more children?"

"No," Diana said with much sadness, "There will be no more children for me. That part of my life is over."

"If I may be so bold, why is it that you don't plan to have more children? I can see how much you enjoyed being a mother."

"Yes, being Geoffrey's mother was the happiest time of my life. I miss him so much at times I can hardly make myself rise from my bed...oh, Lawrence, I'm sorry. I shouldn't have said that. I don't know what it is about you that makes me speak so openly about such private matters."

"It's because you know how I feel about you Diana. You must know."

"Lawrence, I do know, but knowing is all there will ever be. Just as I can never have another child, I can never have another...." Diana stopped speaking and looked out the huge windows with a hint of tears in her eyes.

"Another what, Diana? Another love? I know you and Edward don't have that kind of marriage. I have seen the emotion he feels for another."

Diana gasped. "What have you seen? Edward is married to me. There is no other woman in his life."

Lawrence stood and walked to the window watching the rain. "No, there is no other woman in his life, not in that way. And neither are you. Benjamin is the other person in Edward's life, but who do you have in yours? It isn't fair to you Diana. You deserve so much more. You are young and beautiful and have so much to give. Your life and your youth are being wasted."

"How dare you say my life is wasted! I have a full life. I have the love and affection of two wonderful men. I have much responsibility for the tenants and business of the duchy and my property in Scotland and my English estate. I have my charitable works for the orphans in London. My life is full and it is just the way I want it."

Lawrence came back to the sofa and sat beside her. "Is it, Diana? Don't you long to feel a man's arms around you, his lips on yours, his hands touching you? Lawrence took Diana's hands and tried to pull her close. She resisted and abruptly stood up. "Those things are not for me, Lawrence. They will never be for me. I had the love of a wonderfully strong and loving man once, but he is dead.

And so am I, in that respect. Dead and buried with my Geoffrey." With those words, Diana ran from the room in tears.

Luckily she didn't meet any of the guests as she ran up the stairs. Most of the ladies were napping and the men were playing cards in the library. Just as she was about to enter her bedchamber, Benjamin came out of the door of she and Edward's drawing room. One look at her face and he pulled her into the drawing room hurriedly.

"What is it, Di? What has happened to upset you so?" Benjamin asked as he pulled her into his arms.

At first she didn't answer, just stood in his arms sobbing. Finally, getting control of her emotions, she looked up at him with the saddest eyes he had ever seen.

"Nothing has happened that anything can be done about, Benji." she stated baldly. She could not be compelled to say anything more. Benjamin finally gave up and escorted her to her bedchamber and Barbara's tender ministrations.

The rest of the house party passed without incident. The ball was set to be the last night of the fortnight. The musicians arrived and were taken, by Stephens, to the gallery above the ballroom to set up and get in a little practice. The ballroom was still being prepared and was full of maids and footmen carrying furniture, candles, and flower arrangements. Diana and Barbara were directing where everything was to go.

The ballroom at the Staffordshire estate was huge. It was very ornate with carved wood paneled walls and giant chandeliers holding many candles. Diana and Edward were only expecting about seventy-five guests for the ball, so a lot of the furniture, like the built in upholstered benches along the walls, was being left where it was. The footmen cleared out a large area in the middle of the floor for dancing.

Their house guests made up a third of the guest list. The remainder were members of the local nobility and gentry. Diana had made sure to include political allies of Edward's in the invitations as well. Diana was always looking out for Edward's best interests no matter where they were or who they were with.

No more had been said between she and Benjamin about the events on that rainy day earlier that week. Benjamin had not mentioned it to Edward either. He thought if Diana wanted Edward to know, she would tell him.

Diana had almost completely avoided Lawrence for the rest of the house party. She had been pleasant and polite when she had cause to interact with him, but she had avoided as much interaction as was decently possible. She could see this caused him pain, but in her own mind, she had no recourse.

When all preparations for the ball were complete, Barbara and Diana hurried up the servant's stairs to her bedchamber to get her bathed and dressed for the evening. Diana had chosen her dress with care. Her modiste had not only provided her with the beautiful printed Chinese silk she had worn on the first evening, she had also had an incredible bolt of turquoise colored silk that had been embroidered in sliver thread all over in a lotus flower pattern. The dress was made in the Grecian mode with a high waist and short puffed sleeves. The skirt was narrower than most of her other skirts and she wore only one petticoat under it. The bodice was cut low, but not indecently so. The neckline had silver lace edging, as did the sleeves.

Diana had bought enough of the material to have a pair of slippers made to match her dress perfectly. Barbara had parted Diana's hip length hair in three parts. A middle part for the front section and all the way across her head for the back. She looped the sides up and secured the curls with many diamond pins. For the back section, she brought the curls forward to cover the part and again secured them with diamond pins. Diana chose to wear the Bristol diamond parure with her dress for the evening.

Family legend said that one of the earlier Bristol dukes had found the set while fighting in Spain in the early sixteen hundreds. The legend didn't specify whether he had bought it or stolen it, but either could have been true.

The necklace was a semi-choker that had a looped silver chain. The loops were small around the back and studded with small diamonds from the back to about half-way down the necklace. Then the diamonds got progressively larger and were fitted into the progressively larger loops. The final stone was a huge diamond that hung off the middle of the chain. The bracelet imitated the necklace except for the final stone. Using a different style, the earrings were made in a waterfall pattern of irregularly sized diamonds. There was also a ring that was diamond shaped and paved with irregularly sized diamonds. Diana rarely wore the set. It needed a particularly fine gown to carry it off and she believed her new turquoise Chinese silk would fit the bill very well.

When Barbara had fastened the clasp on the bracelet, the last piece to go on, Diana stood and looked in the mirror. She was very pleased with the ensemble. The deep turquoise brought out the reddest highlights in her auburn hair as did the diamond pins. Just as she picked up her silver lace fan, there was a knock on her bedchamber door from the connecting drawing room. Barbara opened the door to admit both Edward and Benjamin.

Edward had forsaken his peacock colors tonight. Instead his evening suit was all one color, a dark, almost iridescent gray for coat and trousers. His waistcoat was embroidered black on black, his shoes were also black, and his cravat was snowy white to match his ruffled shirt. His blonde curls were brushed back from his forehead with some locks curling around his face. He was very handsome.

Benjamin, as usual, was much more soberly dressed. His ensemble was black with a silver embroidered waistcoat, white cravat and shirt. He was also very handsome. His dark hair was cut short now and he wore it brushed back away from his face where it fell in waves to his collar.

"Edward your outfit compliments my dress perfectly. I wondered why you wanted so much detail about what I was wearing tonight."

"Well, hin, I wanted you to shine tonight and you most certainly do. You look incredibly beautiful. You are even wearing the old pirate's diamonds. You almost never do."

"Now Edward, there is no proof your ancestor was a pirate," scolded Benjamin gently, with a smile. "But you are a vision Di, absolutely a vision. None of the other ladies will even merit a glance when the gentlemen behold you."

"You two are much too kind. I do love this Chinese silk though. I may have to visit Madame le Claire when we get back to town to see what other colors she has it in. It's much too thin for winter wear, but for this terrible summer heat, it's perfect."

The trio soon headed down to the drawing room to greet their guests before dinner. Diana had pulled out all the stops for the last dinner of their house party. When the first course, scolloped oysters, was served, there was much conversation about it around the table. This preparation of oysters was a fairly new one and some of the party hadn't seen it before. The oysters were stewed with butter, flour, garlic, cayenne, parsley, cream, anchovy and nutmeg. Then they were scooped back into their shells, covered with buttered bread crumbs and baked until golden. The aroma was heavenly as was the taste. This dish was served with champagne. Another fairly new twist, as that wine had only just become available again after Boney was finally defeated in 1815.

It was some years before a steady supply of champagne was available to the general public, But since the last duke had foreseen the war with Napoleon, he had laid away several cases of that lovely wine in his cellars on all his estates. The Staffordshire estate also boasted an ice house, so the champagne was chilled to perfection. The second course was filets of beef broiled to perfection with salt, pepper and butter, then topped with a Neapolitan sauce made with horseradish, bay leaf, shallots, cloves, thyme, brown butter, red currant jelly and stock. The filets were served with potatoes au gratin, spinach with cream, and mashed turnips flavored with cream and butter. The meal progressed, course after course with each one just a little better than the last. The dessert course was a huge D'Artois cake decorated with sugared almonds and tiny edible flowers. That course was also served with champagne.

Again Lawrence noticed that the Bristols each took only one glass of champagne and no other wine during dinner. He was beginning to suspect that possibly Edward had a drinking problem or rather had recovered from one. When he had been a man about town a few years ago, he definitely remembered some pretty lurid stories about the prodigious amounts of alcohol Edward was wont to consume and how he had acted. There was definitely none of that evident now. He suspected that Diana had a large hand in that.

After dinner, the ladies didn't adjourn to the drawing room nor did the gentlemen relax with brandy and cigars. All of the guests proceeded to the ballroom. The orchestra was playing softly as they arrived. They were conducted to the ballroom by Benjamin. Diana and Edward stood by the massive front doors to greet their other guests.

After about an hour, their hosts joined their guests. The orchestra struck up a reel and Benjamin lead Diana out on the floor. Because of his former injury, Edward did not dance. After the first reel, Diana was bombarded with requests for dances the rest of the evening. Edward adjourned to the card room as did several of the older gentlemen.

Lawrence was determined to have at least one waltz with Diana. He bade his time after consulting with the orchestra leader as to when the first waltz would be played. Just as Diana was leaving the dance floor with Bernie, Lawrence approached. Diana could not refuse to dance with him without causing a stir, so she simply placed her hand on his and followed him to the floor.

"You look incredibly beautiful tonight, your grace." Lawrence said with a somewhat sad smile."

" I thank you Sir Lawrence for the compliment." Diana said with a small smile of her own. "Are you enjoying yourself this evening?"

"Yes, your grace, thank you for asking." Lawrence shook his head. "Oh, Diana, must we be so formal with each other. I feel I must apologize for the other afternoon. I had no right to speak to you in that way. I am really sorry to have upset you so much."

"Your apology is accepted. Please, I don't wish to speak of it again." Diana said with a very strained look on her face. "Some things are better unspoken and definitely better not acted upon."

"I understand that you do not wish to break your marriage vows, but what about Edward? He made those same vows." persisted Lawrence.

"Edward's conscience is his own. He has upheld his part of the bargain. He married me and because of him my child was not born a bastard nor did my father have to pay for my shame. Edward and Benjamin are my two best friends and I will hear nothing derogatory about either of them." Diana said with asperity.

She started to pull away from him, but he tightened his grip on her waist. She looked up at him with trepidation.

"Please don't go, Diana. I will stop. Please just remember if you should ever need me, I will be there for you. You can write to me and I will come. That is a solemn promise."

Diana didn't respond. When the music ended, she stepped away from Lawrence and hurried from the dance floor. Benjamin had been watching them and hurried to Diana's side. He didn't say anything, but simply put his arm around her and pulled her close leading her to a sofa in a secluded alcove. They didn't speak, they simply sat together while Diana got herself under control.

The evening finally ended much to Diana's relief. The next day all the guests left soon after breaking their fast. When the last carriage had pulled away, Diana looked at Benjamin and Edward and gave a huge sigh.

"I enjoyed the house party, but I can't say I'm not glad it's over. I had no idea how much work a two week party can be." Edward said with a smile. "And I didn't even do half the work that you did, Di. You must be exhausted. What say you we have a very quiet rest of our stay here in Staffordshire? I for one don't even want to think about big dinners or trying to entertain anyone for months.."

"I agree wholeheartedly," said Diana with another sigh.

Chapter 38

The weeks went by quietly and quickly for the trio. Soon it was the end of September and time to go to Bristol Castle for a few months. Then they would travel to the estate in Devonshire after the new year.

The time they spent at Bristol Castle went by quickly. Again this year, they invited Bernie, Michael and Dickey to hunt and spend Christmas with them. This year only Michael and Bernie were able to come. Dickey was spending Christmas with the O'Briens in Ireland. He and Maeve had become engaged in October and planned to marry next May in London. Diana was very pleased that Dickey had found someone to care about.

When Bernie and Michael arrived the first week of December, Michael informed them he and Mary had become engaged just two weeks prior. She and her family were visiting her mother's family for the holidays in Bath. Normally Michael would have joined them, but Mary's grandmother was ill and not up to entertaining too many people. He would see Mary again when they went home to Devonshire for the new year. Edward and Diana invited both their guests to stay with them in Devonshire as well. Michael would be staying at the Sheraton's, but Bernie was quick to accept the invitation.

Again this year, the friends went out and cut down a Christmas tree. The decorations from the prior year were stored in the attic. They were brought down, refurbished and added to in a flurry of activity. Again, Edward and Diana gave the staff Christmas Day off and they all went to their neighbor's home for his annual hunt and ball. On Boxing Day, the tenants and their families came to Bristol Castle.

This year another American tradition was introduced. Ian had sent Diana a bag of popcorn with instructions on how to make it. Corn, or maize as it was known in England, did not grow there, although all grains were referred to as corn, whether barley, oats or wheat. There was no actual maize grown in England.

Diana was intrigued by this new phenomenon. She had cook pop the first batch not long after it arrived. The scullery maids thought the kitchen was exploding when the little kernels began to pop in the heavy pot they had been put into. They ran and hid in the larder much to Diana's amusement. When the noise had abated, cook removed the heavy pot from the stove and took off the lid. The puffy white kernels spilled out with abandon. Diana had cook melt some butter and add it to the dish along with salt. When she first tasted it, she fell in love. She had never had anything so interesting in her life. The kernels that had started as hard, seed-like bits had turned into this wonderful fluffy white treat. She could not seem to stop eating it. Both Edward and Benjamin were like minded on the love of popcorn.

Soon, Diana had to hide the rest of the popcorn in the library to keep everyone from eating it before Boxing Day. She wanted to show it to the tenants and their children. It was such an anomaly, she couldn't wait to see their faces when it started to pop.

Benjamin came up with the idea to make a corn popper to use in the fireplace and worked with the blacksmith to make one similar to the one described in Ian's letter that arrived with the popcorn. They used a cylinder of thin sheet-iron that revolved on an axle in front of the fireplace like a squirrel cage. The drawing Ian had sent was for a fairly small cylinder, but Benjamin had a much larger one made because there were so many tenant's children coming to visit on Boxing Day.

The day dawned very cold, but sunny, with a high wind. The tenants arrived half frozen from their journey. Diana had cook prepare two huge bowls of wassail from the cider she had requested from their Devonshire estate. One was made from brandy and hard cider as well as spices and the other was more child friendly using soft cider and extra sugar and spices.

When the tenants arrived in the grand hall, the staff circulated among them with cups of the hot wassail and trays of biscuits. A jolly time was had by all. When everyone had warmed themselves, Diana lead the children into the large drawing room to look at the tree. They were amazed again at the sight of the huge evergreen decorated with fruit, nuts, and candy, as well as silk ornaments and candles. Gifts were handed round to all the children and coins to their parents.

After the opening of the gifts, the children were called by Diana to the fireplace. Benjamin came in with his invention and set it before the fireplace very near the fire. In just a few minutes of his turning the handle, the corn began to pop. The children had been forewarned so they wouldn't be frightened, but some of the younger ones sought their mothers anyway. When the last kernel had popped, Benjamin opened the cylinder and emptied it into a huge bowl. Butter and salt were added and the popcorn was dished up in small bowls and given to the children and the adults.

The looks of amazement on their faces was priceless to Diana. They all seemed to love the unusual treat and couldn't stop talking about it for the rest of the visit. Diana was very happy that the festivities had gone so well.

Soon it was time for the tenants to leave. The friends were a tired, but happy group. They relaxed in the drawing room admiring the tree while Benjamin popped some more corn just for them. They munched on their buttery, crunchy treat and discussed the highlights of the day.

"Di, you outdid yourself again. We probably have the happiest tenants in all of England." stated Edward with a huge smile on his face.

"They did seem to enjoy themselves, didn't they? Did you see little Mary Dawson's face when the corn started to pop. It was such a mixture of fear and curiosity, it was all I could do not to laugh. She is the dearest child." Diana said with a fond smile.

Watching Diana, Benjamin was struck anew by the thought that Diana was missing out on a lot of life's pleasures by being married to Edward. He felt a deep pain in his heart when he thought of what a wonderful mother she had been to little Geoffrey. Life was so damn unfair, he thought. If anyone should have children, it was their Diana. He wished he could do something about it, but he just didn't know what to do.

The rest of the holiday passed with the usual hunting, eating, and fun that the five of them always enjoyed when together. Soon it was time to get packed to move to Devonshire. The weather in Cornwall was becoming intractable. The old castle was almost impossible to keep warm being so near the water and with so many large windows on the seaside of the building. Diana hadn't felt warm in a month. She, who didn't really enjoy travelling in winter was looking forward to leaving for Devonshire as soon as possible. She had never been to the estate there, but had been told by Edward and Benjamin, it was a much smaller estate than the one in Cornwall and being farther inland, was not subject to the Atlantic Ocean weather like Cornwall was.

Devon was close to Cornwall, so their journey would take less than three days from Bristol Castle to Exeter, where the estate was. The house was truly a house, not a castle. It was very large, having thirty bedrooms and sitting on six hundred acres. Most of those acres were being mined for tin. The rest was used for growing barley and potatoes and for a large dairy. Devon clotted cream was a much sought after delicacy.

On the day of departure, it was raining and very cold. As they travelled further from the coast, the rain turned to sleet and snow. It was extremely cold in the carriage even though they were all wrapped up in their warmest clothes and had rugs, blankets and hot bricks for their feet. The bricks soon became cold and caused more harm than good. Benjamin, who was the warmest of the three, managed to get the bricks from under their feet and stacked them against one of the doors of the carriage.

Diana was shivering with cold. Both the men moved from the opposite seat to sit one on each side of her to try to lend their body heat to hers. It did help somewhat and she was very grateful. Diana was very glad Barbara had insisted on her wearing several petticoats and a wool chemise over her silk one. Even with all the extra clothes, she was still very cold. Diana was relieved when they stopped at an inn for luncheon. Benjamin hopped down from the carriage and rushed inside to see about accommodation for their group.

Luckily, Benjamin was able to obtain a private dining and sitting room for them. It had a roaring fire. Diana went immediately to the fire to try to thaw out. Barbara came in with a tray of hot tea and helped her off with her outer clothes. One of the footmen went out to the carriage and retrieved the bricks so they could again be heated for their feet.

Bernie and Michael were also almost frozen. They were riding in a carriage alone. Diana suggested they all ride in one coach as she, Benjamin, and Edward were all sharing one seat for warmth. They readily agreed and when they left the inn, the five of them were all in one carriage. It was a little crowded, but was a lot warmer with the body heat of five people rather than just three. They also added another small lantern hanging from the ceiling near the door which also helped somewhat.

The rest of the trip proceeded much the same. Around midday on the third day, they reached their destination. Diana was delighted with the house. It was three stories tall and built in the Elizabethan style with gables and mullioned windows. Ivy covered all the walls and being an evergreen, gave the house much character and charm although it was the dead of winter. It also helped to insulate the house, keeping out the cold.

Diana was anxious to have a tour of the house. After changing out of her travelling clothes and bathing, she met with the housekeeper, Mrs. Hodges and the butler, Mr. Stone to have a look at their home for the next three months.

The inside of the house had been renovated a few years before and had all the amenities the friends were used to. There was even a billiard table in the library. A cheery fire was burning in all the rooms downstairs as well as in the bedrooms being occupied by she and their friends. Diana surprised Mrs. Hodges and Mr. Stone by asking to be shone the kitchen and wanting to meet the cook, Mrs. Foster, right away.

The cook was also surprised and delighted to have the young duchess come into her inner sanctum soon after her arrival. Diana also surprised all three with her knowledge of the local foods that were available. She dismissed Mrs. Hodges so she could go about her work. She kept Stone to take her around to the rest of the rooms after she and cook had discussed menus and recipes for an hour or so.

Stone took Diana on a tour of all the downstairs rooms and then she joined the men in the drawing room for refreshments. She had told cook not to bother with a formal luncheon, that they would just have a tray of sandwiches and such in the drawing room. Soon the food arrived on four huge trays carried in by some of the footmen they had brought with them.

A table was cleared and the friends drew up chairs and proceeded to have a small feast on the Irsh sandwiches made with beef, celery and tartar sauce on crusty toast, and ham sandwiches on French bread with spicy mustard and thin slices of cheddar cheese along with an assortment of pickles and olives, and small tasty cakes filled with lemon filling and frosted with royal icing. There was tea and coffee, as well as ale, for those who wished it.

When replete, the friends gathered around the fire and spoke of other friends and inconsequential subjects until it was time to dress for dinner.

Since they were all weary from travelling in the cold coaches, Diana had told the men not to dress formally for dinner, but to be relaxed, Instead of formal evening wear, they all wore trouser suits a la Beau Brummel. Diana wore a pretty gold velvet dress with a high neck and long sleeves. She was still not totally warm after their trip and this dress was made of thick material and was quite warm with an extra couple of petticoats under it. She decided against the skimpy evening slippers she usually wore for dinner. Instead, she wore a pair of short boots in a cordovan brown with a heavy pair of woolen stockings. She had Barbara leave her hip length hair down for a change. It warmed her back with its heavy, curly weight and added extra warmth. It was simply tied back from her face with a gold ribbon that matched her dress.

The house in Devonshire was not nearly as cold as Bristol Castle, but it was still drafty in places and hard to heat to good effect. There were no fireplaces in the hallways and they had stone floors which contributed to the intense cold.

Edward and Benjamin came to fetch Diana for dinner as usual. They were surprised to see her hair down. She rarely wore it that way. It made her look much younger than her almost twenty-two years. She looked as she had at sixteen to them. Michael and Bernie were also surprised at Diana's appearance. If anything, she was even more beautiful in the soft gold dress with her lovely auburn hair hanging in curls down her back. They both complimented her on her appearance.

Diana had asked cook to make something substantial for dinner, but had left the menu up to her. They started the meal with a pie a la St. Teresa which was salmon layered with forcemeat, onions, anchovies, and parsley and seasoned liberally with salt and pepper baked in a buttery, flaky pastry. Next a braised saddle of lamb was served. It was filled with Godiveau, a mixture of ground veal and beef suet seasoned with salt, pepper, nutmeg, chives and parsley, then braised with celery, onion, and carrots. This was served with roasted potatoes and button mushrooms and a wine sauce made with butter and herbs. A salad of hothouse lettuce dressed with lemon juice and oil was next, then dessert. For dessert, cook had outdone herself. She had made a lemon pudding baked in a puff pastry and served with brandied cherries knows as ratifias with a dollop of good Devonshire clotted cream.

When dinner was done, Diana asked Stone to have cook to come to the drawing room. Looking worried and flustered, the plump little woman arrived. She had her hands wrapped in her large white apron and looked exceedingly uncomfortable as she curtsied to the gentle folk.

"Mrs. Foster, I just wanted to compliment you in person on the very excellent meal you prepared for us this evening." Diana said as she went to the older woman and took one of her hands in both her own. "These gentlemen and myself have eaten so much, we can hardly breathe. I rarely fill myself to the brim, but tonight I have done so. I just cannot express to you how wonderful everything you cooked tonight tasted. But, I have to especially comment on the fantastic dessert you made. I have had some excellent meals in London at some of the best homes there, but never have I had a dessert to equal yours."

Mrs. Foster's plump little face was wreathed in smiles and as red as one of her brandied cherries.

"Oh, your grace, how kind you are to say so. I don't get to cook right fancy very often as this old place doesn't see much company nowadays. When Mr. Edward's wonderful Mama visited she always had the place filled to the rafters with folks and I cooked up a right storm."

"Well, we will keep you a sight busier than you're used to for the next few months, Mrs. Foster." Edward said as he came up and took the cook's hand in his. "We plan to have guests several times and one of these gentlemen will be with us the entire time. I look forward to more glorious meals from you and I know they do as well." Edward said with a look toward Bernie with a smile.

Bernie, Michael and Benjamin all joined in the complimenting and by the time Mrs. Foster went back to her kitchen, she wore a huge smile on her face. When she got back, she told the scullery maids and the other servants what had transpired and they were in awe. Rarely did the gentry notice any of the things that were done for them, only the things that didn't get done. This young duke and his lady were quite different it seemed.

The next few days went by quickly. Michael left the day after their arrival to go to the Sheraton's. He was anxious to see his Mary. Diana had sent one of the footmen with a note inviting the Sheraton's to come to dinner on the weekend as soon as they had arrived in Devonshire and had received an affirmative reply.

The weather for their dinner party dawned clear and cold. The Sheratons and Michael were due to arrive around six so Diana had the whole day to prepare for their arrival. She and Barbara met with the head gardener and accompanied by him, visited the greenhouses to see what flowers were in bloom.

They found beautifully fragrant gardenias blooming in one of the greenhouses. Diana asked that several of the potted plants be moved to the house. She consulted with the gardener as to the best places to put the lovely smelling plants and found that sunny window areas were best. They would need to be in a warm room however as they didn't tolerate cold well. There was a domed conservatory at the back of the house and Diana had several plants placed there. She also had one taken to her bedroom and placed on a table in front of one of the windows. Two of the others, she had placed on small tables near windows in the large drawing room.

As there was an abundance of roses blooming also, Diana had many cut and she and Barbara spent several hours placing them in vases to place in the front hall, the dining room and drawing room as well as the bedrooms the Sheraton's would be using, as they were staying the night.

On the tour of the greenhouses, Diana also discovered one used as an orangerie and another as a pinerie or pineapple pit. She asked that several oranges and some pineapples be sent to the kitchens. Diana, a voracious reader, had recently read a book by Captain James Cook about Hawaii and its wonderful fruit, the pineapple. She had never had the opportunity to try the fruit and thought it would make a good addition to the fruit course for their dinner that night.

Around four, Diana had tea with the men and then went upstairs to dress for dinner. Her dress for the evening was a heavy velvet with a full skirt under which she could wear several flannel petticoats for warmth. Being so small, Diana constantly fought a battle with the cold English climate.

Her dress this evening was a dark, hunter green which looked very well with her auburn hair. It was trimmed in cream colored lace around the square neckline and the cuffs of the long fitted sleeves. She substituted her evening slippers for a pair of half boots in dark brown leather with heavy wool stockings. She had Barbara dress her hair in a cluster of curls at the back of her head to keep her neck warm. Even though she was dressing for warmth and comfort, she still looked very stylish.

Soon it was time to go downstairs to greet their guests. Edward, Benjamin, and Diana met Bernie in the drawing room for a drink before the guests arrived. Since it was so cold, Diana had cook prepare some warm mulled wine with some of the oranges from the orangerie and cinnamon sticks, cider, cloves, and honey. It was a very fragrant and warming drink.

When the guests arrived, they were happy to have cups of the warm mulled wine to help warm them from their drive. The drive had only taken two hours, but two hours in a cold carriage could seem like a lifetime, Diana knew.

After some lively conversation and mulled wine, the party moved into the dining room. The party included Lord and Lady Sheraton, their daughters Mary and Abigail, their son, Rory, and Michael. Diana had left the menu up to cook for the dinner party and she wasn't disappointed.

They were served several courses, all featuring recipes specifically from Devon. There was a course of Hogs pudding, a very spicy pork dish, a beef pasty with wonderfully tender beef cooked in a brown gravy with onions, celery and carrots, fried fish with fried potatoes, and several dishes featuring the wonderful Devon cheeses, both soft and hard varieties. For dessert, there were two flavors of ice cream as well as a trifle made with fresh fruit and Devon clotted cream.

The Sheraton's were much impressed with the dinner and complimented Diana several times. She, in turn, told them she could take no credit for the menu nor the food. She had Stone call in Mrs. Foster to receive the accolades she so richly deserved. The round little woman was so red in the face by the time everyone had their say, Diana was worried she might have an apoplectic fit.

Mrs. Foster returned to the kitchen with tears running down her face from happiness.

The ladies left the gentlemen to their brandy and cigars and adjourned to the drawing room. There were only four of them, so they seated themselves on the sofa and chairs nearest the huge fireplace in which there was a roaring fire. The Sheraton ladies had also dressed warmly in velvet for the evening. Mary Sheraton was a fair skinned blond with very pretty blue eyes. Her hair was thick and curly and pulled up into a knot on her head with curls hanging down to her shoulders on each side of her face. She apparently had taken after their mother who had the same coloring and a similarly shaped face. Abigail, the younger sister, however, had taken after their father. She had a ruddier complexion and dark hair. Her eyes were a dark blue. They were both pretty girls, but neither were blessed with even average intelligence. Their conversation, as well as their mother's, seemed to revolve around the weather, their clothes and the local gossip.

Diana soon found herself bored, but did her best to enter into the conversation as much as she could. However, since she had little interest in most of the subjects they touched upon, she was somewhat quiet, even for her.

The men soon joined the ladies and the conversation turned to less mundane subjects. Diana was soon asked to play and sing. She asked Edward to join her and they soon had the company laughing and gay with their sprightly playing and amusing songs. They had been practicing some of the songs they had heard at the theaters in London last season and kept the company laughing hilariously with their very humorous takes on the denizens of the stage as they saw them.

When Edward and Diana ran out of their new repertoire, Edward asked Diana to sing Helen of Kirkconnel. She agreed and soon the entire company was mesmerized by her beautiful voice and expert playing. As usual, she played with her eyes closed, a dreamy look on her face and her lithe body swaying softly to the sad music.

The applause, though from only a few people, was very loud when Diana was finished. Her beautiful face was flushed with both pleasure and embarrassment. She was still not completely comfortable performing in front of people. She still much preferred playing and singing for her closest friends only.

The evening continued with much good camaraderie and laughter. The company split into teams and played charades. Again Diana excelled at the game as she had almost from the first time she played. She was a natural actress and comedienne. The party found much amusement from her shenanigans.

After a very good dinner and stimulating company, it was finally time for everyone to retire for the evening. Footmen came with lamps and candles to light the way to the bed chambers assigned to the guests. Diana had put all the Sheraton's in one wing of the house, but had put Michael into the wing used by she, Edward, Benjamin and Bernie.

The next day dawned dreary with sleet, snow and icy conditions on the roads. Diana insisted that the Sheratons stay another night as the travelling conditions were very bad. The girls were upset about not having more clothes with them and didn't want to wear the same outfits for dinner again. Diana told them she had plenty of clothes and they could borrow something of hers.

The three young women adjourned to Diana's bedchamber after luncheon to see what they could find that might fit Mary and Abigail. There was much laughing and camaraderie as Mary and Abigail tried on several of Diana's dinner gowns. They were of a similar size, but Diana was much shorter. Finally, with Barbara's help, they were outfitted for the evening although they each had a lot more petticoat showing than was the norm, they chose outfits that benefited from that particular look.

When the ladies joined the gentlemen in the drawing room before dinner, there were many compliments given on the dresses they had chosen.

"We can't take much credit." said Mary, "Diana has an incredible collection of the most beautiful dresses."

"Well," said Diana, "Edward is the one to blame for much of my wardrobe. He insists that I buy new things all the time. Sometimes, I cannot make up my mind between two dresses and he just has me buy both. Looking at that dress you're wearing, Abigail, I don't think I have ever even worn it. I had forgotten I had it. It looks wonderful on you, maybe you should keep it." Diana said laughing up at Edward.

"You probably should, Miss Abigail." said Edward with a broad smile. "Diana is no where near the lover of clothes that I am. If I didn't watch her, she would only buy new clothes when the old ones were worn out." he said with a gay laugh.

Diana playfully swatted Edward on the arm as he lead her to the dining room for another wonderful dinner.

Chapter 39

It was a good time for Edward, Benjamin and Diana. They were as happy as they had been since the tragedy of Geoffrey's being killed in what they thought of as Edward's accident.

Unbeknownst to them, the tragedy had not been an accident at all in the real sense of the word. An agent had been sent to kill Diana that day, but his aim was off and he hit Edward's horse instead, causing the animal to bolt. Then the baby was thrust out of Edward's arms when his head hit a low hanging branch.

That agent had been sent by Lady Adelaide Bruce from Scotland. Although her daughter Beatrice had eventually married an English nobleman, he was only an earl, not the duke her mother had set her heart on. The lady had never gotten over what she saw as Edward's defection when he married Diana. She had sworn retribution for what she saw as a personal affront.

When she was informed that Diana's father, Fergus MacDonald's had passed and Diana was back home for the funeral, she saw the young couple's trip back to London after the funeral as the perfect opportunity to exact that retribution. In her sick mind, if Diana was out of the picture, her Beatrice could divorce her earl and marry Edward.

If she had known the circumstances of their marriage, she would not have cared. She would have laughed and been the first to ostracize Diana for being pregnant and unwed. She would have gloried in Diana's disgrace.

Since she was the instigator of the attack on Geoffrey and his valet, she felt she had pulled off the perfect end to the next Duke of Bristol, leaving an opening for her daughter to become a duchess. She had supposed that since Edward had been semi-courting her daughter before he had left Scotland after his first visit with his father and brother, his intentions were serious. She had assumed Edward's intentions were serious although nothing had been said on the subject of marriage. The lady was mentally unbalanced and had absolutely no conscience.

When she was informed by her estate manager, Horace Alexander, that Diana had not died, but Edward had been badly wounded and the baby had been killed instead, she took a perverse pleasure in Diana and Edward's pain. She even put in an appearance at Ainsley Glen after the funeral service for little Geoffrey pretending to offer condolences, but secretly reveling in the sorrow Diana was consumed with. In her twisted mind, Diana deserved to be miserably unhappy for "stealing" her daughter's duke.

One would think the amount of pain Diana and Edward had suffered would have contented Lady Bruce. However, her twisted mind was not content. She consulted with her partner in crime, Horace, to plan further pain for Diana.

Chapter 40

The three friends settled into a routine in their lives. Edward and Benjamin were very busy with Parliament when they were in town. Diana was busy with running the duchy, her estates in Scotland and England, and her charities. The days turned into weeks, the weeks to months and the months to years.

This March, Diana was turning four and twenty. Edward and Benjamin decided they should have a birthday ball for her. A little later in the year, they were finally about to take the trip to the continent they had started planning so many years ago. The duchy business was running very smoothly, profits were increasing every year, and the country was going strong. It was the perfect time to take a few months to see a different part of the world.

The day of Diana's birthday ball was upon them quickly as they had all been so very busy with preparations for the ball and the trip. Many trips to the tailor, the modiste, the haberdasher, the bonnet maker, the glove maker, the shoe maker and so forth, had finally been completed. The first leg of their journey was to begin a week after the ball.

Diana had chosen her dress with much care for her birthday ball. The material was silk and a deep sapphire blue color. The bodice of the dress was fitted tightly over her corset to her tiny waist, with the skirt flaring out into a conical shape over several petticoats. The top petticoat was longer than the dress by a few inches so the delicate white lace on the bottom of the silk petticoat showed under the deep blue of the hem. The hem of the dress also sported rows of the same fine white lace as did the short puffed sleeves. As it was still quite cool in March, she added a white silk shawl with a blue and white paisley print trim on each end. Her shoes were sapphire blue silk slippers and she wore white silk stockings with them. Her hair was arranged in several braids that were wound around her head in an intricate pattern and held with diamond and sapphire pins. She even wore the Bristol diamonds on this occasion.

As was their custom, Edward and Benjamin came through their connecting drawing room to fetch Diana to go downstairs to greet their guests the night of the ball. They were both very appreciative of the way she looked. She blushed under their compliments.

"Thank you both for your kind words, but you both look absolutely splendid yourselves." said Diana as she looked over her two best friends. Benjamin, as was his custom, was dressed in a black evening suit with snowy linen and a white cravat. However, Edward was a peacock in full plume. His evening suit was made up of a pair of silk trousers in a pale pink shade topped with a black evening coat cut high in the front with long tails in the back. His linen was snowy white, but his waistcoat was maroon and his cravat was the same pink silk as his trousers.

Diana walked slowly around Edward with a look of awe on her face. "Only you could pull off this ensemble." she told him with a smile on her face. Edward and Benjamin laughingly agreed and the trio headed down the stairs to meet their guests.

The guest list was huge for this ball. There were any number of dukes, earls, viscounts and lords as well as their wives, fiancees, sisters and friends. Older members of the *ton* sat around the edges of the ballroom gossiping and overseeing the younger set. Every young unmarried lady had a chaperone of some kind as did some of the married ones as well.

Edward and Benjamin had met a young Russian diplomat, Count Ivan Ostrovsky, that they liked very much. The count had invited them to stay with his family in St. Petersburg upon their visit to his country in April. The trio had decided to make Russia their first stop on their trip as they had all been reading The Captive of the Caucasus by Pushkin and were fascinated by the country.

The count, along with several other members of the Russian aristocracy had been invited to the ball. Diana was captivated by their charm and the passion they had for their country and their countrymen.

The evening was a huge success and was enjoyed by all present. The entertainment was the best, the food the finest and the champagne, the best money could buy. Edward was quite pleased at how Diana's ball had turned out. When Diana, Benjamin, and Edward went upstairs for the night, Edward and Benjamin presented Diana with her gift. They had found an amethyst parure which included a necklace, tiara, bracelet and earrings of exquisite deep purple gems of the highest quality. They were set in 24 carat gold filigree and the craftsmanship was incredible. Diana was thrilled with her gift and hugged both men more than once.

The days after the ball flew by. The trio were very excited about their grand tour. Barbara and the upstairs maids were busy practically day and night packing trunks and making sure all Diana's clothes were in perfect condition. Benjamin enlisted the aid of three footmen to help him pack for Edward. He handled his own packing in a few short hours, but Edward actually had more clothes than Diana, though they took up less trunk room.

At last the day came for their departure. The trio would be travelling both by rail , sea, and by carriage. The arrangements had been complicated to take care of, but Benjamin had handled everything for them. Their entourage included the three friends, Barbara, Bertha, two other maids, and four footmen. The footmen were mostly for seeing to the enormous pile of luggage they would need for such a long journey.

The train pulled out of the station at eight in the morning. Benjamin had booked them an entire car for the first leg of their journey. Diana had never ridden in a train and was fascinated by the sites to be seen through the windows. It was a new experience to be travelling in relative comfort. It was still quite cool in England, but spring was definitely on the way as evidenced by the wildflowers just beginning to bloom in the countryside. The train car was heated and the trio was quite comfortable. The train would take them to northern England where they would transfer to carriages to travel to Edinburgh to catch a ship to St. Petersburg. They would be met by their friend, Count Ostrovsky, at the pier in three weeks time.

The train trip took two days. Their carriages met them at the railway station. It took two hours for all the luggage to be taken from the train and packed into the assembled carriages. It was so late in the day, the party decided not to start the next leg of their journey overland until the next morning. Benjamin procured lodgings for their large party and they repaired to the inn to have tea and rest.

The next morning dawned sunny and bright. The next few days went by quickly and the party was soon in Edinburgh. They spent the night in the newly built One Royal Circle Inn overlooking the royal gardens. The Georgian style house was very beautifully furnished including a magnificent painted ceiling in the main drawing room. There was even a wonderful new harpsichord in the drawing room as well. Diana and Edward spent a couple of hours that evening playing and singing.

The ship was due to leave on the morning tide, so the party went to the docks at seven the next morning. They had been assigned three cabins. Diana, Barbara and the two maids shared one, Edward and Benjamin another, and the rest of the male servants the third. The trip to St. Petersburg was to take three days.

Diana, never having been on a ship didn't know exactly what to expect. She was amazed by the tiny size of the cabins. There was hardly room to turn around in the room with four women in it. She determined not to spend much time below decks during the journey. The weather was fine and she wanted to see the ocean so she hurried up the companionway stairs quickly. Diana stood at the ship's rail for a long time, watching Scotland slowly disappear in the distance.

Diana was soon joined by Benjamin and Edward. The three friends stood shoulder to shoulder, with Diana in the middle, watching the sea birds swooping down around the ship. Benjamin and Edward had both been on ships, but those had been short trips across the English channel to France. They were almost as excited as Diana.

The weather held and there were no storms while they crossed the North Sea to Russia. It seemed they had hardly boarded the ship when it was time to depart. The ship had made port late the preceding day and had been at anchor until daylight. Diana and her men had stood on the deck looking at the bright lights of St. Petersburg the evening before. They were all amazed at the size of the city and the amount of the sparkling lights they could see.

The next morning dawned sunny and crisp. It was much colder in Russia than it had been in England. Diana wore a heavy bronze colored velvet gown with several petticoats and a pair of brown boots over two pairs of stockings. She also wore a dark brown velvet cloak with a bonnet and gloves to match. Her curls were confined in a chignon low on the back of her neck with a few curls hanging around her face.

With her tiny stature, her beautiful glowing face, and her shining emerald eyes, Edward thought her one of the most beautiful women he had ever seen. He felt a pang of guilt when he looked at Diana that morning. To think she would never know the kind of love he and Benjamin had, made him sad. He looked over at Benjamin and his heart gladdened.

Edward had matured so much in the last few years. The tragedies in his life, the loss of his entire immediate family, had almost done him in. However, he had finally overcome the guilt and sadness that had nearly weighed him down after little Geoffrey's death. It had been Diana and Benjamin who had brought him back and he owed both of them so very much. Although his slight limp and the pain he often felt in his once badly broken leg were still constant reminders of that awful day, he no longer dwelled upon the accident as he had the first few months after it had happened.

Benjamin was also pensive this day. He looked at Edward, the love of his life, and Diana who was as much a sister to him as any of his own sisters, with so much love in his heart, it actually hurt. Benjamin, who was subject to much introspection, had given a lot of thought to their situation. He also, felt a huge amount of guilt where Diana was concerned. He and Edward had reached a stage in their relationship where their love had grown immeasurably. Diana was at least partially responsible for that. Her easy acceptance of their commitment to each other, her unbiased and unconditional love for each of them, and her practical no nonsense approach to their very unorthodox lifestyle were all integral parts of the reason his and Edward's relationship was where it was today.

He thought, "If only there were a way for Diana to find what we have, then our lives would be perfect." However, knowing Diana as he did, he knew she would never take a lover, so they were at an impasse.

Diana, for her part, wasn't even thinking along the same lines as her two men. She was excited to see Russia. She had read several books about it and longed to see many of the beautiful buildings the books had described. She had spoken to Count Ostrovsky and he had promised he would take her anywhere her heart desired. He was an unconscionable flirt, but seemed harmless to the somewhat innocent Diana.

Chapter 41

Soon the ship had docked. The three friends started down the gangplank and were hailed immediately by the count. He was accompanied by several friends and several servants. There were a line of carriages waiting to whisk the English party away to the Count's family palace on the banks of the Neva River. There was much laughter as they all climbed into the very ornate carriages for the short trip from the dock to the palace.

The Ostrovsky palace was a sight to behold. It was built in the baroque style of the Winter Palace by the same architect, Rastrelli. It was a huge building with some fifty-eight rooms in its three stories. It took up a whole city block near the city center. The drive had taken only about fifteen minutes, but the difference in the dock area and the main city center was like daylight and dark. There were few trees or green areas in the city center. It was building after building on paved courts. The carriages pulled up to the front of the Ostrovsky palace and more servants rushed out of the building to help with the unloading of the people and luggage.

Standing just inside the doors in the very grand hall, was the count's mother and sisters. His father had passed away two years ago, making Ivan the new count. Ivan was still quite young and hadn't settled into his responsibilities as quickly as his mother wished. She worried about his frivolous ways and the amounts of money he spent. The family fortunes were still solvent, but if Ivan kept up his reckless spending and way of life, the coffers might soon be empty. The dowager countess wanted Ivan to marry soon and well, but he had no intention of tying himself down to one woman yet.

Countess Tatiana Ostrovsky was a tall woman with graying dark hair and a high forehead. She was not a beauty, but had an arresting presence and a kind heart. Her daughters, Irina, Katrina and Olga looked much as she did. Ivan, however, had taken after his very handsome father. He was tall and athletically built, with dark curling hair, sparkling blue eyes and an almost perpetually smiling face. He took very little seriously and loved to laugh and have a good time. He was rarely at home except to sleep and change clothes, and sometimes he didn't even come home to sleep, but stayed with one of his mistresses.

The countess hoped the visit by these English people would at least keep him home some of the time. She had been surprised when told by her son that he had invited an English married couple and the man's secretary to stay with them during their Grand Tour. Her son's friends were usually single men like himself who lived to have a good time. This couple, although young, seemed mature beyond their years. The duke was quite handsome in a very English way, but his duchess was extremely beautiful and had a quiet demeanor and a lovely sweet smile. The countess was hopeful they would be a good influence on her Ivan.

As Diana, Edward and Benjamin were shone to a drawing room for refreshments, there was a bustle of activity to get all the luggage sorted and sent to the appropriate rooms. Barbara had taken on that job and was very efficiently directing the Bristol footmen and some of the Russian servants as well.

Barbara, of course, didn't speak Russian, but Diana had supplied her with the words they felt were necessary for several types of situations. Diana had been studying Russian with a tutor for a couple of months, so she wouldn't feel lost when they travelled to that country. She already spoke French, but had taken some lessons in Italian as well. She had a natural bent for languages and picked them up very quickly. Neither Edward nor Benjamin bothered to learn any Russian. They both already spoke French and Edward also spoke quite a bit of Italian. Diana felt it prudent for Barbara to learn some of the languages as well. Barbara had been a very apt pupil and Diana felt comfortable in her handling of the dispersal of the luggage and ordering what was needed for their comfort.

The room the visitors were shown into was huge and extremely ornate. The furniture was made of heavy dark wood and upholstered in dark rich velvets and silks. Most of the chair covers were hand embroidered in flower motifs. The predominant color was a deep, rich red with gold and white accents. There were magnificent marble fireplaces at each end of the room with roaring fires. Diana was obviously cold after her cloak and bonnet had been removed, so the countess lead her to a sofa directly in front of one of the fires. She and her daughters all spoke English and Diana was soon at ease talking to the Ostrovsky ladies. A tea tray was soon brought and the hot drink revived Diana as much as the fire.

When she had first come into the room, Diana had noticed a very remarkable pianoforte. It was made of tulip wood and had marquetry insets in the sides. It was decorated with ormolu cherubs on the front corners and smaller ones down each side. The entire piano was heavily carved with an intricate design including the delicately curved legs and a cross piece between the front legs. The countess noticed Diana looking at the instrument and told her some of its history. The instrument had been made in Germany. Her husband, upon seeing it on one of his business trips, had tried to buy it from the baron who owned it.

The Ostrovsky's had been building their palace at that time and he felt it would look especially wonderful in this room. The German baron was unwilling to sell the piece, but gave the count the name of the craftsman who had made it. He had one commissioned and almost a year later it was delivered by ship from Germany.

Ivan, upon hearing his mother discussing the piano, came over to the ladies. "Mama, you should hear Lady Diana and her husband play and sing. They have a very remarkable talent and incredible harmony together. I had the pleasure of hearing them several times while in London. They are beset by requests at almost every entertainment they go to."

Edward joined the group, "Yes, we are, but it is Di who has the real talent. I don't have nearly the skill in playing or singing that she does. She shows a passion for music that I cannot begin to express. My lovely Di has the voice of an angel.", he said with a fond smile toward his lovely young wife.

Diana, blushing prettily, exclaimed, "Oh Edward, don't be so modest. You have a wonderful voice and are quite a capable pianist as well. I'm lucky to have such a partner as you."

The countess noticed the easy camaraderie between this young couple. However, she did not get a feeling of romance from them. There were no flirting looks exchanged and there didn't seem to be "that" spark between them. She thought, "So, it is a marriage of convenience for them. Too bad." She was hoping for a love match for her Ivan, such as she had had with his father. She and her husband hadn't been in love when they married, but they had affection for each other and mutual respect that had quickly became a deep and abiding love for each other. She knew Ivan must marry soon and produce an heir, but she did hope he would at least have the good luck to find a young woman whom he could love eventually.

After speaking with the English visitors for awhile, the countess and her daughters were happily surprised by their intelligence and their interest in Russia. It seemed they had all read several books written by Russians such as Pushkin and several others, as well as books on Russia by other European authors. Diana, especially, seemed to be well versed in not only Russian fiction, but also history, politics and social issues. The countess, who was herself very well read, was quite surprised at the knowledge of one so young and commented on it.

Edward spoke up, "Diana is the most intelligent and well read of the three of us. She consumes books at an alarming rate. I believe she has read almost every book in the library in the London house and is constantly buying more. I think she's at the booksellers more often than she is at the modiste's, unlike so many of the ladies we are acquainted with. I am very happy to see that you, Countess, also possess that type of intellect. The two of you will no doubt keep us on our toes with many lively discussions while we're here."

Soon the party was called into luncheon by the butler. The dining room was also very large and just as ornate as the drawing room had been. Again, there was a massive fireplace at each end of the room. The table could seat forty easily. As there were only twenty at lunch that day, chairs had been taken from the table and lined against the walls giving each person more room. The colors in the dining room carried over from the drawing room with predominantly reds, golds and whites. The china was also ornate although it was pure white. The fruit pattern around the edges of the plates and bowls was raised and quite beautiful.

The first course was shchi, the wonderfully tasty Russian staple, cabbage soup. The soup contained beef, onions, dill, carrots, pickle juice and of course cabbage and was flavored with garlic, pepper, basil and mushrooms. The soup course was followed by a large, baked beef rump roast cooked with potatoes, carrots, turnips and onions and served with a gravy of pan juices, sour cream and spices. The next course was pelmeni made with finely minced beef, lamb and pork wrapped in a thin yeast bread. They were boiled and then lightly fried in butter and served with sour cream, mustard, horseradish and vinegar. A fish course of smoked salmon mixed with boiled eggs and spices served on toasted bread rounds was served next with the ever present sour cream, mustard, horseradish and vinegar. For dessert, small thin blinis were served with butter and three types of fruit preserves accompanied by tea and coffee.

After such a heavy midday meal, Diana was feeling the effects of travel and very much wanted a nap. It seemed she wasn't the only one needing a bit of rest. The party broke up and everyone went to their rooms. Edward and Diana had been given a suite with two bedchambers separated by a small private drawing room. The countess herself showed Diana and Edward to their quarters. She immediately noticed that the luggage for the two men was in one of the bed chambers and Diana's was in another. She supposed Edward's secretary would sleep in the servant's room on the other side of the bathing chamber as Barbara would sleep in the small room off the closet. She left the English visitors in the connecting drawing room.

"Well, Hin, are you worn out from the journey or all that wonderfully heavy food? I am stuffed and want out of these heavy clothes and into that comfortable looking bed next door for a good rest. Sleeping on a ship is not nearly as comfortable as I thought it would be. The beds were a bit short for men as tall as Benjamin and myself. It will be good to stretch out." Edward said with a laugh.

"Yes, Edward, I, as well, could do with a rest. The food was very tasty, but it was a bit heavy for me. I may not eat another bite until tomorrow." Diana said as she started for her bedchamber door. "You two have a good rest. I will see you before dinner?"

Benjamin said, "We will come get you for dinner. Have a good rest."

Barbara helped Diana strip down to her shift and climb beneath the heavy covers on the massive bed. The bed, as well as all the other furniture in the room, was very heavy and ornately carved of a very dark wood. The bed hangings and curtains were a pale blue silk embroidered with flowers in pastel hues. They brightened up the room considerably since the walls were painted a darker blue. There were two windows in the room, but they had arches built over them and didn't let in much light. When Barbara closed the bed hangings, it was very dark and cozy and Diana fell into a deep sleep almost immediately. It seemed she had just gone to sleep when Barbara was waking her to bathe and dress for dinner.

Diana chose an emerald green silk evening dress with long sleeves. The bodice and new styled puffy sleeves were trimmed in ecru Venetian lace. The sleeves were puffed from the shoulder to about the elbow and then tight to the wrist. The lace was sewn in rows on the fuller part of the sleeve, but none was on the fitted area. The skirt was full from a nipped in waist. The trim on the skirt was 2 rows of ecru braid with an arrangement of pine cones in ecru silk with the silk pine needles in a deep forest green. Barbara didn't need to lace her corset very tightly because Diana had a naturally slim waist although the dress was made with a tiny waist.

Barbara brought out both the topaz set and the smaller emerald set for Diana to choose to wear for the evening. She decided the emeralds would compliment her ensemble the best and chose them.

Barbara dressed her hair high on her head with an ecru lace band around her head and a tiny ecru pine cone resting in her bun. Barbara left long curls hanging around her face and short ones on her forehead. Diana was happy with the effect as she looked into the large oval mirror in the corner of her room.

There was a knock on the door connecting to the drawing room. Barbara opened the door to admit Edward and Benjamin dressed in their evening finery. Benjamin, as usual wore black trousers and coat with a white waistcoat, shirt and cravat. Edward, on the other hand was a vision in gold and royal blue. His gold silk trousers were cut high at the waist and held up by braces. The bottoms of his very snug trousers went under his shoes. His waistcoat was also gold and heavily embroidered with a royal blue paisley print. His shirt was white, but his cravat was royal blue as was his cutaway jacket. The jacket had gold embroidery on the lapels as well as gold buttons and the embroidery extended to the cravat. He had brushed his blond hair away from his face and it curled softly around his face and over his collar. He was the picture of sartorial splendor.

"Oh, Edward, you have outdone yourself this time at your tailor's. Every new outfit is just a little more magnificent than the last.' Diana said as she circled her husband.

Edward's face had a huge smile as he watched her take note of his entire outfit from bottom to top. "I really must congratulate my tailor on this one. I think it may be my favourite of the new batch I had made before our trip."

"I can see why. It is a beautiful color combination and it looks really marvelous with your coloring. Did you choose the colors yourself?" Diana asked with a big smile.

"Oh, yes, Hin. I never let anyone choose my colors for me. I love to see the look on the tailor and his assistant's faces when I tell them what I want. They are always a bit shocked, but never say a word. The mark of a good tailor, I always say."

Diana started to laugh and was soon joined by Benjamin and Edward. Edward's clothes were often a topic for mirth between the three of them. He was constantly trying to outdo Beau Brummel and the other fops of the *ton*. He usually managed it quite well.

The three were still laughing as they left their room to go down to dinner. Ivan, coming down the hallway from his rooms, was struck by the absurd amount of beauty bestowed on these three English people. They were all uncommonly good looking and obviously had the money and style to dress exceptionally well also. These three would bear watching. Ivan was always trying to find new ways to augment his family's fortunes. Perhaps he could interest the duke in an investment of some sort. He would need to speak to his cousin, Anatoly, about this and very soon.

Dinner was another heavy, but very flavorful meal. The soup at this meal was lapsha, a thick hearty soup made of chicken, mushrooms, and milk with the addition of noodles and spices. The second course was kholodets, pieces of pork that had been boiled with spices several times and then jellied in meat fat and served with sour cream, horseradish, and mustard. The third course was pirozhki, a wonderful little yeasty pie filled with chopped beef, mushrooms, onions and rice and served with a horseradish dipping sauce made with mayonnaise and sour cream. The next course was an Olivier salad made with potatoes, chopped pork, onions, boiled carrots, several types of diced pickles, hard cooked eggs and peas. To finish the meal, they were served syrniki, a fried curd fritter served with raisins was served for dessert.

The Russians had not adopted the English habit of the ladies leaving the gentlemen to brandy and cigars after dinner. Everyone sat around the table talking and drinking for about an hour after the meal was finished. They all then adjourned to the drawing room.

Almost immediately, Irina asked Diana to play and sing. Diana looked to Edward and he accompanied her to the piano. In honor of their hosts, they had learned two Russian folk songs from Diana's Russian tutor. They played them first. They were very well received by their hosts. They then sang and played several pieces of both English and Scottish music. Edward then turned to Diana and requested she play Helen of Kirkconell, which was his favorite. Diana smiled at Edward as he stood and took a place behind her. Soon she was lost to the music. She sang the sad words of the ballad in her rich contralto voice as her hands sailed across the keys seemingly of their own volition. Her slim body swayed to the haunting melody as she played with her eyes closed and a dreamy expression on her face.

When the song ended, the room was totally quiet for almost a full minute. Then loud applause brought Diana from her reverie. She looked up to see tears running down the faces of all the ladies present and not a few of the men. They may not have understood all the words of the song, but the meaning of them was evident to all.

As usual, Diana was embarrassed by all the attention, but Edward revelled in it. He was very proud of his little Hin. Over the years, Edward had become more and more proud of his wife. They may not have a traditional relationship, but they did have a very close and loving one.

Edward looked out over the company and was not surprised to see lascivious looks in the eyes of most of the men as they stared at his beautiful wife. He laughed to himself as he thought their desires would never see fruition. He knew his wife. Although he and Benjamin had both told her many times she should take a lover, her strong moral sense would not allow such a thing. Soon, the Russians would find what all other men had found before them. His wife was true to her vows and would not stray.

The next day Ivan had arranged for his English friends to be driven out to one of his estates in the country for a picnic. After a heavy breakfast of three different cereals, buckwheat, oats and rice, cooked in milk and served with heavy cream, sugar and dried fruit along with toasted bread with butter and a variety of jams, the company was loaded into the ornate carriages once again. Heavy fur robes were draped over every one's laps as the temperature was still quite cold. Hot bricks had also been put on the floor for their feet to rest upon. Even with all that, Diana was still cold. She, Edward, Benjamin and Ivan were riding in the lead carriage. When Edward noticed Diana was shivering, he asked Benjamin to sit on the other side of her to give her some of his warmth. As usual, Benjamin was more than happy to comply. Ivan looked at Edward with some surprise. He was not sure he would allow a man as handsome as Benjamin to be that close to his wife, if he was lucky enough to have one like Diana. However, there seemed to be no jealousy between these three.

The journey took about three hours. Diana was fascinated by the beautiful Russian countryside. The grass was just beginning to turn green and wildflowers were just beginning to bloom in the rolling fields they passed. When the company finally arrived at their destination, Diana was enthralled by the lovely dacha on the estate. The dacha was very ornate with many wooden openwork carvings and several different roof lines. There was a pointed structure at the front of the house over a large bay window, a horseshoe shaped arch over the front door and several different grades of roof lines on the house. It was made of wood, but trimmed in brick. It was painted white with brownish, red bricks around the bottom of the house and red trim around the windows and doors. Diana thought it looked like something from a fairytale.

The company, again about twenty people, were led into the dacha by Ivan and his mother. Servants were quick to help the guests remove their cloaks, hats and gloves. In the main room of the dacha, there were fireplaces at each end of the room, both with roaring fires. Diana was very glad of the heat after the long cold ride from the city.

Once everyone had warmed up with warm drinks and hot fires, Ivan led them outdoors for a short walk to their picnic spot. There were several large trees on the property. The area that had been set aside for their luncheon was near a beautiful still pond surrounded by trees. Tables had been set up and servants were rushing around loading the tables with food. The first course was a chicken lapsha, thick with noodles, chicken, onions, carrots and cream and flavored with mushrooms and spices. The lapsha was served with warm yeasty dark rye and pumpernickel breads with bowls of soft butter. The second course was shuba, also known as dressed herring. The herring was salted and chopped, then covered with a layer of chopped beets, then a layer of chopped hard cooked eggs, a layer of chopped onions and pickled cucumbers. This dish was served with a chopped salad made of boiled potatoes, beets, carrots, onions, pickles, white beans, and sauerkraut dressed with sunflower oil. For dessert, they were served vatrushka, a cake made in a ring design. the ring was filled with sweetened cottage cheese and raisins and dried berries. Tea, kvass, and vodka were served with the meal.

Diana, Benjamin and Edward only had tea with their food. They were not used to strong liquors in the middle of the day, but their Russian hosts and their friends downed copious amounts of kvass and vodka. Soon many of them were red-faced and quite loud. The three Brits exchanged concerned looks, but it was soon apparent that none of the Russians was truly drunk. They were merely exuberant.

After the heavy lunch, many of the company returned to the house for naps before going back to the city. The Brits were among them. As the dacha was not nearly as large as the palace, there were limited bedrooms. Countess Ostrovsky asked if Diana and Edward could share a room. To keep down gossip, they quickly agreed to do so. The countess let them know there was a small room en suite for Benjamin.

It was the first time in their six years of marriage that Edward and Diana shared a room. It was a novel experience for both of them. Barbara had accompanied the company with some of the other servants and was ready to assist her mistress in removing her outer clothes for her nap. Edward and Benjamin had waited in the hallway for Barbara to let them know when Diana was ready. When Barbara came out, Edward and Benjamin entered the room. It was an unusual experience for them to see Diana abed. Of course, when she had given birth, they had both seen her in dishabille, but not since. As Diana turned her face to the wall, Benjamin helped Edward undress down to his small clothes and then adjourned to the small anteroom for his own nap. Edward climbed into the huge bed and laughed at Diana's red face.

"Oh, Hin. Who would have thought the first time I shared a bed with a woman, it would be my own wife? None of my old friends would believe it.", he said laughing uproariously.

"Edward, you are incorrigible." Diana said laughing, herself. She had been feeling uncomfortable and embarrassed to have Edward see her in her chemise, but after his comment, she relaxed. With a full stomach and the warmth of the quilts, they were soon both asleep.

When Benjamin came to wake them for the ride back to the city, he was somewhat surprised to see Diana snuggled up to Edward's back. His surprise was nothing compared to Diana's embarrassment when she woke to find herself practically under Edward in the bed.

"Oh, Edward, I am so sorry. I must have gotten cold and gotten close to you for warmth. I do apologize."

"You have nothing to apologize for. I'm happy to have been of service.", Edward said laughing again.

Again, Diana turned her face to the wall while Edward got dressed. He and Benjamin left the room, allowing the waiting Barbara to come in and assist Diana. Soon they were all in the carriages again, on their way back to St. Petersburg.

The days were filled with short journeys to the surrounding countryside for hunting, riding or tea parties or visiting the sights in the city. The nights were filled with dinners, balls, the opera and the ballet. The British friends enjoyed themselves tremendously. The days turned into weeks and the weeks into months. They had originally planned to spend two months with their hosts, but were soon persuaded to stay a month longer. Benjamin got busy and changed their travel plans to correspond.

After nine weeks at the Ostrovsky palace, Benjamin came into his and Edward's room moving at a slow pace. Edward, who was writing a letter at the desk, looked up as Benjamin stood swaying near the door. Edward was instantly alarmed and jumped up and ran to his love.

"What is wrong, are you ill?"

"I'm burning up, Edward. I don't know what is wrong. I haven't felt well all day. Now, I feel so very tired, I can hardly stand."

With that statement, Benjamin slowly began to topple over. Edward caught him under his arms and pulled him over the the bed. Laying Benjamin gently on the bed, he then ran through their connecting drawing room to find Diana. She was also busy with duchy correspondence and sitting at the desk. When she saw the alarm on Edward's face, she rushed into the room where Benjamin was lying on the bed.

"What's happened, Edward? Has he been hurt or is he ill?, she asked quickly.

"He said he wasn't feeling well. He's burning up with fever and he just fainted. Help me get him undressed and into the bed properly. We need to get a doctor as quickly as possible."

"Let me call Barbara and then I will help you get him in bed."

Diana ran into her room where Barbara was seeing to the pressing of her dress for the evening.

"Barbara, quickly, go and find the countess and have her send someone for a doctor. Benjamin is very ill."

"Yes, my lady, right away.", Barbara said as she rushed from the room.

Diana flew back to the other bedroom and helped Edward get Benjamin undressed, down to his small clothes and under the quilts. He had begun to shiver with chills. Diana ran back to her room and pulled more quilts off her bed to cover Benjamin with. Even with the extra covers, he continued to shiver. He restlessly moved his head from side to side and spoke in a hoarse voice, calling for Edward. Edward sat on the the side of the bed and held Benjamin's hand in his. Diana crawled up on the other side and held his other hand. She and Edward exchanged worried looks.

After what seemed hours, the doctor arrived. Dr. Petrovsky was the personal physician to Ivan and his family. He examined Benjamin and then called Edward and Diana out into the hallway.

The doctor spoke English well, and proceeded to explain to them, "This young man has a case of the influenza. It is running rampant through the city right now. Has he been near the docks or some of the poorer sections of the city?"

"He was at the docks two days ago changing our travel plans. We have decided to stay an extra month in St. Petersburg," explained Edward.

The doctor spoke solemnly, "I was afraid of that. The docks and the surrounding poorer sections of the city have been affected the worst. Many people have died from this disease. I am afraid your friend is very ill. I will do what I can for him, but he seems to have a severe case."

Diana and Edward exchanged frightened looks. Diana quickly moved to Edward and took his hand in hers.

"Doctor, what can we do? Will it help to bathe his face with cold water? Is there no medicine you can give him?", Diana asked.

"I will give you a powder for the fever which should offer him some relief. You will need to give him more when the fever comes back. He should be kept warm and given plenty of fluids, especially weak tea, but without milk. Thin soup would also be helpful, if he can tolerate it. Some of my patients are afflicted with vomiting and loose bowels. We will hope your friend is not one of those, as he will need food to keep up his strength. He is young and appears to be in good condition, so we can hope he will pull through. I must caution you however, that other members of the household should be kept away from him. You should probably let one of the servants take care of him to keep yourselves free of the risk of coming down with this disease."

With those words, the Dr. Petrovsky took a bottle of fever powder from his bag. He gave instructions on how to mix it and left saying he would return later in the day.

"No one will take care of Benjamin except you and I", Edward said vehemently. "There's no way I will abandon him to servants."

"Of course not, Edward. I love Benjamin as well. You and I can take turns staying with him. Barbara is very fond of him as well and I'm sure will be more than willing to help too as well as Bertha. I think he needs to be sponged off with cool water. It will help him feel better and help the fever to drop. If you will give him the fever powder, I will go have Barbara arrange for what we will need to care for him. He will not be alone, no matter what.", Diana said fiercely.

After speaking to Barbara, Diana wrote a note to both Ivan and Countess Ostrovsky explaining that Benjamin was ill. She volunteered to move to a hotel so as not to endanger their family with this disease. She sent Barbara downstairs to deliver the notes while she went back into the sickroom with her arms loaded with more linens, towels, and a basin of cool water.

Edward was sitting on the bed holding Benjamin's hand in his and speaking softly to him. Diana was struck anew by the love Edward and Benjamin shared. Edward was almost manic with worry as she was herself. They had lost so many of their loved ones over the years, it was natural for them both to panic at the first sign of illness. Benjamin was their rock. They both depended on him in so many ways, they felt lost now that he was unable to even talk to them. He was delirious with fever, moving restlessly on the bed.

Diana saw an empty glass beside the bed. She set down the ewer of cool water and wrung out a cloth, beginning to bathe Benjamin's face. She continued to tenderly bathe his face until he became still and slipped into a deep sleep. Edward slid off the bed and began to pace around the room. Diana took his place, placing her small hand in Benjamin's much larger one.

Diana and Edward sat vigil at Benjamin's bedside for hours. Barbara came in with a bowl of chicken broth and they tried to get Benjamin to swallow some of it. He was lucid for a short period and said his throat hurt too badly to swallow. They were able to get some of the broth into him, but not much. He did drink the diluted fever powder, however. It seemed to help, but it didn't last long, usually only about 3 hours.

There was a knock on the drawing room door which Barbara went to answer. Ivan was there with his mother and Edward and Diana went to speak to them. They had come to extend the hospitality of their home for as long as was needed. Their only concern was to get Benjamin well and wouldn't hear of moving him to a hotel.

Edward and Diana thanked them profusely and quickly returned to Benjamin. As the night wore on, Benjamin went through cycles of fever and deep sleep over and over. His breathing became harsh and he began to cough. They were able to get him to take a little more broth. He drank cool water whenever he was lucid with or without the fever powder. He seemed to be constantly thirsty, probably because of the fever. Around two in the morning, Edward insisted that Diana go to bed. He told her he would wake her later and get some sleep himself. Barbara led the weary Diana to her chamber and helped her undress. Although Diana was exhausted, she had a hard time going to sleep. All she could think of was both her Geoffreys, her father and Edward's father. They had lost all four of them in a space of less than 3 years. She had also lost her own mother at the age of ten. Death was horribly familiar to her. She couldn't let herself think that Benjamin would die, but she was very worried about him.

Barbara woke her around ten in the morning. Diana bathed and dressed hurriedly and then went to Benjamin's bedside. Edward was in his usual place, sitting on the side of the bed, holding Benjamin's hand. He raised his head when Diana came in.

"I think he's worse, Di. I gave him the powder over an hour ago and it didn't seem to help this time. I haven't been able to get him to take any more broth either. I don't know what else to do.", Edward said with tears in his eyes and a sob in his throat.

Diana went to him and put her arms around him. "You need to get some rest, Edward. Go into my chamber and lie down. I will take very good care of our dear Benjamin. I will call you if anything changes. Have you eaten anything yourself?"

Edward just shook his head in the negative. "I will have Barbara bring you something. You have to keep your strength up too. I'm going to eat in here after I bathe Benjamin. I think he will be more comfortable if I bathe him and change his clothes. I will try to get him to take some more broth as well."

Edward walked dejectedly from the room after giving Diana a fierce hug. During the long hours of vigil, Edward's thoughts had also turned to their lost loved ones. He honestly didn't know if he would make it back from another death. The death of their baby and the pain of his injuries had almost cost him his own life. If not for Benjamin and Diana, he would not have survived. He knew himself and he knew he wasn't strong. He was a better man today than he had been, but he still didn't have Diana's strength.

After Edward left, Diana had Barbara bring in more water and a clean nightshirt for Benjamin. Between the two of them, they were able to get his soiled nightshirt off. Diana took a soft cloth and washed his entire body with cool water. His skin was a frightening shade of red and was extremely hot to the touch.

Benjamin began to shiver uncontrollably when she was bathing him in the cool water. He pulled away from Diana as much as he could trying to escape the cool water. She had Barbara hold him so she could finish. After they got a fresh nightshirt on him, they changed his linens and covered him up with lots of quilts and blankets.

As Diana was turning to hand the cloth to Barbara, Benjamin spoke in a hoarse voice. "Diana, you're here. Where is Edward?"

"I sent him to get some rest. He was with you all night. Would you like for me to get him?"

"No, let him rest. I think he's going to need it. I believe I'm going to die. I have been dreaming of our dear little Geoffrey. I think he wants me to come with him. He seems to be calling to me." Benjamin said with a glazed look in his eyes.

"Hush, now Benji, you are not going to die. I won't allow it. I need you to stay here with Edward and I. We need you and we love you. We couldn't make it without you," Diana said with tears in her eyes and a catch in her voice.

"I may not be able to, Di. I feel so very weak right now. I don't know how much longer I can hang on. I will try though, for you and for my dear, dear Edward. May I have some water? I am ever so thirsty."

Diana gave Benjamin water with the fever powder in it. She also coaxed him to take some more broth. She could feel him slipping away and felt helpless to stop it. She had never nursed anyone with influenza and didn't know what, if any of her home remedies would help. She had Barbara bring her medicine box and some hot water. She brewed a tea of chamomile, feverfew, gentian and honey. She was able to get Benjamin to drink almost the whole cup. After he finished the tea, he lapsed into a deep sleep.

Dr. Petrovsky had been back late the previous evening and came again around noon. He examined Benjamin and thought he seemed a tad better. Diana told him what she had done for Benjamin that morning, the bath and the tea. The doctor told her to keep doing the same and he would be back in the evening.

The doctor looked exhausted and almost ill himself. The epidemic was growing and many people had died, he told Diana in answer to her questions about his own health. He had neither slept nor ate in almost twenty-four hours. Diana insisted that he sit a few minutes and have some food and a hot drink. Barbara went down to the kitchen and brought him a tray. The doctor thanked Diana for her kindness and felt somewhat better when he left to make his rounds of his influenza patients again.

Late in the afternoon, Edward appeared in the room again. He had slept some, had a bath, and something to eat. He looked at Benjamin with his heart in his eyes. It was obvious to Edward that Benjamin was very ill. He feared for Benjamin's life and for his own sanity should anything happen to the love of his life. He honestly didn't think he could survive the loss of Benjamin, who was not only his lover, but his best friend.

He went to Diana and she put her arms around his waist and lay her head on his chest. She said softly, "We won't stop fighting for him, Edward. You and I will not give up on Benjamin. We will do everything in our power to make him well."

"Yes, Diana, we will do everything we can, but will it be enough? What did the doctor say when he was here earlier?"

"He said Benjamin looked a little better. I had bathed him and given him a medicinal tea. He told me to continue to do that and I have. He has had three cups of the tea along with the fever powder and some more broth. He seems to rest afterwards, but it doesn't last long. His fever comes back up and he gets restless quickly. When he gets restless again, I will bathe him again and change his linens. I want to keep him as comfortable as I can."

"Thank you, Di. Thank you for taking such good care of my Benji and for loving him like you do. Not many wives or many women period, would have been as understanding as you have been all these years. You have made both our lives so much easier and so very much better." Edward said with such sadness that Diana was almost brought to tears.

"Oh, Edward. I love you both so much. I can't stand to think….No, I wont even say the words. I won't think that way either. Benjamin will get well. We must think positively, we cannot give up hope." she said with a determined lift of her small chin.

Benjamin began to move restlessly on the bed. Barbara rushed to get more supplies while Edward and Diana started removing his nightshirt. It was easier with Edward's help and they soon had him bathed in cool water, into clean clothes, and his linens changed.

Diana gave him some more tea and broth. She put the fever powder into the tea this time, as Benjamin had such difficulty swallowing. He was lucid for almost half an hour when they were done.

Edward sat on one side of the bed and Diana on the other holding Benjamin's hands. He looked at both of them and said, "I don't want to leave the two of you, but I may not have a choice. I can feel my life slipping away. Please remember that I love both of you so very much. You have both made me so happy over the past years. I had never known that kind of joy and I thank you both for it."

Edward started to cry, then looked at Diana and saw tears running down her beautiful face. He got a tight grip on his emotions and said, "Come on now, old man. What way is that to talk? We can't make it without you, so you must try hard to stay with us. We both love you so much, we cannot think of life without you."

Diana added, "Benjamin, you and Edward are the brothers I never had. I love you both dearly and cannot imagine my life without either of you. You must try very hard to get better."

Benjamin smiled a sad little smile and said, "If love alone could make me well, I would soon be up and around."

Diana and Edward exchanged a sad look. They could tell that Benjamin had little strength left. They encouraged him to rest and he slowly closed his beautiful brown eyes, still with the sad little smile on his face. He was soon sleeping deeply again.

All throughout that evening and night Diana and Edward sat beside their beloved Benjamin. They tried to rouse him several times to give him medicine, but had no luck. Close to dawn, Benjamin took a long shuddering breath and died.

Diana felt as if her heart had been ripped from her chest. Benjamin had been her rock so many times. Without his love and kindness, she felt she wouldn't have survived the death of her baby and Edward's long recovery from the accident. She truly felt as if a part of her had died as well.

Diana knew however, that what she was feeling, Edward felt a thousand times more. Benjamin had been everything to Edward, friend, lover, and helpmate. Diana knew Benjamin's death would have a far reaching effect on Edward and she dreaded the days to come.

Later that day after they had both slept, eaten and bathed, Edward came to Diana's room. The look on his handsome, but haggard face made Diana's heart hurt. He came to her without speaking and put his arms around her. She wrapped her arms around his waist and gave way to the sobs she had been holding back. They cried in each other's arms for a long time.

Finally, when they had gotten control of themselves, Edward spoke in a low sad voice, "Di, I can't bear to think of my sweet Benji being buried here in the cold ground of Russia. I want to take him home. He should be buried near his family at home. I know we have planned this trip for a long time, but I honestly don't want to go on to the Continent without him. What do you think?"

"Oh, Edward, I don't want to leave him here either. He wouldn't want to stay here, he would want to be buried at home. As for the trip, I have no heart for it now. The trip was for the three of us. Without our Benji, we wouldn't enjoy one minute of it. Let's go home as soon as we can."

Edward was in such bad shape emotionally, that Diana took over the plans for their return trip. She enlisted Ivan's help with the authorities to release Benjamin's body. She made arrangements for a casket to be made, but was having trouble with the idea that Benjamin's body would putrefy during the three weeks it would take to get him home. Ivan suggested a porcelain box to house the casket for the trip. The box could be laid on huge blocks of ice wrapped in burlap and sawdust to help delay decomposition.

When Diana approached Edward with the suggestion, his face turned pale and he hurriedly left the room without saying a word. After that, Diana didn't broach Edward with any details at all. She simply made arrangements and then let him know the date they would be leaving.

They boarded the ship three days after Benjamin's death. Edward had hardly eaten or slept in all that time. Diana was afraid he would start drinking, but she saw no signs of it yet except for the first day. She had only been able to get one cabin on the ship. They were lucky to get a ship as quickly as they had. They were only able to do so because someone had to cancel at the last minute. Barbara and the footmen carried the luggage to the cabin. It was terribly small and only had one double bed. Barbara would sleep on the floor, but the footmen would have to sleep in the hold with the seaman.

Edward took one look at the cabin and turned and went up on deck. Diana followed him leaving Barbara to unpack as well as she could with the limited space.

"Edward, I'm sorry I couldn't get two cabins. I know you want to get Benjamin home as soon as possible so I took the only thing they had left."

"It doesn't matter, Di. Nothing matters any more. All I can think of is the empty days, the months, the years to come without my Benji. I just can't seem to care about anything else." Edward said sorrowfully.

"I know, Edward. I miss him terribly. I keep expecting to see his smiling face or hear his voice. How will we get on without him?" Diana said as she tried to keep the tears from starting again. She felt as if she had done nothing but cry for the past three days. When she looked up, she saw tears running down Edward's face. Diana reached for him and he sobbed in her arms as they stood at the rail watching Russia slowly disappear from view.

The trip back to England was the longest three weeks Diana had ever spent. All she and Edward spoke of was Benjamin. They were both lost without him, but for Edward, he hadn't just lost his best friend, but what amounted to his spouse as well. Though they could have never publicly been wed, in their daily lives, they lived as if they were.

Not only was Benjamin the most important person in Edward's life, he had been invaluable in helping with the duchy business.

Diana had depended on his innate business sense and ready availability for the business matters she couldn't handle because she was a woman. She had no idea what she would do now. She knew Edward was in no shape to handle business affairs, she feared he never would be. When she tried to broach the subject of business on the trip home, Edward would just shake his head no and walk away. The only time he spoke at all was about Benjamin.

Edward had come remarkably far since their marriage almost seven years ago, especially in the political arena, but it had been Benjamin who helped Diana most with duchy business. She was reluctant to bring up that aspect of their lives to Edward again and knew she would have to be patient. However, she knew that when they returned to London after the funeral, there would be mountains of paperwork to be seen to and meetings to be attended. Diana decided to wait until they were back in Mayfair to even bring up the subject again. Edward, and she as well, needed time to grieve.

Chapter 42

The interminable sea voyage finally ended. Diana had been able to send one of the footmen, alone, on a ship in steerage that left two days before the rest of the party. She had instructed him to arrange for accommodations in Edinburgh for an overnight stay.

Diana was very surprised when the ship docked to find Edwin Burroughs waiting for them. The footman she had sent ahead, John, had contracted the influenza aboard ship. He had recovered, but been too ill to manage accommodations. He remembered travelling to Ainsley Glen on several occasions and was able to send word to Edwin.

Edwin had hurried to Edinburgh with the Ainsley carriages and more footmen and grooms. They would not need to rent carriages for the journey to the rail head in England after all. Edwin stepped in and took over for the exhausted Diana. He arranged everything for their trip to the rail head. Edwin offered to go with them to Winchester, but Diana declined.

She did however, take him up on the offer of his best footman, Murray, to accompany them on the trip. Then Diana decided to buy him a fast horse and have him ride ahead and catch the first available train to Winchester to inform Benjamin's family of their arrival. Edwin offered one of the Ainsley horses instead, much to Diana's gratification.

She knew that Edwin was needed more at Ainsley Glen this time of year as the mares were foaling, so she declined his offer to accompany them. After thanking him profusely for all his help, she saw him off to go home on the day they started their journey to the rail head. From the rail head, they would travel by rail to Benjamin's old home for his burial. During all the arrangements, Edward had been so overcome with grief, he was no help at all, but Diana had not expected him to be otherwise. She was just very grateful he wasn't drinking.

Diana had never been to Benjamin's home, but Edward had when they were still at Eton. Since his father had lost their fortune, the family had been obliged to move from the family seat to a much smaller house in Winchester. Edward had never been to that house. Diana had written to Benjamin's mother on the day of his death. She had given her an approximate date that they would arrive, but unexpectedly having been able to obtain passage on a ship just three days afterward, they would be arriving almost a week early. Diana was glad she had Murray to send ahead.

At last, almost a month after leaving St. Petersburg, they arrived in Winchester late in the evening. They were all exhausted and wanted nothing more than to sleep. Murray had made arrangements at the local inn for rooms for all of them as per Diana's instructions. The night they arrived, they had a quick supper of bread, cold meat and tea and went to bed.

The next morning Diana and Edward had breakfast together and spoke about Benjamin's family. Edward was in very poor condition, but he was trying bravely to hold himself together for the sake of Benjamin's family. Later that day Diana and Edward made the short journey to the Jenkins' family home. They were saddened to see the terrible state of the house his family lived in.

Edward knew that Benjamin had been sending money home to his family for years and could not understand why their home was in such disrepair.

They knocked on the door and it was some time before the door was opened by a young woman of about eighteen. From her brown eyes, the shape of her face, and dark hair, Diana could tell she was one of Benjamin's younger sisters. Apparently, she recognized Edward from his previous visit some years before. Her eyes filled with tears and she spoke haltingly, "Please come in, your grace. I am Margaret. My mother is in the parlor. Your footman was here a couple of days ago to let us know you would be arriving soon."

Margaret led them into the shabby parlor. Seated before a very meager fire, an older woman sat hunched in a small wooden rocking chair. Her hair was white and her small, thin body was clothed in an old fashioned black gown with a threadbare shawl around her shoulders.

Upon hearing the parlor door open, she turned her head. When she saw that Margaret was not alone, she rose unsteadily from her chair. She spoke in a soft, whispery voice, "Your Grace, please come in and warm yourself at the fire. You too, Lady Diana. You must be chilled to the bone. Margaret, go make some tea, there's a good girl."

"Please have a seat. I apologize for the chairs, but this is all there is I'm afraid. Now that Benji is gone, I don't know how we will make it. He was so good about sending home money. Without him, I would have been hard pressed to feed the girls all these years."

Edward and Diana sat in the rickety chairs near the fire. Edward said, "I am so very sorry about Benjamin. He was my closest friend. Diana and I loved him very much. We will be lost without him as I am sure you will also be."

"Thank you, your Grace. I know he really enjoyed working for you all these years. He talked of you constantly when he came home. He didn't come often, but when he did, he spoke very kindly of you both."

Diana spoke next, "I loved Benjamin as I would have a brother Mrs. Jenkins. He was so much more than a servant to my husband and I. He was our friend and so much more. It breaks my heart to know he's really gone." Diana's lovely eyes had tears running from them in rivulets. She could barely hold back a sob. Edward reached over and took her hand in his to comfort her.

Mrs. Jenkins was surprised at the depth of grief exhibited by these two very distinguished people. People of the nobility rarely paid much attention to their servants. Or so she had observed since she herself had been a maid in the only great house in the neighborhood after her family's fortunes had come so low.

She knew her master would not grieve for her when she was gone, only her daughters would. Her other son, Rupert, after losing all the family funds, had drunk himself to death recently. He had been a bully and took most of the money her sweet Benji sent home for his drink and his women. She just didn't know how she had gone wrong with Rupert. He was the only one of her five children to act so.

Mrs. Jenkins didn't tell Edward and Diana any of this. She kept her troubles to herself. However, she didn't know what she was going to do about her girls now. Margaret was almost eighteen and had managed to go to school until just recently. She most probably could find a place as a ladies maid, but not near home since there was only one great house and no need for a ladies maid there since the elderly countess had recently died. There was only the old master now and he had been letting people go. Mrs. Jenkins still had her job, but didn't know for how long.

She had two younger daughters, Penelope, who was fourteen, and little Susannah, who was only ten. She had hoped to be able to keep them in school, but since she wouldn't have the money Benji sent, she didn't think she could do so any longer.

There were no public schools in England at that time and although the local schoolmistress didn't charge a lot, it was still more than

Mrs. Jenkins could afford on her maid's wages. Thank goodness the house was paid for. She had insisted that Rupert buy it after he had lost their nice estate over a gambling debt. He had sold off their nice furniture to pay for this poor place, but at least they had a roof over their heads.

Mrs. Jenkins reverie was cut short by the entrance of Margaret carrying the tea tray. Edward rushed to take it from her and set it on the small table by the fireplace. He hesitated to even take tea with the Jenkins' family because of their dire financial circumstances. He felt badly for literally taking food from their mouths, but couldn't think of a graceful way to refuse.

He and Diana exchanged a look. He could tell she was terribly distressed at the conditions they had found Benjamin's family in. Benjamin could not have known or he would have done something about it. He knew Diana would agree with him that they must do something immediately to relieve the terrible poverty of these nice people.

Edward said, "Mrs. Jenkins, I don't mean to pry, but Benjamin said you were doing fairly well when he was here a few months ago. I don't want to embarrass you, but your house obviously needs repairs. I know Benjamin was sending money each month. Have you or your daughters been ill?"

"No, your Grace. We are all well. Yes, Benji sent money every month, but up until his death about six weeks ago, my other son, Rupert took most of the money. I am afraid he had a very bad drinking problem as well as a gambling habit. It finally got the best of him and he died. Since Rupert's death, I have had to pay his gambling debts with the money Benji sent. I paid the last just yesterday. The money I make as a maid at the home of Baron Fitzhugh pays for our food and a few clothes, but not much else. I feel terrible telling you this. I am ever so embarrassed, but I honestly don't know what I'm going to do now. I will have to pay for Benji's burial and if he has any debts, I will also need to settle those."

Diana spoke up, "No, Mrs. Jenkins, you will not be paying for Benjamin's burial and he had no debts. We will take care of all expenses. We have already made arrangements for the cemetery plot and the stone. Our man who came ahead took care of all that days ago. As for you, you will no longer need to work as a maid nor worry about your daughter's having food to eat or a decent place to live. Edward and I will take care of everything. We will settle a yearly income of five thousand pounds on you. We will also pay for the repairs and new furniture for this house and provide your daughters and yourself a new wardrobe. We will establish dowries for all three of your daughters with the local bank. When the time comes for them to be married, we will pay for their weddings. It is the least we can do for our Benji. He would have wanted us to take care of his family just as he has been taking care of us these many years."

Mrs. Jenkins and Margaret were flabbergasted to say the least. Mrs. Jenkins started to cry as did Margaret. Diana came to them both and put her arms around them. "You don't need to worry anymore about anything. Edward and I will make sure you want for nothing." She looked at Edward and saw pride for her in his eyes.

Edward, as usual, was amazed at how quickly Diana had assessed the problem and come up with a solution. The amount of money this generosity would cost was negligible to them, but would allow Mrs. Jenkins and her daughters to live very well indeed. He was so very proud of his Hin. He might not be the husband she needed, but he intended to try to be worthy of her, if that was possible.

Edward and Diana took their leave of the Jenkins' family. On the trip back to their inn, Edward was quiet and did a lot of thinking.

When Benjamin died, Edward's first impulse was to get roaring drunk. After they had taken Benjamin's body away, he had sat in their room with a bottle of brandy in one hand and a glass in the other. He had just poured his first drink when Diana came into the room. One look at her grief stricken face had been enough to make him set down the bottle and glass and rush to take her into his arms. She had sobbed for quite some time in his arms. Neither of them had really had time to grieve because of all the arrangements that had to be made to take Benji home. As Edward held Diana, his own grief gave way and tears flooded down his face. He and Diana clung to each other as they poured out their grief for their wonderful Benjamin.

When, finally, their grief subsided, Edward sat back down in his chair and pulled Diana into his lap. She snuggled against his shoulder and heaved a great sigh.

"What will we do now, Edward? I feel as if a huge part of my heart has broken off and will be gone forever. Benji was so much a part of our lives, I don't know how we will continue without him. Haven't we known enough grief in our lives. We have lost everyone we have ever loved." she said with despair.

"No, Hin, not every one. We still have each other. I may not be a traditional husband and we may not have a traditional marriage, but we do love each other. I would not have survived this long without you. You are my strength, as much as Benjamin was. I was about to get roaring drunk, but instead, I think I will just sit here with you and talk about Benjamin long into the night."

Diana was surprised and very pleased. Eward had matured so much in the years they had been married. It was true, they didn't have a "normal" married relationship, but it wasn't so very different than the marriages of most of the *ton*. Most of those marriages were arranged. After the heir was produced, most couples went their own way. Most of the men had mistresses and the women had lovers. They, in truth, lived very separate lives. Sometimes, they didn't even live together. Many wives were confined to a country residence while their husbands lived in their townhouses in London. They saw each other a few times a year.

At least, she and Edward were great friends and lived together in wonderful harmony. They enjoyed each other's company and could find solace in each other during this tragic time. It was more than most couples of the nobility had. Diana was content and told Edward so.

When Diana and Edward arrived at the inn, they went to their drawing room. "Edward, I hope I didn't overstep with what I promised Mrs. Jenkins. I just couldn't stand to see that poor woman so downtrodden. She and those poor girls deserve better than that." Diana said apprehensively.

"No, Hin, you didn't overstep in the least. You did exactly the right thing. I wish my mind worked as quickly and as well as yours. I would have made the same promises if I had thought of it as quickly as you. You always amaze me with your ability to solve problems so quickly and so well. You are the reason the duchy business is doing so well. Under your guidance, all the estates are in much better condition than they ever were. They are all a lot more profitable than even my father could have made them. The amount of money those promises will cost is nothing for us, but it will mean the world to Benjamin's family. He would also be very proud of you. I know he had no idea that his family was living in such squalor. He would have done something about it if he had known. We are just doing what he would have done had he been here."

Diana was very grateful for Edward's words. She had acted without thinking, but she didn't regret her actions. She could not live with herself if she had left Benjamin's family in the state she had found them. She expected Edward to agree with her, but if he hadn't, she would have taken her own money from Ainsley Glen or her English estate and done it anyway.

When she and Edward had married, by law, any property and monies she had then or would inherit would have gone to him. However, Edward had neither wanted nor needed her money. When her father died, Edward had their solicitors place the deeds and bank accounts in Diana's name only. Edward knew her father would have wished that and he wanted to honor Fergus by doing so.

Also, before his own father died, he had told Edward about the estate he had established for Diana and her child. The baby was gone now, but Diana still owned the estate and all the monies it made. She was a very wealthy woman in her own right, even without any monies she would inherit should she outlive him. She would not be able to keep the entailed properties of the duchy, but Edward had purchased four estates outside the duchy and placed them in Diana's name. He had made sure she would never want for anything as long as she lived.

The next few days were a flurry of activity. The first order of business was Benjamin's burial. The local cleric, who had known Benjamin all his life, gave a beautiful eulogy at the graveside. The stone was placed the next day. Diana had this inscription put on it.

"Here lies Benjamin Albert Jenkins, beloved son, brother, and friend. He was much loved and will be sorely missed. "What is a friend? A single soul dwelling in two bodies." — Aristotle

Edward was very touched by the words he saw upon the stone. He knew Diana could not put the words she really wished to for propriety's sake, but he very much appreciated what she had written. He knew Benjamin would have liked it as well.

Again, their borrowed footman, Murray, was an invaluable help. He helped to locate a local builder who could repair the house. He found suitable furniture to fill it and helped to locate a seamstress for the needed clothing.

Edward and Diana, with Mrs. Jenkins, met with the builder and gave him a list of needed changes and repairs. They went over the entire house. Diana suggested many repairs and changes that Mrs. Jenkins or Edward would not have thought of. She truly wanted the Jenkins family to be comfortable and secure.

After the days spent with the contractor, he promised to have all work completed in a month. Diana had Murray arrange accommodations at the inn where the Jenkins family could stay until all work was completed and their house was again ready to be lived in properly.

While the Jenkins were in residence at the inn, their wardrobes would be made. Diana, along with all the Jenkins ladies, met with the seamstress for consultation on what was needed, what fashion plates to use, and materials to be used. The Jenkins ladies were in awe of the way Diana took charge. She decided they would all need complete wardrobes from the inside out. She ordered seven complete outfits for each of them including hats or bonnets, shoes and gloves. Also several chemises, corsets, nightgowns, and petticoats. She requested hair ribbons for the younger girls to match each of their ensembles. She ordered shirtwaists and skirts for every day, pretty dresses for church or social engagements, and a travelling costume for all of them.

Mrs. Jenkins started to protest the latter, but Diana assured her they would be needing them to come to London to visit with she and Edward. She fully intended not to lose contact with Benjamin's family. She owed him that for all the years of his loving care of she and Edward.

Finally the day came when all plans were made and all expenses covered. It was time for Edward and Diana to go home. There was much duchy business that needed seeing to. They had arranged to be gone three months when they thought they were going to the Continent, but that time was soon coming to an end.

Having left their borrowed footman, Murray, behind to see that all was done to their specifications, Diana and Edward again climbed into a train car and began their journey back to London. After three days of hard travel, they finally arrived in London. They sent one of the footman by hackney cab to bring the carriages to the the station to pick them and the other servants up. When the carriages arrived at the Mayfair house, they were greeted by Forbes and the other servants at the door.

After bathing and changing their clothes, they had agreed to meet in the library to discuss duchy business that could no longer be delayed. Diana was very worried about Edward. Yes, he had grieved some for Benjamin, but he had been very quiet for most of their journey home from Russia as well as the trip to the burial and the return home. She feared he would start to drink at any time. She was astounded that it had been almost six weeks since Benjamin's death and he had not succumbed to the temptation to drink. On every other tragic occasion in their lives, the bottle had been his way to cope.

Diana arrived in the library first and sat behind the desk to start on the very large pile of correspondence. Soon the library door opened and Edward entered. She looked up and was struck by the way Edward had aged since they left for their trip to Russia. He was only twenty-eight, but looked years older. She hadn't really noticed until today. The sun was streaming into the library through its many windows and the bright light highlighted the new lines in his face and his loss of weight. He looked tired and haggard.

Since Diana had looked in a mirror when dressing, she knew she also looked much older and very tired. She had recently had her twenty-third birthday. However, she had faced so much tragedy since she was only ten, it was no wonder she looked much more mature than her years.

"Diana, we need to talk," Edward said with a deep sigh. He walked over and sat in one of the chairs facing the desk.

"Yes, Edward. I suppose we do. I was just opening up some of the correspondence from our men of business and the solicitors. There are some problems that may require us to travel to some of the estates very soon. Some things must be handled by us personally."

"Fine, we can do that. That is somewhat related to what I think we need to talk about right now. I have been doing a lot of thinking. Since Benjamin's death, I have lost my appetite for many things, not just food. I don't want to lead the life we lead before. I no longer want to live in London for most of the year. I would rather move to one of the other estates. I don't really care which. Or we can spend a few months at each of them. I really don't care. It's just that every where I look here, I see my Benji. He was such an integral part of our lives in this house, in this city, I just can't face it right now. Maybe in time, but not now." Edward said with finality. He sat with his head in his hands, his shoulders slumped.

Diana came around the desk and put her arm around Edward's shoulders. He leaned his head against her breast and silent tears slipped down his cheeks. She put her other arm around him and he wrapped his arms around her small body. She stood holding him for several minutes.

When he had some control again, she said, "Edward, I think that is a fine idea. I would suggest we travel to the estate with the worst problems first, solve those and then move on. After we have taken care of all the problems, we should visit all the estates including my six. When we have spent some time at each, maybe then we can decide on a permanent place to stay. Or, if we don't find one of them to our taste, we just continue to travel from estate to estate."

"Oh, Hin, thank you so much for being so understanding. I will try to help you as much as I can with the estate business. I don't have the head for business that you or Benji did, but you can bring me up to speed on what I need to know before any meetings I have to attend in your place. It's sad that some men just cannot bring themselves to discuss business with a woman because you are a hundred times better at this sort of thing than I am.", Edward said with a sad laugh.

"Oh, Edward, some men will never have your foresight and understanding where I am concerned. It's better to just humor them and let them think they are superior." Diana said laughing.

It was the first time either of them had laughed in weeks. Maybe it was the beginning of their healing. Diana desperately hoped so. She felt as if she had spent the majority of her short life grieving for the loss of the people she loved.

Chapter 43

She and Edward agreed to take two weeks to make arrangements and get correspondence sent to their men of business about their plans. Edward left their itinerary totally up to Diana. He didn't want to make any decisions right now. He would be happy to just follow wherever she lead him. He knew it wasn't right or fair to put all the load on her small shoulders, but at this point in time he just wasn't capable of doing much else.

Within two weeks, they were ready to go. They decided to travel by carriage since they would need to take so much luggage and so many servants with them. They would need at least four large carriages for the trip. It took about a week to make sure all the carriages were in top shape and another week for the packing.

Quite soon, the day came for their departure. Their first stop would be Bristol Castle. There was trouble with the mines. The price of copper was up, but the length of time it took to get the ore to market was making it difficult to maintain a proper profit level. Diana had been studying the issue before their trip to Russia with Benjamin and their man of business. She had read of a new railway, the Redruth and Chasewater Railway, built by John Taylor.

She thought using the railway to move the ore would be much faster and cheaper. She wrote to Mr. Taylor and arranged a meeting with him at his Wheal Maid mine. She had let him know that she and her husband would both be at the meeting. He had responded with the date he was available, but didn't mention anything about her attendance. She assumed he would not mind meeting with a woman, so she moved forward immediately arranging for their man of business in Cornwall to meet with them as well.

When the travellers arrived at Bristol Castle, they were greeted by Edmonds and Mrs. Smythe. They looked little different from the first time Diana had seen them when she had come to the castle as a just-married, pregnant sixteen year old. She felt a hundred years older now.

Diana had promoted Murray, the footman they had borrowed from Edwin. She had written Edwin and received his permission for Murray to work for she and Edward now. Murray had been very willing to move to London. He had been so very much help with the Winchester trip, they had decided he should be Edward's valet. He was an intelligent young Irishman who had worked at Ainsley Glen for several years and had been trained by Murtaugh.

The day of the meeting with John Taylor dawned bright with sunshine and a cold high wind. It was late spring in Cornwall and the area was beautiful, but it was still quite cold. Diana wore a heavy emerald green velvet dress, high buttoned brown leather boots, and her fur lined cape for the three hour trip to meet with Mr. Taylor. She and Edward had discussed wearing mourning colors for Benjamin, but had decided against it for proprieties sake. He had not been related to them by blood and in the public eye, he was actually their servant, though they had never thought of him as such.

The carriage ride was cold and they were both very glad to arrive at the Wheal Maid mining office. There was smoke coming from the chimney and Diana was longing to stand in front of a roaring fire for a few minutes to warm up. They were welcomed into the office by Mr. Taylor's secretary and led into a meeting room with a large fireplace at one end. After inquiring if they would like tea, the secretary left them. Diana seated herself in front of the fireplace in an upholstered straight chair. Edward remained standing beside her warming his hands. The door opened and their man of business, William Majors, came into the room. He greeted his employers quietly, as was his habit. He was a quiet, taciturn man who took his job quite seriously.

When they had been waiting a very few minutes, the secretary returned with a tea tray, accompanied by Mr. Taylor. John Taylor was a handsome man in his mid forties. His hair was receding, but was still quite curly. He had curls around the sides of his face that gave the impression he was younger than his years. He wasn't nearly as tall as Edward, but had a slim athletic build. He was actually an engineer and had only owned the Consolidated Mining Company since 1815. His railroad was being built now and would open next year.

As he was introduced to the Duke and Duchess of Bristol, he was surprised at their youth and their beauty. The duke was quite imposing. He was tall and slim with curly blond hair and blue eyes. His clothing was quite extraordinary. He affected the Beau Brummel look by wearing a long trouser suit in a bold plaid of grey, green and brown. His linen was white, but his cravat picked up the green hue in the plaid of his suit.

His duchess was a true beauty in every way. She was diminutive in height, but she was exquisitely made. Her clothing was very becoming and well fitting in the latest style, as would be expected of a duchess. Her dark auburn hair, beautiful intelligent green eyes, and heart shaped face were most pleasing to look upon.

Mr. Taylor had not known what to expect when he received a letter from her instead of the duke. He was not used to dealing with a woman where business was concerned, but didn't want to insult the duke in any way by refusing a meeting with her in attendance. He was badly in need of funds to help with the completion of his railroad and hoped to interest the duke in investing.

After some preliminary conversation, the group got down to business. Mr. Taylor was at first surprised at the duchess' grasp of the copper mining business. He soon forgot she was even a woman after she quoted him facts and figures on his railroad and offered a goodly sum as an investment in lieu of shipping the Bristol ore without payment for a period of ten years. The investment would not be paid back in cash per se, but if the railroad netted a profit over and above shipping costs for the Bristol ore, cash dividends would then be paid.

It was a generous offer and was a winning proposition for all involved. Mr. Taylor was most impressed by the duchess' business acumen and sense of fairness. He was, however, much surprised by the lack of participation by the duke. He merely smiled at his beautiful and charming wife when she was finished making her proposal, but added nothing on his own.

The terms were agreed upon. The duchess said her solicitor would send the necessary paperwork and a check on the local bank for the agreed upon amount. All tolled, the entire meeting had taken less than an hour. Mr. Taylor was amazed. Generally, his meetings of this type went on for hours. There was always much discussion and wrangling over money. The duchess had presented a fair and equitable plan and that was that. He wished that all his meetings could be with women from now on. He laughed at himself for his initial reluctance to even have a meeting with the duchess present.

Diana and Edward were soon on their way back to Bristol Castle. As soon as they were in the carriage and moving, Edward turned to Diana laughing. "Well, Hin, you knocked Mr. Taylor off his feet. I could tell at first he was reluctant to have you there, though he was polite. After you made your proposal, his attitude changed immediately. He didn't know what hit him."

"Oh, Edward, I believe you're right. The look on his face when I first spoke up almost made me laugh. I had to try very hard not to. He certainly changed his attitude after I presented my proposal though." Diana said laughing.

"That he did, Hin." Edward said laughing again. Edward had sat on the seat beside her when they entered the carriage. He reached for her and gave her a hug. He kept his arm around her for the rest of the ride helping her to not bounce around quite so much. The roads were horrible after the very rainy winter Cornwall had been through.

The next few weeks were filled with tenant meetings, mine office meetings, and household meetings with Edmonds and Mrs. Smythe. The weather continued to be colder than normal so fires were kept burning in the apartments in use. While they were in residence at the castle, Bertha requested an audience with Diana. She had been acting as an upstairs maid since little Geoffrey's death and Diana hadn't seen her much except in passing. She had made the trip from London to help augment the small regular staff kept at the castle when the family was not in residence.

Diana had her come to the small drawing room for their meeting. Bertha was the same jolly, smiling young woman they had hired here at Bristol Castle almost seven years ago. She had only been seventeen when she was hired, about the same age as Diana.

"Well, Bertha, what can I do for you?" Diana asked kindly.

"Your grace, I would like to ask your permission to marry."

"Why Bertha, that is wonderful. Yes, of course you can marry. You don't need my permission. I am very happy for you. Who is the lucky young man?" Diana asked.

"Well, your grace, that be the problem. His name is Michael Collins and he's a miner here in Cornwall. When we marry, he wants me to stop workin and keep house for him and his Ma. His Pa died in the mining accident that happened about ten years ago. His Ma is getting older now and is sickly, so she can't take care of things like she used to. I would have to leave you, Miss Diana…..oh, sorry, your grace." Bertha said blushing at her blunder.

"Bertha, you have no need to call me your grace. Just Diana would be fine. After all we've been through together, we should be able to use first names with each other. Do you love your young man?"

"Oh yes, I do love him so. We was seein' each other before I come to work for you. We been writin' to each other all these years. Every time we come to Cornwall, we see each other as often as we can. Since we've been back here, I've seen him on every one of my days off."

"Well, then you better marry him and make you both happy. When did you wish to marry, Bertha?" Diana asked with a bright smile.

"We want to marry as soon as we can have the banns read. It takes three times for them to be read in the church and then we can marry the next week. So it will be almost a month from this Sunday since you have agreed to let me go."

"Dear Bertha, you are not a slave here. You can leave at any time. I will regret losing you. You have been a very good servant, but more than that you have been my friend. I would very much like to see you married, if that would be alright. Also, I would consider it a privilege to help you make your dress. I know there is a great quantity of material here at the castle and we do have an excellent seamstress here as well. If you would allow Edward and I to make you this gift."

"Oh, Miss Diana, that would be a dream come true for me. I had thought to try to get a new dress made, but I didn't expect to have it made for me. And surely not by the likes of the Duchess of Bristol. My Ma will be bustin' with pride to see me marry in a fancy dress like the gentry wears."

Diana laughed again. "Oh, Bertha, we will do our best to make sure the dress you wear is indeed fancy. We must meet with the seamstress today and choose a fashion plate. She will need to measure you as well. I will do the embroidery on it myself. I'm not a good seamstress really, but I do love to do the fancy work. Let us go look at the materials in the storeroom and find something to suit your coloring."

Diana took Bertha's arm and led her downstairs to the storeroom off the kitchen. The cook and the scullery maids looked askance to see the duchess and an upstairs maid arm in arm going into the storeroom.

Mrs. Smythe came into the kitchen to speak to the cook about dinner. When she heard the voices in the storeroom, she stuck her head around the door. She was surprised to see Diana and Bertha holding up different bolts of material and holding them near Bertha's face.

Bertha had a rosy complexion, almost black curly hair, and bright cornflower blue eyes. Diana thought one of the darker hues would be better suited to her complexion, but she didn't want the dress to be drab. Finally they found a lovely blue silk almost the color of Bertha's eyes. Bertha was at first shocked that Diana wanted her to have a silk wedding gown, but Diana insisted. She talked her into the gift by telling her she cold use the dress for church and almost any special occasion so it wouldn't be wasted at all. Next the two women went upstairs to the attic sewing room to see the seamstress.

The seamstress took Bertha's measurements and they went over the fashion plates she had on hand. Most of them were years out of date, but Diana knew they couldn't order a new plate from London and complete the dress in the allotted time.

They finally settled on a fitted bodice with short puffy sleeves and a long full skirt by using two separate patterns. There would be a paler blue lace around the neckline and on the bottoms of the sleeves as well as several rows on the bottom of the skirt. Diana would embroider the sleeves and around the bottom of the skirt with tiny pink roses with green leaves and stems between the rows of lace.

Bertha was so excited she could hardly stand still for her measurements. Diana was very happy to have been able to do this small thing for the woman who had been so good to her when her baby died and all the years after. Bertha had loved and cared for little Geoffrey from the day he was born. She had earned a special place in Diana's heart.

When Diana told Edward Bertha was getting married and she was helping with the wedding dress, he suggested they do even more for the young couple. He checked with the mining manager and found that Michael Collins was a hard working young man and had been working for them since he was ten years old. He was now twenty-five and was in line to be made a supervisor soon. Edward asked the mining manager to speed up the promotion if he could and so it was done right away. The promotion meant quite a bit more money each week and less time down the mine shaft.

When the month was up and it was finally Bertha's wedding day, Diana and Barbara went to her mother's house to help her dress for her wedding. The dress they had chosen fit Bertha like a glove. Diana had given her a silk chemise, corset and petticoats to go with the dress. When Bertha was dressed, Barbara went out and brought in a large box. She laid it on the bed and opened it slowly. Inside was a pale blue veil that matched the lace on the dress exactly. Diana had embroidered tiny pink silk roses on it that matched Bertha's dress. Barbara pinned the beautiful creation to Bertha's dark curls and stood her before the little mirror on her mother's wall. She was a vision. Barbara and Diana had tears in their eyes, but Bertha's mother was sobbing. Bertha didn't cry, but the smile on her face was something Diana would never forget.

Diana met Edward outside the house and they walked the short distance to the village church for the wedding. Edward was resplendent in a navy blue trouser suit with a snowy white shirt and a lime green cravat. He now dressed a little more conservatively, but he still had to have his little splashes of color. Diana loved that about him. She had chosen a lemony yellow silk dress with copper lace on the sleeves and hem. Her bonnet was also yellow and had copper leaves on it instead of flowers. They made a striking couple as they walked down the narrow village street to the church.

The ceremony was beautiful to Diana. She hardly remembered her own wedding to Edward. She had been consumed with grief for his brother Geoffrey when they had married. She had been so frightened and felt so alone on that day. She was pregnant and leaving everyone and everything she had ever known behind. She looked back upon that day with wonder. Where had that frightened young girl gone?

She rarely felt frightened these days. She had been very frightened when Benji died because she thought Edward would start to drink again, but it had been almost four months and he was still sober. She missed Benjamin more than she could say, and knew it was even worse for Edward, but he had shown her he was stronger now than he had been when his father died or they lost their little Geoffrey. He had matured into a man she could not only love as a brother, but one she could trust completely. It was a very good feeling.

After the ceremony, there was a party at the home of the newlyweds. Diana was happy to see that Michael's mother seemed to be a sweet woman who liked Bertha and her whole family. Diana had wanted to contribute to the festivities and had cook make all Bertha's favorites. She had also had Edmonds go to the wine cellar and send along some bottles of wine to toast the happy couple.

Diana and Edward did not stay long at the party. Their presence seemed to make some of the villagers a little uncomfortable. They wished the new couple good tidings and made their way down the street to where their carriage awaited. Diana had seen Edward slip

Michael a small purse. When they were riding back to the castle, she couldn't wait to inquire, "How much did you give Michael?" she asked with a smile.

Edward gave a sheepish grin. "It was only twenty pounds. I checked with the mining manager and he said any more would probably make him uncomfortable. It will be enough to give them a nest egg for a rainy day."

"Thank you, Edward. That was very kind of you. I'm glad you did it. I should have thought of it myself."

"Oh, Hin. You did enough. The dress, the veil, the food and the wine. I could see everyone was overwhelmed by your generosity. I don't know what else you could have done to make Bertha's day complete."

"She did look so very happy, didn't she? And she was beautiful in the dress. She positively glowed. I am so very happy for her."

Edward looked at Diana's beautiful smiling face, filled with her happiness for Bertha. He thought of their marriage and it made his heart hurt. He wished he could love his sweet Hin like Michael loved Bertha, but it just wasn't in him. If he could have loved any woman in that way, it would have been her, but he just couldn't feel that way about her. He loved Benjamin still and thought he always would. Yes, he missed the intimacy they had known, but he had no desire to know that intimacy with anyone else now. And he might never want it again. He was too filled with pain right now to even contemplate that part of his life.

Edward and Diana spent the next four months at Bristol Castle. They then moved on to each of their other estates. There were fifteen in all. It took them two and a half years to visit the first fourteen. They saved Ainsley Glen for last.

Chapter 44

They had only been back to Ainsley Glen twice since they had visited little Geoffrey's grave to see his headstone. Each time they had gone, they had spent several hours at the cemetery. Diana's father, the older Geoffrey and their tiny son, Geoffrey were all buried together in Diana's family cemetery near the keep where she had been born and raised. This visit was no different. They arrived at the keep late in the afternoon on Monday, October 24, 1825. It was the day before the anniversary of the elder Geoffrey's death. They had timed their arrival to coincide with the ten year anniversary of his death purposely.

The next morning, accompanied by Edwin Burroughs and his wife, Hannah, they took a carriage to the cemetery. It was just the four of them with a few footmen. Diana had been girding herself for this visit for weeks. She didn't want to break down as she had on her previous visits. She kept telling herself she should be able to control her grief better now.

After all, she was twenty-six years old. She had been married for ten years. She had learned to be content with her life with Edward. They had a wonderful, loving relationship and got along beautifully. She had her work with the duchy business and her own six estates to keep her busy. She still did charitable work when she was in London for the orphans. When she visited her estates she did all she could for her tenants who were will or who had gotten too old to work. She had a full life and she knew it. But the grief was still omnipresent.

As they stood at Geoffrey's grave, Diana stooped down to lay a spray of red roses on his grave. Just at the moment she bent over, a shot was fired from a copse of trees nearby. She heard Edward grunt and suddenly he fell over her knocking her to the ground under him. She could hear him moan and she began to scream hysterically. Diana managed to get out from under Edward and grabbed him holding him against her breast. He had been shot in the head. Blood was gushing from the back of his head, but there was only a small hole in his forehead. Diana was trying to staunch the blood with her dress, but it just kept flowing no matter what she did. She heard Edwin shout and run toward the trees. She didn't want him to go. He might be killed as well. She screamed his name, but he didn't stop. His wife knelt beside her and tried to help her with Edward.

Diana could hear many running feet and much shouting. The footmen who had accompanied them, as well as the driver, were in pursuit of whoever had shot Edward. Diana stopped listening as Edward opened his eyes.

"Edward, oh Edward, don't you leave me too. I need you, Edward. Please, please don't leave me." Diana wailed pitifully.

Edward gave her his old cocky smile and tried to reach up and touch her face. His hand got half way and then dropped. He tried to speak, but wasn't able to form words. In just moments, Edward was dead.

Diana's mourning wails could be heard in the village and many of the villagers came rushing to the cemetery. They were appalled to see their young mistress covered in blood, weeping hysterically over her husband. Diana was not often at Ainsley Glen these days, but she was well loved in the neighborhood and always had been. The villagers rushed to get the priest, Father Andrews, from the church. It was the same priest who presided over little Geoffrey's burial all those years ago. He tried unsuccessfully to get Diana to let go of Edward's body.

Finally, Edwin came back dragging a man with him. He sent one of the footman to fetch the local sheriff. He had two of the other footman take control of the man. They tied him up using some rope one of the villagers ran to get. They all recognized him. He was a local man named Horace Alexander. He was the estate manager for Lord Bruce. No one could imagine why he would want to kill the Duke of Bristol or anyone for that matter.

Once Edwin had disposed of his prisoner, he went to Diana and physically pulled her away from Edward's body. She was completely hysterical by that time and didn't even recognize Edwin. She fought him when he pulled her away, but she was so small she had no chance against a man of Edwin's size. He simply picked her up and carried her to the carriage. By the time he got to the carriage, all the fight had gone out of Diana and she just lay in his arms silently weeping. Hannah got into the carriage and helped him get Diana settled in one of the seats. When Diana realized they weren't taking Edward's body, she began to fight anew.

Edwin held her tightly against him and said soothingly, "Diana dear, I left some men with Edward. He is not alone. I will take you home and come back for him."

"No, no, Edwin. That will not do. That will not do at all. He must come back home with me, now. I cannot leave him. I will not leave him. If he cannot ride in this carriage with us now, then I will stay with him until you return. I will not leave him." Diana screamed and flung open the door of the carriage. She jumped out and ran towards Edward's body. She flung herself down and again picked up his head and put it into her lap. She knew she was hysterical, but she couldn't help it. Every one she had ever loved had been taken from her. She must hold on to Edward for just a few minutes longer. Her sanity depended on it.

When Edwin saw that there was nothing to be done but take Edward back to the keep, he had his men carry his body to the carriage. They lay his body on the floor and then climbed in and moved him to one of the seats. Diana climbed in after him and kneeled on the floor, smoothing Edward's hair from his forehead. Edwin and Hannah squeezed into the other seat and they were off.

Edwin had sent one of the footman ahead to the keep. They were met by Murtaugh, Mrs. Owen and Mrs. Gwen. The women had tears in their eyes. They gathered up Diana and took her inside. She still wouldn't leave Edward. She insisted on helping the other ladies wash and dress Edward's body. She had them dress him in one of his brightest outfits. She knew it would have pleased him to be buried in his usual sartorial splendor. When she had done all she could for him, Diana allowed Barbara to lead her away to bathe and change from her bloody clothes.

While Diana and the ladies were dealing with Edward, Edwin was speaking to the keep carpenter about making a casket. He didn't know if Diana would bury Edward in Scotland or take his body back to England, but he did know they would need a casket in any case. While Edwin was in the barn discussing the casket, his men arrived with Horace Alexander. He had them lock him in the woodshed which was sturdy and had a hasp on the outside of the door.

Soon, the sheriff arrived with the footman that had been sent for him. Edwin showed him into the library. He sent for his wife, Hannah, who was with Diana as the sheriff wanted to speak to all who had been present. Diana came down the stairs with Hannah, her little head held high and her backbone straight. All signs of hysteria were gone, but her eyes were glassy and she held herself with an unnatural stiffness.

After speaking to the three of them, the sheriff requested that Horace Alexander be brought into the library for questioning. He suggested that Diana leave the room, but she adamantly refused.

"I want to be here when you question this man. I must know why he killed my husband. I will not rest until I find out.", she said in a very no nonsense manner.

Hannah left after answering the sheriff's questions, but Edwin stayed to help the sheriff in any way he could. The man that was escorted in by the footmen looked terrible. His shoulders were slumped and his head hung low. He had dark circles under his eyes and his hands trembled uncontrollably.

The sheriff had him seated in a straight chair across from the desk. Edwin had seated the sheriff behind the desk. Diana sat in a chair a short distance away near the fireplace. She was trembling, but her eyes never left Alexander. Edwin and the footmen remained standing near the door just in case the man tried to run. From his appearance, all the fight was gone from him, but Edwin was taking no chances.

"Mr. Alexander, would you tell me why you shot the Duke of Bristol at the cemetery at Ainsley Village this morning?"

"Wasn't supposed to shoot him. Was supposed to shoot her." the man said pointing at Diana. All the men in the room gasped, but Diana made no sound at all. The only response from her was a widening of her eyes.

"And why would you wish to shoot the Duchess of Bristol, Mr. Alexander. Has she harmed you in some way?"

"Not me. I don't even know her at'all. It's me love, me Adelaide, the Lady Bruce, that she harmed. Addie told me to shoot her. She heard from one of her servants that she was coming here to her keep yestiddy. She had me watch her and wait for a chance to shoot her. She wanted the duke for her daughter.

Just like she had me arrange for that other duke fella to die ten years ago, so's her daughter could marry the new duke. But then that didn't work out because he married that woman instead." Alexander said, pointing at Diana.

" So, then she had me shoot at her a couple of years later several days ride from here going towards London, up Warwickshire way, but I missed. I hit the new duke's horse instead. He run off and that poor little bairn died instead. That was no what I intended. You gotta believe me. I watched him be buried from that copse of trees near the church yard. I wouldn't have harmed the bairn no matter what Addie said." Alexander said starting to weep.

It was then that Diana practically flew from the chair she was sitting in. She grabbed Alexander by the back of the coat and shook him like a dog.

"Are you telling me that Lady Bruce had my Geoffrey and my baby killed, you despicable man? Is that what you are saying?", she screamed at him as she shook him over and over with inhuman strength. Edwin ran to Diana and it was all he could do to pull her hands from Alexander.

"And now, you've shot my Edward, you idiotic fool. It should have been me. It should have always been me. Oh my God, oh my God." Diana said collapsing in a heap on the rug sobbing hysterically.

Edwin picked her up and carried her up the stairs to her rooms. Both Mrs. Gwen and Mrs. Owen had heard the commotion and came running behind him. Barbara quickly pulled down the covers on the bed and Edwin lay Diana down tenderly. She immediately turned her face to the wall. Her body shook with her sobs, but she was crying silently now. Somehow that was more terrible. Edwin's heart broke for his little Diana. He stood over her rubbing her back and speaking soothingly to her for some time, but nothing seemed to help.

Finally, Edwin left the room so Barbara and the other ladies could try to get Diana undressed and into the bed properly. The sheriff, Alexander and the footmen were still in the library when he returned.

"Mr. Burroughs, I hardly know what to do. What Lady Bruce has done is horrible, but I'm not sure if I can arrest her. She's a member of the nobility. This fellow I will take to Inverness and lock in their gaol there. He will swing for what he's done, but I will have to talk to the magistrate in Inverness about what to do about Lady Bruce."

Edwin was not surprised. The nobility thought themselves above the law for the most part and common people accepted the situation because they had little recourse against their "betters". But this time, the victim had been a duke of England. A direct relative to the King George IV. Edwin believed she would be made to pay if what Alexander said could be proven.

When Edwin came down for breakfast the next morning, he was surprised to see Diana sitting at the table in the dining room dressed entirely in black. There were no dishes or cutlery in front of her. Her beautiful little face was deathly pale. Even her lips had lost color. The only color in her face were her great green eyes, which were red from crying. There were no tears now. The look on her face was frightening. She looked to be in a rage. Edwin had never seen Diana angry and didn't know how to cope with this new woman in front of him.

"Diana, how are you this morning? Did you sleep at all?"

"No, Edwin. I have not slept. I understand from Mrs. Gwen that you have had a coffin made for Edward. I thank you. We will need to procure several large blocks of ice and a sturdy wagon. We must find a stone or porcelain box to put the casket in to be transported to the rail head. I will take Edward's body back to London as soon as arrangements can be made. With his relationship to the royal family, his funeral will have to be at Westminster Abbey. I do not wish his body to putrefy during the journey, so speed is of the greatest importance. Once the funeral and burial at Bristol Castle is complete, I will return here to seek justice for the loss of every one I have ever loved. That woman, that despicable, scheming woman, will pay, mark my words. She will not get away with this. I will see to it that she never sees another peaceful day if it's the last thing I do" This entire speech was uttered with almost no inflection.

It was if her emotions had died with her husband. Edwin was very worried about Diana. He felt she was barely holding herself together.

"I will go with you, Diana. This is not a journey you should attempt on your own. I know you have your servants, but I think you need a friend with you as well. I can try to ease the way as much as I can for you, if you will permit it."

"Again, thank you Edwin. I would appreciate your help. I have much to do to get the duchy affairs in order when I reach London. Edward's cousin will become the Duke of Bristol now. He is elderly and has no progeny, so he will be the last Duke of Bristol. There are no other surviving male members of Edward's family How sad that such a long distinguished line will end. We have Lady Bruce to thank for that as well." Diana said with the same lack of emotion in her voice that she had when she spoke earlier.

Diana rose and walked to the door. She hadn't eaten nor drunk anything as far as Edwin knew. That was her pattern, as Edwin well knew, when tragedy struck. She would abstain from food or drink until someone made her eat. Edwin knew he would have his hands full trying to deal with her grief, but he could do nothing less. He looked upon Diana as the little sister he never had. He had watched over her since she was born and he would continue to do so as long as he was able. He loved her and always had.

That afternoon, Edwin contacted a local rock quarry to try to obtain a stone container to house Edward's casket. The quarry owner took the dimensions for the casket and had one of his stone masons chisel out a rough stone container large enough. He had it loaded onto a wagon and delivered to Ainsley Glen the next day.

Edwin was able to procure several large blocks of ice which he covered in hay and burlap and put into one of the farm wagons belonging to the keep. The stone container was loaded on top of that and Edward's casket was lowered into the stone container. He had a team of six horses harnessed to the wagon to speed up their progress.

When Edwin returned to the house, he found Diana standing in the hall hugging Mrs. Gwen and Mrs. Owen. Her luggage was piled around her and Barbara and Murray were waiting with her. Edwin saw that his wife had packed his bags as well and was waiting with the others to bid him goodbye. After the goodbyes were said, they all loaded into two carriages and took off for the rail head.

The next few days passed in a rush of activity getting all the people, luggage and the casket moved to the rail head and then to London. Diana hardly spoke the entire time. Edwin and Barbara had to constantly coax her to eat. She would drink tea, but food didn't interest her.

Murray was a godsend to the whole group. He was very capable and seemed to anticipate their needs before they knew what they needed. He was always the one who left the train to procure food and drink at the many stops along the line.

Finally, they arrived in London. Murray left them all standing on the platform while he went to arrange for a wagon and sent a footman to the Mayfair house to have carriages sent for the group.

Before long, a wagon lumbered up to the train platform near the car Edward's casket was riding in. It took ten men to unload the heavy stone container holding the casket. While they rested the container on the edge of the wagon, another wagon came alongside with huge blocks of ice. The ice was loaded first and the stone container set atop it. Diana watched all this with the strangest look on her face. Edwin feared she might become hysterical again, but she did not. There was a representative from Buckingham Palace there to meet the train. She was civil to the man, but that was all. Edwin was very worried about her. She had lost a lot of weight, but the fact that she hardly spoke was the most worrying factor for him.

When they arrived at the Mayfair house, they were greeted by Forbes and the other servants. They were all very distressed by Edward's death. They had all known him since his birth and many had loved him. Of course, they were also concerned for their positions. They knew that Edward was the last of the Westmoreland line. Now a distant cousin would take over the duchy. The servants were not sure if the new duke would reside at the Mayfair house or close it down.

After Diana had bathed and dressed, she called all the servants together in the main hall. "Many of you have worked in this house for many years. I want to assure you that this house will remain open and your positions are not at jeopardy. In the terms of the Duke of Bristol's will, I, as dowager duchess will retain the right to live in this house until my death or until I remarry. Please go about your duties now. I need to meet with Forbes and the cook alone in the library, please."

Diana met with the butler and cook to go over the plans for the guests that would begin arriving at any time. All the cousins, or at least those that were left, would be descending on the Mayfair house in the next few days. Diana had not wanted to inform them of Edward's death until the last possible moment because she wanted some time alone to grieve before she was on display to the cousins and the other members of the nobility. She knew when word got out, there would be a deluge of visitors.

Diana and Edwin had sent footmen to the homes of the cousins who resided in London and mailed notes to the two or three who did not. Diana had also sent notes to their closest friends. Some were in residence in London now, but many were at their country estates as the Season had ended in August.

As was the custom, since Edward was directly related to King George IV, though they were only fourth cousins, his body would lie in state at Westminster Abbey until the funeral could be arranged. Usually, a peer of his stature would be buried in the crypt at Westminster as well, but it wasn't required. Diana was taking Edward to Bristol Castle to lie with his father in the family crypt.

It might take a week to ten days for everyone to arrive that was invited. The funeral would be huge. All the peers of the realm would be included in the invitations. As soon as Diana had notified their solicitors the day of Edward's death, they had informed Buckingham Palace and the wheels had been put into motion. A representative of the king had met their train and taken possession of Edward's body immediately. There was nothing else Diana had to do personally about the funeral now except attend when the date was set. The monarchy would take over now to make sure that all was done correctly according to tradition. It had been the same for Edward's father when he had passed.

Diana might not have to make arrangements for the funeral, but she did need to make arrangements for the trip to Bristol Castle. She dreaded the trip because she knew the cousins would insist on attending. Edward had been so distraught and drinking so heavily,when his father passed, they had not invited the cousins to stay at the Castle except for one night. Diana's father, Fergus MacDonald, had been there to help her with the cousins at that time. Now, she would be alone.

Diana was in the library going over correspondence when Edwin knocked on the door. She called a quick, "Come in." and Edwin came in and sat across from the desk.

"Are you all right?", he asked.

"Yes, I suppose I am for the time being. I have gotten myself under control. The initial shock has passed. I am coming to terms with the situation the best way I know how, by keeping busy. I must get everything in order for Edward's cousin, John Cumberbatch, who is now the Duke of Bristol. I have no idea how a man of his years is going to manage everything that is entailed with running nine estates. I hope he can handle it all."

"Do you suppose he might want you to help him with the duchy business as you have helped Edward all these years?"

"Oh, no, I doubt that very much. Edward's family has frowned on my involvement from the first." Diana said with some asperity. "They don't think a woman should be involved in business in any way. If they knew that it was Benjamin and I who ran everything for almost three years, they would have been fit to be tied. After little Geoffrey's death, when Edward was recovering from the accident…..Well, I guess now we know it wasn't actually an accident, don't we?" Diana shook her head. "Any way, Edward was in no condition to make decisions so I made them all with Benji's help. Honestly, now that Edward is gone, I have no desire to be a part of the duchy business. I have six estates of my own to concern myself with. I'm sure they will keep me very busy in the future."

"Six estates? I didn't know you had six estates of your own. How did that happen?"

"Well, I inherited Ainsley Glen from my father as you know. Also, Edward's father left me a very large estate that wasn't entailed by the Duchy when he passed. Then Edward purchased four more with money his mother left him and had them put into my name. He knew we wouldn't have any other children and his cousin would inherit."

After a very brief pause, she went on. "He didn't want me to be poor. As if I could ever be poor with just the two I inherited from our fathers. But that was Edward. He loved me and wanted to be sure I was very well provided for."

"Yes, I can see he did. I had noticed the last times you were at Ainsley, you both seemed to be pretty happy together. At least until Benjamin died so suddenly. That was very hard on both of you."

"Yes, it was extremely difficult. Both of us loved Benjamin very much." Diana said with a deep sigh.

"Diana, I knew about Edward and Benjamin. I have known since before Geoffrey was killed. I saw them together one night in the barn. I knew what kind of marriage you had. I used to worry about you all the time, but you seemed to make the most of it, and to actually be happy. Therefore I didn't say anything."

Diana was shocked. She had thought only her father had been privy to the true facts of her marriage to Edward. That Edwin had known all these years and never mentioned it astounded her.

"I appreciate your discretion, Edwin. Does your wife know as well?"

"No, Diana, I have told no one. I never even discussed it with your father. I didn't know he was aware of the situation, but I should have guessed. He was very distracted when he came back to the keep after Edward's father died."

"Yes, he was around the three of us quite a bit at that time. He saw some things between Benji and Edward on the day the duke died that horrified him. I think I really shocked him when I let him know I not only knew about their relationship, but accepted it and loved Benjamin myself as a brother. I hope he finally reconciled himself to the situation before he died."

"I believe he did. He seemed at peace when his time came. I believe he was looking forward to seeing his Morna again."

"Yes, I'm sure he was. They had a wonderful loving relationship. I hope they are together and are at peace."

"Diana, I would very much like to accompany you to Bristol Castle for the burial. I understand from what your father told me about the old Duke's burial that the cousins can be a handful. You may need my help."

"Oh, Edwin, you have done so much already.", Diana said with a tired resigned sigh. "But to be truthful, I would welcome your company, not only on the journey, but while we are there for a week or so. I don't plan to stay in Cornwall more than a week. I wish to go directly from there back to Scotland as quickly as possible. I plan to see Lady Bruce prosecuted for her part in the deaths of Geoffrey, my baby and Edward. I have just sent a letter to Buckingham Palace with the details of how Edward died. I am asking for their help in having Lady Bruce arrested for murder."

Edwin was surprised she had acted so quickly. He had thought the tremendous weight of the grief she felt would preclude her dealing with this issue so quickly. He had not realized until now, that Diana had transferred her grief to anger.

The next few days flew past. Diana was often closeted in the library with men of business, solicitors and the like. She had Barbara and some of the upstairs maids busily packing all the new mourning clothes she was having made. She would wear black again for another year. Most of her old mourning clothes were badly out of fashion and had to be replaced. She had an army of seamstresses in the attic sewing all day and into the night to ready everything she would need for an extended stay away from London. Diana had no idea how long it would take for justice to be meted out to Lady Bruce, but she was determined to stay in Scotland until justice was done.

On the fourth day after they had returned from Scotland, Forbes informed her that her friends, Dickey, Bernie and Michael had arrived. She went into the hall and was immediately inundated with hugs and condolences. All three of her friends were now married and had children. They had remained friends with she, Edward and Benjamin over the years, but hadn't seen each other much since Benji died. She and Edward hadn't been in one place very long since that terrible time two years earlier when Benjamin had died of the influenza in Russia.

Diana took the three men into the drawing room and asked Forbes to bring tea for her and wine or whiskey for the gentlemen if they wanted it. She felt somewhat better with her old friends around her. She looked from face to face and recalled old times when they had made her feel much better when she, Edward, and Benjamin had been mourning the loss of little Geoffrey. They had helped

Edward to recover his spirit after the accident for which Diana would always be grateful.

"Diana," Bernie began, "I just don't know what to say. To think Edward was shot to death is just unreal to me. What in the world happened? Was it a highwayman?"

Diana relayed to the three men the tale told to her by Horace Alexander. They were shocked that Lady Bruce was involved.

Michael spoke up, "Has her daughter been waiting all these years to try to trap Edward? I thought a few years ago, I met a Beatrice Bruce who was about to marry the Earl of Canby."

Bernie replied, "She did marry old Canby about seven or eight years ago. He died about six months ago, poor old thing. He was quite old when they married, but she was just a young chit. Married him for his money from what I could tell. She had the coldest eyes I ever saw on a woman. She was beautiful, but only on the outside."

"She was very beautiful. I knew her all my life. The Bruce estate is less than a mile from Ainsley Glen. We were never friends. We had little in common. She was interested in clothes and parties, where I was not. I have no idea if Beatrice even knows what her mother has done, but I wouldn't put it past her to be a part of the whole thing. Bernie is right about her cold eyes. I believe they match her heart." Diana said angrily.

The three men had never seen Diana angry. They were surprised at what she had said. Normally, Diana never said an ill word of anyone. They had always looked to her to take the high road, but apparently, she had changed. Not that any of them could blame her. She had lost almost every one she had loved in her life in the short span of ten years. What woman wouldn't become bitter after such a horrendous turn of events.

The three friends stayed for several hours trying to cheer Diana up. It soon became apparent to them that all she could really think about right now was making Lady Bruce accountable for her actions. They all three promised to do whatever they could to make sure justice was served.

In the following days, Diana received many visitors offering condolences. The cousins arrived en masse on the third day after Diana and Edwin had arrived in London. They made some snide remarks about Scotland being very bad for any of the Westmoreland men that had Diana seething, but she kept her equilibrium and didn't utter the scathing remarks she wanted to. She knew she soon wouldn't have to be around them ever again. That day couldn't come soon enough for her.

Diana found herself becoming more and more bitter as the days dragged on before the funeral. She was very anxious to put all the pomp and circumstance behind her and get back to Scotland to do something about Lady Bruce. She was chomping at the bit, but couldn't hurry the government. After what seemed an eternity, the evening of the funeral arrived. Diana, escorted by Edwin, Michael, Bernie and Dickey, arrived at Westminster Abbey early. One of the ushers escorted them to the front row. Edward's body had been moved from the plain wooden casket they had transported it in from Scotland into an ornately carved casket trimmed in gold filigree. As was the custom, the casket was not open.

The service took four long hours. When it was finally over, Diana and her friends went back to the Mayfair house to receive visitors. It was another four hours before the last of the guests departed. The cousins all made sure to let Diana know they would be there bright and early the next day for the journey to Bristol Castle for the interment.

The trip to Bristol Castle was slower than usual because the wagon carrying the stone container and the casket travelled much slower than the carriages. There were five carriages in the entourage as well as two wagons and multiple outriders. Diana was so very weary by the time they finally arrived at Bristol Castle, she could barely keep her eyes open. Edmonds and Mrs. Smythe had everything prepared for the guests including a late supper. Diana excused herself from supper and simply went to bed.

The next day was dreadfully cold and raining. Diana thought the weather appropriate for the sad occasion. She was burying the very last of the people she loved. Her heart felt as if it had a huge hole directly through the middle of it. She felt as if her soul had leaked out of that hole and nothing would ever bring it back. Diana had the feeling she would never feel anything but sadness and anger again.

After an interminable breakfast with the cousins and her friends, Diana led the way to the crypt under the castle chapel. Edward's body had been carried down when they arrived the previous evening. The priest from the nearby village had arrived earlier to conduct the service. Candles lit the crypt amid the smell of burning incense. Diana felt nauseous from the intense smell of the incense and the closeness of the small space. There were twelve people jammed into a very small area and she was beginning to feel claustrophobic.

Edwin stood by Diana's side and watched her closely. She had been pale when the day started, but now, she was almost completely white. He could see a sheen of sweat on her brow and upper lip. Edwin reached out to steady Diana when he saw her start to waver on her feet. She glanced at him and he saw the intense pain in her eyes as well as fear. Finally the service was over and Edwin was able to lead Diana away to the drawing room. He saw her seated on one of the couches before a roaring fire and tried to keep the cousins away from her by engaging them in conversation.

Michael, Bernie and Dickey also tried to keep them occupied. Diana had told them how they had been acting and the things they had said prior to the services. They knew that Diana was in a very bad place emotionally and didn't need added aggravation.

Edmonds came to Diana to inform her the tenants had come to pay their respects. She went with him to the main hallway to greet them. These were the same people who had been to Bristol Castle for so many happy Christmas celebrations. Some of the children had been small when Diana started the traditions Ian had written to her from America about. Some of them were now working with their fathers and mothers on the farms.

Diana went from family to family and accepted their condolences. She knew their names and asked about new additions to their families or members who weren't present. She asked Forbes to see that refreshments were served to them. When the tenants left, Diana did not return to the drawing room. Instead, she quietly slipped away to the library for a little peace.

While she was sitting behind the desk, the door opened and John Cumberbatch came into the room. Diana raised her head and started to rise.

"Please, Lady, keep your seat. I just wanted a word with you without all those other people around. I know most of them are members of my family, but for the most part, they wear on my nerves."

Diana smiled at the old man. "Please your grace, won't you sit down." she said.

"Your grace. That sounds so foreign to me. I don't think I will ever get used to hearing it. I never expected to be the Duke of Bristol. I never wanted it either. I told Harold he better make sure it never happened when he told me I would be the next in line after Edward and your son when Geoffrey died. I am so dreadfully sorry about your little boy and now about Edward. I was never close to Edward, but I always liked him. He had an independent spirit that I admired. I see that same spirit in you."

"I thank you, your grace. I am probably thought of as too independent by most, but it is the way I was raised and how I have lived my life. I do not believe I could ever be otherwise."

"Nor should you be. It was obvious that Harold and Edward both admired you and respected your opinions very much. Just before he died, Harold told me that you were the driving force that kept the duchy running smoothly while he was so ill."

"Did he now? I'm a little surprised. I knew you had visited him not long before he died, but had no idea he mentioned that. I was just trying to take some of the load off Edward. He was having a very hard time dealing with his father's imminent death. Edward's secretary Benjamin was also a tremendous help during that time. And now he is gone as well these last 2 years."

"You have known much sadness in your very short life. I believe you are only six and twenty, if I remember correctly. That is terribly young to have lost so many people you cared for."

"I may be young in years, but I feel terribly old right now. Being an only child with only a few cousins as family, I am now alone in the world except for my friends. Honestly, I know not what to do." Diana said sadly.

She looked at the new Duke of Bristol with unshed tears in her beautiful green eyes. He thought he had never seen anything more touching than this beautiful young woman who was in such intense pain. She was very strong though. He could tell she would come back from this tragedy as well.

"Well, my Lady, what I wished to discuss with you is what can be done to punish those involved in Edward's murder. I have been informed, not only by your letter, but also by old friends I have in rather high places in the government, that Lady Bruce was very much involved in the plots to kill you. She must be brought to justice immediately."

"Yes, I concur. I plan to leave here in just a few days for Scotland to that end. I have written a letter to King George as well as letters to several members of parliament. So far, I have had no responses, but I understand the wheels of government move slowly. However, I do not intend to sit idly by and wait for these fine gentlemen to act. I plan to insist that the magistrate in Inverness arrest Lady Bruce immediately."

The new duke was impressed by the determination in Diana's voice. He could see the rage in her eyes when she mentioned Lady Bruce. That confounded woman had been the source of almost all her grief. The duke didn't believe she would rest until she saw justice served.

In the next days, Diana noticed a difference in the way the female cousins treated her. She thought she had the new duke to thank for their change of attitude. He obviously had spoken to them. The week finally passed and Diana was able to see all the cousins off in carriages for their journeys home. The new duke was the last to leave. Over the last days, he had asked for Diana's assistance with the duchy business at least for a few months until he could get a handle on everything that was required of him. Diana reluctantly agreed, but again let him know she would only be available by mail or messenger until her business in Scotland was settled.

The next day dawned cold and rainy, but Diana, Edwin, Barbara, and Murray climbed into cold carriages for the beginning of the trip to Ainsley Glen. They had several footmen with them riding horses and on the carriages as well, for protection.

The trip took ten days with the party travelling as quickly as they could. They traded horses every night where they could to increase their speed. Diana was in a terrible rush to obtain justice for her loved ones. Edwin didn't object to the rush. He was anxious to see his wife, Hannah, and their little son. There was also much he needed to deal with as Laird. He had been gone for almost a month now.

Chapter 45

After a long cold ride, they arrived at Ainsley Glen late in the afternoon. As soon as the carriages began to pull into the drive in front of the courtyard, the door opened and Hannah and Murtaugh, along with Mrs. Owen and Mrs. Gwen came out the door. The ladies engulfed Diana in hugs and swept her off to her rooms for a bath and a change of clothes.

Diana was very glad for the journey to end. She was still somewhat in a state of shock from Edward's death. She had not had the time to properly grieve. The formality of the funeral, being inundated by visits from the cousins and member of the nobility, and the rigors of the burial at Bristol Castle had consumed her time and energy since Edward was killed.

The journey to Scotland had given her too much time to think. She went over and over the events in the past. She seemed unable to come to terms with the thought that she had not discerned Lady Bruce's animosity towards her. She did remember the looks she had noticed at the dinner table the night she and Geoffrey had become engaged. She had been so in love, though, she had not given it much thought. She had never been close to the Bruce family. Diana saw them only infrequently at a few social occasions. She had never honestly had a real conversation with the woman.

Diana could not fathom how the woman felt she had harmed her. She did remember Edward's passing flirtation with Beatrice, but she had never thought it was serious. As a matter of fact, she and Edward had never even discussed the Bruce family in any context. Diana was totally mystified by Lady Bruce's actions. She very much wanted to speak to her. There were questions only she could answer.

Edwin was still very worried about Diana. She had resumed eating and drinking somewhat more, but she still had not gained back much of the weight she had lost in the first few days after Edward's death. He hoped being back at Ainsley Glen might help her find some peace of mind. He knew she had been happy there at one time when she was young. Edwin was hoping she could at least find some peace in her old home.

That night at dinner, Diana was very quiet. Hannah and Edwin exchanged glances several times when Diana didn't answer a question that was put to her. Finally, she seemed to realize that Hannah had asked her the same question twice.

"I am so very sorry, Hannah. I can't seem to concentrate on anything this evening. I am weary from our journey. I believe I will retire now if you will both excuse me."

Diana rose from the table after barely eating anything and made her way upstairs to her chamber. Barbara was waiting for her and helped her get ready for bed. Barbara was also very worried about her old friend. She knew how strong Diana was, but she just didn't know if this last tragedy had finally sapped that immense strength.

Diana certainly didn't seem to be recovering her equilibrium very quickly. It was true that after little Geoffrey was killed, Diana had been much worse, at the beginning. However, when she finally overcame the worst of her grief, she had Edward's healing to concentrate on. That had seemed to help her overcome her depression because she had someone depending on her. Diana needed to be needed more than anything.

This time, other than her desire to see Lady Bruce brought to justice, Diana had no one to concentrate her love and energies on. That was the most worrying problem to Barbara, the fact that Diana literally had no one left that she loved.

Chapter 46

The very next day, with very little rest, Diana travelled with Edwin and Hannah to Inverness to see the local magistrate concerning Lady Bruce. Horace Alexander was still in the gaol there. He had confessed and was only waiting for a judge to pronounce sentence on him. He knew he would hang for his crimes, but did not seem to care. Edwin had sent a very trusted footman to keep watch. He was curious if Lady Bruce would visit the prisoner or inquire as to his well being.

Before visiting the magistrate, Edwin left the ladies at the inn they would be staying in. He went to check with his footman. There was literally nothing to report. No one had visited the prisoner and there had been no inquiries about him according to the gaoler. Edwin went back to the inn feeling less than hopeful they would be able to incriminate Lady Bruce. The testimony of a confessed murderer would probably not go far in trying to convince the magistrate of her guilt. Lord Bruce was quite important in the Scottish government after all and had appointed this particular magistrate.

When Edwin told Diana what the footman had said, she was not really surprised. In her mind, if Lady Bruce was cold hearted enough to have someone killed so her daughter could nab a titled husband, she would not spare any thought to the man she had used for her purposes.

Diana and Edwin proceeded to the magistrate's office immediately. At first, they were told by the man's secretary that he could not see them at all. After Edwin reiterated that Diana was the Duchess of Bristol, the man agreed to make an appointment for them for two days hence. Diana was seething when they left the office.

"That man will not do anything. I can see already that Lord Bruce has him in his pocket. I will meet with him, but I feel it is pointless. I need to contact my cousin Robert who is now the Earl. He has connections in Edinburgh. We may have to go there to get anything done." Diana said with disdain.

Edwin agreed and they went back to the inn. They decided to leave the next morning for their trip to the MacDonald estate. It was only ten miles from Inverness, so they made the trip in a couple of hours on horseback. Robert was very cordial when they arrived unannounced. He had received Diana's letter about Edward's death and the circumstances. He agreed with Diana that the local magistrate would do little or nothing. He knew the man and was aware of his close relationship to Lord Bruce. Robert also apprised them of what was being said in the neighborhood concerning the situation.

"I have heard several things from my tenants, my servants and my neighbors whom I questioned after receiving your letter. It is said that the affair between Lady Bruce and Alexander has been going on for years. Lord Bruce is said to have known and been uninterested. Apparently he has a mistress in Edinburgh he has had for years. Lady Bruce at first tried to hide the affair, but in recent years, has been seen in public with the man on several occasions. They have also taken trips together through the years, mostly without a chaperon of any kind." Robert said with disgust.

"Well, proving they had an affair could help, but proving Lady Bruce was the instigator in the attacks may take a lot more proof." Edwin stated.

Diana spoke up. "I, for one, want to meet with Alexander. We need some concrete proof. A witness, or some type of correspondence between the two, something tangible that cannot be denied."

Edwin and Robert agreed. Robert promised to contact his friends in Edinburgh quickly. He had planned to go there on business in a couple of weeks anyway, but would leave the next day instead. For his cousin Diana, he would just make his trip a little earlier than originally planned.

Edwin, Hannah and Diana returned to Inverness to await their meeting with the magistrate. At the appointed time, Diana and Edwin were escorted into the magistrate's office by the secretary they had seen before.

The magistrate, Ian Fletcher, was a short, stout man with a balding head and a pompous air. He seemed defensive almost immediately. When Diana requested a meeting with Alexander, he declined her request. When she pressed the issue, at first he stubbornly refused.

When Diana told him she was headed to Edinburgh next and that her cousin Earl MacDonald had left yesterday for Edinburgh to investigate this situation, he changed his mind. Diana and Edwin quickly surmised the little man feared for his position. After all, magistrates were appointed by the local nobility, so their loyalty lay with them alone. However, they could be removed by the central government in Edinburgh for misconduct.

The magistrate called his secretary and had him escort Diana and Edwin to the gaol which was just next door. The gaol was a two story brick building with an office downstairs and the actual cells on the second floor. When Diana and Edwin arrived on the second floor, they were led to a small cell at the end of a long hallway.

Most of the cells were crowded and the inmates were a noisy, rowdy bunch. Diana blushed at some of the language issuing from the dank smelling cells. There were no bars on the cells, the walls and doors were solid with a small window with no glass in the middle of the door. When the inmates heard steps they jostled each other for a place to see who was going down the hall. When they realized it was a woman, their comments became even worse. The gaoler yelled at them and threatened to cut off their rations if they didn't shut up.

His admonishments meant little to the miscreants. Finally, Diana and Edwin reached their destination. The gaoler opened the door. Diana was shocked at Horace Alexander's appearance. The man was filthy and looked malnourished. He had been beaten at some time in the recent past. He had a black eye, a swollen and split lip, and abrasions on his face and arms. He sat on his filthy cot with his head hanging low and his hands dangling between his knees.

Edwin looked at the gaoler, "What happened to him?"

"Some of the other prisoners didn't take kindly to him lording it over them with all his talk about how Lady Bruce was going to come get him out of here any day.", said the tall, skinny and very dirty gaoler with a nasty laugh. "That's why he's here by hisself. If we didn't move him, he'd probably be dead by now."

Edwin looked at the gaoler with disgust. "Could you bring a chair for the Duchess of Bristol, please? She can hardly sit on that disgusting cot and we may be here for some time.", Edwin asked.

"I guess I could get 'er a chair from downstairs, fer a price, that is."

Edwin reached in his pocket and flipped the man a coin. Edwin's disgust with the man was palpable. Diana felt the same, but their clear disdain didn't seem to register with the uncouth man.

During this exchange, Alexander hadn't even looked up. Finally when a chair was brought and Diana was seated, Edwin spoke again. "Mr. Alexander, her grace and I would like to ask you some questions. Would you be willing to speak to us?"

Alexander raised his head and looked at them as if he had only just realized someone was in the cell with him. "I s'pose so.", was all he said.

Diana could hardly contain herself. She had feared she would want to kill this terrible little man who had wreaked such havoc in her life, but now that she saw him, she just wanted to get what information she could and get out of this terrible place.

Diana said, "Mr. Alexander, it is obvious that Lady Bruce has decided to leave you to face the murder charges alone. We have been told she completely denies any knowledge of the murders, nor does she take responsibility for having told you to commit these acts. What say you to that?"

"Why else would I have done it then? What good would it have done me to kill ye, my Lady? I don't even know ye. I know nothing of ye except what Addie told me. It was all her idea, everything that happened."

Edwin broke in., "Do you have any proof of that Mr. Alexander? Was there anyone else who witnessed her tell you to commit these acts? Is there anything in writing with mention of what she planned for her grace?"

At the mention of something in writing a look of fear came over Alexander's face. He spoke quickly, "No witnesses except maybe one of the other servants at the Bruce estate. Maybe her ladies maid. She was in and out all the time when Addie and me was together. Her name is Lydia, but I don't know that she would talk.

  Addie had me kill the other man I hired to kill the first young man. Him or his man shot one of 'em and he died the next day. The other one, I hit over the head and pushed into the Thames in London after she told me not to leave any witnesses."

Edwin had noticed the quick look of fear on the man's face. He said, "Alright, Mr. Alexander, we will try to speak to this Lydia. What about any written instructions? Did you ever receive any correspondence from Lady Bruce?"

Alexander didn't speak, but sat with his head down and his arms dangling between his knees. Diana could stand it no longer. She jumped to her feet and spoke forcefully to Alexander. "If you have something, you have to tell us! That horrid woman is going to let you hang without so much as a word. She will get off completely free for the murder of Geoffrey, my baby, and Edward. I cannot countenance that. You must help us, please." Diana begged with tears beginning to flow down her cheeks.

Alexander looked up at the beautiful young woman with sadness. He truly hadn't meant to kill her bairn. The deaths of the four men bothered him, but the death of the bairn had given him nightmares for years. Many nights he awoke after nightmares of how the bairn's face looked when the horse bolted and started to run through the woods at breakneck speed. The small boy had been terrified. Alexander started to shake as he saw that scene again in his mind's eye.

"You gotta believe me, I never meant to hurt yer bairn. My horse moved about the time I took me shot and the bullet went astray. I would never harm a bairn on purpose, ye gotta believe me. I dream about that little boy of yers and have for years. For that, I'm truly sorry."

"Well, if you are sorry, then help us!", Diana said with anguish in her voice.

After a few moments of silence, with his head hanging down again, Alexander finally looked up and spoke. "Addie had to go to Edinburgh sometimes with the laird. She would write me letters. She told me to burn 'em, but I just couldn't. I had never had letters in me life until then. I just couldn't burn Addie's words. They meant so much to me. I love her so much, ye see. I've never loved anyone the way I love that woman." Alexander said with tears in his eyes.

Edwin spoke quickly, "Where are the letters, Mr. Alexander?"

"I carried them with me all the time. I didn't dare leave them at my little house on the estate. They were in my saddlebags on the horse I rode to the cemetery. I don't know what happened to the horse after I was caught. Mayhap the sheriff took it. I just don't know. The letters be tied up in a packet with a bit of red ribbon I stole from Addie's dressing table."

Diana looked at Edwin urgently. "What happened to the horse, Edwin? Did the sheriff take it?"

"No, he didn't. Since he came in a carriage, he didn't want to lead it all the way back to Inverness. He left it at Ainsley Glen. He was supposed to send someone to pick it up, but as far as I know, he never did. He probably forgot about it. It was there three days ago when we left to come here."

Diana started towards the door calling for the gaoler. Edwin looked at Alexander and said with a threatening tone, "Mr. Alexander, it would be in your best interests not to tell anyone else about Lydia or about the letters. Do you understand me?"

Alexander bowed his head again looking at his dangling hands. He just shook his head affirmatively. The gaoler came to open the door and Edwin and Diana rushed down the stairs and out of the building. They hurried to the inn to collect Hannah and headed back to Ainsley Glen as quickly as they could go.

Chapter 47

When they arrived at the keep, Edwin jumped down from the carriage first. He helped Diana and Hannah down and they all rushed to the barn. The new stable master was just coming out the door when they arrived.

"Burns, is that horse that Alexander was riding still in the paddock?"

"Why yes, laird. He's in the same spot as he has been.", the man said wonderingly.

"Where is the saddle and tack that was on him?" Diana asked breathlessly.

"Why, your grace, it's in the barn in the tack room. Do you...." he started to say as all three of them rushed past him into the barn.

Burns wondered what all the rush was about. The saddle wasn't going anywhere.

Edwin opened the door to the tack room and rushed inside. There were several saddles in there, but he knew all of them except one. He immediately went to that saddle and untied the saddle bags. He reached inside and found a small packet of letters tied with a faded red ribbon wrapped in a white shirt.

He looked up at Diana. Her face was unreadable, but her eyes glowed with a strange light. Edwin was not sure what she was thinking, but then a grim smile spread across her face.

"Edwin, we must read these letters right away. The evidence must be substantial for us to have Lady Bruce arrested.", Diana said with a fierce tone. "I also want to find the maid, Lydia. We need her testimony as well. Do you think Mrs. Gwen might know of her? I know she knows most of the servants in the neighborhood.", Diana said with asperity.

"She might, Diana. Let us go into the library and read these letters. I will have my father bring Mrs. Gwen to us there."

All three of them hurried to the house. They were met at the door by Murtaugh and he was dispatched to fetch Mrs. Gwen. When they reached the library they found there were nine letters in all. Edwin, Hannah and Diana each took three letters and started to read.

Diana was shocked at the explicit language used by Lady Bruce in the letter to her husband's estate manager. It was obvious they had a very intimate relationship and that it had been continuing for several years. The first of the letters Diana read was dated over ten years ago and it pertained to Geoffrey. It was dated about a month after his death.

In the letter, Lady Bruce praised Alexander for his efficiency in handling the arrangements for Geoffrey to be killed and also for disposing of the only witness, the other brigand who had actually done the killing. Diana could see why Lady Bruce wanted this letter destroyed. She was almost gleeful in the letter. Apparently, she had not heard that Edward had already married Diana when she wrote the letter. She made reference in the letter to what a wonderful life Beatrice would have being married to the Duke of Bristol.

The letter made Diana nauseous. When she finished reading it, she sat back in the chair and put her hand to her head. Edwin noticed her expression and jumped to his feet. "Diana are you all right? Are you ill?"

"This letter, it's so disgusting, it's making my gorge rise. Lady Bruce is insane. She needs to be locked up forever. I don't believe she's totally human." Diana said in a very shaky voice.

"Is there proof in the letter?" Hannah inquired.

"Oh, yes. There is proof, at least where my poor Geoffrey's murder is concerned. I have to assume, if she was this direct about his death, she may have been just as direct about the other crimes she had Alexander commit."

They read the rest of the letters and found four in total that referenced the crimes. One berated Alexander for missing Diana when he hit Edward's horse instead. She was vicious in her condemnation of Alexander. She even went so far as to call him a bumbling fool. She showed absolutely no remorse for little Geoffrey's death. In fact, she gloated about the pain she had caused Diana when her baby died and her husband was badly hurt.

Just as they were finished with the last letter, Mrs. Gwen knocked on the door. When asked about Lydia, she responded that she knew her well. Lydia's mother, Gladys Glynn, had once worked at Ainsley Glen several years ago. When she got too crippled with arthritis to work anymore, Diana's father had pensioned her off. She lived in the village with one of her other children. Lydia no longer worked at the Bruce estate, they were told. She had married one of the local men, who actually worked on an Ainsley farm, and lived in the village as well, very near her mother.

Diana couldn't believe their luck. She wanted to leave for the village right away, but Edwin demurred. They had travelled all day and it was late. He suggested they have dinner and rest, going to the village in the morning. Diana agreed although she could hardly contain her impatience to speak to Lydia.

Chapter 48

The next morning dawned very cold, but it was at least clear. Hannah opted to stay at home, since she had been away from her son for three days. So only Edwin and Diana travelled the short distance to the village. They decided to ride rather than take a carriage even though it was cold. That was Diana's suggestion because it was so much faster to go horseback. She had hardly slept for fear that something would happen before they obtained further proof of Lady Bruce's guilt.

Diana was practically burning with anger. She wanted there to be no question when she and Edwin travelled to Edinburgh to petition the government to arrest Lady Bruce. She hoped to convince Lydia to travel with she and Edwin to testify before the court there.

Diana and Edwin rode up to the door of a small stone cottage much like the others in the village. The yard was neat and there were curtains on the windows. In answer to Edwin's knock, a pretty young woman answered the door holding a small baby in her arms. She looked perplexed to see Edwin and Diana on her tiny porch.

"Can I be helpin' you, sir?" she asked Edwin.

"Are you Lydia who used to be Lady Bruce's maid?" Edwin asked kindly.

"Yes, that's me. I'm no in service anymore though. I have gotten married and aim to stay home with me bairn from now on." Lydia stated, apparently thinking they had come to hire her as a ladies maid.

Diana spoke up, "We're not here about a position, Lydia. We would very much like to ask you some questions about Lady Bruce."

Lydia's face changed immediately. She looked fearful and very nervous. "I don't think I should be talkin' to ye bout her ladyship. She would no like it a bit."

"I'm sure she wouldn't." replied Diana, kindly. "But please, hear me out. We were given your name by Horace Alexander. I'm sure you know who he is. You have probably heard that he shot my husband, the Duke of Bristol about a month ago in the cemetery here."

"Aye, I did hear that. Me husband was down to the cemetery right after it happened and he told me bout it." Lydia said with much trepidation. "I don't know nuthin about that though. I been gone from Lady Bruce's for over a year now. Maybe ye better go. I don't know nuthin."

Diana tried again. "Lydia, Mr. Alexander has confessed to killing my husband. He also confessed to killing my husband's brother over ten years ago and instigating the accident that killed my baby and terribly injured my husband some two years later. He says Lady Bruce told him to kill Geoffrey and then to kill me two years later. He bungled it and shot my husband's horse instead causing my son to be flung off and killed and my husband to be maimed. The shot that killed my husband last month was also meant for me."

"Oh, your grace, I be that sorry about yer bairn and them others, I am. I just don't know what I can do for ye."

Lydia started to turn away and close the door. Diana stuck her hand out and placed it on the young woman's arm.

"Please, won't you speak with us. Can we please come inside and talk to you? This is very important. We have proof of Lady Bruce's involvement, but I'm not sure it will be enough to have her arrested. We need further proof. If you could just take a few minutes to speak to us….." Diana had to give up as Lydia quickly turned away and slammed the door. They could hear her crying on the other side of the door.

Edwin touched Diana's arm. "We should leave, Diana. She obviously knows something but she is entirely too afraid to speak to us. She may have been threatened. Let us go. Maybe we can speak to her mother next. Perhaps she can persuade Lydia to speak to us."

Diana hated to give up and leave, but there was not much point in lingering on the small porch in the cold. Edwin assisted Diana to mount her horse and they rode a few doors down to another small stone cottage. Their knock was answered by an older version of Lydia.

"Laird Burroughs, Lady Diana, have you come to see me husband? He's already in the fields this day."

Edwin smiled at the young woman and shook his head. "No, Jenny, we don't need to speak to Donald. It's your mother we would like to talk to. Is she up for having visitors, do you think?"

"Aye, she would love to have some visitors. Since she can't work, she gets mighty bored just sitting around here. She helps here in the house and with the bairns, but she complains she don't have enough to do." Jenny said laughing and opening the door for them to enter. "Please come on in. She's here sitting by the fire rocking me youngest."

Diana and Edwin entered the small cottage. There was no hall or entryway, the door opened directly into the small common room. It was a combination sitting room, dining room, and kitchen. An elderly woman sat in a rocking chair in front of a sprightly fire. The room was warm and smelled of baking. After making sure they both had seats near her mother, Jenny went back to her bread making.

Edwin remembered this lady now. She had been very quiet, but a hard worker. She had worked in the kitchen with Mrs. Owen as a scullery maid for many years. Diana had been too small when she left the keep to remember her. She had been married to one of their footmen. He had died of a fever when their three daughters were quite small. That is when she had gone into service at the keep.

"Gladys, I don't suppose you remember me. I am Edwin Burroughs, Murtaugh's son. You worked at the keep when I was a boy. You used to give me a cookie or two when I came in from working with the horses."

"Oh, aye, Mr. Burroughs, I remember ye well. I hear ye're the laird now since poor Earl MacDonald passed. And this must be Lady Diana. I helped to care for your mum when ye was born. Ye look much like her."

"Thank you, Mrs. Glynn. I'm sorry I don't remember you. I believe you left the keep when I was quite small."

"Aye, I did. Ye wasn't even out of nappies when I got to the point where I couldn't do much of 'nothin no more. Bless yer Da for what he done for me. Most lairds woulda just told me to get, but not Laird MacDonald. He set me up a pension. I still get it even though he's been dead these many years. I was able to finish raising my girls because of him. We woulda been in the poor house without yer Da. He was a great man, that one."

"Thank you again, Mrs. Glynn. I appreciate those kind words. I agree my Da was a great man. I'm glad he could help you."

Diana looked to Edwin. He said, "The reason we have come to see you today, Gladys, is we would like to ask you to speak to your daughter Lydia for us. We have reason to believe she may know something about Lady Bruce's involvement with the murders of Diana's husband and brother-in-law, as well as the death of her child. We tried to speak to her before we came here, but she appears to be frightened to speak to us."

"Nay, and I don't doubt it. That Lady Bruce is a piece of work, she is. Told my Lydia, she better not talk to no one about the goings on up there at the Bruce place. I heard that Alexander man was the one done the killings. Don't they have him in gaol in Inverness?"

"Yes, Gladys, they do and he will hang for his crimes. We spoke to him yesterday. He's the one who told us about Lydia. He thought she might have heard something that will help us prove

Lady Bruce was the instigator in all the crimes. We were hoping maybe you could speak to her and convince her to talk to us. We would really appreciate it."

"Well, sure and I will. I'll speak to Ronald too. That's her man. He didn't like Lydia workin at that place what with all the goings on between Lady Bruce and that Alexander fella. Soon's they was married, he made her quit. Everyone in the neighborhood knew they was up to no good." Gladys said with asperity.

It was obvious to Diana and Edwin that Mrs. Glynn didn't approve of Lady Bruce. That was to their advantage. She promised to have Jenny fetch Lydia later that day. She said she would send word when Lydia was willing to speak with them.

Diana didn't want to give up yet, but there was little they could do at the moment. They returned to the keep and Diana spent the rest of that morning and part of the afternoon pacing the floor in the library. She read the letters again, and again she was sickened by them. To think that awful woman had sat at their dining table on more than one occasion as Diana and her father had sat at hers. How could anyone be that deceitful? Diana was amazed at the duplicity of Lady Bruce. She appeared to be a lady, but obviously, she was a cretin instead. Or maybe, she was insane. Either way, Diana wanted her locked away so she couldn't harm anyone else.

There was a knock on the library door. Edwin went to answer it. Murtaugh had Ronald Craig in tow. Murtaugh, of course, was privy to all that was going on. He had done any and everything he could think of to help Edwin and Diana in their quest for proof of Lady Bruce's guilt. Murtaugh had an excited look on his face as he ushered Ronald into the library.

Murtaugh said, "Ronald, here, says he's convinced his wife, the wee Lydia, to speak to ye about Lady Bruce. He wants ye to come with him now before she changes her mind. I've sent word to the barn to have yer horses saddled."

Diana ran to Murtaugh and gave him a hug. He was shocked at first, but then she had hugged him often as a child, he shouldn't be surprised to have her do it as an adult, even if she was a duchess now. After a moment, he put his arms around her and hugged her back.

"Da, that's wonderful news. Yes, we will go right away. We don't know how to thank you, Ronald. This is very important to her grace and to me." Edwin said excitedly.

"Nay thanks be needed, Laird. I got my Lydia away from that awful woman as soon as I could. The things that went on in that house is a right scandal.", Ronald said with much feeling.

Ronald had come on foot, so Edwin asked that another horse be saddled for him as well. The three riders wasted little time getting to the village and the Craig house.

Ronald opened the door and strode in calling Lydia's name. She came from the small bedroom behind the main room, again with her baby in her arms. "So, Ronald, ye've brung them, have ye?", she asked with a worried frown.

"Aye, I have. And I want ye to be tellin 'em exactly what ye told me about what went on at that house where ye was a workin'. Ye don't have to be afeared. The Laird and her grace won't be lettin' nothin happen to you."

Lydia went to the small cradle near the fireplace and lay the babe down, covering him with a blanket. She turned to Edwin and Diana with a tentative smile. After inviting them to sit down, she and her husband sat on the settle. He put his arm around her and she sat a few moments wringing her hands before she began.

"I'm that glad to be tellin' ye this even though Lady Bruce threatened all sorts of things if ever I told anythin about what went on in her house. She's an evil woman. I don't think she's right in her head, to be honest. She would rail and rail about how ye," she said pointing at Diana, "stole her Beatrice's chance at a good marriage. But that ain't right 'cause her daughter married a rich old earl and moved away to London years ago. She just couldn't seem to forget that Beatrice hadn't managed to marry one of the Duke of Bristol's sons. It's like the devil was in her mind and wouldn't let go.

Then when Beatrice's husband died three years ago, it got worse. She would natter on and on at Mr. Alexander to do something, so Beatrice could finally be the Duchess of Bristol. She said over and over as how he got it right the first time when he got the oldest son kilt on his way here to marry ye, but how he bungled it right bad when he tried to kill ye on yer way home after ye came to bury yer Da. He tried to talk her out of trying to kill ye again, but she just wouldn't let it go. Mr. Alexander felt terrible for yer bairn dyin', but she sure didn't.

She read all the society pages to see where ye were, your grace. She said since ye hadn't been living in London regular, she would try to track ye by the papers. She was that angry three years ago when she found out ye went to Russia. She couldn't very well send Mr. Alexander there without knowing where exactly ye went.

She did send Mr. Alexander all kinds of places while I was still there, trying to find ye and yer husband. She wanted ye killed so Beatrice could marry him. Beatrice ain't even been home since she got married all them years ago. She has a little son who's the new earl and don't seem to want to ever come home to Scotland again. Lady Bruce has been to see her in London and her country place, but she never comes here."

"When I left there a little over a year ago, Mr. Alexander had been sent to Cornwall because Lady Bruce thought ye might be there. I don't know where else he went after that. When I left that house, I never wanted nothin' more to do with her or nobody else from there."

Diana had a grim smile on her face. "Lydia, would you be willing to travel to Edinburgh with Mr. Burroughs and me. We're going to petition the government to have Lady Bruce arrested for her part in the murders of my baby, my husband, and his brother. I'm sure Mr. Burroughs could see his way to let Ronald accompany us. The harvest is in now. Ronald would continue to draw his pay while we're gone and his job will be here when he comes back." Diana said looking at Edwin.

"Of course, Ronald can be spared from the farm. You can both take in the sights of Edinburgh before we come back. It's a beautiful city as her grace can tell you. What say you, Lydia, Ronald?"

Lydia looked to Ronald, he shook his head affirmatively. Lydia wrung her hands a few more times, then shook her head yes as well. She spoke up then worriedly, "What about me bairn? He canna be away from me now. I need to nurse him."

Diana smiled at the young woman. "That is absolutely no problem. We will have a carriage outfitted just for the three of you. We can have the carpenter build a cradle to fit between the seats. My son travelled much with us in just such a cradle. He was perfectly happy and perfectly safe."

Edwin spoke up, "So, we're in agreement then. We will all travel to Edinburgh as soon as arrangements can be made. Probably in the next two days. Our carpenter will start work on the cradle today. We should be able to arrange everything today and tomorrow and then we will leave the next day bright and early."

"I think you should all come and stay at the keep until we're ready to leave. I would feel better knowing we were all together, until we leave on our journey. Will that be okay with you?" Diana asked anxiously. She didn't want to worry the Craigs, but it was possible Lord Bruce was having she and Edwin watched since they had been to see Alexander. She was sure the magistrate had quickly warned him they were trying to find evidence against his wife.

The Craigs agreed. They had no horses nor wagon, so Edwin went to the local blacksmith and borrowed a team and wagon to carry the young couple and their baby to Ainsley Glen. Diana helped Lydia gather all she would need for the baby, as well as she and her husband for the trip. Soon, they had everything packed in baskets and bundles and were ready to go. Edwin tied the extra horse to the wagon and he and Diana rode alongside it the three miles to Ainsley Glen.

Mrs. Gwen took charge of the Craigs, baby and all, when they arrived. Diana and Edwin adjourned to the library to make plans to get under way for Edinburgh. The plans went smoothly and on the third day, they were all up very early to begin their journey.

Chapter 49

Edwin had hired five local men, to add to the seven footmen in the house as well as four of the stable hands, as guards. He had immediately understood Diana's concern and motivation when she invited the Craigs to stay at the keep until their journey. He too thought Lord Bruce might attempt to stop them from arriving at their destination.

The day before they left, Diana asked Barbara to bring Lydia up to see her. The Craigs had been installed in one of the guest bedrooms and Diana's old crib had been retrieved from the attic for the baby. Diana wanted to do something special for Lydia. She had wondered what she might do when she suddenly thought about a dress she had that would be perfect for her. As a matter of fact, Diana thought to give her several dresses for the trip. She knew the young couple had little money and she had noticed that Lydia had worn the same dress since she first met her. She had only packed one other, a dark blue rather severe dress, apparently her Sunday best.

When Barbara came into the room with Lydia, she still looked frightened and worried. Diana had Barbara go fetch a tea tray and sat Lydia down in front of the fire across from her. It was difficult to get the girl to speak to her, other than to answer her questions with one or two words.

When Barbara came back, Diana asked Barbara to sit with them as well. Lydia looked astonished by that. It was not uncommon for Barbara to have tea in Diana's room with her or to eat a meal with her there, if Diana didn't want to go down to eat. They were friends and had been for years. Barbara had been Diana's only friend when she had first left Ainsley Glen. Barbara had consoled her time and again when tragedy struck and Diana felt she was a part of her family, much as Benjamin had been.

With Barbara there, Lydia opened up a little more. The conversation came around to the journey. Diana said, "Lydia, would you think it terribly impertinent of me if I was to offer you some of my dresses that I don't wear anymore? We are of a like size. It's rare that I find anyone as small as I. Most of my clothes go to waste when I no longer want them. Barbara can use some of them, but she's so much taller, we have to add ruffles to the bottoms for her. Not all dresses really look right with ruffles on the bottoms." at that statement, both Barbara and Diana laughed. They had tried several times to alter dresses for Barbara to no avail. Without matching or co-ordinating material, it was sometimes an impossible task. They told Lydia stories about some of their past mishaps and soon all three women were laughing merrily.

Soon they were at the wardrobe looking over several dresses for Lydia. Barbara helped her off with the dress she was wearing and had her try on a pale yellow day dress made of sprigged muslin. The dress had small green leaves embroidered on it. When she had it on, they led her to the full length mirror.

When Lydia saw her reflection, she gasped. She had never had a dress this beautiful. It had long sleeves that fitted her slim arms perfectly. The bodice was high waisted with a demure neckline, and the skirt had only a modicum of fullness. The dress had lace to match the green leaves on the neckline and around the cuffs of the sleeves as well as three rows on the bottom of the dress. Diana reached into a chest and withdrew a pair of green slippers that matched the dress perfectly.

"Here, Lydia, try these on. I think your feet are the same size as mine. Barbara never can wear my shoes and I have tons of them that I rarely wear."

"Oh, your grace, this is too much. I thank ye from the bottom of me heart, but….Where will I wear these fine soft slippers? I canna see meself doin' me chores in this dress and these shoes," Lydia said with a strained laugh.

"No, Lydia, but you could wear them to church or to a wedding or a party. I know they have parties in the village for holidays. I attended them myself when I was a child with my Da and even later with my friends Ian and Alana. This dress would be perfect for those times."

Lydia looked at herself again in the mirror, smiled, and thanked Diana again. Soon, she had tried on several outfits. Some were practical skirts and shirtwaists that Diana had worn to conduct the duchy business, some were more formal, but all seemed to have been made for her. She and Diana were very much of a like size. Their coloring was different, Lydia was a blue-eyed brunette. Her very thick dark hair was wavy and she wore it in a knot on top of her head. The style suited her because it accentuated her high cheekbones. Her skin was clear and she had bright color in her cheeks. She was a very pretty young woman. The clothes Diana insisted that she take were all in shades that complimented her coloring.

Barbara went with Lydia to carry the clothes to the guest room. They had added some petticoats and chemises to complete her new wardrobe. Diana had even given her some silk stockings, for she had none of her own. Lydia only had heavy woolen ones she had knit herself. Diana felt much better about taking Lydia on this trip to Edinburgh now that she had outfitted her properly.

After breaking their fast with some of Mrs. Owen's wonderful bannocks, scotch eggs, bacon, sausage, eggs, and jam, they were on their way. There were four carriages in all. One for Edwin, Hannah, and Diana, one for the Craigs, one for Murray and Barbara as well as one of the upstairs maids to help with the baby, and the last for the luggage. Diana did not trust the letters to anyone except herself. On the morning they left, she had Barbara bind them to her body with a length of silk as if they were jewels or money. To her they were more precious than either.

The trip would take a little over two weeks since it was a distance of over a hundred and fifty miles between the two places. Edwin had made the trip several times both with Fergus and alone to sell horses. He knew the best inns and private homes to stay in and has sent ahead a rider to make arrangement for accommodations for their first night.

At last everyone was loaded and they were off. It was cold and rainy. Edwin had hot bricks put into all the carriages for their feet. He also made sure there were plenty of blankets and lap robes for everyone. He had the interior lanterns lit as well. They gave out a little heat and helped to dispel the gloom of the dreary weather.

Diana was happy to see that Lydia had dressed in one of the outfits she had given her. She looked very nice in a dark blue travelling suit made of heavy wool. It would help keep her warm. When Diana had woken to the very cold morning, she had sent Barbara to take Lydia a very heavy, dark brown wool cloak. After travelling so very much for so many years, Diana knew Lydia would need it. She was glad to see Lydia was wearing it to start the journey.

Diana and Edwin spent that day and every day of their journey discussing exactly what they could do and who they should see when they arrived in Edinburgh. Edwin knew several members of parliament. He had sold them Ainsley horses over the years. He thought they should approach these men to see what steps needed to be taken to have Lady Bruce charged with her crimes. Diana had sent letters from London to some of her business contacts in Edinburgh. Some of them were merchants and others nobility.

Though she only owned one estate in Scotland, she had done business with Scottish merchants regarding some of her English estates as well as some of the northern duchy estates. Being Scottish born, she tried to use Scottish merchants wherever she could.

She and Edward had also entertained and been entertained by several members of Scottish society during their many travels. Most Scottish big business was headquartered in Edinburgh and she and Edward had travelled there several times over the years.

One of her personal investments, with profits from her six estates, had been in the Royal Mail coaches. She had had the foresight to invest several hundred pounds in the company just a few years back. Edward had also approved her investing a smaller sum for the duchy.

Now fifty coaches a day left Edinburgh. She had received a nice return on her investment as had the duchy and she expected even more in the future. Diana decided to contact everyone she knew in Edinburgh and some she didn't if she could not get Lady Bruce arrested any other way. She was determined to remove this dangerous woman from society before she harmed someone else.

As the days wore on, the party became more and more weary. The roads were in terrible condition this time of year and they were constantly bounced around in the carriages. The weather had been very rainy and was colder than usual. Diana, as usual, suffered from the cold more than others. She thought Lydia might have the same complaint. She also worried about the Craig's small son. She had made sure there were plenty of blankets for the crib the carpenter had installed in their coach, as well as two thick down pillows for him to lie on. She remembered how hard it was to travel when Geoffrey was small and was concerned for all the Craig's comforts.

At each stop, Diana made sure to inquire after the baby, little Ronald, as well as the adult Craigs. She couldn't bring herself to hold the baby, though her arms ached to do so. It just brought back too many thoughts of her own wee bairn, Geoffrey. She had not held a baby since Geoffrey died. She had been around many of them, especially the children of their friends, but she just couldn't allow herself to get physically or emotionally close to any of them, even the tenants children whom she loved. Diana hoped she would get over what she saw as a weakness, but didn't know if she ever would.

As the trip finally wound down and they were almost to Edinburgh, Diana's mind went to Ian and Alana, her friends who lived in America. They now had six children, four boys and two girls. True to their word, their first daughter had been named Diana for her. She longed to see Ian and Alana and meet their children. They corresponded regularly. She had recently received a response to the letter she had written to him upon Edward's death.

> *My Dear Diana,*
>
> *I find I hardly know what to say to you in response to your last letter telling us of Edward's murder by the hands of that madman, Alexander. I cannot even begin to tell you how sorry we both are for your loss. I sincerely hope you are able to bring Lady Bruce to justice. I never cared for that woman, but I had no idea she was so evil.*
>
> *I know you must be devastated at the loss of your husband especially after losing your son and so recently, your good friend Benjamin, as well as your father and father-in-law. What tragedy you have known in your short life.*
>
> *I feel so badly for you. Alana and I have known nothing but joy and prosperity. I feel guilty for all the joy we have had in comparison with all the sadness you have known.*
>
> *Please, if there is ever anything we can do for you, please, please do not hesitate to write to me. We both owe you so much, and I do not mean just the money you gave us to come to this great country. You literally made the life we have now a possibility and we will never forget it.*
>
> *Forever Yours,*
>
> *Ian*

Diana had read the letter several times since receiving it and did so again now. She finished the letter, then sat back in the seat and leaned her head back, closing her eyes with a deep sigh.

Edwin looked up from the papers he was perusing at the sound of the sigh and wondered at the look on her face. She had a wistful, but somehow serene look that he just couldn't fathom. He started to ask after her, but decided to give her some privacy.

There had been little of that on this journey. Accommodations had sometimes been crowded. Diana had to share her room with both the maids almost every night and sometimes Hannah as well. There were times there was only one room available. Edwin had, on those occasions, had to make do with his cloak and a piece of the taproom floor with the other men. At least the inns were warm, unlike the freezing carriages. They should make Edinburgh tomorrow much to every ones relief.

Edwin's thoughts were suddenly interrupted by the sound of a gun shot close to their carriage. He immediately reached under the seat and pulled out the pistols he kept there in a box. Diana reached into her bag and pulled out a double-barreled derringer to Edwin's surprise.

Diana smiled grimly, "Did you think I would come unprepared. I am surprised it has taken them this long to attack us."

Edwin smiled just as grimly, "Well, I know you know how to use it, so please protect Hannah for me, if you will. I'm going to take a look."

With that Edwin opened the window and slowly stuck his head out. There had not been another shot since the first, but he was still very cautious. What he saw did not surprise him in the least. There were five mounted men riding hard to catch up with the rapidly travelling carriage. The driver was using the whip with abandon trying to get the team to pull even faster. His outriders were closing in tighter around the carriage. They had all pulled out their pistols. It was very hard to get off a good shot from the back of a rapidly running horse, but he saw one of his stable hands stand up in the stirrups and turn half way around to fire behind him. He heard a shout and saw one of the attackers fall from his saddle. There was no way Nick could reload on the back of his horse, so he rode even closer to the carriage to offer his own body as protection for the passengers.

Edwin thought to himself, "That young man deserves a raise." Then he aimed one of his own pistols and took a shot at the closest miscreant. He pulled the trigger and after the smoke cleared, he saw another empty saddle and the horse was slowing down now that he was riderless.

Edwin was about the pull his head back in to get his other pistol, when he saw a slim arm come through the small window beside him holding the pistol primed and ready. They traded and he could hear Diana reloading from the supplies in his box. Edwin took aim again and fired once more. Again, he hit his target, though this time the attacker wasn't unseated. He did grab his shoulder and slump over in the saddle. He let his horse slow as well. That was three down and two to go.

Nick shouted, "There go the other two. Guess they ain't so brave without their chums."

Edwin looked and saw that the attackers were no longer following. Hopefully, they would reach the inn they were staying in very soon. Edwin looked back to make sure the other carriages and their occupants had been unharmed. He saw Ronald sticking his head out also and waved to him. Ronald waved back and Edwin noticed he also had a pistol in his hand.

"Now where did Ronald get a pistol? I had no idea he owned one," he wondered out loud.

"I gave it to him." spoke Diana right by his elbow. She startled Edwin and he jumped. She reached out a hand to steady him and said. "I was sure we would be attacked somewhere on this journey. I didn't want Ronald and his family to be unprotected. I loaned him the pair that my Da gave me years ago. I thought they might come in handy. I made sure he knew how to use them too. He had a little trouble loading them at first, but we practiced an hour or so yesterday and he did very well."

Edwin pulled his head back into the coach and reseated himself beside his terror stricken wife. He put his arm around Hannah and patted her shoulder. She wasn't crying, but she wasn't far from it. Diana however, just looked pleased with herself.

"Diana, you never cease to amaze me. You never mentioned a thing to me about it. Why not?"

"You had enough on your mind getting all the men armed and on good horses. It was the least I could do since the Craigs are here because of me. I couldn't live with myself if anything happened to them or their wee one. I made sure Murray was armed also to protect he, Barbara, and Sally. He didn't need any instruction though. That Murray is always surprising me with what he knows. He's quite a smart young man."

Edwin said, "That he is. I realized that when he came to work for us at Ainsley Glen when he was quite young. He learns fast and he rarely forgets whatever he learns. He should go far."

Soon the carriage began to slow. They had made it to their destination and they were all very relieved to have done so. For once, there was enough room at the inn for them all to have rooms. Even Murray didn't have to sleep in the common room with the rest of the men. Diana made sure he had a room of his own since there were plenty available.

The innkeeper blamed the weather on his lack of custom. It had been very cold and the incessant rain had turned to sleet late in the day. Even the taproom was almost empty. The people of the village were staying around their own fires this night. There was plenty of good beef stew and the innkeeper's wife had made fresh bannocks.

Since the taproom was almost empty, Diana joined the rest of the company for dinner that night. She usually had a tray in her room, but she was still a little unnerved by the attack earlier and wanted some company, though no one would have ever known it. They were served by a young woman who looked to be the innkeeper's daughter.

She was pretty blond girl of about eighteen with flashing blue-grey eyes and a merry smile. She flirted shamelessly with Murray, but he paid her no heed. Diana watched the interplay and wondered at Murray's lack of interest. She was a very pretty girl and Murray was quite young, not more than twenty-two. He was quite a serious young man though and didn't hold with much levity.

As a matter of fact, Diana didn't remember ever hearing him laugh. His smiles were rare as well. When Diana thought about it, she realized she knew very little about Murray except that he was very intelligent, a very hard worker, and she trusted him implicitly. He had proven himself time after time. He kept to himself and didn't socialize with the other servants to her knowledge. "Well,", Diana thought, "It's his business who he is friendly with, not mine. He does his job and he does it well. That should be my only concern."

However, she still wondered about him on occasions such as this. She knew he was from Ireland, but he never spoke of his home or family. "Maybe, he's like me, and doesn't have one", Diana thought sadly.

Just then Edwin raised his wine glass and proposed a toast. "Here's to our safety this cold and miserable night. We are warm and well fed and all together, with no one hurt. I appreciate all you did this afternoon when we were attacked. Just a word of caution though. Sleep with your pistols beside you this night. They may not have given up."

Upon hearing the toast, the innkeeper inquired as to what had happened. When he heard the details, he walked to the big front door of the inn and dropped the bar across it. Then he went and barred the back door as well. When he came back, he told the company they need not worry this night. No one had ever broken down that door and this inn was over a hundred years old.

The group was all very tired. Soon after they had eaten and drunk their fill, they all went to their beds. Diana was very happy to have a little privacy for a change. She had been with other people almost constantly for two weeks. She truly needed a little time alone. She was still grieving for Edward and wanted some time to think about him and their lives together.

She and Edward may not have had a traditional marriage, but they did have a very affectionate and loving relationship. They hadn't enjoyed the same level of happiness since Benjamin had died, but they had still managed to find some enjoyment in each other and their work together. They had become closer than ever after Benjamin's passing. They had just been really coming out from under their terrible grief when Edward had been shot. They had been laughing more and planning more for their future together.

Now Diana feared making any plans. It seemed each time she planned very far ahead, tragedy struck again. "Well," she thought, "I have no one else to lose. Everyone I have ever loved deeply is now dead." With that thought, she turned her face to the wall and wept. She hadn't cried in several weeks. It seemed she had been too busy or too exhausted to even cry. Tonight though, she let go and mourned her lost loves deeply.

Chapter 50

The next day found them finally entering Edinburgh. Lydia and Ronald were amazed at the size of the city. Neither of them had ever been more than a few miles from their village. The site of Edinburgh Castle left them in awe. When they saw St. Giles Cathedral , Lydia crossed herself and exclaimed, "Oh Ronald, if Ma could see that, it would bring tears to her eyes. 'Tis that beautiful!" The Craigs continued to be amazed as the carriages pulled up to the Waterloo Hotel. They couldn't believe that they would be staying in such a place.

When Edwin, Hannah, and Diana descended from the carriage, they were met by a wide-eyed Lydia with Ronald and the baby in tow.

"Yer grace, ye canna be meanin' for us to stay in this palace, are ye?"

"Lydia, this isn't a palace, it's an hotel." answered Diana.

"A hotel? What is that?" asked an incredulous Lydia.

"It's like an inn, only bigger and a bit nicer," explained Diana.

Lydia just shook her head. Quickly a doorman and many porters descended on the group to begin carrying luggage into the grand lobby of the hotel. The hotel had opened in 1819 and been designed and built by Archibald Elliott after his design was chosen over James Gillespie and Richard Crichton, both renowned architects of the time, in a contest. The lobby was very grand with sumptuous fabrics on the furniture and much gilding on the fixtures and woodwork. It was very opulent for the time.

Diana and Edward had stayed at the hotel twice before, once in the year it was opened. On that occasion, they had been invited to a ball there and found the experience exhilarating. Edward had become enamored of the cupola in the grand ballroom. There had been a full moon and a lot of stars on the night they were there. Even with the light of multiple candelabras, the light from the moon was easily seen. The room was huge and easily accommodated the several hundred people at the ball. They had both enjoyed the visit and the hotel a great deal and decided then to stay only at the Waterloo when they were in Edinburgh.

After a wonderfully restful night, Diana and Edwin left for the courts just after breakfast. They didn't take Lydia with them on this initial visit. They would bring her to testify when Lady Bruce had been arrested and brought to trial. They had no idea how long the process would take, but hoped to be done with the whole ugly business soon.

Diana took Murray aside and gave him a purse. She requested he take Ronald to a haberdasher and buy him some clothes. She told him to definitely include a warm winter coat and some good shoes. Murray gave her a small smile and headed to the room the Craigs were staying in.

On the way to the courts, Diana and Edwin stopped to pick up a barrister friend of Edwin's, John McTavish. Mr. Mctavish was very knowledgeable about the courts and thought they might profit by speaking to Judge Buchanan. He advised them to wait outside the office of the judge while he went in and presented their case.

They waited for over an hour. Mr. McTavish had taken the letters from Lady Bruce to Horace Alexander in with him. He was also aware they had a witness to several conversations between the two. Finally Mr. McTavish came from the judge's chambers with a smile on his face.

"I believe we have hit on a bit of luck. Judge Buchanan was approached by Lord Bruce recently. Lord Bruce offered the judge a bribe. It offended the judge as he is a completely honest man. That is why I chose him to present the evidence to. Lord Bruce didn't go into detail on what charges might be brought against his wife. He just tried to put a stop to any charges being filed. He made up some convoluted story of bad blood between you, your grace, and Lady Bruce. However, Judge Buchanan was so affronted by the offer of a bribe, that he had Lord Bruce removed from his office before hearing the whole tale."

"Bad blood between she and I? How could that be? I haven't even seen that woman in over ten years. That is just ridiculous," exclaimed Diana.

Edwin patted Diana's hand. He could tell she was very overwrought. "Never mind, Diana, it looks as if we have them running scared if Lord Bruce is trying to bribe judges before we even ask to have charges filed against his wife. He obviously knows she's guilty and is trying to cover up her crimes."

Mr. McTavish spoke up, "Lord Bruce's reputation has suffered some blows recently. He was involved in the MacGregor scandal. He has lost his credibility with a lot of the government officials and many of the nobility as well. He was in the forefront of MacGregor's scheme. Now few people trust him. There have been rumblings about his losing his place in parliament. His wife being tried for murder would probably do him in."

Diana had no sympathy for either of the Bruce's. The MacGregor scandal had left many people without their life savings and some had even lost their lives. MacGregor had sold shares of land in a non-existent Latin American country. Many people had gone to Latin America to find there was no land and no way to live. Many had perished of disease and starvation, some had even committed suicide. She felt Lord Bruce was as evil as his wife if he was knowingly involved with MacGregor, who she felt was guilty of murder. She felt even more angry that he wasn't worried about his wife's welfare, but about himself instead. His utter selfishness astounded her.

Mr. McTavish led them into Judge Buchanan's chambers. The judge was a tall, very slender man with an almost bald head and a stooped physique. What sparse hair he had was mostly white and his eyes a most unusual shade of gray, almost blue at moments, then a deeper slate color at others. He had the gleam of high intelligence in his eyes. His mouth was very thin, almost lipless. He did not smile upon their entrance, but he did stand and gave a small bow.

Mr. McTavish introduced Diana and then Edwin. The judge invited them to sit down. He picked up the sheaf of letters he had been presented. He looked at them several minutes with a scowl on his face. When he looked up, he directed his questions to Diana.

"Your grace, these letters seem to substantiate your claim that Lady Bruce instigated not only the murder of your husband, the Duke of Bristol, but also his brother and caused the death of your child. Her crimes seem to have spanned ten years that we know of. I understand you also have Lady Bruce's former maid with you here in the city. Is that correct?"

"Yes, your honor. We have with us Lydia Craig. She was ladies maid to Lady Bruce for three years. She left her employ a little over a year ago. At the time she left, Horace Alexander was gone to Cornwall trying to find my husband and I in order to kill me. When Lydia left Lady Bruce's employ, she was threatened with her life if she ever uttered a word about the goings on at the Bruce estate.

It seems Lady Bruce conceived the notion that her daughter Beatrice should marry the Duke of Bristol, no matter who held the title. When having Geoffrey killed didn't result in Beatrice marrying Edward, she turned to a different tack. Edward and I married just before Geoffrey was killed, so I became the target. We were also attacked two days ago by several highwaymen. It is my belief they were sent by Lord Bruce. We believe at least two of them were killed and another wounded before they left us alone. You see, we had anticipated such an attack and were prepared."

The judge looked surprised at this information. "Were any members of your party harmed, your grace?"

"No, your honor. Mr. Burroughs here accounted for two of the miscreants and one of our footmen dispatched the other one. All of our carriages carried armed men either inside or atop and our outriders were armed as well."

"That is fortunate," said Judge Buchanan. "Apparently, her man, Alexander, was something of a bungler. He missed you twice according to these letters and what McTavish told me. I understand he has confessed to everything and is just awaiting judgement. I have here a letter that came to my attention from your local sheriff. He seems to feel the magistrate in Inverness may not be inclined to see justice done where Alexander is concerned. He has asked that Alexander be sentenced here instead. What say you to that?"

Diana was quick to respond. "I believe that is a fair assessment of the situation. We recently saw Mr. Alexander. He seemed very malnourished and had been severely beaten. He is the one who told us about the letters and where to find them. He also gave us Mrs. Craig's name and verified she had overheard much while being a ladies maid to Lady Bruce. He has admitted his part in these crimes and seems to feel real remorse, at least for the death of my son.

The magistrate in Inverness, Mr. Fletcher, was very reluctant for us to see Mr. Alexander, but we insisted. He was very dismissive of our claims of Lady Bruce's involvement. We learned from my cousin, Earl Robert MacDonald, that he and Lord Bruce are very close. Mr. Alexander may not have a chance of a fair sentencing in Inverness, if he even survives long enough to go before a judge."

"Well, your grace, I would like to speak to this Craig person. Can you bring her to this office later on today? I believe we must act quickly on this."

"Yes, your honor. Just name the time and we will return with Lydia Craig." Diana said assertively.

The time was arranged and Diana and Edwin took their leave. After leaving Mr. MacTavish at his office, they returned to the Waterloo. Edwin stopped at the desk and asked that luncheon be sent to their sitting room. He then went upstairs with Diana. They stopped at Murray's room and dispatched him to fetch the Craigs. As they sat around the table eating, Diana recounted for all assembled the result of their visit with the judge.

Diana could see that Lydia was nervous about seeing the judge. She reassured her that she would just be asked some questions in the judge's office about what she had seen and heard at the Bruce estate. There would not be anyone else there except she and Edwin. That seemed to quiet some of Lydia's fears.

Diana immediately noticed that Ronald Craig was dressed in a very nice suit of a dark gray material with shiny new black shoes. He had on a new shirt and tie as well. She complimented him on how well he looked. Ronald turned a bright red and mumbled a thank you for the compliment and the clothes.

Diana said, "Well, Ronald, we couldn't let Lydia be the only Craig with a new wardrobe, now could we?

She was gratified to see Ronald and Lydia's smiles at her words.

Shortly after luncheon, Diana, Edwin and Lydia left for Judge Buchanan's office. They picked up Mr. McTavish at his office. When they arrived, they were immediately escorted into the office. The judge could immediately see that the young woman in front of him was terribly nervous. Right away, he tried to make her feel more at ease.

"Mrs. Craig, please tell me, in your own words, what you saw and heard during the three years you were ladies maid to Lady Adelaide Bruce. You need not fear anyone here. What you say will be held in strictest confidence until such time as you may be called upon as a witness for the Crown."

Haltingly Lydia began to tell the judge of the many instances she had overheard Lady Bruce and Horace Alexander discuss plans for Diana's murder. She also recounted conversations the two had about Geoffrey's death and the bungled attempt on Diana, just after her father's death, that resulted in little Geoffrey's death and Edward's debilitating accident. She told of Lady Bruce having her burn letters she received from Mr. Alexander when he was away hunting for Diana in the last year she worked for the Bruce's.

When she had finished her monologue, the judge thanked her for her time and asked her to wait outside. When Lydia had left, he turned to Diana and Edwin and said, "I believe there is sufficient evidence to have Lady Bruce arrested. I have done some investigating and found that she is now here in Edinburgh at Lord Bruce's townhouse. I am sending a constable to arrest her right away. I have also sent a constable to Inverness to have Mr. Alexander moved here for sentencing. I did that before even speaking to Mrs. Craig, based solely on the letter from the sheriff and your testimony to me earlier today".

Diana rose and offered her hand to Judge Buchanan. "Your honor, I thank you very much for your help in this matter. Both my cousin Earl MacDonald and Mr. Burroughs had assured me I would find justice here in Edinburgh. I am very gratified to see they were both right."

As Diana and Edwin left the judges office, she felt such a feeling of relief, she felt weak in the knees and staggered slightly. Edwin caught her arm as did Mr. McTavish.

Edwin exclaimed, "Diana dear, are you all right? You are quite pale and appear weak.".

"I hadn't realized how frightened I was that the evidence would be dismissed as insufficient to arrest the wife of a peer of the realm. To find a judge who was so honest and upright is such a great relief. I am fine now. I think it was a shock is all."

After the group had left Mr. McTavish at his office and returned to the Waterloo, they went, at once, to their shared drawing room and sent for Hannah, Murray, Barbara, and Ronald. The baby was asleep and the maid they brought stayed with him.

When Diana gave the assembled company the news that Lady Bruce would be arrested, Barbara came and gave her a huge hug. They were all soon laughing and talking excitedly. Edwin said, "This calls for a celebration. Tomorrow I propose that we all have a day of sightseeing here in Edinburgh and then a celebratory dinner in the large dining room downstairs."

Ronald spoke up quickly, "I don't know that Lydia and me would be allowed in the dining room, sir. I seen the way people was dressed going in there last night. We wouldn't fit in. Maybe we should just eat here in our room."

Barbara and Murray also made it clear they wouldn't feel really comfortable in the dining room of the Waterloo. Edwin was embarrassed that he hadn't thought about their emotional comfort before suggesting the hotel dining room and his face turned red.

Diana, always one sensitive to other's feelings, quickly concurred that maybe an inn or public house wold be better suited to their purpose and she knew just the one.

She and Edward had eaten at a quaint inn, the Sheep Heid in Duddingston Village, on their last visit to Edinburgh. She thought it would fit their purposes quite well. It was very old and had excellent food. It was also between Hollyrood Palace and Craigmillar Castle, both of which would make excellent sightseeing opportunities.

The plans were set. Murray went down to arrange for supper to be sent to their drawing room. The friends enjoyed a quiet meal and went early to bed. It had been an exciting and satisfying day.

The next day dawned cold, but sunny. The group left the hotel soon after breakfast. They took two carriages with Diana, Barbara, Edwin, and Hannah in one and the Craigs and Murray in the other. They had a wonderful day. They stopped at a public house when they became hungry at midday. Murray, always the purveyor of food and drink, went inside and procured bread, meat, and ale which they consumed in a newly shorn wheat field sitting on the lap robes and blankets they had been using to keep warm on their jaunt.

Later they adjourned to the Sheep's Heid Inn and dined on powsowdie, a rich sheep's head broth cooked with onions, carrots, turnips, chunks of mutton, barley, peas, and celery seasoned with parsley, salt and pepper. Along with the hearty soup, they had bannocks, rye bread, mounds of fresh butter, and a rich ale made by the innkeeper. For dessert they had wonderful buttery raspberry scones with clotted cream.

Chapter 51

By the time they finished at the inn, they were all groaning with repletion. When they arrived back at the Waterloo, they were surprised to find Mr. McTavish waiting for them in the lobby. Not wanting to discuss business in a public place, they adjourned once more to their drawing room.

Edwin could hardly wait for the door to close before asking, "What news McTavish? Has Lady Bruce been arrested?"

With a huge smile on his face, McTavish said, "Aye, that she has. She is in the city gaol right now. From what I could find out from the constable sent to fetch her, Lord Bruce was not at home when they got there, but apparently he had left someone there to run to him if the constable came a visiting. He was at the gaol only minutes after she arrived. He put on a big show and blustered and ranted for most an hour. When he found all his posturing did him no good, he asked to see his wife. That request was granted and then he took his leave. I imagine he went to his barrister to sees what could be done legally. Judge Buchanan has scheduled the trial for next week. He is wasting no time on this matter. Alexander is due here in two days time for his sentencing."

Diana again felt a surge of relief. All day, she had feared that somehow Lady Bruce would, by means fair or foul, avoid incarceration. She was much gratified to think that justice would finally be done for Geoffrey and her baby, as well as Edward. Diana still was not totally convinced that Lady Bruce would be made to pay for her part in all of her heartaches.

The days passed quickly in Edinburgh before the trial. Finally that day dawned. Lydia Craig would be called to testify, but probably not on the first day. Edwin, Hannah and Diana were already seated when Lady Bruce was brought in to the room. She looked terrible. Her eyes were surrounded by black circles, her hair was falling down around her face, and she looked none too clean either. Diana was shocked at her appearance, but felt no sympathy for her.

While they had been waiting for Lady Bruce's trial to commence, Horace Alexander had arrived in Edinburgh. McTavish had again been the bearer of the news. He had been on hand when Alexander arrived. He said the man looked horrible. He was skin and bones and had bruises and cuts all over him when he arrived. Judge Buchanan had ordered that the magistrate for Inverness be removed from his position immediately.

Apparently, Alexander had been beaten repeatedly and deprived of food to try to convince him to recant his story about Lady Bruce's involvement in the crimes. Judge Buchanan had been furious after he interviewed Alexander and had set the wheels in motion immediately for a very speedy trial for Lady Bruce.

Alexander would be sentenced the day after Lady Bruce's trial started. He would be the first to testify for the crown against her. He expected to be hung and was likely right. The penalty for murder was hanging and he had confessed to hiring thugs to kill Geoffrey, being responsible for the baby's death and Edward's injuries, as well as ultimately killing Edward personally. He was also charged with two counts of attempted murder on Diana.

As Diana sat in the court room with Hannah and Edwin, her thoughts turned to Horace Alexander. She would never understand how Lady Bruce could have convinced him to commit these crimes, but she had no doubt that she had. The man's own confession, as well as the letters from Lady Bruce and Lydia's testimony damned him completely. There was no doubt as to his guilt in the matter.

Soon the bailiff called for all to rise as Judge Buchanan entered the room from his chambers. He looked quite different to Diana in his robes and powdered wig, but his voice was readily recognizable. In just a few minutes, Horace Alexander was called to the stand.

He was in hand and leg irons and could barely shuffle to the witness stand with a guard on each side. He was a completely broken man.

When he was asked questions, the audience could barely hear his answers. He hung his head and repeatedly had to be told to speak up. Finally, when asked how he knew Lady Bruce, he raised his head and stared straight at her.

"We been lovers for near fourteen years. I was the manager of the Bruce estate. Poor Addie was stuck in the country most of the time while her husband was here in Edinburgh dallying with first one and then another. Addie got lonely and began to speak to me from that loneliness I s'pose. It wasn't long before we became lovers."

The prosecutor asked then, "When did Lady Bruce ask you to have the young Marquess of Branberry killed and what reason did she give?"

"It was just after she met the Duke and his sons at a ball at Ainsley Glen. Her and her daughter took a trip to London for clothes and such and she had me go along. I was to hire some thugs to ambush the young man in London and make it look like a robbery. She reckoned that killing him would put the other son in line to be duke when the old man died. She wanted her daughter to marry a duke and she decided it just had to be the Duke of Bristol seein' as how he was a direct relation to the king and all. Nothin' less was good enough in Addie's eyes for her Beatrice. The other young man had been to the Bruce estate several times to see Miss Beatrice, so Addie thought she could get them married with no trouble."

The prosecutor walked closer to the witness stand. "And did you hire thugs to do this job of work for you?"

"Addie give me some money, fifty pounds it was, and I hired a couple of East End boys who would do anything for money. They tried to waylay him in town, but he was never alone. He was only there about a week when he headed back to Scotland. I told them to follow him and make the job look like highwaymen done it. We had no idea the young man and his valet travelled with pistols at the ready. They hit the young gentleman, but the valet shot one of them and they ran. The one that got shot died on their way back to London. Addie had me kill the one who got away when he reported back to me. She didn't want no witnesses to what we done. I met him down by the river to pay him and instead hit him over the head with my cane and shoved him in the water."

"What about the second time you were asked to commit a crime for Lady Bruce? Tell us what happened on that occasion and when it was."

"It was about two years after the first time. Lady Diana had married the other son of the duke and that had made Addie madder than a wet hen. When she found out, she started scheming to find a way to get rid of her. When Lady Diana's Da died, she and her husband come to Scotland for the funeral. Of course living in the neighborhood like she did, Addie knew all the comin' and goin's of the gentry.

She told me to follow them when they left Ainsley Glen and hide in the woods and take the first shot at the lady I could get. I done like she said, but my horse moved just when I was about to pull the trigger and I missed the shot. I hit the young Duke's horse instead. He bucked and jumped and took off running through the woods. From where I was hid, I seen that poor bairn's face when the horse started to run. He was afeared somethin awful. I see his little face all the time when I tries to sleep."

At this point Alexander started to cry and hid his face in his hands. It took him several minutes to regain his composure. When he did, he slowly raised his head and continued. "I stayed hid and seen them carry out the young duke and heard Lady Diana screamin' and cryin' about her bairn. Then I seen her walk out of the woods carryin' that little tyke. His neck was broke and I could see from where I was hid that he was dead. I knew the way they loaded the duke, that he was still alive, but I didn't try again. Seein' that poor dead bairn was more than I could take. I regret that part more than anythin' else. That poor, sweet bairn with his head hangin' loose over his Ma's arm and her face all streaked with tears. I just got on my horse and rode for home as quick as I could. Addie was some mad at me, but right then I didn't care." Alexander said, with tears running down his face again as he looked at Diana. One look at the horror on her face and he dropped his face into his hands and sobbed. He was so distraught the judge called for a recess.

Edwin tried to get Diana to quit the courtroom while the recess was going on, but she would have none of it. She had been watching Adelaide Bruce during Alexander's testimony. The woman had actually smiled when Alexander said her bairn was dead. That woman was evil incarnate. Diana would not leave until she had been convicted.

After about twenty minutes, the trial resumed. The prosecutor again stood and asked Alexander more questions about details of the shooting. Then he went on to the most recent incident. "Mr. Alexander, on the twenty-sixth October last, where were you and what were you doing?

"Addie heard that the duke and his wife, Lady Diana, was gonna be payin' a visit to Ainsley Glen because it was the ten year anniversary of the other uns' death. She told me to make sure I hit the right person this time. She wanted me to hide in the copse of woods close to the cemetery and shoot Lady Diana. She said to shoot her in the face if I could."

There were gasps from the people in the gallery, both men and women. The newspapers had made much of the trial of a noble woman and the gallery was packed. The courtroom was filled with the sound of people loudly talking to each other. The judge pounded his gavel and threatened to clear the courtroom if everyone wasn't quiet.

When the courtroom was finally quiet again, the prosecutor said, "Please go on Mr. Alexander. Tell us what happened next."

"Well, I went to the cemetery afore daylight. I waited there like Addie told me to. I saw the young duke and his lady, along with the Ainsley Laird and his wife get down from the carriage and walk over to the graves of the old Earl MacDonald, the young un and the bairn. I had just aimed my rifle at Lady Diana and was pullin' the trigger when she bent over to lay some flowers on the ground. I hit the duke in the head instead. He dropped on top of the lady. I was so shocked by missing her again, I just stood there. Burroughs, him sittin' with the ladies there," Alexander said pointing to Edwin, "Come runnin' to the woods. Before I could get my sense back to get on my horse and run, he caught me. They had some men with them and they had come a runnin' too. Two of 'em grabbed me and took me back to the cemetery. Later they took me to Ainsley Glen and locked me up 'til the sheriff got there."

The prosecutor walked very close to the witness stand. "Mr. Alexander, what you are accusing Lady Bruce of is judged to be the same as murder by our laws. Do you have any proof, other than your word that Lady Bruce was involved in these crimes.?

Alexander looked to Diana and Edwin. He said, pointing to them, "I told them two where the letters Addie wrote me was. I reckon they got them because the judge told me he had read them."

Before Alexander could say another word, Lady Bruce ran to the edge of the box and started to scream at him. "You idiot. I told you to burn those letters. Can you not do anything right? All you had to do was shoot that bitch and everything would have been alright." she screamed while pointing at Diana.

Again the audience in the gallery burst into loud conversation at this damning revelation. Lady Bruce's barrister grabbed her from behind and pulled her back towards him trying to calm her. She fought her way free of him and rushed to the front of the box she stood in. She looked at Diana with so much hatred, several people nearby shrank away from her.

Lady Bruce strained to get over the edge of the box, all the while screaming obscenities at Diana. The bailiff and her barrister both rushed to hold her back. The gallery was in an uproar. Judge Buchanan was banging his gavel and yelling for order.

Diana's face had paled considerably at the beginning of Lady Bruce's tirade. Edwin and Hannah both put their arms around her to comfort her as tears slid down her cheeks unchecked. She said haltingly, "What did I ever do to that woman to make her hate me so? I hardly knew her and that was over ten years ago. I just don't understand."

Finally, order was again established in the courtroom. Lady Bruce was still screaming, but now what came out of her mouth was utter gibberish. She still tried to free herself from the constraints the bailiff and one of the guards had put her in. It was obvious to all that she was completely deranged. Judge Buchanan ordered her removed from the courtroom.

Horace Alexander still stood in the witness box. He was sobbing into his hands. A more broken man, Diana had never seen. Although she hated him for all he had taken from her, she couldn't help but pity him as well. He had been a man easily led and the woman leading him had obviously been insane.

After Lady Bruce was removed from the courtroom, the judge declared the trial at an end. He declared Lady Bruce insane and ordered her to be locked away in Gartloch Hospital for the insane for the rest of her life. He then passed sentence on Horace Alexander. He was to be remanded to gaol and in two weeks time, he would be hung at the gallows in Edinburgh.

Diana, Hannah, and Edwin left the courtroom by a side door. Reporters from the local papers had tried to interview them when they came into the courthouse earlier and they wanted to avoid them if possible. Edwin went to fetch the Craigs who had been waiting in an anteroom until Lydia testified. Murray had come with them and he went to fetch the carriage leaving Hannah and Diana alone in a corridor outside Judge Buchanan's chambers.

The judge walked out of his chambers and seeing Diana, he went to speak to her. "Your grace, I hardly know what to say. I have never seen such an outburst in all my years as a judge. Lady Bruce is insane and probably has been for many years. If it is any consolation to you, I don't believe you had anything to do with the horrible events she put into motion. I have no idea why she hated you so, and I truly doubt if she did either."

"Thank you, Judge Buchanan. I hardly knew her. She was a neighbor while I was growing up, but our families had little in common and didn't see much of each other. I haven't laid eyes on her in over ten years. I cannot imagine why she would want me dead so badly. It is very disconcerting to think someone hated me enough to try to kill me. It is even more disconcerting to know that my baby and my husband died because of the ineptitude of Horace Alexander and the insanity of Lady Bruce."

Judge Buchanan took his leave just as Edwin arrived with the Craigs. The party moved to the nearest exit where Murray waited with the carriage. Diana was exhausted and could hardly wait to get back to the hotel. She said nothing while they travelled to the hotel. She was so emotionally drained, she could hardly keep her head from falling back against the squabs of the carriage.

When Edwin helped her from the carriage, Diana faltered and almost fell. Murray caught one arm and Edwin the other. They left Ronald to help the other ladies out of the carriage and took Diana into the hotel and up to her room. Barbara greeted them at the door of Diana's bedchamber. She took over and led Diana to the bed. The men left and Barbara helped Diana to undress and get into bed. She didn't question Diana, she could see that she was completely done in. She knew Murray would tell her what happened in the court.

Diana lay in the bed with her arm across her dry eyes. She had no tears left to weep. She had shed all of them over the terrible losses she had sustained over the last ten years, the latest, the death of her dear Edward. She felt empty and so very alone. All purpose to her life seemed to be gone.

Chapter 52

London 1827

The weeks and months passed and Diana's mood did not improve. She took care of her responsibilities for her estates from the Mayfair house in London. She also helped Edward's cousin with the duchy business until he felt comfortable enough to handle the work himself.

Since she was in mourning for Edward, she didn't have to accept any invitations and for this she was very grateful. She had no interest in seeing anyone or going anywhere. She had little interest in her estates either, but her sense of responsibility for her tenants would not allow her to stop taking care of them.

Barbara was very worried about her mistress. She tried to think of anything that might help to alleviate the gloom Diana seemed to be permanently mired in. One day about eight months after the trial in Scotland, Edwin came to visit and Barbara hoped he could pull Diana from her depression.

He had come to London to deliver some horses and came to the Mayfair house to check on Diana. She had corresponded with him several times about estate business, but her letters were so cold and unlike her, he felt he had to come in person to check on her. Normally, he would have sent the new stable master to deliver the horses, but checking on Diana was of paramount importance.

When Edwin was announced by the butler, Diana was surprised. She rose from behind the desk in the library to greet him.

"I didn't know you were coming to London, Edwin. You didn't mention it in your last letter."

"I just decided to accompany the horses at the last minute. I felt one of the mares wasn't quite where I wanted her to be and thought I should work her a little more on the journey. I figured I would be here before a letter could reach you. I hope I haven't come at a bad time." Edwin said.

"No, of course not. I was just working on some correspondence. It is nothing that cannot wait. It is very good to see you. Are you well?"

"Yes, Diana, I am well. How are you? You look a little pale and you have lost weight again."

"Oh, I'm fine, Edwin. I just don't seem to have much of an appetite. I suppose I'm pale because I rarely go out. I don't seem to have any interest in going anywhere. And I am still in mourning for Edward for another two months."

"That's true, but you could at least take a walk in your own gardens sometimes. If I remember correctly, they are very beautiful at this time of year, even in smoky old London."

"Yes, I suppose. I just don't seem to have any interest in the gardens either.", Diana said laconically.

Edwin thought he was right in coming to see Diana. She seemed to be immersed in melancholia. He must find some way to bring her out of it. After some desultory conversation, Edwin asked Diana if she had heard from Ian MacAllister lately.

"Oh, yes.", she said in a brighter tone, "I had a letter from him last week. He and Alana have six children now. Their farm is doing very well. He has purchased more land and is raising some new crops. They seem to love America. Did you know his father went to visit them last year? I suppose Angus decided seasickness wasn't enough to keep him away from his son after all. He once told me he suffered from it greatly. He stayed six months and spoiled his grandchildren terribly."

The light in Diana's eyes when she spoke about her friends gave Edwin an idea. He would write to Ian and Alana and see what they thought. He had known the two of them their whole lives as had Diana. Maybe between the three of them they could help Diana start to live again.

After Edwin's visit, Diana's life settled back down to the same old routine. She spent the mornings on estate business and the afternoons brooding or reading. The library was very extensive, but eventually, even she ran out of books she wanted to read and she couldn't persuade herself to visit the booksellers to buy more.

When her mourning period was over, Diana began to accept a few invitations she didn't think she could really avoid. She started working for the orphan's charity again. The ladies she worked with invited her to tea and dinner. She felt she couldn't turn down every invitation, so she accepted a few. Of course, since she had accepted their invitations, she had to reciprocate and have people over for tea and dinner as well. She took no real pleasure in these engagements. Actually, she saw them as a duty and they felt like drudgery.

When Dickey, Michael, and Bernie were in town, she had dinner with them and their wives. She invited them as well, but it just wasn't the same as when Edward and Benjamin had been alive. Diana rarely smiled and never laughed anymore. She didn't play the pianoforte nor sing either. Her friends were very worried about her. They hated to see her waste her life.

She was so very young and beautiful she could have had her pick of the eligible bachelors of the *ton*, but she wasn't interested in any of them. Diana rarely attended a social function such as a ball, but occasionally she felt she had to put in an appearance if the ball was to raise money or awareness for her charity. On those occasions, she turned down all requests to dance and paid not the slightest bit of attention to the myriad young men who tried to catch her attention. She soon became known as the Ice Duchess and that suited her just fine.

The new year of 1827 had come and gone with nothing new in Diana's life. It was the same drudgery as before. Diana's depression had started to lift and she had become restless.

Now, on the second day of February, Diana was sitting behind her desk in the library dealing with the endless correspondence demanded by owning six large estates. She had just finished a letter to the mining manager for her Cornwall estate when there was a knock on the door and Murray, whom she had elevated to the post of secretary, brought in the daily post.

Diana went through the large stack of letters and sorted them as to their importance by the return addresses. She was quite aware of how her estates were doing and could relegate letters from her estate managers as to their importance. Amid the pile of letters, one stood out. It was from her old friend, Ian MacAllister. That one she would open and read right away. Ian's letters always made her feel better. She may not have any close blood relatives, only a few cousins she hardly knew, but Ian was like a brother to her. They had grown up as close as siblings and through the years, they had maintained their relationship, even if only through letters. She opened the letter immediately. Ian wrote:

Dear Diana,

I hope I find you well. We here, all eight of us, are well. I have good news to give you as well. We will be nine in a few months. Alana will bless me with another child in July. We are overjoyed at the news.

Diana, my dear, it is time for you to come and meet our children. They have heard us speak of you so much, they feel as if they know you. It has been too long since we have seen each other.

I know you have much responsibility with your estates, but surely you can take a few months to come see some old friends. I would have you come see what your investment has wrought.

Please say you will come and visit us here in Virginia. We wait with baited breath for your reply.

Yours always,

Ian

Diana sat looking at the letter for some time after reading it. She picked up her pen and wrote a rather short note to Ian. She dashed off another quick note, then jumped up and ran up the stairs calling for Barbara and Murray.

"Barbara, I need you to start going over my wardrobe. We will need to pack almost everything. I will need to buy a few new things as well. Murray, oh Murray there you are. I need you to take this note to the harbor master and post this letter right away. I want to sail on the first ship leaving for America. We need to land as close to Virginia as possible. We will need two cabins, or three if there are enough available. I want you and Barbara to come with me. We will be gone for several months. Is that a problem for either of you?" Diana asked breathlessly.

Barbara had a huge smile on her face and even Murray managed a small grin. They had both been very worried about their mistress, but it looked like the old Diana was coming back to them.

Murray spoke first, "No, your grace, that will be no problem for me. I have always wanted to go to America. I will go right away to post your letter and book our passage with the harbor master." With that, Murray hurried down the stairs calling for his hat and coat. Diana heard the front door close in just minutes after he got downstairs. She smiled to see him so excited and then turned to Barbara.

Barbara smiled at her and said, "Oh, Miss Diana, it is so good to have you back. I have been that worried about you. This trip will do you a world of good. Now, let us go and look at your clothes. There is much to do and hopefully not much time to do it in."

The two women started to pull dresses out of the giant wardrobes in Diana's room. Soon there were clothes everywhere. Diana rang for the butler and had him have all the trunks brought from the attic. She knew she would be gone for several months and would need to take many trunks to hold all the clothes she, Barbara, and Murray would need. She would also need her jewelry and enough money to see them through several months.

After she saw Barbara and two of the upstairs maids started on packing, she returned to the library to write letters to all her estate managers. They would just have to do without her for a few months. She could handle anything really pressing by post, although it would be much delayed. She sent an especially long letter to Ainsley Glen. In it, she asked Edwin to oversee her other estates while she was gone. She sent him all the information he would need to contact her managers. She gave Edwin's name to all her other managers as the person who would be in charge and her liaison while she was out of the country.

Edwin received Diana's letter a few days later. He was very happy to read that she was going to America to visit with Ian and Alana. He could tell from the tone of her letter that just planning the trip was bringing her out of her depression. He knew that the trip itself would bring their Diana back to them. He was surprised that she asked him to oversee her other estates. He had no qualms about doing it, but had thought she would entrust it to her solicitor. It made him feel special that she trusted him with all her property.

Edwin wrote back immediately and sent the letter with one of his stable hands directly to the house in Mayfair. He didn't want anything to keep Diana from leaving as soon as she could.

When Diana received Edwin's answer, she had already booked passage on a ship for two weeks time. She was gratified that Edwin had the forethought to send his response by one of the stable hands instead of relying on the post. She sent a letter back with the man to let Edwin know her departure date and Ian's address. Everything was coming together nicely, she thought. She and Barbara had worn the other maids out packing and sewing and ironing like mad.

Chapter 53

To Diana's great relief, the day arrived for them to board the ship. They would sail on the morning tide so they were spending the night before aboard ship. Murray managed everything in his usual efficient manner. Two carriages and three wagons left the Mayfair house on that day in mid February. Diana had ten trunks when they were done packing, Barbara had two, and Murray one. Diana had insisted they both have a complete new wardrobe. She felt it was high time they both had new clothes instead of Barbara wearing her remade castoffs and Murray just wearing the same two suits all the time.

Once they were settled on the ship, Diana went out on deck to watch the hubbub entailed in getting a ship ready to sail. They were lucky to have found a ship that would dock, in Portsmouth, Virginia. They would then hire carriages and wagons to travel the fifty miles from there to Ian's farm.

Diana had sent a note to Bernie as soon as she had the name of their port city. She knew he had some connections in Portsmouth. She had hoped he could advise her on where to stay there while they arranged for transportation to Ian's. He had been more than happy to do so. She was supplied with the names of a reputable inn and his friend's name in Portsmouth, Mr. Reilly Turner.

Diana was very excited for the first time since Edward died. It seemed strange to her that she was excited at all. She hadn't been excited about anything in a long time. She found herself smiling as she watched the sailors load cargo into the hold of the ship. Edward would have loved this spur of the moment trip to America. He had expressed a lot of interest in going there himself some day. They had even been discussing future trips when he was killed, though America hadn't come up yet.

She felt that Edward would have applauded her courage in undertaking this voyage with only two servants. Diana was not worried about travelling virtually alone. There was no one she needed to impress with an entourage. She would ask Mr. Turner to suggest some men to accompany them on the trip to Ian's. They would need drivers for the carriages and wagons as well as outriders for protection.

The sun began to set and Diana sought her cabin. Barbara and she would share a cabin and they had been lucky enough to get a small cabin for Murray. There was a knock on the door. One of the ship's officers, a Mr. Quimby, extended an invitation to dine with the officers and the captain. Diana accepted. She had met the captain, Mr. Bowie, when she came aboard. She had been impressed by his manner and courtesy.

Mr. Bowie was a Highland Scot and looked the part. He was a giant of a man, maybe the tallest man she had ever seen. He had broad shoulders, muscular arms, and a flat stomach his coat couldn't hide. He appeared to be in his forties, though he was in top physical condition.. He obviously took care of himself and his ship. The ship was clean and from what Diana could observe while on deck, it was efficiently run.

The dinner in the captain's cabin that evening was the precursor for more to come. The food was plain, but very tasty. Wine was served with dinner, but no one overindulged that Diana could see. The officers were mostly young men who had been in the British navy. They had mustered out after the end of the Napoleonic wars had negated the need for a huge navy and found jobs where they could as commercial seamen. They were all polite, although several of them were prone to flirt with her. She was polite to them, but didn't flirt back.

The captain seemed to be watching her surreptitiously. Suddenly, he said, "Ye be born a MacDonald wasn't ye?"

Surprised, Diana replied, "Yes, my father was Earl Fergus MacDonald of Ainsley Glen. "

"I knew it. I thought ye looked familiar. I bought a horse from yer Da when ye were just a bairn. Ye're the spittin' image of yer mam, Lady Morna. Best horse I ever had. I was just startin' out in those days. Hadn't even been to sea yet. Had just left me Da's farm looking to make me way in the world. Yer Da could have took advantage of a green lad, but not him. He sold me a good horse for a fair price. Him and yer mam even had me to dinner. They had the best cook in the county."

"That would be Mrs. Owen. She's still there, though she's training her granddaughter to take over in a couple of years. She's getting on now, but can still make the best bannocks in the entire world."

The captain laughed and shook his head. "That's her alright. I remember that name now that you mention it. "Tis a small world lass, oh, pardon, yer grace." the captain was embarrassed by his lapse in not using Diana's title and his face turned as red as his hair.

Diana laughed and said, "You may call me lass, if you please, Mr. Bowie It reminds me of my Da."

The rest of the evening was spent with Diana and the captain reminiscing about the Highlands. When she went back to her cabin and told Barbara where the captain was from, her eyes lit up. Being a Highland girl herself, she was always happy when she met another Highlander. The next day, Diana took Barbara to meet the captain. It turned out they were from villages just a few miles apart and knew some of the same people. It was indeed a small world.

The days aboard ship soon took on a routine. Not being one easily bored, Diana enjoyed walking on the deck, watching the men work, and watching the ocean pass by. The ship was a three masted schooner and skipped across the waves at what Diana thought was a very fast speed. The only other ship she had been on was the one they took to Russia. It had been a very large, but quite slow ship. Diana much preferred this one, The Mermaid. She thought the name fanciful, but somehow fitting.

The weather was cold, but clear the first two weeks of the voyage. Then one night Diana was awakened by the crash of thunder and the sight of lightening hitting the water near her porthole. The ship was seemingly being flung from one high wave to another by a very high wind. Barbara was white-faced, sick, and shaking. It was all Diana could do to try to take care of her and offer her some comfort. She didn't have time to feel fear herself and surprisingly she didn't feel in the least sick.. After the storm was over, there was a knock on the cabin door. It was Murray coming to make sure his ladies were alright.

Later when Diana had time to reflect on the storm as she strolled around the deck, she found that she hadn't been frightened at all, but exhilarated instead. She wondered at herself. She had never been a thrill seeker, rather she had always been cautious by nature. Edward and Benjamin had teased her about it. Edward, especially, would ride a horse like there was no tomorrow without a thought to the danger he could be in. Diana, being raised around horses was much more adventurous on horseback than anywhere else, but she still didn't like to take chances with herself or her horse. Thinking of horses, Diana's mind went back in time again to Ainsley Glen.

Diana's thoughts drifted to Malmuirra, the beautiful black mare her father had given her. She had been trained by Edwin and although spirited, she was not dangerous to ride, actually she was easy to ride. Diana thought of all the times she and Ian had run their horses full tilt across the moors without a thought, except as to who would win the race. Diana shook her head.

She could hardly wait to see what kind of man Ian had grown into. From his letters, he seemed to have matured much since she had talked he and Alana into running away to America. She wondered at her own temerity, but was glad it had all turned out so well.

Her thoughts then turned to Lawrence Banbury. She wondered if she would see him while she was in America. From Ian's letters she knew he had married some years ago, but his wife had died in childbirth leaving him with a newborn son to raise alone. Thoughts of Lawrence's son automatically brought her little Geoffrey to mind.

He would be eleven years old now nearly twelve. She wondered what type of boy he would have been. She liked to think he would have been like his father, Geoffrey. He had inherited Geoffrey's looks, but had been so young when he died, his personality hadn't been set yet. He had been such a happy, laughing baby. The sorrow of his loss still brought tears to Diana's eyes even though he had been gone for ten years.

Though it had been over twelve years since his father, Geoffrey, had been killed, she hadn't forgotten him in the least. She wasn't sure she was still in love with him, but she did still think of him with love. He was the only man she had ever had carnal knowledge of. She wondered if she would or even could feel those urges again. Sometimes late at night as she lay in her lonely bed, she would replay that one wonderful night in the barn with Geoffrey over and over. She couldn't help but wonder what her life would have been like if Geoffrey had lived.

All these thoughts flitted through Diana's mind as she spent hours standing at the rail of the ship or sitting on a coil of rope watching the ocean slide by. When thoughts of Lawrence would come unbidden to her, she tried to stop them. She had felt such an attraction to him both times she had been in his company. Though she had known him only a few weeks, she couldn't help but wonder what would have happened if she had let those feelings come to fruition. "No," she thought, "I couldn't have lived with myself if I had cuckolded Edward, even though he would have been fine with it."

Sometimes she was annoyed with herself for not giving in to Edward and Benjamin all those years, but then again, she had done what she felt was right at the time. She just wouldn't have felt right sleeping with another man while she was still a married woman. Her parents had not raised her like that and she just couldn't seem to go against all she had been taught as a girl.

Chapter 54

While Diana was ruminating on the past, Murray was trying to learn all he could about America from the sailors who had been there many times. He was excited to finally be going to America. It had been his dream growing up in a Dublin slum. Everything he heard about that country was new and exciting. A man could make his fortune there if he worked hard and saved his money.

Murray had been one of twelve children and his parents had worked hard to just keep a roof over their heads and their bellies filled. Sometimes, their bellies weren't quite as full as they would have liked though. Some of the men in the tenement where he lived were hard drinkers and wasted their money on the drink regardless of whether their kids ate or not.

His father had not been one of those. He worked hard on the docks as a longshoreman unloading ships. His mother was a washerwoman for a family of the gentry. She spent long hours bent over a tub scrubbing other peoples clothes, but she never let her own children go dirty. Somehow, even with fourteen mouths to feed, his parents had managed to provide the money to send the boys to the Jesuit school at least for a few years. Murray had been one of the younger boys. By the time he was old enough for school, money had become even harder to come by because of the potato famine raging over Ireland. His older brothers had taught him to read already, but he hungered for more.

When he found his parents could not afford to send him, he was terribly disappointed, but he didn't give up his dream of an education. Although he was only eight years old, Murray decided he would earn his school money himself. He started badgering the shopkeepers in his neighborhood for any odd jobs he was big enough to do. Soon he was running errands and making deliveries for three different shop owners. He worked from early until late until he had saved enough for his tuition at the Jesuit school for one year, although it took him a year to make enough money.

On his first day of school, Murray caught the attention of Brother John, one of the younger Jesuits who taught mathematics. Brother John was impressed with the young boy's sharp mind and willingness to work extra hard in his class. He was behind the other boys his age, but soon caught up and even surpassed them. When Brother John learned that young Sean Murray had only one year to learn all he could, he decided to tutor him after hours gratis in several subjects.

The boys mind was like a sponge. He almost absorbed knowledge. Even after his year was up, young Sean could be seen climbing the steps late in the day for a session with Brother John. This went on for five years until Brother John had to tell young Sean he could teach him no more as he was being transferred to a school in America. Brother John painted a glowing picture of the new country to Sean.

That's when the American dream started for Murray. He worked very hard and saved his money religiously. He left Ireland at the age of fifteen to try his luck in Scotland. One of his older brothers, Michael, had gone into service in the household of a member of the nobility in Edinburgh and was able to obtain a footman's position for his younger brother.

Again Sean worked very hard and saved his money. He didn't like the master he and his brother worked for. He was an arrogant and hateful man who treated his servants like slaves. He expected perfection at all times and was not averse to using corporeal punishment when he was unhappy with their work.

One afternoon Sean and Michael were set to polishing the andirons on the fireplaces in the bedrooms on the third floor. This floor was not used by the family, they had their rooms on the second floor. These chambers were only for guests and unused most of the time.

The boys were startled to hear noises coming from the room next door. They went to investigate and found their master trying to undress one of the very young scullery maids. She was crying and pulling away from him, but he kept grabbing her by the hair and pulling her back to him while he laughed.

Sean started into the room, but Michael grabbed his arm and shook his head at him. Sean looked at his brother in horror. Was he to let this bastard have his way with this young girl? She was no more than thirteen and tiny besides. Sean jerked his arm away and started into the room. The nobleman saw him and ordered him to leave, but Sean just kept coming.

When he reached the pair, he planted his left fist in his master's gut knocking him to the floor. The girl pulled her dress up around her shoulders and took off running. When the nobleman was finally able to get his breath back, he threatened to have Sean flogged to death. Michael grabbed his brother and pulled him from the room. Sean was screaming curses at the man the whole time.

Michael hustled Sean up to the attic where they shared a room. He grabbed Sean's bag and started stuffing his clothes in it. He went to his own bed and lifted the mattress. He took the money he had saved and gave it to Sean.

"Ye have to go Sean. The earl will do what he says. He'll have the Watch after ye. Ye have to go and quickly."

"Aye, Michael, I know ye're right, but I could not stop meself. The earl is a monster who preys on little children. He should be stopped."

"Aye, and ye're right, but we can't be the ones stoppin' him. He's the one with all the money and all the power and we're the ones with none."

Sean thought of those words over and over as he walked around the streets of Edinburgh. Right then, he decided he would someday have the money and the power and he would stop men like the earl from hurting little girls if it was the last thing he did.

Hunger finally drove Sean to find a public house to have a meal in. As he sat alone at a table, he overheard two men talking at the next table.

"We had better find another footmen since Crawford seems to have run off with that chambermaid at the inn. Mr. Burroughs will be right upset if there ain't enough footmen to help with the horses and the carriage."

"Yeah, Crawford is a fool. Working at Ainsley Glen ain't hardly like workin'. They treat us good and Duchess Diana is hardly ever there. And that Mrs. Owen sure can cook."

Murray couldn't believe his luck. He spoke to the two men and told them he had just left his place of employment because the master was going to America for quite some time and was only leaving a small staff at his townhouse. They took him along to meet Edwin Burroughs who was in Edinburgh on his honeymoon.

After Edwin interviewed the young man, he was impressed with his intelligence and the amount of knowledge he displayed. He had no experience with horses, but he seemed to know all a footman was required to know. Edwin was a little uncomfortable that he had no references, but he was in a hurry and was leaving town the next morning. He didn't want to wait. His gut instinct told him Murray was a good person and would be an asset to Ainsley Glen. He had never regretted his decision and was very happy that Diana had decided to take the young man with her to America and so was Sean.

While Diana reflected and Murray tried to learn everything he could about America, Barbara had a dilemma of her own. She had spent a lot of time aboard ship talking to Captain Bowie. Barbara had been homesick for her little village in the Highlands recently for some reason. Maybe some of Diana's depression had rubbed off on her. After all, she had cared about the same people Diana had been mourning so long.

Barbara had left her village at the age of thirteen to go into service at Ainsley Glen. One of her aunts was a parlor maid at the keep and recommended her for a position as scullery maid. When

Barbara came to Ainsley Glen, Diana had been eight years old and had no need of a ladies maid.

Barbara's innate intelligence and sweet nature had been noticed by the lady of the keep. She had decided to have Barbara trained as a ladies maid for Diana when she was in need of one. Lady Morna knew she would not live long. She wanted her daughter to have a companion who would treat her well and remain with her as long as she needed.

Morna spoke with her husband, Fergus. "Fergus, my love, I have been thinking."

"Ach, that's no a good thing, love." teased Fergus.

Laughing, Morna lay her hand on his arm and said, "You are probably right most times, but not this time." Then she spoke seriously, "I want to have Barbara trained as Diana's ladies maid. She's bright, pretty, and kind. I think we should have her taught to read as well. Diana will need someone to help her when….Well, we both know my health is not good. As it is, I have to lie down most of the day. Diana will need someone to rely on soon, I fear."

"Oh, Morna lass, don't speak so. I canna think on that day. It makes me too sad. How will I ever go on without you?" Fergus asked with tears in his eyes.

"For Diana. She will need you more than ever when that day comes. You must be strong for her." Morna said with a strength she rarely exhibited.

"Aye, lass, you're right. And I will be strong for our sweet bairn. And for you."

In the months that followed, Mrs. Gwen spent hours every day teaching Barbara how to dress a lady, do her hair, which clothes were best suited to each occasion, and all the other myriad things ladies maids needed to know.

In addition, Morna taught Barbara to read. In books, Barbara discovered a whole world she had not known was out there. She had only lived in her small village and at Ainsley Glen in her brief life. She had never travelled farther than the local village since coming to Ainsley.

In books, she could go anywhere in the world and see sights she had never even imagined existed. Barbara became as inveterate a reader as Diana. They shared many hours talking about the books they had read. Barbara became Diana's companion, but most importantly, her friend.

Two years later when the dreaded day of Lady Morna's death arrived, it was Barbara who comforted the ten year old Diana the most. The Laird's grief was almost overwhelming to him. He tried to help his wee daughter, but his pain was so intense, he felt he failed miserably. However, Barbara was a great comfort to Diana and helped her through the loss of her beloved mother. That experience brought the young girls even closer together.

Barbara had never thought much beyond being Diana's maid and companion. Being very shy around men, she never thought she might fall in love or marry. In all the years of travelling with Diana, she had never met a man who attracted her, though there had been many handsome young secretaries and footmen around through the years.

Now, she was beginning to have feelings for Captain Bowie and he seemed to be developing feelings for her as well. Their talks had gone from reminiscences of their childhoods in their neighboring villages to their life experiences. Captain Bowie was easy to talk to and oh, so handsome. With his dark red hair, impressive physique, and laughing blue eyes, he had captivated Barbara's heart.

As the weeks of the voyage sped by, Barbara and the captain quickly came to know each other well. They shared a mutual respect for each other, but more importantly, they had a very strong mutual attraction to each other. On one of the last days of the voyage, the captain and Barbara stood at the rail one moonlit night staring into each other's eyes. His arm was around her shoulders and she leaned against him.

"Barbara, lass, there is something I must say to ye. I have come to know ye and to love ye these weeks. I would marry ye when we reach Portsmouth and take ye back to Scotland with me on the next voyage to meet my family, if ye're willin'. As I've told ye, I have a house in Edinburgh. Ye could either live there and wait for me between voyages, or ye could come with me and sail the seas. I would prefer to have ye with me, but I would understand if ye preferred to stay to home. Life at sea is not for everyone."

"Oh, Richard, I would be ever so happy to be your wife. And no, I would not want to stay to home, but would prefer to be with you wherever you go." Barbara said breathlessly. Then she frowned, "But what will I tell my lady. She depends on me. She is not only my mistress, but my friend as well. She has known so much heartache in her life, I would not be the cause of more. I don't know if I can leave her, even though I have come to love you too." With those words, tears rand down Barbara's cheeks unchecked and the captain wrapped both his big arms around her.

A voice behind them made them both jump and turn swiftly around. "Barbara, I would have you happy. Yes, I depend on you and I love you as the dearest friend I have ever had, but I would never stand in the way of your happiness. I'm sorry if I eavesdropped, but I was walking past and couldn't help hearing you both. You have my blessing if marrying Captain Bowie is what you truly want." Diana said with tears in her eyes as well.

The two women embraced and the gruff captain found his own eyes smarting as he watched his tall beautiful Barbara hugging the diminutive red haired duchess, with both of them crying happy tears.

Plans were made then, right on the deck, for the marriage of Captain Richard Bowie and Barbara McKenzie. Diana wanted to give them a fine wedding. She asked the captain if he could leave his ship long enough to travel with them to Ian's farm. She knew Ian and Alana would be happy to host a wedding for the two. They had known Barbara as long as she had and would welcome a chance to help her begin her new life as a wife.

The captain agreed and the three of them adjourned to the captain's cabin to toast the engagement and discuss arrangements in detail. Diana sent for Murray to join them. She would depend on him for a lot of the arrangements. Murray was happy for Barbara. He had come to like her a lot in the years he had served the duchess.

Captain Bowie had met many of the nobility in his years as a sea captain, but he had never met one like Duchess Diana. She took on no airs, she treated everyone she met with equanimity, and she valued her servants highly. She treated them like friends or even members of her family. He thought she would do well in America, where nobility held no sway with how people were treated. Personal merit was the way of the Americans. If you deserved their respect and love, you got it. Otherwise, you just did not. They were an independent minded lot, those Americans.

Chapter 55

Diana was up before sunrise on the last day of the voyage. Land had been sighted the day before and the captain had told them at dinner that they would make Portsmouth the next day. Diana was excited beyond measure.

Barbara helped her dress warmly as there was a northerly breeze blowing today and it was very chilly for early April. Diana wore a soft brown velvet day dress with long fitted sleeves with a large bows at the shoulders. It fitted her beautifully in the bodice which tapered down to a point just below her tiny waist. The skirt flowed over her hips in a narrow circle over just two petticoats. The dress was trimmed in a wide copper colored ribbon on the sleeves and also just below the point on her skirt. Her hat was the same shade of brown as were her boots. The hat had a wide brim and it was decorated with leaves and greenery, along with the same copper ribbon as her dress. Under her hat, Barbara had dressed her hair in a low chignon with a piece of the copper ribbon around it. She had gained back her weight and the days on board the ship had added color to her smooth ivory skin. She looked very beautiful.

The sun was just coming up as Diana, Barbara, and Murray came up on deck. They could see the Portsmouth harbor clearly. The town itself wasn't very large, but the harbor was and it was teeming with life. There were several ships berthed there, all in stages of being loaded or unloaded. The harbor became larger and larger as they got closer to the dock.

Diana was amazed at the sights and sounds of Portsmouth. She saw people of all kinds on the docks. She saw what she thought must be Indians for the first time. She had read descriptions of them in *The Sketch Book* by Washington Irving and was fascinated by their culture and looks. The people she saw at the dock had very dark hair which they wore long, adorned with feathers and beads. Their clothes were strange to her. They seemed to be made of animal skins and also had feathers and beads of some type attached to them.

For the first time, Diana beheld Negroes. Again, she had read descriptions and Ian had written to her about the slaves that were owned by many Virginia planters and the free men and women who worked on his farm. But actually seeing the dark skinned people for the first time was a revelation to her. It bothered her deeply that none of them looked happy. There were no smiles upon their faces and their posture suggested they were downtrodden and sad. She, who had had servants all her life, would never be able to understand actually owning another human being. She wasn't sure she was going to like America after all.

Suddenly, Barbara tugged at her sleeve. "Look, your grace, that man is waving at the ship. Do you think that it is Ian? He seems too large to be Mr. Ian, though the blond hair is right."

Diana looked to where Barbara pointed and knew immediately it was her old friend, Ian. He was a much larger man now, but it had been over twelve years since she had seen him last, but she would know him anywhere. He was waving his hat in the air with a huge smile upon his face. Diana's face burst into a huge smile and she jumped up and down waving at him. She didn't care if she wasn't showing the proper decorum, she was thrilled to see her old friend after so many years.

As soon as the gangplank was down, Ian rushed on board. Barbara had told the captain that their friend was there and he had welcomed Ian aboard himself. Diana rushed into Ian's arms. He caught her up and whirled her around and around all the while laughing with glee.

When finally he put her down, Diana looked up into his familiar face. She then realized he was familiar and yet strange to her. The years had been kind to Ian, but he had aged some. Of course she had last seen a boy of nineteen and he was now a man of thirty-one. His blue eyes held laugh lines at their corners as did his mouth. His abundant blond hair was just as thick, but he now wore it in a long queue down his back. His skin was brown and weathered by the sun, but he was still the same exuberant Ian she had known and loved as a child and young girl.

Ian laughed as he looked down at Diana's beautiful face. "You haven't changed a bit, lass. You're still the bonniest girl I ever saw next to my Alana. Oh, lass, it's so very good to see you. I have missed your smiling face so much these years."

Diana's smile matched his. "Oh, Ian, it is so very good to see you. Your letters have sustained me in times of trouble, but seeing you in the flesh is wondrous. Are Alana and the children with you? I cannot wait to see them all."

"Nay, lass, with the babe just a few months away, Alana didn't feel she should make the trip. It takes about four days of hard travel to get here from my place. I hope you haven't forgotten how to ride. I've brought you one of Lawrence's horses. He picked her out special for you when I told him you were on your way. I just barely made it here myself. You didn't give me much warning, but it was enough, I got here yesterday. I came horseback, but we can hire some carriages and wagons for you and your servants."

"Oh, Ian, I would love to ride with you. It will be like old times." Just then Diana noticed that Ian was not alone. A tall dark-haired man had suddenly appeared behind him. It was Lawrence Banbury. Diana's heart, which was already racing in excitement, began to beat even more erratically and she almost lost her breath as she met his entrancing grey eyes.

The spark was still there when their eyes met. He, too, looked older, but he was still a fine looking man. Tall and lean with dark hair and riveting eyes, he stood looking down at her with a broad smile upon his face.

Seeing the two of them staring at each other, Ian was quick to understand that there was more to this relationship than he had been lead to believe. He had always thought Lawrence was a friend to both Diana and her husband, Edward. From the way they were looking at each other, it was only Diana that Lawrence was interested in. Ian had a momentary thought that they had been lovers, but he quickly put it aside. Diana would never take a lover while she was married. He knew her too well for that.

Actually, as he looked at Diana, he thought her almost virginal. How could that be? She had born a child and been married for several years. How could she look so innocent, almost like a young girl. There was much Ian planned to discover about his old friend during this visit. Letters were fine, but seeing a person and talking to them for hours was the only way to get the true picture.

When Ian turned to greet Barbara, Lawrence stepped forward and took Diana's hand. "It is so very good to see you again, your grace. My condolences on the death of your husband."

"Thank you, my lord. And mine on the death of your wife. How is your son? Is he with you?"

"Please, no my lord here. In America, titles are a thing of the past. I am just Mr. Banbury here and I find I like it. No, Nathaniel isn't with me. We made the trip very swiftly and I felt it would be too hard on him. He is only five.

Unfortunately, this winter was hard on him. He caught a cold and it went to his chest. I was very worried for a time, but he is beginning to bounce back and become his old lively self. However, I didn't feel comfortable with bringing him this time. You will meet him when we reach Ian's. Alana very graciously insisted he stay with she and children. He loves being at the MacAllister farm. So many other children to play with and so much to keep him entertained."

Diana could see the love for his son shining in Lawrence's eyes. She wanted to ask him more about it, but the captain came over and told them their luggage had been off loaded and they could go ashore now, if they pleased.

Diana turned to Ian then, "Oh, Ian, I have a large favor to ask of you. I do apologize for doing so the minute I get here, but I believe you will be happy to do it when you hear what it is."

"Di, there is nothing I wouldn't do for you, and you know it. Alana and I owe you more than we could ever repay. You are the reason we are so happy and so well off. Now, what is it you want or need. Just say the word and if it is possible at all, it will be yours." Ian said exuberantly while hugging her again.

Laughing, Diana told him the favor wasn't actually for her, but for Barbara and the captain. She explained that they wanted to marry and she wanted to give them a wedding. She asked if the captain might accompany them on the trip and stay until the wedding could be arranged.

Ian, after shaking the captains hand said, "Of course, of course. Barbara is an old friend to my wife and I. We would deem it an honor to host her wedding. If Diana and Barbara both approve of you, sir, then you must be a good man. You are most welcome to travel with us and to stay with us as long as you would like."

Murray walked up to the group then and said, "Your grace, I went ashore as soon as we docked. I found the gentlemen your friend recommended quite quickly. His offices are very near the dock. He has suggested a hostelry where we can obtain carriages and wagons. I have brought a carriage and booked rooms at a close by inn he also recommends."

"Ah, Murray, what would I do without you. As usual you have outdone yourself in taking care of all the details that went right out of my head when I saw Ian. Thank you so much. Let us away then. We can talk more after we're settled in and get something to eat."

The group followed Murray down the gangplank to a waiting carriage. He had also brought a wagon for the luggage. Ian and Lawrence had their horses at the dock and after helping Murray and the captain load the luggage, they rode behind the carriage to the inn. Soon they were sitting at a table in a private sitting room feasting on venison pie and ale.

The conversation was festive. Ian was a little surprised that Diana's servant Murray joined them for the meal. He wasn't surprised that Barbara was there. They had all grown up together. He had expected Diana to have forgotten her democratic ways since she had become a duchess. Apparently, she was the same old Di.

When she was younger, you never knew where you would find her. She might be in the kitchen or the stables. Or she could be at the home of one of her father's tenants helping someone who was ill, in childbirth, or just visiting some of the old people who could no longer work. It looked to Ian as if she had not changed at all. He just couldn't see her lording it over anyone, duchess or not.

Ian also observed that Lawrence had hardly taken his eyes off Diana since they met on the ship. During the ride from the dock, Lawrence was obviously distracted. He answered Ian's comments with a slight shake of his head or a murmured word. All the while, he had stared at the carriage just ahead of them like a man in a trance. Ian found it amusing that his usually businesslike friend seemed to have been thrown off kilter by one little red-haired lass.

Ian also watched Diana, but she was harder to read. He did catch her glancing quickly at Lawrence more than once, but that was all. She was busily asking a million questions about what could be done for Barbara's wedding. She wanted her to have a new dress, something "spectacular", she said.

She wanted to know if Ian had a seamstress on his farm. When he answered that one of his free women who worked for him took care of what sewing Alana didn't do, she pounced like a cat with even more questions about the woman's talents.

Ian finally laughed and said, "Di, she sews dresses and shirts for the children. I don't think she's some fancy couturier. She does plain sewing. This is Virginia, not London. I'm sure she will be able to make Barbara a perfectly fine wedding dress if we can find some suitable material here in Portsmouth."

"Oh, Ian, I'm sorry. I'm just going on and on. But this is important to me. I want Barbara and the captain to have the best wedding I can give them. Barbara is the sister I never had and I have grown fond of the captain as well. As for material, there is no need to purchase any here. I brought a whole trunk full with me. I had no idea what would be available and thought if I decided to stay for some time, I might need some more clothes. Barbara and I have already picked out the fashion plate and the silk."

"Women," Ian laughed, "You might know you two would have already gotten your heads together." He turned to Captain Bowie, "Captain, are you sure you know what you're getting into here. As an old married man, I can tell you they never change. The first thing they always think of when going somewhere is "what will I wear?"

They all laughed with Ian. Then the captain, taking Barbara's hand in his, said, "Aye, Mr. MacAllister, I know exactly what I'm getting into. I believe it's called wedded bliss."

Barbara blushed beet red and again the entire group had a good laugh. The friends soon began to make plans for their trip to Ian's farm. Diana informed them that she would like to begin the journey tomorrow if everything could be arranged. At that, Murray took his leave to begin preparations and gather supplies. Ian accompanied him as well as Lawrence and the captain, leaving the two women alone.

Barbara was quiet for some minutes and then said, "Miss Diana, are you really sure you can do without me? I feel that awful about leaving you here in a strange land all alone."

"Oh, Barbara, I'm not alone at all. I have Ian and Alana and their whole family. I also have Murray who is a miracle worker when anything needs to be done. I will be perfectly fine. I'm sure I can find a girl to do my hair and take care of my clothes at Ian's or I will hire one. You will have a little time to train her to do the things I need done before the wedding. You do know I can dress myself and brush my own hair, don't you?" Diana said laughing.

"Aye, I know you can do it, but you're not used to doing it. That's the thing that worries me. But you're right. If you will inquire of Mr. Ian whether there is someone I can train, I will do my best in the time we have to get her up to snuff."

The rest of that afternoon was spent in making plans for the wedding. Diana was very pleased for Barbara, but she had to admit, if only to herself, that she would miss Barbara very much. They had been together almost every day since they were children. Barbara had been with her during every tragedy she had suffered in her life from losing her mother to Edward's death and had been a big part of her recovery every time.

She honestly didn't know what she would do without her, but she couldn't be selfish. Barbara had the chance to have a wonderful life with Captain Bowie. Diana would not let anything stand in the way of her friend's happiness.

Soon, the men returned and let them know that all arrangements had been made. They could leave at dawn the next day. It would take them probably four to five days travel to reach Ian's farm which was a few miles outside Williamsburg.

That night Diana could hardly sleep from the excitement of finally seeing Ian's farm and meeting his children. She also longed to see Alana again. Alana had been one of her few friends when they were children. Some of the other parents in the area wouldn't allow Alana to play with their children because of her father's drinking. Fergus MacDonald thought they were fools for blaming a small girl for her father's sins. He never denied Diana her friendship with Alana and welcomed the pretty wee thing into his home anytime. He even had Alana learn to read and cipher right along with Diana. She was one of the few girls in the area who could read, write and do mathematics, except for the daughters of the gentry.

When Diana had made it possible for Ian and Alana to elope, she had been very unselfish. She had, in effect, sent away her two best friends, leaving only Barbara for a close companion. And now, Barbara was to leave her too. Diana shed some quiet tears at the thought that after Barbara left her, there would be no one who was that close to her. No one who knew her heartaches and her happiness.

Barbara woke Diana long before dawn to help her dress for the journey to Ian's farm. It was again a very cool day with a brisk north wind. Barbara took out Diana's thickest riding habit, long boots and flannel petticoats and drawers. She also made sure Diana had her thickest cloak and riding gloves.

When Diana saw the mare Lawrence had brought for her, she gasped. She looked so much like the mare her father had given her for her sixteenth birthday, Malmuirra. Diana's beloved mare was at Ainsley Glen. now She had gotten too old to ride, but Diana thought she deserved to live out the rest of her life where it had begun. Edwin made sure she was very well taken care of.

Diana asked Lawrence, "What is her name? She's a beauty. She reminds me of my horse in Scotland."

He replied, "That's what I thought when she was born, so I named her Malmuirra in honor of your mare.", he said with a smile that was meant only for Diana.

Diana's face flushed a deep red and she hastened to mount the mare with Murray's assistance. She was very flustered by not only Lawrence's words, but his tone. It was deep and intimate. The sound of his voice did shocking things to her insides. She was very confused by her reactions to Lawrence. They hardly knew each other really. They had spent a few weeks in each other's company on two different occasions a few years apart, almost always around other people.

Yes, they had been attracted to each other, but they had not acted upon it. Diana couldn't understand her reaction to this man. What made him different from say Dickey or Michael or any of the many other men she had met through the years? Why was it his voice that made her tremble and a warm glow begin in the lower part of her belly?

Diana was soon immersed in looking at the countryside they were passing through. They had left Portsmouth behind quickly. There were a few isolated farms for the first few miles, then there was nothing except deep virgin forest on both sides of the narrow road. Diana recognized a few of the trees like ash, oak and birch, but many were strange to her.

The forest was so thick in places that she couldn't see through the undergrowth. There was sunlight on the road, but it was almost complete shade in the forest. Diana rode between Lawrence and Ian. It felt so good to be on a horse again. She hadn't ridden in quite some time and after a few hours, her body began to rebel. She wouldn't ask for a rest though, she was too stubborn. She knew Ian would tease her unmercifully if she called a halt before it was time for luncheon. The mare had a nice gait, but Diana's lack of recent experience began to be really painful.

Finally they came to a crossroads where a small inn was situated. They dismounted as the carriage and wagons caught up. The innkeeper came out to greet them. He was a very short, rotund gentleman of indeterminate years. What little hair he had was gray, but his round face was pink and young looking. He sported a jolly smile and was very welcoming. He obviously knew Lawrence and Ian as he called them by name. Diana was soon introduced and was amused to find out the man's name was Oliver Pinkman. Since he had a very florid complexion, she felt it suited him quite well.

Mr. Pinkman ushered them into the inn, making sure they were comfortable. He called for his wife and she soon brought out their lunch of cold meat, bread, cheese and preserved peaches. The food was abundant and very good. Diana had been impressed by the bounty to be found in this new country. She questioned Ian intently about the crops he raised and the markets where he took his produce. Ian was somewhat surprised the she seemed to know so much about the business end of farming, however Lawrence was not.

He remembered that while she had stayed with his uncle, she had worked very diligently to take care of duchy business while Edward recovered from his accident. She had spent hours every day closeted with Benjamin answering and sending correspondence regarding the many estates owned by the duchy.

Ian had grown tobacco when he first started farming, but that crop soon depleted the land and prices also started to drop. He had then turned to wheat and sheep. He also raised horses and cattle, but mostly for his own use. Lawrence on the other hand raised mostly horses and only grew feed crops to keep his expenses down.

Lawrence watched Diana as she asked her questions of her friend. She was even more beautiful than she had been when he first met her. The tragedies of her life only seemed to have touched her eyes. They were so very sad. When Lawrence first met Diana she had just lost her child and her husband was gravely wounded. Her eyes had been sad then as well, but she had seemed to snap herself out of her grief and depression fairly quickly.

Ian had told Lawrence about the letter form Edwin Burroughs concerning Diana's long period of grief and depression after Edward's death and the ordeal of Lady Bruce's trial. Ian had also gleaned from her letters that she was not bouncing back very quickly from the latest tragedy to strike her young life.

He had wanted to go to England to be with her, but Alana's newest pregnancy had precluded that. They would have had to stay until after the child was born and Ian couldn't be away from his farm that long. Ian had seven hundred acres in all now and it demanded his full attention most of the time.

Chapter 56

Lawrence, himself, had almost as many acres, though much of his land was pasture. It had taken years to clear all the trees to make those pastures, but he had been able to build a sawmill on his property and sell the lumber for a nice profit. He had sold untold number of board feet to William and Mary College in Williamsburg for the construction of several dormitories to house the students there. That sale alone had managed to make him very wealthy. He had done very well in America and was well satisfied with his life there, but he was lonely.

Lawrence's wife, Amanda, had been rather frail, though quite beautiful. She had been the daughter of a local wealthy tobacco planter. She had been a good wife, but Lawrence had never felt about her as he knew he should. He had determined at a certain point in his life that he required a wife, so he had procured one. The woman he truly cared for was already married and out of reach. Amanda was a quiet, reserved person who maintained his home well and who's connections were an asset to his business. Their marriage bed was for the most part shared as a duty to obtain an heir.

When Amanda first became pregnant, she contracted pneumonia and was deathly ill for several months. Her strength never returned from that illness. When Nathaniel had been born, the midwife nor the doctor could staunch her bleeding and she had quietly slipped away, leaving Lawrence to raise his son alone after only eighteen months of marriage.

Nathaniel was the light of his life. He was everything that Lawrence had hoped for in a son. He was a bright, inquisitive boy with a joyful disposition. He laughed easily and loved deeply. Lawrence had great plans for his son's future.

As Lawrence once again looked at Diana, he caught her eye and they stared at each other for what seemed like an eternity. Ian had been speaking to Barbara and Captain Bowie about his farm, but he noticed the intensity of feeling that seemed to flow from Diana and Lawrence. He had high hopes those feelings might grow. He would love to have his old friend marry his new friend and settle near he and Alana. It would make his already good life just about perfect. He could hardly wait to see Alana and tell her what he suspected about their friends feelings for each other. Alana was a good judge of human nature and he was anxious to see if she agreed with his assessment of the situation.

Barbara was also aware of the emotional tension between her mistress and the handsome Mr. Banbury. Barbara had observed them together before in England and had noticed something then. She had never spoken of it to Diana though, as it was not her place. She knew her mistress well and knew she would never had have an illicit affair while she was married. Barbara had also been privy to Edward and Benjamin urging Diana to take a lover. She knew how moral Diana was and knew she would never do such a thing.

However, they were both widowed now, maybe something would come of it this time. She sincerely hoped so. She wanted Diana to be as happy as she was. She could leave her here in this wild new country with a better conscience if she thought Diana was happy. She hadn't been happy in a long time. "No," Barbara thought, "the poor dear little thing has never been truly happy since her bairn died."

The return of Mr. Pinkman to their table brought Lawrence and Diana out of their trance. Mr. Pinkman thought to warn them of some trouble in the neighborhood recently. There had been a renegade Cherokee who shot at a local farmer and his wife who were travelling on this same road, after he had stolen some horses from them. The Indian had missed, but it had scared the man and his wife very badly.

Ian said, "Well, I don't think one lone Indian would approach us. We have quite a party with us. Between Lawrence, Captain Bowie, Murray, and myself, not to mention the drivers and the other men we hired for the journey, we number twelve armed men."

Murray spoke up, "Don't forget her grace, sir. She carries a pistol whenever we travel and she is a crack shot."

"That she is", laughed Ian. "She used to embarrass me badly when we were young. She could out ride and out shoot me. Lawrence, did you know that our Diana is quite the huntress. Her parents aptly named her. I have seen her take down a stag on the run from a moving horse. Her mother was the same and she taught Diana to shoot when she was very young. They tried to teach my Alana and Barbara, but they neither one had the eye for it."

Barbara laughed and spoke up, "It wasn't that we didn't have the eye. We didn't have the courage. Alana and I were both afraid of guns. I still am."

"My Alana is too, but she has learned to shoot our old blunderbuss just for protection. The last time she shot it in practice, it knocked her down and bruised her shoulder. She told me I would have to protect the family from now on." Ian said laughing even harder."

Diana just laughed along with the rest of the party, but she noticed Lawrence looking at her quizzically. She did have a loaded pistol, actually, she had three. She carried her derringer in her handbag and a la brace loaded dueling pistols in her saddlebags. Her parents had both always impressed upon her the need to be able to protect herself. The times they lived in were not always peaceful.

After their stop for luncheon, the party pressed on at a brisk pace for the rest of the day. They spent the night rough, as there was no inn nor house close to where they were when it began growing dark. They moved only a small distance off the road into a clearing that had obviously seen other travellers. There were signs of burnt out fires in more than one place. The men went about setting up camp quickly before the last of the light failed.

When the fire was burning well, Barbara began preparations for their supper. She made a stew from some of the dried meat with potatoes, onions, and carrots. It was hearty and very welcome on this cool night. After everyone had eaten, Diana helped Barbara clean the dishes with water brought from a nearby creek.

They were all quite tired from their exertions of the day and soon lay down around the fire to try to find their rest. Barbara had made a bed for Diana and herself from cloaks and blankets they had bought in Portsmouth for just this type of night.

Diana hadn't slept on the ground since she was a young girl and had gone hunting with her father and some of his friends. Ian had been on the trip as well. Diana heard Ian's voice say softly, "Just like old times, 'eh Di? Do you remember the night we slept on the moors with our fathers after you snagged that huge stag with only one shot? Your Da was so proud of you, he couldn't stop talking about it. I was that mad at you that night. I bet you didn't even know that, did you?"

"I remember that night well, Ian. And yes, I knew you were angry. You didn't speak to me at all that night and hardly the next day. I didn't know why you felt that way though, you never said." Diana said just as softly.

"It was because my brothers rode me high about a girl out shooting me. They just wouldn't shut up about it."

"That's silly. I out shot them too, or didn't they think of that?"

Ian chuckled softly, "Nay, and neither did I until just this very moment. You always were the smartest one of us. You always seemed to know the why of things."

"Oh, Ian, if only that were true." Diana said softly. Then she turned over and tried to go to sleep. Sleep was far from coming easily though. Diana lay awake for hours wondering why she didn't know the "why" of her attraction to Lawrence. Yes, he was handsome, but so were lots of men. He was intelligent and had a good sense of humor, but again so did a lot of men. She just could not figure it out, so finally she made herself stop thinking about it and was able to sleep, however fitfully.

The next four days followed the same routine. They didn't always have an inn to stop at, so they ate a lot of meals cooked over campfires at night and cold meat and bread during the day. Diana's body finally got used to the riding on the third day, but she was very uncomfortable until it did. Barbara had seen how stiffly she was moving and folded a blanket over her saddle on the second day. It helped some, but Diana was very glad when that day ended and she could get down from Malmuirra again.

Chapter 57

Finally, around noon on the fifth day, the party came over a rise and saw Ian's farm spread in the valley below. He had built a fine house of red brick. It had three stories and many windows that glittered in the sun. Diana could see many dark skinned people working in the fields and around the outside of the house. There were several outbuildings as well as a huge barn painted red to match the brick on the house.

When they started down into the valley, they were spotted by one of the workers who raised a hand and waved, then ran towards the house. Soon Alana and seven very active children came running from the house towards them. Alana was moving fairly slowly and lagged back with the younger children, but the older of the boys met them in just a few minutes.

He cried, "Da, you made it back right quick. We weren't expecting you for another couple of days." He ran to Ian and was hoisted up on Ian's horse for a hug. Ian turned to Diana, "This is my oldest son, Di, this is Angus. I named him for my Da. Da was that proud when he met him when he was here. Say hello to Lady Diana, son."

The boy ducked his head, but then curiosity got the best of him and he looked at Diana and smiled shyly saying, "How do, Lady Diana. I'm pleased to make your acquaintance." He jumped down from the horse then and ran back to join his mother and his siblings with a bright red face.

Angus was a boy of twelve and was tall and strong. He looked very much as Ian had at that age. Diana looked at the brood with Alana and her heart clutched with a surprising spurt of jealousy. She was startled to have that feeling. She had been around other children since her Geoffrey had been killed and they hadn't affected her like this. Why would she be jealous of Ian and Alana's children? "Well," she thought, "I will just have to get over this silly feeling."

With Murray's help, she climbed from Malmuirra and ran toward Alana. She was met with open arms. The two women hugged each other for several minutes murmuring quietly in each other's ears. They finally parted and looked at each other.

Alana thought, "Oh no, Diana looks the same and I look like an old fat cow." Then she laughed at herself and said to Diana, "Ye look wonderful, Di. It's so very good to see ye after all these years. Come and meet our brood. They have talked of nothing but ye since yer letter came."

Diana laughed and said, "Oh, Alana, I almost think I can tell you their names from your letters. Please let me try."

Alana smiled and said, "Go ahead, Di. You young ones line up now."

The children lined up and Diana was amused to see they had lined up according to size making her job even easier.

She started with Angus. "Well, I have already met this handsome young man. This is Angus. And the very pretty young lady beside him is Diana, my namesake. This fine looking fellow here must be Richard, the sweetheart beside him is Bonnie, this little one must be Alec and this handsome baby is Robbie, I bet. That's six, but I see another one," Diana said smiling at the little boy partially hidden behind Bonnie.

" This very fine looking young man must be Nathaniel. I am an old friend of your father's, Nathaniel. It is a pleasure to meet you. It's a pleasure to finally meet you all. Did I get it right, Alana?"

Alana laughed, "Aye, you have them all. How did you remember them all? Sometimes I almost forget their names myself."

Ian came up beside Alana and put his arm around her plump shoulders. He casually lay his hand on her stomach and Diana felt a visceral pain in her gut. What was the matter with her? Was it the fact they had six wonderful, healthy children, or their casual intimacy that made her almost green with envy.

She mentally shook herself and said brightly, "Oh Ian, you have a beautiful family. You and Alana have done well. Six lovely children and this beautiful house in just a thirteen years. You must both be very proud."

"Aye, lass," Ian replied. "We are that proud. But you know none of this would have been possible without your generosity. We owe all this to you. If ever you need anything from us, you have only to ask."

Diana felt awful. Her friends were so kind to her and she repaid them with envy and jealousy. What kind of person was she? She said quickly, "Ian, you and Alana don't owe me anything. Your friendship is all I will ever need and I thank you for it. It means the world to me."

Diana felt, rather than saw, Lawrence walk up behind her. The hair on her arms stood up as well as the fine hairs on the nape of her neck. She didn't understand why she was so very aware of him at all times.

He was holding his son when she turned around. Diana smiled at the small boy and he ducked his head. She looked up at Lawrence and caught him gazing at his son with such love, it hurt her heart to see it. Again, she thought what she felt must be envy. Maybe coming here had been a mistake. She didn't seem able to see all these beautiful children without feeling the pain of losing Geoffrey all over again. She was deeply ashamed of what she saw as selfishness.

When Lawrence glanced at Diana, he saw the deep pain in her eyes. She quickly turned away to introduce Captain Bowie to Alana. Barbara and he had joined the group as soon as the carriage finally made it into the drive. Murray stood outside the group patiently awaiting instructions from Diana. Barbara was hugging Alana and being introduced to the children when Diana went to speak to Murray.

"Murray, would you please see to the unloading of the wagons. I will ask Ian where he wants our things to be placed. If you would also see to paying the drivers and other men when the job is finished, I would appreciate it." She reached into her bag and took out a small bag of gold coins, handing it to Murray.

Ian walked over and led Murray and the other men toward the house with the wagons following. Alana gathered her brood and ushered her guests into the house. She led them into a very large drawing room at the front of the house. It was well proportioned and nicely decorated.

There was a sofa and several armchairs arranged around the huge, ornately carved fireplace where a small fire took the chill off the morning. The wood on the furniture was mahogany and polished to a high shine. The upholstery on the sofa was a dark, mossy green and the chairs were covered in shades of bronze and a deep orange. The fireplace surround was pained a bright white and was the focal point of the room. The walls were plastered and painted a soft green a few shades lighter than the sofa.

There was a fine landscape painting above the fireplace and other paintings scattered on the walls. Several occasional tables were scattered around the room and held objects such as silver candelabras, figurines, and miniatures of the children. The drapes were a soft cream with printed leaves that mimicked all the colors of the furniture from the brown of the wood to the deep orange on some of the chairs. In the center of the room hung a beautiful crystal chandelier.

Diana was impressed with the room. It was very elegantly done. She gave her compliments to Alana, who looked pleased. Alana summoned a servant and ordered tea for everyone. The children were sent to have their tea in the kitchen and the adults settled down to catch up with each other.

Lawrence watched Diana as she conversed with the group. She appeared to be her normal self, but he couldn't forget the look in her eyes he had seen just a few minutes ago. Something was bothering her and he meant to try to find out what it was. He was sure she felt the same attraction that he did. It was obvious from the way her eyes held his when they met by accident.

He meant to act upon that attraction this time. There was no impediment to their being together if it was what she also desired. He felt an intense need to know for sure and had a hard time reigning in his impatience. There had been no opportunity to speak to her alone on the trip from Portsmouth. He intended to try to make such an opportunity soon.

Soon the talk turned to Barbara and the Captain's wedding. Alana seemed thrilled for Barbara and had no qualms about hosting the celebration. She said they had planned to have a gathering soon to introduce Diana to their friends anyway, so they could just combine the two and have a grand party.

She asked if Barbara and Captain Bowie wanted a private ceremony first and the party with the neighbors after. They both agreed a private wedding ceremony was what they wanted. It was decided that the wedding would be in the morning and then that evening, there would be a family dinner with a gathering of neighbors later. A date was decided in two weeks time.

Diana inquired about the seamstress Ian had told her about. Her name was Jeanette and she was originally from New Orleans. She had been the slave of a dressmaker there until her mistress died. In her will, she had set Jeanette, as well as all her other slaves, free. When they got their freedom, they had immediately travelled north together by ship for fear they would be claimed as slaves by someone else. They had somehow ended up in Williamsburg trying to find work. Ian had been looking for more people and had hired all of them.

After Diana's luggage had been brought in, Alana sent a servant after Jeanette. Diana, Alana, Barbara, and Jeanette went up to look at the materials she had brought with her. She and Barbara had tentatively settled on a light blue silk brocade, but were open to suggestions. Jeanette appeared quite young. She was a petite, very dark-skinned woman who wore her hair covered by a tignon, New Orleans style. She had large, very dark brown eyes with long lashes. Her brows were thin and arched delicately over her eyes. Her nose was narrow and slightly elongated and she had a beautifully shaped mouth with full lips. Her figure was full, but she wasn't fat at all. Diana thought her one of the most beautiful women she had ever seen. She was so exotic and different from anyone Diana had ever met, she was fascinated by her.

Jeanette's accent had a distinctly French lilt to it. On instinct, Diana asked her a question in French. Jeanette's eyes lit up and she began to speak to Diana in rapid fire French. Alana and Barbara, neither of whom spoke French, had no idea what was being said. When Diana realized they were being left out of the conversation, she apologized and asked Jeanette to speak English again.

The ladies finally decided on a slightly darker blue silk. Jeanette said it would go better with Barbara's dark hair and blue eyes. They picked out a fashion plate from the ones Diana had brought with her. Jeanette was very excited to see all the newest styles from London and Paris that Diana had brought.

Alana had had no idea that Jeanette had such an eye for style and color. In the few months Jeanette had been with them, there had been no occasion for a fine dress to be made and she spoke little about her life in New Orleans.

She had made clothes for the children and a couple of simple dresses for Alana while she had been there, but nothing else new. She mostly had done the mending which, with six children, was copious. Jeanette seemed thrilled to be working with fine fabrics and styles again. They made arrangements for Barbara's measurements to be taken the next day so the work on the dress could begin.

In the days that followed, everyone was very busy with wedding plans, farming, and showing their guests around. Diana went riding with Ian every morning. Usually, they were accompanied by the Captain, and young Angus. Lawrence had left for home, taking Nathaniel with him, the day after they had arrived. He needed to check on his own place and was expecting a special delivery, but promised to come back in a few days and stay until the wedding.

On the day Lawrence was due back, Ian and Diana were riding alone for the first time as the Captain and Barbara were meeting with the minister and Angus was helping Alana with the younger children's lessons. Ian thought to take this opportunity to inquire about Diana's feelings for Lawrence, but was unable to decide how to broach the subject.

Finally, he just blurted out, "Di, how do you feel about Lawrence Banbury? I see the way you two look at each other. I can almost guarantee how he feels about you, but you're harder to read, even though I've known you forever."

Diana's face flushed a deep pink and she lowered her eyes. She was used to Ian's bluntness, but she was still surprised by his question.

"I honestly don't know, Ian. There are some things that I never told you in my letters. I hesitate to even tell you now because they are so very personal, but I really have no one else to talk to."

"Oh, Di, don't tell me you went against your wedding vows with him?" Ian said, aghast to even think such a thing.

"No, Ian, I did not. If I had, Edward would not have minded. He encouraged me to take a lover for years."

"Edward did what? What was wrong with him? Didn't he stay faithful to you?"

"Oh, Ian. There is so much you don't know about my life. We didn't have a traditional marriage. Be still and I will explain." Diana said with a mirthless laugh as a very agitated Ian began to sputter again.

Diana then proceeded to tell Ian about her love for Edward's brother Geoffrey, that her child had been his and about Edward's long standing relationship with Benjamin and her love for them both.

"So, you see Ian, although Edward had a lover all the years we were together, until Benji died in Russia, I did not. I was not brought up to act like the rest of the *ton*. Honestly, I have only had relations with one man and that was only once with Geoffrey when I was sixteen years old. I know very little about what goes on between husbands and wives or lovers for that matter.

Now, I've embarrassed you and myself, but I just had to tell someone. Barbara knows, of course, and I think Murray knows more than he lets on, but we only got to know Murray after Benji died. He was a tremendous help to us in bringing Benji home and getting him buried and his family taken care of. Edwin Burroughs knows about my marriage, but Edwin is more like an uncle to me than anything else and I couldn't confide in him like I always could in you. I'm that sorry if I've upset you."

"I'm not upset, Di. I think I'm in shock. I have heard of men like Edward and Benjamin, but I have never actually known any. Did you not think what they did was unnatural and against God's laws?"

"I never thought of it in relation to God, to be honest. When Edward first told me, I didn't even understand what he was trying to say. I had never heard of two men loving each other and having…..well relations with each other." Diana said with an extremely red face. "But after I saw them together, how they loved each other and needed each other, well it did seem natural to me. Their love was no different than the feelings I had for Geoffrey.

My Da was scandalized when he figured it out, but when he saw I was really alright with their relationship and that I loved them both, he let it be. I know he was disappointed that I didn't have a love match like he and my Mam had, but he knew I wouldn't break my vows, no matter what."

At first, during Diana's tale, Ian was shocked and angry that his good friend had never known the love of a spouse and had to be alone for all those years. He almost hated Edward for placing her in that position. Then he was ashamed of his feelings. Who was he to be angry at men he had never known. If Di accepted them, then so would he. He still felt it was a damned shame that she had missed out on so much in her life and he told her so.

"Well, I've never known that kind of relationship, so I guess you cannot miss what you've never had. So, you see, when you ask about my feelings for Lawrence, I really don't know because I don't understand exactly what I'm feeling. I know I like him as a person and I see him as a good man, but the other thing…..the feeling I get when he looks deeply into my eyes and sparks seem to fly…. well it's been almost twelve years since I loved anyone like that. To be honest, I sometimes can't remember how it felt.

Geoffrey and I were only together a few weeks and then he was killed. I was pregnant, sick, and unmarried. I was so ashamed of what would happen when everyone found out….what it would do to my Da. Well, when the duke said Edward would marry me and give my bairn a name, I was so relieved, I didn't even really think about anything else. So you see, I'm like a green girl when it comes to men."

Ian didn't know what to say to her. He had assumed that she and Edward were happily married. "After all", he thought, "I thought they had a child together."

She had never written a word about her situation, but then again, how could she. It wasn't something you could put into writing when you were a duchess. Diana had always been more responsible than anyone he knew.

At the age of ten, she had taken over the running of the keep and begun to take care of her father's tenants. She had always been so much more mature than her actual age, even when they were little more than bairns.

It was always she who was the voice of reason when they got up to high jinx. She was the one who kept them out of trouble more times than not. Ian had always been headstrong and anxious to have a good time, it was Diana who was the level-headed one even though she was three years younger than he.

Ian turned to Diana and said, "Well, Di, I cannot exactly explain it to you in words. You know I've never been good at talking about my feelings. But, I would suggest that you just take some time and get to know Lawrence. Maybe if he knew about Edward, he would be patient with you."

"He does know. He discovered the truth about our marriage at a house party the last time he was in England."

Ian was shocked. Lawrence had never breathed a word. He had always asked about Diana and asked to be mentioned to her when Ian wrote to her when he was aware that he was writing. Ian said, "He never said a word."

"Perhaps he felt it wasn't his story to tell. I wish I could have told you myself years ago, but I could never bring myself to write down information that could have caused Edward and Benjamin to be imprisoned and maybe hung. There are just things better left with no written records. They are both dead now. Edward's good name will never be besmirched and neither will Benjamin's. I owe them that and so much more for all the love they lavished on me over the years. They were both wonderful to me and I loved them dearly."

About that time, Ian saw Lawrence's carriage come over the rise. He usually rode over on horseback, but since he was staying until after the wedding, he needed more luggage than saddlebags could carry. His saddle horse was tied to the back of the carriage though.

Diana saw the carriage as well. Her hands clenched the reins so tightly that Malmuirra felt her tension and side-stepped and whinnied. Diana loosened her grip and gave herself a mental shake. She must get over this kind of reaction every time she saw Lawrence or heard his voice. She pasted a bright smile on her face and rode to greet the carriage with Ian.

Chapter 58

The two weeks they had allotted for wedding plans flew by very quickly. The day of Barbara's wedding to the Captain dawned cool and sunny. Ian had told them that most people were married in their homes by the local travelling preacher or a minister from Williamsburg.

Since both Barbara and Captain Bowie were catholic, as was Diana, they had requested their wedding be officiated by a priest. Being there was no catholic church, monastery, nor convent nearby, they had agreed to be married by the local minister. They were all disappointed to find out there weren't many Catholics in Virginia.

Ian and Alana were acquainted with the minister, although they didn't attend his church, and he was willing to come to their home to perform the ceremony.

The ceremony was set for nine in the morning, so there was a flurry of activity getting all seven children up, fed, and dressed in time to attend. Diana helped Alana with the children and then rushed to help Barbara dress.

Jeanette was in the room when Diana arrived. She was putting the final touches on the dress she had worked so very hard on for two weeks. Barbara was nervously walking a path in the rug wringing her hands. Diana went to her and pulled her into a strong hug. It was exactly what Barbara needed.

"Oh, Miss Diana, am I doing the right thing? I feel that awful leaving you here and going off to sea with Richard, but I love him so." Barbara said tearfully.

"Well, there you go, Barbara. You answered your own question. You love him and he loves you. So, yes, you are right to marry him and follow him wherever he goes. I know you will have a happy marriage. I can hardly wait to receive letters about all the wonderful places you will visit with your Captain." Diana said, smiling through her own tears.

Jeanette bit off the last thread and stood up shaking out the dress. "Now, Miss Barbara, you just hesh up that cryin'. I don't want no spots on this beautiful dress I done made you"

And it was a beautiful dress. The bodice was fitted and trimmed on the low, round neckline with flounces of white lace. The very full skirt was also trimmed in the same lace in five rows at the bottom of the gown. The sleeves were three-quarter length and had lace flounces at the cuffs to mimic the bottom of the gown. Jeanette had also made a veil from the same white lace. It attached to Barbara's hair with combs that had been covered in the blue silk. It was one of the most beautiful dresses Diana had ever seen. She complimented Jeanette on her talent and the small woman glowed with happiness to be appreciated so.

When the dress was slipped over Barbara's head and laced up, Diana led her to the dressing table and started brushing her dark wavy hair. Jeanette surprised them again as she took over that task as well. She wove Barbara's waist length hair into several intricate braids. She then took the braids and formed a coronet on top of Barbara's head. She took the veil and fastened the silk covered combs in several prominent places in Barbara's hair so they would be easily seen.

When Jeanette was satisfied, she took Barbara to a full length mirror in Alana's room. When Barbara saw her reflection, she almost didn't recognize herself. She looked like a fine lady, not a maid. Her joy was contagious and soon all the women were laughing like young girls.

Ian soon knocked on the door and told them it was time. Ian was going to walk her to the fireplace where the minister and Captain Bowie were waiting. Diana and Alana preceded them down the stairs together and took their seats in the drawing room. All the furniture had been moved and chairs placed for the wedding guests facing the fireplace. The children had gathered a multitude of flowers for the celebration. Many had been woven into garlands with ribbons and placed on the mantle and above the windows. There were also vases of them on tables around the edge of the room. Barbara hadn't seen the room since its transformation and was awestruck at how beautiful everything was.

Diana was very happy as she watched her closest friend become the wife of what she knew was a fine man. Her eyes met Lawrence's and her smile froze from the intense look in his eyes. It was if they were the only two people in the room.

The moment was broken when Nathaniel pulled on Lawrence's coat and asked, "Do we throw the flower petals now, Papa?"

Lawrence looked down at his little son and said, "Not yet, Nat. When we go outside, we will throw the flower petals. We wouldn't want to mess up Miss Alana's floors, now would we?"

He looked up from his son's serious little face to find Diana looking at Nathaniel with such longing, it hurt his heart. He thought, "That woman needs a child to love. She needs my child."

Lawrence was startled by his thought. He knew that he and Diana had a very deep attraction to each other, but they really hardly knew each other. A few weeks acquaintance with each other, in a mostly formal setting, was hardly enough time to think about spending the rest of their lives together. But, he knew in his heart that she was the one for him. Now he just had to convince her of that. Lawrence could feel her reluctance when they were together. He couldn't put his finger on the cause though.

He had noticed how reticent she was in his presence. He saw fear in her eyes when she felt the spark that jumped between them. After the marriage she had had with Edward it was no wonder she was hesitant to embark on another relationship. He would just need to be patient and give her time. He didn't know how long she planned to stay in America, but he hoped she would be there permanently, with him.

Since the wedding was in the morning and the party in the evening, Diana had arranged for the newlyweds to go to Williamsburg alone for a meal at the best tavern there. It was called the King's Arm Tavern and was highly recommended by both Ian and Lawrence. They told Diana the food was incredible, especially the whiskey and maple-brined pork. Diana had sent Murray to Williamsburg to book a private dining room for the couple.

Diana had a carriage decorated with flower garlands and ribbons and even had flowers put in the horse's halters. The Captain was privy to the plan, but it was a surprise for Barbara. When the service was over and a toast had been drunk to the newlyweds and congratulations given, Diana led the newlyweds outside. Alana had herded the seven children out with their baskets of flower petals in hand first. When the newlyweds came out the door the children showered them with flower petals yelling, "Congratulations" as loudly as their little voices would allow.

Barbara and her Captain were laughing at the children and didn't at first notice the decorated carriage in front of the door. When Barbara saw all the ribbons and flowers, she knew Diana had arranged it all. She turned to see Diana standing in the doorway smiling broadly at the expression on her face. Barbara ran to Diana and hugged her tight.

"Oh, thank you so much, Miss Diana. You have made this day so special for me and for my captain also. I don't know how to tell you what it means to me." Barbara said with tears starting in her eyes.

"No thanks are required. Your happiness is my reward. I am so very happy for you dear friend. And please stop calling me Miss Diana or your grace or Lady Diana in public or in private. You have always called me Diana in private, so please do so in public as well now. You are the lady wife of a sea captain. You need pay obeisance to no one again." Diana said with a gracious smile.

The Captain came and retrieved his bride. He took her hand and lead her to the waiting carriage. The newlyweds took off among a hail of good wishes and laughter.

Ian said, "You would think they were leaving for ever. They are just going to Williamsburg and will be back in a few hours for their party. Come on all of you, there is much to be done to get ready for that party."

With that, everyone scattered to take care of last minute details before the guests arrived in a few hours. Since Alana and Ian had invited some fifty people, they had decided to have the party out of doors. Men had been working for days to build a wooden platform to dance on under the huge oak trees at the side of the house. There were no formal gardens at the house, but Alana had planted numerous rose bushes and flowering shrubs in that area. There were walkways and benches as well in small private areas under the trees.

The dancing platform was outside the planted area, but tables and chairs had been set up among the flowers and shrubs. Each table required candles or a lantern, so several servants were busy filling the lanterns with oil or placing the candles in holders. There were fresh flowers on each table as well.

Diana and the children had scoured the neighborhood for wild flowers as well as asking the neighbors to donate flowers from their gardens. They had been on the flower hunt for two days before the wedding. Alana's pantry and kitchen had been overflowing with blooms.

Diana had thoroughly enjoyed her flower treasure hunt with the children. It had been Angus' idea when he heard Diana lamenting the fact that it was too early in the year for much to be blooming. He told her he knew where there were lots of flowers and on one of their rides, he had shown her a meadow a couple of miles from the house that was filled to bursting with poppies in three colors, red, gold and orange.

After that discovery, Ian had suggested asking some of their neighbors to contribute some flowers form their gardens. He sent one of his men around to get commitments and Diana was very surprised that every neighbor asked had consented to send over flowers on the day of the wedding. Diana was amazed at the variety of flowers and blooming branches that arrived. She particularly loved the branches of the nine bark shrub. The flowers were dense and had a wonderful fragrance. She used a lot of this plant in the garlands that were hung in the house.

There were also a wide variety of roses that arrived. There were all colors and types from floribunda to tiny wild yellow roses the children had discovered on one of their forays into the countryside. The very large long stemmed white roses were Diana's favorite. She combined about a dozen of the white roses with some deep pink azalea branches for the bride and grooms table. Diana and Barbara had spent many hours creating flower bouquets for dinners and balls. It was a pastime that they both enjoyed very much. Diana knew how much Barbara loved flowers, especially roses.

She made a huge bouquet of multi-colored roses for the bridal chamber. She was just carrying the large vase upstairs when the door opened. She turned to see who was there. It was Lawrence.

He saw her on the stairs and headed toward her. She almost continued up the stairs, but it was obvious he wanted to speak to her so she waited. She kept her eyes downcast until he got to the step below the one she was standing on. She looked up then and that spark leaped between them again.

Lawrence heard her quick intake of breath. He reached out to touch her arm and she shuddered. He spoke quietly, "Diana, we need to talk. I know today is not the time with so much going on, but would you please ride with me in the morning. Just the two of us."

Diana almost declined his invitation because she was fearful of the strong emotions he elicited from her. Then, she raised her chin, looking him directly in the eyes and said, "I would like that very much. Shall we say seven?"

Lawrence was pleasantly surprised. He agreed to the time eagerly. He had thought he would have to convince her of their need to talk about their feelings. He said no more then, just gave her arm a gentle squeeze and went back down the stairs.

Diana proceeded to the room she and Alana had prepared for the newlyweds. She placed the bouquet on the table at the end of the bed. She was nonplussed by her easy acquiescence to Lawrence's request for a private ride. "What was I thinking?", she thought, as she sat down heavily in one of the armchairs in front of the fireplace.

Diana had not been alone with a man since Edward died, except Edwin. Edwin certainly didn't count. He was like family. The last time she and Lawrence had been alone in the conservatory all those years ago, he had almost declared himself then. She had been so afraid of her own feelings, she had run from the room.

"But things are different now," she thought, "I'm no longer married. Edward has been dead almost two years. What will I do if he kisses me like he almost did at the house party so long ago?"

Diana had not been kissed in a romantic way since Geoffrey, almost thirteen years ago. She tried to remember how it had felt to be in Geoffrey's arms, but it was just too long ago. She remembered how much she had loved him, but she couldn't recall the feelings he had elicited in her so long ago. She had been so young and inexperienced then. Actually, she was still inexperienced. She thought, " One night of passion in the barn so long ago couldn't be considered experience, could it?"

Diana heard Alana calling her and hurried from the room. Finally all the preparations were complete. Promptly at five o'clock the newlyweds arrived back to get ready for the party. Barbara thought she would be wearing her wedding dress to the party and would just be freshening up. She was shocked when Jeanette walked into her room with a lovely rose pink evening gown in her hands.

The dress was low cut in the front with a square neckline. The sleeves were short and poofy. The bodice was very tight and came to a point just below the waist. The skirt was full and had four tiers of ruffles on the bottom made from the same silk as the dress. There was no lace on the dress, nor bows, but the simple cut was perfect for the shimmering silk material. A pair of silk slippers the same color lay on the bed with a silk chemise, a new corset, and several petticoats.

Barbara was overcome. She said, "When did you find time to make this, Jeanette? I thought this beautiful wedding gown had taken all your time."

Jeanette had a very broad smile on her face. "I didn't make this entire dress alone, ma cher. Lady Diana did much of the work on it with me at night after everyone was gone to bed. She and I sat up together to complete it. She wanted you to have something lovely for your party besides your wedding gown. She is a fine mistress, n'cest pa?"

"That she is. I will miss her so much. She is my friend as well as my mistress. I love her like one of my sisters."

"That is plain to see, as she loves you. I will really enjoy taking care of la petite madame."

"What do you mean, are you going to be Diana's ladies maid, Jeanette? I thought she had decided to use Maisie. I've been giving her pointers on what to do for Diana."

"I know, ma cher, I know. But, la petite, she change her mind. She decide she likes Jeanette better. And for that I am much happy." Jeanette said with a twinkle in her eye. "I will learn all the things I need to know about her in the coming days. I have been maid to the couturier I belonged to in Nawlins. The basics I already know, so not to worry."

Barbara was not really surprised that Diana had changed her mind about Maisie. The young black woman was bright enough, but she had a very docile personality. Diana liked to have people about her who had a bright outlook and good personalities. Since she sometimes fell into a depression over all the tragedy she had felt in her life, she needed that to help buoy her up.

There was a knock on the door. Diana came in already dressed for the party. She wore a beautiful emerald green silk gown trimmed in gold lace and braid. It fit her perfectly and showed off her tiny waist and well-formed bosom. The neckline was a sweetheart style that had the gold braid sewn onto it accentuating her decolletage. There was also gold braid at the waist and around the hem. The gold lace was on the sleeves that were split and went to her elbows where the braid was used to band the full gathered sleeves.

Around her neck, Diana wore her mother's emeralds. The emerald parure was made up of earrings, a necklace, two bracelets, and a ring. Tonight, Diana wore them all in celebration of Barbara's marriage. She rarely wore this much jewelry, but for some reason tonight, she wanted to shine.

In her hands, Diana carried a jewel box. "I have come to give you your wedding gift, Barbara."

"Oh, Diana, the wedding, my wedding gown, the luncheon in Williamsburg today and now this beautiful evening gown are my wedding gifts. I cannot thank you enough for all you have done to make my day special. You are the dearest friend I have ever known." Barbara said with a catch in her voice.

"No crying now. You will make your eyes red and they won't look well with that pink gown." Diana said laughing. "This is something I want you to have. When you wear it, you can remember your old friend. Now let's get you dressed. Your new husband is all ready and waiting for you downstairs."

When Barbara was laced into her dress and Jeanette had worked her magic on her hair, Diana came up behind her and clasped a fantastic diamond and pink topaz necklace around her neck. Barbara had never seen this piece. The center was a huge pink topaz surrounded by brilliant diamonds. The chain also had smaller diamonds all around it. It nestled perfectly between Barbara's breasts. Diana also handed her a pair of matching earrings.

"Oh, Miss Diana, this is too much! Wherever would I wear something like this on board a ship. I cannot accept something so very expensive." Barbara cried.

"Oh, but you can. Do you remember what my Grandmother MacPherson told me. A woman should always have something of her own in reserve just in case. You can never tell what will happen in life. Consider this necklace and the earrings a nest egg for you and the Captain. Should you want to leave the sea at some time in the future, you could sell this set and finance a new way of life.

Barbara, if ever you should need anything, please do not hesitate to let me know. You know I have more money than I could ever use and I am still making more every day from my estates. I have more jewels than I can ever wear. Please accept this gift in the spirit in which it is offered. It's my way of making sure you will never be without." Diana said with tears in her eyes.

Barbara agreed and the two friends went down the stairs to greet the guests who were beginning to arrive. As they started down the stairs, Captain Bowie looked up. He couldn't believe the vision his new bride looked in the pink gown. Her fair skin was glowing, her dark hair was swept up in a beautiful style and her eyes sparkled with love as brightly as the diamonds around her neck and on her ears. He felt himself a very lucky man. After all the years of being alone, he would never be again. He had found his soul mate in Barbara.

There was someone else watching as the two beautiful women came down the stairs. Lawrence almost lost his breath when he beheld Diana. She looked incredibly beautiful. The vibrant green of her dress made her red hair almost glow. The jewels around her neck and wrists and dangling from her ears added even more sparkle. He could hardly wait for their ride in the morning. He had much to say to this tiny Scots beauty.

Ian and Alana had Diana and the newlyweds stand in the receiving line with them, as well as Lawrence. Diana was a little surprised that they asked Lawrence, but later Ian told her Lawrence had contributed the meat for the dinner party as well as all of the wine, and some of the ale and beer.

It seemed that Lawrence had an extensive wine cellar, unlike Ian, who was not a wine drinker and cared little for it. Actually, Ian and Alana drank very little spirits, other than ale sometimes with their meals. Ian told her they had just never acquired a taste for strong spirits.

Since Diana, because of Edward's inclination to over imbibe, had drunk very little spirits herself, she hadn't even noticed that it was rarely served in the two weeks she had been there.

There were twenty couples at the party along with a multitude of children. It seemed in America, there were few adult only parties.

Diana had become comfortable with Ian and Alana's brood, as well as Nathaniel Banbury. She had spent much time wandering the countryside in the last couple of days gathering flowers with all of them. She tried not to show special attention to any one of the children, but she had a special soft spot in her heart for Nathaniel.

He was an engaging child. He had Lawrence's dark hair and coloring, but his face was that of an angel. His dark blue eyes were large and expressive. His skin like silk and his cheeks rosy. He almost always had a smile on his little face, after he became used to Diana and her friends. His sunny disposition was hard to resist as well as his intelligence. Diana found herself drawn to him more and more.

The party was a resounding success. Diana enjoyed meeting all the neighbors and also Ian and Alana's friends from Williamsburg. She was much gratified to meet Mr. Benefield and his very pleasant wife, Marie. He had been a mentor for both Ian and Lawrence. She was somewhat surprised to find he was a man in his early forties. For some reason, she had imagined him to be a much older man. Carl Benefield was not an especially tall or large man, but his personality was such he seemed larger than life. He was quick to smile and quick to laugh and he enjoyed story telling immensely.

After speaking with Mr. Benefield for a few minutes, Diana was amazed at the vast amount of knowledge he had about the American frontier. She asked him, "Were you born in this country, sir? You seem to know a great deal about America and especially Virginia."

"Why, yes, I was, my lady. I was born not ten miles from here on the farm I now own. My father was the overseer on the place. When he died from a logging accident, I took his place. I was young for it, but the owner liked me and decided I could do the job. I was all of nineteen when I took the job. I had thirty slaves under me at that time and the farm owned three hundred acres of land. Since I bought the farm fifteen years ago, I freed the slaves and hired them to work the place. A few years later, I bought another five hundred acres and hired more freedmen."

"Mr. Benefield, from what I have read of America, your attitude on slavery, especially here in Virginia is quite different from most of the other planters in this area. I applaud that attitude. I could never own another human being myself. I find the whole concept wrong."

"Well, my lady, after watching the slaves my father oversaw, and then doing the job myself, I started to think how I would feel if I was a slave. I didn't like the way it felt. When the opportunity arose to buy the place after the owner's untimely death, I couldn't in good conscience treat others as I would not want to be treated. Our slaves were always well treated and none were sold during the time I was there. That, however, is not the case most of the time.

I have seen families split up on the auction block, children as young as five or six taken from their mothers, husbands and wives separated, and many siblings torn apart from each other. I have heard the mothers wail for their children deep into the night at the slave pens in Richmond. It is a sound I never want to hear again."

Diana was disturbed by the images this story put into her head. She, who had lost a child to death, could sympathize with these poor women who's children were taken from them, never to see them again. To lose a child, in her opinion, was the hardest thing a woman could ever face.

When the dancing started, Diana found herself dancing a reel with Lawrence. The music was performed by three black men. There was a violin, a guitar and a drum in the trio. All three of the men were wonderful performers. They also sang wonderful harmony when the dancers took a break. The party went on well into the night and everyone had a wonderful time.

Diana was much sought after as a dancing partner. She was light on her feet and loved to dance. Ian and she even performed the Highland sword dance. Normally women didn't participate in this dance, but Fergus MacDonald had taught it to Diana when she was a child and had encouraged her to keep it up when she was older. She hadn't done the dance since she was sixteen, but she had never forgotten it.

When Ian went into the house and brought out his father's sword wearing the kilt of MacAllister plaid that Diana had brought him, he teased Diana until she agreed to perform the dance with him. She laughingly told him she had no ghillies, but he said neither did he, but they could dance anyway. Ghillies were the shoes traditionally worn to perform the dance. There were no bagpipes either, but the musicians were consulted and appropriate music was soon decided on.

The pair danced for almost thirty minutes to the shouts and clapping of all assembled. Some of the guests were of Scottish descent themselves and revelled in seeing an old custom from home performed so well by Ian and Diana.

When they were finally done, Diana breathlessly said to Ian. "Oh, no more of that Ian me lad. I haven't danced the Highland reel since you and I did it at the Michaelmas fete the year before you and Alana left. I didn't know if I would remember all the steps, but they came back to me almost as soon as the music started."

Alana came up to the two very tired dancers, "Aye, I remember that fete. Diana, your Da insisted that you be allowed to do the sword dance even when all the other men were dead set against it. Your Da was a braw man, he was. He was more of a father to me than my own Da. I mourned when you wrote he had passed. A kinder man never lived than Earl Fergus MacDonald."

Diana looked at Alana with unshed tears in her eyes, "Thank you, Alana. He was a braw man. He cared for you too. He was kind and good and true. And oh, how I miss him."

Ian put his arms around both women and said, "Now no tears you two. This is a party, a celebration for Barbara and her Captain. Come let's go see what the newlyweds are up to."

Ian whisked them away to see the bride and groom. They were sitting at their special table gazing into each other's eyes. Diana was lifted from her melancholy moment by the look on Barbara's face. She looked so very happy, Diana couldn't feel any sadness tonight.

Chapter 59

The next morning dawned bright and cool. The days were beginning to be warmer and warmer, but the nights were sometimes almost cold here in Virginia. Jeanette had taken out one of Diana's heavier riding habits for her ride this morning. It was a deep, rich brown color as was the hat and boots. The somberness of the outfit was relieved by the pale yellow blouse she wore under her riding coat as well as the jaunty yellow feathers in her hat. Jeanette had pulled her hair back and tied it with a yellow ribbon at the nape of her neck. The deep auburn tresses cascaded down her back to her hips curling at the ends.

Lawrence was already in the barn when Diana arrived. He had never seen anyone as lovely as Diana this morning. Malmuirra was saddled as was the large black stallion Lawrence had ridden on the trip from Portsmouth. He was a splendid animal. His name was de Groot and he was seventeen hands high with high muscular withers and a proud neck. His mane and tale were long and full.

Diana had never seen his breed before and had asked Lawrence where he was from. He had told her the horse was from the Netherlands and was a Friesian. Lawrence had found him in Richmond on a buying trip. His owner, one Hans van Guilder, had come to America to raise Friesians, but his mares had both died on the ship coming over from injuries they received during a bad storm. Down on his luck, Van Guilder had been forced to sell de Groot for passage money home. He had lost his taste for the new country after losing his beloved mares. He didn't want to sell de Groot, but had no other option.

When Diana inquired on the meaning of the horse's name, Lawrence had told her de Groot meant "grand" in Dutch. She thought the name fit him perfectly. Lawrence thought the name unwieldy and usually just called the horse Groot. Diana was anxious to see the foals he had sired. Lawrence told her he had sired two colts and four fillies in the four years he had him.

When Diana arrived at the barn, Lawrence greeted her warmly and helped her mount Malmuirra. When she inquired where they were going on their ride, Lawrence told her it was a surprise. They left Ian's farm and headed west. About four miles down the road, they turned off the main road onto a well used, but smaller road. About a mile down this road, they turned off again and rode through a fine white wooden gate.

The property they turned onto was covered in pasture for the most part and fenced with a white three board fence. There were crops growing in the distance, but, they seemed empty so early in the morning. As they travelled further down the lane a house came into view. It was a three story white painted wood house with a wide porch running along both the bottom and second floors. It was trimmed with black shutters and had six columns holding up the porches.

The house was surrounded by huge trees. There was a formal garden on each end of the house and a circle drive in front. Not terribly far from the house were a barn and two large stables. These were also painted white with black trim. The home and property obviously belonged to someone with great wealth. The grass was beautifully trimmed and the gardens were immaculately kept. Everything looked bright, fresh and clean in the morning sun.

"Who's house is this, Lawrence?" Diana asked.

"It's mine. I wanted you to see Groot's offspring. I had them brought up to one of the stables along with their dams. I bred him to different types of mares to see which had the best result. I cannot decide which is better because they all look good to me. Maybe you can help me decide before I breed him again. I respect your opinion on horses very much."

Diana was gratified by his words. Men rarely sought out a woman's opinion. Diana had been faced with so much male opposition when she tried to take care of duchy business, it was a rare treat to find a man who didn't question a woman's knowledge or business sense.

When they arrived a the first stable, Diana was taken to a paddock behind the building to observe the six foals and their dams. They were of varying ages, but she thought the two larger ones were 3 year-olds, the next 2, two year-olds, and the smallest probably not weaned from their dams for very long. The colors of the horses left no doubt as to their sire. They were all black. Some had other markings as well, unlike their pure black father. One of the older colts had a white blaze on his forehead and four perfect black stockings. The filly was the smallest and also had white stockings, but no blaze. Each of the young horses was very well built and quite tall for their ages.

Lawrence lifted Diana from her saddle. As he was letting her down, he held her close to his body so she practically slid down him. It was an extremely intimate thing to do. Diana blushed a deep pink and looked up at him quizzically.

Lawrence smiled down at her and said, "I have been wanting to hold you this close, literally for years. Since I have seen you again this time, the desire to hold you has grown every day. I've thought of little else since I saw you standing on that ship in Portsmouth."

Diana didn't know what to say or how to react. Her heart was pounding so loudly she thought Lawrence must be able to hear it. As she raised her eyes again to him, the look of naked desire in his eyes was hard to ignore. Diana gasped as his head came down towards her. His lips touched hers very gently at first.

It was as though Diana were drowning. She could not breathe. She gasped again as she tried to pull air into her lungs. Lawrence deepened the kiss, moving his lips slowly over hers. The spark that Diana had felt between them turned into a raging fire. Her hands, seemingly of their own volition, crept up his chest and around his neck. His hair was so soft at the nape of his neck, she couldn't help but tangle her fingers in it. Lawrence angled his head to take her mouth more fully with his.

The kiss deepened again. Diana felt Lawrence's tongue touch her bottom lip and she gasped again. Taking that as a sign of Diana's approval, Lawrence placed his tongue inside her mouth to mate with hers. Before she even knew what she was doing, Diana reached out with her tongue and touched his lip. He groaned. The kiss went on for a long time getting deeper and deeper until Diana couldn't tell where her mouth began and his ended. She had never been kissed so thoroughly in her life.

Geoffrey's kisses had been for an inexperienced sixteen year old girl. Lawrence's kisses were for a woman. Finally Lawrence raised his head and gazed down into Diana's flushed face. She opened her eyes then and looked at him with a startled expression. She touched her mouth with the tips of her fingers as if she could actually feel the kiss he had given her with her fingers.

"Diana, I have wanted to do that since the day I met you. I know you would not have welcomed that kiss the other two times we saw each other because you were a married woman. Now that you are a widow, may I dare to hope that there is a chance for us to be together?"

"I…. I don't know know what to say. I have never felt…..I don't have any…. What just happened, Lawrence?" Diane said looking up at him with wide eyes.

"I kissed a beautiful woman and she responded to that kiss. That is exactly what happened. I want us to really get to know each other now, Diana. To spend time together, to talk for hours, to share our dreams, our wants, our desires with each other. I want to know who you really are. Are you the beautiful, cool duchess, the smart business woman, the daughter of a famous horse breeder, or all three wrapped up in one delectable package?"

Diana looked up at him again. "I would like to know you as well. We have spent very little time together in reality. We have been in formal social situations and casual social situations, but we have spent very little time alone. Perhaps that is what we need to do, spend time together to see if there is a chance for us."

Lawrence was heartened by her reply. He could see she was still shy with him. Obviously, she had little experience with the romantic aspects of a relationship. From what he had gleaned from prior conversations with Diana and his uncle, he had learned that she and Geoffrey had had little time together before his death. And she had also been extremely young when they were together. He would give her time, if that is what she wanted and needed. They would have the rest of their lives together if he had his say in the matter.

They spent the rest of the morning looking over Groot's offspring and their mothers. Diana recommended breeding Groot with the mares that were the mothers of the two year-olds as she felt they had retained more of their father's traits. She also recommended Lawrence send to the Netherlands for at least two Friesian mares so he could breed purebreds. She felt he would realize a greater profit from the purebreds. Lawrence thanked her for her assessment. He had also thought of trying to obtain more of the Friesians to raise purebreds and he was happy his idea was reciprocated by Diana. He knew she knew horses probably as well or better than he did.

Lawrence took Diana on a tour of his holdings. She was amazed that he had accomplished so much in a few years. When he told her his land had been all forest, except for the meadow where the house was when he bought it, she was even more amazed at the transformation he had wrought. It must have taken an enormous amount of work to clear all those hundreds of acres.

Before going back to Ian's farm, Lawrence took Diana on a tour of his sawmill. His mill had a water wheel for power and had been built on the part of the James River that ran through his land. She was intrigued by the machinery and how everything worked. Lawrence was surprised at how quickly she understood the concept of how the machinery worked and the profit a mill like his could produce. The difference between a mill and manual labor was about eight to one in the production of board feet per day. She asked many intelligent questions about how many board feet could be produced per day and how much the finished boards fetched at market. Lawrence was intrigued at Diana's business acumen and her very quick mind.

Chapter 60

After the short ride back to Ian's farm, they had lunch with their friends. Ian had proposed a lazy day after the late night they had at the wedding celebration. Everyone agreed that they were a bit weary after all the preparations for the wedding and the party. After lunch, everyone went out to the garden to relax and watch the children play a game of bowls.

It was a warm sunny afternoon and soon even the children became sleepy and wanted to rest. The servants had brought out blankets and chairs for every one. Diana and Lawrence were seated on a blanket together close to where the children played. Nathaniel, who had lost the game he was playing, wandered over and sat between them.

When Nathaniel began to yawn, without thinking, Diana reached over and pulled his head down in her lap. He nestled against her and was soon asleep. She absentmindedly smoothed the dark hair off his forehead as she watched him sleep. "He is such a sweet little boy." she thought. She glanced up to see Lawrence watching her. He had a very tender look on his face.

"Nat has really taken to you, Diana. He doesn't usually warm up to people so quickly." Lawrence mused.

"Well, he's such a bonnie little lad. Who wouldn't fall in love with him? He always has a smile and seems to get along very well with the other children."

"Yes, he loves coming here. It gets lonely for him at Banbury Place. He plays with the servant's children sometimes, but he really needs a brother or sister. I would love to have more children some day." Lawrence waited for Diana's reaction, but it wasn't the one he wanted to hear.

Diana felt her heart drop with those words. She had been told after little Geoffrey's birth that she probably wouldn't be able to have any more children. It hadn't mattered then, because she was married to Edward and they certainly wouldn't be having any children. She hadn't even thought about Lawrence wanting more children. She should have, he was still a young man.

Diana became very still and her face drained of color. Lawrence didn't know what was wrong, but he could tell that she was upset. She stopped smoothing Nathaniel's hair and sat up straighter. It looked like she wanted to jump up and run away. If Nat's head hadn't been in her lap, she would have done just that.

Finally, she knew she had to tell him. She couldn't let their relationship go any further without him knowing that more children might not be possible for them. Diana opened her mouth to explain when Ian walked over and threw himself down on the blanket.

"I hear you went over to Lawrence's place today to see his foals, Di. They are impressive aren't they? I have been trying to talk him out of that three year-old stallion for the last six months. He would make a great addition to my little herd. I could get some really good foals from him. My children are growing up fast. They will be needing horses before I know it. Angus is already wanting a horse he can call his own. We both had horses at a younger age than he is now."

"Yes, Ian, we certainly did." Diana said quietly.

Ian was perplexed at her lack of excitement at the beautiful horses she had seen. He knew Diana's love of good horseflesh and could not understand her reticence now. Had Lawrence said or done something to offend her? He sincerely hoped not. His wish was for the two of them to grow to love each other, marry and live near he and Alana. He wanted his friends to both be happy and he thought they would be very happy together.

Later that evening, Lawrence caught Diana alone about to descend the stairs for dinner. She looked especially lovely in an evening dress of dark blue velvet with white lace around the neck, sleeves and hem of the skirt. Her hair was caught up in back with a white lace bow, holding the heavy red mass in place.

"Diana, please may I speak to you?" Lawrence asked.

"Yes, Lawrence, I also wanted to speak to you. There is something you need to know."

They went downstairs and walked outside onto the large porch. After they were seated in the rocking chairs there, Diana turned and spoke to him. "Lawrence, something you said this afternoon has made me believe you may see a future for you and I. If so, then there is something about me you must be told."

Lawrence was very apprehensive about whatever revelation Diana was about to make, but he had to know. "Yes, Diana, I would very much like to have a future with you. I need and want a helpmate and wife and Nathaniel needs a mother. I can see he has grown very fond of you, as I have always been."

"Nathaniel is part of the problem," Diana said seriously. "I have begun to care quite deeply for him. As you said earlier today, he needs siblings and you want more children. I may not be able to give you what you and Nathaniel need and want." Diana hesitated, the tears she didn't want to shed coming into her eyes. She gulped and said, "When my Geoffrey was born, there were some complications. I was told I might not be able to have any other children."

Lawrence was struck dumb for a moment. He had feared she would tell him she didn't want to be a mother to his child or didn't want children of her own. What she was telling him was in some ways worse. He did desperately want more children and he truly thought Nat would benefit from having siblings as well.

Then he thought about what he would be giving up if he didn't pursue the relationship with Diana. She was kind, warm-hearted, and generous to those she loved. She had a great sense of humor and was very intelligent and strong. In other words, she was everything he wanted in a wife. The fact that she might not be able to have children was horrible, but it was not the end of the world. After all, he had Nat, and if they couldn't have more, well one would just have to be enough.

Taking Diana's hand, Lawrence said. "That is disturbing news, Diana, but it doesn't have to mean that we cannot some day marry and have a happy life. If you should be unable to have another child, I will be disappointed, but it won't stop me from loving you. I am lucky enough to have a son, and a fine one at that. If I must be content with only one child, then I will be content, as long as I have you as well."

Diana was distressed. She pulled her hand from his and turned away. "You say that now, but how will you feel in a few years?

The bloom of love sometimes wears off. I'm not even sure what I feel is love. It's been so very long since I have loved a man, I'm not sure what it feels like. I know I care for you and your son, but is it love? I just don't know."

Lawrence reached for her and caught her by the shoulders turning her around. She had her head down and he could see the tears trembling on her long dark lashes. "Diana, I know it has been a long time for you. You were only sixteen when you fell in love. But, I truly believe in time you will learn to love again. I am willing to give you that time. Please say you will give me a chance."

Diana looked up into Lawrence's eyes. What she saw there both gratified and frightened her. She saw what she thought was love shining from those eyes, but how could she be sure? It was unlike her not to be able to make an important decision, both well and quickly. She knew she needed time, so she said, "All right, Lawrence. I plan to stay here in America for several months. We will get to know each other and I will get to know Nathaniel better and we shall see what happens. That is the best I can promise."

Lawrence felt a great relief. At least she was willing to try. That was all he could ask. He said, "That's wonderful news. I am so very happy you have decided to give us a chance. I won't pressure you, but I will try my best to convince you to stay here permanently and become my wife."

To Diana, the next two weeks sped by. It was soon time for Barbara and her Captain to say goodbye and return to their ship. On the morning of their departure, Barbara came into Diana's bedchamber soon after she had risen. Jeanette was doing her hair in front of the dressing table mirror.

Barbara looked sad and happy at the same time. When Jeanette was finished, Diana stood and hugged her old friend. "Barbara, I want you to be happy. I want you to enjoy travelling with your Captain all over the world. And I don't want you to worry about me or wonder if I am sad. I have finally come out of my time of melancholia. Being here with Ian and his family has done me a world of good. I plan to stay here for several months."

Barbara smiled and looked down into Diana's beautiful face. Her eyes were still sad, but there was a different look in them now than when they had arrived. She sensed some hope for the future in her former mistress.

"I believe a certain gentleman and his young son might have something to do with that also, am I right?"

"Yes, you're right. I am becoming more and more fond of Mr. Banbury and Nathaniel. Who knows what the future will bring? For you, I hope it brings much happiness and some bairns too." Diana laughed at the expression on Barbara's face.

"You sound like Richard. He wants a houseful of bairns." Barbara said laughing.

The two friends made their way downstairs. Standing at the bottom of the stairs were Ian, Alana, and all their children as well as Lawrence and Nathaniel. Even the taciturn Murray had appeared to bid the newlyweds goodbye.

After many hugs and kisses, Barbara and her Captain were finally loaded into the carriage that would take them back to Portsmouth. Ian had insisted that several of his men go as outriders. Murray was also riding with them to pick up the post and some supplies for Diana and Ian. The newlyweds were bound again for England, so they were taking the letters she had written to Edwin and her managers.

Diana was very quiet in the days after Barbara's departure. Lawrence knew she grieved for this latest loss, much as she had the loss of so many people in her life. He gave her space and even stayed away at Banbury Place a couple of days with Nathaniel although it was less than an hour's ride away.

Diana and Ian had kept up their early morning rides. Sometimes alone and sometimes with Lawrence and Angus. Sometimes, even Murray went along.

Murray had been trying to learn everything he could about America since they arrived. He peppered Ian and Lawrence with questions when no one else was around. Both of them recognized something of themselves in the young man. He was obsessed with making his fortune and believed that America was the place to do so. He was still very attentive to Diana's needs and wants, but he was also looking in the area for a place with a few acres to buy. He knew next to nothing about growing crops, so he spent hours talking with the black freedmen who worked Ian's farm. He learned what crops did best in this area as well as when to plant and how to tell if there was a problem with insects or disease. He would go back to his room later and write down everything he had learned that day. He didn't want to chance forgetting this important information.

Murray had diligently saved his money over the years and had managed to accrue two hundred pounds. That was an enormous amount of money for the times, since footman only made about twenty-five pounds per year and valets about fifty. He had made that type of wage until after Edward's death when he had been promoted to secretary and started to earn seventy pounds per year. Murray had done without almost all creature comforts other than those offered by his employers and all entertainment for all the years he had worked.

When Murray found that property was selling for $1.50 per acre in the area, he was flabbergasted. He had thought land would cost him much, much more. With what he had saved he could buy a hundred acres and still have enough left to hire a couple of helpers, seed, and to cover living expenses until his first crop came in. Murray was ecstatic.

Murray scouted the nearby area in his off time. That time was considerable since Diana rarely needed him these days. She had told him his time was his own unless she needed him for a particular reason, yet she kept paying his wages at the rate of a secretary while they were there. Murray felt bad about taking the money because he felt he hadn't earned it, but Diana said he had more than earned it even before they came to America.

Murray found an abandoned farm about three miles from Ian's place in the opposite direction from Branbury Place. There was a small house on it and a somewhat dilapidated barn. The house was sturdy and there were no leaks in the wood-shingled roof. The barn needed shoring up, but there were plenty of trees on the land he could use for lumber.

He had asked around Williamsburg every time he was there for anyone who wanted to work. He was finally directed to two freedmen who were brothers. They were working at an inn as hostlers, but really wanted to work the land again. He had everything in place. He just had to speak to Diana about his plans and make sure she would release him from his duties.

Ian had been taken into Murray's confidence. He excused himself to speak to his foreman one morning when they were riding, leaving Diana and Murray alone. Murray started to speak several times and then stopped. He couldn't find the words. He felt he was abandoning his mistress in a strange country.

Diana, sensing his unease, finally asked, "What is it, Murray? You seem to be trying to speak to me, but having trouble finding the words. Have you met a young lady?" Diana teased.

"No, Lady Diana, nothing like that. It is something much more important to me."

"More important than a pretty girl? Well, tell me what is troubling you, Murray?"

"I've found some property near here that I want to buy. It has about a hundred acres cleared off, but very overgrown right now. It has a little house and an old barn. I want to farm here in America. I have found a couple of men willing to work for me that are experienced farmers. They have the experience I don't. It's been my dream for years to buy my own place and work until I have the money to send for my family." Murray rushed to say.

Diana was surprised. She hadn't known Murray wanted to farm nor had she known he had a family to send for.

"Do you have a wife and children, Murray? I didn't know you were married."

"Oh, no Lady Diana. I've no wife. It's me Da and Mam I'd be sending for, along with whatever brothers and sisters want to come. We're all grown now, but some of them may want to come to America. If I can help them, then that is what I will do. There is nothing for them in Dublin. With the potato famine and the costs of things, they barely scrape by. And my parents are getting older. I would have them come to me and not have to work at all."

Diana was touched by what Murray told her. She knew so little about this handsome young man on whom she had depended so many times. She felt she had taken advantage of him to a degree. He had helped her untold times and all she had ever done was buy him a few clothes, pay his passage to America and pay his wages each quarter. She was ashamed at what she saw as her own selfishness.

"Murray, do you know I don't think I have ever heard your first name. What is it?"

"Tis Sean, Lady Diana, Sean Andrew Murray."

"Well, Sean, I think this is a grand idea. What can I do to help you? Can I pay the rest of your wages for this year to help you along with your plans? I feel I owe you that much and more for all the help you have been to me.

I don't know what I would have done without you after Russia or after we came back to London for that matter. When Edward was killed, you were there again to help out any way you could. I don't know if I have ever told you, but I really appreciated everything you did for me."

Murray's face flushed a bright red. Hesitantly, he said, "There is no need to thank me, your grace. You have paid my wages regular like from the start. You even gave me a grand raise when I took over as his grace's valet and again when you promoted me to secretary. Even though I have not been much of a secretary since we came here, you have continued to pay me that same wage. It is more than enough that you have already done. I couldn't take wages for the rest of this year without working for them. It would not be right."

Diana smiled at him and said, "Well, then, I will have to just invest in your farm, if you will let me. You can pay me back with your profits whenever you can. I would suggest you buy more than one hundred acres. I would suggest you buy at least four hundred. I will advance you whatever money you need to buy the land, bring your family over, build houses for them, hire help, and get your farm started correctly. You are one of the most intelligent, hard-working young men I have ever met. I know my investment will be repaid and in a timely manner."

"Oh, your grace, I couldn't do that. What if I couldn't pay it back. I would feel terrible if that should happen. Mr. Ian has told me farming is a gamble, but one worth the time and trouble."

"I know all that. Do you think the tenants on my estates always have their rents to pay me. In the lean years, I wait, just as I would for you. No one can predict weather or insects or disease. I know what I'm getting myself into. I have six estates and all of them are profitable, but not all the time. Farming is a long range investment. You of all people know I have the money. Why shouldn't I help someone I consider my friend."

"Your friend, oh your grace, I am but a lowly Irishman from Dublin. I could never consider myself your friend."

"And what was Barbara? She was just a young girl from a poor Scots village when I met her. Do you deny I loved her as a friend?"

"No, your grace, you treated her as a sister."

"Yes, well I thought of her as a sister. And although I haven't known you as long nor as well, I feel a real kinship to you. I trust you and respect you. I would deem it an honor to help you get your farm started and your family brought here in America to be with you. I, of all people, know what is is like to live without the people you love. I would not have you do that any longer than absolutely necessary. Please say you will write to your family and have them come here right away."

With tears in his eyes, Murray looked at the grand lady he had thought of as his mistress, but also, as something much more. He had admired her strength and her kindness for these past years very much. Now to have her make all his dreams come true in what amounted to a moment, was almost more than he could comprehend.

Finally, after some moments of soul searching, he shook his head. "Aye, your grace, if you want to do this for me, it shall be done. I will write to my family today."

Diana thought a moment, then said. "I wonder if Captain Bowie has set sail as of yet. If we could catch him, he could take your letter and maybe even bring your family back on one of his voyages. That way we would know they would be well taken care of on the voyage. I have read of some pretty terrible passages for some people."

Murray thought a moment, then said, "I doubt we could catch Captain Bowie as he told me he was sailing the day after we got to Portsmouth. However, some of his sailors told me of other good ships that make the voyage all the time. I might be able to catch one of them to carry my letter to my parents. Da would get ahold of the others. They are mostly still right there in Dublin. I have no idea what it would cost to get them all here. It might not be possible after all." he said with a deep sigh.

"Well, our passage was only twelve pounds for the three of us. That is not too much. They charge less for children. Do any of your siblings have children?"

"Aye, all the married ones do. And all are married except me and my brother John. There were twelve of us all told. That's a lot of wee ones to think of too." Murray said even more dispiritedly.

"Ah, Murray, don't despair. However much it is, I will pay it. If we have to hire a whole ship, the Murray clan needs to come to America if they wish to. They will have better lives here in

Virginia, than in Ireland with all the troubles that are happening there now. Don't worry yourself so about the money. It will all work out. Once you have your family here, you will have a lot of help on the farm. The more help, the better the profits."

Murray could see there was no arguing with Lady Diana. When she set her mind on something, she would carry it through if at all possible. Finally, he just smiled and agreed with her.

In the days that followed, Diana was caught up in helping Murray obtain his land and starting the process to bring his family to America. Lawrence was heartened to see her striving so hard to help her servant get a good start in this new country. It made him feel that Diana was becoming more affable toward staying in America herself.

Chapter 61

One morning when Diana went to the barn to saddle Malmuirra, Lawrence was the only one of her riding companions who was there. The other horses usually ridden by her friends were still in their stalls.

"Are Ian, Murray, and Angus not coming for a ride this morning?" she asked Lawrence.

"I asked Ian and Murray to allow us to have a ride alone today. I wanted to speak to you privately."

Diana said no more, she just went and saddled her horse. She hoped that Lawrence wasn't going to rush her into an answer about their relationship. She had begun to learn more and more about the man he was. She liked what she had learned, but she still didn't know her own mind when it came to the question of marriage. There was much to consider.

On one hand she was excited about the prospect of being married to a man like Lawrence. On the other, she was actually worried about what would be expected of her in the marriage bed. Having only had very limited experience in that area, she was almost virginal in her outlook. She had enjoyed making love with

Geoffrey, but it had been painful, though he told her it wouldn't be after the first time. Unfortunately, they only had that one time, so she had no real knowledge. She wanted to know so many things, but she had no one to ask.

If her mother was alive or if she had a sister, she would talk to them about these things. She thought about asking Alana, but she was hesitant. They had been very good friends when they were young, but Alana had changed a lot, as had she. They still liked each other very much, but they didn't have the closeness they had as girls. Intimate questions such as she had would be difficult to ask and to answer. Diana just didn't know what to do.

Then there was the consideration of moving permanently to America. She owned six estates in Scotland and England. Her tenants depended on her for their livelihoods. She could sell the estates, but she was fearful of how her tenants might be treated by a new owner. She was ever mindful of how many in the *ton* treated people they saw as menials. She was very hesitant to turn her people over to someone else. She had worked very hard over the years to make sure her people were taken care of properly.

She could continue to own the estates and manage them from afar, but that would put a considerable strain on Edwin as he was the hands on administrator while she was gone. She would have to consult with him as well. She didn't know if he wanted that type of responsibility on a permanent basis. So many questions and absolutely no answers.

All these questions and more plagued Diana as she and Lawrence rode through the countryside. She paid little attention to where they were going. Before she knew it, they were turning up the drive to Banbury Place.

She turned to Lawrence and asked, "Are you showing me more foals today?"

"No, I wanted to show you my home. I thought you might like to see it and I wanted to speak to you privately in a comfortable setting."

Again Diana was apprehensive about the conversation they were about to have. She feared not having answers to the questions she thought Lawrence might pose. However, she had been very curious about the beautiful house that lay before her.

As they dismounted, a groom came to take their horses. Lawrence led her up the steps and into the house. The front hall was large and very well decorated. There were beautiful large paintings on the walls, the floors were highly polished wood, and the walls were wainscoted half way up with a dark wood polished to a bright lustre. The walls above were plastered and painted cream. The ceilings had elaborately detailed plaster moldings with a beautiful crystal chandelier in the center.

Lawrence led Diana into a large drawing room done in shades of blue. The walls were plastered and painted a lovely shade of cornflower blue, the trim around the doors and windows was white as was the large fireplace. The drapes were a darker sapphire shade as was most of the furniture in the room. It had a definite masculine feel to it, yet it was very attractive and comfortable.

There were two large sofas upholstered in damask fabric in a blue and white print flanking the fireplace. Other chairs in shades of blue were scattered around the large room with small tables. There was a large Turkey carpet on the floor over the shining wood. It held all the blue shades of the room as well as some crimson and gold.

Then Diana's eyes widened. In the corner near one of the floor length windows was a beautiful pianoforte. It was made of fruitwood and had elaborate carving all over it, even on the legs. She was drawn to it although she hadn't played since Edward died. As she ran her fingers over the ivory keys, she looked up at Lawrence and said, "I didn't know you played, Lawrence."

"I don't, Diana. I bought this for you. I ordered it when Ian told me you were coming to America and it was just delivered a few days ago. I had a piano teacher from Williamsburg come out and tune it. Play something and see if he did a good job, please."

Diana was astounded. Lawrence had ordered this instrument even before she arrived. Were his feelings for her so strong that he would invest all this time and money without having even seen her again? Her thoughts were turbulent as she sat down on the bench and ran her fingers over the keys again. She began to play a piece she knew by heart by Handel. It was a soft, dreamy piece of music and it began to soothe her nerves.

When she finished that piece, she noticed there was music on the piano. She was very surprised to see it was "Helen of Kirkconnel". She looked up at Lawrence wonderingly.

"I remembered how you looked and sounded when I heard you play and sing that song at your house party in Stratfordshire. It was one of the most beautiful moments of my life. Would you consider playing and singing it now?"

"Thank you, Lawrence. That is kind of you to say. It is one of my favorite pieces. I haven't played in a long time, nor have I sung. I hope I am up to your memory."

Diana began to play the song and soon her beautiful contralto voice filled the room. Soon her eyes closed and her body swayed slowly to the music as she sang of love and heartbreak for Helen and her lover. When she was done, she slowly opened her eyes, her hands idle on the keys. She was surprised to find Lawrence standing beside her. She had not heard him move, nor sensed his presence, she had been so lost in the music.

There were tears in Lawrence's eyes as there were in Diana's. He sat beside her on the bench and put his arms around her pulling her head down onto his shoulder. They sat that way for some minutes. Diana raised her head and said simply, "Thank you."

Lawrence didn't answer. He slowly lowered his head and touched his lips gently to hers. "I should thank you," he said. "You have given me the greater gift. The piano was nothing without you here to play it. You have an amazing talent, Diana. Your voice brings a song to life with the emotions you feel when you play and sing it."

"I love to play and sing, but I haven't felt the inclination in a long time. My life was pretty much meaningless after Edward was killed, until I came here to America."

"Dare I hope that Nathaniel and I have something to do with that?"

"Yes, you and little Nat have much to do with it. Now, come and show me the rest of your home, please." Diana said brightly. She didn't want to get into a conversation about their relationship right then. She was frightened of her own feelings and limitations.

Diana complimented Lawrence on the room. He thanked her, but said he couldn't take all the credit. He had had help from Mrs. Benefield in selecting the furnishings and color scheme.

As they toured the rest of the huge house, their conversation was almost entirely on the rooms they looked through. Nothing personal was spoken of again until they came to the library. It was filled with books and comfortable chairs. It also boasted a large fireplace, but the surround and mantle was of polished oak as were the walls and shelves. There were two walls of only bookshelves. One wall was taken up with shelves and the fireplace, but the outer wall was almost entirely floor to ceiling windows. The drapes were a deep crimson and they were pulled back to let in the warm sunshine.

There were ornaments around the room which all looked to be of a personal nature. It was obvious that Lawrence had travelled and collected items from his visits to foreign countries.

Lawrence seated Diana in one of the chairs near the windows overlooking the paddock and barn, then sat opposite her. Diana began to fidget with her riding gloves. She was sure that the conversation would now become uncomfortable, but she was wrong.

They discussed horses, crops, workers and much more. Lawrence told her tales of his travels to Turkey, Rome, Paris, and beyond. She told him of her time in Russia before Benjamin became ill.

She became more and more relaxed until Lawrence said. "Diana, I feel we have grown much closer over the last few weeks. I feel I know you better and I hope you feel the same?"

Nervously, Diana said, "Yes, I feel I know you better as well."

"Could you see yourself living here in America?"

"I have given it much thought, Lawrence. I really like this new country. It offers people a chance to spread their wings. There is a much more democratic way of life here. A person can attain a good life here whether they are born into wealth or not.

It is also very beautiful and so large and fertile. There seems to be endless possibilities here. However, I have much responsibility in England with my estates. It would be very difficult to administer them from such a distance for an indefinite time."

"Have you thought of doing as I did and selling your estates?"

"I have, but I fear the new owners would not be as considerate of my tenants and holdings as I have been. My people are very happy under my stewardrship and have told me so countless times. I have made numerous improvements to how things are done on each estate to make my tenants lives better and also to increase my profit margin. I would feel terrible if I sold the estates and my tenants were treated badly or dispossessed by the new owners."

"I'm sure that is a valid consideration. However, if you screened the new owners very carefully, you shouldn't have that concern. Have you thought to offer the properties to people you know well there?"

"No, actually I hadn't considered that possibility. I could write to several of mine and Edward's friends to see if they might be interested or know someone who is reputable who might be interested. I would never sell Ainsley Glen though. It has been in our family for hundreds of years. I don't really worry about that estate however. Edwin Burroughs is a fine manager and a really good friend. He is more like family than the few cousins I have."

They were quiet for a few minutes as Diana thought over writing to Bernie, Dickey, Michael and a few others about her English estates. Lawrence rose from his chair and went to stand by the fireplace. After several minutes of contemplation, Diana looked up at him. He was staring at her with a look she couldn't quite comprehend.

"What is it, Lawrence?

"When we were speaking a few minutes ago, you only mentioned your estates as an impediment to you living in America. Do you have no emotional ties to England?"

"No," Diana answered emphatically. "There is no one in England that I am tied to in any way other than friendship."

"And what about America? Are there people here you are tied to emotionally? Other than Ian and his family, I mean?"

"I feel very close to Murray, he has been very good to me. But I don't think that is what you mean, is it Lawrence?"

"No, Diana, that is not what I mean. I am referring to Nathaniel and myself. I think you know how I feel about you. These last few weeks have just reinforced my earlier feelings for you. I am terribly attracted to you physically, but even more than that I find you to be a wonderful person. You are kind, giving, generous, and loving. I see the way you look at Nat and Ian's children.

Nat needs a mother and I believe you need children." At the look on Diana's face, he quickly added, "I remember what you told me. I know you believe you may not be able to bear another child. And if that is the way it turns out, then so be it. I love and respect you for you, not for how many children you can produce. I won't lie and say I don't want other children, but if we cannot have them together, I can live with that."

"But I'm not sure I can. To know that you are longing for more children and I am unable to give them to you would weigh heavily on my mind. I fear that over time, you may become less than content with just one child."

"Diana, I cannot predict the future. All I can tell you, and I assure you I am being very honest with you, is that I love you now and I cannot see myself losing that feeling for you. I can only see it grow stronger over time. I can understand your reservations. After all, we have not really known each other very long. What I would propose is a courtship. If after six months you feel the same way, I won't ask you again to marry me."

"Six months is not very long, but it is a lot longer than I knew Geoffrey before I fell in love with him, or Edward, for that matter before we married." Diana sat quietly for a few moments, then looked up directly into Lawrence's beautiful grey eyes. "I will agree. There are things I need to sort out for myself, but if I haven't been able to do that in six months, then I probably never will be able to." Seeing the question in Lawrence's eyes, she quickly said, "No, I cannot speak to you of these issues, it is not something I think I can discuss with a man."

Lawrence was confused by this turn in the conversation. He could not imagine what Diana was so concerned about, if the subject of more children had been settled. He decided to let it go.

He went to Diana and drew her up from the chair. He put his arms around her and slowly lowered his head. "Thank you for agreeing to my courting you. You have made me a very happy man today."

He had been wanting to kiss her again for so long. His mouth gently touched hers. Diana felt that electrical charge again as soon as his lips touched hers and she gasped. Then she felt his tongue enter her mouth and tentatively touch hers. Her breath almost left her completely and she gasped for air again. The feeling that had started in her lips swiftly spread to her breasts and then down, down, down into her lower abdomen. She pressed herself closer to him. Even through their layers of clothes, she felt his erection.

Diana didn't know what to do or how to act. Lawrence deepened the kiss. His mouth was no longer tentative, but questing. His tongue searched for hers. Everywhere his tongue touched excited a stronger response from the rest of her body. She felt alive all over. Her knees began to weaken and she reached up and clasped

Lawrence's muscular upper arms to support herself. Then somehow her hands were in the hair at the nape of his neck. It felt so very soft and thick.

Lawrence's hand came around the front of her body between them and touched her breast. She uttered a small cry, though it wasn't a cry of alarm. She felt many things at that moment, but alarm was not part of it. Again, she thrust her body closer to his. Her hips, of their own volition, moved against him in an age-old rhythm. His hand cupped her full breast and his fingers kneaded her nipple. She thought her breast would burst the confines of her clothes from the feelings his fingers elicited. She wanted him to touch her bare skin. She wanted all of him to touch all of her.

Lawrence unbuttoned her riding coat and reached inside to touch her breast through just her thin blouse and chemise. The feeling was exquisite, but still not enough. She rubbed her breast against his hand. Lawrence was still kissing her and Diana felt her whole body responding to his lips, his fingers, and his body as it was pressed tightly to hers. She wanted more, so much more.

Diana brought one of her hands from Lawrence's neck to his chest and rubbed her hand across the hard muscles there. He groaned deep in his throat. She reached inside his coat and rubbed her small hand down the front of his shirt across the small nub there under his shirt. Again, he groaned. Diana felt a sense of power she had never known. How had her simple touch produced such a response from this handsome man? She was intrigued. "Did he feel the same things she was feeling?" she wondered. How could just a touch produce these longings she felt all over her body?

Lawrence unbuttoned a few buttons on her blouse. He pushed it aside as well as her chemise. As soon as his hand touched her bare skin, Diana thought she would explode. The pressure in her lower regions became almost too much to bear. She had never felt such longing.

Lawrence lowered his head to her breast and teased her nipple with his teeth and tongue. Again, Diana thought she would explode. He pushed her blouse and chemise out of the way exposing both breasts. He kneaded one breast while he suckled the other. Diana's head went back and her body bowed toward him. Her feet almost left the floor. She was standing on the very tip of her toes now.

Keeping his mouth on her breast, Lawrence swept her into his arms and sat down in his chair with her on his lap. She could feel his erection prodding her bottom through the skirt of her habit. She wiggled her bottom to get more comfortable and Lawrence shuddered at the contact. As Lawrence put more pressure on her breast with his mouth, Diana's head fell back and her body arched to give him even more access. He supported her shoulders with his left hand and his right hand slid from her riding boot under her skirt to her knee. She sucked in a deep breath and involuntarily drew up her knee. His hand fell from her knee and started up her thigh to that most secret of places. This time it was Diana who shuddered.

Lawrence's fingers trailed fire along her inner thigh to the curls at the apex of her body. One of his fingers parted her curls and very lightly stroked the small nub there. Diana almost screamed, but caught herself in time and only uttered a sharp cry. As Lawrence's finger kept up its exploration of her core, his mouth was suckling first one breast and then the other. Diana felt she was on fire all over her body.

Her body stiffened as Lawrence slid his finger inside her. She expected the pain she had felt when Geoffrey made love to her so long ago, but all she felt was pleasure. She relaxed and moved her legs farther apart to give him better access. When he inserted another finger inside her and used his thumb to rub the tiny nub, she lost all control. Her body moved on its own against his hand. Her breath came out in sobs as she strained for her release.

When her release came, she could not contain the little scream that issued from her lips. But Lawrence didn't stop, he continued to slowly slide his fingers in and out of her using his thumb to caress the nub that gave her so much pleasure. Before she knew it, she was spasming again and then again. Diana had never felt such intense pleasure.

Finally, Lawrence withdrew his hand and held her tightly as she collapsed against him. She looked up at him in wonder. He smiled down at her and kissed her gently.

"Somehow, I knew you would be passionate, but I had no idea you would respond so wonderfully to my touch." Lawrence said softly. When Diana's face flushed a dark pink from embarrassment, he said, "No, my darling, please don't ever be embarrassed about what we do together. That is one of the most wonderful parts of being loved. When you respond so eagerly and completely to me, it is a great gift and I thank you for it."

Diana looked down for several moments and then she looked into Lawrence's eyes. All she saw there was truth. She said hesitantly, "This is the part of loving that I have so little experience with. I....I, well, I don't even know how to talk about the....that...Well, you know what I mean. I didn't know if I could respond.

I was very emotionally upset when Geoffrey and I made love.....and it hurt so badly at first. Geoffrey was very patient with me, but we only made love once and just a few weeks later, he was dead. I was very young and then I found I was carrying a bairn and I thought my world would end. I have never been with a man again. It has been almost thirteen years."

Lawrence could hardly believe what he was hearing. He had thought Geoffrey and Diana had been true lovers. He had no idea she was practically a virgin. No wonder she was so reticent about what she felt for him. She had no frame of reference from her past to rely on. He saw he would have to take it very slow with her.

Lawrence slowly rearranged her clothing. He then held her close and told her about all the wonderful things two people in love experienced in the marriage bed. Then he told her something very private because she had confided so completely in him.

"Diana, you know that Nathaniel's mother and I were only married a little over a year, don't you?" When Diana shook her head yes, he continued, "Well, she did not enjoy the marriage bed. She was very delicate and not an entirely healthy person, even before she began to carry Nat. She was often so indisposed I slept in a separate room, so as not to disturb her. She never responded to my touch the way you do. So, you see, that is why I consider your response such a great gift to me."

Diana was confused. "You know so much though ,Lawrence, how did you learn all of that if your marriage wasn't…..complete?"

"I am not nearly so young as you, my sweet. I had mistresses in London over the years. However, those women weren't in love with me nor I with them. What we had was a business relationship. I bought them clothes and jewels and paid their rent and they gave me….well, what I needed at the time. Most of them were quite skilled, so I learned a thing or two over the years."

Lawrence expected Diana to be shocked or maybe even angry. Instead, she looked up at him with a mischievous grin and said, "I'm glad you did."

Lawrence laughed delightedly. This woman was one of a kind. Although practically an innocent, she did not begrudge him the pleasures he had known before he met her. She was rare. He hoped that whatever impediment she had seen to their marriage was gone. He wanted to marry Diana as soon as it could be arranged and begin their lives together immediately.

"Diana, was this the problem you needed to sort out when we spoke earlier?"

Shyly, she looked down and then brought her eyes back to his face. "Yes, I wasn't sure if I could be a true wife to you. I knew I felt a great attraction to you, but I honestly didn't know if I could respond to you the way I thought you would want me to."

"And are you satisfied now that we won't have that particular problem in our marriage?"

"Oh, yes, Lawrence, I am very satisfied," she said with another saucy grin.

"No, my love, you have only been satisfied in one way, there are many others we will try. I intend to make your satisfaction my life's work." Lawrence said with a low chuckle. Diana's face flamed a brilliant pink again. She was such a delight. Provocative one moment and innocent the next. What a life they would have.

Epilogue

Less than a year later, Diana sat on the front veranda of Banbury Place embroidering a small white dress. She heard hoof beats and looked up. Ian came cantering up the drive on Blaze, Groot's son. He had finally talked Lawrence into selling him the three year old a few months before.

He slid from the horse and walked up on the veranda smiling at Diana. "How's the little mother today," he asked with a grin.

Diana scowled at him and patted her huge stomach. "I am quite well, thank you, though I have to admit I'm a little uncomfortable. This baby seems to be growing at an alarming rate."

Ian frowned and looked down at her stomach again, "What does Dr. Peterson say?"

"He says that we are both fine and he hopes there will be no complications. What else can he say. We won't know until it's time for her to be born."

"Her, who says it's a girl? It might be a fine big strapping lad, like we had last year." Ian said with a grin.

"He is a fine lad, Ian. He'll be walking any day now. Your little Donald has really grown since he was born last June. Not even ten months old and pulling up on everything. He keeps poor Alana running to keep up with him," Diana said laughing.

Alana had delivered a fine, big boy making five boys and two girls for the MacAllisters now. Ian hadn't stopped smiling for a month after he was born. Diana thought about her Lawrence and the baby she carried. For some reason, she just knew they were having a girl. She hoped Lawrence would be as proud of their little girl as Ian was of his son. He had told her he didn't care about the sex of the baby. He just wanted her and the baby to be well. Nothing else mattered.

"Where is Lawrence, this fine morning? I wanted to speak to him about maybe trading him some of my corn crop for some of his fine alfalfa hay. My horses seem to favor it over the hay we cut in our meadow."

"He's gone to Williamsburg to buy some supplies and get the post. He took Nat with him. So, you will have to be content with just my company today, unless you have time to wait."

"Well, Di, your company has always been enough for me. We had a letter from Barbara last week. Did you have one as well?"

"Yes, I did. It was wonderful hearing from her. I am so pleased that she and the Captain will be here to visit in the next few months. I long to see her."

"As do we. I can hardly wait to show her Donald and all the others as well. They have all grown so much. And you will have someone to show off as well. Have you thought of a name for her yet?"

"We're leaning toward Catherine for Lawrence's mother with maybe my Mam's middle name of Elizabeth. It's a mouthful though. What do you think?"

"That is a mouthful, but you would honor both of your mothers. I think your Da would like that."

"Yes, he probably would. Little Geoffrey had a whole host of names and one of them was Fergus for Da." Diana suddenly gasped and bent over holding her stomach.

Ian jumped up from the rocker where he had been sitting and rushed to her side. "What is it, Di, is it the bairn? Isn't it too soon? Aren't you due in two weeks?"

Diana couldn't answer any of his questions because the pain in her abdomen was so very bad. It finally began to ease up and she looked up at Ian. "I don't think she wants to wait for two weeks. I believe my daughter is impatient and wants to be born now. Can you help me into the house, Ian. I'm not sure I can walk on my own."

"Of course, of course." Ian was very flustered and practically pulled Diana off her feet helping her from the rocker.

"Easy does it, Ian. I don't want to fly into the house. Just give me your arm now."

Ian proffered his arm. Diana put a lot of her weight on his arm and slowly went inside the big house. Just as they got through the door, Jeanette could be seen hurrying down the stairs.

"I's had a feelin' that little one was comin' today. Mr. Ian, you gonna have to carry Miz Diana up the stairs. She got no business walkin' up all them steps. I'll go get some hot water and rags. You know which room is hers and Mr. Lawrence's doncha?"

"Yes, Jeanette. I know where to go." With that, Ian swept Diana up into his strong arms and carried her up the stairs. When he came to her closed bedroom door, he paused and she turned the door knob for him.

Once they were inside, Ian went to the large canopied bed and gently lay Diana on the counterpane. She was sweating by now and holding her stomach as another contraction almost doubled her over.

"Oh, Ian, what are we going to do? I think this baby is coming right now. I can feel her trying to get out. Can you ride for Dr. Peterson? He's all the way into Williamsburg and that's almost two hours away. I don't know if I can wait until he gets here."

"Di, I don't think you can wait either. Alana's first pains were never this close. Does Jeanette know what to do or one of the other women who work here? I helped Alana with our first, but she had an easy time of it. What if something goes wrong? I won't know what to do." Ian fretted as he stalked back and forth by the bed.

Jeanette came rushing back into the room with her arms laden with sheets, towels, and a kettle of hot water. "Mr. Ian, you best go for the doctor now. I'll take care of Miz Diana until he gets here. I ain't never birthed a baby, but I'll sure try to do what's right."

"Jeanette, do any of the other women here know what to do? Is there a midwife among the workers?"

"No, Mista Ian, there ain't no one that I knows of. Bessie from Mr. Benefields's place helps our women when they needs her."

"Benefields place is almost as far as Williamsburg. Di, do you want me to go get Alana? She's helped with some births at our place and she has certainly been through it enough to know what to expect. I can get her and be back in an hour."

Diana's face was red and she was holding her stomach and panting. She looked up and almost laughed at Ian's expression. Then another contraction hit her really hard and really fast.

"We don't have an hour, Ian. This baby is coming now. Jeanette, come and get these clothes off me and get me into a night rail. Ian, turn your back, but don't leave. You have more experience than either of us, you have to stay and help."

Ian was terribly nervous. He knew that Diana had almost died having little Geoffrey and that was with a skilled physician in attendance. He knew what to do if the birth was normal, but if it wasn't he might kill Diana with his ignorance. His breathing came hard and his hands were shaking.

While Jeanette stripped Diana's clothes off between contractions, Ian shed his coat and waistcoat and washed his hands in the basin in the room. Diana's contractions were coming almost non-stop now. Ian could hear her moans as Jeanette tried to get her into a night rail. Finally Diana told him he could turn around.

Diana was in an almost completely upright position bolstered by many pillows. Her knees were up and she looked to be straining terribly.

"Don't push yet, Di. Let me see what's happening."

Jeanette held a sheet up to give Diana as much privacy as she could. When Ian looked, he saw dark hair and a lot of blood. His heart started to race and his hands started to shake uncontrollably again.

"Di, this baby is coming and I mean now. You need to push as hard as you can on the next contraction." Ian looked up and Diana's face was pouring sweat and she was gasping from the pain. Jeanette sat behind her on the bed holding her shoulders. Suddenly, Diana screamed and bent forward with Jeanette's help.

Ian looked down just in time. He caught the baby girl just as she slipped from her mother's body. He cleaned off her little face with a towel, but she didn't seem to be breathing. He lifted her by her tiny legs upside down and started to pat her little bottom. Before his hand touched her, she screwed up her little face and let out a hearty yowl.

Diana relaxed back upon the pillows with Jeanette's help. Her face was wreathed in smiles. Ian wiped the baby off a little more, cut the cord with the knife Jeanette had brought, and handed her to her mother. As soon as Diana started to talk to her, she quieted. She was beautiful. She seemed to have Diana's facial features with Lawrence's dark hair. She was small and perfect.

Suddenly, Diana groaned. Jeanette reached for the baby and lay her on the bed. She lifted Diana's shoulders again. Ian and Jeanette thought Diana was delivering the afterbirth when another tiny head appeared between her legs. This one slipped out just as easily as the first.

A boy this time. Ian didn't need to even clean his mouth or face. He was screaming almost as soon as he was clear of his mother. He was larger than his twin. He had Diana's red hair and Lawrence's features. He almost made two of his sister in length and outweighed her a couple of pounds. These were definitely not identical twins.

Ian looked up at Diana. He had thought she was happy before, but now she was absolutely radiant. He wiped off the boy, cut the cord, and handed him to his mother. As before, as soon as he heard Diana's voice, he settled down and started to nuzzle her chest.

Ian and Jeanette laughed. "That young'un is hongry, Miz Diana. He wants to eat now, not later."

"I believe he does, Jeanette. And apparently, so does his sister." Diana said as the other baby began to howl again.

Later, after the bed was changed and Diana had been cleaned up, Ian came back into the room. She was holding both babies and they were both asleep. Diana had tears in her eyes as she looked at her little twins.

"Oh, Ian. Who would have guessed there were two. I thought I was just having another large baby like Geoffrey was. I knew the baby was very active, but I never expected two. What in the world will Lawrence say?" And with those words Diana started to laugh. Soon Ian, after taking her son from her arms, joined her.

That is how Lawrence and Nathaniel found them when they got home a few minutes later. Both shaking with barely suppressed laughter. Lawrence looked from one to the other in wonder. They each had a sleeping baby in their arms and were almost doubled over with the laughter they were trying to hold in.

Diana looked up and saw her two loves looking at her like she was crazy. She tried to stop laughing, and finally got control of herself.

"Lawrence, come and see your son and your daughter. It seems we have twins. Now we have to come up with another name." For some reason, this statement brought on her laughter again. "What a wonderful conundrum! Having to have two names instead of one."

The End

Made in the USA
Charleston, SC
15 August 2015